A Stain on the Silence

PRAISE FOR ANDREW TAYLOR

'Taylor is a major talent' *Time Out*

'The most underrated crime writer in Britain today'
Val McDermid

'The master of small lives writ large' Frances Fyfield

'An excellent writer' *The Times*

'Andrew Taylor is a master storyteller' *Daily Telegraph*

'A sophisticated writer with a high degree of literary
expertise' *New York Times*

'As Andrew Taylor triumphantly proves . . . there is still room for
excellence' *Irish Times*

'Like Hitchcock, Taylor pitches extreme and gothic
events within a hair's breadth of normality'
Times Literary Supplement

'What's rare and admirable in Taylor's fiction is his painterly and
poetic skill in transforming the humdrum into
something emblematic and important' *Literary Review*

BY THE SAME AUTHOR

Caroline Minuscule

Waiting for the End of the World

Our Fathers' Lies

An Old School Tie

Freelance Death

The Second Midnight

Blacklist

Blood Relation

Toyshop

The Raven on the Water

The Sleeping Policeman

The Four Last Things

The Barred Window

Odd Man Out

An Air that Kills

The Mortal Sickness

The Lover of the Grave

The Judgement of Strangers

The Suffocating Night

Where Roses Fade

The Office of the Dead

Death's Own Door

Requiem for an Angel

The American Boy

Call the Dying

A Stain on the Silence

ANDREW TAYLOR

PENGUIN BOOKS

PENGUIN BOOKS

Published by the Penguin Group
Penguin Books Ltd, 80 Strand, London WC2R ORL, England
Penguin Group (USA) Inc., 375 Hudson Street, New York, New York 10014, USA
Penguin Group (Canada), 90 Eglinton Avenue East, Suite 700, Toronto, Ontario,
Canada M4P 2Y3 (a division of Pearson Penguin Canada Inc.)
Penguin Ireland, 25 St Stephen's Green, Dublin 2, Ireland
(a division of Penguin Books Ltd)
Penguin Group (Australia), 250 Camberwell Road,
Camberwell, Victoria 3124, Australia (a division of Pearson Australia Group Pty Ltd)
Penguin Books India Pvt Ltd, 11 Community Centre,
Panchsheel Park, New Delhi – 110 017, India
Penguin Group (NZ), 67 Apollo Drive, Mairangi Bay, Auckland 1310, New Zealand
(a division of Pearson New Zealand Ltd)
Penguin Books (South Africa) (Pty) Ltd, 24 Sturdee Avenue,
Rosebank, Johannesburg 2196, South Africa

Penguin Books Ltd, Registered Offices: 80 Strand, London WC2R ORL, England

www.penguin.com

First published by Michael Joseph 2006
Published in Penguin Books 2007
2

Set in 12.5/14.75pt Monotype Garamond
Typeset by Palimpsest Book Production Limited, Grangemouth, Stirlingshire
Printed in England by Clays Ltd, St Ives plc

ISBN-13: 978-0-141-01860-7

For Cheryl and Sue, with love

'Are you sure it's here?' the sergeant says.

'Yes.' I watch the other man picking his way among the saplings and the stones. 'There used to be one further up, but that fell down long before I came here.'

The other man drags away a fallen branch and swears as a bramble sucker rakes its thorns across the back of his hand. He works the blade of the spade under a corner of one of the stones, which has been roughly squared. It tapers slightly so perhaps it came from the vault or even from the arch over the entrance. He tries to lever it up but it's too deeply bedded into the tangled roots and impacted rubble. They won't get far with a single spade. They really need a mechanical digger.

The sergeant cocks an eyebrow at me. He's at least ten years younger than I am but, like so many policemen, he believes himself centuries older in the ways of the world.

'Listen, sir,' he says. 'When it comes down to it, we haven't got a great deal to go on. And it's hell of a long time ago.'

'You've got the fish necklace.'

'Which you have to agree is a long way from conclusive. There's no way of telling if it's the same one.'

Blood near the gate, I think, and the sound of thunder on a fine day? Doesn't that count for anything?

'We can't even be sure where it was found. Particularly as one witness is no longer with us, and the other was a kid when it turned up. And why here exactly?' he goes on. 'It's a big place. Could have been anywhere, surely.'

'Because this was special,' I say, as I've said many times before to this man and to his colleagues. 'This was a secret.'

'If we find nothing, it's not going to make things look any better. Have you thought of that? And even if we do find something, it's –'

I sigh. 'Nothing's going to make things look better.'

'No one likes time-wasters, you know.'

'I'm trying to help you. That's why you brought me here. Haven't you got a metal detector in the van? That might save time.'

He doesn't like my telling him what to do. 'If you're right, there's a hell of a lot of earth and stone on top. Even if there is something worth finding down there, we won't get a peep out of it.' He lights a cigarette – a Marlboro Light, as it happens – and turns away to stare down the slope at the stream. He gets out his phone and moves further away from me.

Wood pigeons coo. There are still a few bluebells in the green shade on the opposite bank of the stream. Bluebells mean constancy, Felicity said, everlasting love. And I hear her voice: 'The trouble is, I don't know who I'll marry.'

A few minutes later, a detective constable appears on the path, carrying the metal detector on her shoulder. I watch the three police officers consult in a huddle among the ruins. The sergeant glances at me. The woman turns on the metal detector. They have the sense to use it near the edge of the stones, where there is almost certainly a thinner layer of debris above the former ground level.

Less than a minute later they have a very sharp signal.

2

The man with the spade comes over. He digs, and the other two try to help by pulling branches and stones out of his way. It's a warm afternoon and it's getting hotter in this little valley, despite the trees and the stream. The air isn't moving.

'I can see something, Sarge,' the woman says, crouching. Her fingers scrabble among the stones. 'I think it's a wheel off a bike.'

A BMX bike. My phone rings. I take it out of my pocket and move away from the sergeant. I know he's watching me. I glance at the caller display and press one of the keys.

'Jamie,' the voice says. 'Jamie, it's me.'

I

Jamie.

That was when it had begun again, nearly three weeks earlier: Rachel told me that someone had phoned the office and asked for me as Jamie. No one had called me that since I was sixteen, with one exception. At the time I was in my early twenties, a student, and very drunk in a pub near King's Cross. I met a man who thought my name ought to be Jamie. He sensed he had riled me, and he kept on using it, Jamie this, Jamie that. I ignored him but he wouldn't stop. He came closer and his voice rose higher and higher. *Jamie, Jamie.* In the end I headbutted him and broke his nose.

I squeezed the phone tightly. After a pause that lasted both a heartbeat and a third of a lifetime, I asked Rachel whether she was sure.

'Yes.' Her voice had an edge of curiosity. 'I've never heard anyone call you Jamie before so it stuck in my mind. And the second time she said it again. Jamie.'

'She phoned twice?'

'Once just after lunch and then about twenty minutes ago to see if you were back.'

With my free hand I worried at a spot of dirt on the gear lever. I remembered a lane between a fence and a high hedge, a place where no birds sang in the

4

unbearable silence. I remembered a fish sparkling like a silver stain in the sunshine.

'James? Are you still there?'

'What was her name?'

Rachel breathed heavily and I heard the rustling of paper on her desk. 'Lily – Lily Murthington.'

'Oh, yes,' I said. 'I know. And the number?'

I found a pen. Rachel reeled off a telephone number and I scribbled it down on a copy of yesterday's *Independent*. It was a landline number with an outer-London prefix. She was only a few miles away.

'She said it's a switchboard, you have to ask for her.' Rachel paused, then added with a little gasp of excitement, 'And she said to tell you not to hang about because she might not be staying there much longer. Are you coming back to the office?'

'There's no point now. I'll go straight home.'

'Shall I email the agenda for Monday?'

'If you must.' My voice sounded quite normal, at least to me. 'Any other messages?'

There weren't. I said goodbye and broke the connection. It was Friday afternoon, the end of a long, hard week. I had been working on site in Queen's Park, assessing what needed to be done to convert a redundant chapel into retail premises. If I set off now, I would miss the worst of the traffic crawling out of London on Western Avenue. Instead I stared through the Saab's windscreen at a line of parked cars.

God help me, I had assumed the ghost was dead and buried. Out of sight, out of mind. I said the ghost's name, Lily, trying the unfamiliar shape in my mouth and finding it no longer fitted there. She still called herself Murthington, which suggested that she had not remarried. Who cared? I didn't want her to exist under any name. Had she known where I was all the time? Did she know where I lived as well as where I worked? And, above all, why should she want to break the silence? And why now?

I picked up the phone again. I had no choice. If Lily had found out where I worked, she could also find out where I lived. I couldn't risk her pestering me at the office or – far worse – at home.

The phone rang so long that I almost gave up. At last a woman answered: 'St Margaret's.'

'May I speak to Mrs Lily Murthington?'

'I'm afraid not. The doctor's with her at present.'

I hesitated. 'When would be a good time for me to call?'

The woman misunderstood me. 'You can come any time until about six thirty.'

'I meant when should I phone her.'

'Whenever you want. She's got a phone in her room but we tend to monitor her incoming calls because she's not always well enough to receive them. Whatever you do, though, I wouldn't leave it too long.'

'So she's very ill?'

'Oh, yes. I'm sorry, I assumed you knew.'

'Yes, but I wasn't sure how bad it was.' I had slipped into the lie without noticing. 'She's an old friend, you see, but we've been out of touch for a while. Listen, where are you exactly – can you give me directions?'

The woman gave me an address in Wembley. 'You

can't miss it – there's a church next door to us. Red brick with a little spire, and a car park beside it. Shall I tell her you're coming?'

'Yes, please do.'

'And who shall I say?'

I said, 'Tell her it's Jamie.'

The first thing I noticed was the sign by the entrance. It wasn't a hospital. It was a hospice, a modern building shoehorned into a small and expensively landscaped garden. Inside there were exposed bricks, gleaming expanses of pale wood, a small exhibition of monochrome photographs, and big windows that filled the place with light. The reception desk stood at one angle of a cloister running round a little court-yard where a fountain played. The staff had been trained to smile.

When I got there it was a little before six o'clock. I asked for Lily Murthington. The receptionist asked me to sit down on one of the leather sofas arranged in a U-shape round a coffee table. She murmured into a phone and a few minutes later a nurse conducted me down a corridor filled with the soft sun of early evening. We passed half a dozen doors, most of them open. I glimpsed old and shrivelled people lying on beds or slumped in chairs. They were dwarfed by the shiny equipment and the brightness of the flowers, and seemingly hypnotized by the chatter of televisions.

The nurse slowed, allowing me to draw level with her. 'She tires very quickly. I should think ten or fifteen minutes will be enough.' She stopped outside a doorway. 'There's a visitor for you, Lily.' She smiled at me, as if in encouragement.

I went into the room. A woman was sitting up in the high bed, staring at me. She was very thin and very pale. Her face and even her arms looked strained and lopsided: it was as though a giant had gripped her in an enormous hand and squeezed, and when he let go, she had lacked the elasticity to return to her former shape. The brown eyes seemed larger than before because the surrounding face had shrunk. I do not think I would have recognized her if I had not known whom to expect.

She raised her right hand a few inches above the blanket. 'Jamie.'

'Lily.'

The nurse cocked her head. 'Anything I can get you? A cup of tea?'

'No, thank you.' Lily smiled up at her. 'I'll ring if I need anything, I promise.'

The nurse smiled back and left the room. Lily was good at making people like her. It had always been one of her talents. Almost everyone succumbed at some point, even Carlo, I think, right at the beginning. The only person who never liked her was Felicity.

I said, 'I'm sorry you're not well.'

She shook her head and her hair, thinner now but still dark, trembled round her skull. A layer of grey showed at the roots. I had never known exactly how old she was and in the past I hadn't asked, perhaps because I didn't want to know. At least fifteen years older than me? Twenty? Sometimes it had seemed more, at others much less.

'I wanted to see you.' She frowned. 'You don't look as I thought you would.'

'Why do you want to see me?'

'Sit down. It's tiring looking up at you.'

I sat in the low chair by the bed, which brought the level of my head below hers. I was suddenly angry. 'You wouldn't see me before. God knows, I tried. So why now?'

'There was no point, and it wouldn't have been right. But now there is a point.'

To say goodbye? In my mind I stared back at us across a gulf of a quarter of a century. I didn't want to remember. I didn't want to see Lily. I'd said goodbye to her many years ago. All I wanted to do now was to go home and pour myself a large glass of red wine.

'Because you're ill?'

'That's not the reason,' she snapped.

I stared at her. 'I'm sorry you're like this. Truly. And – and I'm sorry for what happened. But we can't change it, you know, we can't change anything. So there's nothing to talk about. It's all over.'

'No, that's just it.' She struggled to sit up. 'It's not over.'

'Of course it is.'

She lay back against the pillows. Her eyelids drooped. For a moment I thought she was about to fall asleep. Then she said, 'Hugh's dead. Had you heard?'

'No, I hadn't. I'm sorry.'

'You've not tried to find out what happened to us?'

'No.' I spoke more loudly than I had intended. 'Why should I?'

'Hugh was sorry for you,' Lily said, after a pause. 'Of course, he never knew the truth.'

Nor had Lily, come to that, not the whole truth. Anyway, I didn't want Hugh Murthington's pity. I had liked him, and I felt guilty for what I had done to him. 'Is there anything I can do for you?' I asked.

'Not for me.' She grinned unexpectedly, another twist in the twisted mouth. 'I didn't want you to come here for me. I wanted you to come for your daughter.'

I stared at her. At first I thought I must have misheard. She shook her head slowly, as if to reject that possibility. I held my tongue. I have learned over the years that it is always better to say less rather than more and when in doubt to say nothing, if nothing will do.

My daughter, a voice said in my head. *My daughter*.

'You didn't know,' she went on slowly, speaking as if each word cost her an effort. 'I realize that. You couldn't have. I didn't know either, not when I last saw you. And afterwards it was too late.'

At last I found my voice. 'What about Hugh? Why can't it have been his?'

'It?'

'I'm sorry. She.'

The broad mouth twisted again, but this time there was no trace of humour in it. 'Her name's Kate.'

I wasn't surprised. The only surprise was that I remembered her saying, all those years ago, that she liked the name Kate.

'I was quite sure she wasn't Hugh's for the most obvious reason in the world,' she was saying. 'I had to pretend that she was premature, which involved a lot of juggling with the dates.'

'I'm not sure you should tell me this, for her sake or mine. We should forget it.'

Lily shook her head. 'She needs a father.'

'She's got one. Hugh's her father. I'm sure he made a very good job of it, and it's better to leave it at that. I don't think there's any need to drag me into her life at this stage. Or at any stage.'

'You've changed.'

I looked out of the window. I saw a square of grass and a bird table, beyond which was a leylandii hedge. I wished I hadn't come.

'She needs you,' Lily said.

I didn't turn round. 'Nonsense.'

'I'm no good to her. She's got no one else.'

'I can't believe that. She must be – what? Twenty-three, twenty-four? She's not a child. I'm sure she's got scores of friends and relations.' I hesitated. 'She's got Carlo.'

'Carlo's part of the problem.'

'You haven't told me what the problem is.'

There was silence in the overheated room. A couple of nurses passed across the open doorway. They were laughing at something but one glanced in and smiled at us.

'She's in trouble,' Lily said. 'That's why she needs your help.'

'I'm sorry but it's nothing to do with me.'

'She's got no one else. And, Jamie —'

'What?'

'You owe me something. You owe us all something. Don't you think so?'

I looked at her. Perhaps my face showed the hatred I felt.

'You owe me,' she repeated. 'Don't you?'

'We both made mistakes,' I said. 'I don't owe you anything.'

Lily lifted the glass beside her. Her hand was trembling so much that she spilled a few drops of water.

'Let me.' I stood up and took the glass from her. Feeling as awkward as a teenager, I held it to her lips. She put her finger to the base of the glass to steady it as she sipped. Her skin brushed mine. I glanced at her face, and found her looking at me.

'Not quite the same, is it?' She pushed aside the glass. 'Touching me, I mean. Nothing's the same. I'm scared to look in the mirror.'

'What's she supposed to have done?'

'The police believe she killed someone.'

'I don't think I heard you properly.'

'I haven't much energy so don't waste time. They believe Kate killed someone. Or if they don't now they soon will.'

'Who?'

'His name's Sean. They used to live together. She was going to marry him but then she changed her mind.'

I said, in a tight little voice, 'If there's been some sort of accident, the best thing for her to do is to find a solicitor and then go to the police.'

'You don't understand.' Lily sounded weaker now.

'I'm sorry, but I understand more than enough. Tell her to find a solicitor and go to the police.'

'It's more complicated than that.' Her head swayed on her narrow neck. 'She needs time to decide what to do, and somewhere to catch her breath. And then there's the problem of Carlo.'

I shook my head and stood up.

'Jamie,' Lily said. 'Please, Jamie.'

I stared down at her.

'You owe me something,' she said. 'Remember?'

She stretched her hand to a book, a biography of a dead actress, which was on the table by the bed. She pulled out a white envelope that had been marking her place. Its flap was unsealed. She fumbled inside and took out a tarnished fragment of very fine chain with a scrap of metal hanging from it. I glanced at it and looked away. Lily let her hand drop to the white sheet, and curled her fingers round the chain.

It can't be, I thought. *It can't be.*

'Do you recognize this?' Lily asked.

'No,' I said, and looked away.

'It was Kate who found it. Isn't that strange? It was when she was a little girl. We went for a picnic by the stream. You remember? There were some ruins, and that's where it was, among the stones. No point in saying anything, I thought, not then. Far too late. Better to let sleeping dogs lie. Kindest thing for everyone.'

'I have to go now,' I said. 'Goodbye.'

'But now it's different,' I heard Lily saying as I left the room. 'You said it was a fox, didn't you, Jamie? But it wasn't.'

2

Lily had been right: it was different now, and it was also true that I owed her something, and that it was the sort of debt you can never finish paying. But she didn't know that she had destroyed the last shred of hope, that now I could no longer pretend there might be another explanation.

When I was younger I wanted so badly to find a scapegoat for what had happened. Anyone but me. Carlo was the obvious candidate. In the darkest time, blaming him became a sort of lifeline, and it was good to have one to hold on to even though the other end wasn't attached to anything. Of course, it wasn't really Carlo's fault, though it's true that he introduced me to Lily.

I first saw him in September 1976. I was nearly thirteen, and he was five months older. He had already been at the school for a year, but this was my first term. I am not sure when or how we became friendly. Friendships often grow imperceptibly. You realize that they have begun only in retrospect.

Carlo and I played in the same teams, we slept in the same dormitory, we liked the same TV programmes and bands. He lived in Chipping Weston with his father and his younger sister. One of the things that brought us together was that he had no mother.

Both she and the child she was carrying had died in childbirth, though I didn't know about the baby until much later. But it gave Carlo and me something in common: my father was dead, the victim of a car crash in Birmingham on the last Friday before Christmas in 1970.

I liked it when Carlo talked about his home, his father and sister. Not that he did so very often – a boarding-school is a self-contained place, especially for boys of our age, and we were bound up in its events and rituals. But when people talked about their home lives, it was as though they were travellers who had returned from exploring an exotic foreign country: their stories were touched with the glamour of the unknown. My own home and family existed in theory rather than practice. I was hungry for the reality of other people's.

I remember a Saturday afternoon near the end of my first summer term. Carlo and I were sitting on the boundary that ran round the perimeter of the cricket field, watching the school's first eleven being beaten by the visitors. Those of us who weren't playing in one or other of the school teams were obliged to watch and clap at appropriate moments. We lay on the grass in the shade while white-clad figures moved like sunlit ghosts. It was a tedious way to spend an afternoon but oddly restful too. Carlo and I lay side by side and lobbed sentences between us.

'I'm getting an electric guitar at the end of term,' he announced.

'Jammy bastard,' I said. 'What sort?'

'A Fender Strat.' He plucked a piece of grass and pretended he was smoking it like a cigarette. 'Brand new. With a practice amp.'

'It's not your birthday. What's your dad up to? I thought he didn't like any sort of music since Beethoven.'

'It's not from him,' Carlo said. 'It's from Lily.'

'Who's she?'

He turned his face away. The tips of his ears reddened. 'A friend of my dad's.'

'Are they – you know?'

'I don't know. Probably. She was around quite a lot in the Easter holidays, and I met her again at half-term.'

'Ooh-er,' I said, trying to sound lascivious. Then: 'What's she like?'

'OK. Quite nice, really. She's a nurse. She's giving my sister this amazing doll's house. It's because they're getting married, her and my dad.'

I wondered how long he'd known this. 'You going to be a bridesmaid, then?' I asked. 'Are you going to hold her flowers?'

He kicked me in the shin and we scuffled discreetly for a moment where we lay on the grass.

Afterwards he said, 'Lily.' He let the word linger. 'She says I have to call her that. Lily, like my dad does.'

'Lily,' I repeated, in the soppiest voice I could manage, rolling my eyes and placing my hand upon my heart. 'Lily, darling!'

*

The footsteps behind me were a woman's, light and fast. I pressed the remote control as I crossed the car park and the Saab's lights flashed in welcome. I stopped. The footsteps behind me stopped too.

A woman said in a low, husky voice: 'Hey. You're Jamie, right?'

I turned and stared at her. She hadn't been in the hospice's reception so she must have been waiting outside. It had been raining during the afternoon and her blue waxed jacket was still damp round the shoulders. She looked younger than I'd expected – if I hadn't known better I would have said that she was still in her teens. She was small and slight, brown-eyed and dark-haired like her mother, with a generous mouth and high cheekbones. She was attractive. I liked that, which I suppose was a form of vanity. If I was going to have a daughter wished on me, I preferred her not to be ugly.

'Kate,' I said.

'You've seen my mother?'

'Yes.'

'Then you know –'

'I don't want to know anything,' I interrupted.

'It's too late. You already do.'

'That doesn't matter.'

Kate came closer to me and said, more quietly, as though afraid her mother might hear: 'She's dying.'

'I'm sorry.' I wasn't sorry at all, not really. I just felt uncomfortable.

'Did she tell you about Sean?'

I edged towards the car. 'Yes.'

'Did you believe her?'

'I wondered if she knew what she was saying.'

'Because of the drugs?' Kate glanced over her shoulder, a fugitive's reflex. 'I wish to God she'd made the whole thing up.'

'If you're in trouble, the best thing for you to do is to see a solicitor. That's what I told her.'

She looked up at me. 'All I need is time. A little breathing space.'

'She said the police think you killed someone.'

She flinched. 'But I didn't.'

I said nothing. Silence is safer.

'I'm not asking for –'

'I can't help you.'

'But you're my *father*.'

'No,' I said. 'I'm not getting involved.'

'Why? Have you got children of your own?'

'No.'

She stared at my hands, at the ring on my finger. 'But you're married, right? Are you afraid your wife might –'

'I just don't want anything to do with this, or with you. Is that clear enough? Find a solicitor.'

I climbed into the car and locked the doors from the inside. I started the engine. Even if Lily had realized the significance of what was in the envelope, she couldn't have told Kate because Kate would have used the knowledge just now. And Kate wouldn't know what it meant unless someone told her. No one else could even begin to understand its meaning – not now. Except, of course, Carlo.

Kate could have stood in front of the parking space and blocked me. But she moved to one side, waited and watched. I drove slowly out of the car park. As I turned into the road, I glanced into the rear-view mirror. She was still waiting, still watching.

I thought I was handling everything perfectly well. I thought I was still in control. But I don't remember driving home to Greyfont, the route I took or even what I thought about. There's a gap in my memory. There must have been a lot of traffic on the A40 and the M40, with everyone rushing out of London for the weekend. I must have thought about what had happened, about Lily and Kate. I must have thought about Nicky.

But I do remember turning into the driveway, the sound of the tyres leaving Tarmac for gravel. I switched off the engine. Nicky's Mini Cooper was parked exactly parallel to the boundary fence. The kidney-shaped patch of grass needed cutting.

My home looked like somebody else's. We had lived there for less than three months and I still found it hard to think of it as mine. It was about eighty years old, a solid, detached house built of red brick, which had expanded during the intervening decades to the side and back. There was nothing about it to like and nothing to hate. It looked as if it had what it deserved, as if it belonged to careful, comfortable people living respectable suburban lives. It was a sensible house, a good place to bring up a family if you happened to have one.

There was a Raku bowl on the sitting-room windowsill. It was one of Nicky's favourite possessions. I looked at it now, and its curves reminded me of the first time I had seen Lily naked, the neat little waist and the swell of the hips, the most alluring shape in the world.

I forced myself to leave the sanctuary of the Saab. The hall smelt like a stranger's. I noticed the clean paintwork and the lack of clutter, the way the colours in the picture on the wall harmonized with the flowers on the table below it. Perhaps we'd tried too hard to make it attractive, homely. All we had achieved was something tastefully sterile, like an operating theatre in a private hospital.

Nicky was in the kitchen at the back of the house, sliding a dish into the oven. Her bag was on the table, her coat draped over the back of a chair. She was wearing navy jeans and a pale blue polo-necked ribbed jersey that emphasized her waist. She looked five or ten years younger than she was.

She closed the oven door and straightened up. 'Your supper's in there. It's an aubergine and mushroom bake. It should take about half an hour.'

'You're going out?'

'My book group.' She smiled. 'Don't you remember?'

'I thought that was next week.'

'It was, but we had to change it. It's all been a bit of a rush because I was late back from work.' She glanced at her face in the mirror on the dresser, and pushed back a stray hair. 'There's salad in the fridge.'

'Thanks. What is it?'

'What's what?'

'The book.'

'Henry James. *The Turn of the Screw.*' She pulled a face as she picked up her coat. 'Horribly spooky. You're later than I expected.'

'Something came up. I was going to come straight back from Queen's Park but I made the mistake of phoning the office first.'

She pecked my cheek. I smelt her familiar smell and felt the touch of living, healthy skin.

'You're tired,' she said.

'A long day. You know.'

'Are you feeling OK? You look cold.'

'I'm fine. But it's getting quite chilly out there. Not like May at all.'

'Have a bath – that'll warm you up. I'll be back about ten.'

Like a doting husband, I walked Nicky to the front door, kissed her, and waved as she drove away. I went upstairs and changed into jeans. The suit Nicky sometimes wore to work was hanging on the back of the bedroom door. Her colleagues usually wore jeans but Nicky thought appearances mattered.

Afterwards, I fetched a bottle of Burgundy from the rack in the garage. I uncorked it and carried the bottle and glass into the sitting-room. I wanted to drink too much tonight, partly because of Lily and partly because of the tarnished scrap of metal in the white envelope.

It was almost time for the Channel 4 news. I wanted to know if there was a report of a man named

Sean being murdered. Whatever happened, I knew that later this evening I'd be trying to track down more details on the Internet. I didn't feel guilty about refusing to help Kate – it was what anyone would do, anyone with an atom of sense – but I admit I was curious. Part of me hoped that the whole thing was a pack of lies, that Lily and Kate had been playing an elaborate joke or fabricating the story to manipulate me for reasons unknown.

As I picked up the remote control, there was a tapping on the window. I looked towards the source of the sound. Kate was standing outside, her face pressed against the glass.

My first reaction was anger mixed with relief. At least Nicky had gone out. I put down the remote control. Kate was still staring at me. She looked like a refugee or a beggar or a prospective burglar. Her face was expressionless. She might have been examining an empty room. I felt another spurt of anger. This was no better than emotional blackmail.

But I couldn't leave her there. She was at the front of the house, overlooked by two of our neighbours and easily visible to anyone passing along the road. Someone would notice, someone would wonder – someone might mention the strange woman to Nicky. People who lived in Greyfont prided themselves on their community spirit.

When I opened the front door, cold air eddied into the hall. Kate was waiting for me on the step. It had started to rain again and the collar of the blue jacket was turned up. There was a long rip in the left sleeve and a smudge of white paint on the shoulder. She looked unkempt – not at all the sort of person who lived in Greyfont, or not in our road.

'Go away,' I said. 'I don't want to see you.'

'I just need a little help.'

'It's not possible. Please go.'

'It's not much to ask. In the circumstances.'

I said nothing.

'Is your wife out?'

I nodded. I wondered what would have happened if she had called while Nicky was here. I would have liked to find out how Kate had discovered where I lived, where I worked, but I knew it was better not to start a conversation. In the long run it would be better for everyone if I kept her at arm's length. I began to close the door.

'All I want is somewhere to stay for the night,' she said, in a gabble. Her forehead was shiny with perspiration. 'Time to work out what's best. It's not much to ask.'

'Please go, or I'll have to phone the police.'

'You really want to phone the police?'

I said nothing. I thought about Lily and the little tarnished chain and wondered what the police would make of it all.

Kate put her foot on the threshold. 'I don't think so. And if you shut that door on me, I'll just wait here till your wife gets home.'

'I wouldn't be so sure of that.'

'Sure of what?'

'That I won't phone the police.'

24

'I didn't kill Sean,' she said. 'And there's one more thing you should know.'

I hesitated a moment too long. Kate undid the jacket and opened it. Underneath she was wearing jeans and a loose white T-shirt, which she smoothed over her belly and hips. The soft material flowed over and round the gentle hump below her breasts. 'I'm pregnant,' she said.

3

You could say that this is a story about lost children. The world is crowded with their absences. Sometimes we lose children because we love them too little, sometimes because we love them too much. We lose them to drugs, or to faceless men with obscene desires, or to those arbitrary catastrophes that punctuate the most orderly lives. Sometimes we're too careless, sometimes too watchful, too rich or too poor. Most often, though, we lose them to their own mysterious futures, which have no room for us.

Lily was almost certainly pregnant when I first met her. That was in May 1978, when Carlo took me to Chipping Weston for the first time. She had been married to Hugh Murthington for nearly a year.

We'd had a half-term holiday when the boarders were allowed to go home for a long weekend. They were occasions I dreaded, whether I went to my grandmother's or stayed at school. My grandmother lived not far from Hastings in a bungalow among an army of similar bungalows about two miles from the sea. She saw few people and most of them were over seventy. When I was there I felt I was living at the edge of the world among a race of zombies, about as far from the beating heart of humanity as it was possible to be.

To go to my grandmother's at half-term was bad but to remain at school was worse. There were usually others in the same forlorn position, though rarely more than half a dozen. One of the married teachers would take responsibility for us. There would be outings, perhaps picnics, visits to the cinema. We watched a lot of television and were jollied into playing games, like rounders and Monopoly, that most of us believed we had outgrown.

You would have thought that our abandoned condition would bring us together, comrades in adversity, but it rarely worked that way. Even to each other we were pariahs. The boys who were left behind were always the ones I didn't like or who were the wrong age, had the wrong interests or didn't like me. We knew ourselves for what we truly were – lost boys: the ones who weren't wanted, the ones who had been mislaid. Afterwards, we suffered the exquisite torture of hearing what the fortunate majority had done when they returned home to their families at half-term.

So when Carlo asked me to stay for half-term I was glad to accept, though I tried to conceal this from him. The weekend had an air of celebration about it, too, because the Sunday would be Carlo's fifteenth birthday.

We left school after breakfast on Friday morning and took the train to London. This was the familiar part of the journey for me: I took it when I went to my grandmother's or, less frequently, when I went to the airport on my way to my mother and step-father. In London, however, we caught the Underground to Paddington, then boarded a train going to towns I had never been to before.

Chipping Weston, nearly two hours from London, was folded among hills. The train approached through a winding valley, threading its way through a disorderly maze of contours and following the course of a weed-choked canal. The slate roofs and stone buildings slipped in and out of view as though the town were trying to hide and making rather a bad job of it.

Carlo was smoking a cigarette as quickly as possible, hoping to finish it before the train drew into the station. He looked up as it crawled along the edge of the platform. 'God, what a boring place this is,' he said. 'Almost as bad as school.'

There was no one to meet us. We picked up our bags and walked through sun-baked streets that climbed up and down the hills. The warmth and exercise made me sweat, and I wondered whether Carlo's family would be repelled by my smell. If they weren't, I thought, they would probably find the two spots on my forehead offensive instead. I was fourteen, and ready to be unwanted.

The Murthingtons lived in a Victorian suburb to the west of the town. Their house was in a broad, curving road lined with London planes. The houses were set back from the road behind iron railings and dusty shrubberies. Each had a short driveway with enough space to take a couple of cars. Most were shabby but there was something solid, spacious and settled about the neighbourhood. My grandmother's bungalow belonged in a different world.

The Murthingtons' house was built of dirty yellow brick beneath a slate roof, the openings for windows and doors framed by improbably Gothic arches. It looked oddly incomplete, as though it formed only a single wing of what had been designed as a much larger building: municipal offices, perhaps, or a modest lunatic asylum. It stood at a right angle to the road, with the front door facing the garden at the side.

After the sunshine, the hall was cool and dark. A pitch pine staircase stretched into the gloom above our heads. We dumped our bags at the foot. Carlo poked his head into one room, then led me down a long hallway into a big kitchen at the back of the house.

'I suppose we'd better go and say hello.' He opened a tin on the table, took out a couple of biscuits and tossed one to me. 'They're probably down the garden.'

We found them sitting in deck-chairs outside a little summerhouse tucked into the angle where two walls met. The branches of an ash tree formed a green canopy overhead and the lawn was dappled with shadows. Carlo's step-mother, Lily, was playing cards at a wicker table with his little sister. Felicity was still wearing the white blouse and navy-blue skirt of her school uniform. She looked at us, smiled shyly, blushed and stared down at her cards.

Lily stood up, kissed Carlo and shook hands with

me. 'Lovely to see you both. Did you have a good journey?'

Carlo grunted ungraciously.

Her perfume seemed very strong – an uninvited intimacy like someone flaunting themselves in their underclothes. I noticed Felicity was staring at me.

'Charles dear,' Lily went on, 'your father hoped to leave work early but he must have been held up.'

So that was the first time I saw her. Later I used to wish that the meeting had had more of an air of importance. In view of what happened afterwards, I came to feel, it would have been more appropriate if her beauty had immediately dazzled me, or if Fate had underlined the significance of the occasion with a clap of thunder or a small earthquake. Later still, I wished I had never met her at all.

'So, what are you boys going to do now?' Lily asked. 'Would you like some tea?'

'Is there any Coke?' Carlo said.

'In the fridge. Is that what you'd like too, James? There's squash or milk, or –'

'James'll have Coke,' Carlo informed her.

I nodded.

'Can I have one, too?' Felicity asked.

Lily laughed and said Felicity had a perfect sense of timing. The girl glanced at her step-mother and for an instant I glimpsed something in her expression that was at odds with this snapshot of happy family life. In May 1978, Felicity was ten years old, almost eleven, but sometimes she looked older and sadder than she had any right to look.

'Why don't you two go and get the Coke and bring me some orange juice at the same time?' Lily said to Carlo. 'I want a word with Jamie about something.'

'It's James,' Carlo said.

I stared at the ground. Carlo and his sister went back to the house.

Lily patted the chair beside her. 'Come and sit here. I'll try to remember to call you James, but you look much more like a Jamie to me. Now' – she leaned towards me, drawing me into her confidence – 'I want to ask your advice. It's Charles's birthday on Sunday. His father and I were thinking of having a family outing. Do you think he'd rather go to the cinema or to a bowling alley?'

I muttered that I wasn't sure. She refused to let me get away with that, however, and manoeuvred me into saying that I thought Carlo would prefer to go bowling.

'And what about afterwards?' she continued. 'We thought we'd go out for a meal. Is steak and chips still his favourite?'

I was more relaxed now. 'Carlo was saying on the train that he could spend the rest of his life eating pizza.'

'Pizza? Great – that's settled. Luckily Felicity likes it too, and she hates steak.' She smiled at me. 'Carlo? Is that your name for him?'

I nodded, suddenly awkward again. 'Everyone calls him that.'

'It's rather nice. Charles sounds a bit formal.' She put her head on one side and grinned. 'A bit snooty.'

Carlo and Felicity were returning with the drinks. He was walking ahead very rapidly, and in silence, with Felicity almost running after him, chattering.

'Well done, Carlo,' Lily said. 'You remembered the ice.'

He put down the tray without saying anything, glanced at me and then away. She never called him Charles again, not in my hearing. The name stuck to him. Soon Felicity was calling him Carlo too, and her friend Millie, and at last even his father.

I think now that Lily liked to give people names. It was a way of drawing them into her circle. It gave her a special relationship with them, perhaps even a form of power over them. That's why she called me Jamie, and it didn't matter to her that nobody else did. She appropriated Carlo. She turned Carlo's father, Hugh, into Hughie. Outwardly, at least, he was a stern, formal man and the pet name sat awkwardly on him, like a party hat on an undertaker. Carlo told me later that, in the early days, Lily had tried to call his sister 'Fee', but Felicity became so angry about this that she had been forced to stop. Felicity was always Lily's failure.

I don't remember a great deal more about the first weekend I spent with the Murthingtons. Everything was overshadowed at the time and in memory by what happened on Sunday evening. But memory is selective and perhaps as liable to change as everything else.

Sunday was Carlo's birthday. In the morning it was raining, which everyone said was unfair after all the fine weather we'd been having. I gave Carlo a tape of Elvis Costello's *My Aim Is True*. I knew he liked it because he rubbed it with his fingers over and over again, almost stroked it, which was what he often did with something he liked. Lily gave him clothes, and Mr Murthington a music centre with a turntable, a cassette player, a radio and a couple of free-standing loudspeakers. I was envious but pretended not to be.

Felicity presented him with a book, a biography of Eric Clapton, and Carlo said how wonderful it was, just what he wanted, although I knew he wasn't interested in dinosaurs like Clapton any more or in the music they played. She had also made him a card, and she stood watching him as he opened it, her eyes huge and blue in her pinched white face. On the front was an ink and crayon drawing of a long-haired man in dark glasses playing a red Fender Stratocaster.

After lunch we piled into Mr Murthington's Rover SD1 Vitesse. The car impressed me, as Carlo intended it should. He murmured that it had cost over fifteen thousand pounds. 'It's the manual model,' he said, with an almost equally impressive assumption of expertise. 'Much sharper acceleration than the automatic, of course. It's even got central-locking.'

We drove down to Swindon, where the ten-pin bowling centre was. Carlo and I had been bowling before and were at least half familiar with the sport. Felicity was eager to learn, if only to emulate Carlo.

But she found the bowls much heavier than she had expected. Her first throw ended up half-way down the alley, stranded in the gully along the side. I thought she was going to burst into tears but she didn't. She chewed her lip and hugged herself instead. Carlo said that, as it was his birthday, he made the rules and she could have her go again.

Mr Murthington and Lily hadn't played before either, and they didn't really want to play now. They tried to conceal this from everyone, even each other. Mr Murthington retreated into himself and became even quieter, calmer and more abstracted than usual. Lily manufactured an ersatz excitement and pretended to be overjoyed when at last she knocked down a single pin. Carlo tried to jolly things along, for Felicity's sake as much as for his own, but he couldn't keep it up for ever.

I don't know what pushed him over the edge. It might have been the sight of his father looking surreptitiously at his watch. It might have been Lily clapping vigorously and crying, 'Hooray, darling!' when Felicity knocked down two pins, thereby attracting glances from the people using the alleys on either side. Or it might have been the heat – it was very warm in there – or the monotonous muted thuds and rumbles of the bowls or the rubbish they were playing on the jukebox. Anyway, quite deliberately, he let the bowl he was carrying slide through his fingers. He jumped aside before it hit the ground. He had been standing next to Lily. The bowl missed her foot but for an instant her face went perfectly blank and her mouth hung open. As it hit the floor, she sprang to one side like a startled deer and stumbled on an empty Coke can. She fell awkwardly, and the air rushed out of her lungs with a great gasp of surprise.

'Sorry,' Carlo said. 'It slipped.'

Mr Murthington helped Lily to her feet. Everyone was very nice to each other. We carried on for a little longer, but Lily said she was tired and went to sit down. She fussed over her tights, which had laddered. Mr Murthington joined her and they talked, his head close to hers. All the enjoyment had gone out of the afternoon, not that there had been much to begin with. Nobody disagreed when Mr Murthington suggested it might be time to go and find some pizza.

We trailed back to the Rover, but we didn't find any pizza. Lily murmured something to Mr Murthington. He turned to the three of us on the back seat and said Lily wasn't feeling well, perhaps we would go back to Chipping Weston after all.

No one spoke on the drive back. Lily gave a little cry. Mr Murthington glanced at her. She leaned towards him and said something I couldn't hear above the noise of the engine. We drove on. Lily moved continuously in her seat as if she couldn't get comfortable. At one point I thought I heard her moaning but I wasn't sure.

I felt uncomfortable – not because of what Carlo and Lily might be feeling but because I was witnessing it. It was a private matter, not for strangers, and with the effortless egocentricity of the adolescent, I imagined they were blaming me for the afternoon's problems. I stared out of the window at the outskirts of Chipping Weston and wondered whether they were all wishing I were somewhere else.

But we didn't drive back to the house. A few minutes later we reached the broad main street of the town. Mr Murthington pulled over to the kerb and braked. With the engine still running, he turned to the three of us on the back seat, Felicity in the middle, Carlo and me on either side. 'Lily's a bit under the weather,' he said, in a heartier voice than I'd ever heard him use before. 'Um – I might take her down to the hospital and have her checked over. Nothing to worry about, but it's always wise to make sure, eh?' He took out his wallet and removed a couple of notes, which he handed to Carlo. 'Why don't you get yourselves some fish and chips or something? Go and have a – a feast at home. I'm not expecting any change.'

'There's ice-cream in the freezer,' Lily said faintly. 'And a chocolate cake in the larder.'

The three of us scrambled out of the car. We bought food and took it home. The evening that followed had a dream-like quality. In the absence of Lily and Mr Murthington, the house became unfamiliar, even threatening. Felicity stayed up much later than she normally did. Mr Murthington phoned from the hospital to say that everything was fine but they were keeping Lily in for a night just to make sure. He would be back in an hour or two.

Carlo told Felicity to go to bed – and to make sure she had a bath and did her teeth.

'Yes, Carlo,' she said, with a meekness she never showed to Lily.

When she was upstairs, Carlo raided the sideboard in the dining-room and poured us both large vodkas, which we topped up with Coke.

'Vodka's better than Scotch,' he said, with a worldly air I envied. 'They can't smell it on your breath.'

We clinked glasses solemnly and I wished him a happy birthday. 'Is she going to be OK?' I asked. 'Lily, I mean.'

Carlo swallowed a third of his drink. 'I couldn't give a fuck.'

Glasses in hand, we strolled round the garden, still full of the long twilight of early summer, and smoked cigarettes. Afterwards we gave ourselves more vodka and put Elvis Costello on the music centre. Soon I had drunk enough to feel unsteady. Carlo suggested a nightcap and I became even unsteadier. When at last we went to bed, Mr Murthington had still not returned.

At breakfast, Mr Murthington said Lily was fine but she needed a rest in hospital. 'Um – women's trouble,' he murmured, staring at his cornflakes. 'It may be better if you boys go back to school on the earlier train – there's one at ten thirty-five.' He smiled at Felicity. 'And you're spending the day at Millie's, aren't you? I don't have to worry about you.'

Lily sent her love, he went on, as an afterthought. Carlo winked at me and sent his back. I muttered something about thanking her for her hospitality.

Mr Murthington took us to the station but didn't wait for the train to come.

'Trust that woman to ruin my birthday,' Carlo said, as his father drove away.

'What's wrong with her?'

'She's a bitch.'

'No – I mean why's she in hospital? The bowl didn't hit her.'

He shrugged and stared down the line. The train was a small black dot, growing slowly louder and noisier. Neither of us spoke.

Once we were on our way, Carlo took the Clapton biography out of his bag and opened it. I picked up a *Daily Mail* that somebody had left on a seat across the aisle. I read about terrible things happening in other parts of the world. We travelled most of the way to London in silence. It was only when we were on the Underground that the shadows of Chipping Weston dropped away and everything was normal again. We talked about music and football and how, when we were rich, we were going to build the perfect stereo system together.

I never found out for sure what happened to Lily in the bowling alley but I can guess. From something she let slip later, I know she had had a miscarriage in the first year of her marriage. It seems more than likely that when Carlo dropped the bowl it triggered a sequence of events that led to her losing the baby.

A commonplace family tragedy – up to fifty per cent of all pregnancies end in loss, most of them during the early stages and often before the mothers even know they are pregnant. Miscarriages happen all the time.

Millions upon millions of lost children. And one was Lily's.

4

I had to bring Kate into the house. If I left her on
the doorstep, it would increase the chance of someone noticing her. There was, of course, the possibility
that someone had already seen her, or that they would
see her when she got into the car with me, but there
wasn't much I could do about that. So she sat on the
chair in the hall while I wrote a note to Nicky and
found the car keys. She folded her arms across her
chest, and looked around her. 'It's a nice house, Jamie.
You and your wife must be very happy.'

'How did you find me?' I said.

'Carlo told me your name the other night. I found
you on the web.'

Her answer just gave me more questions to ask. I
remembered the aubergine and mushroom bake. I
turned off the oven and left my supper to cool,
uneaten. The smell made my mouth water. I scooped
up my jacket and took her out to the car. Once inside
the Saab, we would be screened by the tinted glass
of the windows.

'Where are we going?' Kate asked, as I started the
engine.

'Somewhere you'll be safe for the time being. That's
what you want, isn't it?'

She put her right hand on the steering-wheel,

forcing me to look at her. 'If you take me to the police, I'll make sure it all comes out. Everything.'

Everything? But what did she mean by everything? No one knew everything, not even Lily, not even Felicity. Not even me.

'I mean it,' she said.

'It's all right.' I pretended to alter the heating controls so she couldn't see my face. 'I'm not taking you to the police.'

'And it mustn't be a hotel or anything like that.' For the first time her voice had an edge of panic. 'There mustn't be people.'

'OK,' I said gently, as though she were a fractious child. 'As a matter of interest, though, why not? There's a hundred places in London where they never really look at you, as long as you pay your bills. And if you pay cash –'

'No.' Her fingers tightened round the steering-wheel. 'I don't want to be with anyone. I want to be alone.'

'Why?'

'Because – because someone might see me. I can't take the risk, not yet. I need to change how I look. I need to know what's happening. And I need time to *think*.'

'In that case, I've got an idea where you can go, but I'm afraid it won't be very comfortable.'

'That doesn't matter.'

'We'll have to stop on the way and buy a few things. You'll need some food and a toothbrush, that sort of thing.'

41

I expected Kate to ask where I was taking her, but she didn't. I drove first to a big branch of Tesco. I made her stay in the car. She noticed me taking the keys from the ignition. As I was walking away, she opened the car door. 'Jamie?'

I stopped.

'Would you get me a packet of cigarettes and a lighter?'

'What sort?'

'Marlboro Light. Thank you.'

It was the first time I had seen her smile. I went inside and bought the lighter and the cigarettes. She had made no other requests so I used my imagination. I bought water, fruit, milk, cereal, cheese, ham and a torch. I remembered toothpaste, a toothbrush, soap and toilet paper. I joined a queue at a checkout but had to go back for picnic plates and plastic cutlery.

As I waited to pay, I found myself glancing round for the cameras. I read somewhere that ten per cent of the world's CCTV cameras are in Britain: the average person is photographed three hundred times a day. These are not reassuring statistics if you are aiding and abetting someone suspected of murder. I paid cash and felt like a criminal on the run.

Kate was sitting in the car just as I'd left her. I put the shopping into the boot beside a down sleeping-bag I had last used in Ireland the previous summer. She said nothing when I slid into the driver's seat.

'Are you OK?' I asked.

'I feel —' She broke off and looked directly at me.

'If you really want to know, I feel naked.' Suddenly she smiled again. 'It has its good side. It's like being a child again, I suppose. A baby. I don't own anything. I don't have many choices to make.' Her voice wobbled. 'If you wanted the short answer, though, I'd have to say I feel like shit.'

I gave her the cigarettes and lighter, which earned me another smile. 'Smoke if you want.'

I started the engine and drove out of the car park. Kate ripped the Cellophane from the packet but she didn't light a cigarette. For a few miles neither of us spoke. I glanced surreptitiously at her more than once, and I caught her doing the same to me. *I may have a daughter. She may be in the car beside me.* For the first time the full realization hit me, so hard that I couldn't find any other words to say, even to myself.

Kate was the first to break the silence. 'So, where are we going?'

'London – to an empty building in Queen's Park. Rather primitive, I'm afraid, but it's vandal-proof. You shouldn't be disturbed, at least not by humans.'

'Then by what?'

I shrugged. 'I don't know. It's been empty for a while. There may be rats or cats.'

'I see.'

I glanced at her. 'Unless you'd rather go to a hotel or a bed-and-breakfast. It's not too late to change your mind.'

'No. What do you do, anyway?'

'I'm an architectural engineer. The company I work for maintains the infrastructure of buildings.'

'Like the drains and stuff?'

'And the electricity and the water supply. And the insulation, the ventilation and the heating system. We don't actually design the buildings, but we design and take care of all the things that make a building work.'

We drove another mile in silence, crawling along Western Avenue towards the great grey heart of London. The evening was overcast. The rain had stopped, apart from the occasional flurry of drops against the windscreen. I expected her to ask more about where we were going, but she didn't. In the end, I said, 'I'm taking you to an old chapel. I went round it today so I've got the keys. There's a room at the back with a sink and a lavatory. The odds are that no one will go there for weeks.'

'A chapel,' Kate said. 'Is it old?'

I thought she probably meant, 'Is it spooky?' 'Not as chapels go. It looks like a glorified Scout hut. Even in its prime, it can't have held more than a hundred and fifty people. And I doubt there's been a service in it for forty years.'

'What are you doing there?'

'It's a change-of-use job. The architects have been in, and we've been in, and now we have to sort out the planning permission before it goes to tender.'

The chapel was in a side road between Kensal Vale and Kilburn. The area was largely commercial now, and there weren't many people about at this time. I parked the car fifty yards up the street. We walked quickly to the chapel, carrying the sleeping-bag and the shopping. I ignored the main doors and made for the tall gate at the side, which was faced with corrugated iron and topped with loops of rusting barbed wire. It took me a moment to find the right key from the bunch the agents had given me. Kate was nervous, looking up and down the road, her breathing fast and jagged.

I found the key, and the gate swung back with a creak, opening into a damp alleyway running between the wall of the chapel on the right and a tall chainmesh fence topped with more barbed wire on the left. Beyond the fence was the gated car park of a small office block, closed for the weekend.

We slipped into the alley. I shut the gate behind us and locked it, then led the way down the path, Kate's footsteps keeping pace behind me. I could do anything to her, I thought. Here she was, a small, attractive young woman, trusting herself to a middle-aged man she had met only a few hours ago, alone with him in a place without witnesses where no one would come for weeks.

At the far end of the alley was a doorway with a boarded-up window. The door was secured with a five-lever lock and a Yale. More minutes crawled by as I fumbled for the keys. Kate breathed noisily behind me. I tried to work as quietly as possible. Even here people might be listening. I knew from long and often bitter experience that empty buildings were not always as empty as they seemed.

The second lock yielded. I pushed open the door and stooped to pick up the carrier-bags. The room was small and narrow. It smelt of damp and rot and the charred ghosts of old fires.

'Shut the door,' I murmured. Kate obeyed and the room became entirely dark. I switched on the torch and its wavering beam found her white face. 'At least you can have a light,' I said, feeling like an inadequate host trying to emphasize the virtues of the accommodation on offer. I put down the carrier-bags and blundered along the room to a door at the end. 'The sink and the lavatory are in here. Not very clean, I'm afraid, but the water's still on. Try not to use it unnecessarily. I'm not sure who's in earshot.'

Kate said nothing. I turned and let the beam of the torch play up and down the room. In its spotlight we saw empty cans, a pile of old newspapers, and the blackened remains of a wooden kitchen chair. In the wall on the right was a third doorway, also smoke-blackened. It was padlocked shut.

'Someone squatted here for a while,' I said. 'There was a fire. That was when they boarded up the window, and put on the extra locks.' I found the key for the padlock and opened the door. 'That's the chapel itself. Be careful about light. Don't use the torch in there. There isn't a blackout.'

'I don't want to see it,' Kate said. 'I can feel it.'

It was not a rational thing to say but I understood what she meant. You could sense the cold, musty silence in the chapel, the empty space, the smell of decay, the smell of a place unloved and abandoned. I shut the door and re-fastened the padlock.

'We'd better make you comfortable.' I sounded

falsely jolly. 'I'll put the sleeping-bag here, shall I? Food and drink in that bag, loo rolls and so on in the other. I'll leave you the torch, of course.'

'When will you come back?'

I thought quickly. Nicky and I had planned to go to the garden centre in the morning. I'd have to find a way of postponing it. 'In the morning. I'll try to get here between ten and eleven.' I hesitated. 'We'll have to have a proper talk then. You'll have decided what you want to do, I expect.'

Kate laughed, almost a giggle, a sound that teetered towards hysteria.

'Well, then.' I handed her the torch. I felt the warmth of her hand as her skin brushed mine and for an instant I felt a twinge of desire, as unexpected as it was unwanted, because she was so completely at my mercy in this place. Power is an aphrodisiac. Nobody knew she was here. I could do anything to her.

'Jamie?'

I sucked in my breath. It was as though her mother had spoken. Not just that she'd called me Jamie but the way she'd said my name. Something in my body responded faintly to the timbre of her voice. The ghosts of old emotions touched me. I felt edgy, desperate and unsatisfied – *sixteen again*. 'What is it?'

'Can I ask you a favour? Another.' Kate was calmer now, and she moved away from me. 'Can you buy me a phone on the way here tomorrow? I'll pay you back, I promise.'

I wondered how she would manage that. I said, 'OK.'

It was easier to say yes than no. Time was moving on. Nicky would be back before me, which had a number of unwelcome implications.

I jingled the keys. 'I'm going to have to lock the gate at the end of the alley. I suppose at a pinch you could always climb over. I won't lock this door, though.' I ran the torch beam over it. 'You can put the Yale down when I've gone, and there's a bolt.' I worked it to and fro to make sure it was still usable. 'It's not too late to change your mind. You don't have to stay here.'

'I'll be all right.'

I shrugged, then realized she probably hadn't seen the movement.

'Jamie – do you mind if I call you that, by the way?'

'Of course not.'

'Thanks for everything. Anyway, you need to go home. I'll be fine – see you in the morning.'

I gave her the torch and she shone the beam on my face. It was deliberate. As I walked down the alley, it occurred to me that perhaps she'd been searching for a resemblance between my face and hers. If I'd found my father after twenty-five years, that's what I should have wanted to do – to gaze into his face for as long as I could in the hope of finding a reflection of myself. Whether I would have done it is another matter. But a lost child is always on the lookout for a parent.

My father had left little of himself behind, besides his genes, a handful of unreliable memories and a creased photograph. All the rest is silence.

I was seven when he died. The photograph shows a slim, dark man with a slim, dark moustache and what seems like very long hair. It had been taken on his wedding day, and he is wearing a suit with wide lapels and an even wider tie. My mother is in a very short dress and a hat with an enormous brim. In the photograph she is gripping his arm with both hands as though she is afraid he might blow away if she doesn't hold on tight.

I don't have a direct memory of my father's clothes, face or hair. But I remember the feel of the moustache, the way it tickled my skin when he kissed me goodnight, and how he often smelt of sour masculine things, like alcohol and sweat, cigarettes and aftershave.

He worked for a wholesaler's firm specializing in office products, especially stationery. It was based in Bristol, where we lived, and his territory covered much of the West Midlands. That was why he was in Birmingham on the last Friday evening before Christmas in 1970. It was about half past six in the evening, and he was hurrying home. A white Transit van ploughed into the side of his red Capri as he was driving down the Bristol road. The driver, who had been celebrating his last day at work since half past eleven in the morning, wasn't wearing a seatbelt. He was killed too.

The most important thing I remember about my father, with blinding clarity, is that I loved him. Love seems a pallid, inadequate word for what I felt. It was a form of adoration. I can't remember his face but I can remember waiting at the gate for him to come home. If it was raining, I watched from the front window. I carried his empty briefcase about the house and pretended I was him. When, suddenly, he was no longer there, I persuaded myself that he was away on a longer trip than usual. Although I was told many times that he was dead, I clung to this belief as the weeks became months. Day after day, I waited at the gate or watched from the front window.

Before we married Nicky once said to me, when she was asking about my childhood, that the further back you go, the more fictional memory becomes. We create myths and legends from the debris of our past. She said we make patterns to keep the chaos from overwhelming us.

So I don't know for certain that my parents' marriage was unhappy. I think I remember feeling uncomfortable if I was in a room with the two of them, and raised voices as I lay in bed at night. But I may have invented all that. It may have been a hypothesis that I constructed to explain what happened afterwards, a hypothesis that subsequently solidified and became indistinguishable from fact.

When she met my father, my mother had been a secretary working for the sales director of the company that employed him. After he died, she brushed up her typing and shorthand speeds and went back to work. Gran came to live with us, to look after the house and me. My mother found employment with a local construction company, which did a lot of contract work in Saudi Arabia. That was how she met the man who became my step-father.

Ed was an American engineer spending several months in England because his company and my mother's were working on the same project in Jeddah. He and my mother became friendly but she rarely asked him back to the house. On the few occasions when I met him, it was on neutral territory, like a restaurant. He seemed infinitely tall and remote. His American accent made him unreal and mildly glamorous. He was also very generous. I had no objection whatsoever when my mother said she and Ed were going to get married. It seemed rather a good idea.

It proved a good idea for my mother but less so for me. Ed's job took him all over the world. While he worked on the project of the moment – a dam, a hospital, an office block, a freeway – she lived in a compound with all the other American employees. Surrounded by barbed wire, and with the perimeters patrolled by armed guards, these were green enclaves, studded with single-storey houses arranged with military neatness along miniature suburban roads. The inhabitants drove everywhere, even if it was only a hundred yards – to the PX store, the bridge party, or the little open-air cinema.

I hated it. And I also hated my step-brother from Ed's previous marriage: Danny, three years older than me. He once stole my clothes when we went swimming in a neighbour's pool and made me run home in my swimming trunks. He laughed at my accent and my ignorance. He put salt on my cereal and stole my pocket money to buy cigarettes. At night he gave me Chinese burns in the bedroom he was forced to share with me.

Ed ignored me wherever possible. As far as he was concerned, I wasn't really there. Eventually he and my mother decided there wasn't much room for me in their busy and otherwise satisfactory lives. This was especially obvious when my mother became pregnant with the first of the three children that she and Ed were to have together. I was an unwanted reminder of another relationship.

It seemed like an eternity but it was less than a year after my mother's remarriage that she and Ed made up their minds to send me to school in England. They persuaded themselves that this was the best thing they could do for me. The sad thing is that they might well have been right. Money was not a problem. Ed's employers paid for most of my upbringing – for my education and the return flights once a year between the UK and wherever my mother and Ed were living.

I remember my first day at boarding-school, when I wept among the lank, dusty bushes at the bottom of the housemaster's garden. I decided then that the best way to survive was to cut myself off. My father was dead, and so, for most of the time, to all intents and purposes, was my mother. I told myself I no longer loved her and after a while I believed it. It was better that way. If someone is effectively dead, they cannot hurt you.

All this helps to explain why Carlo Murthington was so important. It wasn't only him I liked: it was his family as well. They weren't perfect but for most of the time they seemed to live together in reasonable harmony, which was more than my own did. Lily was step-mother to Carlo and Felicity, as Ed was my step-father, but she never stopped encouraging them to like her. They talked to each other.

The second time I went to stay in Chipping Weston was at the end of the summer holidays in 1978, after I had returned from visiting my mother and step-father and their other children in Turkey. For me, the highlight of the visit was when Mr Murthington took Carlo and me to Rackford.

Hugh Murthington was a tall, thin man who, as a boy, must have been very fair. Now his complexion had weathered to a mottled red and the bright hair had turned wiry and grey. He seemed very old to me – at the time he was probably in his fifties. He had a small moustache that gave him a military air at odds with his hesitant speech. Not that he said much. Carlo made a joke of this and if he wrote to me during the holidays would sometimes refer to his father under the codename CTCL, which stood for the wartime slogan 'Careless Talk Costs Lives'. Carlo's grandfather had been a partner in the town's auctioneers, and he had left his son comfortably off. Hugh Murthington still worked in a vague and not very arduous capacity for his father's firm, but he also pursued business interests of his own.

He had bought the decommissioned RAF airfield at Rackford as a long-term investment. The first time we went there was on a Sunday afternoon. The Rover Vitesse had just been cleaned, and its metallic blue paintwork gleamed in the sun. Mr Murthington drove on to the larger of the remaining runways. He stopped and switched off the engine. He turned round to Carlo and me, sitting on the back seat. Carlo was pretending to be blasé about the outing – he was reading a magazine, whistling under his breath and rolling his eyes at the same time. He had been there before, of course, and treated the occasion with the disdain he felt it deserved.

'All right, boys,' Mr Murthington said. 'Um – your turn now.'

Carlo went first. He chugged along the runway in second gear and only stalled twice, once when he mistook the brake for the clutch, and once when he accelerated, changed up to third gear and tried to break the land-speed record, whereupon Mr Murthington hauled on the handbrake.

Then it was my turn. While Carlo laughed unkindly in the back seat, Hugh Murthington taught me how to find first gear, second gear and reverse. He showed me how to balance the clutch against the accelerator. He allowed me to drive fifty yards, very slowly and mainly in first gear, charting a wavering course like a nervous kangaroo. I was terrified and exhilarated, and by the time I'd finished, my shirt was soaked with sweat. I was also amazed that he trusted me enough to let me drive his car.

'Well done,' Carlo's father said afterwards. 'Your first try? Um, not at all bad.'

He was a kind man, Hugh Murthington, and in some ways I wish he had been my own father.

5

Nicky was already home when I got back from Queen's Park. She was in the sitting-room, watching the news with a glass of wine. I could tell she was in a good mood.

'How was Henry James?' I asked.

'Scary. What happened to you?'

I had been deliberately vague in my note to her, saying simply that I had had to go out. 'You remember that place I went today? The old chapel they want to turn into a carpet warehouse? Someone thought some kids were trying to break in. The police had our office number – Rachel was working late and phoned me. I've still got the keys so it was easy enough to pop over. But the traffic was heavier than I thought it'd be.'

'And had they?'

'Had they what?'

Nicky looked puzzled. 'Had they broken in, the kids?'

'No, luckily not. False alarm. There's an alley at the side, and they'd climbed over the gate but they hadn't got any further. Still, we may have to review the security.'

I went into the kitchen to fetch myself a glass of wine and retrieve my supper from the oven. Nicky and I watched the rest of the news. There was nothing about a dead man called Sean. Afterwards we watched something else, but I cannot for the life of me remember what it was. All I could think of was Kate and the unanswered questions she had brought with her.

Nicky went to bed before I did. I went into the little room I used as a study and switched on the laptop. I searched for the name 'Sean', looking for an entry that included at least one of the words 'died', 'murder', 'death', 'murdered'. I asked the search engine to return pages written in English and in any format. I wanted pages that had been updated in the last three months. This brought up nearly two million hits, many of them emanating, as I should have predicted, from Ireland. I ploughed through the first couple of hundred and found no Seans whose death appeared to have a plausible connection with Kate. I had not realized that the worldwide web contained so many dead Seans.

My next problem was how I was going to explain my absence tomorrow to Nicky. In the event, I was lucky — or so I thought at the time. When I got upstairs, she wasn't asleep but reading in bed. 'What's this?' I said. 'The next one for the book group?'

She looked at me over her glasses — she had recently taken to wearing them for reading, and I thought they made her look voluptuously prim. She held up the paperback so I could see the jacket. It had a photograph of a little girl, monochrome and forlorn. 'That reminds me,' she said. 'I know we were planning to go to the garden centre tomorrow but would you mind if I gave it a miss? Miranda asked if I'd go up to London with her. She wants me to help her choose a dress for a wedding.'

'Of course not. When will you be back?'

'I'm not sure. She's picking me up at about ten. We should be back by early evening. We'll have to be – I think they're going out. Anyway, I'll phone.'

So the deceit was easy. In the morning it was sunny, and Nicky and I had a leisurely breakfast in the conservatory. After she had left, I went into my study and phoned the hospice. I asked to speak to Lily Murthington. The nurse said she had had a bad night and was sleeping now. She didn't want to disturb her.

I had told Nicky I might go for a walk so she wouldn't be surprised if she phoned the house and found I wasn't there. I drove to a supermarket, not the one we'd visited yesterday evening, and withdrew some cash from an ATM. I felt both ridiculous and paranoid as I took these precautions. Either they were unnecessary or they were inadequate, but they were like touching wood or crossing my fingers: a way of tipping my hat respectfully to the supreme power of Fate.

I bought another packet of Marlboro Light, a phone and an in-car charger. On the way to Queen's Park, I listened to the news on both national and local radio stations. There was no mention of a young man called Sean, living or dead. I didn't want to ask Kate for information because the more she told me the more I should be involved with her. But I had to know what was going on – for my own protection, and for Nicky's. At the back of my mind was the tarnished chain that Lily had shown me.

I parked several streets away from the chapel. It was a Saturday morning, and there were plenty of people about. I tried not to glance over my shoulder as I unlocked the gate to the alleyway beside the chapel. After all, I had a perfect right to be there – I was a keyholder, with a legitimate purpose for visiting the place. It wasn't enough to reassure me.

The alley was damp and airless. The noise and smells of the street dropped away. I walked to the end and tapped on the door of the little room at the back. I heard nothing. I tapped again and said, as loudly as I dared, 'It's me, Jamie.'

The name 'Jamie' slipped out by accident. It seemed to belong to someone else, not to a respectable architectural engineer but to a wild boy who had taken risks and paid the price, and was now taking even more risks.

A bolt scraped on the other side of the door.

'Kate, it's me,' I whispered.

The door swung backwards and I stepped quickly into the room. She closed it gently and for a moment we were alone in the darkness. I heard her breathing. The atmosphere was thick with stale cigarette smoke. Mixed with it was the faintest hint of perfume, perhaps soap.

Kate switched on the torch. In the artificial light, she looked pale and unhealthy. My eyes struggled to adjust. The smoke was making them smart. She was still wearing the blue waxed jacket. I wondered whether she had taken it off. 'How did you sleep?' I asked.

'I didn't – not much.'

'I rang the hospice this morning. Your mother had a bad night, too.'

Kate took a step towards me. 'You talked to her?'

'They wouldn't let me. She was asleep and they didn't want to disturb her. I left my number with them.'

'Have you got a phone?'

'For you? Yes, but it's in the car. It needs charging.'

The torch in her hand dipped and my shadow swooped along the wall. I wanted to see her properly, and also to breathe fresher air. I said, 'Let's go next door. There's natural light and a few chairs.'

'If you want.'

I unlocked the connecting door. Most of the windows in the chapel had been boarded up but there were two fixed lights in the roof and another over the main door to the road.

'Avoid the wall on the left,' I said. 'It's not safe underfoot.' The chapel had a sprung floor and on that side the ends of the joists were rotten. 'We shouldn't be overheard if we talk quietly.'

I led the way down the chapel to a pile of wooden chairs with elm seats and racks for hymnals. I found two that were usable. Kate and I sat facing each other and a couple of metres apart. It was a formal arrangement, as though we had business to transact.

It was much colder in the chapel than it was outside and the high space was filled with pale, grubby light. Kate wrapped the jacket around the bulge of the growing baby, fumbled in her pocket and brought out the packet of cigarettes. She stared at me. Then she sighed, shook out a cigarette and lit it.

'I need to know more,' I said. 'What happened to Sean? There was nothing on the news.'

'There wouldn't be, not necessarily – not if they haven't found the body yet.'

'What's his surname?'

She seemed not to have heard me. She bit her lower lip and blurted out a question of her own: 'You know Chipping Weston?'

'I used to. I haven't been there for years, since I – I knew your mother.'

There was silence, short but uncomfortable, while we both thought about that.

'I grew up there,' Kate said. 'My mother still lives in the same house. I mean, she did, until she and Dad got too ill. They leased a flat in Ealing to be nearer hospitals. That's why she's in St Margaret's. She's given up the lease on the flat now but she's still got the house, and I've been living there off and on over the last few months. Are you sure you want to hear all this?'

'I don't think I've got much choice.'

'Wouldn't it be safer for you not to know?'

I wondered whether she was right. I said, 'But I want to know. And if I'm going to help you, I need to.'

She inhaled. 'Carlo did it,' she said, in a flat, dull voice, and the smoke drifted out of her mouth and nostrils.

'Carlo did what?'

'Carlo killed him, of course. Killed Sean. Bloody Carlo, the prodigal son. My brother — except he's not my brother, of course. That's the whole point. That's — that's *important*.'

'You're not making much sense.'

She smiled and, to my surprise, I smiled back at her. 'I'm sorry. I keep forgetting there's so much you don't know. I'm not thinking straight. Until my father died, I hardly knew Carlo.'

'Your father.'

She blushed. 'I can't stop calling him that. He thought he was my father, and I thought he was too. I still do.'

For a moment, neither of us moved or spoke. I listened to the rumble of traffic outside. Someone sounded a two-tone horn. Music rose and fell as a car went by with its windows open.

'When did he die?' I asked. 'Hugh, that is.'

'In October last year. He had a stroke in the summer, and he never really got over that. My mother had been diagnosed with breast cancer by then. She had a lumpectomy, then radiotherapy and chemo-therapy.' She wrinkled her face. 'But there were secondaries, first lung and then bone.'

'Who's the father of your baby?'

She blinked. 'Sean.'

'Your mother said you were going to marry him.'

'That was earlier. I met him in London. I was temping, and I met him through work.' She glanced at me, then away. 'And things sort of went on from there. We lived together for a while. But after my father died, we quarrelled.' She laughed without humour. 'Sean always wanted his own way. It's one of the things I used to like about him, actually. He seemed so certain about everything.'

I looked at her belly. The pregnancy wasn't showing much. 'When did you break up with him?'

'October. But it was the other way round – he broke up with me.' Kate's eyes widened. 'Oh, I see what you mean. He came down to Chipping Weston after Christmas. That's when I got pregnant. We had a sort of reconciliation.' She patted her stomach. 'But it didn't last.'

She stubbed out her cigarette. I waited.

'He didn't want *me*, anyway,' she said. 'He was out for what he could get.'

'He needed money?'

'He did by then. He used to have it coming out of his ears – he earned at least ten times what I did. He had this amazing flat near Covent Garden. The trouble was he spent it all, and the flat was only rented. So when they fired him, he didn't have anything to fall back on.' Kate rubbed her forearm as though feeling for old bruises. 'Results were down, and he had a row with his boss. He actually hit him. And the sort of job Sean was doing, it's a very small world. Word got out. He knew it wouldn't be easy to find another job, even if business got better. So that suddenly made me attractive again. In financial terms, that is – until he found out the truth.'

I remembered the house, the partnership in the auctioneers' firm, the investments. 'He thought your father had left you something?'

Kate shook her head. 'He knew my father had been fairly well off. But things hadn't been going so well the last few years. Anyway, there was nothing for Sean. What's left of Dad's estate will come to me and Carlo in the end, but Mum has a life interest.'

When you're young, I thought, everything seems permanent, from your own youth to other people's money. 'Who's the executor?' I asked.

'Carlo. Anyway, Sean went off, and I didn't see him again until earlier this week when he came back to Chipping Weston.' She traced the outline of the packet of cigarettes in her pocket. 'And Carlo was there. You don't know about Carlo yet, do you?'

'How can I?'

She shivered. 'I didn't see much of him when I was growing up. He was married for a while and they used to live quite near us. But after the divorce he moved away. He lived all over the place – Canada, Africa, the States.'

She paused, as though she was expecting me to say something. I stared at the floor.

'Things changed after Dad's first stroke,' she went on. 'Carlo came back. First it was just a visit, and then, after the funeral, he decided to stay. He's living in London now.' She hesitated, and I had the sense that she was on the brink of telling me more. But she shook her head violently as though shaking away unpleasant memories. 'He never liked my mother, you see – that was why he stayed away. He never liked me, either.'

'Did he know?'

'About you and my mother?'

I nodded. Even now I found it hard to put it into words.

'He does now. I don't think he did before. But maybe he suspected.' Kate ran her tongue along her lips, as if her mouth was dry. 'Have you heard of Rackford?'

'The airfield?'

She nodded, licking her lips again and feeling for another cigarette.

'What's Rackford got to do with this?' I said loudly, far too loudly.

Surprised, she stared at me. 'Because that's what they both want, Sean and Carlo. They want the old airfield.'

'Why?'

Kate wasn't listening. 'Except Sean doesn't want anything now.' She gave a high, nervous laugh. 'But in a way he's got it because that's where his body is. He's at Rackford, Jamie, and he's waiting for the police to find him.'

Every time I stayed with Carlo at Chipping Weston, apart from that very first time, we went to Rackford. Mr Murthington would take us, or sometimes Lily. In those days most of the land was let to a farmer in the village. He had ploughed some of the ground. Whenever I see a field of oilseed rape glowing improbably yellow in the early summer, I think of Rackford.

Rape was still a novelty in England during the 1970s. Mr Murthington explained that the farmer was methodically breaking up the ground to grow wheat. Year after year, as more and more of the former airfield came under cultivation, the patches of rape moved from one area to another. Its vivid colour was exotic and its smell – a combination of oil and fresh urine – faintly disturbing. Even now, the strange, ambiguous scent takes me back to Hugh Murthington's Rover Vitesse.

The farmer used some of the less fertile ground for grazing. Along the western boundary of the airfield, where the land began to rise, there was an irregular strip of ground so broken up that it was little good to anyone. It was enclosed by the airfield's perimeter fence only because it bordered the lane, and it would have been more trouble than it was worth to leave it out. There was a side entrance to the airfield here – if you walked briskly, you could reach the village in ten minutes, or even less if you cut through the fields behind the church.

Most of this wasteground was filled with a patch of woodland lining the sides of a steep little valley. A stream ran – or, rather, strolled – along the bottom, and near the banks in the spring were cuckoo pints, wild garlic and wood anemones. Here, too, were places where ferns grew, natural bedding, their leaves curling like green intimacies in the spring, then growing broad and dusty in the summer. On the far bank, the land rose sharply towards the fence and the lane beyond.

Before the Second World War, the land at Rackford had been the property of a local farmer, who had made a tidy profit when he sold it to the Ministry of Defence in 1940, and whose son subsequently paid Hugh Murthington a token rent to use it for agriculture once again. When I knew the airfield, in the late 1970s, the longest runway had been broken up and sold for hardcore. But the smaller runways and the perimeter road were still there.

Many of the buildings survived – the control tower, the two hangars and an untidy cluster of Nissen huts and single-storey brick buildings. The farmer used the larger hangar for storing winter fodder, rusting farm machinery, tractor tyres worn smooth and all the rubbish a working farm accumulates. The other buildings were sliding towards ruin.

Hugh Murthington had bought the airfield in the early 1970s, when a property developer had lurched into bankruptcy. From his point of view, the most important thing about it was the road access. Sooner or later, he explained to Carlo and me, this would make the land soar in value. The main road ran east–west a few miles south of Rackford. A broad minor road led north towards the village, passing what had once been the main entrance of the airfield, still with its guardpost and padlocked gates. In the long run, he was right about the significance of the road access but, of course, by that time it was far too late for him to profit by it.

The second time I went to Rackford, it was winter, January 1979, in the last week of the Christmas holidays. There had been a hard frost overnight and it was a cold, brilliant day. The sun made the hard edges of the buildings gleam and there were puddles of black ice in the potholes of the runway.

The plan had been that Hugh Murthington would take us, but at breakfast that morning he had had a phone call: a pipe had burst at his office, and he had to deal with it. So Lily said that she would drive us instead. I sat in the front of the Rover with her. Carlo was in the back behind me, and Felicity bounced up and down beside him. As we turned into the airfield, we saw a fox trotting with fluid elegance not far ahead of us. It was at least a yard long, its coat rich and glossy. Ears cocked, it glanced back. The white tip of its tail twitched and then the fox slipped without haste into a dense patch of brambles.

Lily allowed all of us to drive that day, even Felicity. It was her first lesson. We pushed the driver's seat as far forward as it would go. Even so, she had to perch on the edge to reach the pedals, with Carlo's coat wedged between her little body and the seatback, and my coat underneath her so she could see through the windscreen. The Rover jerked and stalled repeatedly. In the end Felicity hammered the steering-wheel in her frustration.

'Don't worry, darling,' Lily said. 'That's how everyone starts.'

'But I'm not everyone,' Felicity shouted. 'I'm me.'

Lily laughed, which made matters worse. It was not only that she laughed but how. When I came to know Lily better, to study her, I discovered that she had a small repertoire of laughs. This one had ended in a discreet gurgle and was accompanied by the arching of the eyebrows. She used it especially with those she felt she could safely patronize.

Felicity blushed, and her pale complexion cruelly betrayed the rush of blood. Carlo muttered something under his breath. He leaned forward and put his hand on his sister's shoulder.

'Handbrake on,' he said, in a low, monotonous voice. 'Good. Press down the clutch. Put the gear in neutral. No, find where you can wiggle it from side to side – yes, that's it. Now start the engine again. Good.'

The touch of his hand and the calm instructions quietened her. She obeyed. Carlo taught her how to lift her foot slowly off the clutch until she felt the biting point. He was good with mechanical things, and with Felicity too. All the impatience and surliness he showed towards Lily and his father dropped away. Felicity would have done anything he asked of her.

Lily watched with a smile fixed on her face. Soon Felicity, under Carlo's instructions, was edging along the runway in first gear. A few minutes later, he talked her into changing up to second. In another five seconds, she stalled, but by then it no longer mattered. 'Good girl,' Carlo said. 'You're a quick learner.'

When it was my turn, Lily made a determined effort to redeem herself as a driving instructor. She rested her arm on the back of my seat and told me what all the controls did, what all the dials were for. I had never been so close to her. I saw a tiny mole on the side of her neck and noticed how her lashes curled, which I now realize may have had something to do with art rather than nature. Her perfume – I learned later that she always wore Chanel No. 5 – seeped into me: it was a smell that, like the oilseed rape, both repelled and attracted. When at last I started the engine, I forgot the car was in gear – it bucked as the engine stalled.

Lily touched my shoulder. 'Silly boy. Come on. Try again.'

Felicity giggled.

Lily rounded on her. 'Do be quiet, dear. You'll distract Jamie. After all, you know how difficult it can be.'

Despite my own experience, I had assumed that adults had a duty to love and protect the children in their care. In those days it never occurred to me that liking or disliking could come into it. I realize now that Lily must have disliked her step-daughter, that perhaps she repaid hatred with hatred.

I was a slow learner. Unlike Felicity. And most unlike Carlo.

Carlo terrified Kate. She made that very clear.

'He killed Sean at Rackford.' She turned her head to look at me. We were sitting side by side in the decaying chapel, and I was growing colder by the minute. 'It was only yesterday but it seems like weeks ago.'

'How did he do it?' I said. *Why did it have to be Rackford?*

Kate stroked her belly with both hands, an unconscious movement, as though she wanted to reassure the person who was growing inside. 'Just lost it and went for him. I saw him do it.'

'I don't understand. Why?'

'Carlo started hitting me and Sean tried to stop him. So Carlo knocked him down. Then he kept hitting him and kicking him, and there was all the blood.' As the hands stroked the belly, Kate's voice wavered in volume and quality like a poorly tuned radio programme. 'I told you – he just lost it. He's always scared me. Carlo, I mean. Even before Daddy died.' She looked quickly at me out of the corner of her eyes, something her mother used to do, and her shoulders lifted and fell with the smallest of shrugs, simply to show that she knew I had heard it too: *Daddy.* 'There was blood all over the place,' she went on. 'And Carlo said, "And now I'm coming for you. If the police don't get you first."'

'What did he mean by that?'

'That he was going to make it look like I killed Sean.'

'Are you sure Sean was dead?'

Kate screwed up her face and rocked to and fro, her whole body nodding. The chair was digging into my back. I stood up and stretched. Her eyes followed

71

my movements. I felt very tired. I like problems to have boundaries or at least a framework for describing them. But Kate's were messy and shapeless. There was no telling where they began or where and how they would end.

'You don't know what Carlo's done,' she said, in time with her nodding body. 'You just don't know what he's capable of. I do.'

'There's something else? Something you're not telling me?'

She did not reply. She rocked to and fro like a child in a swing.

'You have to do something,' I said. 'You can't stay here.'

She lowered her head to stare down at her hands and her belly. I prowled up and down the chapel, avoiding the holes in the floor and the piles of rubbish. According to Kate, she had seen Carlo kill Sean yesterday. So how had she got up to London? At some point she must have phoned her mother, who had then phoned me. If Kate didn't have a mobile, where and how had she contacted Lily?

Kate still had a jacket but surely she must have had some sort of handbag as well. Where was it? What else was she leaving out? It struck me then, with full force, how vulnerable I had made myself. Did Kate want more than help? Did she want a scapegoat as well? We're used to trusting people. In most relationships, we make assumptions about the nature of those we meet, and generally the assumptions are more or less correct. But take away those assumptions, take away trust, and all that's left is chaos.

She shook yet another cigarette from the packet and lit it.

'Surely you shouldn't be smoking,' I said, before I could stop myself. 'Not if you're pregnant.'

'At present it doesn't seem very important. All right?' She blew a smoke-ring, angling it so it wobbled across the air towards me. The hand holding the cigarette was trembling. 'I – I need to know if they've found Sean yet.'

'Who? The police?'

She nodded. 'If they haven't, everything's easier, and it's only Carlo I have to worry about.' She wrinkled her nose. 'Only Carlo,' she repeated. 'Christ.'

I watched the coils of cigarette smoke writhing like blue snakes above her head. 'There was nothing on the national news this morning,' I said. 'And I couldn't find anything on the web last night.'

'That's something.'

'But I didn't know Sean was at Rackford then. And you still haven't told me his surname.'

'It's Fielding.' Her eyes narrowed. 'Would you go there for me?'

'What?'

'Would you go to Rackford?'

I stared at her. She seemed perfectly composed now. I was the one in danger of losing control.

'Not to the airfield,' she went on. 'There's no need for that. You could just drive through the village, maybe have a drink at the pub. Did you ever go there?'

'Yes,' I said. I remembered the Eagle. I remembered Carlo with the baby punk in the yard. I'd wanted to be sick but there hadn't been time. 'And I don't particularly want to go back.'

'But no one would have any idea who you are. You'd soon know if the police were around. You'd hear if they've found a body.'

Which body? 'And if they have?' I said.

'I'd have to think again. But if they aren't there, maybe you could fetch a few things for me from home – from Chipping Weston, I mean. It shouldn't be a problem, if you're careful.'

'Then what?'

'Then I'd leave.' Kate flicked ash on the floor. 'I'd be out of your life for ever. You'd never see me again.' She smiled at me. 'How's that for an inducement?'

'It certainly has its attractions.'

Neither of us spoke. We avoided each other's eyes. She had found a father to replace the one she had lost, only to learn that he didn't want her. I wondered whether that mattered to her. It would have mattered to me.

At last she dropped the cigarette and ground it out under her heel. 'But you'd have to be careful if you go,' she said. 'Do you think you'd recognize him now? When did you last see him?'

'Carlo?' I knew the time, the date and the place of our last meeting. I remembered what he had said, too: *Christ, what a mess. It's a fucking nightmare.*

'It was years ago,' I said. 'He was seventeen. What does he look like now?'

74

It was a capitulation, and Kate knew it.

'He's taller than you, and heavier. He's got a beard. Close-cropped. So's his hair, and they're both going grey, although the beard's less grey than the hair.' She closed her eyes as though visualizing him. 'But he's in good shape for his age. Looks as if he works out.'

I tried to mesh her description with my memory of the Carlo I had known: a tall, slim boy with wide shoulders, floppy hair and a sharp nose. I remembered his hands, which were large, with powerful, agile fingers: a guitarist's hands, he used to say. He had been very good at Chinese arm-wrestling.

'The other question is,' Kate went on, 'would he recognize you?'

'That's assuming I go, of course.' It occurred to me that Kate might be off her head, and that perhaps the story was a fabrication from start to finish. After all, Lily was hardly a trustworthy witness now – if, indeed, she ever had been. I smiled and pretended a confidence I didn't feel. 'Anyway, would it really matter if Carlo saw me? Even if he recognized me, what's he going to do about it?'

Kate took a deep breath and let it out slowly. 'You really don't understand, do you, Jamie? Even now. Carlo's not like me and you. He'll do whatever he wants. And what he wants to do right now is kill me.'

6

I suppose I was always a little scared of Carlo. It was one of the things that made our friendship interesting. With most people you know how far they will go when you push them. But with Carlo it was hard to be sure. His boundaries were more elastic.

At school this gave him a dark glamour, which made his liking for me all the more flattering. Once I was fighting with another boy in the changing-room. It wasn't serious – just a squabble over a disputed towel, an excuse for a mock duel. But Carlo came out of the showers and misinterpreted what was happening. Naked and dripping, he grabbed the boy by his collar and his waistband and rammed his head against the wall. The boy was concussed and needed three stitches. Carlo was punished, of course, but the incident increased his prestige.

Sometimes he worried me. After Felicity's first driving lesson, for example, he was like a baited trap waiting for a mouse. The hatred he felt for Lily would have to find an outlet, but I didn't know how or where. All I knew was that I had a dull ache in my stomach and would have preferred to be somewhere else, even in my grandmother's bungalow.

In the afternoon, Carlo and I went to the high street and prowled through shop after shop. We were adrift in the limitless boredom of the adolescent. At length we wandered into a café near Woolworth's where we drank Coke, ate greasy chips and fed the jukebox. The place was full of local teenagers who glanced at us with wary eyes and talked with lowered voices. Carlo said little, but I knew he was tense, waiting for whatever needed to happen.

Our table was beside a window that had steamed up. In an attempt to divert Carlo's attention, I rubbed a peephole in the mist and began to make scurrilous remarks about the passers-by. Eventually he rubbed another and joined in. It was growing darker outside, and even colder.

I was the first to see Felicity. She was standing on the opposite pavement, her back to the window of a shop selling washing-machines. She was clutching a parcel and chatting with a couple of boys. She had the parcel in the crook of one arm, and a little white handbag looped over the other.

'Look,' I said. 'Your sister's over there.'

Carlo enlarged his peephole. As soon as I spoke, I realized I had misread the situation: Felicity wasn't chatting – she was being interrogated.

'What's she carrying?' I asked.

'It's a present. She's going to Millie's birthday party this afternoon.'

Even as Carlo was speaking, the taller of the boys lunged at the parcel. Felicity pulled away, turning to evade him, which brought her face to face with the other boy, who stood over her with his hands on his hips.

Carlo swore. He stood up and ran from the café. I scooped up our coats and followed. By the time I reached the doorway, Carlo was almost across the road. A cyclist rang her bell and screamed at him.

The taller boy pulled Felicity's parcel, and his friend tugged the handbag. Carlo cannoned into the smaller one and knocked him into the shop doorway. The other boy's reactions were too slow. Carlo caught him by the throat with his left hand and punched his victim's ear with the right.

I ran across the road.

'Get the fucker,' Carlo said, as he hit the taller boy full in the face.

I dropped the coats, shoved the younger boy against the side of a phone box and punched his nose. His friend shouted something and broke away from Carlo. The two sprinted down the road. Carlo snarled and gave chase.

'Help him!' Felicity shouted in my ear. 'Go on.'

I ran after them. We stampeded along the pavement, scattering shoppers. Our quarry turned into a small park. Carlo swung through the gates in their wake. I hesitated and glanced back. Felicity had picked up the coats. She waved me on.

I had never before been inside that park. It was dusk already, and the streetlights cast a dull yellow glow over the grass and the leafless trees. I heard shouting at the far end away from the lights and road. I ran towards the noise.

I found Carlo in the children's playground. He was underneath the infants' swings with the smaller of

Felicity's attackers. There was no sign of the other. The boy was lying on his side on the Tarmac underneath the iron frame and curled into a foetal huddle. Carlo crouched over his body, hammering it with his fists. Neither said a word. Carlo grunted. The boy cried, gasped and wept. I took Carlo's arm and tried to drag him off. He pushed me away.

'Hey – that's enough,' I said. 'You don't want to kill the little bugger, do you?'

'Why the fuck not?'

The blows continued. The boy on the ground was screaming, calling for his mother. I glanced round, afraid we were attracting attention, afraid of the police, afraid most of all that Carlo might really kill the boy.

'Come on,' I whispered. 'Felicity's over there.'

For a second or two, Carlo's fist stayed in mid-air, poised above the squirming, moaning body. The boy must have been a couple of years younger than us. I caught sight of his face, which gleamed with dark moisture – blood, I suppose, mucus and tears.

Carlo sighed. He stood up. He looked towards the gates, where Felicity was waiting. He turned back to the boy and gave him a kick in the ribs. Then he bent down and spat in his face. The boy muttered something moist and gurgling. Carlo kicked him in the head and the boy howled like a dog.

I touched Carlo's arm. 'Felicity's waiting.'

The Eagle was in Lower Rackford. I drove into the car park at the side. The last time I'd been here was the night the fox was killed, the night Felicity cried. I couldn't help looking towards the corner at the back, beyond the toilet block. There was a line of wheelie-bins there now. That was where Carlo had taken the baby punk, another thing that had happened that evening.

The pub's main block was two storeys high and separated from the road by a strip of garden. Smaller, single-storeyed extensions projected from the ends. At the back, at right angles to the road, were two roughly parallel rows of outbuildings. Over time the stone tiles had settled on the timbers beneath and the cluster of roofs had acquired shapes and curves that seemed organic, almost animate.

I got out of the Saab. The car park contained a sleek herd of Jaguars, BMWs, Mercedes and sparkling SUVs. The shape of the place was the same but much else had altered. While time had been moving forward elsewhere, at the Eagle it had apparently been moving backwards. I remembered metal windows and pebble-dash rendering. Now there were wooden sashes and casements. The door to the bars was flanked with a couple of brass coach lamps.

Inside, framed on the wall, was an eighteenth-century bill of fare. On the floor were flagstones where I remembered a purple carpet with ranks of orange flowers. What had once been the public bar was now a restaurant. Every table was full. In the lounge bar, the jukebox and the fruit machine had been swept away in favour of oak settles and Windsor chairs. Wooden casks squatted behind the bar and blackboard menus hung on unplastered stone walls. Despite the warmth outside, a log fire burned in a grate that had not existed at my last visit a quarter of a century ago.

The people in the bar went with the cars outside. No one took any notice of me, which was another thing that had changed. When Carlo and I had come here, pretending to be eighteen, conversations had faltered and people glanced at us, then away. In those days we drank vodka if we could afford it and cider if we couldn't.

I asked for mineral water and wedged myself into a corner at the end of the bar. I sipped my drink and let the conversations around me ebb and flow. I dipped into a discussion about Henrietta's new pony, another about a planning dispute over an extension, and a third about what Ursula had said of Giles's asparagus last night, and how terrible it was.

But there was nothing about a body at Rackford airfield.

I stared out of the window at the children making life hell for the parents in the beer garden at the front of the pub. The airfield was a little over a mile away from the village. If a body had been found, if the police had been there, everyone would have been talking about it. Yes, on the whole, no news was good news. It meant that by the end of today I should have Kate off my hands and, with luck, that I should never again have anything to do with the Murthingtons. It was less than twenty-four hours since Lily had come back into my life, yet I could hardly remember a time when I had been free of her.

Had I ever been truly free of her? Lily's death wouldn't mean the end of it either, not necessarily – because now there was another reason to be afraid: she might have told Kate at least some of the truth.

I needed a distraction. Through the window I noticed a little post office and general store across the road. After I had finished my drink I went over there to buy an Ordnance Survey map. I sat in the car and unfolded it.

RAF Rackford had had a typical wartime layout: three intercepting runways, forming a pattern like a folding campstool in profile. Across the top had run the broad main runway, intersected near the ends by the tops of the cross made by the two lesser runways below. All three were linked by the wavering line of the perimeter road, from which protruded the frying-pan shapes of the aircraft dispersal areas scattered around the edge.

I found the patch of woodland on the west of the site with the thin blue thread of a stream running through it. According to Kate, Sean was somewhere down there. Well, there was a coincidence. Beyond the woodland one of the lanes from Rackford zig-zagged along the western boundary of the airfield and eventually joined the main road to Chipping Weston. I laid the palm of my hand on the map, obliterating both woodland and lane. 'You don't exist,' I said aloud. 'Not now.'

I folded the map and started the engine.

Fortunately there was more than one way to get to Chipping Weston from Rackford. I took the shorter route, a B road that skirted the eastern boundary of the airfield and passed the main entrance.

The road was wider than I remembered. There were roundabouts where before there had been only crossroads. Hedgerows had vanished. The fields on either side had become larger. I felt oddly aggrieved: it was as though someone had been making un-licensed alterations to my own past. I drove fast, keeping my eyes on the Tarmac and white lines in front of me. The airfield's boundary flickered along the edge of my vision like a soundless and almost monochromatic cine film, a home movie from some-body else's childhood.

After a few miles I joined the main road from Oxford and, after another mile, turned left towards Chipping Weston. I drove down the old London road – the town was now bypassed by the trunk road to the north. Familiar buildings appeared like ghosts. Among them was the Newnham House Hotel, sprawling among a rash of new houses on the left-hand side. It was a large, red-brick Victorian place, which had sprouted modern wings since I had last seen it. Once it had seemed the height of sophisti-cation. Now it was just another chain hotel with a gym, a swimming-pool and a very big car park.

The nearer I came to the Murthingtons' house, the worse it was. There was a chance that someone might notice me or the car. Perhaps I shouldn't have gone to the Eagle or called at the village shop. Once you start worrying about the possibility of unpleasant consequences, it's not easy to stop.

I turned into a side road and found myself driving along the boundary of a cemetery. I had never been there before. There was parking on the road so I pulled over and switched off the engine. It was as safe there as anywhere.

I left the shelter of the Saab and walked in a broad arc round the southern part of the old centre of the town. I found a callbox and phoned the Murthingtons' number – it was the same number, though prefixed with a sixth digit. The phone rang on and on. The ringing stopped and the voicemail's standard recorded message began to play. I put down the receiver. I had lost my chance of a last-minute reprieve.

In the Murthingtons' road, some of the old houses had gone, replaced by newer, smaller ones. Gardens had been subdivided. Although more and more families had been crammed into the space, the road had acquired an air of glossy affluence. Wherever they looked, I guessed, the owners of these houses saw double: two kids, two cars, two homes, two foreign holidays a year.

The only house that was out of place was the Murthingtons'. Since I had last seen it, it had become shabbier, more ramshackle: slates were slipping over the bay window and one of the bedroom windows at the side of the house was broken. In the garden, the shrubs had grown enormous and the lawn had run to seed. The house wasn't quite an eyesore but it was getting there. If houses were fairy-tales, then this one was *The Sleeping Beauty*, its heroine grown older and no longer beautiful.

I walked rapidly down the opposite pavement. Children were playing in back gardens and someone was having a barbecue, a late lunch or an early supper. A man was mowing his lawn two doors up. He paused and waved to me. I waved back and hoped he would not remember my face. As I passed the Murthingtons', I glanced over the road at the house and garden. There were no cars in the driveway, and the curtains were drawn across the downstairs windows at the front. It looked empty, just as Kate had said it would be.

At the end of the road I turned left. Sixty yards further down, on the left, was a path surfaced with Tarmac between tall creosoted fences. When I had known it as a teenager, it had been a narrow, muddy track bounded by hedgerows running between the backs of the gardens of the Murthingtons' road on the left and open fields on the right. The fields and the hedges had gone but the path was still there.

'Some of the people in our road put gates in,' Kate had told me. 'Ours is the fifth on the left.'

I met no one. At the fifth gate, I stood on tiptoe and glimpsed the thick, fresh greenery of trees in early summer.

'Put your hand over the top of the gate,' Kate had said, 'and feel to the right, round the post. There's a key hanging on a nail.'

It was a Yale, the metal warm from the sun. I

opened the gate and slipped inside. I left the key where I had found it and advanced slowly up the garden, like a soldier moving through potentially hostile jungle. The path was still there – cracked stone slabs running through a forest of weeds where once there had been a vegetable garden. There was a little potting shed with a greenhouse leaning against its side. Two of its glass panes were broken, and nothing green grew inside except weeds. I remembered this place too well and I was a little afraid of it. It contained a ghost who hated me.

People still came this way – the path was clear and, where it passed under an iron-framed archway, the box hedge had been cut back. The cuttings were lying in the lee of the greenhouse, brown and brittle.

On the other side of the archway was the ash tree. This was where I had first seen Lily. One of the branches had fallen off – years ago, by the look of it – and landed squarely on the roof of the wooden summerhouse.

The shrubs and trees were so high that this part of the garden had become a green tunnel. I glimpsed the chimneys and slates of neighbouring houses, but no windows. The remains of the lawn rose to my knees. The tips of the grasses had tiny purple fronds, and among them were wild flowers – clover, vetch, cow-parsley and the drying stalks of cowslips.

'You'll find a spare key to the front door underneath the bowl of the little birdbath near the shed,' Kate had said. 'The shed by the scullery. You just lift up the bowl of the birdbath and the key's on the –'

'I know,' I had said. 'There's a hollow in the base. That's where they always kept it.'

The key turned easily. Someone had recently oiled the lock. I remembered Carlo oiling locks, both there and at school. He always planned ahead if he could, and oiled locks made it easier to slip in and out late at night without anyone knowing.

I turned the handle, pushed open the door and stepped from the overgrown, sunlit garden into the stillness of the house. Once inside I closed the door and waited while my eyes adjusted. I listened to the silence of the house and felt the thudding of my heart.

Slowly the details emerged. The hall was smaller than I remembered but I had expected that. A faded runner stretched across black-and-white tiles to the foot of the stairs. There were splashes of colour on the tiles, where the sun filtered through the stained glass in the fanlight of the front door. I heard, very faintly, noises from the outside world – a child wailing, a car on the road. Inside the house, everything was quiet – more than quiet: the silence had a thick, smothering quality, grey and feathery like dust.

As the seconds slipped by, my pulse slowed. There was an odd smell in the house, dry and papery, with an unpleasant underlayer of sweetness, and beneath that something worse. Stacked along the right-hand wall was an irregular inner barrier made up of news-papers, piled into stacks, each leaning against the wall and its neighbours. There must have been years of news in those crumbling pages. Two or three of the piles had bellied out under their own weight and collapsed across the strip of carpet.

I don't know how long I waited. The silence of the house settled around me like a blanket, the sort that stifles rather than comforts. In the end panic pushed me forward, the sense that if I didn't move now I would lose what little courage remained.

I edged past the wall of newspapers. Some time after my last visit to the house, the dark-stained stairs had been painted white, although the paint had mutated now to a blotchy yellow. An island composed of black plastic sacks rose like shiny volcanic rock in the middle of the floor. Old clothes dribbled from their open mouths.

The drawing-room door was ajar. I edged inside. It was here that I truly appreciated the scale and the nature of the changes. The Murthingtons' house had always been untidy – as a teenager, I had thought its casual clutter much more distinguished and homely than the spotless order of my grandmother's bungalow – but it looked as if in recent years the Murthingtons had simply stopped caring. The drawing-room was now like an overcrowded second-hand furniture shop. Smaller objects were heaped on every horizontal surface including the floor. A chesterfield with a broken back supported an old-fashioned tin bath containing a pile of sheet music. The shelf above the fireplace housed a collection of clocks and china ornaments, as well as a cut-glass vase crammed with brown stalks. A pile of overcoats had been dumped over the wing-backed armchair where Hugh Murthington used to sit.

The same story, with minor variations, was repeated throughout the house. Carlo's father had been a man who collected things, and there's a fine line between collecting and hoarding. It was clear that in his later years he had found it hard to stop acquiring and even harder to throw anything away. Lily's casual approach to housekeeping, which had seemed endearingly carefree, had turned into something darker: a surrender to chaos. I wondered how long the two of them had been living there alone.

In some rooms, however, there were pockets of order, as if Kate or Carlo had tried to introduce limited areas of tidiness. The desk in Hugh's study, for example, was clear of everything, including dust, apart from a photograph in a silver frame, in the corner of which was a small card. I went closer. The photograph was a head-and-shoulders shot of Felicity grinning up at the camera. The card gave the address of St Margaret's Hospice.

Someone had also made an effort in the kitchen. The big Belfast sink, though stained by decades of use, was clean and smelt of bleach. The draining-board was empty apart from a mug and a plate. Yesterday's paper – the *Guardian* – lay folded open on the table.

Slowly I mounted the stairs. The runner was beige in colour and years of use had worn a dark track through the centre of it. My limbs seemed heavier than usual, my movements slower. The stairs creaked.

If someone was in the house, they would have heard me by now. The air smelt unclean. The higher I went, the warmer the temperature and the worse the smell.

On the landing, I paused. A passage led to the back of the house. Another flight of stairs climbed into a deeper darkness. The panelled doors were all closed. I pushed open the one on my right.

The room had belonged to Lily and Hugh. It was large and high-ceilinged with two big windows, both with pointed heads, looking through overgrown trees towards the road. But the furniture made it cramped. There were three tall wardrobes, all with clothes hanging from their doors and sides. One of the two dressing-tables still held a man's brushes and a strop for a cut-throat razor. Shoes, mostly in boxes, filled the gap between the end of the bed and the window, and these at least were tidy, the corners squared off, drawn up in ranks like soldiers on parade. A pile of hatboxes towered between two of the wardrobes. A zimmer frame and a commode stood beside the high double bed with its dark wooden headboard.

Two other bedrooms opened off the main landing. They had both silted up with clothes, magazines, suit-cases and cardboard boxes. But the smallest bedroom was different. It was set apart from the others at the end of the passage, next to the bathroom. According to Kate, this was where Carlo slept when he stayed there. The room had once belonged to Felicity but there was no trace of her now.

Here, as nowhere else in the house, I felt I was truly a trespasser. I was also aware of panic nibbling at the edges of my mind. This was so clearly a room whose owner intended to return. Everything was very clean – scoured, scraped and polished until not a speck of dust or dirt remained. The single bed was made up. A radio stood on the bedside table. A big backpack was leaning against the wall behind the door. Carlo had not been particularly tidy as a boy but now he appeared to live in surroundings that were almost monastic in their organized simplicity.

I glanced into the bathroom, which was empty, and again surprisingly clean. The bath was still the Victorian one with the high sides of scarred enamel and iron legs with claw feet. I walked back quickly to the main landing and up the attic stairs.

This had been Carlo's domain – a bedroom with a sloping ceiling and two dormer windows, with a tiny boxroom lit only by a skylight next door. One Christmas holidays we piled the contents of the boxroom against one wall, thereby clearing just enough floor space for ourselves and our guitars. We referred to this as the studio and played music under its sloping ceiling with religious solemnity. Music was our secret cult and in this airless little room we worshipped the gods of punk with the fervour of the newly converted.

But there was no trace of this now, and had not been for years. It was obvious that Kate had spent her childhood and her teenage years in the attic. An archaeologist of the individual would have been able to find layers relating to every stage of her life, from infant to student. Overlaid upon this older and longer period of occupation were glimpses of the adult. The bed was unmade – the duvet thrown on the floor, the sheet twisted and crumpled, the pillow still dented by the head that had rested on it. On the dressing-table stood a mug half full of what looked like herbal tea and an ashtray containing a solitary butt. The room was untidy but in a different way from the rest of the house, suggesting the mess had been made recently and in haste. I wondered who had been responsible for that.

I was in sight of the end at last, which made me hurry. Originally Kate had asked me to pack all of her clothes but I had persuaded her against this. It would make me far too conspicuous, whether I brought the car to the house or simply walked off towing suitcases. Besides, I had added, I would pay for her to buy new clothes, then no one could circulate an accurate description of what she was likely to be wearing.

Her passport and other papers, she had told me, were zipped into the inner pocket of the smaller of two suitcases. The suitcase was there but its inner pocket was empty.

While I considered what to do, I dropped a couple of T-shirts and a change of underclothes into a nylon overnight bag with a shoulder strap. I had arranged with Kate that I would phone her only in an emergency because the call would leave a record. But now I had no option. She answered on the first ring.

'It's me,' I said. 'Look –'

'Have they found him?'

It took me a moment to realize whom she meant. 'No, I don't think so. Not yet.'

'Thank God.' She drew a long, shuddering breath.

'I'm at the house now. The trouble is, some of your things are gone. The important stuff.'

'Any sign of him? The – the other one.'

'No. But his things are in his room.'

'Shit.'

There was a silence.

'I'm leaving,' I said. 'He could be back at any moment.'

'No – wait. You could have a look for them. He might have –'

'There's no point. You know what this place is like. It could take years to search.' The revulsion in my voice took me unawares. Suddenly angry, I went on: 'I'm leaving. That's that.'

'If they're still there, they'll be in his room.'

'I'm going.'

'Please, Jamie.'

I hesitated.

'Is his backpack there? He always brings it when he comes. That's where it'll probably be. It's all I need – the building-society stuff and the passport.'

It occurred to me that perhaps the risk was worth running for my sake as well as hers. Sean hadn't been found yet. Nothing incriminated her so she was free to go abroad, to go anywhere as long as it was away from me. But once Sean was found, it would be too late.

'I won't spend long,' I said. 'Just a couple of minutes. If that.'

'Thank you.'

93

I rang off and went down the attic stairs. It seemed incomprehensible that I'd ever liked this ugly, over-crowded house, as incomprehensible as my obsession with Lily. I walked down the passage into the bedroom that had been Felicity's and now was Carlo's.

The backpack was enormous. It had a wealth of outside pockets and I decided to start with those. There was one held with Velcro at the top of the main flap. I pulled it open. It contained a map – the same edition of the Ordnance Survey map I had bought in Rackford earlier that day – and also a manilla enve-lope, foolscap size, folded in two, the flap unsealed.

I pulled out the contents and wished I hadn't. I found myself looking at another photograph of Felicity, this time when she was older, self-conscious and wearing a dress that was probably new and the reason for the photograph. Her long hair hung beside her pale face. Adult features were just beginning to emerge from the gentle, rounded contours of puppy fat. She was almost beautiful, not a word I'd associ-ated with her before. I didn't want to look at her.

Beneath the photograph was a homemade card. I was standing near the window and I angled it towards the late-afternoon sunlight. 'For Daddy – happy birthday, with lots of love and hugs from Felicity.'

I turned the card over. Felicity had done a picture for her father, just as she had for Carlo on his birthday on my first visit to Chipping Weston. Technically, it was surprisingly good in many ways. It showed a group of flowers carefully drawn in ink, with deli-cate dabs of watercolour that even now made them glow. Yet the composition was oddly stiff. She had lined up the flowers in a row with no apparent thought to the effect they made together. They didn't belong with each other.

I was about to slide the card and the photograph back into the envelope when I heard a sound from outside. I glanced out of the window. I was in time to catch only a flash of movement at the edge of my vision. Someone had just turned into the little porch.

Carlo, I thought. At last.

I stuffed the envelope into the bag and slipped out of the room. I heard the sound of the key turning in the distant lock. If Carlo came straight upstairs, he would meet me on the landing. If he went somewhere downstairs first, he would hear me moving about or on the stairs.

I backed into the bathroom, because that put more space between us. I bolted the door and glanced at the window over the basin. It was the original Victorian sash with stained glass in the lower half. A memory came back to me – Carlo and I together in the bathroom: we were teasing Felicity. We'd locked the door and she was on the other side, banging on the panels, almost weeping in her anxiety to join us. Carlo had winked at me. 'Hang on a moment,' he called out to her. 'I'm going to make James vanish. I'm going to flush him down the bog. Then you can come in.'

He pulled up the lower sash. 'There's a way down over the shed roof,' he whispered. 'She doesn't know.'

I had climbed on to the sloping slate roof of the scullery. I heard Carlo flushing the lavatory and gently closing the window. Then he let Felicity into the bathroom – and into the secret, too. He would never tease her for long.

I was too desperate for caution. The window went up with a screech. I glanced down, wondering where to put my feet. And that was when I saw the blood.

The shock made me catch my breath. For an instant I forgot the desperate need to hurry. A white plastic bucket was standing on the floor, tucked between the basin and the bath, full almost to the brim with blood. Something pale and slimy floated just below the surface.

For Christ's sake. Brains? Intestines? What the hell is Carlo –

I snatched a toothbrush from the jar on the side of the basin and poked its handle into the bloody mess. I fished up the cuff of a pale blue shirt, dripping with watery blood.

Relief hit me like a blast of warm air. Then I heard rapid footsteps somewhere in the house – on the stairs? the landing? – and another form of panic set in. I clambered on to the side of the bath and poked a leg through the gap. I pushed my head and shoulders through, then the other leg. I let go of Kate's overnight bag and it slid down the slates, snagged for a moment on the guttering and vanished. I slithered down the roof.

When I had done this before I had been fifteen, lighter, smaller and much more supple. My adult body

96

was cumbersome and fragile. A slate gave way beneath me. My foot jarred against the guttering and for a moment I thought that that, too, would give way. But it held. I dropped down four feet to the flat roof of the shed below. I grabbed the bag. The roof cracked and sagged beneath my weight.

On the far side of the shed, in the corner where its back wall met the boundary fence of the garden, there had been a compost heap. It was still there but now it was covered with a dense forest of nettles. I sucked in a breath of air and launched myself into the green leaves. I landed awkwardly. My ankle twisted. My leg gave way. I fell head first to the path below. Grunting with pain, I staggered down the long, overgrown garden.

A terrified grey squirrel scrambled up the trunk of the ash tree and vanished among the leaves. As I reached the gate I heard the bathroom window close and, somewhere in the distance, the seesaw wail of a police siren.

7

During the drive back to London I checked the rear-view mirror repeatedly. On the eastern side of the Oxford ring road, a few miles before the motorway began, I stopped at a pub where I ordered a cup of coffee and phoned Nicky. When her voicemail cut in, I said I hoped she was having fun, and I'd see her soon. It didn't occur to me to worry about her. My mind was on other things.

I didn't want to talk to Kate. But before I left the pub I texted her: 'No luck. C came back.'

The motorway unrolled before me, a grey carpet stretching all the way to London. Most of the traffic was coming the other way. Thoughts scurried around my mind like a pack of monkeys. For a moment those monkeys were more real to me than my hands on the steering-wheel and the vehicles in the other lanes: I saw their little black hands gripping the bars, rattling them, trying to get out. Then I stopped being metaphorical and thought instead about Felicity's photograph and the bloody shirt soaking in the white bucket. I thought about Lily lying in her room and holding the tarnished chain with the twisted shred of metal attached to it.

All the while, I watched the cars behind me, fixing on first one, then another. I slowed, I speeded, I changed lanes. I passed the Greyfont turn-off and drove on to London. When the motorway petered out, I pulled over and phoned the hospice. A pleasant, concerned voice told me that Lily Murthington had woken up in the afternoon and had some food. She seemed happier in herself, the voice said, and in less pain, but now she was sleeping again. No, if I wanted to pay her a visit it would probably be better to do so in the morning.

I drove to Queen's Park and left the car in a side road. At a general shop I bought two egg-mayonnaise sandwiches and, as an afterthought, a packet of Marlboro Light. I took my time walking to the chapel, following a roundabout route and using shop windows as mirrors. I entered a pub by one door, walked rapidly through the bars, glancing about me as though looking for a friend, and left by another.

Paranoid logic is irrefutable. If I could not see a pursuer, it did not mean that one was not there; if anything, it confirmed his or her fiendish cunning. I walked past the chapel once, then again. Only on the third time did I decide it was safe to go in. I unlocked the gate, went rapidly up the path, and tapped on the door of the little room behind the chapel. There was no answer. I pushed the key into the lock. To my surprise, the door opened.

The room was empty. The inner door on the right was ajar. Panic spurted through me. I kicked the door fully open. The main body of the chapel was as bright as I had ever seen it. Sunshine streamed through the grimy window above the doors to the road. The skylights glowed golden. There was more than enough light to see the stained floorboards, the crumbling plaster, the dust that swirled lazily in the air and the huddle of chairs at the end. There was more than enough light to see that I was alone.

I walked slowly towards the chairs. Beside the one where Kate had sat there was a heap of squashed cigarette butts and some ash, which formed a grey smear the size of a dinner plate. In places I could see the swirls and curves that Kate's fingers had made. She hadn't had a pen or anything to write on so she'd used the ash as her paper and a fingertip as her pen. Only two words were written there.

Sorry. Goodbye.

I ground the ash under my heel until the message was gone, until all that remained of Kate was a little pile of cigarette ends. It was better that way.

By the time I reached Greyfont it was after half past six. I drove slowly along our road and turned into the drive. Nicky's Mini wasn't in front of the garage. She must have come back and gone out again. In a way I was glad – I wasn't looking forward to explaining how I'd spent my day. I didn't like having to lie to her, even by implication.

Inside the house the air was cool and musty. I switched off the burglar alarm and went into the kitchen. There was no sign of an evening meal.

To my surprise I found the trousers Nicky had been wearing folded neatly over the back of a chair in our bedroom. So she'd come back and gone out again. I picked up the phone by the bed, intending to ring her. When I put the receiver to my ear I heard the broken tone indicating a new message on the voicemail. I punched in the access number. Then Nicky's voice, thin and remote, was speaking rapidly, saying words that at first I didn't understand: 'James, it's me. I can't believe what you've done. I need time to think about it, about what I'm going to do. I'll be away for a night or two.'

The message ended abruptly, as if she had slammed down the phone. I played it again, then again. I phoned her mobile. It was switched off and I went straight through to voicemail: 'Nicky, it's me. Can you call me? Where are you?'

Nicky had come home to change. It occurred to me that if I worked out which clothes she had taken, I might get an idea of where she had gone. I opened the wardrobe and pulled out drawers.

It didn't take me long to realize that I had the wrong sort of mind for this. I vaguely recognized some of the clothes and shoes I saw but it did not follow that I was aware of the ones that weren't there. I glanced round the room. I noticed one absence – her novel was gone from the bedside table.

My head buzzing, I went back downstairs. It occurred to me that my message must have sounded curt to her, as curt as hers to me. I picked up my mobile from the table, leaned against the wall and began to text her. 'Please call.' I'd already said that on the phone so I deleted it. 'I can explain.' That sounded unduly defensive. I knew I had a good deal to defend but there was no point in making a tactical error at the outset. In the end I wrote, 'I love you,' and pressed the send key before I had time to change my mind. I couldn't think of anything else to say to her.

An idea slipped into my mind. Nicky had taken her novel with her, the current book-group selection. She had gone up to London today with Miranda, another member of the book group. So Miranda might know something.

I found their number on the pad in the kitchen and phoned them. Their baby-sitter answered – Miranda and Dave had gone out to the Furstons' round the corner. I grabbed my jacket and left the house. Nicky and I knew the Furstons, though not as well as Miranda and Dave did because we didn't have children. In this neighbourhood, children act as the principal form of social glue, binding together the most ill-assorted couples in an unending round of competitive hospitality.

The Furstons were having a party. As soon as I turned into their road, I smelt the barbecue and heard the sound of raised voices and laughter. I rang the front-door bell and one of their children answered the door. This one was a girl, and she scowled at me from beneath a long, straight fringe. 'Is your mum in?' I asked unnecessarily, as I could hear the shriek of her laughter from where I was standing.

The child, who couldn't have been more than ten, clung to the edge of the door and said nothing.

'I'm James,' I reminded her. 'I live round the corner. I'm looking for Miranda Hammett.'

'Round the back,' the child said, and shut the door in my face.

I took this as an invitation and went through the gate beside the double garage. Guy Furston was the director of marketing for an IT company. The children went to the prep school in the next village, and his wife described herself as a homemaker. They ran three cars, and in the two years since they'd lived there they'd converted the loft, built an enormous conservatory on to the sitting-room at the back and added a swimming-pool.

This was where the barbecue was – on the patio area that spread from the hardwood doors of the conservatory to the sparkling blue waters of the pool. Elton John throbbed and warbled in the conservatory, mingling with what sounded like an episode of *The Simpsons* from one of the upstairs windows. A dozen people were talking and drinking. Guy was arranging steaks, burgers and sausages on the barbecue. He saw me coming and waved an uncooked sausage in my direction.

'James! Come and join us – beer? Glass of wine?' He was a big, efficiently sociable man with a smile that split his fat red face in two. 'Nicky with you?'

'Actually, I wanted a word with Miranda. She and Nicky went to London today.'

'I know. Dave said he didn't realize you could cram that number of carrier-bags into an M-class Merc. Probably a world record. After all, the poor girls only had two thousand litres of luggage space to play with.' He laughed, spreading his arms in uncomplicated enjoyment of his joke. Then he bellowed across the pool to Miranda, who was standing in the evening sunshine with a glass in one hand and a bottle in the other. 'James wants a word with you. Why don't you get him a drink while you're at it?'

Miranda broke off her conversation and gave me a little wave. I watched her walking along the edge of the pool. Her long, flowery dress billowed like a tent on the move. She was a heavy woman, and growing heavier. Her pretty features were framed by artfully cut hair lifted by blonde highlights, and they were sinking slowly into thickening jowls. There was no surprise in her expression. I guessed she had been expecting me.

She pecked my cheek with soft, heavy lips, and her hair swung forward, revealing glimpses of grey and ginger at the roots. She nodded at the table where the drinks were. 'What would you like?'

'Nothing, thanks. I was wondering if you'd seen Nicky.'

'Not since we got back from London. Is she coming here? She didn't say.'

'I thought you might know where she was – she's not at home.'

She brayed with laughter. 'You mean she's vanished?'

'No, of course not.'

Miranda smiled. 'But you don't know where she is?'

'She came home, got changed and went out in the car. She must have forgotten to leave a note. I wasn't there, you see – I've been out all day.'

'Have you tried phoning?'

'Of course. Her battery must be flat or something.'

Miranda shrugged, which sent a ripple through the floral tent. 'All I know is I dropped her off at yours at about half past five. She didn't say if she was going out or not.'

'Was she OK?'

Her smile slipped. 'She was fine. All things considered.'

'How do you mean?'

'Well, the thing is, James, she's a bit upset. Naturally.' There was no mistaking the malice now. 'As you would be, wouldn't you?'

'I don't understand.'

'If it was Dave, I'd go after him with the frying-pan. But Nicky's different.' Miranda sipped her wine. 'We're good friends, you know, me and Nicky – she tells me quite a lot.'

'I'm sure she does. So what was the problem today?'

'You were, of course.'

'I really don't understand what you're getting at.'

Miranda gave another metallic laugh. 'Come on, James, there's no point in pretending. If you don't want people to notice when you play away from home, you'll have to do it a bit more subtly than that.'

I stared at her. Late one evening, at a party just after our move to Greyfont, Miranda had made a pass at me. I'd backed away as if she'd stung me and muttered something about needing to ask Nicky something. I wondered whether she disliked me because of that.

Suddenly she stretched out the hand holding the glass and touched my arm. A few drops of wine slopped on to my sleeve. 'You OK?'

'Yes. I think there's been a mistake.'

'Well, that's something for you to sort out with her, isn't it? But it's only fair to say you're going to have an uphill job.'

'What did she say? Tell me exactly what she said.'

Miranda waved a finger in front of my face. 'It's been going on for a while, hasn't it? And then, of course, Dave saw you with that girl yesterday evening. I mean, that's what really did it – letting her come to the house. All very surreptitious, I gather.' She glanced slyly at me with little eyes wedged in folds of fat. 'I had to tell Nicky, you do see that? I mean, us girls have to stick together.' She took another sip of wine, examining me over the rim of the glass. 'Dave said she was a pretty little thing, your young lady. Ravishing – that was his word. Mind you keep her away from him. I don't want him straying.'

I nodded, I didn't trust myself to speak, and turned to go. Guy shouted something about sausages. Dave barged into me and laughed as if I'd made a joke. But Miranda hadn't finished: her voice pursued me as I escaped from the patio. 'You know what they say, James? Sauce for the goose is sauce for the gander. It works both ways, doesn't it?'

*

It was a long evening. I went home and poured myself a glass of the Burgundy I had opened the previous evening. I took the glass and the bottle into the garden. I didn't want to stay in the house. It was heavy with silence, pregnant with Nicky's absence.

Time stretched. I sat on a wooden bench in the last of the evening sun beside a little herb garden that Nicky was making. Felicity had liked flowers, gardens and plants, and so did Nicky. I looked at lovage and parsley, chives and rosemary, garlic and thyme. I didn't think much about Carlo, Kate or Lily. I didn't wonder about what had happened at Rackford or whose blood was in the bucket. Instead I thought about Nicky. I listened for the phone, which didn't ring, and tried not to glance at my watch too often. I was a failure as a husband in more ways than one, but at least I had been faithful. With Nicky that had come easily.

I tried to phone her. Once again I went straight through to voicemail. So I wrote her another text: 'It's not what you think, I promise. We need to talk.' But I deleted it without sending. There was no way round the fact that I had lied to her about Kate. Nicky was right to be angry. She was only wrong about the reason. Much as I loved her, though, I couldn't tell her the truth. Because if I did, one thing would have to lead to another. I would need to explain about the Murthingtons and Chipping Weston, and then she would have a far more powerful reason to leave me. It was better left alone, dead and buried. And there was another reason for silence: I had no right to involve Nicky in Kate's problems.

I drank another glass, then a third. In the end the cold drove me back inside the house. I forced myself to eat a slice of toast and a slab of cheese. While I ate, I watched the news in case there was mention of a body near Lower Rackford. Sean still hadn't been found. I almost wished he had been. At least the waiting would be over.

Miranda's parting words turned and twisted in my mind. Were they a broad hint that Nicky had found consolation with someone else? Or had they been merely an instinctive attempt to correct an imbalance of injury?

The wine bottle was empty. I considered opening another but a shred of sanity held me back. Nicky might ring. I needed to have at least some of my wits about me. I staggered upstairs and stood in the shower. I held my face up to the showerhead so the water washed down my cheeks. The tiled enclosure was slippery and seemed to sway as if it was floating on a choppy sea.

I would have liked to cry. I could not remember crying since that first day at boarding-school when I had wept in the housemaster's garden and told myself that I would no longer love my mother. I knew what would happen if I didn't find a way to deal with Nicky's absence: it would turn into something sad, sour and hard, just as it had when my mother and step-father packed me off to school in another country.

But perhaps, in the long run, that would be better than the alternative. If I cut myself adrift from Nicky, if I stopped loving her as I had my mother, then at least one of my problems would be solved. It wouldn't matter if she thought I was having an affair. It wouldn't matter if I was or, indeed, if she was. The trouble was, I did love her. And I didn't want to stop.

It was still early – not much more than ten o'clock – when I left the shower. I went to bed because I couldn't think of anything else to do. I lay with my head on a pillow that smelt faintly of her perfume and thought about how we had met, when I had been working in London and she was still living in Winchester. The first time I saw her was at the house of a client, a man with more money than sense who had bought a half-ruined Jacobean mansion on a whim and was trying to find out whether it could be made habitable again. There were dead sheep among the brambles in the garden and no mains services. Most of the land had gone and an industrial estate had grown up on the other side of the garden wall.

The client had wanted everything done in a hurry. Nicky, who worked for a firm of interior decorators, had been summoned about three years prematurely to advise on colour schemes. After the client had driven away to his next appointment, she and I had had lunch in the local pub. Then we picked our way through the ruined garden, trying to imagine what it had once looked like. We compared notes on the sanity of our client and discovered that we were both intending to see the same exhibition that weekend. The following Saturday afternoon, I contrived to bump into her at the Barbican.

I knew from the first weekend that Nicky was different. I wanted to be with her when she woke up in the morning with her eyes gummy from sleep. I wanted to share the Sunday newspapers with her. If I had to trail round a supermarket, I would rather do it with her than with anyone else. I wanted to buy a house with her and make it into a shared home, something I had never had since my father died, a home I shared on equal terms with other people. At the end of all my long days, I wanted to drive into the sunset with her. It was that complicated and that simple.

We got to know each other slowly. We spent a lot of time walking, looking at buildings and gardens, sitting in parks and restaurants. And all the time, in those early months, we were talking. I had never talked so much about myself. I unlocked doors in my mind that had been shut since childhood. I was amazed at Nicky's power to liberate me and amazed at my own willingness to let her.

But there had to be a limit. Some doors remained closed, as much for her sake as mine. It wouldn't have been fair to ask her to share the burden of what had happened all those years ago. Besides, I thought that if she knew, she would no longer want to be with me. So I told her about school, my parents and my step-father, but I said little about the Murthingtons. I mentioned Carlo's name once or twice – it would have been hard not to – but only in passing.

'How could your mother bear to send you away?' Nicky said. 'It's weird. Have you ever asked her why she did it?'

I shook my head. 'I haven't talked to her for years.'

'Don't you want to?'

'I don't even know whether she's alive.'

Nicky laid a hand on mine. We were sitting on a bench near the summit of Primrose Hill and London rolled away from us, wave after wave of brick and concrete, Tarmac and glass, surging towards the distant shore of the horizon.

'I'd never send a child to boarding-school. What's the point in having them if you send them away?' Nicky's eyes were large and serious. 'What do you think?'

'I agree.'

She worked a finger into the gap between two of mine. Our hands curled together on the warm bench. 'Do you think we should have children? You and I?'

'Oh, yes,' I said. 'We must have children.'

I dropped a kiss on to her warm hair. It seemed to me that she had given me a chance I had never had before. I couldn't mend what was broken. But at least, with Nicky's help, I might make something that was whole.

Despite the wine, I couldn't sleep. The hours crept by. I lay on the double bed with the curtains drawn. I shuttled to and fro between two sets of terrors. When I wasn't thinking about what had happened at Rackford, I was creating scenario after scenario that showed in graphic detail what Nicky was doing now.

She was sitting up in bed in a big, anonymous hotel reading her novel for the book group, the one with the little lost girl on the cover. She was lolling on a faceless friend's sofa, eating chocolate and watching a DVD. She was in an airport departure lounge, waiting for her flight to be announced. Worst of all, she was writhing under another body in the oldest dance of all.

Slowly I slid into the trance-like state between sleeping and waking, where thoughts merge imperceptibly with dreams. But I didn't dream of Nicky. Instead the logic of the sleeping mind led me back to Lily – not as she was now but as she had been then.

It was half memory, half dream, the summer of 1979, when I had spent the last ten days of the holiday at Chipping Weston. Carlo was already sixteen, and my own sixteenth birthday was only a couple of months away. Lily took the three of us – Felicity, Carlo and me – to a falconry centre near the Malverns, where the green hills shaded into the blue horizons of Wales.

Felicity enjoyed watching the peregrines and goshawks swooping at the lures, and examining the birds on their perches, and so did Lily. Carlo and I, however, were at an awkward age: too old to take a child's pleasure and too young to take an adult's. We trailed behind the others in sulky silence. When the tour of the centre had finished, we had a late lunch in the picnic area beside the car park. Carlo and I spread a rug in the shade of an oak tree. Lily and Felicity unpacked the contents of the ice-box and the picnic basket.

Looking back, I realize that Lily had gone to some

trouble, although at the time none of us was very grateful when she produced sausage rolls and pâté, ham and chicken, several sorts of salad, bread, crisps, cheese and fruit. We ate quickly and in silence, washing the food down with fruit juice and Coke. Lily had also brought the remains of a bottle of Frascati that she and Hugh had shared the previous evening. She ate little but drank quickly – first one glass, then another, then the half-inch at the bottom of the bottle.

After lunch, she shook the crumbs from the rug and lay down on it. She said she was going to enjoy the sunshine for a few minutes. Felicity tugged at Carlo's hand, pulling him to his feet. She wanted to go back to the shop attached to the centre to buy souvenirs. He pretended to be angry and chased her, shrieking with laughter, across the picnic area in the direction of the shop.

I lay on my side in the grass. My head rested in my right hand and with my left I plucked idly at blades of grass. I glanced at Lily on the rug. She was lying on her back, her eyes closed. Her cheeks were pinker than usual. The picnic rug had a pattern of red-and-white checks, and her cheeks were almost the same colour as the red checks.

I stared at her. She was wearing a pale green cotton dress. It was sleeveless and came above the knee. Her legs were bare and there were sandals on her feet. For the first time, it seemed to me, I was seeing her properly – as herself, rather than as a figure in Carlo's background defined only by his relationship to her.

There was no reason for this – or, rather, nothing for which she could be held responsible. After all, I had seen her before in poses that were far more obviously alluring – in a bikini, for example, or in a nightdress. It wasn't her doing. It was mine. None of this would have happened if it hadn't been for me. It was my fault.

I looked at the faint sheen of sweat on Lily's forehead. I noticed the soft dark hair on her neck just behind the ear. It was as fine as a baby's. I watched her breasts rise and fall as she breathed. There was a slight breeze, enough to send the occasional ripple through the hem of her skirt. I stared at the place where the dress ended and the legs began, almost willing the breeze to grow stronger, to push the light cotton higher up the leg.

Something changed.

At first, I didn't know what was happening to me. I had heard people at school talk about this, usually with a knowing laugh. I had read about it in books and seen it on the screen. But it had never happened to me. I was simply not prepared for it. For several minutes I didn't recognize it for what it was.

Though I had recently eaten I had a sensation curiously close to hunger. I felt something in the back of my throat, too, an anticipation, an excitement, as if a momentous event was just round the corner. I couldn't tear my eyes away from Lily. She drew me towards her, like a falling body to the earth, and I could no more resist the force of her gravity than I could live backwards in time.

Running footsteps pounded across the grass. Felicity shrieked with laughter.

I was acquiring an erection, which was increasingly obvious as it pressed with painful urgency against the crotch of my jeans. Lily opened her eyes and stared at me.

8

Sunday morning. It was dawn and I had a headache from the wine. I had slept for an hour or two. My body felt brittle. A well-placed blow could have shattered it into a million pieces. I lingered in bed because it was easier than getting up.

The red digits on the LCD display changed from 05:59 to 06:00. I panicked – I hadn't checked my phone: Nicky might have texted me in the night or, if she hadn't, she might have emailed. I rolled out of bed, tripped on the rug and stubbed my toe.

But there were no messages on the phone. I went downstairs to my study and switched on the laptop. Emails were waiting, but not from Nicky. Afterwards I checked the news. Still nothing about a body at Rackford.

I closed the laptop. Beside it on the desk was the brown envelope I had stolen from Carlo's backpack during the abortive trip to Chipping Weston. I slid out the photograph and the card. There was Felicity, eternally poised between child and woman, doomed always to be neither one nor the other. I glanced at the card, with its row of brightly coloured flowers strung across the front like a line of washing. 'For Daddy – happy birthday, with lots of love and hugs from Felicity.'

It made me feel worse than ever. I had another shower because I felt unclean. The morning crawled slowly by. At eight o'clock I tried to phone Nicky. At eight thirty I tried again, and at nine o'clock too. I called Kate's number. She wasn't answering her phone either.

I needed to do something. I wrote a message for Nicky and left it on the kitchen table. I drove to Wembley. The hospice car park was full. The reception area was thronged with Sunday visitors.

'Yes, go on in,' the nurse said. 'Lily's had quite a good night but she's finding it hard to concentrate.'

'Is she worse?'

'It's not so much that – it's the medication.'

'Has her daughter managed to visit?'

'Not that I know of. But her son came yesterday afternoon.'

'Her son?'

She looked sharply at me.

I said quickly, 'Oh, of course – her step-son, you mean. Carlo.'

'Try not to excite her,' the nurse went on, as we walked along the corridor. 'I think he did. I'm sure he didn't mean to. But Lily was quite agitated after he left.'

Lily was sitting up in bed with her arm attached to a syringe driver. The biography was no longer on the bedside table. When she saw me, her face brightened. 'Jamie.' She held up her cheek for me to kiss. With the nurse looking on, I lowered my head and brushed the dry, wrinkled skin with my lips.

'Come and sit here.' Lily touched the arm of the chair beside the bed. 'I want to see you.'

The nurse left us. Lily smiled at me, and the ghost of her old charm reached out and touched me. 'I'm so glad you're here,' she whispered. 'You're the only one I can trust.'

This was a technique she had always used. She made you feel special. She made you feel that there was no one in the world who could do whatever it was as well as you could. She made you feel unique and wonderful.

'How are you feeling?'

She waved the question aside with a hand that was all skin, bone and tendon. 'Carlo came, I think,' she said, in the same hissing voice. 'He scares me.'

'Did he try to hurt you?'

'No, not that. He doesn't want to hurt *me*.' She frowned, groping in the cloud-filled recesses of her memory. 'She phoned, Kate did. She said you were helping. I knew you would, Jamie, I knew I could trust you. Only you.'

Carlo must have come in the early afternoon, I thought, before driving down to Chipping Weston where he had flushed me out of the house. I glanced about the room, hoping to see the book with the white envelope in it. *Surely she hadn't shown it to Carlo?* 'What did he want?' I said.

'Kate, of course.' She stared at me, and the brown irises of her eyes were enormous, the pupils reduced to minute dots. 'He's going to kill her, you see.'

'I'm sure that's not true,' I said gently.

She shook her head. 'He wants me to stay alive until she's dead because then he'll get it all. Everything from Hugh, I mean.'

'Did she say where she is?'

Lily looked blankly at me. 'She's with you.'

'Not any more. I found her a place to stay but she left yesterday afternoon. No warning. I went there and found she'd gone.'

'Why?'

'I don't know.' In fact I thought that Kate might have calculated that if the body hadn't been found, no one would be looking for her. Yet. So in the meantime it was safe for her to leave.

Lily yawned. She poked a fingertip into a nostril, then took it out and stroked her cheek with it. She yawned again. Her eyelids were closing. I moved a little closer, hoping to catch sight of the envelope. I cleared my throat. 'Maybe Kate told you where she was when she phoned?'

Lily blinked.

'Try to think. Lily, you must think.'

She rubbed her clawlike hands together. 'I – I'm not sure.'

The harder I pressed, the vaguer her replies. Her memory had become treacherous: it allowed her to lurch from time to time, from place to place. In the end she gave up all pretence of listening to me. She rested her head on the pillows and closed her eyes. I sat back in the chair and watched her sleeping. Except she wasn't quite asleep. Slices of brown iris showed between the lids.

'Hugh,' Lily said, opening her eyes wide. She smiled. Then her face crumpled and she frowned.

'Not Hugh,' I said. 'I'm Jamie.'

Her head nodded, a heavy, dying flower on a brittle stalk. 'Look after Kate. Promise me.'

'I'll – I'll try.' As I spoke I thought of Nicky, and my need for her was so extraordinarily painful I almost cried out. 'But I don't know where she is.'

'At Sean's?'

I frowned and whispered: 'But Sean's dead.'

'His house. She lived there for a bit.'

'Where is it?'

Lily thought – for so long that I wondered whether she'd forgotten the question. 'I don't know.' She gave another wave of the fleshless hand. 'I used to know. I've forgotten.'

'I expect you wrote it down somewhere,' I suggested, without much hope.

But she nodded. 'Of course I did. It's at the back of my diary.'

'And where's your diary?'

She wasn't listening. 'I'm tired, Hughie, so tired.'

'I know. The diary – where is it?'

Lily blinked. 'It's bedtime, Hughie.'

The lids slipped over the eyes. She turned her face away from me on the pillow. Her breathing became heavy. She began to snore.

The door was wide open and every few seconds someone would pass along the corridor. I stood up, slowly and quietly. The snoring continued, growing louder. With my eyes swinging between Lily and the corridor, I sidled round the bed. I stooped over the locker beside it. The door creaked when I opened it. The snoring stopped. I straightened up and pretended to stare out of the window. The snoring did not start again but in a moment the breathing resumed its regular rhythm.

I turned back to the locker. There was no sign of the biography, but a blue suede handbag was on the bottom shelf. I eased open the catch and rummaged quickly through the contents. A black appointments diary was in a side pocket. I flicked through its pages, which were mainly blank. At the back was a section of addresses and phone numbers. Carlo's wasn't among them, but the name Sean Fielding was halfway down the second page. He lived in St Albans: 9 Laburnum Lane. As I was trying to memorize the phone number, Lily stirred. She opened her eyes.

I smiled at her. 'Had a nice rest?'

'Did I drop off?'

I put the diary into the open mouth of the handbag and closed the locker door with my knee. 'You nodded off for a couple of minutes.'

'I do that all the time now. It's so silly. Sometimes I don't know if I'm waking or sleeping.'

'I'd better go. I don't want to tire you.' I lifted up the glass, which was on top of the cupboard. 'Would you like some water?'

'Thank you.'

She leaned against me. I slid my right arm round her and supported her. She took several sips. Water dribbled down her chin. I dabbed it dry with a tissue.

'Thank you,' she said, and sank back against the pillows.

At that moment I saw the book. It had slipped between her arm and her body, and most of it was concealed by the folds of her nightdress. 'Shall I move your book? It can't be very comfortable there.'

'No,' she said. 'It's all right where it is.'

Her eyelids closed and her breathing slowed again. I looked down at her. For a moment I forgot about Nicky and Kate. I forgot about the tarnished chain in the white envelope and the address in my memory. For a moment there was only Lily. Lust had evaporated and love had run dry. But something remained – a connection, perhaps, or a responsibility; a sadness for what had been and what might have been.

I bent down and kissed her cheek. I wished her a gentle death.

In December 1979 I went to stay with the Murthingtons at the beginning of the holidays. Since the previous summer I had spent a surprising amount of time thinking about Lily and constructing dramatic situations designed to make her realize how wonderful I was. I didn't want to think about her while I was at school but I found I had no choice in the matter. I even encouraged Carlo to talk about his family in the hope of eliciting scraps of information about her, however small and inconsequential. I needed something to feed on.

But it didn't mean anything. I told myself that over

and over again. I couldn't fancy Lily, not really. It would be too sick and weird for words. After all, she could have been my mother. She was *old*.

Life, I already knew, was full of private embarrassments and secret fears. You just had to keep quiet about them and pretend that they didn't exist, and hope that sooner or later they wouldn't matter. My mother didn't want me. My penis was smaller than anyone else's in the history of the world. I would never pass my A levels. I was terrified that my grandmother would die, and sometimes I had nightmares about finding her dead body in the bungalow. So Lily was just another item for the list. Something to grow out of as quickly as possible.

During that visit to Chipping Weston, Christmas spread like an infection throughout the house. The freezer filled up with mince-pies. Cards dangled on ribbons attached to the picture rails. Wrapping-paper, Sellotape and scissors appeared and disappeared all over the house. The sitting-room, the hall and the stairs were laden with golden and silver streamers. The landing windowsill became the setting for Felicity's nativity crib with scenery and figures she had painted.

Lily seemed hardly to notice me, except as another pair of hands to help with the preparations. There was something ruthless and single-minded about her desire to ensure that Christmas conformed to the rigorous expectations she had of it. She sent Carlo and me to dig up the tree from a damp, sunless corner of the garden beyond the summer-house. We lugged it into the house, scattering a trail of earth down the hall and into the sitting-room. Felicity took control of decorating it, spurning any advice from Lily but graciously accepting Carlo's assistance and even mine. Carlo was co-operative but less than enthusiastic.

'I mean, for God's sake,' he said to me afterwards, 'all that bloody holly. And the mess the tree makes, you wouldn't believe it. I hate Christmas. Everyone buys everyone else presents they don't really want, and they spend about four weeks wrapping them up. Why don't we just give each other money? And, Jesus, you should be here for Christmas Day. They couldn't make more fuss about lunch if it was a blood sacrifice with a couple of underage virgins. And on Christmas Eve we all have to go to the midnight service at church. It's full of people like us who never go for the rest of the year. It's pathetic. Bloody hypocrites. Why do they have to pretend it's so wonderful when it's not?'

But it sounded wonderful to me – what Christmas ought to be. When I spent Christmas with my mother, my step-father and their family, I was a stranger, the boy perpetually on the wrong side of the window with his face pressed up against the glass. It was slightly better at my grandmother's, where I was going this year, because my expectations were so low as to be almost invisible. We would pull a solitary cracker and chew our way through a roasted turkey roll. Afterwards my grandmother would go to sleep in front of the television while I slipped into my room or outside for a quick cigarette in the garden.

In the meantime, being in the same house as Lily wasn't easy. There were two main problems. First, I discovered that she still had a profoundly unsettling effect on me. I tried not to look at her too often, which was hard. Second, it was painful to discover that the real Lily was so far removed from the obliging woman in my carefully nurtured fantasies.

On my last evening at the Murthingtons', I met her coming out of the sitting-room. She stopped, and I stopped too. 'That's for you.' She held out a small parcel. 'For Christmas.'

I looked from the present to her unsmiling face and back again. I felt my skin growing warm. Her cheeks were flushed too, perhaps from the wine she had drunk at supper. 'Thank you,' I said, and my voice emerged as a strangled whisper.

'Jamie.'

'What?'

'Mind you don't open it until the day itself.' She rested her fingers lightly on my arm and the hairs rose on my skin. 'Promise.'

'I – I promise.'

'Good boy.'

She raised herself on tiptoe. Still holding my arm, she brought her face up to mine and kissed my lips. I was too surprised to kiss her back. She released my arm and walked away. I heard her saying something to Hugh in the kitchen.

That was the first time Lily kissed me. They say

you always remember the first time. In every kiss is the ghost of that first one – the first, I mean, that expressed something other than duty or affection. The first that tasted of desire.

I reached St Albans at lunchtime. Laburnum Lane was part of a former council estate. As it was Sunday there were plenty of people about but none paid me much attention. Most of the semi-detached houses were now privately owned. Owners had expressed their individuality with doors and windows, coats of paint and extensions. The gardens offered a guide to the rich variety of human life.

Some houses, however, were still trapped in an unwholesome past. If Sean's, number nine, had had any money invested in its exterior over the last ten or fifteen years, it kept its secret well. I drove past it, parked round the corner and walked back.

The garden contained weeds, discarded food wrappers, a dustbin without a lid and two bicycles, neither of which had any wheels. I pushed open the gate and walked up the cracked concrete path to the front door. I tried the bell but nothing happened. I thought I heard a child crying inside but the sound might have come from a neighbour's. I rapped on the door with my knuckles.

Nobody came to ask what I wanted so I followed the ribbon of concrete round the side of the house. The back door was open, and just inside it a small child, naked except for a pair of shorts, was sitting on the floor with his legs spread out before him. A litter of discarded objects surrounded him – a plastic bath book, a wooden spoon, a handful of large, brightly coloured plastic bricks and a soft purple object, which bore a faint resemblance to a monkey. The child was crying in a half-hearted way – not from pain or sorrow, I guessed, but because he could think of nothing better to do.

When he saw me looming over him outside the door, the crying stopped. He looked up at me with round blue eyes and his mouth opened in astonishment. Behind him was a grubby kitchen in need of a complete refit. I tried the effect of a smile. The child stared blankly at me and his mouth opened wider. I nudged the door further open with my foot.

'Hey!'

I turned in the direction of the sound. A sturdy woman was walking quickly towards me. She had short dark hair and wore a paint-stained T-shirt and jeans. She looked in her late twenties or early thirties. 'What do you think you're doing?'

I smiled at her. 'Sorry – I hope I didn't surprise you. I tried knocking and ringing the bell but there was no answer. Maybe I've got the wrong house.'

'More than likely.'

Some of the hostility had gone. I don't sound or look like a debt collector or a burglar, which probably counted in my favour. Another child appeared behind the woman – this one was definitely a girl of four or five. She clung to her mother's T-shirt and stared at me. There was a ring of chocolate round her mouth.

'So who do you want?' the woman said.

'I'm looking for Sean Fielding.'

'He's not here.'

'So he does live here?'

She nodded. 'But if you've come about the car, I might as well tell you you're wasting your time.'

'The car?'

'The one in the paper this week.'

The girl yanked her mother's T-shirt. 'It's not Daddy's car, it's yours.'

'In theory,' the woman said. 'It's Daddy's, really. Anyway, I don't think anyone will want to buy it now.'

'What's happened to it?' I asked.

She glanced at me. 'Someone took the wheels off and set it on fire. So now it's not a car. It's a piece of scrap metal somewhere in Peckham.' She detached the child's hand from her T-shirt. 'Don't do that, Maisie.'

'I'm sorry,' I said. 'I've come at a bad time.'

The woman's mouth was a thin straight line. 'Where Sean's concerned, it's always a bad time.' She ruffled the little girl's hair. 'Still, we'll manage.'

'I haven't come about the car, actually.'

She bent and gave the child a gentle push towards the doorway. 'Go and look after Albert, darling. He wants to play with you.'

The girl went into the house, squeezing herself against the wall, as far away from me as possible. She tried to pick up her brother, who shouted until she stopped.

'Why do you want him?' the woman said quietly. 'Does he owe you money?'

'No. It's not him I'm looking for, really – it's a friend of his. Her mother's ill.'

Albert howled with rage. Maisie had taken the monkey.

'Play nicely, darling,' the woman said, without much conviction. Her voice hardened. 'Her? Is it Kate?'

I nodded.

'It's my monkey,' Maisie said. 'Albert stole it. He's a thief.'

'Are you a friend of hers?'

I said carefully, 'I hardly know her, but I used to know her mother quite well. That's all.'

Albert lost interest in the monkey. He fell silent and chewed a plastic car.

'I don't know where the cow is, and I don't care.'

'What about Sean?'

'Your guess is as good as mine. I thought he was here. The first I knew was when I had a call from the police about the car – it's still registered at my address and in my name. I tried to ring him but I couldn't get an answer so I thought we'd better come over.' She wrinkled up her face. 'He was going to sell the car and split the proceeds with us. Some hope. With Sean, it always goes wrong.'

'Any idea where he might be?'

'Somewhere with Kate? Maybe she's living in Peckham, these days. Bit of a comedown.' Her voice was jerky now, the words coming in spurts as though pumped out under pressure. 'I thought she was ancient history as far as Sean's concerned. She wasn't going to hang around after he got fired. Not her style at all.'

I glanced into the kitchen. The children were playing in a more or less co-operative manner with the purple monkey, the plastic car and an empty cereal packet. 'I didn't realize that Sean –'

'Was married with two kids? Nor does he, half the time. That's the problem. And Kate never gave a toss anyway. If it wasn't for her, we'd still be together.'

'What happened?'

For a moment I thought she would tell me to mind my own business. Then she shrugged and said, 'You really want to know?'

I nodded.

'You won't get the truth from Kate so you might as well have it from me. The first thing you need to know about her is that you can't believe a word she says. Come and sit down – if you can find a chair you can trust in this tip.'

For an instant I was surprised she had invited me into the house. Then I grasped that she didn't really care any more and she was desperate for someone to talk to. We went into the kitchen and squatted on stools at the table. Maisie and Albert scrapped and scuffled like a pair of puppies around our feet.

Her name was Emily, she said, and she had met Sean Fielding at university when she was in her first year and he was in his third. Two years later, she had married him. It had seemed like a good idea at the time because she had been pregnant with Maisie.

Sean was working for a firm in the City. They invested other people's money. His face fitted; the timing was right. His employers showered him with promotions and bonuses. Soon the Fieldings could afford to buy an early-Victorian farmhouse with five acres in south Cambridgeshire. Sean leased a flat in Long Acre with a garage in the basement for the Lotus. It was more convenient if he had an early start at the office, which he increasingly did. Emily spent most of her time with Maisie in Cambridgeshire. A woman came in five days a week to help with the cleaning and the more mundane side of the house-keeping, and a firm of contract gardeners kept the garden in trim.

'I suppose I thought it would always be like that,' Emily said. 'I'd never known any different, not since I left university. I used to worry about whether my soufflé would rise when we had people round for dinner. Or whether we'd get Maisie into the right pre-prep school.'

I didn't have to prompt her much. Bitterness fuelled her, and perhaps loneliness too. She wasn't really interested in why I was there, except in so far as it might affect herself and Sean. She had enough problems of her own without worrying about other people's.

'But it started to fall apart after Albert was born. I sort of lost interest in Sean. I took him for granted, I suppose. What I didn't know was that he was having a hard time at work. The market had changed.

Suddenly he wasn't the favourite face in the office any more.'

Beneath us, the children wriggled through the forest of legs – the chairs', the table's, Emily's and mine. Albert tripped over my foot, fell on his face and started to wail. Emily bent down and scooped him up. Still talking, she held him against her and patted his back until he quietened.

'Sean wasn't very good at handling that. He needs to feel loved – don't we all? Spoiled rotten by his bloody mother, that's his problem. If he doesn't feel loved, he does stupid stuff. He was making mistakes, and that made everything worse. Then he started losing his temper. It was just before that he'd started seeing Kate.'

'How did they meet?'

'She worked for one of his colleagues. Must have thought she had a meal ticket for life. Well, she had a nasty shock in September. Sean got the sack. They told him to clear his desk by the end of the after-noon, and don't bother coming back. He phoned me with the news but I was out, so he left a message. I tried to call him back but he wasn't answering so I picked up the kids and went up to town. I turned up at the flat and there was Kate.' Emily shrugged. 'The bastard didn't know what had hit him.'

The Fieldings' lives had disintegrated in a matter of weeks. Sean had lost his job. He had lost his wife and children because of the girlfriend, and he lost the girlfriend because he'd lost his job. He lost the flat because he couldn't afford the lease. Neither he nor Emily had had much in the way of savings because they had always lived up to their income.

'And Kate was always going on at him too. He didn't know what he'd let himself in for.' Emily glanced across the table. 'Tell you one thing, I feel sorry for Kate's mother. That girl's weird. Seriously weird.'

Sean had sold the Lotus. He and Emily put their home on the market. Once the mortgage was paid off there was just enough money for Sean to put down a deposit on this house and for Emily to put down a deposit on an even smaller one in Bedford.

'We keep in touch, of course,' Emily said. 'For the sake of the kids. Give him his due, he's quite fond of them as long as he doesn't have to spend much time with them. Anyway, the divorce hasn't come through. Both the cars are in my name – it's cheaper to insure them that way.' She picked at a congealed smear of tomato sauce on the chipped Formica top of the table. 'Are you sure he's seeing Kate again?'

'I think so.'

But if Kate was right, Sean wasn't seeing anyone or anything. He would never see his children again, and they would never see him. Emily lifted Albert from her lap and lowered him gently to the floor. Maisie hugged him fiercely and hit him with the purple monkey, which made him giggle.

'What do you think?' I asked.

Emily rested her elbows on the table. 'I can't help wondering if he's gone off for good. With her, I mean.'

'Why?'

'If she whistled, he'd go to her – no question. When I saw them together he was always watching her. Like a dog, you know. A dog that's worried it's going to be left behind. And there's nothing to keep him here, is there?' She hesitated. 'I had a look round. I can't find things like his passport. Or his bank stuff. I phoned his mum but she hasn't heard from him and that's odd. They're really close – he told her he'd been sacked before he told me.' Her face quivered. 'I – I just hope he's OK. He's such a bloody fool. He needs someone to look after him. He's like a kid in some ways. Maisie's got more sense than him.'

She gave me her telephone number in case I heard any news of him, and I gave her my mobile number in return.

'And another thing,' she said, as I was leaving. 'He's not answering his mobile. That's not like him.'

When I left the house, she was still sitting in the kitchen. The children were getting fractious but I think she was waiting for Sean.

I drove home to Greyfont. Emily's Sean seemed to bear little relation to Kate's. They might almost have been different people. And I was no nearer to finding Kate, let alone Sean. I was just more confused. If there was more than one version of Sean, perhaps there was more than one version of Carlo.

Before I reached the motorway, I pulled over and phoned first Nicky, then Kate. Neither answered. I phoned the hospice. The woman on the switchboard told me that Lily was asleep. I asked her to say that Jamie sent his love and that I would be in touch.

It was mid-afternoon before I turned on to the patch of gravel outside our house. Nicky's Mini Cooper was parked outside the garage.

9

Nicky said, 'There's someone else, isn't there?'

'No. No, there isn't.'

We were upstairs in the bedroom. She had two suitcases open on the bed, the big blue one we took on holiday and the smaller one we used for weekends. She was carefully folding shirts, skirts and trousers and putting shoes in bags.

'You haven't been talking to me for weeks. For months, even. Not properly – not since we moved here. I thought you might be seeing someone else but I wasn't sure, not till this weekend.' She slipped a new toothbrush into the smaller suitcase. 'Now it all makes sense.'

'It makes nonsense. Where do you think you're going?'

'It's not nonsense. And where I'm going is no concern of yours.'

I glared at her and she glared at me.

I tried to throttle back my anger. 'I'm sorry if –'

'I don't care if you're sorry or not. You lied to me. It's the one thing I thought you'd never do. I can put up with your moods and your silences but not lying. I thought you understood that.'

'There's been a mistake.'

'You mean you've made a mistake.'

'No. I mean you're jumping to the wrong conclusion.'

'I don't think so. Where were you on Friday?'

'I told you, I was working.'

'Not according to Rachel.'

'You asked *Rachel*?'

Nicky put a towel in the big suitcase and concentrated on smoothing away the wrinkles. 'Of course I did. I often talk to her. You probably haven't noticed but we're quite good friends.'

'That's spying.'

'Don't be stupid. I haven't tried to conceal it. Anyway, I like her, and she's your assistant. She sees more of you than I do, so it makes a lot of sense.'

'But why didn't you mention it?' I asked.

'You never asked. You never *noticed*. Which did not surprise me. You spend most of your life hermetically sealed in a bubble. She tells me a damn sight more about what's going on at the office than you do.' She picked up two pairs of shoes and considered them. Then she held first one pair, then the other against a dress that was already in the suitcase. 'And you weren't working. That's a direct lie. Rachel said you phoned in and –'

'I was working before that.'

'Before what? Before you went off to your lover? Is that what you call her? Or is she your bit on the side? Your young woman? Did you know Dave Hammett saw you on Friday night with your – your young woman? Is that why you like her, by the way?

Because she's young? Younger than me? Because she can have –'

'She's not my young woman,' I interrupted. 'And I don't –'

'Then who is she?'

'She's – she's just someone I'm helping. I will explain, I promise, but not now. I can't.'

'Is she called Lily? Rachel said she kept ringing the office on Friday, that she sounded quite upset.'

'That's someone else. An old friend who's very ill. In fact, she's dying.'

'So that's another person I haven't heard of. What else haven't you told me?'

Nicky continued packing, her movements deft and methodical. My head hurt. I dropped my jacket on to the bed and went into the bathroom. I opened the cabinet and took out the paracetamol.

'Miranda says she's very attractive, according to Dave. Very sexy.' Nicky had pursued me and was standing in the doorway. 'Whatever her name is. She said Dave was quite smitten.'

Nicky's face was still beautiful, but bleak. I told myself that jealousy corroded not only other emotions but also how the sufferer thinks. Nicky feared this: therefore it existed. My apparent affair with Kate had taken on independent life.

'This has been coming for a long time, hasn't it?' she went on. 'You know what really hurt? That you let her come here, to our home. This house was meant to be special, remember?'

I poured myself a glass of water and popped one

of the capsules out of the foil. 'Look, this business is something out of the past, long before I met you.'

'Does that make it any better – assuming what you say is true? The point is, it's not in the past, it's now, and it's affecting you and me.'

I swallowed the second capsule. 'It's over.'

'Is it? Not for me.'

'I'm not having an affair. I never have and never will.' I followed her back into the bedroom. 'This was about something else.'

She closed the lid of the smaller suitcase, snapped the locks and straightened up. She stared at me like an accuser, like a judge. 'We started to go wrong a long time ago, didn't we? You know why.'

I looked away.

'I need time to think,' she said. 'I'm going away for a few days to work out what to do. But I tell you one thing, James. I've had enough. I can't go on like this.'

At that moment my mobile gave two sharp bleeps. Someone had sent me a message. Nicky swung round as though the sound had stung her like a wasp. She picked up my jacket and patted the pockets until she found the phone. She stabbed at the keys and stared down at the tiny screen. Her face changed. Still bleak, still cold and now, I thought, suddenly much older.

'You see?' She tossed the phone down on the bed. 'You bastard. It's not over.'

When Nicky had gone I went downstairs and sat in the study, a small room that contained nothing but a desk, a chair, a filing cabinet and bookshelves. I sat at the desk, flipped open the laptop and switched it on. Immediately in front of me was a framed photograph of Nicky, smiling.

While the computer was humming and churning, I opened the envelope I had taken from the Murthingtons' house in Chipping Weston and pulled out the contents. I put the photograph of Felicity, the eternal girl-woman, on the desk with the floral birthday card beside it. Why had Carlo put them into his backpack? Why now?

I took the phone out of my pocket and put it beside the card. I tapped a key. The phone beeped and its screen came to life. Kate's message was still there.

'Sorry to leave like that. You were great. Will call. Love K xxx.'

Not many words but quite enough to be going on with, certainly enough for Nicky to misinterpret.

I logged on and ran a search linking Sean Fielding with Rackford. Nothing came up.

What did I have to go on? I brought up the word-processing program and made a list.

Lily was dying.

She said Kate was on the run from the police because it looked as if she'd killed Sean, her former boyfriend.

Kate was certainly acting like someone on the run – she was so paranoid that I wondered if she was mentally unstable.

Kate said Carlo had killed Sean. According to her, Carlo hated Lily and Kate because of what Lily and I had done all those years ago.

Carlo was capable of violence. Or, at least, he had been as a teenager.

Emily hated Kate. Emily thought Sean had done a runner. Emily said he had put up his car for sale, but that the police reported it had been stolen and wrecked in London.

Now the land at Rackford was potentially valuable, Kate said, and Carlo wanted it all. I wasn't sure of the legal position and, in any case, it would depend on the terms of Hugh Murthington's will. But if he had left his estate in trust while Lily was alive, then on her death to be divided between Carlo and Kate, what would happen if Kate predeceased her mother? Would her share of the estate be transferred automatically to Carlo? If that was true, perhaps Kate was right to be paranoid.

And Lily had shown me a tarnished fragment of very fine chain with a scrap of metal hanging from it.

Looking at the list in front of me, I realized I was taking a lot on trust. I couldn't be sure that Emily was telling the truth. I wanted to believe Lily because she was dying and Kate because she was so desperate. But I wondered whether I wanted to believe them both for another reason, because on some level I felt I deserved to pay the price for what had happened all those years ago.

I highlighted the text and pressed delete.

If I could turn back the clock, I would return to the point just before everything went out of control, in other words to the moment when Lily had kissed me in the hall at Christmas. It was the first hint that she might be interested in me. Previously I had taken it for granted that what I felt could never be reciprocated in a million years. Indeed, I wasn't sure what I did feel. I had no words for it, or rather none that seemed to fit. I had no experience, no means of calibrating what was happening except the romanticized half-truths I'd picked up from films and books.

Lily had kissed me when she gave me the Christmas present. In my more rational moments I wondered whether I had misunderstood the implications. After all, I had no experience of how women worked. Perhaps it was the sort of thing a friend's mother might do out of the kindness of her heart. She might have thought I was lonely and needed cheering up. She might have been trying to fill the gap left by my own mother's absence.

But the rational moments were relatively few and far between. At school, in the months that followed the Christmas holiday, I thought about Lily constantly. Every night, as I lay in the darkness of the dormitory, I would replay the memories like a video: the first time I saw her, in the garden under the ash tree with Felicity when she had called me Jamie; the time she lay on the grass after the picnic and I watched her sleeping; and, most often of all, the kiss in the hall. Sometimes I went further than that, and made up my own stories, my own videos, which left me breathless and unsatisfied. Ignorance was not bliss. It was a nightmare.

The present she had given me acted as a constant

reminder. I couldn't wait until Christmas Day to open it. I tore off the wrapping paper when I was on the train to London. She had given me a watch with bold Roman numerals on a bracelet of expanding stainless steel. Heavy and obviously expensive, it clung to my wrist like a shackle. When no one was looking I would fondle it, even kiss it, and think that perhaps Lily had done the same.

As the weeks went by, I waited on tenterhooks for an invitation to stay during the Easter holidays, but I had to wait until nearly the end of term before Carlo asked me. We were smoking what we hoped was dope one Sunday afternoon when he mentioned it. I took my time answering, sucking at the joint and blowing out the sweet, acrid smoke before I said yes, I thought I could manage it. I added, 'Are you sure your dad and Lily won't mind?'

He grinned evilly at me. 'They think you're a good influence. If you come to stay I've got someone nice to hang around with, which gets them off the hook. They think we spend our time solving maths problems and reading Shakespeare. And if you weren't there I'd be chasing girls, smoking dope and getting pissed.'

'"Once more into the breach, dear friends, once more",' I recited. 'Do you want the roach?'

So I went back to Chipping Weston during the Easter holidays of 1980. I was sixteen and a half. Carlo and I had been friends for so long that we took each other for granted. Not just Carlo – his family treated me almost as one of themselves, as a cousin, perhaps, rather than a nearer relative.

At Chipping Weston, I became a spy. I didn't want to but I had no choice. I did what I had to do and hoped that, whatever the reason for it, this strange and embarrassing state of mind would soon pass. In the two weeks of the Easter holiday, I watched Lily constantly and surreptitiously. I noticed what she was wearing and where she went. I speculated endlessly about what she was thinking and feeling.

Once I saw her in the hall as I was coming down the stairs. She was wearing a dressing-gown and it had fallen open slightly at the neck. For an instant I saw her left breast. I glimpsed the darker pink of the nipple. She turned away and, tightening the belt, continued telling Felicity why it was sensible to keep your room tidy.

The glimpse of Lily's breast haunted my waking life and sometimes I saw it again in my dreams. What I felt for her had nothing to do with love. It was something inside me – in my belly, in my throat – something that yearned to escape but didn't know why or where it would go if it did. It was an aching obsession, an appetite that was almost impersonal in its nature, as inexorable as hunger but far less explicable.

Love implies a concern for the beloved's well-being. I didn't wish Lily any harm, but her happiness was irrelevant beside the urgency of my need for what only she could give me. I knew it must all come down to sex, but I didn't understand how or why. My enthusiastic exploration of masturbation and pornographic magazines seemed to inhabit a different universe, sunlit and straightforward. Why did I want *her*, for God's sake, when there was a world full of girls out there? It made no sense.

I tried with increasing desperation to engineer situations where Lily and I could be alone. Hugh Murthington, Felicity or Carlo always intruded. Nor did Lily help me. It was as if she had erased that kiss in the hall from her memory. Perhaps I had made a terrible mistake – and it really had been a friendly, aunt-like kiss that had somehow missed its way and found my lips. Perhaps I'd imagined the air of furtiveness, the secrecy. Perhaps my own desire had been so intense that I had seen it reflected in her eyes.

I saw everything refracted through my hunger for Lily. For example, I noticed that Mr Murthington was very busy, and that he seemed abstracted – he was even quieter than usual at meals, and in the four months since Christmas he seemed to have aged as many years. I remember thinking that Lily looked young enough to be his daughter, which lent a faint respectability to how I felt about her. I liked Hugh Murthington, what I knew of him, and I didn't want to injure him, but if to all intents and purposes he was Lily's father rather than her husband there was less to worry about. The logic of lust makes strange flights of reason.

One of the hardest things to bear was when Lily talked to me and others were there. She asked me about school, about my family. She was interested in the music I was listening to – or rather, perhaps, she pretended to be – and my plans for the future. I dared not look at her while I replied. I was terrified that my face and my stumbling words must give away my feelings not just to her but to everyone else in the room.

I almost longed for the holiday to be over. The driving lessons at Rackford were particularly bad. Lily was so close to me when I was at the wheel. Sometimes she touched my hand or brushed against my leg. Carlo was always in the back seat, and usually Felicity, sometimes her friend Millie as well. At that time, Millie was a plump child who talked only to Felicity and laughed when Carlo said anything. It didn't occur to me until much later that she and I might have had something in common.

On the Thursday after Easter, while Hugh Murthington was at his office in town, Lily decided that she wanted a trunk down from the loft. She asked Carlo and me to help her.

'She probably keeps the bloodless bodies of her victims up there,' Carlo murmured in my ear.

We carried a step-ladder upstairs from the shed. Carlo grumbled about having to help but he'd never been in the loft before and the grumbling was more for show than anything else. The loft was at the back of the house, over the bathroom, Felicity's room and the passage from the main landing, and the hatch was in the bathroom ceiling.

Felicity, who was in her bedroom next door, was practising the recorder. She was working her way through 'On Top of Old Smoky'. Her music teacher was going to give a record token to the girl who made

146

the most progress in playing the recorder over the holidays. Felicity and Millie were both desperate to win the prize, and both of them practised religiously every day, sometimes simultaneously and in the same room. Even now when I hear a recorder I think of Lily – of the agony of wanting someone so badly and not being able to have her. I think of Felicity too.

Carlo was first up the ladder. He pushed aside the hatch and hauled himself into the darkness beyond. His legs dangled through the opening. A shower of dust floated down to the floor.

'Is there a light?' he called down, his voice muffled.

'I don't think so,' Lily said. 'Hang on, I'll get a torch.'

Her arm brushed mine as she left the bathroom – but with a step-ladder in the middle of the floor there wasn't much space. She gave me a half-smile, as if in apology. I climbed up the ladder and poked my head and shoulders through the opening. Carlo was at the far end of the loft where the light from the hatch barely reached.

'Bloody hell,' he said. 'There's a wasps' nest. It's enormous.'

My eyes adjusted. The loft was like a tent, its sloping roofs hung with cobwebs and grey with dirt and dust. A central gangway stretched into the shadows where Carlo was. On either side were the unwanted remnants of family life – suitcases, trunks and boxes; rolls of carpet; stacks of magazines tied up with yellowing string; pictures in heavy old frames that no one wanted to look at any more.

'Jesus,' Carlo said, 'it's bigger than a football. There's enough room for a whole fucking army of them.'

I heard footsteps beneath me and looked down. Lily had returned to the bathroom. She passed up the torch to me. I turned it on. The beam slid up the gangway, climbed Carlo's crouching shadow and came to rest on a dirty white globular shape clinging to the angle where the roof timbers met a chimney breast.

'It's huge,' I said.

'What is?' Lily said below.

'There's a wasps' nest,' I said.

'I don't think it's live,' Carlo said. He scrambled back to the hatch. Even in the centre of the loft, where the gangway was, there wasn't room to stand up and he had to crouch. In his excitement, he almost snatched the torch from me. He crawled back to the nest.

'Be careful,' Lily called up.

He ignored her. I turned towards the sound of her voice. She was staring up at me. Felicity was still playing the recorder.

'Jamie, could you come down a moment?' She sounded breathless, almost on the edge of panic. 'There's a daddy-long-legs in the basin.'

'Are you OK?' I said, climbing down the ladder.

'I know it's stupid. It's just that I can't stand them.'

I edged past Lily and scooped up the insect. She gave a little cry, half fearful, half admiring. I opened the window and dropped the daddy-long-legs on to the sloping roof outside. I turned. Lily was beside me. 'Thank you,' she whispered. 'Is there something in my hair? Another? I felt something moving.'

I took a step nearer and looked carefully at her dark hair. Lily shivered. She was wearing a cream silk shirt and I was aware of her breasts just inches away from me. I felt the warmth of her body. My breathing was rapid and growing faster. The recorder played on. Carlo was still moving at the far end of the loft.

'Nearer,' she commanded. 'You'll see better.'

Her hands rested on my shoulders. Suddenly there was no longer a space between our bodies, and there was nothing aunt-like about her now. Her hands slipped down my arms and joined behind my back. She moistened her lips, and their flesh gleamed pink.

'I think it's gone now,' she said, in a voice that was almost normal. 'I can't feel it, anyway.'

Carlo was muttering to himself. Felicity was now practising 'The Skye Boat Song', repeating the first four bars of the tune over and over again and making at least one mistake each time. Lily Murthington was kissing me, and I was kissing her.

10

Nicky had gone. When I woke up on Monday morning, the sun was shining, sending a bar of golden light across the ceiling. For two or three seconds it felt good to be alive. Then I remembered what had happened. I pushed my hand across the bed and felt a cool sheet where a warm body ought to have been.

It was the start of the working week. I got up and checked the phone for messages that weren't there. Over coffee I skimmed through my emails. There was nothing of even the slightest interest, apart from the one that Rachel had sent late on Friday afternoon containing the agenda for that morning's meeting.

There was nothing I could do, nothing that would bring Nicky back to me, nothing that would resolve the problem of Kate. In the end I walked to the station and caught the usual train into town. I needed a distraction of some sort, something to fill the front of my mind, and work was as good as anything. I reasoned that Nicky would expect me to go into the office. She knew how to contact me there. If Kate needed me she would phone the mobile.

The office was in the tangle of streets south of Smithfield market. The contents of my in-tray and the ritual exchanges of office life filled the hour and a half before the meeting began. Rachel broke with tradition and brought me a cup of coffee, usually something I did for myself unless I had a client with me. I wondered whether she knew or had guessed that Nicky had left me. It depended on the nature of the friendship between her and Nicky. What else was there I didn't know? Once you allow doubts into your life they don't trickle, they come in a flood.

I never said much at these weekly meetings. I said even less today. Afterwards Rachel, who had been taking the minutes, followed me out. 'Are you OK?' she asked.

'Fine, thanks.' I turned away to pour myself a glass of water I didn't want.

'You seem a bit under the weather.'

'You know how it is – that Monday-morning feeling.'

She looked at me curiously. I was uncomfortably aware of her intelligence probing my weaknesses. Perhaps she was even trying to help. For the first time it occurred to me that she knew me better than I knew her. I certainly hadn't realized how friendly she and Nicky had become.

As if catching the echo of my thoughts, Rachel said, 'Nicky said something about you working late on Friday.'

I sipped water. 'That chapel in Queen's Park – I forgot to do some of the measurements. I had to go back.'

'She thought I'd said something. You know, when you phoned in. Something that made you late, I mean.'

'Crossed wires,' I said. 'Which reminds me, I

dictated the draft report on the chapel while I was there. Would you type it up and marry it with the plans? We'll need it in presentable form by Thursday.'

I tried to work but it was impossible to settle. In the end I went out early for lunch. In the street, I passed a delicatessen I occasionally used and the sight of its window gave me an idea. I sometimes bought things for supper there on the days that Nicky was working. Monday was one of her gallery days. It was just possible that even now she might be in Kew. She took her responsibilities seriously. It was one thing to leave me, I told myself bitterly, but quite another to leave her job.

I took the tube to Kew. I didn't want to phone in case she refused to speak to me. The gallery where she worked was on the main road north of the bridge. Once it had been a greengrocer's shop. Now the ground floor had been turned into a long thin display area with a small office at the back.

That was where I found Victor, with his feet on the desk. He was eating an overripe melon and the juice was running down his chin. Mahler's *Kindertotenlieder* was on the stereo, a choice of music I could have done without. Victor was wearing a pair of very short shorts, which showed off his thin, slightly bowed legs, a short-sleeved shirt and a pair of glasses with large, heavy rims. Nicky said he resembled a frog and she was right. He gazed at me with the beginnings of a frown.

'I'm James,' I said, as I said every time I saw him. 'Nicky's husband.'

'Of course. I know. Sit down, lad, don't just stand there.' Victor came from Yorkshire and believed he had a professional obligation to speak bluntly. 'What are you doing here?'

I wished he'd turn off the Mahler. 'Nicky's not in?'

He glared at me, swung his legs off the desk and wiped his chin with a paper handkerchief. 'Of course she isn't. Why on earth do you think she might be?'

'Maybe there're crossed wires,' I said, using what seemed to be becoming my formula of the day. 'I must have misunderstood something she said.'

'More likely you weren't listening.' He hesitated. 'She's off work this week. I'm surprised you don't know.'

'Like I said, crossed wires.'

He grunted. 'What have you been doing to her?'

'I beg your pardon?'

Victor waved a finger at me. 'She was upset. She phoned me yesterday evening and I knew she was. I can always tell. I feel it here.' He laid his hand over his heart and patted himself approvingly. 'I've a strong sense of intuition. Have you had a row?'

Suddenly I was tired of pretending. 'Something like that.'

'You bloody fool. A woman like that, it's bound to be your fault. I'd marry her myself, like a shot, if she'd have me. If I was that way inclined.' He pushed back his chair and stood up to his full height of five foot three. 'Well, she's not here, is she? Where are you going to look next?'

'I don't know.'

'You could ask some of her friends.'

'Which friends?'

Victor poked his tongue into his cheek. 'She does have them, you know. Too many, if you ask me.' He stared aggressively at me, as though I had tried to contradict him. '"I pay you to work," I tell her, "not to provide a floorshow of your social life." That was after the other day, when that Miranda woman descended on us.'

'Miranda Hammett?'

'Could be – I don't recall.'

'When was this?'

'Tuesday.' He registered that I hadn't been aware of it. 'You know what women are like when they get chatting. Like sparrows in your back garden. Tweet-tweet-tweet. Drives you mad if you have to listen to it for long. And Nicky kept trying to get hold of that man on the phone. My phone, I might add. He was meant to be meeting them here too.'

At last *Kindertotenlieder* stopped. In the sudden silence, I said, 'Who was the man?'

Victor glanced into the mirror over the fireplace and put his head on one side. His eyes met mine in the glass. 'How should I know? He didn't come here in the end.'

'Do you know whose friend he was – Miranda's or Nicky's?'

'I don't know anything.' Victor rubbed his chin with the handkerchief again. 'No, I'm wrong. I do know one thing. Miranda and Nicky were saying he'd be much better looking if he shaved off his beard.'

*

'I'm in a hurry, James,' Miranda said. 'Can't it wait?'

'No,' I said. 'It's about Nicky.'

She stopped beside the driver's door of her enormous Mercedes off-roader, the keys jingling in her hand. 'Haven't you found her yet?'

'I saw her on Sunday.'

Miranda's eyes were blank behind her sunglasses. 'But she's gone off again, is that it?'

'I'm not quite sure where she is.'

'Sorry, I can't help you.' She opened the door and hauled her heavy body behind the wheel. 'Wish I could but there it is. Now I must rush.'

'Wait.' The window was open and I rested my hand on the sill. 'Maybe she's with a friend.'

'Maybe. Everyone needs friends.' She turned her head and looked at me. 'Well, most people, anyway.'

'I went to Nicky's gallery at lunchtime. Victor said you'd been there on Tuesday, and that you and Nicky were meeting a friend.'

Miranda started the engine and gave a high laugh that went on for too long. 'Charlie? Yes, he's in the book group too.'

She revved the engine, which rumbled menacingly. 'Sorry, James, you'd better ask Nicky. Look, I really must go – I've got to fetch the dry-cleaning, and then I've got to pick up the kids from school. There'll be hell to pay if I'm late.'

The Mercedes crept down the drive. I walked with it for a few paces. I still had my hand on the door.

'Just one thing.' I hated the note of pleading in my voice. 'What's his other name? Where does he live?'

The Mercedes reached the end of the drive. The driver's door was so near the gatepost I had to let go to avoid being crushed. Miranda said something, perhaps in reply, but the words were drowned by the thunder of the engine. She pulled into the road and accelerated away. She didn't wave.

I walked back to our empty house. Increasingly paranoid questions flickered through my mind like a silent movie. I knew they were paranoid but once you start asking questions, it's hard to stop, and they made a vile kind of sense. Was there a friendship between Nicky and Charlie, even an affair? Could Charlie even be Carlo? Had Carlo targeted Nicky because she was my wife? If so, how much had he told her? Because if Carlo had told her everything, it would have given her another, perhaps stronger, reason to leave me.

But no one knows everything. I didn't know what any of the Murthingtons were up to, or Nicky. The only thing I knew for certain was that I was scared.

I tried Nicky's mobile again. I went straight through to voicemail. I left a message, more urgent than before, begging her to ring for her own sake. I texted her too. I couldn't even warn her.

I thought about going to the police. But what could I tell them? Women leave their husbands every day. There was no question of her being compelled to go. I didn't have a shred of evidence to encourage them to take me seriously.

But if Kate was right, and Carlo had killed Sean, then what was to stop him killing Nicky too?

*

I drove to the hospice, buying flowers at a service station on the way. A nurse I recognized was chatting with the receptionist.

'Lily's awake. Do you want to go straight through?' She looked at the flowers I was carrying. 'Freesias – my favourite.'

'They're Lily's, too,' I said. 'Or they used to be.'

I walked along the corridor to her room. The door was open. She was propped against the pillows. Her unopened book and a glass of water stood on the table over the bed. The news was on the radio but I don't think she was listening. I hesitated in the doorway and watched her drifting through an internal space whose geography I couldn't begin to imagine.

She caught sight of me and frowned.

'Hi,' I said, suddenly as awkward as I'd been at sixteen. 'How are you?'

It took her a few seconds to recognize me. 'Still here.'

I bent down and kissed her cheek, which seemed the natural thing to do. 'I brought you some flowers.'

'Freesias. Nice.' She smiled, drawing back thin, bloodless lips. 'You remembered.'

'What shall I do with them?'

'Vases in the wardrobe. Water in the shower-room.'

I put the freesias in water and stood the vase on the windowsill.

'No,' Lily said. 'Put them here.' She touched the edge of the table in front of her. 'I want to see them. I want to smell them.'

I obeyed her. Her eyes followed my movements.

The pupils were black pinholes. She smiled at me, her lips lifting to reveal long, yellowing teeth set in receding gums. 'I was dreaming,' she said. 'Though it didn't seem like a dream. I was remembering when I met Hugh. He seemed so old.'

I said, 'I've got a problem. I didn't know who else to come to so I came to you.'

'He was wearing a dark blue pinstripe suit and carrying a rolled-up umbrella. I wouldn't be surprised if he had a bowler, too. Even then he looked about twenty years behind the times. As if he'd wandered out of an Ealing comedy and got lost in the future.'

'Lily, I really need to –'

'He was making me old. That's why I liked you, you see. You made me young. And you were very sweet. So was Hugh, but that was different.'

She wasn't looking at me any longer but at the freesias. She began to hum. There wasn't any tune to it but by the way the sounds were spaced I thought it might be 'You've Lost That Loving Feeling' by the Righteous Brothers. She used to like that song. I wished I hadn't come. I wished they hadn't given her so much morphine. I picked up the biography of the dead actress. The humming stopped abruptly.

'No, not oysters,' Lily said. 'I don't like seafood.' She smiled, this time with her lips closed and her eyes swung slowly towards me. She blinked. 'Jamie. It is Jamie, isn't it? You've changed. Yes, thank you – I might read for a bit.' She held out her hand.

I gave her the book. 'Have you heard from Kate?'

She shook her head slowly from side to side, rolling

it to and fro against the pillow. 'Not for a day or two, I think. But you're looking after her. She's – she's your daughter.'

'She went away on Saturday,' I said. 'I don't know where she is now.'

'You must find her.' Lily's hands scratched the blankets on top of her, trying to get a grip. 'She needs you to look after her.'

'Kate can take care of herself.'

'Don't be silly. You will look after her.' Her voice was rising in volume. 'Promise me you will. Promise me. You owe her that.'

I leaned forward and took her hands, trying to quieten her. 'I promise,' I said.

'And you'll find her? You'll keep her safe from Carlo?'

'Yes. Actually, it's Carlo I want to talk about.'

'He never liked me. I thought he wouldn't come back. But he wants the money.'

'Where is he?'

'Carlo? Oh, he upset Hugh so much, going off like that after the divorce. Hugh never really got over it. It was so unkind.'

'It's just possible that Nicky may be with him. With Carlo. That's why I want to find him.'

Lily frowned at me. 'Who's Nicky?'

'My wife. She's got hold of the wrong end of the stick about Kate and she's gone off. And I can't get hold of her.'

It was no use. Lily's mind was following its own train of thought. 'He and Felicity used to gang up against me. And I tried so hard with them – it wasn't my fault their mother died. I was only trying to make their father happy. What's wrong with that?'

'I need to find Carlo now.'

'Find him? Whatever for?'

I had learned cunning. 'For Kate's sake.'

Lily's face began to shake as if a small earthquake were taking place inside her skull. 'He's trying to hurt her,' she whispered.

'I want to stop him. But I have to find him first. Where is he?'

She shrugged. 'He's come home now. He wants everything. That's why he's come.'

'I know he's come home. But where –'

'I expect he's at home.'

I leaned forward and took her left hand in both of mine. 'Lily? Where's home for Carlo?'

'Where it always was.'

'In Chipping Weston? But he's not living there, is he? Where's his real home?'

She was drifting away from me. 'I do like freesias.' She touched one and smiled. 'Is she nice?'

'Who?'

'Your wife, of course. Nicky.'

11

Freesias. I learned about freesias from Hugh
Murthington. I don't think I'd even heard their name
before. It was near the end of the Easter holidays
and he had had to go to London for something connected with business. When I knew him, he seemed
always to be busy but to achieve little. I suspect that
by this time he was losing considerable sums of
money. Years ago, he had promised to buy Carlo a
car when he passed his test – an MGB. But one night
last term, when we were very drunk on a bottle of
rum, Carlo had told me that his father said there
might be a bit of a delay.

'It's business, you see,' Carlo had said, with a wave
of the hand that somehow implied he was privy to
enormous financial secrets. 'You get good years and
bad years. Upturns and downswings. We're in a bit
of a downswing now because of the fucking unions
and the change in the interest rate.'

That morning in Chipping Weston, Mr Murthington
beckoned Carlo and me as he left the house, briefcase
in hand, umbrella hooked over his arm. When we were
in the garden, he took out his wallet, removed a five-
pound note and gave it to Carlo. 'Yes – ah – I'd like
you to look in at the florist's. Will you do that for me?'

Carlo nodded.

'Will you buy some freesias? They said they should have them in today.'

'What do you want me to do with them?'

'They're for Lily. She's – she's particularly fond of them. I thought you boys could give them to her.' He hesitated, his hand on the gate, and looked back at us. 'Say they're from you. No need to mention me, eh?'

He strode down the road. From the back, Hugh Murthington looked quite different – purged of diffidence and uncertainty: he was upright and commanding, a leader among men, albeit one made in a rather old-fashioned mould.

Carlo watched his father, his face expressionless. 'Our little way of saying thank you,' he said. 'Say it with bloody flowers.'

Felicity tagged along when we went into the florist's. The freesias were waxen, yellow and purple. While Carlo was paying, I held the bunch. I had never really looked at flowers before, not as things in themselves. If I had thought of them at all, it was only as a colourful nuisance, the cause of mysterious adult obsessions and irrational prohibitions. Those freesias made me feel oddly uncomfortable. They were sensual, and part of their power derived from the fact that they looked unnatural: they were artificial like lipstick, impractical like high-heeled shoes.

Carlo pocketed the change and led the way out of the shop. Outside on the pavement, Felicity tugged at his arm. 'Can we have some hot chocolate? We don't have to go back yet, do we?'

'OK by me.' Carlo glanced in my direction and raised his eyebrows.

'I don't mind,' I said.

'We could go to the Hot Pot.' Felicity's face was pink with the urgency of desire. 'Millie says it's ever so nice.'

'It's miles away,' Carlo said, 'and I bet it's expensive.'

'I'll pay. Honest, I will, whatever it costs. I'll pay for all of us.'

The Hot Pot was a recently refurbished coffee shop attached to the Newnham House Hotel. Last night at supper, Lily had mentioned a rumour that David Essex had spent a night there incognito just before Christmas, which might have increased the Hot Pot's allure for Felicity: both she and Millie were in love with him. The hotel was on the London road, at least a mile and a half from where we were standing.

'It's not just the money,' Carlo said. 'Anyway, we can use the change from Dad. It's the distance. And then there's these bloody flowers. I don't want to carry them around all over the place. I don't want to look like a bloody pansy.'

'I'll carry them,' she said. 'What's a bloody pansy?'

'A man who carries flowers in public. And don't swear. If you carry the flowers you'll drop them or something. Anyhow, they'll get in the way.'

I pushed my hands into the pockets of my leather jacket. 'I'll take them back to the house, if you want.'

'You'll be ages,' Carlo said.

'No, I won't. Not if I walk fast. Anyway, I need

to get my baccy. I forgot it.' The fingers of my left hand curled round the packet of Golden Virginia tobacco in my pocket.

Felicity smiled at me as if I'd given her a present. 'We'll walk slowly, James. You'll probably get there almost as soon as we do.'

'Are you sure?' Carlo said.

I shrugged. 'No problem.'

'You'll give her the flowers?'

'If you want.'

'They're from both of us, OK? And don't say my dad gave us the money.'

I nodded. Carlo handed me the flowers. I walked away quickly. At the corner I looked back. Carlo and Felicity were walking slowly in the opposite direction, very close together, her face turned up to his.

It was a crisp, fine morning, with wisps of cloud moving rapidly across a pale, pure blue sky. Besides the jacket, I was wearing new jeans and zip-up black boots. I thought I looked cool, or at least as cool as nature and opportunity allowed. I walked faster and faster. My breathing was ragged. I didn't know what I wanted any more or what I hoped for. It was as though someone or something had taken control of my will. This wasn't the sort of thing I did. Whatever it was I was doing.

The closer I came to the house, the more unreal I felt. Lily had kissed me twice. The first time might have meant nothing but the second couldn't by any stretch of the imagination have been what someone might expect to receive from a schoolfriend's mother.

I felt dizzy when I thought of the warm, slippery writhing of her tongue in my mouth, the pressure of her breasts against my chest, my hands running over the smooth curves of her hips. I wanted it to happen again and I was terrified it might.

The door was unlocked, which meant that Lily was at home. I heard a clatter of plates from the kitchen.

'Mrs Murthington?' I called, and my voice emerged as a breathless squeak.

The clattering continued. I opened the kitchen door. Lily was standing at the sink, her hands in pink rubber gloves streaked with foam. She was wearing a loose white cotton top over jeans. She had pushed her hair back behind her ears but some strands had escaped.

Her eyes widened. 'Jamie — you gave me quite a shock.'

'Sorry.'

She shook her head, smiling. 'Are the others with you?'

'No, they're going to the Hot Pot.'

'Very posh. Looking for David Essex?' As she was speaking, she dried the gloves on a tea-towel and stripped them off. They made a sucking noise as she peeled them away from her skin. 'Why aren't you with them?'

'I'm going there now.' I held up the freesias. 'I said I'd bring you these on the way.'

'From you?'

'From — from me and Carlo. As a sort of thank-you for everything.'

Her face had lost the smile. 'They're my favourites.'

'I know.'

While we were speaking, we had come closer together. I'm not sure how that happened. The edge of the kitchen table jarred against my thigh. I gave Lily the flowers and her hand touched mine as she took them. She wasn't looking at them: she was looking at me.

'That's sweet of you. You're a clever boy, aren't you?' She sniffed the flowers. 'I love their smell. Don't you?'

She held the bunch. I bowed my head over it. The flowers smelt like my grandmother's garden when a long dry spell had been followed by a shower of rain. Lily touched my hair. I gasped and shied away as if she had pricked me with a pin.

'So soft. It's like a baby's.' Her fingertips trailed behind my ear and followed the line of my jawbone. 'That's soft, too.' She dropped the flowers on to the table. She lifted my hand to her cheek. 'Is it softer than mine?' she murmured.

'No.'

My senses were unnaturally alert, sucking in information as indiscriminately as a vacuum-cleaner. The washing-machine began to spin. The fanlight of the window was open and the curtain was swaying in the draught. There was a faint smell of fresh coffee. I noticed the fine lines at the corners of Lily's eyes. I felt her breath, warm and sweet, on my skin. I was aware of her breasts underneath the thin cotton.

She raked her fingernails down my throat. I cried

out. She pulled at the neck of my shirt and drew me towards her. We pawed at each other's clothes. My jacket fell on to the floor. I tried to tug her top over her head but her arms were in the way. She clawed at my belt. I had no idea what I was doing except that I was in a desperate hurry.

Lily pulled her mouth from mine. 'No. Not here.'

She took my hand and we ran like children into the hall and up the stairs. She led me into the room where I slept. We didn't even bother to close the door.

What followed was short and desperate, messy and unsatisfactory. I had no idea that sex was such an awkward business. Ignorance and urgency made me clumsy, and we were both in a rush. Afterwards we scrambled back into our clothes. I was almost crying with frustration and shame.

Lily patted my arm. 'Don't worry.'

I tried to kiss her but she wouldn't let me. I followed her downstairs.

'You'd better get going,' she said rapidly. 'Carlo and Felicity will wonder where you are.'

I shrugged. I didn't care about them. I didn't care about anything.

She glanced at her watch. 'Oh, God, look at the time. I'd better take you in the car.'

I went into the kitchen to fetch my jacket. While I was there I picked up the freesias – we must have knocked them off the table. They looked bedraggled and several of the flowers were crushed. I left them beside the sink.

We drove across town in silence. Lily pulled into a side road fifty yards from the Newnham House Hotel. I fumbled for the door handle.

She stroked my leg. 'Next time, Jamie,' she whispered. 'Thanks. Thanks for the flowers.'

I lunged at her but she pushed me away. I walked quickly to the hotel. Carlo and Felicity had found a window table in the Hot Pot. For a moment, I hesitated in the doorway and, in a sudden fit of panic, surreptitiously checked my flies. Part of me wanted to swagger, part of me wanted to run away and hide.

Carlo looked up. 'You took your time. What are you having?'

'Coffee. Black.'

I sat down, took out my tobacco and began to roll up.

'You gave her the flowers?' Carlo asked.

'Yeah.' I licked the edge of the paper.

'What did she say?'

'She said thanks.'

Felicity pursed her lips. 'Is that all? You'd think she'd be really pleased, wouldn't you? It shows how cold-hearted she is. She doesn't deserve those flowers.'

'Yeah, well,' Carlo said. 'Anything to keep Dad happy.'

I don't know how I got through the rest of the day. Everything had a dreamlike quality, as though I were an observer in someone else's reality. My mind found it almost impossible to grasp what had happened. Lily and I had, after a fashion, made love.

Therefore I was no longer a virgin. I had done it – now, after years of speculation, I knew what it was like. I had seen and touched a woman who had had no clothes on. And I wanted to do it again.

But it had happened so fast. Was it always like that? I wondered whether women took their pleasure instantly, at the moment of penetration, or even just before. Everyone said they weren't like men but the notion of women taking pleasure at all was not an easy one for me to understand. And was it always so disappointing for the man?

When we went home at lunchtime, Lily asked if we'd had a nice morning. Carlo grunted at her. Felicity laid the table, when asked to do so. Carlo and I took out the rubbish. Lily didn't look at me and I tried not to look at her. The flowers were in a cut-glass vase on the kitchen table.

'Thanks for the freesias,' Lily said to Carlo. 'How did you know they were my favourite?'

Late on Monday afternoon, I drove out of London in brilliant sunshine. But as the motorway cut through the Chilterns, the showers started. The rain continued on and off until I was on the other side of Oxford. I pulled into the first empty lay-by I could find. When I got out of the Saab, the air was full of the smell of freshly watered earth – heavy, dark and pregnant with possibilities, like the scent of freesias.

I walked up and down. A few feet away from me, cars and trucks roared and made the ground tremble. I phoned both Nicky's mobile and the Murthingtons' house. I didn't expect anyone to answer either phone. Nobody did.

It was almost six o'clock by the time I reached the outskirts of Chipping Weston. I drove straight to the house and turned into the driveway. I could no longer see any point in concealing my movements. On this occasion, in fact, I positively wanted to be seen. I wanted confrontation. I would have liked to hit someone, perhaps Carlo. What I really wanted, though, was to find Nicky.

The key was not in its usual hiding-place underneath the birdbath. I hammered on the door and rang the bell. No one came. I tried again. A couple of minutes slipped by. I walked slowly along the side of the house, peering into each of the ground-floor windows. In the kitchen, the *Guardian* was no longer on the table, and Kate's blue jacket was draped over the back of a chair. The plate and the mug on the draining-board had been joined by another mug and an upturned teapot. I didn't like the look of that second mug.

I tried the door of the shed at the back of the house. It was unlocked. The interior was cool and smelt of rusty metal and decaying paper. Apart from the area immediately inside the door, the space was filled to the ceiling with cardboard boxes, scraps of wood and redundant machinery. I recognized a lawnmower I had once pushed and a doll's pram that had belonged to Felicity. Next to it was an elderly BMX bike. The metal frame was dull and scratched but the tyres were pumped up and the chain had recently been oiled.

The past ambushed me. Once there had been two BMX bikes, Carlo's and Felicity's. This one had been Carlo's. I didn't know where Felicity's bike was, of course I didn't. No one did. Felicity's bike was –

There was a noise behind me. Fists clenching, I swung round. Kate was standing on the path, barely three yards from me. I stared at her face and the shock of what I saw squeezed the breath from me. I was back in the present, and it wasn't much better than the past.

'What happened?' I said.

She opened her mouth as if to reply but said nothing. She was holding a rusty garden trowel in her right hand, raised as if she was about to hit me with it. Her face was streaked with blood: most of it had dried but some was still vivid and fresh. The skin round her left eye was swollen and discoloured.

'Kate.' I took a step towards her.

'Jamie,' she croaked. She lowered the arm. The trowel slipped through her fingers and clattered on to the path. I leaped forward and put my arm round her. Her small body slumped against mine. For a moment neither of us spoke. She was trembling, but gradually she brought the shaking under control.

'I – I thought you were Carlo,' she muttered into my chest.

'He did this? He attacked you?'

She began to shiver again. 'He went for me like an animal. Hitting me. Scratching.'

'But why?'

'Because he hates me.' She pointed down the path

beside the house. 'I was by the door. He must have been round the back. He just came at me. I ran into the road and he didn't dare follow.'

'Is he there now? Inside, I mean?'

'I don't think so. I saw him drive off.'

'If he is in, he's not answering the door.' I pulled away from her and tried to get a better look at her face. 'I'll take you to hospital. You need checking over.'

'No.' She squeezed my arm. 'I'm OK. Really.'

She drew away from me. I stared at her. The bruise would probably discolour further but the eye itself looked undamaged. I wasn't sure if the scratches on her face were superficial or not. The blood made it hard to tell. 'Did he hurt you anywhere else?'

'Just my face.'

More questions were bubbling into my mind but now was not the time to ask them. 'We need to get you cleaned up.'

'We could go inside.'

'Here?'

'Why not? It's my home.'

'Listen,' I said. 'If Carlo —'

'He's not here. I told you, I saw him driving off. And he won't dare come back if you're here too.'

I still didn't like the idea. The house might be a trap as well as a refuge. But the alternatives were even less appealing. At present the priority was to get Kate away from prying eyes and find out how badly she was hurt. A pretty, pregnant young woman with a bruised and bloody face would attract attention.

'Please,' she said. 'Please, Jamie. I just don't want to see people. I want to be here, at home.'

'All right.'

She pushed her hand into her pocket, pulled out a Yale key and gave it to me. I unlocked the door, thinking how odd it was that she should ask my permission to go into her own house. Odder still in that Kate did not strike me as a timid woman – quite the reverse. One question wouldn't wait.

I glanced back at her. 'Was Carlo alone?'

'What? Of course he was.'

'Was he alone in the car as well?'

'As far as I know. Who did you think might be with him?'

I didn't answer. I opened the door and the still, stuffy air of the house enveloped me. For a moment I stood listening on the threshold.

Kate rushed past me. 'It's OK. I told you, he's not here.'

'Wait. I'll bolt the door. Then I'll check the house.'

She allowed me to do that at least. In the kitchen, there was fresh milk in the fridge and an unopened packet of teabags on the worktop. Carlo's backpack had gone from Felicity's bedroom. The white bucket was still in the bathroom next door but now it was empty. Someone had removed the shirt, scrubbed out the bucket and left it to drain upside-down in the bath.

'You see?' Kate said, when we reached the attic. 'He's not here. It's quite safe.'

'When was he here?' I asked. 'In the house, I mean.'

'I'm not sure. Earlier today, I suppose.'

'I don't understand what he was doing.'

'That's because he's a bloody law unto himself.' She was trembling again. 'I'm freezing. I'm going to have a bath.'

I went downstairs. On the ground floor, I walked through the rooms again, checking the doors and windows. I heard Kate's footsteps overhead, first running up to the attic, then down to the bathroom. The questions buzzed in my mind like flies, aimless and persistent. If she was so scared of Carlo, if he'd beaten her up a few hours earlier, why did she want to stay here? Surely it was the first place he would look.

The house was as secure as I could make it. In Hugh's study, I tried to phone Nicky again. There was no answer. I wanted her and the strength of the desire was as nagging as a stitch. More than that, even, I wanted to know that she was safe. I checked the voicemail on the home phone. There were two messages for her and none for me. One message was from Victor at the gallery and the other was from Miranda, both asking her to phone.

After a quarter of a century, my ears were still attuned to the language of the plumbing. I heard the faint sound of Kate's splashing in the bath and the groan the hot-water pipes made when the water was flowing. The house was strange, shabby and uncomfortable, too full of memories and objects that no one in their right mind would want. But it was familiar. I rather wished it wasn't but there was nothing I could do about that. The house was like

Kate: it gave me no choice. If there had been a choice, I had made it a long time ago and now I was living the consequences.

When Kate came downstairs I was making tea in the kitchen. She wore a faded blue dressing-gown with a pink rabbit on the breast pocket. Her hair was wrapped in a towel. She might have been about thirteen, if you edited out the bulge in her belly and the marks on her face.

'You look better,' I said. 'Do you want some tea?'

'Sounds good. With sugar.'

She sat at the kitchen table and found her cigarettes and lighter in one of the pockets of the waxed jacket. She stacked them in front of her.

I put the lid on the teapot. 'Turn your face to the window,' I said. 'I want to see you better.'

She twisted her head and raised her chin, pretending to pout like a model. I stooped over her and examined the damage. I had been standing on the same spot when Lily had dropped the freesias on the kitchen table.

I touched Kate's chin with my finger. Her eyes swivelled towards mine but she did not respond to the contact. I tilted her face to one side so it caught the light better. The bruise was on the outer corner of the left eye. It was beginning to turn purple. A scratch raked diagonally down her right cheek, its surface now scabbing over, and there was a shorter but deeper one on the left side of her face, just below the cheekbone. The wounds were clean. She smelt powerfully of disinfectant.

'I'll live,' she said.

I released her chin and went to pour the tea. She lit a cigarette. When I sat down, she glanced at me and smiled. For a while neither of us spoke. We might have been sitting side by side at the kitchen table every day for years. We might have been father and daughter, together since birth.

Kate tapped my arm to attract my attention. 'Jamie?'

'What?'

'I'm so tired. And I'm scared. What am I going to do?'

12

At the end of the Easter holidays, the day before Carlo and I went back to school, Lily took the three of us to Rackford for another driving lesson. By now Carlo handled the car quite skilfully as he drove sedately up and down the runways and along the perimeter road. He was capable of avoiding the major hazards, which were potholes and rabbits. I was a slower learner. The car still stalled unexpectedly when I pulled away or veered off the runway when I changed gear. I was furiously but secretly jealous of Carlo's expertise. I also begrudged the fact that Felicity was nearly at the same level as me. It was unfair – she was a girl, and still a child.

It was one of those warm, heavy days you sometimes get in April, an unexpected foretaste of full summer. The sun hung heavily in a bright blue sky. Despite the green shoots, the earth looked baked and tired and the heat bounced off the concrete. It was hot in the car and the sweat gathered between my shoulder-blades and left damp smudges on the fabric of the seats. Lily was wearing a blue shirt-dress. Her legs were bare and the straps of her sandals criss-crossed up her calves.

Carlo and I sloped off for a cigarette while Felicity had her turn.

'Jesus,' he said, as we crouched in a clearing among the brambles, sucking frantically on our rollies. 'This is so boring. I wish we were back at school.'

'Come off it.'

He scowled. 'Lily's really getting on my tits. I don't know how Felicity stands it, all year round.'

I said nothing.

Carlo spat. The spittle crash-landed on a handkerchief-sized square of dusty earth amid the brambles, roots and rough grass, where it squatted like a grey, shiny slug. 'She's a pain,' he said. 'Makes me want to puke. The way she laughs, that smile of hers.' He glanced at me through narrowed eyes. 'You think she's a pain, too, don't you?'

'Of course she is.'

In saying this, I didn't feel I was betraying Lily. Whether she was a pain or not was irrelevant to me. I was addicted to her. But I wasn't sure I liked her. What had liking got to do with it? In those days I hardly thought of her as having an independent personality.

Carlo squinted through the smoke at me. 'What are you doing in the summer? Going to your mum's?'

'Some of the time. But I'm going to Gran's first.'

'Maybe I could come too – to your Gran's, I mean. Do you think she'd ask me?'

'You wouldn't like it.'

'I won't know till I try, will I?' He gave a gasp of laughter. 'Me and your gran might be soulmates.'

'You'd be bored out of your skull. But I'll ask her, if you want.'

'Good.' Carlo dropped the cigarette butt on to the

dry earth and manoeuvred it with his toe into the spittle. 'That's settled, then.'

I stubbed out my own cigarette and we walked towards the runway. Behind his back I silently mouthed every swearword I could think of. I had received so much hospitality from Carlo and his family over the years that I could hardly object to a return fixture. On the other hand, having him to stay at Gran's would have been bad at any time. For me, Gran and her bungalow were something to be ashamed of in every way — socially, psychologically, materially and financially. I felt inadequate enough as a human being without having to put her on display to Carlo. And it was true that there was nothing to do there except watch TV, read books, walk half a mile through boring suburban streets to the nearest shop, which didn't even sell Golden Virginia — in any case, the woman who owned it knew Gran and had a nasty habit of reporting my purchases to her.

Now there was another, even stronger reason not to go there: the thought of not seeing Lily next holidays made me feel physically ill. If I couldn't be with her, I didn't want to be with anyone, even Carlo.

The Rover was coming up the runway towards us. Felicity was driving and she was revving the car too high in too low a gear. We waited for them in the shadow of the control tower. The car slowed as it approached us. Felicity braked hard. The engine stalled. The car juddered. The driver's window was down and I heard Felicity saying, in a cold, clear, calm voice, 'I hate driving.'

She and Lily joined us beside the control tower.

'So, who's next?' Lily said brightly.

'James,' Carlo said, although it was his turn.

Felicity touched her brother's arm. 'Can we go down to the stream? Please?'

Carlo yawned. 'OK.'

'But why, darling?' Lily asked.

'Because there's lots of flowers there.'

'Well, I suppose so. But don't get muddy, will you? You've got your best sandals on.' Lily glanced at me. 'So, it's your turn, Jamie. Maybe we should have a look at the Highway Code. It's about time you got to grips with the theory.'

Carlo and Felicity walked away. Lily watched them for a moment, then climbed into the front passenger seat. I opened the driver's door and got behind the wheel. My body felt weak and a little unreal, as though it was fighting a fever. Lily opened her handbag and took out a copy of the *Highway Code*. She turned her head towards me again and we looked at each other. We were so close that I could make out the down on her cheek.

'The seats are so uncomfortable and the car's like an oven,' she said. 'Perhaps I should test you somewhere else. Somewhere in the shade.' She pointed through the windscreen at the huddle of Nissen huts beyond the control tower. 'In one of those, do you think? The one over there might still have some chairs in it.'

I swallowed. 'OK.'

Lily picked up the *Highway Code* and got quickly

out of the car. She walked away briskly, leaving me to follow. The material of her dress was thin and soft. A woman's walk can be the sexiest thing in creation: I couldn't tear my eyes off her hips swaying from side to side, rocking gently across the direction of travel. She went directly to the second hut on the left. So, this was not a spur-of-the-moment decision. She had known exactly where she was going.

She opened the door and went inside. When I joined her, she was standing at the far end near a window opaque with grime and cobwebs. The hut contained a long metal table and a calendar for 1954. The air was warm and dry.

'God, it's hot.' She took hold of one end of the table and abruptly abandoned her role as driving instructor. 'Help me with this.'

We pushed the table against the door. She smiled at me and held out her hands. I went blindly towards them. This time it lasted longer. I remembered the cool metal on bare skin, the roughness of the concrete floor.

'I wish I was a cannibal,' I said. 'I want to eat you all up.'

She bit me. Our bodies rose and fell together, like complementary parts of a perfectly designed machine. At the same moment we cried out. At the same moment we lay still. When I looked into her face, her eyes were as blank as smoked glass in a car window.

Afterwards she touched my cheek. 'We must hurry.'

We went back to the car, moving furtively like

scouts in hostile terrain. My jeans were smeared with
dirt from the table but Lily's dress seemed spotless.
We were just in time. As I closed the driver's door,
Carlo and Felicity came into view two hundred yards
away at the other end of the runway.

'Start the engine.' Lily pulled down the sun visor
and examined her face in the mirror mounted behind
it. 'You can drive over and offer them a lift. Check
your mirror first, then signal and move off.'

There was hardly any food in the house except for a
few rust-spotted tins in the kitchen cupboards. I wondered when Kate had last had a proper meal.

'We need to go to a supermarket,' I said.

'There's a Waitrose,' she said. 'Go back to the
bypass, then come into the town from the west. It's
faster than going through the centre.'

'You'd better come with me.'

'Like this? You must be joking.'

'You can get dressed.'

'I'm not going out like this in public. I look like a
battered wife. Everyone will think you've been
bashing me about.'

'You could stay in the car.'

She shook her head. 'I'm tired. I don't want to
have to get dressed. It's all right, I'll lock up and put
the bolts across. He won't want to make a row because
the neighbours would hear.'

'That didn't stop him beating you up.'

'That was different. He lost his temper. Can you
get me some grapefruit juice?'

'I'm not leaving you here by yourself. It's as simple as that.'

We glared at each other. For an instant a suspicion eddied in my mind: surely she wouldn't really want to stay here alone if Carlo had attacked her only an hour or two ago. But Kate had a habit of doing the unexpected. Or perhaps it was vanity.

Suddenly she smiled and touched my arm. 'You sound like a father.'

'I mean it. I'm not leaving you here.'

'All right, I'll come. I'll wrap a scarf round my face and lurk in the car.'

Fifteen minutes later we drove over to the other side of Chipping Weston. I left Kate smoking in the car. My mouth watered as I wandered up and down the aisles of the supermarket. Since Friday lunchtime I had survived on coffee, wine and the occasional snack. With increasing urgency I plucked items from the shelves and filled the trolley with food and drink.

The place was crowded. The queue at the checkout tested my patience to its limits. I found myself trapped between two trolleys at the end of a long line. One contained a toddler who was full of rage against the universe. The other supported a very old lady with an irresistible desire to teach me the finer points of her shopping technique.

'I wait for the special offers, that's the secret. You can save pounds and pounds. My daughters gave me a freezer for Christmas so it's no trouble. Most of the ladies know me and sometimes they . . .'

It was then that I noticed a young woman with

short dark hair on the far side of the store. She had just come through the checkout nearest the exit and was carrying a bag in either hand. She hesitated at the sliding doors.

'The best time to come is around now,' my instructor was saying, 'or perhaps a little later, because that's when they go round the perishable stuff and put the reduced stickers on the ones that are nearly out of date.'

For an instant I glimpsed the woman's face in profile. Emily Fielding? It was hard to be sure because she was wearing different clothes and there was no sign of Maisie and Albert.

'Excuse me,' I said to the old lady. 'I can see a friend of mine over there. I need to have a word with her.'

But it was no use. The old lady continued talking. The toddler continued howling. I used the trolley to force my way out of the gridlock, but by the time I reached the sliding doors, Emily had disappeared. A line of cars was streaming steadily on to the main road, and one was probably hers.

I returned to the queue, which had grown longer since I had been away. The toddler had been placated with chocolate and the old woman had found another pupil. I couldn't be certain that I had seen Emily Fielding. I reminded myself that I hardly knew her. I was hungry, worried and scared. All in all, I wasn't a reliable observer. I wasn't a reliable anything.

When I reached the Saab, Kate's eyes gleamed at the sight of the supermarket bags. I had bought a

French stick and she fed us with handfuls of it as we drove back to the house. We went into the kitchen and continued eating. We stuffed the food into our mouths – bread, cheese, ham, olives and fruit. Kate drank half a litre of grapefruit juice, straight from the carton. It was a picnic without table manners, without conversation. I didn't mention Emily to her, then or afterwards. If I was wrong about seeing her, there was no point. If I was right, I needed time to think about the implications. When I had eaten enough, I put on the kettle. I spooned coffee into the cafetière.

Kate lit a cigarette. 'Can I have tea?' she said. 'I can't stand the taste of coffee at present. Everything's upside-down. I never used to like grapefruit juice either.'

I reached for the teapot. 'How are you feeling?'

'Better. Much better. The bath helped, and the food even more.'

'So, what was Carlo up to? Why did he go for you like that?'

She tapped ash into a saucer. 'He lost it. This isn't just about money, you know. He hates me. I don't know – it's like I'm a symbol of all that's gone wrong in his life. Everything from his mother dying onwards.'

'What was he doing here? And why were you here too?'

'Why shouldn't I be here? This is my home.'

'That's what your mother said. I suppose it's Carlo's home too.'

She began to empty the remaining carrier-bags. 'I came back because I wanted to collect some clothes. Some of Mum's jewellery too. I don't want to leave that sort of thing lying around for Carlo to grab. I thought I'd be safe if Sean hadn't been found. I was just going to pick up the stuff, then go back to London and lie low for a bit. I'd have phoned you, honestly.'

I wondered whether she was telling the truth, and also why I cared.

'The trouble was,' she went on, 'Carlo was here too.'

'For God's sake,' I said, suddenly angry. 'I don't believe it. Why run the risk of coming back here? You must have known that Carlo –'

'I'm not going to let him frighten me away for ever. Besides, I checked – I phoned the house. I looked through the windows.'

'You said he drove away. Was his car in the drive?'

'He'd parked in the road.'

'You didn't notice on your way in?'

'I don't notice cars much. Anyway, he was in the back garden.' She winced. 'I told him he was a vicious, mean-minded prick and he said I was a greedy little bastard. But that was just warming up. Sort of like the adverts before the main feature.' She grinned at me.

I smiled back. I wasn't sure that Kate was my daughter, but there were many things I liked about her and her sense of humour was one of them. Maybe this was one of the side-benefits of having children – when you grew to like them as well as love them, when pleasure and biology marched together side by side, just as they should in the moment of conception.

'I need to know more,' I said. 'Your mother kept going on about him wanting everything. And why did it all come to a head on Friday?'

'Because I found a letter from a property developer. It came here by mistake – it should have gone to Carlo in London. My mother's not even dead yet and Carlo's already trying to sell the airfield. He had a meeting set up for Friday morning, at Rackford, and he hadn't told me about it. He was planning to sell the place over my head. So I phoned Sean, got him to come and pick me up. I thought I'd give Carlo a little surprise in front of witnesses.' Her lips trembled. 'And I did. And then he gave me a surprise too.'

'He's full of surprises.'

She nodded, avoiding my eyes. She lined up items of shopping on the table top – pasta, oil, soup, coffee – adjusting their positions so they made a crescent-shaped curve. 'But what about you?' she said suddenly. 'How come you just turn up out of the blue when I need you?'

'I was looking for Carlo.'

What happened next unnerved me. My throat constricted, as though it was attempting to force back a tide of emotion welling up from deep inside me. Something of this must have shown in my face. Kate frowned. She put down a shrink-wrapped pack of apples and came round the table to where I was standing by the kettle. Neither of us spoke. She took my head between her hands, stood on tiptoe and stared at me as though I were a book she wanted to read.

'What is it, Jamie? Something's happened, hasn't it?'

'Nicky's gone,' I said. 'Maybe Carlo's got something to do with it.'

Kate's brown eyes had amber flecks in them. Her hands were dry and warm. Her smell was familiar, a blend of soap and talcum powder, a reminder of childhood, of a time before everything went wrong. 'What?' She released my face. 'What's he up to?'

'There's someone called Charlie in her book group. She never mentioned him. Does Carlo ever get called Charlie?'

'Not that I know of.'

'Apparently he's got a beard. Like Carlo.'

'So have lots of men. Jamie, this doesn't make any sort of sense.'

I shrugged. A shrug is a convenient response in that you let the other person provide the interpretation. If Carlo knew what I knew, and what I suspected Lily knew, he would have a very good reason to want to hurt me through Nicky. But I didn't intend to share this with Kate.

'Are you sure he's got your wife?'

'No,' I said, 'and in a way that makes it worse. I can't be sure of anything. The last time I saw her, yesterday, Nicky said she wanted some time by herself. She thinks we're having an affair.'

'Us? You and me?' Kate gave a snort of laughter.

'She's not been in touch. She's not answering her mobile.'

'So? She's pissed off with you. She doesn't want to talk. You're reading way too much into this. There's nothing to show that Nicky isn't by herself. I can't see why Carlo would want to go after her. And I don't see why this Charlie has to be Carlo.'

I let out my breath. 'You're right. Probably.'

'Of course I am.' Kate smiled at me. 'Jamie, don't look so worried. Dads are meant to be cosy and re-assuring, OK? I know you've not had much practice but it's never too late to learn.' She saw me smiling back. 'That's better.'

I sat down. Nothing had changed but I felt a little less miserable than before. 'Your mother thought Carlo might be here.'

Kate sat down opposite me. 'She said that to you yesterday?'

'Today.'

'How is she?'

'No real change. She's comfortable, but rambling a bit.'

'You're taking your new responsibilities seriously. Me and Mum.'

'One of the nurses said that Carlo went to see her on Saturday afternoon and she had a bit of a setback after that.'

'We should get him banned from visiting. We should –'

'Your mother thought you might have gone to Sean's so I went there first. That was yesterday.'

189

'Sean's? But how did you know where he lived?'

'His address was in your mother's diary. Kate, I met Emily.'

'At Sean's?' Her face was full of hard lines and sharp angles, like a fox's. 'What was she doing there?'

'Looking for him. Apparently the police phoned her and said they'd found his car. It had been stolen. It turned up in Peckham. Someone had set it on fire.'

Kate reached for her cigarettes. 'I left it in Harlesden on Friday afternoon with the keys in the ignition before I came to your house.'

'Why did you leave it?'

'Because it tied me in with Sean.' She shook out a cigarette. 'Jamie, I was in such a state I couldn't think. You understand? Like you with Nicky? I drove up to London in his car on Friday afternoon. He'd driven me over to Rackford in the morning, you see, and when Carlo killed him, I made a break for it.' She was shaking so much she couldn't get the cigarette into her mouth. 'It was either that or let Carlo kill me.' Then she straightened her spine and looked at me with startled eyes. 'So you met Emily? You talked to her?'

'A bit.'

'I hope you didn't believe a word she said.' Kate managed to find her mouth and light the cigarette. She inhaled twice, holding the smoke in her lungs. 'I'll tell you about Emily. She made Sean's life hell. She was always wanting things. That was what cost him his job. And when he didn't have a six-figure income she just didn't want to know him.'

'She put a rather different slant on it.'

'She would, wouldn't she? Had she got the children with her?'

I nodded.

'I feel sorry for those two. She takes them everywhere. Have you noticed how mothers with little kids use them to get their own way? You can't teach Emily anything about emotional blackmail.'

'Emily thought that some of Sean's things had gone. His bank stuff, ID, that sort of thing. She said it looked like he was planning to go away, maybe for good.'

'Maybe he was. He didn't want to pay child support for the rest of his life. He wasn't cut out to be a dad. I always knew that if we ever had kids, I'd end up a single parent. But I didn't expect it to happen this way.'

She was trembling again. I got up and put my arm round her. She nestled against me. We stayed like that for a minute, perhaps ninety seconds. I thought about the baby that was living inside her clean, pink body, feeding and moving and growing as a child should. It was a child that would lack a father, just as I had done, or as Carlo and Felicity had lacked a mother.

'You can't be sure that Sean's dead,' I said. 'He might have gone back to his house after you last saw him. Maybe Carlo's the reason he's gone away.'

'He's dead,' Kate whispered, trembling more violently than before. 'I know he is. I saw him, he was covered with blood. He wasn't moving. I know what Carlo's like.'

I thought about that, and I remembered Emily saying that Sean hadn't been in contact with his mother, and how that had surprised her. I said, 'If the police find Sean's body, the evidence will point to you?'

'Yes. I think so.'

'Thanks to Carlo?'

'Yes. I told you.'

'So if they don't find the body, or if the evidence isn't there, you're off the hook?'

'In theory. But what about Carlo?'

I didn't know the answer. All I could do was hold Kate until she stopped trembling.

13

Part of me assumed I was still in the normal, pre-dictable world where two and two made four, I went to work five days a week, and Nicky was beside me when I went to sleep and when I woke up. Another part wondered whether I had slipped without real-izing round a mental corner and arrived in a place where nothing made sense.

That night I used my old room at the Murthingtons' house, although I didn't do much sleeping. Before we went to bed, Kate and I checked the doors and windows. Afterwards, as she climbed the attic stairs, I noticed a claw hammer in her hand.

'Just in case,' she said.

My bedroom smelt of stale perfume. Every surface was grey and feathery with dust. The air was cold and had the dead, sad quality you find in rooms where nothing happens except the passing of time. The floor was a jumble of suitcases and furniture, and everywhere there were possessions large and small that were too old or battered to use but too good to throw away.

The top of the single bed was covered with clothes, men and women's, some on hangers, some in carrier-bags, some loose. I dumped them on top of a treadle sewing-machine in front of the empty fireplace. I didn't undress but lay down with a blanket over me for warmth. I thought about Nicky most, but also about Carlo, Kate and Sean, about Lily dying in the hospice and about a younger Lily lying with me on this bed. If the room had a memory, the shapes of our warm, naked bodies were imprinted there. Nothing could be forgotten, nothing could be eradicated, nothing could be changed.

For the first time in twenty-five years, for the first time since I had decided to remake my life without the Murthingtons in it, I could not see a way forward. I did not have a plan for the future. I wanted my old life back and I hadn't the faintest idea how to get it. Most of all I wanted Nicky. My need for her was a form of hunger. I clung to the idea, as an article of faith, that it was better to be hungry for Nicky, even to starve for want of her, than never to have the hope of eating.

At two o'clock I turned on the light and tried to read. There was a pile of yellowing paperbacks on the shelf above the fireplace. I remembered some from previous visits. I opened one and found myself looking at *C. Murthington* on the flyleaf. I turned the pages and found the first chapter.

But the words wouldn't hold my attention. It was almost with relief that I heard Kate's footsteps coming slowly and carefully down the attic stairs. She passed my door and continued along the passage to the bathroom. A few minutes later the lavatory flushed. Her footsteps returned. They stopped and she tapped on my door. When I told her to come in, she opened the door a few inches and slipped through the gap, as though she was trying to make herself as small as possible.

She was still wearing the dressing-gown. In the harsh electric light, the bruises and scratches on her face looked like garish imitations of what they really were, like the accidental by-products of a child playing with a paintbox. She was carrying the hammer. An absurd fear flashed into my mind that she would hit me with it.

'Do you mind if I come in?'

'It's not easy to sleep, is it?'

She picked her way through the debris on the floor. 'It's not just that. I need to pee all the time. The baby's pressing on my bladder.'

I drew up my knees, making room for her on the end of the bed. She sat down and balanced the hammer on top of the pile of clothes over the sewing-machine. It seemed impossible that such a childlike person should have another life growing inside her. She hugged her belly and rocked gently to and fro.

'I expect you'd like to see your mother soon,' I said.

The rocking stopped. 'I'd like to, of course, but that's where Carlo will expect me to go.'

'It didn't stop you coming here.'

'I know.'

'Then you're not making sense.'

'Don't be angry.' She glanced at me and her face was now thin and worried. 'It's – it's not just that.

I'm scared of Carlo but this is something else. I – I don't like people who are ill. It makes me feel – Jamie, I hate to see her dying. I don't think I can bear it. Should I go and see her?'

'I can't tell you that.'

'But what does she want?'

'Most of all she wants you to be safe. If you went, you might not catch her in a lucid moment. She's in and out of consciousness. At one point she thought I was your –' I broke off and smiled at her '– your father. Hugh.'

Kate rubbed her eyes like a sleepy child. Then she nodded at the window. 'Do you think Carlo's out there? In the garden, I mean, watching us. Waiting for the right moment.'

'I don't know about that either.'

'There's him and there's Emily. It's strange when you know there are people who hate you. Really hate you.'

'When did you last see Emily?'

'Just before Sean and I split up.' Kate wrinkled her nose. 'But she phoned me once or twice after that. Just to remind me of what she thought of me.'

I was on the verge of asking whether she'd been to Sean's house after she left the chapel but she forestalled me. 'Jamie, I've got this huge favour.'

'OK.'

'Promise you'll think about it even if you don't say yes right away.'

I nodded.

'I need to go back to Rackford. Will you take me?'

'What – now?'

'Tomorrow. I'm not sure I could find my way in the dark. Listen, it's my one chance. If I go back to where – where Sean is . . . My handbag's there. If I can just get it, there'll be nothing left to link me to his body.'

'Except that you used to live with him and you're eventually going to own the place where he's found. And that's leaving aside the chance that someone saw you with him, or that you left something else behind.'

She tossed her head. 'I can't help that. But I can help my bag being there.'

'I don't think it's wise, Kate. Once you start tampering with the evidence –'

'I just –'

'You'd only make matters worse. And you're tired and upset and this is the middle of the night. It's not the best time to make a decision. No one thinks straight in those circumstances.'

'Don't say no,' she hissed. 'Please.' She leaned towards me, her face sharp and grey like old carved stone. 'Don't say no.'

I sat up. Her vehemence alarmed me. 'OK. I won't make up my mind, and you won't make up yours. We'll talk about it tomorrow. How's that?'

Suddenly she was a child again, made of flesh and blood. She rubbed her eyes. 'All right.' She slipped off the bed and picked her way across the room to the door. 'And, Jamie?'

'What?'

'Thank you. Goodnight.'

The door closed behind her and I listened to her bare feet padding up the stairs. I dropped the paperback on the floor and turned off the light. I lay there in the darkness. I didn't know whom to trust. I had no idea who was telling the truth or when they were telling it. I didn't even know whether Kate was my daughter or not. As far as the Murthingtons were concerned, I had only two certainties: that Lily was right when she'd said I owed her something, and that Kate was scared and pregnant.

That was another reason I missed Nicky – she had a way of making things clearer. I remembered her saying when we were in the process of buying our house and I was afraid that the seller would withdraw at the last moment, 'You know what your problem is, James? You never trust anyone. You never just shut your eyes and jump because you're always afraid someone will take away the safety net.'

At last it was Carlo's turn. Short of feigning illness or making a scene, there was no way he could get out of driving with Lily that afternoon. I'm not sure he wanted to. He loathed Lily but he liked driving.

I hoped Felicity would go with them. I wanted to be alone with my memory of what had happened in the hut. Like a miser I wanted my privacy, so I could count every single golden coin in my hoard. I wanted to relive what I'd seen and smelt and heard and tasted. I was the holder of secret knowledge and I revelled in it. I knew now that those first fumbles in the spare bedroom at the Murthingtons' house were not really what sex was about after all. I pitied people like Carlo and Felicity, who did not know how wonderful it could be, who had not experienced it.

But Felicity had other ideas. 'Come on, James – Carlo promised you'd help.'

'Help with what?'

'The den, silly. We're building a den.'

I glanced at Carlo. He was watching me. I couldn't tell what he was thinking. I was instantly afraid that he knew or guessed what Lily and I had been doing, that somehow it had marked my face like a smudge of lipstick.

'I can't do it by myself, you see,' Felicity went on, in a sweetly reasonable voice. 'We need to get branches across the stream. It's a two-person job.'

'Try not to get too muddy, dear,' Lily said to Felicity. 'It's not just your best sandals. Those are your new jeans as well.'

Carlo sighed in a gusty, melodramatic way. He opened the car door and got behind the wheel.

'See you later,' Lily said, aiming the remark some-where over our heads. 'We'll honk twice when we've finished and you can come up to the road.'

Carlo started the engine and drove off, working his way up through the gears with a smoothness I envied. Felicity and I took the path leading from the runway to the section of the road near the western boundary of the airfield. At first neither of us spoke. We crossed the perimeter road near the airfield's side entrance. Felicity dived into the belt of trees and bushes separating it from the fence along the lane.

The track zigzagged downwards, following the logic of four-footed animals rather than two-footed ones. Felicity went first. I sniffed my fingers. They smelt of Lily. There was another surprise – I had not realized that even smells could be charged with eroticism.

'Look,' Felicity said. 'There's a wood anemone. Isn't it sweet?'

I grunted.

'And see that tall green one with the purple-spotted leaves? That's called lords-and-ladies. Or cuckoo pint.'

'How do you know all this stuff?'

'Mum used to tell me the names.' Felicity looked back over her shoulder. 'My real mum. Flowers are interesting.'

I grunted again. Felicity was no longer looking at me, which was a good thing because I thought I might be blushing. The first Mrs Murthington was rarely mentioned, or not in my hearing. The mother of Carlo and Felicity was not quite a taboo subject but she came close to it.

The ground levelled out. There were few trees down here. The bottom of the valley was clearer than I remembered – the last time I had come, with Carlo at the end of last summer, the ground had been thick with bracken that masked much of the stream. Now I could see that the water followed a wavering course and, except in the narrowest parts, it was only a few inches deep. On the other bank the slope of the land rose much more steeply than on this one. Felicity came to a stop beside the widest part of the stream. We had water on three sides – we were inside a bend shaped like a horseshoe.

She pointed. 'There's my den.'

On the other side of the stream a shelf of land was shaped like an orange segment. Behind it the ground rose almost perpendicularly. The shelf was about three yards wide and no more than two yards deep at the maximum. An untidy pile of branches filled one end.

'Carlo started building a sort of frame,' Felicity said. 'Can you see? He's pushed that curved branch into the bank at the back – that will be the doorway – and that long straight branch on top goes all the way from the opening to the back. We've just got to get more branches, pile them up and make a wall and a roof.'

I took out my rolling tobacco and began to make a cigarette. 'It's not very big.'

'Big enough to sit or lie in.'

'What are you going to use it for?'

'It's a den. I can do anything there. Anything I want to.'

'OK.' I licked the edge of the cigarette paper and folded it over. 'What do you want me to do?'

'You haven't got time for that now, James. Can't you smoke it afterwards? Carlo says we must get it weathertight by the time we leave.' Felicity nodded across the clearing at an uprooted birch, the casualty of a miniature landslide. 'He broke off some of the branches. We need to get them over the stream.'

'It's too wide to do it there. We'll have to get across where it's narrower.'

'That's why there have to be two of us. I'll get on the other side and you can pass the branches over. Then, if you go round to where the den is, I can float them down to you on the current.'

It was a sensible plan, in its way. Felicity worked hard and expected me to do the same. It wasn't long before we were both wet and muddy from the knees downwards. When she judged we had enough materials, we constructed the den itself, building up the walls and roof with branches. All the while, the sound of the car's engine ebbed and rose in volume as Carlo drove round and round the perimeter road and up and down the runways. I knew he was driving faster than usual.

'Look – there are some bluebells.'

I glanced across the stream. Half-way up the bank a clump grew underneath the branches of a beech.

'They're the first I've seen.' Felicity sounded unusually excited. 'Do you know what they mean?'

'Spring is here?'

'No – what they *mean*. Flowers have meanings, didn't you know?'

'Sort of symbolic? Like horseshoes mean good luck?'

Felicity stared across the stream. 'They mean constancy,' she said, in a quiet voice, 'everlasting love.'

'Say it with flowers,' I said, trying to make a joke of it, echoing Carlo the other day. 'So, what do freesias mean?'

'I looked them up the other day. They mean innocence.'

I laughed and turned away to put another branch on the roof of the den.

'So I don't know why they're Lily's favourites,' Felicity went on. 'Do you like her, James?'

'I don't know,' I muttered. 'She's nothing to do with me. Pass me that branch.'

Felicity handed it to me. 'It's funny that everyone gets married sooner or later.'

'Some people don't.'

'Most people do. I suppose – I suppose I might one day.'

'I expect so. What do you want to do about the doorway?'

'Just leave the opening for now. We'll find something we can drag across it. Or bring a blanket or something from home. The trouble is, I don't know who I'll marry.'

I smiled at her. 'You'll find out.'

The car's engine stopped. There were two blasts on the horn.

'Come on,' I said. 'We'll finish it later.'

'Yes,' Felicity said. 'We've got plenty of time.'

The phone woke me. I hadn't been asleep for long and I was down in the depths of a dream from which I was glad to escape. Half awake, I rolled off the bed. The phone rang on. *Not the mobile.* So it couldn't be Nicky – she didn't have the Murthingtons' number.

I blundered from the room, across the landing and

into the big front bedroom. There was a telephone on the side of the bed that had been Hugh's. Perhaps Nicky had got the number from Directory Enquiries. But it was far more likely to be someone else.

I picked up the handset. All I heard was the faint background hum of an open line. I covered the mouthpiece with my hand in case my breathing was audible at the other end. I waited. Seconds crawled by.

'Kate?' It was a man's voice. 'Kate, are you there?'

I said nothing.

'Kate?'

'Who's speaking?'

The man at the other end put down the phone. I broke the connection and dialled 1471. I listened to the recorded voice telling me that I had been called today at 07.45 hours and the caller had withheld their number.

I listened but there was no sound of movement in the attic. I wasn't sleepy any more. I phoned Nicky and the call was transferred directly to her voicemail.

I wandered downstairs and prowled through the ground floor of the house. Nothing had changed. There was no sign of Carlo or anyone else. Sunlight filtered through dusty windowpanes. The fears of the night receded. In the kitchen I filled the kettle and plugged it in. The room smelt of stale tobacco. I opened the back door. The long grass was silvery with dew. I stood on the doorstep and took a deep breath of morning air.

Then it hit me. The back door had already been unbolted.

I knew I had checked all the locks and bolts before we went to bed last night. The lock was another self-closing Yale, and I had put the catch down so it couldn't be opened from the outside. But the catch was up now.

In the garden, a grey squirrel scrambled up the trunk of the ash tree and ran out along one of the branches. Birds sang. The door of the shed was ajar. It was possible we hadn't closed it yesterday afternoon. I pushed the door open. For a moment I thought the interior of the shed was unchanged. Then I realized my mistake. Carlo's BMX bike was gone.

I closed the shed door, went back to the house and walked upstairs, first one flight, then the next. I stopped outside the attic door and knocked. There was no answer. I hadn't expected there would be. I opened the door and went in. The bedroom was empty, and so was the little boxroom next door. The duvet had been pulled up. Kate's suitcases were still there. Some of the clothes she had worn yesterday were on the chair in the corner. The dressing-gown with the pink rabbit was hanging on the back of the door. There was nothing to show where she had gone or when she would be back. Or whether she planned to come back.

Suddenly I discovered I was angry. I was tired of being manipulated and taken by surprise. I was tired of not knowing whether Kate was telling me the truth. Self-pity washed over me. I was being treated abominably by everyone. Kate was the worst offender but she wasn't the only one. I'd had enough. Most likely she had gone to Rackford to look for her handbag. Well, she could do what she wanted without any help from me. The sooner I left this house the better. If I was going to be unhappy I might as well be in the comfort and privacy of my own home.

I gathered up my belongings, locked up the house and left. Things weren't any better now, but at least they were simpler. When I reached Oxford I drove into the centre, bought a paper and had breakfast in a café near Magdalen Bridge. The place was full of chattering students who weren't much younger than Kate. Food made me feel more cheerful.

I was on my second cup of coffee when the phone rang. I lunged at the mobile, missed, knocked it on to the floor and spilled my coffee. A girl at the next table picked up the phone for me. It was still ringing. But it wasn't Nicky's number on the display, or even Kate's.

'James? Is that you?'

It took me a moment to place the voice. 'Yes, Victor, it is.'

'At last. A real person. I thought I was the only one left in this poor bloody universe.' He sounded older, and more querulous, on the phone and his Yorkshire accent was more pronounced: he had become a caricature of himself. 'If I hear another recorded message I'll go mad.'

'Nicky's not with you, I suppose?'

'Of course she's bloody not. That's why I'm ringing. I want to know where she's put the VAT return.'

'I'm afraid I can't help you. She's —'

'It's most inconvenient, lad.'

'The thing is, I'm not sure where she is, and her mobile seems to be out of range.'

Victor snorted. 'It's a funny sort of marriage you've got. Is there anyone I can ring who might know? What about these other numbers?'

'What numbers?'

'On this list of hers. I found it in the drawer of her desk. That's how I got yours. They're not work numbers, I can tell you that. I just hope she doesn't spend all the time ringing up for a chat when I'm not here. I don't pay her —'

'Who else is there?' I interrupted, and I must have raised my voice because the girl at the next table looked at me curiously. 'What are the other names?'

'That Miranda woman.'

I took a deep breath. 'Is someone called Charlie there?'

'No. But there's a Charles. Charles Browning. Will he know where she is? Shall I give him a ring?'

'No,' I said. 'I will. I want a word with Charlie.'

14

If God exists, He must be lonely, for even a little knowledge cuts you off from those who do not possess it. So omniscience must leave you with no one to confide in.

When I went back to school for the summer term of 1980, I was lonely. Over the years I had gradually acclimatized myself to the institution. But now it had become alien. I still conformed to its rituals. I did what was expected of me. But I was detached from the place and its inhabitants. They had become part of my past. I was like the grown-up joining in the games at a children's party, the only one who knew that they really didn't matter.

Real life lay somewhere else, somewhere as yet ill-defined. All I knew for certain about my real life was that it would have to contain Lily and lots of sex. I was desperate to finish school. At the time I thought I had well over a year of it left, and it stretched ahead of me like an endless wasteland. What I didn't know was that I had already begun my last term.

I think Carlo sensed something had changed. One day he started to talk about our plans for the summer. We had just had lunch and were walking away from the school dining-hall.

'Why don't we go abroad?' he suggested. 'As well as to your gran's, I mean.'

'I thought you wanted to have driving lessons.'

I was confident that this tactic would work. Carlo had turned seventeen in May, and had immediately applied for a provisional driving licence. His father and Lily had given him a course of ten lessons for his birthday, which he was going to take over the summer. I knew, because Carlo had told me on many occasions, that he was particularly keen to pass his test because then he could be much more independent at Chipping Weston, and he wouldn't have to rely on Lily to drive him when he wanted to go anywhere. I also knew, because I knew Carlo, that he wanted to be the first in our year to pass his test, and that being first mattered to him in a way it rarely did to me.

'I want to get away,' he said. 'That's more important.'

'Don't you want to spend some time at home?'

'I'm sick of Lily. She's always bloody watching us.'

'Where would we go?'

'Who cares? Somewhere with lots of girls. Ibiza, maybe, or a Greek island.'

'It'd cost money.'

'My dad wouldn't mind.' He raised his eyebrows. 'And wouldn't your mum be only too glad to fork out a hundred quid or so?'

I shrugged. 'Maybe.'

'What's got into you?'

'Nothing.'

Carlo stopped and stared at me. 'I could always go with someone else, you know.'

Usually at this point we'd wander off and have a cigarette. But not today. He scowled and walked rapidly away without another word.

This left me with a practical problem. Carlo was no longer the most important person in my life. Now that I was older, now that Lily had changed my entire universe, he had become no more than a means to an end. But in that way he was still important. If I wanted to go back to Chipping Weston, if I wanted to see Lily again, I would have to woo Carlo. I didn't care. They say that love – if that's the right word – is blind. What I realized then, at the tender age of sixteen, is that love is amoral as well. Or at least the sort of love I felt.

I was entirely cynical. I even took a sinister pleasure at the almost immediate success of my programme of manipulation. I offered Carlo a cigarette when it was his turn to offer me one. When we played the guitar together, I encouraged him to do the lead vocals. I let him copy my physics homework.

When I wrote the obligatory weekly letter to my mother, I mentioned the idea of going to Greece with Carlo. In her reply, my mother was unexpectedly enthusiastic. It would be ideal, she wrote, if we were to go in the second half of the holiday, perhaps during the last two weeks in August. That was when she, my step-father and their children were flying to Seattle to spend some time with my step-father's parents, and to help them celebrate their golden wedding. My mother thought I really wouldn't enjoy that very much so it would be nice if I could do something I really wanted to do with Carlo instead. After all, I would be nearly seventeen by then, and she knew she could trust me to behave responsibly.

One problem solved – but there was another, more difficult one to deal with. This was the danger that we would spend most of the rest of the holiday at my grandmother's. When Carlo decided to be obstinate, it was hard to shift him. My mother and my grandmother, who were both aware of how much hospitality I'd had from the Murthingtons over the years, had agreed to this without hesitation. I tried pointing out the drawbacks to Carlo.

'No,' he said, 'it'll be fine. We'll lay in some booze and fags on our way down. She can't expect us to stay in the house all the time, so we can walk down to the seafront. There must be some sort of nightlife down there in summer.' He rolled his eyes and intoned in a deep, solemn voice: 'And girls.'

Nothing I could say dented Carlo's enthusiasm for my grandmother's bungalow. As far as he was concerned, it might have been in outer Siberia. Its main attraction was that it wasn't his home in Chipping Weston.

As the term drew towards its end, it was a measure of my increasing desperation that I even prayed to the God I had never really believed in. As if to show how wrong I had been all these years, the prayer was answered. Just before the end of term, my grandmother tripped on her back doorstep and broke her left leg in two places. She would still be in hospital at the beginning of the holidays and would probably go from there to convalesce in a nursing-home. There was even a question of whether she would be well enough to return to the bungalow and live an independent life, let alone invite teenage boys to stay. I felt guilty enough to sell three of my least favourite records and use the proceeds to send her a bunch of roses by Interflora.

When Carlo heard the news he said, 'Oh, shit – can't we go by ourselves? Sort of look after the house while she's in hospital?'

'I can ask,' I said, safe in the knowledge that the answer would be no.

I was right. And God continued to be obliging: Hugh and Lily said I'd be welcome to come to Chipping Weston for the first part of the holiday. Carlo reluctantly accepted the need to make the best of a bad job. He fixed all of his hopes on the second half of the holiday, when we were going to Greece. Lily had arranged this on our behalf. We were to spend a fortnight in Lindos on the island of Rhodes. We would share a villa room. A schoolfriend in the year above had been to Rhodes the year before. He told Carlo the Dutch chicks were really hot and a lot of them went around topless. Also, cocktails were as cheap as cups of tea.

'Fuck me,' Carlo said, not once but many times. 'I can't wait.'

I did my best to appear excited. It seemed to me

that Carlo was behaving like a kid – he was excited in the way a child is excited on Christmas Eve, expecting something magical and unreal. The anticipation I felt, for Lily and Chipping Weston, was something altogether darker and more urgent. It wasn't a matter of enjoyment and I believed I had no more choice in the matter than the moth does when it flies towards the candle flame or the lemming when it heads for the cliff edge.

But I did have a choice. I know now that there is always a choice.

Nicky's Mini Cooper wasn't outside the house when I got home midway through Tuesday morning. But, then, I hadn't expected it to be. I hadn't expected there to be a message from her either, and there wasn't. I felt grubby, as though the dirt and dust of the Murthingtons' house had got under my skin. I shaved, had a shower and found clean clothes. I put on the kettle and made yet another pot of coffee. Then, when I could put it off no longer, I went into the study and sat down at the desk. I pulled the telephone directory from its shelf and flipped it open. I took out the piece of paper on which I had written the name and number that Victor had given me.

Charles Browning. The number was a landline. And the area code was the one for Greyfont.

I could have phoned on my way from the café in Oxford. But it's easy enough for someone to say on the phone that another person is not there, even if that person is in the same room as them. And if I'd talked to Nicky, it's always easier to put the phone down on an unwanted caller than to show him the door.

There was a Browning, C. J., listed in the residential section of the phone book, and he had the same number as Nicky's Charlie Browning. He lived at 3 St Ann's Lane, which was in the old part of town near the church. Early nineteenth-century terraced cottages, I remembered, two up and two down, most with extensions at the back and some with converted roof spaces; the front doors opened directly on to the street. They weren't cheap – nowadays nowhere in Greyfont was. They were the sort of houses that attracted single professional people or young couples with two jobs and no children.

I was scared about what I might find there so I found a reason to delay going. I remembered I had a job. I phoned Rachel's direct line at the office.

'Hi – it's me.'

'James! How are you?'

'Fine. Well, no, not really, not a hundred per cent. So I'm afraid I won't be in for a day or two. Maybe longer.'

'Are you OK?'

'Nothing a little rest won't cure. Gareth will cover for me if there's anything you can't handle.'

'Have you seen a doctor?'

'No. It's not like that.'

'I think you should. What does Nicky say?'

'She's away, actually.'

Rachel did not reply.

'I wondered whether she'd phoned you.' I risked a lie. 'She said she might.'

'No, she hasn't. James, are you sure you're OK?'

'Yes, of course.'

There was a short, uncomfortable silence. I didn't know how much Nicky had told Rachel.

'I'd better go,' I said. 'There's someone at the door.'

Once the lies start, they come easily, and the more you lie the more easily they come. The only person at the door was me and I was leaving, not arriving. I grabbed my jacket and keys from the hall and set off for the centre of Greyfont. I walked quickly. My mind was blank. I didn't have a plan. I met no one I knew, which was just as well because I couldn't have found anything to say to them.

St Ann's Lane sparkled in the morning sun. Number three was near the far end. There were pansies in the window-boxes and the front door was painted eggshell blue. Just beyond the single window on the ground floor a covered passageway ran through the terrace to the gardens or yards behind. Screwed to the wall beside it was a painted sign: CHARLES BROWNING. After the name were the letters MSTAT, a qualification I didn't recognize.

I rang the doorbell. I waited for what seemed like three years and rang it again. Still no one came. I tried to peer through the ground-floor window, but it was covered with an off-white linen blind. I walked down the passageway, which was paved with old bricks. Behind number three there was a tiny yard full of shrubs and flowers in pots, and at the far end, a modern single-storey building with long clean lines that should have clashed with the setting but complemented it.

A man was standing on the other side of a half-glazed door at its left-hand corner and his face was a blur through the glass. The door opened. He was tall and fair, with a neat little beard and narrow, sloping shoulders. Neither his face nor his figure had any resemblance to Carlo's, apart perhaps from the beard. An ambiguous feeling, somewhere between relief and despair, swelled inside me.

'Yes? Can I help?' The voice was light and pleasant. It sounded as if it had started life in Manchester but hadn't been home for some time.

'I'm looking for Nicky.'

His face changed. His mouth lost its smile and a couple of frown lines appeared on his forehead.

'You are Charles Browning?'

He nodded.

'Nicky's my wife,' I said, and took a step nearer to him.

'Yes, I guessed that. You must be James.' He was standing very still and looked relaxed. Perhaps dealing with aggrieved husbands was part of his everyday life. 'She's mentioned you.'

'You're in the same book group, I understand?'

'That's right. That's where we met.'

'Do you know where she is now?'

He said nothing.

'Is she here?'

'No, she's not.' He smiled. 'Come and see for yourself.'

He locked the door of the single-storey building and walked slowly down the path. When he passed me he came so close that I saw the silver threads in the fair hair at the temples and smelt a hint of after-shave.

He led me into a large, airy kitchen and through an archway to the sitting-room at the front of the house. It was an uncluttered room. Bookshelves filled the alcoves on either side of the fireplace. The only pictures on the walls were monochrome photographs of flowers. A couple of sofas faced each other across a coffee-table. He waved at the nearer. 'Do sit down.'

I stayed on my feet, looking around. Nothing was particularly expensive – most of the kitchen's contents had come from IKEA – but it was a home that someone had planned with care and affection.

'You're Charlie, aren't you?'

He scratched his neat little beard. 'Yes. That's what my friends call me.'

'Nicky does.'

'Not just Nicky. Lots of people.' He smiled at me again. 'I was half expecting you.'

He sat down on the other sofa and nodded at the one opposite. This time I took him up on the offer.

I gestured around the room. 'What do you do?'

'I teach the Alexander Technique.'

'You teach people how to stand? Give them exercises?'

'That sort of thing.'

'You teach Nicky?'

He shook his head.

I stared at him. Charlie Browning was being far too nice. He should be asking me to leave rather than giving me quiet reasonable answers. I wanted to smash the coffee-table over his head. Or possibly over my own. So here was the man that Nicky liked – sensitive, kind and caring; nice enough looking, as far as I could judge these things, and at least five or ten years younger than me. Equally disturbing was the fact that I had constructed a paranoid fantasy over the last few days on the strength of a similar first name, a beard and my own insecurities. It was hard to believe that I had allowed myself to entertain the possibility that Charlie Browning might be Carlo Murthington.

Charlie cleared his throat. 'I don't want to hurry you but I have an appointment in a moment.'

'I've been trying to get in touch with Nicky.' I waited but he said nothing. 'She's not been returning my calls,' I went on. 'I think she's switched off her mobile.'

'Maybe she wanted a breathing space.'

'Has she come here?' The question came out almost as a snarl.

'Yes.'

'When? How long?'

'On Sunday. That's when she arranged to use our cottage.'

There was a pause long enough for a couple of heartbeats. I repeated, like a parrot. 'Our cottage?'

'It belongs to my partner and me.'

Neither of us spoke for a moment. Then Charlie got up in one slow, fluid movement and went into the kitchen. While he was out of the room, I glanced at the spines of the books nearest to me. Paperback fiction mainly, with a couple of shelves of larger-format books below. I recognized two that Nicky had read in the last few months, including *The Turn of the Screw*.

Charlie came back with an unframed colour photograph in his hand. It showed a dark, compact man lying on the sofa where I was sitting. He was smiling at the camera and showing rather a lot of chest hair. Charlie was standing behind the sofa, leaning over it and holding the man's hand.

'Your partner,' I said slowly. 'I see.' Apparently I had been even more of a fool than I'd thought. 'I – I want to find Nicky. Can you tell me where the cottage is?'

'I'm sorry. No.'

'She's my wife.'

'It wouldn't be fair to her.' He hesitated. 'But I'll pass on a message if you'd like. Would that help?'

I should have liked to strangle Charlie until he told me where the cottage was. On the other hand, if I tried, I should probably discover he was a martial-arts expert as well. In the end I said, 'Would you tell her I'm worried about her and I miss her? Ask her to ring my mobile if she can't get me at home.' I wanted to add, 'Tell her I love her,' but I felt awkward saying this in front of a stranger.

Charlie put the photograph of his partner on the mantelpiece. 'I'm sorry to hurry you but we'll have to say goodbye now.'

I stood up. He opened the front door that led directly from the room to the street. Neither of us offered to shake hands.

'Thanks,' I said. 'I'll be in touch.'

'Look after yourself,' he said. 'This must be a very difficult time.'

I didn't reply. It's humiliating to be on the receiving end of someone else's compassion.

Charlie Browning closed the front door behind me. I turned right and walked down the lane towards the church. A door slammed. I glanced towards the sound and saw Miranda climbing out of her enormous Mercedes. She lowered herself heavily to the ground and waddled across the lane. She was wearing tight white trousers and a pink top that told me altogether more about her figure than I wanted to know.

'Hallo, sailor. Fancy seeing you here.'

'You knew about Charlie all the time,' I said. 'Didn't you?'

She opened her little eyes as widely as they would go. 'Didn't Nicky mention? That's funny. I've been doing the Alexander Technique for ages. It was me that brought Charlie to the book group.'

15

At the hospice, Lily was sleeping. I sat beside the bed and watched her. The freesias were still in the vase, which was now on the windowsill. They were beginning to look the worse for wear. Nobody had brought Lily any other flowers. I wished I had remembered to buy more. I should have liked to search the room for the chain but she was sleeping too lightly for that, and people were coming and going along the corridor. But perhaps the chain didn't matter any more. It only mattered if you knew what it had been, what it meant.

I had come here partly because I didn't want to stay at home. Our house felt like a prison. Nicky and I had moved into it three months earlier and promised ourselves it would be a place for a new beginning. It had turned into a place for an ending.

At least Lily couldn't ask me too many awkward questions. She was lying on her back. Her mouth was open and her right arm rested on her chest. The sleeve of her nightdress had ridden up. The arm was very thin now and surprisingly hairy. Even in the last few days she had altered. The window was open and everything was very clean but still there was a hint of decay in the atmosphere. She was dying quietly, and alone.

I got up to go. The chair creaked and Lily opened her eyes.

'Jamie.' She licked her lips, which were dry and flaky. 'I was dreaming about Hugh. Isn't that funny?'

I held a glass of water for her and supported her with my arm while she drank. A tall thin clergyman passed across the open doorway. Lily glanced at him. 'Is that Hugh?'

'No, it's not,' I said. 'Hugh isn't here.'

'Hugh's dead.' Lily pushed the glass away. 'I wish he wasn't.'

I put the glass down. 'I must go. I only dropped in to see how you were.'

'Much the same but worse.' She bared the yellow teeth in what I think was a grin. 'Hugh never really got over it.'

I knew at once what she was talking about. 'I'm sorry.'

'But Kate helped, of course. She was the only one who could make him forget. Not for long, but it was something. I want Kate, Jamie. Where is she?'

'I don't know.'

'Tell her she must come and see me. She's my daughter.' Lily sniffed and frowned. 'Have you found your wife yet? What's her name?'

'Her name's Nicky. No, I haven't.'

'Hugh said marriage is for life. You shouldn't just give up on it if it goes through a sticky patch. He's such a nice man, you know. He's somewhere here. I know he is.'

Lily stared at the doorway, as though willing Hugh Murthington to stroll into the room.

'Why did you choose me?' I said. 'For Christ's sake, why did it happen?'

'You and me? Because you changed. It was very sudden. One day you were just a boy, and then suddenly you were something quite different. And you were *young*. I couldn't stop it happening. Because I wanted someone young. That was the one thing Hugh couldn't be. I think he was born aged thirty.'

I said, because I suddenly needed to know: 'Tell me, was I the only one? Or were there others? Was I just one of a series?'

But I was too late. Though her eyes were still half open she was no longer aware of me. For a moment I wondered if she had died. Then I saw the muscles at the corners of her mouth were twitching. I had asked her a similar question a long time ago and I had never understood what her answer meant.

I left her sleeping and drove back to Greyfont, to the house that wasn't a home. I wished I had someone to talk to. I had colleagues and business partners, and people who shared the same interests as I had. Before I'd met Nicky there had been lovers as well. But I had never had anyone to talk to except Nicky.

At home, I planned my afternoon. I was going to mow the lawn. Then I was going to dig the long flowerbed at the far end of the garden, which was trying to revert to primeval jungle. It would be boring, back-breaking work but at least at the end of it I should be tired, perhaps tired enough to sleep properly. I went upstairs to change. I had pulled on a

T-shirt and was zipping up a pair of jeans with holes in the knees when the doorbell rang. I ran barefoot down the stairs. I don't know why I ran. I knew perfectly well that if it was Nicky she would let herself in with a key. I opened the door.

A strange man was standing in the middle of the driveway, staring up at the house. He brought his eyes down to me – slowly, like a panning camera. He was tall, with very short hair and a very short beard. He wore a grey suit, a white shirt and a bright blue tie. He was carrying a briefcase made of shiny black leather, like his shoes. For an instant I thought he'd come to sell me something I didn't want, like double-glazed uPVC windows or the keys to the Kingdom of Heaven.

'Hello, James,' Carlo said.

He looked tanned and fit. He was Carlo but he was also someone else. Our shared past had evaporated, leaving only a sour sediment behind.

'Aren't you going to ask me in?'

I wouldn't have known his voice. It was the sort you hear every time you turn on the radio or the television – a voice without tribal or geographical roots apart from a hint of outer London.

I said, 'Who told you where I live?'

'It's not much of a secret. Your company lists you as a director on its web page. You're in the phone book. You answered the phone at Chipping Weston this morning but you weren't there when I called round at the house. This was the obvious place to come next.'

I held open the door. Carlo stepped into the hall. He glanced round it, his face indifferent yet attentive, like an estate agent's. I led the way into the sitting-room. I offered him a chair but he prowled up and down, looking at the pictures and the ornaments. I stood on the hearthrug and waited. I was acutely conscious of the disparity in our sizes. I wished I was wearing shoes. My bare feet felt vulnerable.

Carlo came to rest at the window overlooking the drive. He touched Nicky's Raku bowl with the tip of his forefinger and turned back to me. 'Nice place. I expect you're pretty comfortable.'

'I get by.'

'More than that, I should think. No kids?' He waited and, when I didn't reply, went on: 'Except our Kate, of course. Or rather your Kate. Yours and Lily's.'

'What do you want?'

He ignored the question. 'I never liked her, you know. She never felt like my sister. Not one little bit. Not surprising, really.'

When in doubt, I thought, say nothing. Nothing does less damage.

'I only found out on Thursday,' Carlo went on. 'And you want to know how?'

Again I made no reply.

'Felicity told me.'

A shiver ran through me as though I'd been touched unexpectedly by something cold. 'I don't understand.'

'That's your problem.'

'It was all a long time ago, Carlo. We – we were different people then.'

'You don't get out of it that easily.' He picked up the Raku bowl and held it to the light. He turned it this way and that as though studying the glaze. 'Where is she?'

'Kate? I don't know.'

'She's a sly little bitch. You want to be careful with her.' He added, with an odd emphasis on the words, 'You can't believe a thing she says.'

'Is this true about Rackford?'

'Is what true?'

'That it's potentially much more valuable than it was.'

Carlo nodded. The bowl gleamed in the light. He ran his finger round the rim.

We no longer had anything in common but a shared past. Over the years he had become a creature of my memory, someone who was never more than seventeen; someone who was, in a sense, my creation. Now I had a large, angry, middle-aged man in my sitting-room. To all intents and purposes he was a total stranger. But he was also Carlo.

'Look,' he said suddenly. 'It's just not fair. Rackford was my father's. He bought it before he even met Lily. He left it to his children. But Kate wasn't his child so she's got no earthly right to it.'

'I don't know if a lawyer would agree with you.'

'Sod lawyers. I'm talking about what's right.'

'You can't be sure. Your father thought Kate was his. Perhaps she was.'

He shook his head. 'I'm having a test done. Not that there's any doubt about it.'

'And your father accepted her as his. Surely that's the point?'

Carlo did not reply. He stroked the inside of the bowl with a fingertip, working his way down in a spiral. Then he sighed and relaxed his grip on the rim. The bowl slipped from his fingers, fell to the floor and shattered.

He looked up at me. 'Oh dear. Sorry.'

I glanced sideways. We had an open fire sometimes and there was a poker in the hearth. I remembered how Carlo had behaved at the ten-pin bowling centre on his birthday. I remembered the boy he had beaten up in the park. Carlo would suddenly snap and become quite another person when his anger reached a certain level. I had always assumed that he couldn't know the whole story of that last afternoon at Rackford. But I was no longer sure.

'What exactly do you want?' I said.

'To warn you. Kate's planning something. She'll probably try to use you.'

'Planning what?'

'Work it out. When she was a kid she was greedy. She hasn't changed. She wants it all.'

'Rackford? She says the same about you.'

He picked up a vase from the bookcase. I tensed.

'Are you married?' I asked. 'Have you got children?'

He sighed. 'No children. I'm not married now either. I tried it once but it didn't work out. And you?'

Carlo put down the vase on the bookcase. He

walked slowly across the room to the door. Shards from the Raku bowl crunched and crumbled beneath his feet. In the doorway he stopped and looked back.

'Yes,' I said. 'Her name's Nicky.'

So Carlo and I went down to Chipping Weston in the summer of 1980. Occasionally, even now, I find myself imagining that somewhere in another universe there exists a version of me who didn't go down to Chipping Weston that summer. It wouldn't have taken much, after all – if my grandmother hadn't fallen on her doorstep, for example.

I know now that to expect too much is dangerous. On our first evening at Chipping Weston, Lily was wearing jeans and a sweatshirt, and her hair was scraped back from her face. She was slim and sexy and apparently uninterested in me.

'Felicity's just got a brace on her teeth,' she said to Carlo and me when she collected us at the station. 'Try not to mention it. She gets terribly self-conscious about how she looks. And I've got you a present for her. You can pay me back later. She doesn't know I bought it, by the way.'

Lily gave Carlo a little package wrapped in silver paper and tied with a purple ribbon. Carlo grunted. Felicity's birthday had been at the end of June and he had failed to buy her a present. Lily had volunteered to deal with it for him.

Carlo gave Felicity the present as soon as we got to the house. Her face turned pink with pleasure. She ripped off the wrapping paper and found a small box made of rosewood. Inside it was a silver pendant in the form of a leaping fish. In a way, the fish was like Hugh Murthington's freesias – another gift with a deceptive provenance and unintended consequences.

'It's gorgeous,' she said, and hugged him. 'It's beautiful.' She made him fasten the chain round her neck and admired herself in the hall mirror. 'I'm going to wear it always,' she said. 'For the rest of my life.'

'What a lovely present,' Lily said, edging away from me. 'Well done, Carlo.'

That evening I hardly exchanged a word with her. I spent more time talking to Hugh Murthington than anyone else.

'Ah, James,' he said, shaking hands, frowning as though quarrying my name from the depths of his memory. 'How is your – your grandmother coming along?'

I said she was as well as could be expected. He plied me with further questions about her, about my parents and my plans for university. If I had been a better person, his kindness would have made me feel guilty. Instead it made me impatient. He was nothing more than yet another obstacle between me and his wife.

I hoped at least for a kiss from Lily and tried to manoeuvre myself into situations where this might be possible. But she seemed to take an almost calculated pleasure in treating me as a sort of appendage to Carlo. I tried to steal a moment after supper but Lily avoided being alone with me and in any case I had reckoned without Black Maria.

Felicity, now thirteen, had recently learned to play

Hearts, the card game whose object is to avoid winning tricks containing cards of the hearts suit. She especially liked a version called Black Maria, in which the queen of spades is an extra penalty card. Each heart is worth one negative point but the queen of spades scores thirteen, which makes it as undesirable as all the hearts together.

We played Black Maria on the first evening – and every day after that, while I stayed at Chipping Weston during that last summer. Felicity was a persistent child. Unfortunately the game requires a minimum of three players, which meant there was rarely an occasion when either Lily or I was not playing. And Black Maria wasn't just a game. It became an elaborate joke designed to ridicule Lily.

'I know why you like this game,' Carlo said to Felicity on the second evening, when he and I were playing with her after supper.

'Oh, no, you don't.' She stuck her tongue out at him. 'Why?'

'Because it's Black Maria. She's nasty by nature and thirteen times as unlucky as anyone else.'

He stared at her, his face blank and innocent, and she stared back. They started laughing at the same moment.

I looked from one to the other. 'Is this a private joke or can anyone join in?'

'Black Maria,' Felicity said, in a stage-whisper. 'She eats babies for breakfast.'

'And raw snails,' Carlo added.

'And cat's poo.'

At that moment the door opened and Lily came in. 'What are you laughing about?'

'Nothing,' Carlo said. 'James was telling us a joke.'

'Dad and I are going out now. I'll leave the Millers' number on the hall table in case you need us.'

Carlo grunted. Felicity gave no sign that she had heard. I glanced at Lily. She was wearing a dress and high heels. I smelt her perfume. As the door was closing Carlo began to hum a tune from *The Sound of Music*. It was called 'How Do You Solve A Problem Like Maria?'

Still humming, he selected a card and put it down on the table. It was the nine of clubs. I had to follow suit so I put down a ten. Felicity gave a whoop and slammed down the queen of spades.

'Your trick. Poor old James.' It was the third time in three rounds that I had been left with the queen of spades. 'You just can't get away from Maria.'

She began to laugh, and Carlo joined in. I laughed with them, although I didn't like losing any more than they did, and I didn't like the way they were looking at me.

So Maria became our codename for Lily, which gave both of the others much pleasure. Felicity constructed a fantasy Maria to extend the joke's potential. At breakfast the following morning, for example, she confided to Carlo that Maria smelt.

'Really?' he said. 'Yes, now you come to mention it I suppose she does.'

'It's very bad,' Felicity went on. 'And getting worse.'

'Pooh.' He held his nose. 'What a stink!'

She began to giggle and both she and Carlo glanced at me.

'Who's Maria?' Lily asked. 'Anyway, perhaps she can't help her body odour.'

'Just a girl I know,' Felicity said. 'Not a very nice one. I don't think she washes very much. Madame Stinker has only herself to blame.'

'That's not very nice, dear. How would —'

'Can we go to Rackford today?' Carlo interrupted. 'I need all the practice I can get.'

Carlo had become deadly serious about his driving. If we had to spend the first half of the summer at Chipping Weston, he was going to use the time to pass his test and he had arranged to take the lessons he had been given for his birthday. He had booked a driving test, too, four days before we were due to fly to Rhodes.

The first lesson was scheduled for the afternoon of our third full day at Chipping Weston. I hoped this would give me an opportunity to be alone with Lily but Felicity ruined that plan. First she wanted a game of Black Maria, which involved all three of us, and then Lily sent us out to buy vegetables. I was furious.

Felicity and I walked into the town centre together. On the way we met her friend Millie. Since I had last seen her at Easter Millie had acquired small but unmistakable breasts, twin mounds that poked at her shirt, creating an oddly enticing gap between two of the buttons.

'This is James,' Felicity said, laying her hand for an

instant on my arm. 'You remember him, don't you?'

'Of course I do.' Millie giggled. She was no longer plump, either – she was much taller than Felicity, and her long red hair framed a face with green eyes and a big mouth. She grinned at Felicity. 'How could I forget?'

'We're just doing a bit of shopping.'

She giggled again. 'I like your pendant. Is it new?'

'Carlo gave it to me for my birthday.' Felicity touched the silver fish. 'It came in its own wooden box. Where are you off to?'

Millie said that she was going home but she was thinking of going to the cinema later in the afternoon. 'Do you want to come?' Her eyes flicked from Felicity to me and I realized with a shock that I was included in the invitation. 'Maybe Carlo'd like to come too?'

'What's on?'

'*Kramer vs Kramer*.'

'I've seen it. Anyway, we've got things to do, haven't we, James?'

Felicity glanced at me and I nodded automatically. For the first time I noticed that she was wearing eyeshadow and very pale lipstick. I hadn't known that she used cosmetics. I was sure she hadn't been wearing makeup when we were playing cards. She must have put it on just before we came out. It looked rather odd with the brace on her teeth.

'See you, then,' Millie said. 'Maybe I'll come round later.' And she smiled at me and swung her hair across her face like a veil. 'Nice seeing you again, James.'

'OK.' Felicity touched my arm again. 'Let's go.'

It seems so obvious now. But at the time I was almost wilfully blind. That summer I found myself spending almost as much time with Felicity as with Carlo. I didn't have the first idea what was going on in her head. I knew she sometimes made me uncomfortable. I knew I didn't particularly want to be with her. But what I didn't know, not then, was that in some sense she had fallen in love with me.

16

My mobile rang while I was sweeping up the fragments of Nicky's Raku bowl. I ran to answer it. It wasn't Nicky but a nurse from the hospice.

'I'm afraid Lily's taken a turn for the worse,' she said.

'I'm sorry,' I said, then wondered what I was sorry for.

'We'd like to get in touch with her children but we're not having much luck with the numbers we've got.'

'What are they?'

She recited the Chipping Weston number, followed by those of two mobiles I didn't recognize. I scribbled them on the cover of the phone directory. 'I've got another for her daughter,' I said. 'If you hold a minute I'll try it.' I used the landline to call the mobile I had given Kate. There was no answer. I left a message and went back to the nurse.

'Lily's really not at all well,' she said. 'I know you've already seen her today but is there any possibility you could look in again?'

'Is she – is she conscious?'

'Drifting in and out. She keeps asking for Hugh.'

'Her husband. He died last year.'

'I know.'

The nurse said nothing else. I listened to the silence that filled the house like a cloud of feathers, to the expectant silence at the other end of the line. Lily had been the sort of woman who accumulates friends and admirers. Now all she had left was a daughter who was afraid to see her, a step-son who hated her, and me. I glanced at my reflection in the hall mirror and saw a thin, pale man who looked faintly familiar.

'All right,' I said. 'I'll come over.'

The traffic was heavy and it was after six by the time I reached Wembley. At the hospice, Lily was asleep. Small and shrunken, she lay on her side with her knees drawn up and a drip trailing away from her like a thin, plastic tail. She didn't look quite human any more. It was as though she was in the process of migrating into another species. The biography of the dead actress was no longer on the bedside table.

I had bought her another bunch of freesias on the way, which was just as well because the old bunch had gone. Once I had found a vase for them, there was nothing else to do so I sat down and gazed at the figure on the bed. But I didn't think about her. Instead I drifted into my mind and thought about Nicky.

I had left a note on the kitchen table at home in case she came back. It said where I had gone and also gave her the name of the patient I was visiting. I tried to visualize Nicky's face, as though by doing so I might will her into existence and bring her through the doorway. It was surprisingly hard to remember her features. It was as though I knew her so well I no longer saw her face but something beyond it, something closer to the essence of her.

'Jamie.'

I got up and stood by the bed. Lily stared up at me but I wasn't sure whether she saw me. I touched her shoulder. 'Can I get you anything?'

'Jamie, where's Kate? You were going to fetch her.'

'I can't reach her. I don't know where she is.'

Lily began to cry. They were the weary tears of old age that slid almost unnoticed from the corners of her eyes. Sobbing takes effort, and effort was now a luxury she couldn't afford.

'I want Kate,' she said. 'She's my daughter.'

'I'll try to find her. I promise.'

'But it's too late. I can't bear it any more. Will you do something for me?'

'If I can.'

'Hurts too much now,' she said. 'I've had enough.'

'I'm sorry,' I said. 'I wish —'

'I want to go. I can't wait for Kate any more. I want you to put a pillow over my face.'

'What?'

'A pillow over my face.'

'Don't be foolish.'

Her lips curled into something that was almost a smile. 'Not foolish. Not for me. I asked them to give me something, but they won't.'

'You can't do that,' I said. 'And I won't help you.'

'Why not?'

'It's obvious.'

'I wouldn't have thought it would bother *you*.'

I noticed the slight stress on the last word. 'Well, it would.'

Her lips curled again. 'I need Carlo.'

'Carlo? Why?'

'He'd do it like a shot. Been wanting to for years.'

I said nothing.

'He'll kill somebody one day, if he hasn't already. And he damn nearly did before, didn't he?' Her voice was becoming slurred now. 'So, why not me?'

'What do you mean? Who was it?'

She didn't reply. Pain twisted her features. Her eyes closed. Gradually her face relaxed.

'Who did he nearly kill? What happened?'

Her chest rose and fell. Each intake of air made a soft, wheezing sound, but when she breathed out the flow of air seemed to hop and skip like a shallow stream flowing over stones.

I shook her shoulder gently. 'Lily. Wake up. What happened? What did Carlo do? It's important – for Kate's sake.'

The eyelids fluttered but remained closed. She said something else I couldn't distinguish. Then she added, quite clearly: 'Kate knows. And Millie, of course.'

Two hours passed. In that time Lily said nothing more, or nothing that I could understand. People came and went – I was rarely alone with her for more than a few moments.

The nurses were kind but professionally reticent. Lily was balanced between living and dying and the scales were swaying, first one side up and then the other. People die as they live, in ways unique to them-selves. A Church of England priest came and sat with us for a while. When she left the room I followed her into the corridor.

'Do you think Lily knows what's happening?' I asked her. 'Is she really asleep?'

'I don't know,' she said, 'but people are often like this. Neither one thing nor the other. I like to think there's a rhythm to it, that they go when they're ready.'

I said nothing.

'You look tired.'

'It's a difficult time.'

'She's in good hands.'

'I think I'll go home,' I said. 'I've got things to do.'

I drove back to Greyfont, thinking about Carlo rather than Lily. At home, the driveway was empty and the grass still needed cutting. Inside the house, I turned on the heating and checked the voicemail for non-existent messages. Five minutes later a frozen pizza was thawing in the oven and I was sitting at the kitchen table, drinking wine and watching my laptop flicker into life. I logged on. The only emails I had were from work, and I didn't bother to open them.

I fired up the search engine. I found nothing relating to 'Charles Murthington'. Could I trust what Lily had said? It was certainly plausible. If Felicity's friend Millie knew about it, it must have been some-thing that happened at Chipping Weston. I couldn't remember Millie's surname, if I'd ever known it.

I thought of what Carlo had done to the boy by

the swings in the playground all those years ago, the one who had bullied Felicity, and to the other boy at school, the one who had jostled me in the changing-room. But Lily hadn't known about those episodes, or about the girl at the Eagle on the night the fox died. So whom had Carlo nearly killed? And when? The threat of violence, usually concealed, had always been part of Carlo's charm. You knew it was there, part of his fabric, something hard and awkward like a knot in the grain of a plank. People don't change: they just find new ways to be themselves.

Why hadn't Kate or Lily told me before? As soon as I'd framed the question, I glimpsed a possible answer. I was their reluctant helper at the best of times. Perhaps they had feared that telling me more about his history of violence would make me even less enthusiastic.

Too late to think about that now. I felt queasy with fear. During the evening I drank most of the bottle of wine and forced myself to eat a third of the pizza. I went to bed early. At the back of my sock drawer was a packet of mild sleeping tablets that the doctor had given me a couple of years ago and I had never used. I swallowed a couple before I turned out the light.

I'm not sure I needed them. I slipped into a dream-less sleep and stayed there for seven and a half hours. When I woke up, I drew back the curtains. It was a grey, windy morning and the sky was spitting with rain. Somehow my sleeping mind had made a decision. It was still early, before nine o'clock. I didn't bother to shave or eat breakfast. I drove into the centre of Greyfont, the old village, and parked in the lee of the churchyard wall. I turned into St Ann's Lane. Most of its residents would have left already for work. At Charlie's house, blinds covered the windows at the front, upstairs as well as downstairs. Tucked up against the guttering was the metal oblong of a burglar alarm.

I rang the doorbell and waited. Nothing happened. I rang the bell again. Just to be sure, I tried phoning him. I stood on the doorstep with my mobile and listened to one phone ringing in my ear and another somewhere in the house. After a while Charlie's phone stopped and his voicemail cut in. I broke the connection.

The street was still empty. I walked swiftly down the passageway leading to the little gardens at the back of the terrace. The curtains were drawn across the windows of the studio. There was an outside tap beside the back door and a crowd of plants in pots clustered round it, like chickens waiting to be fed. I tried the door. It was locked. I peered through the kitchen window but a Venetian blind covered most of it. All I could see was a stretch of worktop and the edge of the sink.

It was a dead end. Even if there hadn't been a burglar alarm, I doubted I had the courage to break into somebody else's house in broad daylight. As I turned to go, my eyes ran over the dustbins beyond the tap. I hesitated, rubbing the stubble on my chin. Then I raised the lid of the nearer one. It was empty.

I replaced the lid and opened the second. It contained a black plastic sack, neatly secured with a double knot.

I didn't give myself time to think. I bent down and pushed my fingers under the knot. I hooked the bag like a fish. I put the lid back but in my haste I let it slip from my hand. It fell with a clatter on to the concrete path. I left it there and plunged into the gloom of the passage.

A door opened behind me. There were footsteps. A woman said, 'Hey – you! What d'you want?'

I didn't look back. At the street, I turned right and fixed my eyes on the church tower at the far end. As I walked, the plastic sack swung to and fro as though it was trying to escape me. It banged against my leg. I thought I heard footsteps pursuing me. Panic rose like nausea. I broke into a run. At the end of the lane, I didn't look back. I flung the rubbish bag on to the floor of the car. I started the engine but it stalled when I tried to move off. I heard myself swearing with a childish violence that even in my panic-stricken state amazed me. At my second attempt I managed to drive jerkily down the high street. An old man shouted at me and I realized I had jumped a red light at a pedestrian crossing.

The neighbour had seen me mainly from behind. She might have glimpsed my face in profile, but only for an instant. That was what mattered. As for the rest, I was wearing jeans and a dark coat with the collar turned up against the rain. There wasn't a great deal to describe. Anyway, I told myself, it was unlikely that the police would be interested in the theft of a bag of rubbish. These were reassuring arguments and made perfect sense. Nevertheless, when I reached home, my pulse was still racing and my hands were clammy.

I took the black sack into the garage and set it down in the middle of the concrete floor. I put on a pair of rubber gloves and teased apart the knot. I spread out sheets of newspaper and emptied the contents on to them.

There are people who make their living by going through other people's rubbish. I suppose you must get used to it, this intimate acquaintance with the waste-products of someone else's life. I picked my way through crumpled tissues and eggshells, torn packaging and emptied tins. There were papers, too – mainly flyers and junk mail. I studied them all. There was a rash of special offers at the local supermarket; someone was pleased to inform Charlie that he had been pre-selected for a ten-thousand-pound loan; and someone else was full of excitement about a plan to pedestrianize part of the centre of Greyfont. It was no good. All I'd achieved by going through Charlie's rubbish was to make myself feel physically and emotionally grubby. I began to shovel the debris back into the sack.

But the loan letter caught my eye as I picked it up again. Not the letter itself but Charlie's name above his address. In particular, what caught my eye was the middle initial, which was X. It was sufficiently unusual to distract me for an instant. Xavier? Xerxes?

But the X was probably a mistake. He had been Browning, C. J., in the phone book.

X. A single letter was all it took. The second glance gave me time enough to see the rest of the address. I sat back on my heels and made myself read the words very slowly, just to make sure I hadn't invented them: *Mr C. X. Browning, Wyesham Cottage, Larks Hill, Farleigh Pemberton, Bath, Somerset.*

Charlie's cottage, the one he shared with his partner, the cottage he had lent to Nicky. I abandoned the pile of rubbish on the garage floor and went back to the car with the letter in my hand. I found Farleigh Pemberton in a road atlas. I could be there in ninety minutes.

My instinct was to start the engine and go. But I forced myself to return to the house and make toast and coffee. After breakfast, I looked up Farleigh Pemberton on the Internet and discovered that its population was fewer than two hundred, that the church was late medieval, that the post office had closed two years ago, and that there was a farmers' market on the first Friday of every month. While I was on-line, I checked to see whether there was any news of Rackford. There wasn't.

It was still raining when I left Greyfont. I took an overnight bag containing a change of clothes and my laptop. The traffic was heavier than I expected. I cut down to the M4 and drove westwards. The weather seemed to mirror my state of mind. More than once I considered turning round and going home. Even if Nicky was there, she might not want to see me. And, for all I knew, she was long gone. She was not a person who vacillated.

The rain became heavier. The wipers slapped to and fro. The wind was blowing out of the south-west and throwing the rain against the windscreen. I switched on the heater. It felt more like February than May. But part of me wanted the journey to go on for ever.

I turned off the motorway and drove south first towards Bath, and then east into a network of smaller and smaller roads. At last I came to Farleigh Pemberton. The village was strung out on the side of an escarpment that faced west. Most of the houses were tucked below the road. A few, however, were on the higher ground, linked to the road by lanes carved into the hillside like old men's wrinkles, and running with rivulets of grimy rainwater.

Larks Hill was one of these deep-cut lanes. At the end of it, near the top of the hill, a five-bar gate was set in a tall yew hedge. I stopped the car in front of it and got out. On the other side of the gate was a stretch of gravel with a trim little garden to the left and a low stone cottage on the right. Nicky's Mini was parked on the gravel. Next to it was a Renault Mégane.

For a moment, I leaned on the gate, and studied the place. Rainwater trickled down my neck. There were cast-iron grilles over the cottage windows and enough hanging baskets to stock a small garden centre. An ornamental wheelbarrow with a cargo of pansies stood by the front door, and on the lawn was the sort of well that had nothing to do with water. A puddle the shape of Italy had formed on the gravel, and the rain was making the water dance.

I heard the sound of a car in the lane. I turned slowly. A black VW Golf came round the corner. The driver braked sharply when he saw the Saab. He switched off the engine and got out. It was the man I had seen in the photograph at Charlie's house in St Ann's Lane: the man who was lying on the sofa, smiling and showing his chest hair. Today he was wearing a shiny black leather jacket and he wasn't in a good mood.

The Golf's passenger door opened. Nicky climbed out. She was wearing jeans and a black moleskin coat that fitted snugly over her hips. She frowned at me. 'What are you doing here?'

I didn't answer, partly because the answer was obvious and partly because the words had dried in my throat. I had forgotten how beautiful she was, how elegant, how delicate.

'Well?' she prompted. 'What do you want?'

Charlie unfolded his long, thin body from the back of the car. He smiled at me. 'Hi.'

I ignored him. 'I want you to come home.'

Nicky shook her head. 'I'm going on holiday.'

I took a step backwards. I stared at her and tried to find the right words. There were raindrops in her hair.

'We're going to drive down to Montpellier.' She glanced at the man in the leather jacket. 'We're just about to leave.'

'You're going to France with these two?' I said.

'Why not?'

Charlie reached into the car and found a black umbrella. He opened it and held it over Nicky. He said, 'Jason's got a friend who's lending us a house. There's plenty of room. This is Jason, by the way.'

I nodded at Jason, and he continued to scowl. 'Your car's in the way,' he said. 'Would you move it?'

'I'd like to talk to Nicky.'

'That depends on her.'

'I'm not sure we've got time,' she said. 'And I'm not sure I want to talk to you.'

'Please.'

'Whatever you're going to do,' Jason cut in, 'can you move that car out of the way? I'm getting soaked.'

'Anyway, there's nothing to say,' Nicky said.

'There's everything to say. Can't we talk in private?'

'I didn't say we could talk at all.'

'We do need to get out of the rain,' Charlie said gently.

Nicky combed the wet hair from her forehead with her fingers. 'I'm not talking to you.'

'For God's sake —' I began.

'I don't trust you any more.'

'Just a few words. That's all I want.'

'And I want to get the car inside so I can load it up without getting even wetter than I am,' Jason said.

'He's right, you know,' said Charlie, the voice of reason. 'No point in getting wetter than we need to.' He unlatched the gate and pushed it open. 'James, if you drive over there, near the steps up to the lawn, that will give Jason plenty of room to turn and reverse up to the front door.'

Nicky glanced at him. 'You think I should talk to him?'

He didn't answer.

She turned back to me. 'Two minutes.'

While I was parking, Nicky and Charlie went into the cottage. Jason manoeuvred his car back to the front door. He caught up with me in the porch.

'You know something?' he said. 'I hate Charlie's lame ducks.'

The cottage wasn't large: one room deep and perhaps two or three rooms wide. A vase of lilies stood on the hall table and filled the air with a heavy funereal perfume. The wallpaper had Regency stripes. The cottage wasn't like Charlie's house and it didn't fit with what little I knew and guessed about Jason. But people are full of surprises.

'You can go in there.' Jason nodded to the room on the left, a sitting-room with pink peonies on the three-piece suite.

At that moment, Nicky came out of the room on the other side of the hall. She had shed her coat and somehow found time to tidy her hair. She followed me in and sat on a hard chair in front of a bureau. I stood by the window and looked at the rain.

'I've not decided what to do,' Nicky said. 'That's why I'm going to France with Charlie and Jason. I need time to think.'

She had left the door open. Charlie and Jason were moving in and out of the hall with bags and boxes.

Jason was explaining something about timetables with mind-numbing thoroughness.

'Nicky.' I stopped and glanced at the open door. 'Nicky, it's very difficult to say anything like this.'

'Why? Because of them? You don't think they're interested enough to listen, do you?'

'Yes.'

'Then don't say anything at all.' She started to get up. 'Anyway, there's nothing more to say.'

'Nicky. I love you.'

Her head jerked towards me as though tugged by an invisible rein. But she sat down again.

I said, 'You must let me try and explain. I know I haven't handled this well but if I could make you understand —'

'That's the trouble,' she interrupted. 'I do understand, and how do you think it feels? You felt like a change. Your old model's not quite what it was, it's showing its age. And it's got a big drawback you didn't know about when you got it. A fault in the design. So you've moved on to something a little more up-to-date.'

'It's nothing like that.'

'That's what it amounts to.' She sounded harder and sharper than I had ever heard her before. 'A sordid little mid-life crisis.'

'That's nonsense.'

'Maybe you've given it a pretty name, like falling in love. But really it's just one of those things that middle-aged men are always doing. Like — like getting high blood pressure or turning into pompous old bullies. And the real losers are the poor bloody women they're married to.'

'You needn't lose anything. Especially not me.'

'I know. In a way it's my fault. I can't give you what you most want and maybe that's the real reason. But do you know what's worst? I feel such a fool. I'd actually persuaded myself you were different, that you weren't like the rest.'

Jason was on the phone now. He was postponing an appointment with his dental hygienist.

'Can't we talk alone?' I said to Nicky. 'Please.'

Nicky sighed and knotted her fingers together and studied them. I realized with a lurch of dismay that she wasn't wearing her wedding ring.

'Nicky. Darling. You're what I most want.'

She looked at the bureau, not me.

'The Monday morning's out,' Jason said. 'Afternoon?'

'I'm not sleeping with her,' I went on. 'She's not my lover.'

'I don't even have a name for her.' Nicky turned to face me again. '"Love K." That's what it said on the text message. "Sorry to leave like that. You were great. Will call. Love K." Kiss, kiss, kiss.'

'It's not what you think.'

'Miranda was right about you. All men are bastards and it's just a matter of how much and when they reveal it.' She shook her head. 'It would be funny if it weren't so sick.'

'No,' Jason said. 'I can't do the Tuesday, either.'

'Her name's Kate,' I said. 'According to –'

'You always did like the name Kate,' Nicky said. 'I remember you saying that if we had a daughter maybe we should call her –'

'That's it. That's just it.'

'That's what?'

'All right, then,' Jason said. 'If there's nothing else it'll have to be four thirty.'

I moved away from the window and stood beside the bureau. I looked down at Nicky and said quietly, 'According to her mother, Kate is my daughter.'

17

It was Lily who had originally put the name into my mind, and it was such a tiny, insignificant thing that I had failed to erase it along with everything else. The four of us were in the car, on our way to Rackford. Carlo and Lily were in the front and Carlo was driving because now he was seventeen he had his provisional driving licence. Felicity and I sat in the back with as much space as possible between us. Felicity was telling Carlo about a friend of hers, who had just acquired a baby sister called Kate.

'I rather like the name Kate,' Lily said, over her shoulder. 'It's one of those names that never go out of fashion.'

'Like Maria, you mean?' Felicity said.

Carlo snorted. The car veered towards the nearside of the road.

'Careful,' Lily said. 'We nearly went up on the kerb.'

'All right,' Carlo muttered.

'And put the windscreen wipers on. It's starting to rain.'

'I don't like the name Kate much,' Felicity said. 'It's almost as bad as Maria. Sounds nasty and angry, like the one in the film.'

'The film?' Lily said.

'*The Taming of the Shrew.*' Felicity looked and

sounded smugly superior. 'Shakespeare, you know.'

Carlo drove on. We left Chipping Weston behind and threaded our way through the network of lanes north of the town. Hugh Murthington had taken Felicity to see the Zeffirelli film of *The Taming of the Shrew* because she was due to study the play the following term.

'Ow,' Carlo said.

'What is it?' Lily asked.

'Nothing.'

From where I was sitting I could see the side of Carlo's face. He had poked his tongue into his cheek and the skin was puckered at the corners of his mouth and eye.

'Toothache again?'

'Just a twinge. That's all.'

'You must see the dentist,' Lily said.

'It's all right,' Carlo replied. 'I'll have some aspirin when we get back.'

'No, you must have it seen to,' Lily persisted. 'Think what it would be like if it got worse when you were in Greece. You wouldn't know what to do.'

'Don't fuss,' Carlo said. 'It feels fine now.'

The car began to slow. He indicated right. We turned into the airfield entrance and drove past the ruined guardpost.

'Look!' Felicity said. 'There's a fox – near the control tower.'

We all looked. No one else saw it.

'It was there,' Felicity said. 'It was. I'm sure it was.'

'We saw a fox here once,' I said. 'Ages ago.'

She smiled at me. 'Yes, we did. I was there too.'

Her mouth was full of jagged teeth like white rocks roped together by the silver wire of her brace. 'It was my first lesson.'

I nodded. 'I remember.'

'Yes,' she said, still smiling. 'Just the four of us. You, me, Carlo and Dad.'

'Your father wasn't there,' Lily said. 'It was me.'

All of us drove that afternoon but Carlo most of all. After all, he needed the practice. It wasn't much fun for the rest of us because he paid obsessive attention to each manoeuvre. I had not realized that so much could go wrong with parallel parking, reversing round corners, three-point turns and emergency stops. And it was not enough for Carlo to get them right. They had to be perfect.

Even Felicity started snapping at him. As far as I was concerned, the real torture was that I was so close to Lily and yet, for all the good it did me, she might as well have been in another country. I was sitting immediately behind her. I could have leaned forward and nuzzled the nape of her neck. I could have stretched my hands over her shoulders and touched her breasts. Even the thought of these things, impossible though they were, aroused me and I had to keep my jacket draped across my lap so the signs of this were not obvious to Felicity. The rain continued, though it was never much more than a half-hearted drizzle. As the afternoon wore on, I became increasingly hot and uncomfortable – increasingly angry, too: it was as though the Murthingtons had somehow banded together to make me feel ridiculous.

Felicity said, 'This is so boring. Can I go down to the stream for a while?'

'But it's raining, dear,' Lily pointed out.

'So what? A little water won't hurt me. Anyway, it's not raining very hard.' She turned to me. 'Do you want to come?'

'OK.'

Felicity's face broke into another smile, all teeth, brace and pink gums. By then I think I would have agreed to anything that enabled me to get away from Lily. I didn't particularly want to go with Felicity but if we went down to the stream at least I could have a smoke. Carlo drove us round the perimeter road to the entrance on the western side of the airfield.

'We'll honk when we need you back,' Lily said.

Felicity and I climbed out of the car and followed the path through the belt of trees to the stream. The bracken had grown since the spring and the bottom of the little valley was green and crowded with vegetation. On the other side of the water was the ledge with Felicity's den.

'It's come on a bit since last holidays,' I said. 'Your den, I mean.'

Felicity glanced at it. 'I suppose so. I don't use it much nowadays.' She made it sound as though the den belonged to another era in her life, one that was unimaginably far removed from now. 'Are you going to have a fag?'

I nodded.

'Can I have one?'

I stared at her. 'I didn't know you smoked.'

Her thin shoulders rose and fell. 'You do now. Can you roll it for me?'

The rain had stopped. I took out my tobacco and squatted down. I was conscious of her watching me while I rolled the two cigarettes. Vanity made me work a little harder than usual to make the white cylinders neat and even. As I was licking the gum on the second cigarette I looked up at her. She was still staring at me. In that instant it struck me what an intimate thing this was, rolling someone else's cigarette. When Felicity put this in her mouth, I thought, my spit would mingle with hers. That was a repulsive idea. But if it had been Lily's mouth rather than Felicity's, the prospect would have excited me.

'Are you sure you want this?' I said. 'They're not good for you.'

'You smoke them. So does Carlo.'

'We're older.'

She said nothing. Her mouth was a tight, straight line. She held out her hand for the cigarette. I gave it to her and lit our cigarettes from the same match. When she bent over the flame the silver fish round her neck swung forward and brushed my cheek. She screwed up her face when she drew in the smoke and held the cigarette gingerly, between the very tips of her fingers. She did not inhale.

The packet of Golden Virginia was nearly empty so the tobacco I had used for our cigarettes was dry and powdery. A shower of burning shreds fell from the end of her cigarette. Two or three burning flakes landed on the front of her pale blue shirt.

'Look out,' I said.

Felicity brushed them away. But she was too late to prevent one burning a small, dark-rimmed hole in the material.

'Oh, bugger,' she said. 'Oh, shit.'

It was the first time I had heard her swear like that, too. I wasn't sure I liked the new Felicity. I preferred the old one, the predictable child.

I relit her cigarette. We stood there smoking, watching the water dripping from the leaves and the clouds moving sluggishly across the sky. I didn't want to look at Felicity, or talk to her. She smoked silently, as children do, and with obvious concentration, as though engaged in some religious rite designed to appease an obscure god. She smoked fast, too, so she had finished before I had half smoked mine. She flicked the butt into the stream. The current caught it. It slid across the surface of the water, turning slowly, and came to rest on the opposite bank.

'Do you want to see something?' she said. 'Something I found the other weekend.'

'What is it?'

Her eyelids fluttered. 'You'll have to come and find out.'

She set off along the bank downstream. There wasn't a path – it was a matter of scrambling through the gaps between the bracken, the brambles and the saplings. Still smoking, I followed her. Her bottom swayed from side to side. She was beginning to walk like a woman. I stopped to tie my laces. When I looked up again, Felicity had vanished.

I called her name. There was no answer. I made my way further along the bank. The hems of my jeans were getting wet. The stream curved into a sharp, right-hand bend. The land on my right rose more sharply. I walked on.

I heard Felicity laugh. She was above me somewhere. I scanned the trees and bushes that masked the slope. A second after my eyes had noted it, my mind registered a variation in tone and texture. There was something up there that looked like stonework, a fragment of wall. Roughly squared blocks of limestone were bound together with ivy. Not much of it was visible.

'James. Up here.'

I couldn't see her. I worked my way up the slope towards the stones. I found traces of her – footprints in the mud and downtrodden nettles. As I drew nearer, I discovered that the stones formed a low archway that seemed to lead into a tunnel to the depths of the earth. Mortar crumbled and oozed from the joints between the stones. There were brambles on either side of the archway and ivy trailed down from above so the opening was much smaller than the archway itself and there was little light within. I took a step towards it. 'Felicity?'

She didn't answer. I was suddenly afraid. Suppose there was some sort of mine or pit in there. Suppose she had fallen. Suppose she was lying hundreds of feet below me in the darkness with her bones broken.

Suppose she was dead. In the same instant that these thoughts flashed through my mind I saw myself blamed for the terrible accident, my life blighted because I had allowed Felicity to fall to her death.

'James.'

She was standing in the green frame of the archway. Only her top half was visible, which meant the ground inside was lower than outside. She was smiling, the whiteness of her teeth bright in the green gloom, and holding out her hands.

'What do you think? It's much better than the den we made, isn't it?'

'What is it?'

'I don't know. A sort of cave, I suppose.'

'Can't be. It's man-made. I think it's a kiln.' I wasn't entirely sure. 'A sort of oven.'

'There was another higher up the slope but it fell down. It's covered up with bushes now.'

I pushed aside one of the bramble suckers and peered into the dark interior. It was smaller than I had expected, walled and roofed with the same stone as the archway itself. There was a strong and unpleasant smell I couldn't identify. The roof was curved and, like the walls, tapered towards the back where the space ended in a crude apse. Roots poked through from the trees and bushes above. As my eyes adjusted I saw roughly squared pieces of masonry on the earth floor. The roof was slowly collapsing.

'For Christ's sake!' I seized Felicity's wrist and yanked her back into the open air. 'That ceiling could come down at any time.'

'What would you care?' she said, sounding angry. 'What?'

'What would you care?' she repeated.

'Of course I'd bloody care.' My mind had instantly replaced the falling-into-a-pit nightmare with an alternative version in which Felicity lay buried alive, her body mangled beyond recognition by the pile of masonry on top of her.

'Would you care?' she said, in a softer voice. 'Would you really?'

I was still holding her wrist and the bones felt tiny and delicate. She was looking at me with a peculiar intensity that made me uncomfortable. The brace glinted in her mouth. Her cheekbones were beginning to poke out and her face was no longer soft and rounded like a child's. At that moment, half to my relief, half to my annoyance, we heard the sound of the horn.

'Oh, shit,' Felicity said softly.

I let go of her wrist. Without a word we made our way down to the stream and walked along the bank in single file. I turned left up the path leading to the perimeter road.

'James,' Felicity said, behind me, 'you won't tell anyone, will you?'

I glanced back. 'About what?'

'About the cave. Or whatever it is. And about what happened. Even Carlo.'

'Why not?'

'Oh, because I want it to be a secret, and –' The horn sounded again. 'Can't she bloody shut up?' she added, with a sudden spurt of anger. 'She must know we heard her. Bloody Maria.'

We plodded upwards in silence. The car was parked at the side of the perimeter road with its engine running. We climbed into the back. Lily was in the driving seat. I knew, though I'm not sure how, that she was furious. It was something to do with the way she was sitting, the set of her head on her shoulders.

She rammed the gear lever into first. 'You took your time.'

'We came as soon as we heard,' Felicity said.

Lily turned to her for the first time. 'Look at the state of you. What have you been doing? Rolling in the mud? Isn't it about time you started to grow up?'

Felicity said nothing but the colour drained from her face. She seemed to shrink into the seat, as though making herself as small a target as possible. Carlo said nothing: usually he would have found some way to defend Felicity. I said nothing because I was hideously embarrassed, I didn't know what to say and I didn't want to draw Lily's anger towards me.

Lily looked more closely at Felicity. 'And what's that on your shirt? It's not a burn hole, is it?'

Felicity hugged herself.

'Have you been smoking?' She glanced at me with cold, remote eyes, then back at the girl. 'Have you? I want the truth, Felicity.'

No one spoke. I longed to be somewhere else. Lily glared at her step-daughter. My throat was dry. Felicity licked her lips and I glimpsed the jagged teeth and brace.

'It was me,' I said, and the words came out in a whisper.

'What?' Lily turned the glare on me.

I cleared my throat. 'It was me who was smoking. Felicity wasn't.'

Carlo let out his breath. Felicity stared at her knees.

'A bit of tobacco fell on her shirt,' I went on. 'That's how the hole got there. So it was my fault. I'm sorry. I'll pay for a new one.'

Lily's foot must have slipped off the clutch. The car jerked forward. The engine stalled. She muttered something under her breath and turned to face the front.

'Easily done,' Carlo said, to no one in particular. 'I've done it myself sometimes. Stalled, I mean.'

I didn't turn my head but I could see Felicity at the edge of my range of vision. I saw her hands relax and draw apart, her arms fall to her sides.

Oh, fuck, I thought. What have I done? Oh, fuck.

Nothing more was said about the cigarette burn, then or later. During the drive back to Chipping Weston, in fact, nobody said anything at all. For the rest of the day, I waited for something to happen. I was convinced that Lily or, more probably, Hugh Murthington would tell me that they were sorry but the trip to Rhodes was cancelled and I would have to go home immediately, wherever home might be – the school, perhaps, or over to the States to my mother and step-father.

But everything went on as before. Lily behaved to me as she had throughout the holidays, as though I were a semi-detached extension of Carlo, not quite family, not quite friend, not quite adult, not quite child, not quite anything. Felicity didn't say anything either, although sometimes I found her looking intently at me in a way that made me uncomfortable. Hugh Murthington was just as he always was – vaguely benevolent but with at least half of his attention elsewhere.

After supper, Carlo and I walked into the town and went to the Black Lion, where the landlord was relaxed about the ages of his younger drinkers. When we went out to pubs, Carlo and I bought rounds alternately, a routine we adhered to strictly and carried over to the next session. This evening it was my turn to buy the first round but he insisted on buying me a large vodka and a packet of Golden Virginia.

'There's no need,' I said, as he put the drinks and the tobacco on the table.

'This is like a birthday,' he said. 'So it doesn't count.'

I pushed the tobacco across to him. 'Thanks.'

Carlo sat down and took a sip of his drink. He opened the packet and began to roll a cigarette. 'Was she?'

'Was she smoking? Yes.'

'Bloody hell. They start younger and younger.'

'She asked me to roll it for her.'

'She's just a kid. Is she smoking dope too?'

'I don't know. No sign of it.'

'Oh, fuck.' His hand flew to his cheek.

'What is it?'

'Bloody tooth. It's OK.'

'Listen,' I said, 'I could have said no, but what was the point?'

He shrugged. 'If she's going to smoke, she's going to smoke. But why did you say it was you?'

'I don't know.' I thought about what had happened in the kiln that afternoon, about the way Felicity had stared at me with that strange expression when I held her wrist. 'I felt sorry for her, I guess. Do you think Lily will tell your dad?'

He frowned as he lit the cigarette. 'I doubt it. She doesn't like going to him about us. It's like a – what do you call it?'

'A confession of failure?'

'Something like that. Anyway, you're OK. They like you. They wouldn't want to change their minds about you being a good influence on me.'

He laughed and soon it was my turn to buy us a drink. The alcohol helped, as it often does for a time, and it was good to sit with Carlo on a small, masculine island, surrounded by a sea of chatter, tobacco smoke and loud music. They were playing an old song by 10CC on the jukebox – 'I'm Not In Love'. It seemed to say everything I felt. I wasn't in love with Lily. I just happened to be obsessed by her – or, rather, by my desire to make love to her. That's all, I told myself, I'm not in love, I'm not in love.

When the pub closed, we walked home slowly. The air was still warm. The clouds had cleared. It was a fine, dry night and despite the yellow haze of the streetlights you could glimpse the stars.

'Maybe we'll sleep on the beach when we're in

Lindos,' Carlo said. 'With a couple of girls to keep us warm, eh?'

We wandered, a little unsteadily, through the streets. The Murthingtons' road was less well lit than the town centre. There was a crescent moon like a bright fingernail. We stopped in a patch of shadow a few doors away from the house so we could finish our cigarettes.

'Fucking Maria,' Carlo said. 'She's really got it in for Felicity.'

I flicked away the cigarette end, an arc of sparks swallowed by the blackness of the hedge.

'We've got to do something.' Carlo swayed towards me. 'Teach the bitch a lesson.'

I shivered. 'How?'

He prodded my chest with a finger, forcing me to step backwards. 'Got to be careful, though. Because of Dad. But can't let the bitch get away with it.'

His voice was thick and slurred, the words tumbling over each other, like rocks in a landslide. He sucked hard on his cigarette and flung it on to the pavement. He ground the butt under his heel.

'I don't see what you can do,' I said.

'Nor do I. Not yet. But I know what I'd like to do.' He touched my arm, gently this time and his voice fell to a whisper. 'I wish she was dead.'

He staggered on and I followed him. When we reached the Murthingtons', the usual miracle happened: suddenly we found ourselves capable of appearing sober, at least for short periods. Felicity was already in bed. Hugh and Lily were watching television. We went upstairs, played our guitars for half an hour and went to bed early.

Time passed. I heard Hugh and Lily coming up to bed. I wondered whether they would have sex. Slowly the house settled. The more I tried to sleep, the more awake I became. It was hot, which didn't help, and neither did the possibility that Lily was making love with her husband. I threw off first the blankets on my bed and then the top sheet.

As time went by I thought more and more about Carlo's threats against Lily. I wasn't sure how seriously to take them. Carlo had a tendency to go one step further than everyone else. I sometimes thought he wasn't quite sane. Nor was I, of course – not where Lily was concerned.

At a little after one o'clock I got out of bed. I stood by the window, to one side so I could see more of the garden. The moon had moved and, though it was so small, it cast a grey light over the trees, grass and flowerbeds and gave them a faintly luminescent quality, like pearls or wet shells. I pulled on a T-shirt and jeans, then checked that I still had tobacco and matches in my pocket. I picked up my sandals, tiptoed round the end of the bed and opened the door.

Houses at night are different from their daytime selves: their spaces fill with silences into which noises drop like stones in a pool. The air is cool and still. Houses at night become the homes of unfamiliar dreams. Maybe, I thought, I would meet someone else on Rhodes, someone who would take the place of Lily, someone who wouldn't hurt so much.

The landing window was uncurtained. There was enough light for me to pick out the head of the stairs. I moved slowly across the carpeted floor. I could have found my way in complete darkness. I knew the Murthingtons' house as well as I knew anywhere, certainly better than I knew any of my mother's homes. If I was careful I should make very little noise on the stairs, so long as I avoided the third step down and the second step from the bottom.

I took the precautions automatically. My mind was elsewhere, bouncing unsteadily on the turbulence of the last few days, perhaps helped by tiredness and the alcohol in my system. I padded down the hall and into the kitchen. I unbolted the back door and slipped outside. I did not put on my sandals until I was on the grass, which was already wet with dew. I walked across the lawn to the little summerhouse where I had first met Lily and Felicity. By the time I got there, my feet were cold and wet.

The summerhouse was a grand name for what was no more than a rectangular wooden platform, perhaps three yards wide and two yards deep, which formed the base for a three-sided shelter with a pitched roof. The fourth side was open and faced the lawn. I perched on the narrow bench that ran round the inside of the walls and began to roll a cigarette.

The cold and the dark made my fingers clumsy. I couldn't see what I was doing. More by luck than good judgement, I managed to create a misshapen cylinder. I was just about to light it when I heard the click of the back door.

I pushed myself back into the shadows, into the corner furthest from the moonlight. In front of the summerhouse, the lawn shimmered: it seemed to shift and move like mist. For the first time I noticed there were two lines of darker smudges on its surface – my footprints in the wet grass.

One moment the lawn was empty. The next moment she was there, moving slowly towards me, treading in my footprints. The light was so poor that at first the figure was little more than a blur. But I knew at once it was Lily. She came closer and closer. I held my breath. Suddenly a blinding light filled my eyes. My fist curled around the unsmoked cigarette. I wanted to run away.

'Jamie.' Lily lowered the torch. 'What are you doing out here?'

'I couldn't sleep.'

'I thought you might be sleepwalking.'

I shook my head, forgetting she couldn't see me in the darkness. 'Sorry if I woke you.'

'You didn't. It's too hot. I couldn't get to sleep.'

'Nor me.'

She stepped into the summerhouse. 'It's cooler here. Were you coming out for a smoke?'

'I – well –'

'Oh, come on, Jamie.' She giggled softly, a low, throaty sound that ran down my spine like a small nocturnal animal. 'You and Carlo stink of tobacco. You're always nipping off for a smoke. You can hardly miss it.'

For a moment neither of us moved or spoke. I

wondered whether Lily would mention Felicity and the burn on her shirt. Instead she sighed.

'What is it?' I asked.

'I don't know. It's a bit chilly, isn't it?'

'There's the rug over there.' In the darkness I waved towards a wicker basket that stood in the far corner. 'You know, the picnic rug.'

I wondered whether she really did know – whether she remembered. The picnic rug was made of heavy cotton with a red-and-white checked pattern. We had used it when we had the picnic at the falconry centre the previous summer. The first time I had seen Lily properly, as opposed to Carlo's step-mother Mrs Murthington, was when she was lying on that rug at the falconry centre. I had thought she was asleep until she opened her eyes and caught me staring at her.

I opened the basket and pulled it out. It was heavier than I expected and slightly damp. I shook it out and draped it over Lily's shoulders. She stood there with her head bowed and her hands dangling at her sides, like a child allowing a parent to dress her. Our roles had mysteriously reversed. In the near-darkness of the night, she had become another person, someone smaller and more vulnerable than her daytime self.

'Why?' I asked.

'Why what?'

'Why haven't you been – why haven't you been talking to me this holiday?'

I was standing in front of her now, still holding the rug because otherwise it would have slid from her shoulders. I did not see her shrug but I felt it.

'Talking?' she said. 'Is that what you call it?'

'It's not fair. I'm going mad.'

'No, you're not, Jamie.'

I brought my face close to hers. 'Is there someone else? Is that what it is?'

She drew in her breath. 'I'm cold, Jamie. Wrap me up.'

Her arms glided round my waist. She drew me towards her. Her fingers dug into the small of my back and pulled apart, as though she were trying to tear the flesh from my spine, to fillet me like a kipper. Our mouths collided. I tasted blood. The rug fell to the ground. She was wearing a cotton nightdress. Her thin body rubbed and twisted against mine.

She pushed me into the back of the summerhouse, as far away as possible from the pale shadows on the lawn. Between us, somehow, we spread the rug, lay down and wrapped it over us. I pulled at the neck of the nightdress and heard the sound of tearing cloth. She fumbled at the waistband of my jeans.

I don't know how long we took. I remember crying out because Lily was holding me so tightly, and her hushing me by covering my mouth with the palm of her hand. I remember how the smell of her was unlike it usually was, because we were making love at night, whereas before we had always made love in the day when her face was made up and she wore perfume. I remember the hardness of the wooden floor, the way the rug rubbed like sandpaper against my skin and the desperate urgency of it all.

I was no longer cold. We pushed the rug aside. My

clearest memory of all is of Lily on top of me, rearing up like a pale grey ghost in a pale grey world that was only one remove from darkness. For an instant I felt as though a winged beast had trapped me with her wings and I would never escape. Then she made a wordless sound, a groan wrenched from deep inside her, and her body crumpled.

Afterwards we dressed in silence. I didn't know what she was feeling or even whether I had satisfied her. She stepped down on to the lawn.

'Is that it?' I hissed.

She stopped. 'I need to get back.'

'But aren't we going to talk? Aren't we –'

'There isn't time.' She was barely visible now, reduced to a shadow. 'Wait five minutes and then go to bed.'

'Do you do this often, then?' The words burst out of me before I knew they were in my mind. I hadn't realized I felt so abandoned, so angry.

'What do you mean?'

'All this.' I waved my arm in a gesture I hoped embraced the summerhouse, the rug, the hardness of the floorboards and the ritual that had just absorbed us. 'You know – having boyfriends. Making people fuck you.'

'No,' she said quietly. 'No, you stupid boy. How can you be so stupid?'

18

When the mobile rang I was only five minutes away from the M4 and driving too fast through the rain. I braked sharply and pulled into a lay-by. An articulated lorry swept past me, flashing its lights and sounding its horn in a long, sonorous reproof.

The other lorry, the road monster, sounded its horn on our way back from Rackford on the night of the fox, the night of the baby punk, and that was also the evening when Felicity cried, the only time I saw her cry.

I braked again, harder, and the Saab came to a stop, rocking on its suspension. The phone, still ringing, shot forward from the seat beside me on to the floor. I scrabbled among old newspapers and empty mineral-water bottles. It was still ringing when I found it.

'James?' Nicky said.

'What is it?'

'I've changed my mind.'

'So we can meet?' I said. 'You'll let me explain?'

'What?' Her voice was very far away. 'What?'

'The line's breaking up.' I opened the door and got out of the car. 'Is that better?'

'A bit. I'm not making any promises, James. All I'm saying is that I'll come and talk to Kate. Then I'll probably fly down to Montpellier tomorrow. What's the address?'

'It's in Chipping Weston. I'll take you there.'

'No. I want to drive myself.'

I said, 'I'm not exactly sure where Kate is.'

'Really? That's very convenient. So maybe I should go with Jason and Charlie after all.'

'No, don't – the odds are she'll be staying at her parents' house.'

'Her parents?' Nicky said, with a hint of sarcasm.

'She wasn't there this morning,' I rushed on. 'Or if she was, she wasn't answering the phone. But it's the obvious place to start. She – she's probably left a note.' I hardly knew what I was saying. I would have said anything to keep Nicky on the phone, to keep some sort of future for us, even if it only lasted a couple of hours.

'Anyway,' Nicky said, 'we're going in two cars.'

'All right. We could meet at a service station and go on from there.'

'What? Service station?'

'The line's breaking up again. Can I phone you back?'

'No – I'm at the cottage still. I'm using Charlie's line. The battery on my mobile's flat.'

'Meet me at Membury services on the M4,' I shouted, as though by raising my voice the quality of the connection between us would magically improve.

Nicky said something I couldn't hear and broke the connection. I stood in the rain staring at the phone, while the traffic streamed past me almost within touching distance, heading for the motorway. At least we were talking again. At the cottage, when

I'd told her who Kate was, she had told me to leave. I tried to explain but she wouldn't listen. She'd walked out of the room, and a moment later Jason had ushered me off the premises.

When I reached the M4, I made myself take the slow lane and settled down behind a pair of caravans. There was no point in hurrying. If Nicky had phoned from the cottage, I would be at Membury long before her.

At the service station, I parked the car, left a note for Nicky on the windscreen and went inside the building. I bought an in-car charger for Nicky's phone, a sandwich and some coffee. It had stopped raining so I took my lunch outside. I stood by the main entrance and watched the cars drifting in and out of the parking area, and the people drifting in and out of the cars. Too much time went by – enough for another cup of coffee and a lot more worrying. When at last the Mini Cooper nosed into the car park, it was after three o'clock. I glimpsed Nicky, pale and ghostly, hunched over the wheel. She parked several ranks away from the Saab. I waited for her to get out but she stayed inside the car.

I walked towards her. When I reached the Mini, she was still sitting in the driver's seat. Her eyes were fixed on the car parked in front of hers. She had been expecting me to come to her, I thought, and she had no desire to meet me half-way. I stopped beside her window, which was open.

'I nearly didn't come,' she said, without looking at me.

'I was beginning to think you wouldn't. I'm glad you did.'

'You know what really scares me? That you're lying again. That this woman isn't your daughter after all.'

I rested my hand on the sill of the window. 'What I said at the cottage was the truth. But not the whole truth.'

Nicky transferred her gaze from the windscreen and stared up at my face. She looked older than I'd ever seen her look before. Something turned inside me. I had made her look like that.

'You mean there's more?' she said. 'Or just more lies?'

'Kate's half-brother is someone I was at school with. That's how I knew the family in the first place. Kate says he's trying to kill her.'

'James, you can't seriously –'

'He's got a history of violence,' I said. 'Kate thinks he killed her ex-boyfriend. There's quite a lot of money at stake. And when I saw her on Monday her face was covered with scratches and bruises. He attacked her – that's what she said.'

'For God's sake! Don't be such an innocent. If there was any truth in all that she'd go to the police.'

'There's a reason she can't go to the police.'

'I'm sure there is. The reason being she's telling a pack of lies.'

'Kate says it looks as if she killed the boyfriend, not Carlo.'

'Carlo,' Nicky said, dangerously calm. 'He's the brother?'

I nodded.

'Either you're lying or she's taking you for a ride.'

'I'm not lying. Nicky, there's one more thing.'

'Just the one?'

I ignored the sarcasm in her voice. 'It's the only other thing that's important now. Kate's pregnant.'

There was a silence. Nicky lowered her head. She said something but I couldn't make it out. I asked her to repeat it.

She fiddled with the neck of her shirt. 'I said, that's all I needed. Are you sure that wasn't a lie too?'

I hesitated. 'She's about five months gone. So it's showing.'

'Well – either you take me to see this woman right now or I'm going to Montpellier on the next flight I can find. What's it to be?'

'Shall we drive in convoy?' I said.

'OK.'

'This is for you.' I passed the phone charger through the window. 'I don't want to lose touch.'

She tore at the packaging. 'That may not be up to you.' She hesitated and, at last, raised her head. 'You know, James, even if all this is true, all this nonsense, I don't understand why you've got involved. It really doesn't make sense. This woman you used to know phones you up out of the blue. OK, she's dying, and maybe you've got some sort of sentimental attachment to her. But that doesn't explain it, does it? Why you're acting like this – it's just not like you.'

'I – I suppose the fact that Kate's pregnant –'

'That's unkind, and you know it. And it's not

the truth, either.' Then she raised her voice and mimicked me: '"Or if it is the truth, it's not the whole truth."'

She was right. I said nothing. Then, right on cue, it started to rain again, more heavily than before. Within thirty seconds my hair was running with water and the shoulders of my jacket were dark and wet.

'We'll finish this later,' Nicky said. 'You're getting soaked.'

'But you'll come?'

'Yes. But for God's sake, go and find your car.'

Pursued by the rain, we drove north through the afternoon. On the road I phoned Kate's mobile twice but there was no answer. I wasn't sure whether to be glad or sorry. At least, I thought, even if Kate isn't there I can show Nicky the house. Words are treacherous, slippery things. But you can't argue with a house. You can't misinterpret something made of bricks and mortar and slates. The house might not prove the truth of what I had claimed but at least it would be a form of independent testimony.

We reached the A40 and joined a line of lorries moving sedately westwards. I kept glancing in the rear-view mirror to make sure that Nicky was still there. I was gambling my future with her. I had no way of knowing whether I would be successful. More than that, I had no way of knowing what constituted success. Not now – because the rules had changed. The one thing I did know was the nature of failure: if I lost the gamble, then I would lose Nicky.

By the time we got there, Chipping Weston was

crowded with cars and people going home. We turned into the Murthingtons' road. At the house, I pulled into the driveway and Nicky parked on the road. The landing window was open. I got out of the car and checked the birdbath where the spare key was kept. It wasn't there. I went into the porch and rang the bell.

Nicky came to stand beside me in the porch. 'No one in?' She said it in such a way that suggested she hadn't expected there would be. 'So what do we do now?'

I rang the bell again and didn't reply. We listened to the silence. After a moment, she touched my arm but there was no need because I had heard it too – footsteps on the other side of the door. Nicky drew a slow, deep breath.

Then came another sound, quieter than the first. Somewhere in the house a child was crying.

I hate it when children cry. I saw Felicity crying only once. It was in the evening, a few days before Carlo was due to take his test. By that time, of course, she was hardly a child but she still cried like one, letting the emotions run unchecked through her and making no attempt to wipe her eyes. She even stamped her foot.

It was a Friday and the three of us were alone in the house. Millie's parents had taken Hugh and Lily to Cheltenham to see a play at the Everyman Theatre, and afterwards they were going out to supper. We had already eaten our meal and were sitting in front of the television.

As usual I was thinking of Lily. We had made love twice more since the time in the summerhouse. On one occasion we had done it during the day, writhing and panting on the sitting-room carpet while Hugh was at work and Felicity and Carlo were visiting a friend of their mother's – their real mother. On another, when Hugh was spending the night in London, she had come to my room in the early hours and woken me.

'Wake up,' Carlo said. 'Let's go for a drive.'

I blinked. 'Now?'

'Why not? We'll drive out to Rackford.'

'You want to go to the airfield?'

'Don't be stupid – it's Friday night. Party time. We'll go to the Eagle and have a drink.'

'We could go for a drink in town instead. Then we could walk.'

'I want to go to Rackford.'

'But you haven't passed your test. You wouldn't be insured.'

'You sound like my dad,' Carlo said, with a grin that wasn't entirely friendly. 'No – you sound more like Lily.'

'Black Maria, you mean,' Felicity said. 'Yes, let's go to the Eagle.'

Carlo turned to her. 'I wasn't talking to you.'

'But I want to come.'

'You can't. Anyway, they wouldn't let you in. You're too young.'

'I could sit in the car. And you could bring me a drink and some crisps. Please, Carlo.'

He shook his head.

'I'm not sure this is a good idea,' I said. 'What happens if the cops stop you?'

'They won't. They're not going to stop me unless I'm driving dangerously.'

'Or if you have an accident.'

'Are you saying I'm not a safe driver?'

'No. I'm just saying –'

'You're chicken,' Carlo interrupted.

'I'm not. I'm –'

'Prove it.'

We stared at each other. I sensed that something more was at stake than whether we drove to the Eagle and had a drink. I couldn't put it into words then but I can now. Carlo was testing my loyalty as well as my courage. Also, he wanted to shock me and perhaps Felicity as well. The ability to shock people is, after all, a way of exercising power over them.

'Please,' Felicity pleaded. 'I'll do the washing-up when it's your turn.'

Carlo didn't look at her. 'No.' He hit my arm with his open hand, and the blow was a little too hard to have been merely playful. 'Well? Are you on?'

'If you don't take me, I'll tell,' Felicity said.

Carlo towered over his sister. 'If you tell anyone we've taken the car – *anyone* – I'll never talk to you again. Got it?'

The brother and sister stared at each other. Felicity's mouth opened. Her face crumpled, as though the bones had turned to jelly. That was when she started to cry. Carlo watched her for a moment.

He made no move to comfort her and neither did I.

He turned back to me. 'Are you coming?'

Felicity stamped her foot. 'It's not fair!'

Carlo ignored her. He raised his chin and stared down his nose at me. 'Well?'

'What the hell? All right.'

Felicity shrieked, 'I hate you. I hate you both.' She ran out of the room. We listened to her feet pounding up the stairs. Her bedroom door slammed.

'Women.' Carlo grinned at me as though we were the best of friends again. 'Christ. They're all the same.'

'Shouldn't you go up? See if she's all right?'

'No point. She'd just start yelling again. We'll let her cool down in her own time.' He tapped my arm again but this time his touch was gentle. 'Come on. I'll buy you a drink.'

It was a fine evening, and to the west the sky was streaked with red. Carlo drove to Rackford with great care. We didn't speak. When we reached the village, he didn't turn into the pub car park but left the Rover on the street.

'Don't want to get boxed in,' he said, elaborately casual.

I knew that really he was doubtful of his ability to manoeuvre the car in tight spaces. I followed him into the Eagle. The place was heaving with people, most of them young. It took us some time to reach the bar. We ordered Carlsberg Special Brews and drank them in a corner by the fruit machine.

There was too much noise for us to be able to talk easily and perhaps we hadn't much to say to each other. Instead we smoked furiously, sipped our beer and eyed the girls. In one corner of the bar it was somebody's birthday party.

'Christ,' Carlo shouted in my ear. 'I wouldn't mind a bit of that one.'

'Which one?' I shouted back.

He nodded towards the birthday corner. 'The baby punk with big tits.'

Baby punks were what we called people who played at being punks, the ones who kept the spikes and chains and safety-pins for weekends, and who scrubbed themselves up and smoothed themselves down for schools or offices on Monday morning. The girl in question was probably fifteen or sixteen. She wore a frayed denim skirt, a torn T-shirt and a leather jacket festooned with chains. She had a pink, plump face and someone had sprayed golden glitter over her hair. I didn't fancy her, but she had indisputably large breasts. The leather jacket was so skimpy that it enhanced rather than concealed them.

Carlo's lips moved. I couldn't hear him but I knew what he was saying: *She isn't wearing a bra.*

He was right about that too. I bought another round. The noise, the smoke and the alcohol were making me dizzy. Carlo kept glancing at his watch in the intervals between staring hungrily at the baby punk. I was only half-way through my second bottle when he suggested it was time for us to go.

I finished the lager and followed Carlo towards the door. As we threaded our way through the crowd we came close to the birthday corner. Carlo leered at the baby punk. She ignored him. But she looked up at me over the rim of her glass and smiled. Despite the breasts, she wasn't much taller than Felicity. The glitter on her hair and shoulders looked like golden dandruff.

Carlo and I came out into the yard at the back of the pub. By now it was twilight and the air was cool. The noise and light of the pub receded. The yard was full of parked cars and shadows.

'I need a pee,' I said, and sheered away to the gents', which had a separate entrance from the bars. No one else was in there, which was a relief, because I had drunk the lager too quickly and thought I might be sick. I waited, swaying, for several minutes, willing the nausea to pass.

I heard a faint scream, swiftly muffled.

I staggered outside. For an instant I thought the sound must have come from someone in the bar. But I heard movement beyond the toilets, on the far side of the yard where the shadows clustered most thickly. 'Hey?' I called. 'Where are you?'

There was no answer, but the movements continued and I thought they sounded urgent and violent. *Someone's beating up Carlo.* I ran across the yard. There wasn't much light but there was enough for me to see Carlo pushing someone against the wall. He was grunting and snarling – but quietly, which somehow made it worse. I heard the chink of metal on stone, and suddenly I knew exactly what was happening, and to whom.

'Stop it! For Christ's sake!' I grabbed Carlo's

shoulders and pulled him away. He resisted for an instant, then went slack. The baby punk was pressed against the wall. Her skirt was round her thighs and her breasts, no longer covered by the T-shirt, poked out like a pair of pale bombs.

'Quick, come on.' I broke into a run, pulling Carlo after me. I expected the baby punk to scream. But she didn't. She started crying instead.

I had to remind him to put on the lights. He wasn't used to driving in darkness; and twilight, with its treacherous, shifting shapes, was even worse. We left the village and drove fast along the narrow, winding road that ran round the western boundary of the airfield. The other road was faster, but that would have meant turning the car round. There hadn't been time for that.

'Fucking cock-teaser,' he said. He was panting like a thirsty dog.

'What happened?'

'She came out after me. She was asking for it. Then she pretended she didn't want it.' Carlo glanced at me. 'Sometimes they do that. They like you to be rough.'

'Slow down,' I said, fumbling to fasten my seat-belt.

Carlo accelerated. The Rover plunged onwards. 'It'll be dark by the time we get back,' he said.

'I hope Felicity's OK.'

'Of course she bloody is. You didn't mention my name, did you?'

'In the pub? I don't think so.'

'Then we're OK. That stupid girl can't do anything.'

'Do me a favour,' I said. 'Just think about driving.'

Carlo was hunched over the wheel. I hoped he was right about the baby punk. We came round a shallow left-hand bend on the wrong side of the road. A fox was standing in the middle of the lane directly in our path.

'Fuck,' muttered Carlo, and swerved.

For an instant I saw the fox clearly in the headlights, which were on full beam. For no good reason, I automatically assumed it was the one we had seen at Rackford earlier in the summer. Its eyes blazed, reflecting the headlights. Still looking at us, it started to run, moving towards the airfield's perimeter fence.

The car lurched on to the narrow verge. The driver's side scraped along the hedge. But Carlo was going too fast and the fox was running too slowly. There was a jolt as the nearside front wheel went over it.

'Oh, Christ,' Carlo said. 'Oh, shit.'

I turned in my seat. The headlights had dazzled me. I wasn't sure whether I saw or imagined a small patch of darkness on the roadway behind us. It was only a glimpse. Almost at once we were careening round a right-hand bend, and Carlo was fighting for control of the car. Afterwards the lane straightened. He cut the speed to less than thirty m.p.h. We passed the side entrance to the airfield.

'Bloody thing,' he said. 'Nothing I could do. Shit. Stupid animal.'

'Maybe it's OK. Just a bump.'

He didn't reply. Neither of us suggested that we should go back to see if the fox was alive. I thought that if it wasn't dead it was dying. I thought about how quickly it had happened, how quickly the ginger fur, the flesh, blood and muscle, the blazing eyes and the fluid movements had been converted to a ragged smudge of shadow on the Tarmac. I wanted to be back inside the Murthingtons' house with the car parked blamelessly outside.

Carlo was having trouble managing the head-lights. Several cars flashed us and one lorry honked its horn, a long, deep, booming sound like an outraged sea monster. By the time we turned into the Murthingtons' driveway, my back was sticky with sweat. But at least I was no longer feeling sick.

Carlo turned off the lights and switched off the engine. 'There,' he said, and his voice trembled slightly. 'Safe and sound. Told you it wouldn't be a problem.'

We got out of the car. I wondered whether there was blood on the bumper or the wheel arch but I didn't want to look. Carlo glanced at the side of the house. All the upstairs windows were in darkness. 'Felicity's asleep.'

'Maybe you should go up and check,' I suggested.

He unlocked the door. 'Or maybe you should,' he said over his shoulder. 'She likes you.'

I followed him into the house. 'You go. You're her brother.'

He stopped in the hall and stared into my face. He

smiled, as though what he saw there was a source of amusement. There were flecks of golden glitter on the shoulder of his shirt.

'OK,' he said. 'But it's been quite an evening. Let's celebrate. Why don't you get some glasses and some ice? I fancy a vodka.'

When he came down, we took the drinks out into the garden so we could smoke.

'Was she asleep?' I asked.

'Yeah.'

'She got really worked up.' I wasn't sure which girl I meant, Felicity or the baby punk, or perhaps both.

'Women. She'll be fine in the morning. You'll see.' He took a swallow of his drink, and suddenly his mood changed. 'She's been acting really weird lately. Have you noticed?'

I turned my head so he couldn't see my face, which was ridiculous because it was too dark to see it properly in any case. 'What do you mean?'

'Always uptight about something. Did you hear her yelling at Lily the other day? I mean, that's understandable, everyone should shout at Black Maria, but Felicity went way over the top.'

'She's growing up,' I said.

'She's just a kid.'

I let a silence grow between us. Felicity was using makeup more often, especially when she was with Millie. She had started wearing a bra since the Easter holidays.

'Shit,' Carlo said. 'Everything's changing. Dad's looking about sixty-four. Felicity's acting like a keg of dynamite. Lily's even more of a bitch than usual.' He hesitated, then said, in a lower voice that seemed not to have quite as much breath behind it as it needed, 'Even you're different.'

I turned so I could see the glow of his cigarette, his dark profile and the gleam of his glass. 'Everything's the same as it always was.'

'I don't know.' He sounded almost ashamed of himself, which was not an emotion I associated with Carlo. 'You just seem – not like you were before. It's not Lily, is it?'

'Lily? Of course not. Why should it be?'

'No reason.' The cigarette tip burned brightly and I saw his face, intent and red as the devil's. 'I just thought maybe you liked her.'

I crossed my fingers behind my back. 'She's a cow. Black Maria. The queen of the bitches.'

Carlo was standing so close I felt his breath on my cheek. 'Just wait till we get to Rhodes, eh? All those chicks. It's going to be great.'

'Yeah, it's going to be great,' I echoed, and thought of Lily splayed out before me, but then the picture was spoiled because she turned into the baby punk against the wall.

'So, things are OK?'

He was making me uncomfortable. 'Sure they are – of course.' I saw lights moving along the hedge that bordered the road. 'Look out, I think that's your parents.'

We flicked the cigarettes into the darkness and carried our glasses into the kitchen. We finished what was left in them and rinsed them in the sink. I heard footsteps in the hall.

'Nothing's changed,' Carlo said under his breath, as though trying to convince himself. 'Nothing's changed at all.'

But Carlo was wrong. More than one thing changed that night.

At about two o'clock in the morning, Lily scratched like a cat on my door. I hadn't expected her because Hugh wasn't away. We went into the moonlit garden and across the lawn to the summerhouse. For the first time I couldn't do anything. My body, the one thing I thought I could rely on, betrayed me.

'It doesn't matter,' Lily whispered. 'It really doesn't matter.'

I heard her speaking but I listened only to the silence around the words. She held me in her arms and stroked me but still nothing happened. I was helpless again, reduced to childhood.

'You're just tired, Jamie,' she said. 'It doesn't matter.'

But of course my failure mattered. So did the baby punk up against the wall and the fox in the lane. So did Felicity crying. Everything mattered.

'Don't worry,' Lily said, easing herself away from me and standing up. 'It happens. Next time it'll be fine. I'm going back to bed. Give me five minutes, OK?'

I didn't reply. She loomed over me, dark against the grey of the sky, and the world was silent and full of misery. She sighed and walked quickly across the grass to the house. I waited for as long as I could. At last, when I could bear the cold no longer, I went back into the house and climbed the stairs.

On the landing, I thought of Lily and Hugh, side by side, perhaps touching each other, within a few feet of me. A sour rage washed over me. I wished they were dead, like the fox. I was about to slip into my room when I heard a sound, the sort of click the lock of a door makes when it closes. It came from the back of the house – the bathroom, perhaps, or Felicity's room.

Yes, Carlo was wrong. Something changed that night and nothing was ever the same again.

19

The Murthingtons' house hadn't changed much in twenty-five years, apart from growing older and dirtier and more crowded. But there was one innovation I hadn't noticed on my last visit: the fisheye lens of a spy-hole set in the door. Someone was looking at us. I heard bolts rattle. The door opened a couple of inches, then stopped. It was on the chain. The child's crying increased in volume. A face appeared.

'Hi,' Emily said. 'I can't remember your name.'

'James.'

'I'm still looking for Sean. You haven't seen him, have you?'

'No. May we come in?'

'Who's this?'

'My wife. Nicky, this is Emily.'

The crying stopped as the distant child began to shriek instead. 'Mummy! Carry me!'

The door closed. I waited for the bolts to shoot home. Instead there came the rattle of a chain.

'Who's Emily?' Nicky hissed. 'Another of your young women?'

The door opened again. Emily was lopsided because she was carrying Albert on her left hip. He was holding her hair, and in his other hand was a wooden spoon, which he was waving to and fro very slowly and regularly like a metronome.

'Do you at least know where Kate is?' she said, in a voice that wobbled.

'No, I don't. May we come in?'

Emily nodded listlessly and stood back. She was wearing blue dungarees and a torn T-shirt. She hadn't brushed her hair recently and her complexion had the pale, slightly grubby quality that faces acquire when their owners spend too much time indoors eating the wrong sort of food and thinking the wrong sort of thoughts.

'I'm looking for Kate too,' I said. 'How did you get in?'

'I broke a window at the back.' She glared at me, challenging me to object. 'We found some food. And chocolate biscuits. You liked those, Albert, didn't you?'

'Tick,' said the little boy. 'Tock.'

'I *need* to find Sean,' Emily said loudly, as though explaining something so obvious it shouldn't need to be spelled out. 'The car broke down and I haven't any money. I had to go somewhere.'

As she was speaking, she turned away and began to walk down the hall to the kitchen. We followed. By the time we got there the crying had stopped. Maisie had emptied out what looked like an entire packet of cornflakes on to the kitchen table. Some had fallen on to the floor. She was cramming them into her mouth with both hands.

'Oh, Maisie,' her mother said.

The child continued eating.

'Will you please tell me what's going on?' Nicky murmured to me.

But Emily had heard. 'You don't know either? Nor do I.'

'Then why are you here?' Nicky said, in a voice so gentle it made the question inoffensive.

'Because this is where Kate Murthington lives.' Emily looked at me. 'Have you told her?'

'Not about you.'

'She broke up my marriage,' Emily said to Nicky. 'I'm trying to find my husband and remind him he's still got some responsibility to our children. And to me, if it comes to that.'

'She's still living here?' I asked. 'You've seen her recently?'

'She was here on Monday. She tried to scratch my eyes out. Her things are upstairs so I presume she's still living here.'

'Kate attacked *you*?' I said.

'Yes – on Monday. She's *vicious*,' Emily added, as though stating an inalienable truth to one of her children.

I remembered the scratches and the bruise on Kate's face. Kate had told me that Carlo had attacked her – but had it been Emily? And who had attacked whom?

'I thought I saw you on Monday,' I said. 'At the supermarket on the other side of town.'

She nodded. 'We stopped on the way home.'

'What happened to your car?'

'I don't know. It's completely buggered, I can tell you that. It's in a car park off the high street. We drove over from Bedford this morning, and I stopped there to get us a drink. But when I tried to start the car again, it made this horrible noise and smoke started coming out of the engine. So we walked here. No one answered the door and – Maisie, stop doing that.' Emily swooped on her daughter and lifted her away from the table. She began to heap the remaining cereal into a pile. Meanwhile the cornflakes on the floor crunched beneath her feet. 'Oh, God,' she said. 'Kids make such a mess. You can't leave them alone for a minute.'

'Let me help,' Nicky said. From somewhere she found a dustpan and brush and began to sweep up the cereal.

One of the lights of the kitchen window was broken and there were shards of glass still in the sink. I cleared them away and cut a piece of cardboard to make a temporary cover for the broken pane. I pulled out the overflowing pedal bin that festered under the sink and took it outside to empty into the dustbin, which was also overflowing.

Five minutes later, a degree of order had been restored. Nicky put the kettle on and we sat round the table. If any of us thought it strange to be doing this in somebody else's house, none of us said so. Albert sat on his mother's knee and continued to murmur, 'Tick, tock,' but more quietly than before. Maisie practised writing on the back of an envelope she had found on the worktop. She wouldn't look at us. She was pretending we didn't exist.

'What are you going to do?' I asked Emily.

'Wait for Sean. I know he's been here. And he must be coming back.'

'What makes you say that?'

'Because his jacket's over there.' She looked towards the corner by the door, where there was a chair against the wall. A blue waxed jacket was draped over the back. Her face crumpled. 'We both got one – we bought them in Cambridge. I was pregnant with Maisie. And I know it's his because of the tear in the left sleeve. He did that when he was pruning one of the apple trees at the farm.'

I picked up the jacket. It was definitely the flyweight Barbour Kate had been wearing when I first met her; I recognized the tear in the sleeve and the smudge of paint on the left shoulder.

'So I knew he must be here,' Emily said. 'That's why I broke in. And I was right.'

I glanced back to her. 'How do you mean?'

She delved into the bib of her dungarees and pulled out three scraps of paper, which she put on the table, slapping them down one by one, as though showing her cards in a game of poker. 'These were in the pockets.'

They were slips from automated teller machines. On Sunday, someone had drawn two hundred pounds out of Lloyds TSB's Chipping Weston branch. The second withdrawal, also for two hundred, had taken place yesterday at a cash machine in Paddington. The third, for a hundred and again at Chipping Weston, had taken place this morning. There was now £39.53 left in the account.

'See?' Emily tapped the table with her fingertip. 'That proves it. And he told me he was broke. I mean, Christ, we could live for weeks on five hundred quid.'

'So it's definitely his account?' Nicky said.

Emily nodded. 'I'm staying here till he comes back.'

'And if he doesn't?'

'I'll wait till he does. We'll camp outside on the pavement if we have to.'

'Poo,' Albert said. 'Tick, tock. Poo.'

Emily peered down the back of her son's waist-band and glanced at Nicky. 'I'll take him up to the bathroom. It's a bit messy.'

Maisie abandoned her drawing and clung to the leg of her mother's dungarees.

'Is there anything we can do?' Nicky asked.

Emily shook her head. 'Albert's very unsettled, aren't you, darling? It's all the stress. He's forgotten everything he ever knew about toilet training.'

She left the room with Albert in her arms and Maisie, still attached to the dungarees, trailing after her. Nicky and I listened to their dragging footsteps on the stairs.

'There's a lot you haven't told me,' Nicky said. 'Too much.'

'There hasn't been time.'

She looked at me, her face unsmiling. 'So, is the husband alive?'

I shrugged. 'Sean's jacket doesn't prove anything. Kate was wearing it when I first met her.'

'And Sean's the ex-boyfriend? The one the brother's meant to have killed? But if Emily's right, it looks as if he's been here. And it also looks as if your precious Kate has been telling you a lot of lies.'

'Not necessarily. It's –'

'You're not trying to tell me Kate was attacked by both Emily and Carlo, are you? Though from what I'm hearing it's more than likely that Kate was the one who did the attacking.'

'I don't know what to believe.'

Nicky got up. To my surprise she stretched out her hand and touched my shoulder. 'You look bloody awful, too. I don't know what Kate's up to, or what you're doing with her, but I do know that it's not agreeing with you.'

'I've told you the truth,' I said. 'I can't do anything else.'

'You can show me the house.'

'What?'

'Show me the house,' she repeated. 'It doesn't matter if Kate walks in – you're her father, aren't you?'

The question had a mocking edge. It didn't need an answer. I opened the door to the hall.

Nicky paused in the doorway. 'Are you really telling me the truth?'

'As far as I know it myself.'

She grimaced. 'You should have been a lawyer.'

We walked slowly through the crowded, dust-laden rooms. Nicky stared without comment at all the possessions that were no longer worth possessing. She looked out of place, a stranger in a country with inexplicable rituals and a lower standard of living than her own. The last room on the ground floor was Hugh's study. Nicky glanced at the photograph of Felicity but she didn't ask who the girl was. She picked up the card with the hospice's address and flicked it between her fingers.

'All in all, your Kate doesn't seem much of a victim to me,' she said. 'More of a hellcat.'

'It's complicated.'

'I'm worried about Emily and those poor children.'

'Emily's not much more than a child herself.'

Nicky nodded.

I smiled at her. 'So we can agree about that, in any case.'

She didn't return the smile. 'I don't think you should leave her here.'

'I don't think we've got much choice.'

'But Kate's already attacked her once. And you say that brother of hers is violent. Do you think it's true what Emily said, about having no money?'

'I only met her on Sunday, at Sean's house in St Albans. She says they used to be quite well off. Then Sean started having the affair with Kate and a little later he was sacked. I don't think either of them has much money now. Emily thought he'd come back for his passport. She couldn't find his bank stuff either. So the implication is that either he decided to disappear or someone wanted to make it look as if he had.' I shrugged. 'But it's their lives. It's you I –'

'But it's not just them, is it?' Nicky interrupted. 'It's the kids.'

'What do you think we should do?'

She said nothing for a moment. Then: 'It's your problem.'

'It's a mess.' I waited.

'You can't just leave them here. Not the children. We could contact social services.'

'Once they get involved, God knows what would happen. They'd probably notify the police, for a start.'

'So it's back to you.'

'What are you suggesting? That we take them home with us?'

She shied away from that idea. 'No, I was thinking – perhaps a hotel. Just for a night, so the kids can calm down and everyone can take stock. Have you got a better idea?'

I stared at her, wondering whether I should take her words at face value or treat them as ironic. But Nicky was always serious about children.

'There's a place called the Newnham House Hotel on the London road,' I said slowly. 'We used to go there for coffee.'

'You and Lily?'

'No. I went with Carlo.' I didn't mention Felicity. 'The thing is, will Emily agree?'

Nicky nodded. 'Leave her to me.'

'Thank you,' I said.

She was already in the doorway. 'I'm not doing this for you. It's for the children's sake.'

'I know,' I said, and I heard the bitterness in my voice. 'I know.'

By the time I had left the others at the Newnham House Hotel, the rain had petered out and the sky was a fresh, clean blue with wispy streaks of red cloud in the west. It was one of those clear, bright May evenings that seem to go on for ever.

Nicky and Emily were putting the children to bed. We had taken a family room for Emily and the children and a double for Nicky and me. I drove up to the main road, then north, following the familiar route to Rackford. At the entrance to the airfield I slowed, but at the last moment I couldn't face it. I went on to the village and parked outside the Eagle.

Before I left the car, I called the hospice and asked how Lily was. No change, they told me. She had spent most of the day asleep. No one had come to see her.

Suddenly I was ravenously hungry. I went into the bar. The place was much less crowded than it had been on my previous visit. I ordered a chicken salad and a glass of red wine from a well-maintained blonde with faded, puzzled eyes. While I waited for the food to come I nursed the wine at a table in the corner of the room – the corner where the baby punk had sat with the birthday party.

Three indeterminately middle-aged men were celebrating the end of the working day near the window. A young couple talked in an undertone, their heads almost touching, at a table next to mine. At the bar, two elderly men were sipping whisky. They

wore well-cut tweed jackets and neatly pressed cor-
duroy trousers; they had unlined pink faces and
scanty but neatly trimmed hair — they might have
been brothers. Everything was ordinary. No one was
talking about a murder.

The food came. The chicken was leathery and taste-
less. I ordered another glass of wine to go with it.

'House prices,' said one of the old men at the bar.
'That's the big unknown.'

'It's the traffic that's the problem,' the other replied.
'The village is crowded enough as it is. More houses
mean more cars.'

'It's not just a matter of houses. If the golf course
goes through, every Tom, Dick and Harry for miles
around will be coming here. More traffic. They'll
all be in a hurry. You mark my words, there'll be
accidents.'

'The golf course, though.' The other man drained
his glass and slid cautiously off the stool, holding on
to the bar for balance. 'That can't be bad, not for
house prices. It'll add a few thousand on.'

The two walked out unsteadily. A little later, I said
to the woman behind the bar, 'So, you're getting a
golf course?'

She wrinkled her forehead. 'There's talk of it. New
houses, too.'

'Where are they going to go? I wouldn't have
thought there was much room in the village.'

She jerked her thumb in the direction the old men
had taken. 'Over the hill. There's an old airfield up
there.'

'Have they got planning permission?'

'Not yet. Haven't even applied. But they'll probably get it if they do.' She laughed, automatically cynical. 'Sooner or later. If they grease the right palms.'

'Good for trade if it goes through.'

She smiled at me and leaned forward across the bar top, resting her elbows on the counter. 'So long as they're nice houses. We don't want any riffraff here. This is a nice village.'

I smiled warily back. 'I'm sure it is.'

'I've seen you before, haven't I? Weren't you in a few days ago?'

I nodded.

'On holiday, are you?'

'Not exactly.'

'On business, then.'

'Family business.' I finished my drink and stood up, abandoning the salad. 'What do I owe you?'

For an instant, the woman looked surprised, as if I'd failed to live up to expectations. I paid the bill and left. I had been a fool to go back to the Eagle, I decided, and a fool to strike up a conversation with a woman who remembered me from my last visit. When I drove away, I turned left out of the village rather than right, so I wouldn't pass in front of the window of the bar and risk the woman seeing the car.

But turning left brought me back to the airfield, and this time I was approaching it on its western side. For the first time in twenty-five years I drove along the lane where Carlo had killed the fox. It still zig-zagged, a left-hand bend and a right-hand bend. The fox had died between the bends. I accelerated hard into the second bend and the nearside of the car scraped the hedge. I felt the prickle of sweat along my hairline and in the small of the back.

I've done it. I've done it.

The hedges were higher on the right, and on the left, where the airfield was, the tangle of vegetation that sloped down to the stream had grown into a small forest. The lane had been resurfaced, and the fresh Tarmac overlaid the memory of blood. The side entrance, the one we used if we were going directly from the airfield to the village, was blocked with coils of rusting barbed wire. A buzzard hung in mid-air, wings outstretched, floating in defiance of gravity.

I skirted the boundary of the airfield and worked my way round to the main entrance on the eastern side. A clump of brambles masked the location of the guardpost. I pulled over on to the concrete apron. Further in there was a gate, new since my last visit, which was standing open. Without giving myself time to think about it, I let out the clutch. The car crawled through the gateway, jolting in and out of potholes.

The surface of the perimeter road had deterior-ated and most of the runways had vanished beneath the spreading tide of green and brown. The buildings were still there, but at some point the control tower had caught fire and only blackened wall remained. The surrounding land had been sown with what looked like cereal crops.

I parked beside the tower and got out of the car. It was very quiet – apart from the ticking of the Saab's cooling engine, the only sound was the distant murmur of traffic on the main road. I walked from one building to the next. All the doors had gone and I didn't see an unbroken window. In the Nissen hut where Lily and I had once made love, the metal table was still there, coated with rust. The calendar for 1954 had disappeared. I remembered how Lily had walked in front of me into the hut that afternoon, and how her hips swayed under her dress; and I remembered what we had done inside. But it no longer seemed very important. Revisiting the past diminished it.

Revisiting the past . . .

I went back to the Saab and drove round the perimeter road to the western side of the airfield, to the patch of woodland that sloped down to the stream and then up to the boundary fence along the lane. I left the car on the disused access road leading to the blocked side entrance. The path to the stream was still there, though narrower and less clearly defined than before. I followed it downhill.

In the little valley at the bottom, the stream was shaded oppressively by the bushes and trees on either side. I struggled along the bank to where Felicity had shown me the stone arch. I knew exactly what it was now – a primitive kiln, probably late-eighteenth or early-nineteenth century, where they would have made quicklime.

Revisiting the past . . .

But the past was no longer there. A pile of masonry marked the site of the kiln. Saplings and bramble shoots sprouted among the stones. In front of the ruin, the ground was relatively clear beneath the overhanging branches on either side. There was a cider can and a crisp packet, so old that the weather had bleached away the colours and made them ghostly. Someone else had been here more recently, perhaps several people – the ground underneath the archway and just in front of it was muddy, churned up by the movement of feet. There was nothing as straightforward as a footprint. I saw no sign of Sean.

Slowly my eyes adjusted to the green gloom under the trees. I scrambled higher up the slope and found another heap of stones, probably the remains of the second kiln, which Felicity had mentioned but I had never seen. On my way back, a speck of white caught my eye. It was the remains of a cigarette caught in the angle between two of the fallen stones. I stooped and picked it up. Just above the filter was the word Marlboro.

Kate smoked Marlboro Light. So did a lot of people. But, unlike the can, the butt had not been here long. I dropped it on the ground and wiped my fingers on my trousers.

I walked back to the stream. I felt an unexpected and perhaps undeserved sense of achievement. I hadn't found Sean and I hadn't found Kate. On the other hand, it was a relief not to have stumbled over

Sean's corpse. I had confirmed Kate's story that a developer was interested in the airfield and discovered a possible trace of her at the kiln. Also, perhaps most importantly, I had driven down the lane where Carlo had killed the fox and I had come back to the airfield, back to the stream and the kiln. I couldn't wipe out the past – I couldn't rewrite the memories and reroute the chain of cause and effect. But something had changed. Kate had done me a favour without intending it. There was nothing to be frightened of any more. The past was over. Maybe, I thought, maybe one day I can tell Nicky what happened. Maybe.

I followed the bank of the stream to the point where the path climbed up towards the perimeter road. The sun was low in the sky and some of its rays had found their way through gaps in the foliage. Bars of gold slanted across the stream where it curved into a bend. I glanced across, following the light to the opposite bank. I saw the spot where Carlo and I had helped Felicity build her den in that strange time when she was neither child nor teenager. Nothing remained of the den now and the ledge on which it stood had either been eroded or buried since I had last seen it. But there, outlined in the shaft of sunshine, was a square of cherry red, as vivid as blood against the browns and greens surrounding it.

On the other side of the stream, no more than five metres away from me, was what looked for all the world like a small red handbag – a simple rectangular shape with two loop handles. One loop had caught the end of a branch. The bag dangled above the water, close to the opposite bank.

In that instant, the bar of sunlight shifted. Where the handbag had been there was only a patch of shadow.

20

At the Newnham House Hotel, the first person I recognized was Carlo. The second was Nicky. They were sitting opposite each other in the bar that opened out of the reception area and drinking white wine. Nicky was laughing at something Carlo had said.

She was laughing because she was really amused, not because she was trying to be polite or because she couldn't think of any other response. Carlo looked relaxed too, and he was smiling. There seemed nothing left of the hard, dour man who had broken the Raku bowl in the sitting-room of our house in Greyfont. Instead I glimpsed someone who had once been my friend.

Slipping the red handbag under my jacket, I made a U-turn and headed for the door. I went back to the car park, where I locked the bag into the boot of the Saab. When I returned to the bar Nicky and Carlo were still where I had left them, and she was still laughing. I walked towards them. At almost the same moment, they looked up. I watched their faces change. Carlo pushed back his chair and stood up, holding out a hand. I shook it. He had an uncomfortably firm grip.

'Nice to see you,' he said, with an affability wholly at odds with his behaviour at our last meeting.

'I was about to phone you,' Nicky said.

I looked at Carlo. 'How did you find out we were here?'

'The neighbour saw you and your car. He mentioned a Saab. It wasn't hard to put two and two together.'

I knew, without quite knowing how, that he was lying. 'But how did you find us here – at the hotel?'

He glanced at Nicky and smiled, inviting her to share his amusement at my scepticism.

'Emily,' Nicky explained. 'The neighbour heard her saying something to the children as we were leaving. He was in his garden on the other side of the hedge. Something about a hotel, and that it wasn't far.'

'So I thought I'd ring round on the off-chance,' Carlo said, signalling to the barman for another glass. 'Might have known you'd try the Newnham House.'

'Where's Emily?' I said.

'Upstairs with the children. She and Albert are a bit under the weather.'

The barman brought me a glass. An uneasy silence settled over the table. The three of us hadn't any small-talk. The strangest of strangers are those you once knew well.

Carlo cleared his throat. 'I was saying to Nicky – I've come to apologize.'

'What I really find amazing is that you haven't mentioned him until today,' she said to me.

'You came to apologize,' I said to him, my voice sounding harsh in my ears. 'What for?'

'For barging in on you the other day. I was under

a lot of strain.' He turned up the palms of his hands and studied them. 'I'm afraid I wasn't very diplomatic.'

I thought of the Raku bowl and nodded.

'I also wanted to say sorry that you had been dragged into our little family dispute.'

'I know about Lily,' Nicky said. 'James told me this afternoon.'

He smiled at her. 'Whatever happened between James and my step-mother is ancient history. I only found out myself on Thursday. I came across something that gave me the hint when I was going through my father's things.'

He paused, and I waited for him to drop Felicity's name into the conversation. He glanced at me and I thought I saw malice in his eyes.

'A hint was all it needed, really,' Carlo went on. 'I think on some level I already knew. Kate and I have always been like chalk and cheese – and, looking back at that last summer James had with us, it's no surprise. All the signs were there, but I didn't know how to read them.'

'It must have been terrible,' Nicky said.

Carlo shrugged. 'It's a long time ago.'

'Do you think your father knew?' she asked.

'I'm not sure. It's quite possible he didn't. He was very fond of us all but he wasn't an observant man. Anyway, it all came to a head last Thursday,' Carlo continued, directing his words to Nicky. 'I haven't seen much of Kate lately – I'm living in London these days – but we happened to coincide here. We don't see eye to eye about my father's estate and then this business with Lily came up, and that was the last straw. We had a row.'

'By her account, you terrified her,' I said.

'She terrified me,' Carlo said. 'She's a little vixen when she's angry. And I must admit, if she's not my father's daughter, I find it hard to see what moral right she has to a share of his estate.'

'The fact that he treated her as his daughter? That's ignoring the very real chance that she is his child.'

'As to that, we'll soon know.' He turned back to Nicky. 'I'm having a DNA test done. Not so much for the legal side of it – I don't think it would be of much use in a court of law – but for my own satisfaction. I like to know where I stand. Especially where my family's concerned.'

After a pause I asked, 'And how does Kate feel about the test? You can't alter the fact that she's grown up thinking you both have the same father.'

'She doesn't know I'm doing it,' Carlo said. 'Unless you've told her.'

'Why are you two like this?' Nicky asked.

'Like what?' I said.

'Like a couple of dogs trying to pick a fight.'

'You're right. This isn't helping anyone.' Carlo raised his glass. 'So, let's have a toast. To sweet reason.'

Nicky picked up her wine and looked at me.

I left my glass on the table. 'What's going to happen?'

'With what? With Kate?' Carlo was still looking at Nicky. 'I wish I knew – I don't even know where she is.'

'She thinks this is about Rackford.'

'The old airfield? And why should she think that?'

'She said she saw a letter from a property developer. A letter to you.'

'It's true I've had a preliminary discussion about what we could do with the land, but it's no more than that.'

'Who've you been talking with?'

'I don't think we need to go into that now.'

'And what about Sean?'

'The boyfriend? I assume that's his wife and children upstairs. Was she the one who broke the kitchen window?'

'Yes,' I said. 'But what about Sean?'

'What about him?'

'You didn't see him on Friday? At the airfield?'

'I didn't even realize he and Kate were still an item. Are they?'

I gave up that line of questioning and tried another angle. 'As I understand it, your father left his estate to you and Kate, but Lily has a life interest.'

Carlo nodded.

'What happens if one of you predeceases her?'

As I asked the question, he was taking another sip from his wine. He coughed and put the glass down.

Nicky said, 'James, are you sure you –'

'If Lily dies first, we divide the estate into equal shares,' Carlo said. 'But if one of us predeceases her, then the other gets the lot when Lily eventually does die.'

'And what happens if one of you dies before Lily, and that person has a surviving child?'

His lips moved. He was trying to smile but his muscles weren't co-operating. 'Then that child would inherit the parent's share.'

'And neither of you has any children yet – is that correct?'

'Perfectly.' Carlo leaned forward and rested his elbows on the table. He was smiling now, back in control. 'Kate's been letting her imagination run away with her. She was always inclined that way. She was asked to leave one of her schools because she had a habit of making up stories. Anyway, I don't see what you're getting at. Lily's dying. There's no debate about that. After she's gone, and I'm afraid it probably won't be long, Kate and I will see what we can do with Rackford. It's all quite straightforward and above board.'

Carlo made it sound so reasonable. And perhaps he was right. Perhaps Kate had let her imagination run away with her. It wasn't as if I had discovered Sean's body at Rackford. All I had found was a cig-arette butt and a cherry-red handbag. If Emily was to be believed, Kate had lied to me about Carlo attacking her. And, also if Emily was to be believed, Kate had had a far more predatory relationship with Sean than I had understood from Kate's version of it. The only thing I didn't doubt was Kate's preg-nancy. I had seen the curve of her belly and the glow on her skin.

'Anyway,' Carlo said, 'I'm so glad we've all had a chat. And I hope we've cleared up some of the problems.' He smiled at Nicky. 'We must all have dinner some time. I'll give you my card.'

He took out his slim black wallet and produced a business card, which he slid across the table. The card described him as a marketing consultant and gave an address in Hendon.

'You know what puzzles me,' I said. 'It's that you got in touch with me, out of the blue, at the same time. All of you – you and Kate and Lily.'

'No mystery there.' Once again, Carlo seemed to be talking to Nicky rather than me. 'In a manner of speaking it was my fault. As I told you, I had come across your company on the web and seen your name, and just gone from there. You know how it is – you get curious about people you used to know. And then on Thursday, when all this blew up, I blurted it out to Kate. So it's my fault you got involved. Sorry.'

He shook hands with us again, smiled at Nicky and patted me, briefly and awkwardly, on the shoulder. 'I'll be in touch,' he said. 'And if you need me for anything, my phone number's on the card.'

Nicky watched him leave the bar, walking through Reception and out of the revolving doors at the front of the hotel.

'Well?' I said. 'What do you think of him?'

'I rather liked him. He seemed straightforward. It was nice to hear a bit of plain speaking.' She paused. 'Nice-looking, too.'

I sat down and picked up the glass of wine. 'He's up to something.'

I was grateful that at least Carlo hadn't mentioned

Felicity. On the other hand it also made me wary. Sooner or later, Nicky would have to know. I didn't want Carlo to be the one to tell her so the sooner I told her the better. I turned over in my mind the words I would use. I was about to open my mouth when one of the reception staff came into the bar area and made her way towards our table.

'There's a message from Mrs Fielding,' she said to Nicky. 'She phoned down and asked if you could go up to her.'

I stood up but Nicky shook her head. 'You might as well stay here and finish your drink. I'll phone down if we need you.'

I watched her walking through the lobby to the lifts. When she was gone, I went through the french windows at the end of the bar and walked round to the hotel's car park. The important point, I thought, was that I hadn't found Sean's body at Rackford. I had found the handbag and the cigarette butt, both of which supported the rest of Kate's story, but the significant thing was the absence of Sean. He might still be alive. His fight with Carlo might never have happened.

In that case, was I looking at this whole business from the wrong angle? Was it some sort of conspiracy between Kate, Carlo and perhaps Lily with me as its intended victim? The ownership of Rackford might have nothing to do with it. Maybe some or all of the Murthingtons simply wanted to destroy my life.

I opened the Saab's boot and took out the handbag

I had found at the airfield. It was a jaunty affair –
rather like a small, squashed leather bucket. The top
was held together by a zip which had been open when
I found it. I emptied the contents on to the floor of
the boot and felt the bag's lining. There was nothing
there. I worked my way through Kate's possessions.
There were crumpled paper handkerchiefs, a phone
without any charge on it, and a bunch of keys, which
looked as if they belonged to the house. A foil-
wrapped stick of sugar-free chewing-gum had wedged
itself into the bristles of a small hairbrush. A blue
leather purse contained a collection of receipts, five
debit and credit cards and a driving licence. The driving
licence was one of the newer sort with a photograph
of the holder. In the miniature picture, Kate looked
improbably pretty, like a Barbie doll or a face on a
television screen. There was no cash whatsoever.

I put everything except the phone back into the
handbag and tucked it into the box of tools I kept
in the boot. I went back to the hotel. On my way
upstairs, I asked the receptionist to have the phone
charged for me.

Nicky was not in our room. Her suitcase was on
the bed but she hadn't unpacked it. I called the extension for Emily's room. Nicky answered.

'Everything OK?' I asked. I heard a child wailing
in the background.

'Albert's got an upset tummy,' she said, in a res-
olutely cheerful voice. 'I'm giving Emily a hand.'

I heard Emily shouting something. 'Anything I can
do?'

'Not really – oh, wait a moment, maybe there is. I don't suppose you'd like to read Maisie a story?'

'Of course I will,' I said, without enthusiasm.

'I'll bring her along to our room. She's got a book with her. And afterwards she may want to have a little sleep on our bed.'

'Of course.' I liked the way Nicky had said *our bed*. I cast around for the sort of hospitality that might appeal to a small child. 'Would she like a drink of something? Shall I look at the room-service menu?'

Nicky gave a snort of laughter. 'A fruit juice from the fridge will be fine. Not a Coke, though. If she wants milk, you could phone down for it.'

A little later there came a knock on the door. I was unexpectedly nervous. I wasn't used to being responsible for a small child and I wasn't sure how you did it. Nicky led Maisie into the room. Maisie was carrying a green plastic satchel, a grubby white blanket and the purple monkey I had seen at Sean's house. She stared up at me as if she didn't like what she saw.

Nicky presented me with a book whose cover showed a youthful wizard standing on tiptoe to stir an enormous cauldron. 'James will read to you now,' she said to Maisie. 'He'll get you a drink if you want, but you must remember to do your teeth afterwards and then you'll have a rest. Mummy or I will come and fetch you in a bit.'

The child wandered into the room and stopped in the middle of the carpet. Nicky jerked her head at me, summoning me into the corridor.

'I'm afraid Emily's in a bit of a state. On top of everything else, Albert's got rampant diarrhoea and I think she's going down with it too.'

'What about you?'

'I'm fine.' In fact, Nicky looked more cheerful than I had seen her for weeks. 'The toothbrush is in the satchel, if you need it. Do try and encourage Maisie to get some sleep. The poor kid's exhausted.'

When I went back into the room, Maisie was standing at the end of the bed with the blanket and the purple monkey pressed to her mouth. She was wearing pyjamas whose colours had faded from too much washing. The top was too short to cover her plump little belly. I had a moment of complete panic. 'Well,' I said brightly. 'I suppose we'd better do some reading.'

Maisie said nothing.

I piled the pillows at the head of the bed. 'We'll sit here. We'll be more comfortable.'

There was no response so I put my arm round her shoulders. She allowed me to steer her. I thought I would have to lift her up but at the last moment she decided to climb on herself. I covered her with the duvet. She wedged the satchel against her body and pinned it in place with her arm.

Sitting next to Maisie seemed a little too intimate for the length of our acquaintance so I sat on the side of the bed. All the time she held the purple monkey and the blanket up to her mouth. I wasn't sure but I thought she was probably chewing her fingers.

The youthful wizard turned out to be very good at finding things because he had one spell that made invisible objects visible and another that operated as a sort of occult sonar. He was a nauseatingly smug child who, according to the illustrations, wore an oversized green dressing-gown and carried a wand like a policeman's truncheon. The story lasted ten minutes, and by the end of it I was exhausted.

Unfortunately Maisie was not asleep. She was still staring fixedly at the book, with the monkey and the blanket against her mouth.

'Would you like to shut your eyes for a bit now?' I suggested.

She muttered something I couldn't catch.

'What was that?'

'Again.'

'You want me to read the story again?'

'Yes. With the pictures.'

This involved a certain amount of rearrangement. I sat beside her on the bed and held the book so she could see the pictures. The weight of my body drew her towards me, and it would have been natural for her to nestle against me. But she pulled away.

I began to read. As the story progressed, I was aware that Maisie was drawing slowly closer. She examined each picture carefully and on two occasions grunted furiously when I tried to turn over before she had finished her inspection. First the blanket slipped away from her mouth, then the purple monkey.

When I had finished the second reading, I suggested again that she might like to settle down. She said she wasn't tired so I offered her a drink. Her eyes gleamed when I opened the minibar. Before I had time to object, she seized a can of Coke, opened it and retired to bed with the purple monkey, the blanket and the book.

While she drank, she turned the pages. She turned again and again to a picture of the wizard's house, a small pink building with a tower. It nestled on the slope of a mountain, its windows overlooking a lake in which the wizard had found several items his neighbours had lost.

'Do you like the lake?' I said, to break the silence.

She nodded.

'What do you like about it?'

'Granny lives near a lake.'

'Really? What's it called?'

She shook her head. 'It's a nice lake. It's much bigger than this one. It's as big – as big as America.'

'I'm sure it is.'

'It's the biggest in the world. Daddy took me there.'

'That must have been nice.'

'We went to see Granny. We went in a boat on the lake.'

'So Granny's your daddy's mother not your mummy's?'

Maisie nodded. 'Mummy hasn't got a mummy. Or a daddy.' For the first time she looked directly at me. 'I know a secret.'

'What's that?'

'I can't tell. It's a secret. It wouldn't be a secret if I told you.'

'But if you told me and I didn't tell anyone it would still be a secret.'

She thought about this specious suggestion, which seemed to satisfy her. She leaned towards me and her hair brushed my hand. 'Mummy doesn't like Granny. She told me.'

'Do you like Granny?'

'She smells funny. But it was nice being with Daddy. It was just us, him and me. And it was nice on the lake.' She twisted on the bed and hugged the purple monkey to herself. 'I've got a picture.'

'Have you? Can I see?'

She dug out the green satchel, which had become entangled with the duvet. She opened the strap and emptied a jumble of toys, crayons and crumpled drawings on to the bed. The envelope was there too – the one she had been using to practise writing in the Murthingtons' kitchen. She had written her name, Maisie, all over it in letters that staggered up and down in a variety of sizes.

'Nice writing,' I said.

I turned the envelope over. There were more Maisies on this side, and I admired those as well. I also noticed that the envelope was addressed to Mr Charles Murthington at the Hendon address on the card he had given us earlier this evening. The postage mark on the envelope was dated at the beginning of last week and had the company logo of Tarborough's beside it.

Tarborough's. I knew the company – we had even done some work for them over the years. They were London-based with a head office near Moorgate.

Maisie squealed with triumph and dug out a dog-eared colour photograph from among the drawings. She passed it to me. It showed her with a man I had never seen before in the stern of a small boat on a stretch of grey water. Maisie was on the man's lap and she was wearing a yellow lifejacket. He had his arms wrapped round her and his chin resting on the top of her head. He had a round face, gold-rimmed glasses and a receding hairline. It was hard to get an impression of his size from the photograph but I thought he was probably small.

'So, that's your daddy?'

'Yes.' Maisie lifted the purple monkey to her mouth and began to chew her fingers again. She added something I didn't catch so I asked her to repeat it.

'We're going to go back one day,' Maisie said. 'We're going to sail from side to side in a big boat. There's a monster that lives in the lake. And Daddy says we're going to find it.'

21

For years I thought of myself as a monster. You can't change the past: you can only try to forget or forgive what you were, what you did. I tried both tactics, first one then the other, but neither worked.

There are few things more obtuse than a teenage boy with sex on his mind. Looking back, I remember that Felicity didn't smile much in those last few days and that she spent a lot of time by herself. When I was with Lily, however, she often contrived to be with us. Jealousy feeds on what causes you pain. It also makes you preternaturally observant. A scorned woman is no less terrifying, no less vulnerable and no less perceptive if she is only thirteen years old.

I overheard Lily and Hugh talking about Felicity while they were having tea in the garden on Sunday afternoon. They were sitting on the lawn in front of the summerhouse, the scene of my humiliation on Friday night. Lily was doing most of the talking, as was usual when she and Hugh were together. Carlo was having an extra driving lesson at the time, at vast expense because it was Sunday, and Felicity was spending the day at Millie's house.

I didn't mean to eavesdrop. I had been into town by myself to buy tobacco from the garage shop. I came through the gate at the back of the garden so I could have a quiet smoke in the old vegetable garden where nobody grew vegetables any more. I was on the other side of the hedge from the Murthingtons, no more than five yards from them. I had no idea they were there until Lily began to talk as I was rolling a cigarette.

'Felicity will need some clothes before school starts,' Lily said. 'I thought I'd take her to Cheltenham or perhaps Oxford.' There was a pause. 'Of course, London would be better.'

Hugh muttered something I couldn't catch.

'I can't help that,' Lily replied. 'Growing up's an expensive time. At least she'll be worth it in the long run.'

'What do you mean?'

'In a few years' time she'll be quite an elegant young woman. Clothes will look good on her.'

'Oh, Lord. Boyfriends.'

Lily laughed. 'Not for a while. Anyway, my bet is she'll be more elegant than sexy. So perhaps the boys won't go for her.'

I thought the last remark had a touch of complacency about it. A silence followed, broken by the chink of china.

'You mustn't be so possessive,' Lily went on, sounding amused, though Hugh hadn't said anything. 'She's not going to be your little girl for ever. Just be glad you're not Millie's father.'

'Why? Nothing wrong with Millie, is there? Rather – ah – rather clumsy, poor kid, but –'

'Early developer,' Lily said. 'You just wait. She'll soon have boys round her like wasps round a spoonful of jam. It won't last – she'll be running to fat by the time she's in her twenties. That sort always does. But not Felicity.'

I licked the gum on the edge of the paper, rolled the cigarette and slipped it into the pocket of my shirt. Hugh said something else I couldn't hear.

Lily laughed. 'Jamie? Well – who knows?'

Overhearing that conversation made me feel uncomfortable, as though I was at fault. In a sense I felt guiltier about listening to Hugh and Lily chatting than I did about making love to Lily. I suppose eavesdropping on a conversation between a friend's parents was something I'd been brought up to think of as socially inappropriate, while what I was doing with Lily had nothing to do with society. It was hidden away, a thing apart that existed in a different place from the rest of my life, a place without rules.

I turned, intending to retreat as quietly as possible to the gate. That was when I saw Felicity. She was standing in the gap between the hedge and the greenhouse. Her hand was pressed against her mouth and her eyes were fixed on me. She was wearing Carlo's present, the silver chain with the fish pendant. The chain round her neck looked like a piece of Christmas tinsel decorating a plucked bird hanging in the butcher's window. I had no more wish to touch her than I would an uncooked chicken.

Felicity stared at me in silence.

What strikes me now is how callously I behaved towards Hugh Murthington. At the time he seemed barely important. In retrospect, to make matters worse, he was clearly such a nice man. I never heard him raise his voice, I never saw him act unkindly. There's a dark irony in that if he hadn't been so considerate I would not have gone to Rackford on the day before Carlo's test.

We were due to fly to Rhodes at the end of the week, on Saturday. Carlo's driving test had been booked for Tuesday. It was arranged that Lily would take us both out for a drive on Monday afternoon: I would drive at the airfield for a little and Carlo would practise on the roads.

In the morning, however, Carlo's toothache grew suddenly worse. It had been troubling him all summer but he had tried to ignore it. He never admitted it but I think he was afraid of the dentist. By Monday he could no longer endure the pain and Lily made him an emergency appointment for the afternoon.

Hugh came home for lunch. It was a hurried meal, partly because of Carlo's appointment and partly because Felicity was due at Millie's house by two p.m. She left while we were clearing up, and I saw her wheeling her BMX bike past the kitchen window. She was wearing a white T-shirt, which showed off Carlo's fish. Hugh waved to her and she waved back.

'Ah – what about James?' Hugh asked, when Felicity was out of sight. 'Will you still take him out for a drive?'

'I hadn't really thought,' Lily said.

'No reason not to,' he said. 'I'll be around if Carlo needs someone.'

'I suppose so.' She sounded unenthusiastic. 'It's very hot.'

I didn't dare look at her.

'And Felicity won't be back till this evening,' Hugh went on. 'If Carlo wants a drive later on, I'll take him out. If he feels up to it.'

Lily glanced at me. 'What do you think, Jamie? Maybe you'd rather stay here?'

I stared at my plate. I knew she didn't want to go. 'No, thanks,' I said. 'I'd rather have a driving lesson, please. If you don't mind.'

On the way over to Rackford, neither of us spoke. It was very hot. Lily turned on the radio, and classical music poured out of the speaker, preventing conversation. I stared sideways at her with fascination, longing and loathing. *Why hadn't she wanted to come this afternoon?*

We drove on to the airfield. The runways quivered in the heat. The Rover drifted round the perimeter road and glided to a halt beside one of the dispersal bays near the western boundary, not far from the stream and the side gate to the lane. Lily turned off the radio. Without a word we got out of the car. I heard the distant throb of a tractor engine. Somewhere in the trees, wood pigeons were cooing.

'I've got a bit of a headache,' Lily said. 'Do you want to drive?'

'You know what I want,' I said, and my voice was thick, heavy and sticky like black treacle.

'Jamie.' Lily waited in silence until I had turned to her. 'This can't go on.'

I looked at her across the roof of the car. 'Why can't it go on?'

'Because I'm married to Hugh and you're Carlo's friend. Because you're sixteen and I'm old enough to be your mother. That's why.'

'Doesn't matter. None of that stuff matters.'

'It does. I shouldn't have let things get this far.'

I knew Lily was right, and not just for those reasons. But it didn't matter. I walked round the car to where she was standing by the driver's door. I gripped her arm between elbow and wrist. She flinched, just a little. I enjoyed that. But I didn't want to be like Carlo with the baby punk so I let go of her. 'We can't just stop,' I said.

'We can.' Her colour was high and she was breathing hard. 'We should never have started in the first place.'

'Lily – please. Just once more.'

'No. We should –'

'We could go down by the stream. I know some-where really private. No one would ever see. You must.' I was gabbling and the sweat was running down my face. I knew that it was over, that we would have to stop. I didn't care. I just wanted her now, and I wanted her all the more because this had to be the last time. I wanted to take her down to the kiln and make it last for ever. 'Please, Lily. It'll be so good, I swear. Once more. Just once.'

'Stop it,' she said. 'Sooner or later you're going to meet a girl of your own age and you'll want to be with her. You'll probably find someone waiting for you on Rhodes.' Her mouth twisted. 'You don't want someone like me. You're young, Jamie. You've got it all in front of you.'

'I don't want anyone else. I want you.'

'Don't be silly. Let me go.'

I realized I'd taken hold of her again. I let go of her arm. I hated her. She made me feel stupid. She was treating me like a child. She rubbed the bare skin where I had gripped her. She was still breathing hard.

'Well,' she said brightly, 'shall we go home or do you still want to do some driving?'

I felt a surge of rage at the unfairness of it all. Lily had wanted me to make love to her, had wanted me to be an adult. Now she'd had enough and she expected me to return to being a child. Shaking with anger I opened the driver's door and slid behind the wheel. I twisted the key in the ignition and watched her moving through the heat to the passenger door. I touched the central-locking switch and the locks slammed home.

'Jamie.' She rapped on the window, which was an inch or two open. 'That's enough. Don't be stupid.'

'I'm not a child,' I said.

'What are you doing?'

'Going for a drive,' I snarled. 'That's what you want me to do, isn't it?'

'Jamie, just calm down. That's enough. All right? You've made your point.'

I'm not a child.

I let out the clutch. For once I had perfect control, and the Rover moved slowly and smoothly forward.

Lily was still holding on to the door. First she walked, then she broke into a run.

'Jamie,' she shouted. 'Stop. We'll talk.'

I didn't reply. In my head I was saying over and over again: *I'm not a child, I'm not a child*. I changed up to second gear and suddenly she was gone. I accelerated, changing up to third. Exhilaration flowed into me. I changed up to fourth. I was going faster than I'd ever driven before. I followed the perimeter road to the main gates. I slowed, changed down and drove past the ruined guardpost.

I'm not a child. If Carlo can do it, so can I.

The exhilaration changed into something dark and bitter, an emotion I had never tasted before. I was going to make Lily squirm, I thought, I was going to show her who was boss, show her I wasn't a kid to be pushed around. I decided to drive round the airfield, up to the village and back. She'd think I'd left altogether. She wouldn't know what to do. But then I'd turn up at the airfield, driving perfectly. I'd slow down beside her and ask, oh-so-casually, if she'd like a lift. Then I'd say that if she wanted a ride, there was a price to pay. And there would be nothing she could do about it.

I'm not a child, I'm not a child, I'm not a child.

I drove into the lane without stopping to see if anyone was coming. I pressed the accelerator. Driving was easy. I followed the twists and turns of the road. The Rover roared past the airfield's side entrance. *I'm not a child*. On the left was a high, unkempt hedge and on the right the rusting boundary fence.

Everything was noise and movement. The car slid over to the right and careered round a sharp left-hand bend.

This is where Carlo hit the fox. Oh, Christ –

In front of me was an old green tractor parked against the hedge. In front of the tractor was Felicity. She was running, trying to get away from the oncoming car. But she hadn't expected the car to be on the wrong side of the road. I swung the wheel to the left. Her mouth was open but the noise of the engine drowned all other sounds.

I'm not a child.

A moment later I saw the silver fish quite distinctly. It was an instant of extraordinary clarity. Sound and movement stopped as though someone had thrown a switch and the surrounding details dropped away. All that was left was the fish, like a silver stain on Felicity's pale skin, a stain that could never be removed.

Nothing else. Just the silver stain on Felicity's skin, in the middle of an immense silence.

22

My heart lifted when Nicky came back into the room. It was nearly midnight and I was lying on the bed with the laptop open in front of me.

'I'm not staying,' Nicky said. 'I promised Emily I'd go back.'

'You're going to sleep in her room?'

'There are twin beds. It's a family room so there are a couple of smaller beds for the kids.' She picked up her bag, which she still hadn't unpacked. 'I know we should talk but she really does need me.'

'What's wrong?'

'She's in a dreadful state. On top of everything else she's gone down with whatever Albert's got.'

I closed the laptop. 'And Maisie?'

'Fast asleep.' Nicky hesitated at the door. 'You did a good job.'

I felt ridiculously pleased and tried not to show it. 'She's a nice child. What do you intend doing?'

'I don't know. Where's Kate? That's why you brought me here, remember?'

'I wish I knew. Lily needs her too. The best thing I can do is look for Sean.'

'You think he's alive?'

'I went to the airfield but I didn't find his body. If he's alive it changes everything.'

'He hasn't got any money,' Nicky pointed out. 'Not if Kate's been using his cards.'

'But I found Kate's handbag there. At the airfield.'

'Why didn't you say?'

'There hasn't been time, remember? Her mobile was in it, and her wallet. But no cash. So he could have taken that.'

'But I thought you'd already tried his house.'

'I didn't search it.' I pushed the laptop away from me and sat up. 'I told you – Emily said Sean's passport had gone. And what she called his bank stuff.'

'You think he's abroad?'

'Maybe. Or he could have gone home to Mum. If he's alive, Nicky, then Kate's off the hook. And so am I, and so's Carlo, and we can all go back to normal.' I decided not to mention the conspiracy theory, not yet. 'I'd also like to know what really happened on Friday, and he's probably the only person who might be able to tell us.'

'If he's alive.' Nicky put down the bag and perched on the end of the bed, poised for flight. 'Emily said she'd already tried Sean's mother.'

'That doesn't mean Sean's mother was telling the truth. Her name is Fielding, by the way, initials L. M. She's a widow and she lives near Inverness.'

Nicky raised her eyebrows. 'You've been busy.'

'Maisie went up there with her dad. Just the two of them. According to Maisie, Emily doesn't like Granny. Maybe it's reciprocated.'

'How did you trace her?'

'Maisie said she lived near Loch Ness.' I touched

the laptop. 'It's easy to find a residential address if you've got a surname and an area, and if the person isn't trying to be discreet. Mrs Fielding's been on the electoral roll up there for the last three years. And her landline number is in the memory of Kate's mobile.'

'You seem very sure he's there.'

'Not really. But if he's alive, he has to be somewhere. Maybe he's the sort of man who needs a woman to look after him. And the best person to do that is always your mum.'

I paused. Into the silence came an unwanted snapshot of my own mother: her image was grubby now and blurred, like someone seen through a dirty windscreen on a misty day. Nicky was looking at me and there was something in her face I didn't want to see.

'And then there's the passport,' I went on quickly. 'Sometimes you need photo ID for internal flights in the United Kingdom. Something official like a passport or a driving licence. If Kate's got his bank cards, maybe she's got his driving licence too. So perhaps he went and fetched his passport from St Albans. Luton airport's only a few miles away. There are direct flights to Inverness. The airline insists on photo ID.'

'It's a long way to go on what's probably a wild-goose chase.'

'Have you a better idea?'

'You could go and have another talk with Carlo.'

'I don't think he'll tell me anything. Or nothing I want to know.'

Nicky sighed. 'He's the first person I've met who

knew you when you were a boy. I asked him what you were like. He said it was all too long ago. It was hard to remember. But he said he trusted you. And then he said he felt he'd never really known you.'

I picked at a loose thread on the duvet cover.

'Believe me, I know how he feels,' she went on, letting out her breath in a great rush of exasperation. 'I just wish you'd talk to me sometimes. And I wish I knew what you were really up to.' She opened the door. 'We'll talk in the morning.'

'I'll probably leave about seven.'

'Then phone me from the airport. If you want to.'

'I will,' I said.

In the event I was up at five thirty and left the hotel a little after six. There wasn't much point in staying in bed when I couldn't sleep. I drove through steadily thickening traffic to Greyfont, where I picked up clean clothes, checked the mail and listened to the messages on the phone. One was from Rachel. She wanted to know when to expect me in the office. Colleagues and clients had been asking. She sounded worried and her voice was uncharacteristically tentative, as if she was unsure of the response she would get and whether she would like it.

I drove to the airport. After I had checked in, I called Nicky from the departure lounge. She had been up for most of the night with either Emily or Albert. I didn't ask what her plans were. There was a fragile truce between us, based on other people's needs. I thought if I pressed her too hard it would fly apart.

Next I phoned the hospice. Lily was still sleeping. There was no change since yesterday evening. Finally I rang Rachel.

'How are you? Are you better?'

'Yes,' I said, belatedly remembering that I was supposed to be ill. 'But not out of the woods yet. I'm afraid I can't come into the office for a few days. You'd better cancel my appointments for the rest of the week.'

'But they're –'

'It can't be helped. And there's something I'd like you to do for me.'

'Where are you?' Rachel asked.

I ignored the question. 'You know Brian Valden?'

She was there at once: 'The guy at Tarborough's? He's on the board now, isn't he?'

'That's the one. See if you can find me a number for him – a mobile for preference, or his home.'

'OK.'

'And text it to me. And, Rachel, I'd rather the people at Tarborough's weren't aware of this. So don't go through the switchboard or call his PA.'

I knew this would strike her as unusual but not necessarily strange. There was often a need for confidentiality in our work, usually because our clients demanded it. I thanked her and rang off.

Time in departure lounges moves more slowly than elsewhere. I bought a paper but was unable to concentrate on other people's news. Kate's phone was in my overnight bag. I dug it out and switched it on. She hadn't bothered to protect it with a password.

Once again I scrolled through her contacts. There were thirty or forty names on the list. Carlo's home number was there and so was his mobile, as were St Margaret's Hospice, Sean's house in St Albans and Mrs Fielding's in Scotland. I checked the call register. No calls had been logged since the previous Friday. Before that, in the fortnight before she had lost the phone, Kate had used it mainly to stay in touch with Sean, the hospice, Carlo and a mobile number she had labelled 'Regine'. She hadn't saved any text messages but one from Regine had arrived on Saturday while she had been at the chapel. 'Got to stay till Thursday. Bloody builders. Can we make it Friday instead? XXXXXXX.'

The Inverness flight number came up on the screen. I turned off the phone and joined the queue waiting to board. During the flight, which lasted a little over an hour and a half, I had the newspaper open in front of me but I didn't read much. I tried not to think either. I was going to Inverness on the strength of a hunch that Maisie had planted in my mind the previous evening. There didn't seem much point in thinking about it because the more I thought the less plausible it seemed. On another level, I knew I had to keep moving because I was afraid of what would happen if I stood still. My life at present was like riding a bicycle. If I stopped pedalling for long, the bike would drift to a halt and fall over, taking me with it.

But if Sean was alive, everything changed.

The plane arrived a moment or two after one

o'clock. The weather was fine. As we were coming in to land, the country below looked cleaner, greener and somehow more clearly defined than the fields around Luton.

I had phoned ahead to hire a car. Now I was there, I was suddenly in no hurry to find out whether I was making a fool of myself. I drove into Inverness, where I bought a map and had lunch in a pub where they were playing country music and where the main activities were drinking lager and staring at strangers.

I switched on Kate's mobile, opened the address book and found Regine's name. I pressed the call button. The phone didn't ring. It went straight through to voicemail – an anonymous woman recited a recorded announcement. I couldn't understand a word of it – I think she was speaking Spanish. I didn't leave a message.

After lunch I drove south-west out of town on the A82. A mile or two outside the city, the Caledonian canal and the river Ness flowed into the north-eastern tip of the loch. The road hugged the western bank. I drove with the windows down. The water was a long slash of blue between the road and high ground on the far side. Suddenly life seemed not just cleaner but simpler too. Nicky and I had once had a holiday up here. I remembered smoking endless cigarettes to keep off the midges, the brightness of the stars, and early-morning air that tasted as though it should be bottled and sold in Harrods and Bloomingdale's.

After I turned off the A82, the road narrowed and began at once to climb. It was fenced on either side.

Beyond the fences were fields, rough grazing studded with outcrops of rock and, behind them, the dark green shadows of conifer plantations. I passed a scattering of houses, most of them isolated, set back from the road, and a small, reed-fringed loch whose water was the sheer, blinding blue of the sky.

The road came to a junction. I took the left fork. The road wound on, mile after mile. Just before another plantation of pines, I came to the mouth of a track on the left-hand side. Tightly confined by fences, it ran down for a hundred yards to a white-painted cottage, its little garden backed by the dark curve of the forest.

I drove cautiously towards it. A long time ago someone had surfaced the track with coarse grey stones. I pulled up in front of the house. No one was visible. An elderly Nissan Micra was parked in an open shed that leaned against one gable wall of the cottage. I switched off the engine and climbed out. It was very quiet, as though the place were holding its breath. I felt I was being watched.

The front door was painted pink but most of the colour had leached out of it. I knocked and waited. No one came. I knocked again. This time I heard footsteps inside. A woman opened the door. She was small and broad, with long grey hair scraped off a wide face and held at the back with a comb. She wore a paint-stained fisherman's smock with black trousers and sandals below. Her feet were grubby and her toenails looked like jagged, yellowing teeth. She could have been any age between sixty and eighty.

'I'm working,' she said.

'I'm looking for Mrs Fielding.'

'You've found her.' Her accent was English, Home Counties with a hint of the West Country in the background.

'I need to have a word with your son.'

'He's not here.'

She began to close the door. She hadn't asked me my name or what I wanted with him or why I had turned up unannounced on her doorstep.

'Do you know where he is?'

'No.'

My eyes went past her, over her right shoulder to the whitewashed wall behind. A painting of a little girl with a watering-can hung there. 'That's Maisie,' I said.

The door stopped moving. 'What?'

'Isn't that a picture of Maisie?'

The woman stared at me. I saw something in her face that had not been there before, a sort of hunger. 'Who are you?' she said.

'I'm a friend of Kate's mother.'

'Kate. I see.' Mrs Fielding looked as though she would have liked to spit on the ground.

'I'm not here for Kate.' I glanced to the east, the way I had come. I couldn't see the water from there. 'Maisie showed me a photograph of herself and your son. They were in a boat on the loch, looking for Nessie.'

She flushed. 'I took that photograph.'

'She misses her dad. That's why I came.'

There was a pause. Then Mrs Fielding stood back, opening the door wide. 'I suppose you'd better come in.'

I followed her across the tiny hall into a long, low room, also painted white, with a small fire burning in the granite hearth at the far end. The place was simply furnished with a table and a couple of sofas. The air smelt of woodsmoke and cigarettes. The walls were hung with paintings in a variety of frames.

'Where are they?' Mrs Fielding asked.

I turned back to her. 'At present your grandchildren and Emily are staying with my wife and me.' That wasn't quite the truth but it wasn't far off. 'I need to talk to Sean about what happens next.'

'But why are they with you? Emily's got a home of her own.'

'She's having a difficult time,' I said. 'There are problems with money –'

'That girl couldn't manage a doll's house,' Mrs Fielding said. 'The only thing she can do with money is spend other people's. Why Sean ever –'

'The thing is, we need to decide what's best for the children.'

'What's all this got to do with you?'

'I told you, I'm a friend of Kate's mother. She's very ill.' I bent the truth once again, this time a little further: 'And she's very concerned about the children. Your grandchildren, I mean.'

'She probably feels guilty about the effect her daughter's had on them.'

'Emily's been trying to get in touch with Sean,' I

went on, 'but he's not at his house. And he's not answering his phone either. His car was stolen and ended up a wreck in London so, naturally, she's concerned. And then there's the question of the children's welfare. As you say, Emily's not a good manager, but at least she's their mother. Believe me, if social services have to be called in, it won't do the children any favours.'

Alarm flared in Mrs Fielding's eyes. I glanced round the room. The afternoon sun was slanting through one of the windows: it reached the fire and reduced the flames and the smoke to pale, wispy wraiths. The sunlight touched the mantelpiece, too, and picked out a packet of Marlboro Light. I turned. There were two placemats on the table, each with a scattering of crumbs beside it, as if two people had sat down to lunch and nobody had yet cleared away.

'I just want to speak to him for a moment,' I said softly. 'For the children's sake. That's all.'

'He should have brought them here,' she hissed. 'If he had had any sense at all, he would have brought them to me.' Muscles worked in the leathery cheeks. Her mouth twisted as though she was chewing something vinegary. 'Maisie, especially – that child loves it up here.'

'Maybe they will come,' I said. 'They have to go somewhere.'

She sighed. 'All right. I'll see if he'll talk to you. No promises, though. You'd better wait here.'

Mrs Fielding left me alone. Unable to settle, I walked up and down the room. Excitement surged through me. I'd found Sean and he was alive. At last there was a glimmer of light, a chance I might find out what was really happening.

I looked out of the window but there was no sign of anyone. While I waited, I examined the pictures, searching for clues about the Fieldings' lives. Other people's dreams are always mysterious. Most of the paintings were portraits of people with stiff, unconvincing faces and lifeless bodies. The colours were dull. The frames had been hung without thought to their combined effect. I wondered whether Mrs Fielding had dragged herself up to the Highlands in the hope that the place would make a proper painter of her.

I recognized some of her subjects. There were two portraits of Albert and four of Maisie. There was one of Emily and Sean together and, to judge by their clothes, it might have been based on a wedding photograph. I counted no less than six portraits of Sean, one of which showed him as a boy and another as a slim, sulky teenager.

A door opened in the back of the house. Mrs Fielding came back alone. I waited.

'He asked if you'd come outside,' she said abruptly. She turned, and I followed her into a kitchen beyond the living room. 'He doesn't want me listening in,' she flung back, over her shoulder. 'He's afraid of what I'll say.' She pointed accusingly at the back door, which was standing ajar. 'He's over there.'

I went outside. The sun was on this side of the house and for an instant the light dazzled me. The area immediately in front of the door was paved with slabs of what looked like granite. On the left, a lawn sloped down gently from the cottage. On the right, the ground rose at a sharper gradient towards the plantation.

Sean Fielding was standing against the fence that separated this upper area of the garden from the trees. His dark green shirt and olive army-surplus trousers blended into the browns and greens behind him. For a moment I could hardly believe he was real, and not a trick of the light.

I walked slowly towards him. There was little trace of the sulky teenager. He was a compact man, already running to fat, with one of those round faces in which the flesh begins to drown the features as middle-age approaches. He had fair, ragged hair and he hadn't shaved for a day or two. What I noticed most of all, though, was his posture: although he was still, there was nothing relaxed about him. As I drew closer I stared at his face, half hoping and half fearing to see something that supported Kate's story of Carlo attacking him.

'Sean,' I said. Surnames seemed redundant in this context. 'I'm James.'

'My mother said you're looking after Maisie and Albert.'

'My wife's giving Emily a hand with them.'

'Why?'

There were several possible answers to that. I said, 'Emily's broke and Albert's ill.'

He didn't pursue it. 'So you're a friend of Lily's?'

He gave a yelp of laughter. 'In a manner of speaking. Kate told me you're her father. Does my mother know?'

'I haven't told her. But that's why I'm here.'

'Where is she?'

'Kate? I don't know. Do you?'

He shook his head. 'I hope I never see her again. But I thought Emily and the kids were out of this. I thought they were safe.'

'When you disappeared, they came to Chipping Weston to look for you.'

'Oh, Christ. The stupid cow.'

'Emily thought you'd be with Kate.'

'We've not been together for months.'

'What about Christmas?'

'What about it?' He grimaced and, for a moment, bore a startling resemblance to his mother. 'Kate fancied a quick one for old times' sake but that's all it was.'

'Your choice or hers?'

'Hers. I didn't hear anything from her after that until Thursday last week when she rang me up. Friday, really – it was in the early hours. She was at her parents' house in Chipping Weston, and she was scared shitless. Which made a change.' He glanced at me. 'You know Carlo?'

'Yes.'

'And you know he'd found out that Kate's not really his sister – that you're her dad? And now he wants all of his father's estate, not fifty per cent.' Sean swallowed. 'He's angry. Know what I mean?'

'Yes,' I said impatiently. 'I know all that.'

'I tell you, she was fucking terrified. Which I guess wasn't surprising if what she said was true.'

He hesitated. He was on the verge of adding something but evidently thought better of it. It struck me that Kate wasn't the only one who was terrified.

'Why did she phone you?' I asked.

'She wanted me to come down and fetch her because she hadn't got a car. But when I got to Chipping Weston she said we had to go to the airfield. Have you been there?'

Again I nodded.

'It could be worth a lot of money if they build on it. That's what Carlo really wants. He'd fixed up a meeting with a developer there on Friday morning – Kate had only just found out about it. She wanted to go too. She wanted a witness, in case things got nasty. So we drove over there and met Carlo.'

'Was he expecting you?'

'No.' Sean stared at me but I think he was seeing someone else. 'Anyway, the whole thing was a waste of time – Carlo said the guy had phoned to say he couldn't make it.' Sean licked his lips. 'And he and Kate started arguing again. He hit her. I tried to stop him and he beat me up.'

I looked at Sean – small, out of condition, reluctant to be involved. Carlo was a big, powerful, angry man.

'I lost a tooth somewhere along the line and there's a bruise on my jaw. There was a hell of a lot of blood – but some of it was his: I made his nose bleed. I think a couple of ribs are fractured – anyway, they're bloody painful. And there's another bruise on the back of my head. Look.'

Sean came closer and displayed his injuries to me. One of his front teeth was missing. Now I was closer I could see that his lower lip was swollen, and there was a bruise under the stubble on his jaw. He parted his hair with his fingers, revealing a larger bruise and a patch of broken skin among the hair roots at the back of his head. 'That's the one that must have knocked me out,' he said, with pride in his voice. 'I probably hit a stone or something when I went down. But I don't remember any of that. I do remember telling Kate to run. Next thing I knew, I woke up and I was alone. I had a bloody awful headache and I was lying on top of Kate's handbag.'

'You were brave.' I watched him preening himself. 'Where did this happen exactly?'

'I told you – at the airfield. Near where we parked.'

'Yes – but where exactly?'

'Near a stream, which was in a little wood on the edge of the airfield. It wasn't far from one of the entrances. That was where we parked, just off the lane. You couldn't drive into the airfield that way any more but you could get through a gap in the fence. Kate must have run back to the car and driven off. The trouble was, my jacket was in the boot, and my wallet and phone were in the pockets.'

'But you had Kate's bag.'

'Just as well. The phone was dead – she'd forgotten to charge it – but I took the cash. I needed money to get away. It was her fault I was there in the first place.' His eyes wouldn't look at me. 'But I didn't go at once. I was in too much pain, and I didn't know whether Carlo was still around. So I cleaned myself up as best I could in the stream. Then I hid in the wood and waited a couple of hours.'

'Where exactly?'

He frowned. 'Under the trees near some ruins.'

The lime kiln. I remembered where I had found the cigarette end and the handbag. Everything fitted. Everything came back to the lime kiln, sooner or later.

'I walked into the village and phoned for a taxi to take me to the station,' Sean went on. 'I told the guy I'd fallen off my bike. I went straight home, got a few things and came up here.'

'Kate's been using your bank account.'

He laughed, and for a moment I almost liked him. He laughed so hard his whole body shook.

'What's so funny?' I asked.

'Because it's typical of her and it's typical of me. I never changed the PIN number, you see. It was the date we first met. Our special anniversary. She knew that. That's what comes of being sentimental – you get ripped off. She'd never make that mistake.'

'What are your plans?'

He shrugged. 'I've stopped having plans. They don't seem to be much help. I've given them up.' He was talking faster and faster, the words bumping into one another. 'I used to have a spreadsheet for everything. Everything in my life was planned. But it didn't work, not after I met Kate. In the last twelve months I've lost my job, my home, my wife, my kids. And for a while last Friday I thought I was going to lose my life. I tell you one thing, though – I'm not going anywhere near Carlo or Kate ever again. They're off their fucking heads.'

Neither of us spoke for a moment. Someone was using a chainsaw half a mile away. I looked back at the cottage. I thought I saw movement at one of the windows.

Sean said softly: 'At least I've stopped wanting her now, since Rackford. Sometimes I felt I was addicted. Do you know what I mean?'

I thought of Lily all those years ago. 'Yes. I do.'

'I didn't want her but I had to have her. The bitch.' He glanced at me. 'Sorry – she's your daughter.'

'And Maisie's yours. She misses you.'

His face brightened. 'How is she?'

'She seems OK. A bit confused, maybe. She showed me a picture of you last night – the two of you in a boat on the loch.'

He smiled. 'I remember it.'

'Maybe you should talk to Emily,' I suggested. 'About the kids.'

His eyes became slits. 'Maybe.'

I took out my wallet and gave him a card. 'There's my number. I'll tell her where you are.'

'I can't stop you doing that.'

'What I'd really like to do now is find Kate. You know she's pregnant?'

'She made damned sure I knew. She says it's mine.'

'And is it?'

'Who knows?' He didn't sound very interested.

'I need to find her before Carlo does.'

'She's not worth it.'

'The baby is.'

'Not to me.' He stared at me, mouth slightly open, and a muscle jumped below his left eye. 'Anyway, I told you – I've no idea where Kate is and, frankly, I couldn't care less. I just don't want to get involved.'

I looked past him, up into the trees. A red squirrel was perched on one of the pines, perhaps thirty yards away from us. I had never seen one before because they were extinct in most of the country. I took it as a good omen. 'Tell me,' I said. 'Who's Regine?'

He blinked. 'Who?'

'Someone Kate knows. Regine.' I spelled the name.

Sean's face was blank with willed incomprehension. 'Never heard of her.'

'Maybe it's a shop or something.'

'I haven't the faintest idea,' he said.

'A Spanish friend?'

'God knows.'

I knew he was lying. The squirrel skipped along a branch and leaped on to a neighbouring tree. It climbed up the trunk, higher and higher, until it vanished. I said goodbye and began to walk down the slope to the cottage. After a few steps I glanced back. Sean was standing where I had left him. 'You said Kate was terrified on Thursday night, and that it wasn't surprising if what she said was true.'

I waited but Sean said nothing.

'What *did* she say?' I said, and took a step towards him. 'Why was she so scared?'

He flung up his hands, palms out, as if he was trying to push me back. 'I thought you knew. She said Carlo raped her.'

23

Perhaps, I thought on the plane back to London, Sean had been lying. Or perhaps Kate had lied to him – after all, lying seemed to come naturally to her. The trouble was, I thought they were both telling the truth.

It was Friday morning. As the plane cruised noisily through the blue world above the clouds, I argued the matter out with myself yet again. Neither Kate nor Sean could know what I knew – about the boy in the school changing-room; about the other boy who had bullied Felicity; and, most tellingly of all, about the baby punk at the Eagle. They didn't know about Nicky's Raku bowl either. The notion that Carlo had raped a pregnant woman was unexpected but it fitted a pattern that was familiar to me. It also explained why Kate was so terrified of him. I remembered our conversation in the chapel, and how I had wondered even then whether she was holding something back.

Kate screwed up her face and rocked to and fro, her whole body nodding. 'You don't know what Carlo's done,' she said, in time with her nodding body. 'You just don't know what he's capable of. I do.'

If actions speak louder than words, then what the rape said was this: *You are no longer my sister. You are in my power. I hate you.*

If I was right, the next question was: how far would Carlo go? What distinguished the sort of violence that came with such frightening ease to him from the sort that ended in murder? Or was there no distinction at all? Was it simply a matter of degree? After all, most murders are not only domestic affairs but also by-products of something else, as unplanned as a pregnancy after a one-night stand with a former lover.

First things first. Rachel had texted me Brian Valden's number. I had called him before leaving Inverness and set up a meeting later in the day. When I got back to London, I phoned the hospice. Lily wasn't well, they told me, which was their way of saying she was worse. She was asking for her daughter. I said that I'd do my best to bring her and I would come myself as soon as I could.

A few hours later, I walked through blazing afternoon sunshine along the north side of Fleet Street. I turned into the Gaunt Tavern and was swallowed into its gloom. The place was a superior drinking-hole, once the haunt of journalists and now much patronized by lawyers. At present it was in the brief lull between lunch and early evening. I searched the labyrinth of rooms arranged on either side of the low, stone-flagged hallway. There was no sign of Brian so I ordered a glass of water and sat at a table with a view of the entrance.

While I waited, I rang Nicky. She hadn't phoned me since yesterday and I hadn't phoned her. She answered on the second ring. She was still at the

Newnham House Hotel with Emily and the children. She hadn't seen Carlo. 'I'm taking them home,' she said.

'To Bedford?'

'No – to Greyfont. Just for a day or two.'

'You make them sound like stray kittens.'

'Would you mind?'

'No.' I glanced at the clock behind the bar. 'But it's no answer, is it? Not in the long term.'

'Of course it isn't,' Nicky said. 'But I'm not talking about the long term. I'm talking about the short term. That's what matters.'

'OK. If that's what you want. To go back to Carlo –'

'What about him?'

'There's something I heard. He may be dangerous.' I heard Nicky sigh with what sounded like impatience. 'I'll explain later. But try to avoid him, if you can. And don't be alone with him.' I saw Brian in the doorway. 'I've got to go.' I waved at Brian and he shambled towards my table, then veered away in the direction of the bar. 'One last thing, does the name Regine mean anything to you?'

'No.'

'Will you ask Emily? It's someone or something to do with Kate.'

We said goodbye. Brian was leaning on the bar counter, examining the list of wines chalked on a blackboard. He was a big man who carried a lot of weight although he wasn't fat. He had a red face, rumpled hair and the perpetually surprised expression of someone who has just awoken from a deep sleep. He shook hands without taking his eyes from the blackboard.

'What are you having?' I said.

'The Chilean Cabernet Sauvignon? If I remember rightly, it slips down quite nicely.'

I ordered a bottle and we took it to the table. Brian drank most of his first glass in one mouthful. He sat back on the settle, thrust his feet under the table and loosened his tie. 'Thank God for the weekend,' he said. He glanced at me over the rim of his glass. 'You look as if you could do with the break, too.'

'You know how it is,' I said, hoping he didn't.

He cocked an eyebrow. 'My spies tell me you've been off work.'

'One of these bugs. It's on the way out now.' I guessed that he had tried to phone me at the office. 'How's the family?'

'How should I know? The children just want me to sign cheques nowadays and, anyway, they live with their mother when they're not drinking themselves senseless in the cause of higher education.' He spoke without rancour, even with a trace of amusement. 'You don't have kids, do you? Wise man.'

We drank a couple of glasses apiece and talked about nothing in particular. I didn't know Brian well but I realized he didn't want to be hurried. And both of us were aware that he owed me a favour – last year I had worked over a weekend so that he could complete a time-critical contract that Tarborough's had on the Isle of Dogs. Gradually the conversation meandered to a discussion of the chancellor's last budget and its possible implications for Tarborough's and my own company.

'Too early to tell, really,' Brian said, 'but we're slowing down on new projects for the time being. Unless the funding's in place.'

'I heard a whisper that you were looking at a site near Chipping Weston.'

'Oh, yes?'

'A bit outside your normal range, isn't it?'

'And yours, perhaps.' He smiled at me and his face disintegrated into folds and wrinkles. 'Are you fishing? Between ourselves, we're a long way from putting it up for tender.'

'This isn't work, not for me. A friend has an interest.'

'Ah.' He topped up our glasses. 'I take it we're talking about the same place?'

'A former airfield near Chipping Weston. Golf course, housing development.'

'That's it. Good road access, mainline railway station in Chipping Weston, and they tell me the demographics look good.'

'Planning?'

'The council's playing cautious but they'll probably come round in time. It's broadly in line with the county structure plan. But it's very early days. I believe we've only had a few preliminary discussions. So, you know the owner?'

'Not exactly. I know someone who has an interest in it.'

Brian rubbed his finger down the stem of his glass, considering the distinction. 'Not my project. As far as I recall, the landowner contacted us off his own bat.'

'Charles Murthington?'

He nodded. 'But you're saying that someone else has an interest?'

'The land's part of an estate held in trust. Murthington's the executor.'

'I think we knew that.'

'But were you aware that there are two residuary legatees, with equal shares in the estate? Murthington's one of them.'

He reached for the bottle. 'How very interesting. Who's the other?'

'His half-sister.'

'Your friend?'

I sidestepped the question. 'There's not much love lost between them.'

'You don't mind if I pass this on?'

I shook my head.

'I wonder if that explains it,' Brian went on. 'I seem to remember there was a site meeting set up at the end of last week. Apparently the chap cancelled at the last moment.'

'Murthington cancelled? Not someone at Tarborough's?'

'It was definitely Murthington. Very last minute, too. One of my colleagues wasted his morning on the M40 and he wasn't happy.'

We drank in silence for a moment. So, Carlo hadn't

expected Kate to come to the airfield; he hadn't known that she knew about the proposed meeting, and almost certainly he was unaware that she had been in touch with Sean. Suppose he had got to Rackford first. Suppose he had seen them arriving. His instinct would have been to cancel the meeting because the last thing he would have wanted was Kate queering his pitch with Tarborough's. No wonder he had been angry.

'As I say, it's all at a very early stage,' Brian said. 'If there's a possible problem with ownership it may not be worth the effort of pursuing. Not in view of the last budget.'

'Yes,' I said. 'It's not really the climate for risk-taking, is it?'

Brian grinned and raised his glass in a silent toast. 'Better safe than sorry. Plenty of other fish in the sea.'

The phone in my jacket pocket gave two bleeps. Someone had sent me a text message.

Regine Wilder's skin resembled cracked, tan-coloured leather in need of polish. She had shoulder-length platinum blonde hair with grey roots, and her lipstick was the colour of blood. I thought her mouth pouted naturally rather than from petulance.

'Yes?' She glared up at me. She wore a long, tight-fitting dress made of some shiny green material. She was carrying a packet of Marlboro Light in one hand, and in the other a half-smoked cigarette.

'May I see Kate, Mrs Wilder? Kate Murthington.'

'She's not here.' Regine began to close the door in

my face, just as Mrs Fielding had done the previous afternoon. 'Sorry.'

'She's either here or you know where she is.'

The door slammed in my face. 'Bugger off,' Regine said, on the other side. 'I know your sort.'

'All I want to do is –'

'If you don't go now, I'll call the police,' she said, in a voice that ran out of breath before the end of the sentence.

'I'm going to give you my phone number.' I found a card, crossed out the office numbers and wrote my mobile number on the back of it. 'Ask her to ring me, all right? This is for her sake, not mine.'

There was no reply. I fed the card through the letterbox. I walked down the steps from the front door and glanced up at the façade of the neat terraced house. No one was visible at the windows. I began to walk in the general direction of Clapham Common. I felt oddly relieved.

Then I heard Kate call my name. I turned. She was on the pavement outside Mrs Wilder's house. I walked back slowly. She was wearing a loose dress that made her seem more pregnant than before. I stopped at the gate. She kissed my cheek.

'You've been drinking,' she said.

'Just a glass or two.'

'How did you find me?'

'Your phone was at Rackford. At the airfield.'

She held on to the gate and swayed.

'It's all right,' I said. 'It was in your handbag. The handbag was there but Sean wasn't.'

'Then what's happened to him? Have they found the body?'

'He's alive and well and living with Mum. I saw him yesterday.'

Her face changed. 'He's in Scotland? With the Loch Ness monster? The rat. He could have let me know.'

'He's trying hard to pretend you don't exist. I don't know who terrifies him more, you or Carlo.'

Carlo. The name hung in the air between us.

Kate touched my arm. 'It's good to see you. I – I just thought it would be safer for everyone if I wasn't around. I'm trouble, you know? I don't want to be but I am. But I still don't understand how you found me. Did you phone Regine? She didn't say.'

'I didn't talk to her. I just listened to a Spanish voicemail message. No – you've got Emily to thank. She remembered Regine's surname, and the road she lived in. She said she came here once.'

'It was just after she found out about me and Sean. Regine rents out the basement flat and I lived there for a bit before I moved in with Sean. I wasn't here when Emily came. She had a go at Regine but she didn't get very far.'

'Why come back here now?'

'I had to go somewhere safe, somewhere where no one knew where to find me. No one ever came here except Sean and Emily, not even Mum. And Regine's always been kind to me. I'd have come before if she hadn't been in Spain.' She opened the gate. 'You'd better meet her properly.'

I followed her into the house. There were two large

suitcases in the hall. Regine was smoking a cigarette in the little sitting-room on the left of the front door. The three-piece suite and the television had been designed for more spacious surroundings. Kate settled with a sigh into an armchair and waved me towards the sofa.

Regine looked hungrily at her and sucked the cigarette. 'Well, who's this, then?' she demanded.

'He's my dad,' Kate said.

'I thought your dad was dead.'

'He is. Jamie's my biological father. I didn't know about him until last week. No one did, except my mum. And he didn't know about me.'

Regine glanced at me through a haze of smoke. 'Why have you come?'

'Kate's mother asked me to. She's very ill.'

'You never told me,' she said. 'Kate, why didn't you say?'

Kate reached for the cigarettes on the glass-topped table beside Regine's chair. 'I didn't want to worry you.'

'What's wrong with her?'

'She's dying,' I said. 'Cancer. She's in a hospice.'

'I can't believe you never told me.'

Kate lit the cigarette and tossed the match into the ashtray. 'You've got enough on your plate.'

'Yes, but your *mother*.' Regine seemed shocked, even hurt. 'Where is she?'

'Wembley,' I answered. 'I've come to take Kate to see her.'

For a moment I thought Kate would refuse. But

Regine was nodding, as though what I had said was the most natural and sensible thing in the world, which in a way it was. Kate opened her mouth. I expected her to protest but instead she blew one of her smoke-rings.

'You need something to eat before you go,' Regine said. 'Or a drink at least. What about a nice cup of tea and a sandwich?'

Kate shook her head. 'I'm all right,' she snapped. 'Don't fuss.'

Regine winced. I wondered how often this had happened before, not just with Regine but with other people, Sean included, and perhaps Lily and Hugh. Kate made people love her, and then she hurt them. But it would never happen with me, I thought – I knew what was happening: I had a choice.

'I've got the car,' I said. 'I've parked a few streets away.'

'I'm taking Kate to Spain with me,' Regine said, seemingly out of the blue. 'I've got a villa in Marbella. Now the builders are out it's really nice. She can get a bit of peace and quiet, and there's a pool. Be good for her and the baby.'

Kate said nothing. I had the feeling this had been said before and it was being said again for my benefit.

'Of course, you'll want to do what you can for your mum first,' Regine went on. 'But the place is waiting when you're ready.'

Kate stubbed out her cigarette. 'I'll get my bag, then,' she said.

Regine and I sat in silence and listened to Kate's

feet on the stairs. Regine fiddled with the gold bangles she wore on her right wrist. Her face was like a painted wooden mask but the faded eyes were alive and swimming with moisture. 'She's in trouble, isn't she?'

'There are family problems.'

'That brother of hers? She told me about him. Nasty piece of work.'

'It's a difficult time for all of them.'

'She's a sweet girl. People can be so unkind.' Regine patted her hair and the bangles slid down her thin brown forearm. 'Money, eh? It brings out the worst in people. I'd like to help her. I'd like to take her away from all this.'

'I know.' I hesitated. 'But first she needs to sort a few things out.'

'I haven't got any children of my own, you see,' she said, as though I had asked her a question and this was the answer. 'Me and Keith – he was my husband – we weren't able to have them. We'd have liked to.'

There were footsteps on the stairs. We both stood up and went into the hall.

'You look as if you've come to arrest me,' Kate said. She smiled but it wasn't quite a joke. She kissed Regine on both cheeks. The older woman clung to her. 'I'll be back soon, sweetie,' Kate said. 'You look after yourself.'

'You're coming home this evening, aren't you?' Regine said, looking from Kate to me.

'I don't know.' Kate gave her a hug and released

her. 'There may be a few things to sort out for my mum. I'll phone and let you know.'

I said goodbye. Regine's hand was small and dry, and trembled slightly in mine. I knew that as we walked silently away she was standing on the doorstep, watching us. Kate didn't turn round, didn't wave.

24

I opened the passenger door of the Saab and Kate eased herself carefully inside. Scented air wafted out. She looked up at me, smiling her thanks. 'You've been buying flowers,' she said.

I could smell them even on the pavement. 'Freesias.'

'Mum's favourites.'

'I know.' I closed her door, walked round the car and opened the driver's door. Inside, the smell was overpowering. I let down the windows.

'I can't say I like them myself,' Kate said suddenly. 'They're so waxy they look unreal. And the smell makes me think of rotting fruit.'

I remembered what Felicity had told me all those years ago. 'In the language of flowers they stand for innocence.'

Kate drew in her breath sharply. 'You're full of surprises. Carlo knew about the meanings of flowers too.'

I wondered whether the language of flowers had a word for rape. 'I saw him the night before last. He's in Chipping Weston.'

'What's he doing there?'

'Passing through.' I started the engine and edged into the traffic. 'Looking for you, probably. A lot's been happening since you left. Talking of which, why did you leave?'

'You mean on Tuesday morning?' Her voice was wary. 'I'm sorry, Jamie.'

We drove in silence for a few minutes. The smell of the freesias slowly diminished.

'You could have let me know you were OK,' I said.

'I wanted to, honestly. The thing is, I thought it would be safer if I had nothing to do with you. Safer for you, I mean. I thought Regine was coming back on Tuesday morning – she had a flight booked. If you wouldn't take me, I couldn't go to Rackford to look for the handbag. So I took the bike down to the station, caught a train to London and came here. The trouble was, the house was all shut up and I didn't have Regine's mobile number – it was in my phone.'

The story fitted with the ATM slips that Emily had found in Sean's jacket at Chipping Weston. According to the second slip in the sequence, someone had withdrawn money in London on Tuesday. And according to the third, the next withdrawal had been in Chipping Weston.

I said, 'And then you came back to the house.'

'How do you know?'

'The jacket.'

'I had to go somewhere,' she said, in a voice that was almost a wail. 'I knew I had Regine's number in Spain in an address book in my room. I wanted to pick up more of my things. And – and there was also my mother's jewellery. I didn't take it last time, and I didn't want Carlo to get his hands on it.'

I kept my eyes on the line of cars moving sluggishly in front of us along the Upper Richmond Road.

'Why don't you say something?' she demanded. 'For Christ's sake, I'm trying to tell you the truth.'

'But you haven't told me the truth,' I said. 'Some of the time you've told me lies. You told me Carlo attacked you on Monday afternoon. But he didn't. It was Emily. And for all I know you attacked her and she was just defending herself.'

I remembered how Kate's face had become sharp and startled when I'd mentioned meeting Emily at St Albans. She hadn't expected me to talk to Emily, and she must have been calculating the implications at desperate speed.

'All right,' she said. 'That was a lie, and I'm sorry. The thing is, I needed your help and that seemed the best way to get it. I thought Emily would just be a complication – I didn't even know you'd met her. And when I did find out it was too late. Anyway, in a sense it wasn't a lie.'

I blinked. 'What do you mean?'

'Because Carlo really is out to get me. You know that.'

'Oh, come on. That doesn't begin to justify it. And it doesn't explain why you ran away from me, either.'

She made a muffled sound, half sob, half groan. Then she said, 'I know it makes me sound as if I'm just out for what I can get, but it's not like that, I promise. I'm trying to be honest with you now. I'm just trying to do the best I can for me and the baby.

That's all I care about. That's all I've ever cared about.'

I risked a glance at Kate. She wasn't beautiful any more. Her face was red and her features were distorted. I felt an enormous tenderness for her. She was one of those people who roll like grenades through the empty rooms of other people's lives. She was capable of doing untold damage and probably would. 'I'm not trying to judge you,' I said.

She sniffed.

Neither of us spoke for some time. We turned right and drove up to Kew Bridge. On the other side of the river, we passed the gallery where Nicky worked. I caught a glimpse of Victor, still in his shorts, arranging a sculpture in the window. He looked inherently improbable, like a creature from another galaxy in your garden shed.

The traffic was even worse on the North Circular. The tired air smelt of diesel and Tarmac. The city was sweating. We crawled in fits and starts through a series of roadworks. Kate lit another cigarette.

'Have you found your wife yet?' she said.

'Yes.'

'And?'

'Nicky's more or less convinced that you and I are not having an affair.'

'So it wasn't Carlo who took her?'

'He had nothing to do with it. She's met him now, though.'

'I don't understand.'

'It's a long story and I don't think I understand it either. We met on Wednesday evening in Chipping

Weston. She rather liked him. If she had to make a snap choice about whether to believe you or him, she'd probably go for him.'

'What's he up to?'

'I don't know.'

There was too much to talk about and not enough time to say it. And I didn't know how far I could trust Kate. We had to take this one step at a time. Most of the decisions could wait until after Lily had seen her.

'So he didn't kill Sean?' she probed, unwilling to let it go. 'That's good, I suppose. But he still wants me out of the way. And the baby. Because if Mum dies after me, and the baby's already been born, then my share will go to the baby.'

Was that another reason for raping her? In the hope of inducing a spontaneous abortion? But this was already the second trimester of the pregnancy so the baby should be well established, its hold on life as secure as –

'I've made a will, it's all sorted,' Kate said suddenly. 'It's with my bank. Barclays, in Chipping Weston.'

'I don't know,' I said. 'For what it's worth, I think he may be potentially violent. But I don't think he's the sort of man who would sit down and plan how to kill somebody.'

'He could easily do it on impulse, though. He might just lose his temper. He knows the advantages of having me out of the way, and he's always hated me. It wouldn't take much, would it? He just has to lose his temper and let it happen.'

'Is that what happened last week? When he realized you weren't his sister?'

Kate said nothing. Her fingers played with her cigarette packet.

'Did he lose his temper then?' I asked.

'Yes. Of course he did.' She turned her head towards me. 'Oh – I see. You've been talking to Sean. He told you.'

'But is it true?'

'That Carlo raped me?' She let out her breath in a rush. 'Yes.'

'Why didn't you say? Why didn't you go to the police?'

'Because he was clever. There were no marks. He came into my room. He wrapped me in the duvet. He – he made sure there was nothing left behind.'

I said, as gently as I could, 'So, it would have been your word against his.' Allegations of rape were notoriously difficult to prove, and perhaps this one, with its extraordinary ramifications, would have been harder than most.

'I kept thinking what it would do to Mum,' Kate said, in a high, wavering voice, 'if she heard.'

'You could have told me.'

'I didn't want to tell anyone,' she shouted. 'Why are you so stupid? It's gross. It leaves you feeling like shit. Can't you understand that? The last thing I wanted to do was talk about it. I wish I hadn't told Sean. I wish –'

'Kate, stop this. It's better that I know. But we'll talk about it later. See your mother first.'

She lit a cigarette. The traffic crawled along a few more hundred yards while we breathed foul air and thought foul thoughts.

'She's worse, isn't she?' Kate said. 'I can tell by the way you're speaking about it. I hate hospitals and places like that. I hate seeing her ill.'

'It'll be all right. Everything will be all right.'

'Are you sure?'

'Yes.'

I glanced at her face. She was looking happier, I thought, which was absurd. She had taken my assurances at face value. Then I realized that it wasn't absurd at all: in a sense, it made me responsible for ensuring that what I had said was no more than the truth. When you help someone they put themselves in your power but at the same time, and by the same transaction, you put yourself in theirs. It's the classic weapon that the weak use against the strong, that the child uses against the parent.

After Hanger Lane, we drove in silence up to St Margaret's. I found a space in the hospice car park and turned off the engine. Kate angled the vanity mirror and tried to repair her makeup with a paper handkerchief.

'You should go in alone,' I said.

Her eyes widened. 'I thought you were coming to see her too.'

'I am. But later. If she's awake she'll want to see you. She won't want me there.'

'And if she's not awake?'

I shrugged. 'Even so. She's your mother.'

'You won't be long?' She bit her lower lip. 'You won't be long – promise?'

'Five minutes or so.'

She picked up her bag. 'I don't like these places. I really don't.'

Kate struggled out of the car, the extra weight making her ungainly. I watched her walking across the car park and through the doors. My mind was clogged with images I didn't want to see. Carlo could well be twice as heavy as Kate. The duvet must have trapped her like a net.

I twisted round and scooped my jacket from the back seat. I patted the pockets, looking for my phone. Just as I found it, I glanced through the windscreen.

A woman came out of the hospice. She tottered with surprising speed across the car park and gestured imperiously at a silver M-class Mercedes, which obediently flashed its lights at her. She wore a tent-like dress covered with little flowers and high-heeled sandals that seemed too fragile to bear her weight. Her face was partly concealed by dark glasses.

She hauled herself into the driving seat of the Mercedes. Despite the glasses, there was no mistaking her shape, the way she walked or the car she drove. The engine growled. She manoeuvred the heavy vehicle out of the car park and turned on to the main road. She passed within a couple of metres of the Saab but she didn't turn her head.

Miranda Hammett had just paid a visit to St Margaret's Hospice.

*

The smell of the freesias was growing stronger and stronger. The heavy scent was suffocating me. I wrenched the door handle and scrambled out of the Saab. I felt dizzy, almost drugged. I leaned against the car and phoned Nicky. The call was answered on the third ring but the voice belonged to a strange woman. 'Who's that?' I said, suddenly on the edge of panic. 'Where's Nicky?'

'It's Emily. Nicky's driving. Who is it?'

'James. I need to speak to her.'

A few minutes later, Nicky phoned me back. 'What is it? Emily said you sounded as if you'd been running.'

'I'm fine,' I said. 'Are you OK?'

'Of course I am. We're on the way to Greyfont now.'

'I'm at the hospice.'

There was a pause. 'Seeing Lily?'

'No, not yet. I'm in the car park. I let Kate go in first.'

'Kate's with you?' Nicky's voice was cold.

'I found her at Regine's. Listen, the hospice is called St Margaret's and it's in Wembley. Kate went in a moment ago, and I was sitting in the car, just about to phone you. And Miranda came out.'

'Miranda? Miranda Hammett?'

'Yes. She just climbed into her car and drove off. She didn't see me.'

'But what was she doing there?'

'I wondered if you knew. Does she know someone who's a patient?'

'I talked to her yesterday, and the day before,' Nicky said slowly. 'She didn't mention it. Would you like me to ask her?'

'No need. *You* didn't say anything to her, I suppose?'

There was a silence at the end of the line. Then: 'Are you asking if I sent her to spy on you?'

'No,' I said, and my voice sounded feeble to me. 'At present I don't know what to believe. But please don't mention this if you talk to her.'

'OK. But I really don't like it.'

'Nor do I.' Suddenly Felicity was in my mind, sauntering about because she belonged there, an unwanted ghost who had earned her place the hard way. 'Nicky – when I see you, there's something I need to tell you.'

'If you and Kate –'

'It's nothing like that. I promise. It's about a mistake I made a long time ago.'

'Can't you tell me now?'

'No. Sorry, I've got to go.'

I told her I loved her but I'm not sure she heard because she broke the connection. I picked up my jacket and the freesias, locked the car and went into the hospice. I asked after Lily.

'Her daughter's with her now,' the receptionist said. 'She's having quite a busy day.'

'She's had other visitors?'

'Her daughter-in-law was in a little earlier. You've only just missed her.'

For the second time that evening, the earth shifted uncomfortably on its axis.

'That's nice,' I said, clinging to my character as an old family friend and wondering who had been telling lies to whom. 'I'll try not to tire her. Is she in the same room?'

The receptionist nodded. 'I see you've got her some more freesias. She loves freesias, doesn't she? She'll be so pleased.'

You could tell the receptionist was pleased as well. Lily might be dying, she might be one among many patients, but still the staff knew her likes and dislikes and wanted to please her. There was a shelf of books near the desk, donations from patients, and among them I noticed the biography of the dead actress, the one Lily had been reading.

'Isn't that Lily's?' I said.

'It was – her daughter-in-law said she'd finished with it.'

I walked along the corridor, feeling curiously calm. I paused in the doorway of Lily's room. She was lying back with her eyes open, her head and shoulders propped against a stiff mound of pillows. She seemed to have grown less substantial, as if time and illness were gradually diminishing her, reducing the flesh, bringing the bones nearer to the surface, nearer to their final dissolution. Kate was sitting beside her, holding her mother's hand in both of hers.

Lily looked up and saw me. She frowned. But she raised her other hand, beckoning me in.

'I can come back later,' I said.

'No – stay,' Kate said. She had been crying. 'I'm not being much use at present.'

'Freesias,' Lily said, in a voice that rustled like the wind in dry grass. 'How lovely.'

'I'll find a vase,' Kate said, and stood up.

I pulled up a chair to the other side of the bed and sat down. 'How are you?'

Lily ignored the question and ignored me. She watched Kate moving around the little room, finding a vase, filling it with water.

Suddenly she sighed and looked at me. 'At least we did something right.'

I glanced at Kate, then back to Lily and smiled. The urgency I felt, the fear, the confusion, dropped away. The company of the dying makes you view life through the other end of the telescope. Kate put the vase of freesias on the table at the end of the bed where Lily could see them. She returned to her chair. Once again she took Lily's hand.

'I gather you had another visitor today,' I said.

Lily glanced at me. 'Who?'

'Miranda.'

'Oh, yes,' Lily said. 'Miranda.'

'Really?' Kate sounded surprised. 'I didn't know she was still around.'

'I haven't seen her for years.' Lily frowned. 'She just turned up. She was asking after you, darling.'

'What did you tell her?'

'I think I said I hadn't seen you. I can't remember. I can't remember what I said. Or if I just thought it.'

'How do you know Miranda?' I put in.

'She used to be married to Carlo,' Kate said. 'It was ages ago. They divorced when I was a kid.'

'That's the trouble with marrying young,' said Lily, her voice suddenly vigorous and authoritative. 'She was only just eighteen, and Carlo wasn't much older.'

'I remember the police coming round and talking to you and Dad,' Kate said. 'I remember thinking I ought to feel sorry for her.'

Lily's mind was elsewhere. 'She's put on a lot of weight. I always said she would.'

'I didn't realize they were still seeing each other,' Kate said. 'You'd think she'd never want to clap eyes on him again.'

'She was besotted with him.' Lily fought to retain her concentration. 'She's married again now, and they've got children, but she's never quite given up on Carlo.' She made a dry, malicious sound that was almost a laugh. 'He nearly killed her once, you know.'

'Broke her nose and her arm,' Kate said, glancing at me. 'And pushed her out of a first-floor window. Didn't he injure her spine as well? He was drunk and he thought she'd been carrying on with someone.'

'But she wouldn't press charges.' Lily stared at her right hand, as though she hadn't seen it before. 'Worshipped him like a dog,' she muttered. 'Still does.'

I leaned forward, elbows on knees. 'Miranda is Carlo's ex-wife? I had no idea he even knew her.'

Lily's brown, incurious eyes met mine. 'But you know her too, Jamie. Don't you remember Miranda Miller? You know – Millie. Felicity's best friend.'

25

I tried to summon up the memory of Millie's face and impose it on Miranda Hammett's. I couldn't do it. There's a huge gap between a thirteen-year-old child and a middle-aged woman. Anyway, I hadn't noticed Millie much in the old days – apart, of course, from the last time I'd seen her, which was at the hospital.

She had been Felicity's friend, after all, much younger than Carlo and me, a nonentity, at worst a minor irritant. I remembered wondering whether some of the guilt had rubbed off on her. After all, Felicity had been going to spend the whole afternoon with her and something must have happened to change her plans. Perhaps they had quarrelled.

According to Millie, when I saw her at the hospital the following Wednesday, Felicity had decided to go home because she had a headache. The story was that she cycled away into that hot August afternoon, and that was the last Millie saw of her – the last anyone saw of her.

But I saw her – just for an instant – when I drove round the bend of the lane, too fast and on the wrong side of the road. There she was, open-mouthed, with the green tractor behind her. The sunshine sparkled on the silver fish that dangled from the chain around her neck.

I'm not a child.

After that, the rest is darkness. I wasn't wearing a seat-belt. When the Rover hit the tractor, the impact flung me forward. It drove my forehead into the windscreen, and my ribcage into the steering-wheel. The edge of the rear-view mirror caught the corner of my eye. I deduced this after the event from the nature of my injuries. I don't remember the crash or its immediate aftermath. That is quite normal. In some cases the memory returns, but often it doesn't – and not in my case.

'Open the door,' someone was screaming. 'Open the door.'

Lily was next to the car. She was hammering on the window. I opened the door and she pulled me out. I wasn't in pain, not then. She was crying, and my blood was on her dress. There were cuts on my face and hands from the broken glass.

'You stupid boy, you stupid, stupid boy.'

The engine had stalled. I watched Lily reach into the car and turn off the ignition. I propped myself against the warm metal and felt the blood trickling down my face.

I heard a faint rumble, a ripple of sound in the hot, heavy air. Then everything was silent. Not even the birds were singing.

'That's all we bloody need,' Lily muttered. 'A bloody storm. What happened?'

'Felicity –' My mouth was full of blood and I choked as I said her name. I stopped and swallowed. The blood tasted of salty metal. 'Fox,' I said firmly. 'There was a fox.'

There was blood on the side of the Rover Vitesse, and blood on the ground by my feet. There was even blood on the other side of the lane, by the side entrance to the airfield. Puzzled, I staggered towards it like a sleepwalker, leaving a trail of blood behind me with every step. How had my blood got all the way over there? I leaned against the fence and stared down at it. More of my blood dripped down to join what was already there.

Something nibbled at my memory, then slipped away when Lily spoke. 'I was driving,' she said sharply. 'Got that?'

'What?'

The sounds failed to make sense. Nothing made sense. She took my arm in both hands and shook me. There was an explosion of pain in my shoulder. I yelped. 'Listen to me,' she said, bringing her face very close to mine. 'I was driving.' Her mouth was a jagged pink hole. 'Listen to me, Jamie. I was driving. Do you understand?'

I rubbed my cheek. 'All right.' I looked at my hand. There was blood on my fingers. The watch that Lily had given me for Christmas was still on my wrist. There was blood on that too.

'We were going to buy something to drink in the village. We came round the corner and found some idiot had left the tractor in the way.'

'You were driving? You were?'

'Yes. You bloody fool. Otherwise the insurers won't pay up and you'll be prosecuted. So who was driving?'

'You were,' I said.

'And what happened?'

'Some idiot left the tractor there. You went up the back of it.'

'Good boy. It was nobody's fault, except maybe the tractor driver's. There was nothing we could do. *And I was driving.*'

'The tractor,' I said, looking at the blood. 'The tractor.'

'Yes, the tractor,' she repeated. 'It was in the way.'

Lily made me say the words after her until she was sure I had understood them. She had analysed the situation quickly, and she tried automatically to minimize the damage by moulding the truth into a shape she believed would suit us better. On one level, I am sure, she would have preferred to say that I was driving but that would have meant admitting that she had lost control, that she was no longer the responsible adult. And once she admitted that I had been driving, there would be the risk of further questions, of the details about our relationship emerging, of my blurting out the sort of truth that couldn't be moulded.

But at other times I wonder whether she did it for me – whether she was trying to spare me the consequences of my actions. The possibilities aren't mutually exclusive. People aren't simple: they do things for more than one reason. In my more cynical moments I think that for her truth was an entirely plastic commodity, infinitely adaptable to her changing requirements.

The sequence of events immediately afterwards is blurred. There was a white-faced man, the tractor driver – I think he was the son of the farmer who rented the land at the airfield. He drove away on the tractor, the engine whining like a mad thing, to the nearest telephone.

Later the police came, followed by an ambulance, which took us to a hospital near Swindon. By that time the anaesthetic of shock was wearing off. I had broken my collarbone and several ribs. My face was bruised and cut, and I was concussed. I had a blinding headache. They put me in a ward full of men who coughed and groaned and spat; and somewhere in the background a television chattered to itself.

At one point, Hugh Murthington was stooping over me. His face was thin and very pale, corrugated with wrinkles. I shut my eyes because I couldn't bear to see him. When I opened them, he had gone and the headache was worse.

That night, it was as though I had been thrown into a black well where there was neither light nor movement nor thought. I woke with a thick head and a dry mouth. I thought I heard thunder. It might have been a dream, but it was still enough to wake me up.

The sky was full of light but no one was awake in

the neighbouring beds and I wasn't sure how to call a nurse. For some reason it seemed desperately important to discover what time it was. I opened the cupboard by the bed and found my watch. The blood had dried to a rust-coloured stain. The glass was broken and the hands were no longer moving. Time had stopped at 3.19 in the afternoon.

At times like this you rely on the kindness of strangers. Later in the morning, one of the nurses told me that my friends hoped to come and see me soon but a problem at home was holding them up.

Just after lunch, Hugh Murthington peered through the porthole of the door at the end of the ward. I watched him striding towards my bed, where he perched like a sad grey bird and stared out of the window at a sky so blue it belonged over a Mediterranean island. I tried to speak to him but he wouldn't listen.

'Ah – James. Um. How are you feeling?'

He said kind things in a flat, dull voice. Everyone sent good wishes. He was so sorry I had been involved in the accident. But there was something else he needed to talk to me about.

'It's Felicity,' he explained. 'She – well, she's disappeared.'

'I don't understand.'

'Nor do we. She didn't come home from Millie's yesterday. I don't suppose you've any idea . . . ?'

'No,' I said. 'I thought – I thought she was at Millie's.'

'Yes – we all did. Anyway, we've had to call the

police. Do you think they could have a quick chat with you? Just in case.'

There were two officers, a man and a woman, both in plain clothes. The sweat was pouring off me. After they had asked how I was, the officers wanted me to confirm what they had already been told about Felicity – what she was wearing, where she was going, what had been on her mind recently.

The policewoman said, 'Does she have a boy-friend?'

'She's just a kid,' I said.

'Someone said she rather likes you.'

'She's just a kid,' I repeated. 'It's not like that.'

The policewoman smiled. 'When they're that age, it's all in the mind most of the time, isn't it?'

'Yes,' I said, flattered.

'So you didn't have an argument? Something that could have upset her? It might have meant more to her than to you.'

'No. Everything was fine. I've known her for years. She's – she's like a kid sister.'

'I see.'

She smiled, and so did her colleague. They thanked me for being so helpful and went away.

The next time I saw Hugh Murthington was later that day, Tuesday, in the evening. He came over with Carlo.

'Any news?' I said.

'No, I'm afraid not. Not as far as Felicity's con-cerned. No sign of her or her bike. But I – I'm afraid I've got some rather sad news for you.'

I gaped up at him.

'I'm so sorry. We had a phone call from your mother. Your grandmother's died.'

'Oh,' I said. 'Oh.'

'Your mother's flying home now, and if you're up to it, she'll come and fetch you tomorrow. There'll be the funeral and so forth.' He swallowed, and for a dreadful instant I thought he was about to start crying. 'At times like this, families have to stick together.' He held out his hand. 'But I'm sure we'll see you soon.'

While I was still trying to find words, he marched away, radiating soldierly purpose, until he reached the door, where he blundered blindly against the frame and stumbled into the arms of a passing porter. I never saw him again.

'Christ, what a mess,' Carlo said, when we were alone. 'It's a fucking nightmare.'

'Felicity?'

'She's just buggered off.'

'I hope she's OK.'

We couldn't find words to say to each other. In a moment he mumbled goodbye and wandered off in search of his father. I was relieved when he went. Too late, I remembered that his driving test had been booked for that day.

My only other visitor was Millie, who came on Wednesday morning. I was sitting in a chair by the window. I had my eyes closed because it hurt to have them open. I heard footsteps beside me. I opened my eyes, expecting to see a nurse. Millie was standing very close to me and the rust-coloured hair swung on either side of her face.

'What are you doing here?' I asked, too surprised even to try to be polite.

'Mum's come to see my auntie.'

'Any news?'

'About Felicity? No.' She took a deep breath. 'I just want to say I hate you.'

'That's not –'

'I told those cops, you know. I said that was why she was in such a mood on Monday. It was because of you.'

'Listen, I was –'

'Don't you know how she feels about you? Why can't you be nice to her? If she's dead, it's your fault.'

She turned on her heel and stormed out of the ward. I realized she had spoken loudly enough for people in adjoining beds to hear what she had said. Everyone pretended not to have heard, and I pretended that I didn't know they had heard.

In the afternoon, my mother arrived. She looked tanned and glossy, a creature from another planet. She drove me to my grandmother's bungalow. I sat in the back, pretending to doze. We didn't speak a single word during the journey.

Carlo and I didn't go to Rhodes. He rang me once at my grandmother's bungalow, and we exchanged a few letters. The Murthingtons were in a terrible state. No one had seen Felicity leaving Chipping Weston. Nothing connected her with Rackford on the Monday afternoon she disappeared. There were several unconfirmed sightings of her – one in Glasgow, two in Manchester and one in Brittany – but they came to nothing. The BMX bike didn't turn up. The local police force sent an officer to interview me again: he covered the same ground as the others.

I didn't think too much about it. There was no point. I convinced myself I couldn't be sure I had seen Felicity in the lane beside the airfield. Even if she had been there, she'd obviously gone somewhere else. Telling the police wouldn't help them find her. It would just let everyone know that I'd been driving the car by myself, and that Lily and I had lied.

Lily didn't try to get in touch – either in the hospital or afterwards. She had cut me out of her life. So I had to cut the Murthingtons out of mine. I did not go back to school. I couldn't, because of Carlo, and I made such a fuss that my mother agreed to let me leave. I went to London to finish my A levels at a sixth-form college in South Kensington. My mother arranged for me to live in Hammersmith, at the house of a friend of a friend. It was a business arrangement. The friend of a friend rented me a room, made me breakfast every day and left me alone for the rest of the time. That suited everyone.

I never told Carlo where I was living in London. He had the address of my grandmother's bungalow, and he wrote to me there. In December, my mother at last succeeded in selling the bungalow and I didn't give my address in London to the new owners. I didn't send Carlo a Christmas card. If he sent me one, I didn't receive it.

I worked harder than I had ever worked in my life. I had nothing else to do. In that year I reinvented myself as someone who had never been to Chipping Weston, who had never known anyone called Murthington. In that year I learned to live with my own company. I learned to keep silent.

One summer while I was at university I went to Crete with a girl whose name I can't now remember. She was studying classics and she liked visiting ancient sites. I remember a ruin on a headland. I don't know what it had once been. Stone walls baked under an unbearably hot sun. The girl wandered round with a camera. I sat in a patch of shade beneath an olive tree. I smoked a cigarette and watched a lizard sunning itself on a rock.

I heard a distant rumble. The ground shook slightly. I looked up at the sky, which was a serene and cloudless blue. I heard the girl calling my name, and as I stood up she came running towards me.

'Did you hear it?' she gasped. 'A whole chunk of wall fell down. Just like that. No warning. It was only a couple of yards away. Jesus, I could have been killed.'

'It sounded just like thunder,' I said.

Lily's mind was drifting away from us.

'Mum? Do you want to feel my bump?' Kate picked up her mother's hand and placed it against her belly.

'What?' Lily said.

'It's the baby.'

'What baby?' Lily closed her eyes and began to snore quietly.

'Mum –'

I touched Kate's arm. 'It's the morphine. She needs to rest.'

Kate put her mother's hand gently on the bed. She stooped and kissed her cheek. At the touch of her daughter's lips, Lily stopped snoring for a moment and nodded, as though agreeing with an inaudible proposition. Kate glanced at me and, after a moment's hesitation, I kissed Lily's forehead. She did not react. She smelt of urine and decay. The skin was waxy.

At the doorway, Kate glanced back at the little figure on the bed. 'Mum?'

Lily did not respond. Her eyes were open. The top of her nightdress was unbuttoned. Her neck looked as though a child could snap it by flicking a couple of fingers.

Kate left the number of her mobile at Reception and asked them to call her if there was any change. She seemed composed until we reached the car park. Then she began to cry quietly as we walked side by side across the Tarmac. She got into the car, folded her hands across her belly, bowed her head and continued to weep. After a moment I leaned across and found her a paper handkerchief in the glove compartment. She wiped her eyes and blew her nose.

'Why does it have to be like this?' she said at last. 'Why can't they just switch us off like a light?'

I thought of Felicity, alone in her darkness.

'What's up?' Kate said suddenly. 'Jamie?'

'It's OK.'

'I wish I'd gone to see her more,' she said. 'I should have done, shouldn't I?'

'You've seen her today.'

'I can't stand it when people are ill, when they're dying. When I was young, Carlo used to tell me stories where everyone died. They terrified me. I had nightmares for years.'

'He knew you were scared?'

She nodded. 'That was the whole point of it. He's always had it in for me. I could never be good enough for him – I couldn't be Felicity, could I, the one who disappeared? Besides, he hated Lily, and I was Lily's daughter. Once he shut me in the cupboard under the stairs, in the dark, and left me there for a whole afternoon. I was three years old. It was Felicity's fault.'

'How come?'

'I'd found an old recorder that used to be hers and I was trying to play it. That was what set him off.'

I groped for a change of subject, anything to escape the ghostly echoes of 'The Skye Boat Song' and 'On Top of Old Smoky'.

'Where do you want to go? Regine's?'

'It's too far. They might need me.' She glanced at the hospice and gave a little shiver. 'How about a hotel or something?'

'Do you want to come to Greyfont for an hour or two? It's nearer than Regine's and if there's a call I can drive you or you can borrow the car.'

'What about Nicky? Won't she mind?'

'The sooner you meet her the better. One thing, though – Emily's there with the children.'

Kate laughed, a harsh, jarring sound. 'Then maybe it's not such a good idea.'

But I wanted Nicky to discover for herself that Kate was who I said she was. There was also the point that Kate needed company. I said: 'Let me ring her – Nicky, I mean. See what she thinks.'

I got out of the car to make the call. Kate let down the window and lit a cigarette. I walked to and fro while the phone rang on and on. When Nicky answered, she sounded harassed. I explained the situation.

'You can bring her if you want,' she said.

'What about Emily?'

'There's no need for them to meet, not if it's just for an hour or so. Emily's upstairs in the bathroom being sick. Whatever she had has come back with a vengeance. She wouldn't notice if the roof fell in.'

I heard the television in the background and a child shrieking. 'Are you OK?'

'I'm fine,' Nicky said. 'We may need a new carpet in the sitting-room but that's a minor matter. I can't stay and chat, I'm afraid, because I'm trying to borrow a cot for Albert. He's decided he's afraid of beds.'

I said goodbye and returned to the car.

'That's all right.'

Kate brushed a fleck of ash from her leg. 'So, what's Emily doing there?'

'She's staying for a day or two with the children. She's run out of money and her car's broken down. She's not well so you probably won't see her.'

'Doesn't Nicky mind having her to stay?'

'It was her idea.'

Kate looked at me but said nothing. Nor did I. I wasn't going to explain, not to her.

She gave me a hint of a smile. 'You're very loyal.' She dropped the cigarette out of the window. 'Which is just as well for me.'

26

Nicky's Mini Cooper was parked, as neatly as ever, in front of the garage doors. I let the Saab roll to a halt beside it.

'I'm nervous,' Kate said. 'It seems stupid at a time like this, but I am.'

So was I. I unlocked the front door and we went into the hall. From the sitting-room came the sound of music, full of synthetic excitement and gaiety, of hurdy-gurdies and fairgrounds. A discarded beaker and a small pile of crisps had been deposited on the antique Caucasian saddlebag I had given Nicky for her last birthday. A trail of Lego led from the kitchen to the sitting-room door.

Albert ran into the hall from my study. He was wearing nothing but a pair of pants and a single sock. He hugged the newel post and stared at us with huge, worried eyes.

'A man's come!' he howled. 'Nicky!'

Nicky appeared behind him. She swung him up and rested his little body across her hip. He laughed and touched her cheek with a small hand smeared with a brown substance that I hoped was peanut butter.

I kissed her other cheek. 'Nicky, this is Kate.'

The two women shook hands. I watched with an

unexpected sense of anticlimax. Albert's legs curled round Nicky's hip and he dug his heels into her waist. Still laughing, utterly confident that she would keep him safe, he arched away from her body like a bareback rider at a rodeo. *Ride her, cowboy.*

Nicky glanced down from Kate's face to the curve of her belly. 'How's your mother?'

Kate grimaced. 'Not very good. I'm sorry to turn up like this.'

'The more the merrier. Although I hope James has warned you – we've got Emily and her children here, and Emily's not very well.'

Kate nodded.

Nicky drew Albert back to her side, tucking him under her arm. She swayed, her body automatically rocking him, and turned back to me. 'By the way, Miranda's here too. She's –'

'*Miranda?*'

'I told you – Albert needs a cot. She brought one round.'

Nicky's face changed. She was looking over my shoulder. I turned. Miranda Hammett was coming down the stairs.

'James. Hi. I see you've found Nicky at last. That's nice for you.' She reached the hall and said to Nicky, 'I've put it up. It's a bit stained in places but there's nothing wrong with it. A cot's a cot, eh?'

She stopped abruptly. She had just seen Kate standing beside me.

'Hi, Miranda,' Kate said. 'I haven't seen you for ages.'

'Millie,' I said quietly. 'Millie Miller.'

Miranda opened her mouth, then closed it.

I smiled at her. 'Why didn't you say?'

She wriggled her heavy body and laughed; for an instant I glimpsed the red-haired girl with the two little mounds beginning to grow on her chest. 'I didn't want to stir up old memories,' she said. 'You know how it is. Some things are best left, aren't they?'

'But now you've changed your mind.'

'Yes. Especially since this afternoon.'

Albert buried his head in Nicky's shoulder. Kate had her hands on her hips and a scowl on her face. Somewhere upstairs a lavatory flushed.

Nicky looked at me. 'I don't understand. What's going on?'

'Miranda lived in Chipping Weston when she was a girl,' I said. 'I've only just found out. She was a friend of the Murthingtons, and I knew her slightly. Everyone called her Millie because her surname was Miller. I didn't know her real name was Miranda.'

'She married Carlo,' Kate said. 'My brother. But it didn't last.'

I continued, speaking to Nicky, 'But she and Carlo still see each other. That's how Carlo found me.'

'Is this true?' Nicky said.

Miranda shrugged.

'It explains a lot,' I went on. 'I think she told Carlo that Kate had come here on Friday evening. And she must have told Carlo that we'd gone to the Newnham House Hotel on Wednesday. But long before that she did her best to stir up trouble between you and me.'

'That's balls,' Miranda said. 'I don't know what you're talking about.'

I remembered when she came to see me in hospital, twenty-five years ago. *I just want to say I hate you.* I said to Nicky, 'For her this is a sort of revenge.'

Nicky murmured in Albert's ear: 'Why don't we go and find Maisie and see if she'd like to watch cartoons with you?'

The child nodded. He had two fingers stuffed into his mouth. Nicky carried him into the sitting-room. I heard her talking to Maisie. Miranda picked up her bag from the hall table.

'Well,' she said, to no one in particular, 'anyway – I must be going. The children will –'

I leaned against the front door. 'We need to talk.'

'We shall. But not just now.'

I guessed she wanted to see Carlo first, to show him the chain, which was almost certainly in her bag. 'Wait till Nicky comes back.'

'That may not be a good idea,' Miranda said.

'And why's that?'

'Because she may hear something you'd rather she didn't.'

'About what?' said Nicky, coming back into the hall.

Miranda smiled in triumph. 'About Felicity.'

'Who?' Nicky looked confused, then suspicious.

Miranda pointed at me. 'He knows all about her, don't you, James?'

'Carlo's sister,' Kate said to Nicky. 'She would have been my half-sister but she disappeared before I was born. It's terribly sad, of course, but that's all. What does it matter now?'

'Of course it matters,' Nicky said. 'What happened?'

'It was in the summer holidays – she was spending the afternoon at Miranda's house. They were best friends. She cycled off and no one ever saw her again.'

'But there's more than that,' Miranda said. 'Much more.'

'Wait,' Nicky said. 'Let me get this straight. Are you saying you recognized James when we moved here?'

'Yes. But he obviously didn't recognize me and I didn't see why I should tell him. I thought I'd see what sort of man he'd turned into.'

'What about Carlo?' I asked. 'Did you tell him?'

'I mentioned it, yes. He agreed with me – best not to say anything. To be honest, he didn't have very good memories of you, the way you left him high and dry, the –'

'You're still in love with him,' I said. 'Had that got anything to do with how you acted?'

'Oh, for God's sake!' Miranda tossed her hair away from her face. 'You're letting your imagination run away with you.'

'So Dave knows about this, does he?'

She flinched but said nothing.

I turned back to Nicky. 'Miranda made a pass at me a couple of months ago. You remember? When we went round to the Hammetts' and the Furstons were there? She tried to grab me in the hall. I thought she was just drunk and that the best thing for all concerned was to forget about it.'

'I don't see why I should stand here and be insulted,' Miranda said.

Nicky looked at Miranda. 'So getting friendly with me was all —'

'No. It wasn't like that.' She had the grace to look embarrassed. 'All right, at first it was, but not later. I've nothing against you. Quite the reverse. And you ought to know the truth about James and Felicity. I can't believe he's never mentioned her.'

'It's best to leave it,' I said.

Nicky shook her head. 'I'll be the judge of that.'

'No one knows what happened to Felicity,' I said. 'After she disappeared, there were sightings in Manchester, Glasgow and —'

Miranda's breath hissed between her teeth. 'She never went more than a few miles away from home. And if it wasn't for you, I reckon she'd still be alive. I went to see Lily this afternoon and she told me something very interesting.'

'About what?' I said.

'My mother is dying,' Kate shouted. 'She's off her head on morphine and God knows what else. She doesn't know what she's saying.'

You can argue with the words of a dying woman, I thought. But you can't argue with a tarnished chain and its pendant.

'You were driving the Murthingtons' car in the lane near the airfield,' Miranda said. 'You were on the public road and you were all by yourself. You were only sixteen and you didn't even have a provisional licence.'

Nicky touched my arm, then snatched away her hand. 'I want you to tell me what happened, James. I want *you* to tell me.'

'Felicity was in love with you,' Miranda put in, as if that made it worse. 'You were so nasty to her. Sometimes she –'

I looked at Nicky. 'Felicity was only twelve and –'

'Thirteen, actually.'

'– I hardly had anything to do with her.'

'Because you were only interested in Lily,' Miranda put in.

'She was giving me a driving lesson at Rackford,' I said. 'It's an old RAF airfield, and Hugh Murthington owned it. Carlo was at the dentist that afternoon. Felicity was meant to be at Millie's. Lily said it was over between us, that we had to stop. I lost my temper. I drove out of the airfield and into the lane. I was trying to scare her, I suppose. I came round a corner and there was Felicity straight in front of me. I couldn't avoid her.'

'Oh, God,' Nicky said.

I dared not look at her face. 'A tractor was parked at the side of the road. The car smashed right into it. I blacked out. When I woke up, Lily was there, and she said we had to say she'd been driving. Because of the insurance, because she was afraid everything would come out. And there was no sign of Felicity.'

Blood near the gate to the airfield, the sound of thunder on a fine day?

'I didn't even know she'd disappeared until the next

day. I was in hospital then. I was concussed, and my memory was patchy. I thought I'd imagined seeing her or she'd just walked away.'

'Isn't it amazing?' Miranda said. 'Just listen to him. I can't believe he never told you. I think you hit her. I think you and Lily did something with the body. And I know that because –'

'Stop it,' Kate said. 'I can't stand this any more. You're a bloody hypocrite. I'm glad my father can't hear all this shit that's coming out of you.'

'Your father?' Miranda laughed. '*Your* father? That's a joke.'

Kate advanced on Miranda. She was much smaller but Miranda took a step back. 'My father had his own way of dealing with things. So do I.'

Miranda scowled. 'Felicity tried to tell him about Lily and James. Did you know that? She painted a card for his birthday. Carlo found it a week or two ago in his father's things. He didn't understand what it meant but I did. That was when we knew how far they'd gone. That's when we knew about *you*.'

'The card? The one on your desk in the study?' Nicky put her hand on my arm. 'With flowers in watercolour?'

'That's the one,' I said.

'So it was you who stole it?' Miranda said. 'Carlo thought it was Kate. He was furious.'

Nicky ignored her. 'Maisie found it. She said it was pretty.'

'It is.'

'I had a book about the language of flowers when

400

I was a kid,' Miranda said. 'I've still got it, in fact. It's Victorian – it belonged to my great-grandmother. Felicity borrowed it just before she died, and Lily gave it back to me afterwards. But I didn't see the card until Carlo found it.'

Nicky slipped into the study. Through the open door of the sitting-room came the chatter of the television. Maisie laughed. Albert was singing to himself, a song without words and a very simple tune, three notes repeated over and over again. When Nicky came back she had Felicity's card in her hand.

Miranda came to stand beside her, and Kate moved to her other side. The three women read the message inside the card, then studied the picture like a panel of judges assessing an entry for an amateur painting competition.

'That's a lily,' Nicky said. 'The one on the left.'

'Yes, it reads from the left, I think,' Miranda said, confidence flowing back into her voice. 'The lily's obvious enough. But it's yellow, and that's important, too. A yellow lily stands for falsehood or gaiety. We can guess which it meant here.'

'What's next to it? An azalea?'

'Yes – a sort of rhododendron, sometimes called rosebay. It means beware or danger. And next to it there's a variety of mimosa, acacia. That's secret love in this context.'

My mouth was dry and my knees were weak. Felicity was in the hall with us. The ghost of a thirteen-year-old child had come to accuse me. A child who had once loved me.

'She was quite good, wasn't she?' Nicky said. 'I know the scale's all wrong and there's no real perspective but the colours are lovely, and it's so delicately done. What about this one? It's a bit like Solomon's seal.'

'Jacob's ladder,' said Miranda. 'It means come down.' She looked at me. 'Perhaps you used to meet downstairs at night, and she saw you. But it's more than that. It's the clincher.'

'Jacob,' Nicky said, in a high, strained voice. 'In other words, Jacobus, which is, of course, the Latin for James.'

'And the last one,' Miranda went on, 'is colt's foot, which means justice shall be done. I think she was planning to tell Carlo or her father. Maybe she was going to tell her dad when she gave him the card. But by the time Hugh's birthday came round she was gone.'

'It's all crap,' Kate said, drawing away from the other two women. She folded her arms across her chest and glared at Miranda. 'Total crap. For all we know you painted it yourself. I mean, what was the point of Felicity doing it? Dad wouldn't have known what it meant. And I don't think Felicity even knew about my mother and Jamie.'

I saw Felicity's face with hallucinatory clarity – the watchful eyes, the long hair framing adult features emerging from puppy-fat. I blinked and she vanished.

'James.' Nicky was beside me. 'What is it?'

'Felicity did know about Lily and me,' I said, 'but she couldn't tell Carlo because they'd quarrelled. He made her cry, and that was just before she found out. So she did the card for Hugh instead.'

I closed my eyes and I was with Felicity again on the last Sunday afternoon of her life, back in the ruined vegetable garden behind the summerhouse; and Lily Murthington was talking to her husband about children growing up, about Carlo and Felicity, about Millie and me. But by now I was no longer eavesdropping on their conversation, and neither was Felicity.

I hurry away. I know Felicity is following. She catches up with me at the garden gate and follows me on to the path beyond. The gate closes behind her with a click, and I remember another sound, the one I heard on Friday night when I came in from the summerhouse after failing to make love to Lily.

I turn to face Felicity. The silver fish is resting on her flat chest. She is carrying a book, an old hardback with a red cover and a torn spine.

'Hi,' I say, and for the first time I am anxious about her. I am aware of the need to win her over. 'I thought you were at Millie's.'

'I came back.' She hesitates and then adds, with an emphasis I do not understand, 'I borrowed a book from her.'

'I've just bought some more tobacco. Do you want to go and have a smoke somewhere?'

Felicity wrinkles her nose as though she smells something that disgusts her. 'I saw you from the bathroom window,' she says. 'You and fucking Maria in the moonlight. You fucking lying bugger.'

27

I opened my eyes and found Nicky looking at me. I had no idea what she was thinking, whether this would be an ending or a beginning.

'You never told me,' she said softly. 'You never told me about Felicity. You never told me *anything*.'

'I didn't want to lose you.'

'I need to sit down,' Kate said suddenly. 'Sorry – would you mind?'

'Yes, of course – we'll go into the kitchen.' Nicky avoided my eyes. 'I'll just check on the children and Emily. Why don't you see if the others would like something to drink?'

In the kitchen, Kate asked for herbal tea, and Miranda for white wine. Kate sat down at first but after a moment she went out into the garden so that she could smoke a cigarette. Miranda stayed at the table, her face stiff with disapproval, and watched Kate through the window. 'I just don't understand how people can smoke when they're pregnant,' she said. 'The poor baby. There's no excuse.'

I set down the glass of wine in front of her. 'I don't understand how people can do a lot of things.'

'And I wonder what Nicky will think about Kate's baby.' Miranda picked up the glass. 'What with her not being able to have children. So sad.'

'It always struck me as strange,' I said, 'the way you got friendly with Nicky so quickly. And all your other friends have kids. Now I know.'

'Poor Nicky. So brave of her, trying to make a new start in Greyfont. But such a waste.' Miranda took a swallow of her wine. 'I never liked you when we were young,' she said, in the same conversational tone. 'You were so stuck up, so conceited. Nothing changes, really, does it?'

I didn't reply.

'If I was Nicky I'd leave you. It's the best thing she can do.'

I turned aside to fill the kettle. It is easier to face anger than malice. Malice has a way of finding your weaknesses.

'You can't expect her to stay,' Miranda said. 'Not now.'

Kate's mobile started playing a tune, penetratingly audible through the half-open window. She fumbled in her bag and moved further down the garden to take the call.

While her phone was making its insistent noise, the doorbell rang. I turned off the tap and put down the kettle. I was half-way across the kitchen when I heard Nicky's footsteps in the hall and the sound of the front door opening.

'Oh – hi,' she said.

A man's voice replied.

'You'd better come in,' she went on. 'We're in the kitchen.'

'Nicky!' Emily called down the stairs, and her voice

was wavering on the edge of hysteria. 'Can you give me a hand? Sorry, I've made a bit of a mess.'

'You phoned him,' I said to Miranda. 'You told him to come here.'

She smiled at me. I wanted to strangle her.

Carlo's big body filled the kitchen doorway. He glanced from me to Miranda. 'You've seen Lily?'

'Yes,' Miranda said. 'James knows. I've told him about the card.'

Carlo's eyes slid back to me. Nicky was climbing the stairs.

'And I've found Kate for you, too,' Miranda went on, and now her voice was soft, almost pleading.

I glanced through the window over the sink. Kate was standing by the herb bed that Nicky had planted and she was talking into her phone. I moved a little closer to Carlo so he wouldn't be able to see her through the window.

'Best of all, though, we've got something else.' Miranda sounded breathless. 'From Lily. We've got proof.' Her face blazing with triumph, she stabbed her finger in my direction. 'It was him. It was James. He killed Felicity.'

'You?' Carlo said. '*You?*'

'No. It wasn't like that at all.' I spread out my hands. 'You remember the car crash? Felicity was there. She was in the middle of the lane. It was like you and that fox.'

He stared at me. 'But Lily was driving.'

'No. I was. She wasn't there. I'm sorry.'

'Why?'

'Why what? Why am I sorry? Isn't that obvious?' I felt a sustaining spurt of anger. 'Or do you mean why was I driving? I was driving because I was angry with Lily. I wanted to upset her.'

'But Felicity –'

'Lily didn't know Felicity had even been there. She can't have been badly hurt. I think she ran off, and I don't know what happened to her after that.'

Blood near the gate to the airfield, the sound of thunder on a fine day?

'He's lying,' Miranda said. 'You can see it in his face. He killed her, and then Lily helped him hide the body. And now we've got proof. Look at this. It's Felicity's fish, the one you bought her.'

The one that Lily bought for Carlo to give to her.

Miranda opened her bag and took out the white envelope. She emptied the tarnished chain and pendant on to the palm of her hand and held it out to Carlo. His face intent, he rubbed the fish between thumb and forefinger as though trying to bring it back to life.

'Lily said Kate found it years afterwards – at the airfield,' Miranda went on. 'Lily wasn't making much sense by then, but I'm sure she said that.'

Carlo put the fish on the table and took a step forward. For a moment I thought he was going to lunge forward, grab me by the neck and shake me. I remembered him in the playground at Chipping Weston, towering over a smaller boy while he kicked and punched him for Felicity's sake. I remembered him naked and dripping in the changing-room at school, ramming a boy's head against a brick wall, doing the wrong thing for the wrong reason. I was terrified, and he knew it, and he knew that I knew it.

'Why did Lily take the blame?' he asked.

'Because if it came out that I was driving on a public road, she'd have been blamed anyway and the insurers wouldn't pay up. Because she was afraid that the truth would come out about us.' I paused. 'And because she didn't want to hurt your father and you.'

'That's a joke.'

'I promise you she had no idea Felicity was there that day. Not till Kate found the chain, and that was years afterwards.'

'So that was why you went away. That was why you left school. You felt guilty.'

I bowed my head. Of course I felt guilty, then and now. But now I also felt angry – specifically with Carlo. I hated him. There's nothing like injuring someone to make you hate him, and when you're afraid of him too, you hate him even more.

'You can't hide from the truth,' Miranda said smugly.

'Shut up,' Carlo said.

She shied away as though he'd threatened to hit her. She looked down at her hands. They were cupped round the wine glass, which was now almost empty. Carlo gave a shout of laughter.

'What is it?' I snapped. 'For God's sake, what's so funny?'

'You've no idea how ironic this is. That's what's so funny. So what really happened to Felicity?'

'I think she had an accident. I think she came to Rackford to spy on Lily and me. She had a special place she showed me once, an old lime kiln near the stream. Kate found the fish in the ruins. So I think Felicity left her bike in there. And I think she went back there after the crash, and the roof collapsed on top of her.'

'Just like that?'

'It was dangerous. It could have come down at any time. I told her.'

That was why Felicity went there. Because I'd told her it was dangerous. Maybe she wanted the roof to fall in. Maybe she made it fall in.

I shook my head. 'Anyway, no one looked for her there because no one had any idea she was at Rackford.'

'No one except you.'

'I didn't even know she was missing until twenty-four hours later.'

Carlo walked slowly towards me. I was aware of many things all at once – the distant sound of the television, Nicky's feet moving across the guest-room immediately over the kitchen, Miranda raising the glass towards her lips, and above all Carlo himself, his height and breadth, and the way the bones of his face stood out as though the skin that covered them was thinner than it ought to be.

'Yes, it's ironic,' he repeated, drawing nearer. He ran his left hand along the worktop, his fingertips palpating the surface, searching blindly for cracks and stains. It reminded me of how he'd touched Nicky's Raku bowl with a fingertip, caressing the glaze, just before he let it fall to the floor and shatter.

'Are you planning to share the irony with us?' I asked.

'I was coming to tell you you were off the hook. I had the report today.'

'What report?'

'The DNA test.' He came to a halt in front of me, and now his fingertips drummed a miniature tattoo on the marble worktop. 'You'd forgotten, hadn't you? It wasn't even important enough to remember.'

'Of course I remember, but I've had other –'

'I paid extra to have it done by express,' he interrupted. 'Five working days. They phoned this afternoon and confirmed it by email.'

I turned aside, plugged in the kettle and switched it on. I moved with infinite caution like a drunk pretending to be sober. 'And?' I said.

'You don't have a daughter after all. There's something like a ninety per cent probability that Kate and I have a parent in common.'

Miranda slammed down the glass on the table. Wine slopped over the brim. 'So he's not Kate's father? Hugh was?'

'I'm afraid so,' Carlo said.

I stared at him. 'You're afraid? Why?'

'Because it complicates things in one way and makes them too simple in another.'

'It's certainly more complicated. It means that when you raped Kate last week, it was incest as well.'

'What?' Miranda said. '*What* did you say?'

'You killed Felicity,' Carlo said. 'Is that simple enough for you? It is for me.'

I took a step backwards. The movement gave me a clear view through the window and down the garden. Kate was still talking on the phone. I couldn't see her face. I wished I could think of a way to warn her.

'I didn't kill her,' I said. 'It was an accident.'

'The point is,' Carlo went on, fingertips still tapping on the worktop, 'I had it the wrong way round, didn't I? I thought you'd given me a sister. A fake one, of course. A fraud – a sister I didn't want. But now it turns out you're not Kate's father after all. You didn't give me a sister. You took one away from me instead. My real sister – the one I did want. *You killed Felicity.*'

'It was an accident.' My voice sounded shrill. 'I wish I could go back and change it, just as I wish I could turn back the clock and stop you raping Kate. But I can't. What do you want me to say?'

He didn't answer. He rocked to and fro between the balls of his feet and his heels. He smiled. Then he hit me.

It was a backhanded blow with the left hand. He wore a ring on his wedding finger and I felt it smack against my cheekbone. My body slammed against the worktop. I knocked over the kettle. Lukewarm water splashed over my arm, flooded across the marble and poured on to the tiles below. I tried to scramble backwards, away from Carlo, but my feet slipped away from me. I lost my balance and sprawled on the floor. Carlo kicked my ribs. I curled into a ball, trying to minimize the target. He stamped on me twice more and then he crouched and punched my face.

'You keep out of it, Kate,' I heard Miranda screaming. 'Fuck off. You're not wanted.'

Carlo knelt on me with his full weight and placed his hands round my neck. He looked at me, his face serious but also calm, as though I were an algebraic equation that it was important to solve. His hands began gently to squeeze.

'It's the hospice,' Kate said – not loudly but I heard her clearly, despite the blood pounding in my ears.

The fingers tightened round my neck. I tried to struggle but Carlo had pinned me into the angle between the floor and the line of cupboards below the worktop. He trapped me like a lover.

'My mother's dead,' Kate said. 'They phoned to tell me she's dead.'

'Good,' Carlo said. 'Good, good, good.' He banged my head against the floor in time with the words.

'No,' Miranda shouted. 'No.'

Through the pain, I thought, Thank God, Miranda's trying to stop him.

Carlo's weight collapsed on top of me. The air rushed from my lungs. Everything was black.

Miranda screamed. Feet ran down the stairs. Nicky, I thought, keep Carlo away from her. And I tried to say the words aloud but Carlo's chest was pressing down on my head. He coughed and spluttered. I squirmed and saw a patch of daylight and part of the door of the cupboard. A fine red spray had appeared on it.

'James,' Nicky said. 'James — where are you?'

I summoned up all my strength and wriggled away from Carlo. Water was soaking into my clothes. It wasn't only water. There were streaks of dark red, of pink, of a variety of shades between them. I raised my head and tried to take in what had happened. Kate was standing over me, her hands wrapped around her full belly. Miranda was still screaming. I wished she would stop. I couldn't think with all the noise.

Carlo lay beside me in an untidy sprawl. He was coughing and choking. More blood spattered out of his mouth. His legs jerked and his feet tapped on the floor in a petulant, ineffectual dance.

A knife with a black handle jutted out of his back, a little to the left of the spinal column. It had come from the block beside the kettle. I recognized the welt of scarred plastic on the handle where I had left it by accident on a cooker hob and turned up the heat, in another life long before we moved to this house. It was the one with the biggest blade, long and tapering, which we used for carving.

'It won't come out, Jamie,' Kate said, shouting to be heard over the noise Miranda was making. 'I tried to pull it out but it just won't come.'

The blade had penetrated the ribcage. It had hit the lung and probably the aorta or the heart itself. Now the ribs and muscle spasm gripped it like a pair of pliers, holding it in the wound.

Carlo gasped. His body twitched. Then at last he stopped moving. For an instant the room filled with blessed silence.

Miranda shrieked, her voice rising higher and higher. Nicky closed the door. She slapped Miranda first on one cheek, then the other. The screaming modulated into a wailing sigh.

'You must stop,' Nicky said. 'You mustn't frighten the children.'

'How can you say that?' Miranda sobbed. 'Kate's mad, she's out of her fucking head.'

I climbed slowly to my feet, holding on to a chair for support. There was blood everywhere now, and it was spreading across the floor, a red tide.

Nicky took my arm. 'Are you all right?'

I was looking down at Carlo. 'I think so. Nothing hurts.' I knew the pain would come later, when the anaesthetic of shock receded, just as it had after Felicity died.

'I didn't mean to do it,' Kate said, in a small voice. 'Honestly. I was just trying to stop him hurting you. He was going to kill you.'

Honestly?

'She picked it up and stabbed him,' Miranda said. 'With both hands – I saw her. You all did. She came rushing in from the garden and killed him. Why don't you call the police? She's –'

'Shut up,' Nicky said. 'Just shut up.'

'It was an accident,' Kate said. 'I had to stop him somehow. He was going to kill Jamie.'

'You've got what you wanted now, haven't you?'

Miranda said, in a voice that had shrunk to a ragged whisper. 'Your mother's dead, and so's Carlo. It's all yours now, the house, Rackford, everything. It's so fucking obvious. Can't you see it?'

No one answered her. The red stain spread further and further across the tiles. Miranda groaned and fell to her knees beside Carlo. She shook his shoulder. I think she was trying to shake him awake. I tried to calculate how many inches of the blade were buried in his body. Five? Six? Who would have thought that Kate had all that strength?

'Jamie,' she said urgently. 'It *was* an accident. You do believe me, don't you?'

Nicky was moving towards the door. 'The children. They mustn't come in. I'll take them up to Emily.'

'Children first,' I said. 'You take them up and I'll phone for an ambulance.'

'Jamie.' Kate hugged my arm tightly against her, and I felt the gentle curve of her belly. 'You won't leave me, will you? Whatever happens, you won't leave us?'

'No, of course I won't,' I said.

My wife was at the door.

'Nicky?' I said. 'Nicky?'

But it was too late. She had gone.

'An accident,' Kate murmured. She sounded drowsy. 'Honestly.'

But, honestly, who did you really kill him for? For me or for you?

Still on her knees, Miranda looked up at her. 'You're a murderer.'

415

'I'm not,' Kate said. 'I was just trying to make him stop hurting Jamie, wasn't I?' She turned her face to mine. The amber flecks glowed in the brown eyes. 'An accident, Jamie, an accident.'

Writing *A Stain on the Silence*

It used to be said of Harold Macmillan that as prime minister he marched steadily towards the left, with his eyes to the right. During the last ten years I have sometimes felt that as a crime novelist I have been lurching steadily forwards with my eyes looking backwards over my shoulder. From the middle of the 1990s, after *The Four Last Things*, all my novels have been set in the past, mainly in the 1950s. *The American Boy* was set in the early nineteenth century.

Steadily the urge grew on me to write a book about a place that barely existed when I wrote *The Four Last Things* – this brave new world of ours where mobiles chatter and trill like birds, CCTV cameras perch on every corner, and people go Googling on svelte laptops that no longer need to be attached to the rest of the world with wires.

Some authors methodically prepare for the novels they write by researching, planning, visiting locations and assembling material. Others, including me, go about it in a less rational way. The first drafts of my novels evolve rather as a plant grows. Like a gardener, I can do a certain amount to facilitate the process – to extend the analogy, I can prepare the soil, water the seedling and pray for the right sort of weather. But, also like a gardener, I have to accept that there are elements I cannot control. (The rearing of children and the writing of novels have much in common.)

The title came first: my wife heard it on the radio, an unattributed phrase floating on the ether. Thanks to the helpful staff of the Scottish Poetry Library, I eventually tracked it down to a remark made by Samuel Beckett on several occasions near the end of his life. For him, he said, his work was the only thing that made life worthwhile, his way of leaving a stain on the silence. My immediate reaction was to think that, for many people, the stain on their silence is the children they leave behind them. This led to the next thought: what happens if for some reason those children go missing?

Suddenly I had a theme. Though the novel's setting is contemporary, its dilemmas are as universal as love and death. I knew it would be a book about children and parents, and especially about missing children. Children go missing in many ways. Their parents may lose them. They may lose themselves. They may fall victim to one of the anonymous predators that stalk through every parent's nightmares. They may even be missing without having been born, when their potential selves haunt the minds of those who might have been their parents.

Two more ingredients came to the surface of my mind. Both of them were triggered by true stories. The first was a report in the press about a murder trial in which a woman was accused of killing her lover. The case turned not so much on the forensic evidence as whether you believed what the woman said. The real-life outcome was irrelevant to my purpose. What mattered was the issue of credibility: are you inclined to believe what an attractive woman says, for all the wrong reasons?

The second story concerned a middle-aged man looking back to an affair he had during his schooldays. He had barely hit puberty. The woman had been in her twenties. He had not seen her since their affair had been discovered, and she had been sent away. For the moment I ignored the legal and moral dimensions of the relationship. The question that came into my mind was this: what if the woman had been pregnant?

Out of all this came *A Stain on the Silence*. The novel starts with three very simple questions: what if a childless man in his forties discovers that he has a daughter, the result of an affair twenty-five years earlier? What if the daughter herself is pregnant? And what if she's on the run for murder?

That's all I had at the beginning – the story gathered itself in the writing, like a snowball rolling down a hill (and in this case a snowball pursuing a rather erratic course). Now another novel is rolling down another slope. I know the title – *Bleeding Heart Square* – and I know at least one of the themes, two of the settings and many of the characters. Almost certainly, there will be no mobile phones in this book, and no laptops either. But I can't be absolutely sure. Not until the snowball reaches the end of its run.

Andrew Taylor

ANDREW TAYLOR

THE BARRED WINDOW

It is 1993 and Thomas Penmarsh has lived in Finisterre, the house by the sea, all his life, sleeping each night in the room with the barred window. He's only 48 but has been an old man since one evening in 1967 when he lost everything he valued.

Yet now his controlling mother has died, leaving him master of the house and of his own destiny. So when Esmond, his cousin and childhood confidante, comes to live with him Thomas is overjoyed – Esmond always looks after him. But is Esmond all that he seems?

'A psychological tingler with more than a touch of the Daphne du Mauriers' *Independent on Sunday*

THE RAVEN ON THE WATER

Back in 1964, in the wild and overgrown garden of a Somerset vicarage, Peter Redburn and his best friend Richard had spent a golden summer holiday playing out their special game – a private world of secret rituals and oaths of loyalty.

But the boys' peace was suddenly threatened when an unwelcome new playmate introduced sinister elements of a mystical religion into their innocent game. Then, one terrible night, the childish dreamworld turned into a nightmare.

'Like Hitchcock, Taylor pitches extreme and gothic events within a hair's breadth of normality' *The Times Literary Supplement*

He just wanted a decent book to read …

Not too much to ask, is it? It was in 1935 when Allen Lane, Managing Director of Bodley Head Publishers, stood on a platform at Exeter railway station looking for something good to read on his journey back to London. His choice was limited to popular magazines and poor-quality paperbacks – the same choice faced every day by the vast majority of readers, few of whom could afford hardbacks. Lane's disappointment and subsequent anger at the range of books generally available led him to found a company – and change the world.

'We believed in the existence in this country of a vast reading public for intelligent books at a low price, and staked everything on it'
Sir Allen Lane, 1902–1970, founder of Penguin Books

The quality paperback had arrived – and not just in bookshops. Lane was adamant that his Penguins should appear in chain stores and tobacconists, and should cost no more than a packet of cigarettes.

Reading habits (and cigarette prices) have changed since 1935, but Penguin still believes in publishing the best books for everybody to enjoy. We still believe that good design costs no more than bad design, and we still believe that quality books published passionately and responsibly make the world a better place.

So wherever you see the little bird – whether it's on a piece of prize-winning literary fiction or a celebrity autobiography, political tour de force or historical masterpiece, a serial-killer thriller, reference book, world classic or a piece of pure escapism – you can bet that it represents the very best that the genre has to offer.

Whatever you like to read – trust Penguin.

read more
www.penguin.co.uk

Essential Components of Nursing Care

Nursing Process

KEYWORDS

The following words include nursing/medical terminology, concepts, principles, and information relevant to content specifically addressed in the chapter or associated with topics presented in it. English dictionaries, nursing textbooks, and medical dictionaries, such as *Taber's Cyclopedic Medical Dictionary,* are resources that can be used to expand your knowledge and understanding of these words and related information.

Care plan, types:
  Case management
  Clinical pathway
  Computerized
  Individualized
  Standardized
Clinical record, parts of:
  Admission sheet
  Consents
  Flow sheets
  History and physical
  Laboratory/diagnostic test results
  Medication administration
   record
  Health-care provider's orders
  Progress notes
Data, sources of:
  Primary
  Secondary
Data, types:
  Objective
  Subjective
Data collection methods:
  Auscultation
  Examination
  Inspection
  Interview
  Observation
  Palpation
  Percussion
Functions of the nurse:
  Dependent
  Independent
  Interdependent

Goal, components of:
  Achievable
  Measurable
  Realistic
  Time frame
Inference
Intervention skills:
  Assisting
  Collaborating
  Coordinating
  Managing
  Monitoring
  Protecting
  Supporting
  Sustaining
  Teaching
Nursing diagnosis:
  1. Diagnostic label
  2. Related to factors: contributing
     factors, etiology
  3. As evidenced by: signs and
     symptoms, defining characteristics
Nursing process:
  Assessment
  Analysis
  Planning
  Implementation
  Evaluation
Outcomes:
  Actual
  Expected
Reasoning:
  Deductive
  Inductive

NURSING PROCESS: QUESTIONS

1. During which of the five steps in the nursing process does the nurse determine whether outcomes of care are achieved?
   1. Implementation
   2. Evaluation
   3. Planning
   4. Analysis

2. When considering the nursing process, the word "observe" is to "assess" as the word "explore" is to which of the following words?
   1. Plan
   2. Analyze
   3. Evaluate
   4. Implement

3. Which statement is related to the concept that is central to the nursing process?
   1. It is dynamic rather than static.
   2. It focuses on the role of the nurse.
   3. It moves from the simple to the complex.
   4. It is based on the patient's medical problem.

4. Which word **best** describes the role of the nurse when using the nursing process to meet the needs of the patient holistically?
   1. Teacher
   2. Advocate
   3. Surrogate
   4. Counselor

5. Which word is **most** closely associated with scientific principles?
   1. Data
   2. Problem
   3. Rationale
   4. Evaluation

6. A pebble dropped into a pond causes ripples on the surface of the water. Which part of the nursing diagnosis is directly related to this concept?
   1. Defining characteristics
   2. Outcome criteria
   3. Etiology
   4. Goal

7. A nurse teaches a patient to use visualization to cope with chronic pain. Which step of the nursing process is associated with this nursing intervention?
   1. Planning
   2. Analysis
   3. Evaluation
   4. Implementation

8. Which action reflects the assessment step of the nursing process?
   1. Taking a patient's apical pulse rate every 2 hours after being admitted for an episode of chest pain
   2. Scheduling a patient's fluid intake over 12 hours when the patient has a fluid restriction
   3. Examining a patient for injury after a patient falls in the bathroom
   4. Obtaining a patient's respiratory rate after a nebulizer treatment

9. A nurse is caring for a patient with a fever. Which is a well-designed goal for this patient?
   1. "The patient will have a lower temperature."
   2. "The patient will be taught how to take an accurate temperature."
   3. "The patient will maintain fluid intake adequate to prevent dehydration."
   4. "The patient will be given aspirin every eight hours whenever necessary."

10. Which should the nurse do during the evaluation step of the nursing process?
    1. Set the time frames for goals.
    2. Revise a plan of care.
    3. Determine priorities.
    4. Establish outcomes.

11. During which step of the nursing process does determining which actions will be employed to meet the needs of a patient occur?
    1. Implementation
    2. Assessment
    3. Planning
    4. Analysis

12. Which information supports the appropriateness of a nursing diagnosis?
    1. Defining characteristics
    2. Planned interventions
    3. Diagnostic statement
    4. Related risk factors

13. Which is the primary goal of the assessment phase of the nursing process?
    1. Build trust
    2. Collect data
    3. Establish goals
    4. Validate the medical diagnosis

14. Which **most** directly influences the planning step of the nursing process?
    1. Related factors
    2. Diagnostic label
    3. Secondary factors
    4. Medical diagnosis

15. A nurse collects information about a patient. Which should the nurse do next?
    1. Plan nursing interventions.
    2. Write patient-centered goals.
    3. Formulate nursing diagnoses.
    4. Determine significance of the data.

16. When two nursing diagnoses appear closely related, which should the nurse do **first** to determine which diagnosis most accurately reflects the needs of the patient?
    1. Reassess the patient.
    2. Examine the *related to* factors.
    3. Analyze the *secondary to* factors.
    4. Review the defining characteristics.

17. Which is the **primary** reason why a nurse performs a physical assessment of a newly admitted patient?
    1. Identify if the patient is at risk for falls.
    2. Ensure that the patient's skin is totally intact.
    3. Identify important information about the patient.
    4. Establish a therapeutic relationship with the patient.

18. A nurse evaluates a patient's response to a nursing intervention. To which aspect of the nursing process is this evaluation **most** directly related?
    1. Goal
    2. Problem
    3. Etiology
    4. Implementation

19. A nurse concludes that a patient's elevated temperature, pulse, and respirations are significant. Which step of the nursing process is being used when the nurse comes to this conclusion?
    1. Implementation
    2. Assessment
    3. Evaluation
    4. Analysis

20. When the nurse considers the nursing process, the word "identify" is to "recognize" as the word "do" is to which of the following words?
    1. Plan
    2. Analyze
    3. Evaluate
    4. Implement

21. A nurse is collecting subjective data associated with a patient's anxiety. Which assessment method should be used to collect this information?
    1. Observing
    2. Inspecting
    3. Auscultation
    4. Interviewing

22. A nurse assesses that a patient has slurred speech and a retained bolus of food in the mouth. The presence of which additional patient assessments should be clustered with this group of signs and symptoms? **Select all that apply.**
    1. _____Dyspepsia
    2. _____Coughing
    3. _____Drooling
    4. _____Gurgling
    5. _____Plaque

23. Nurses use the nursing process to provide nursing care. These statements reflect nursing care being provided to a variety of patients. Place the statements in order as the nurse progresses through the steps of the nursing process, starting with assessment and ending with evaluation.
    1. "Did you sleep last night after I gave you the sleeping medication?"
    2. "The patient's clinical manifestations indicate dehydration."
    3. "The patient will have a bowel movement in the morning."
    4. "What brought you to the hospital today?"
    5. "I am going to give you an enema."
    Answer: _____

24. A nurse is caring for a patient with a urinary elimination problem. Which are accurately stated goals? **Select all that apply.**
    1. _____"The patient will be taught how to use a bedpan while on bedrest."
    2. _____"The patient will experience fewer incontinence episodes at night."
    3. _____"The patient will transfer independently and safely to a toilet before discharge."
    4. _____"The patient will be assisted to the commode every two hours and whenever necessary."
    5. _____"The patient will experience one or less events of urinary incontinence daily within 6 weeks."

25. Which human responses identified by the nurse are examples of objective data?
Select all that apply.
   1. _____Irregular radial pulse of 50 beats per minute
   2. _____Wheezing on expiration
   3. _____Temperature of 99°F
   4. _____Shortness of breath
   5. _____Dizziness

26. Place the following statements that reflect the analysis step of the nursing process in the order in which they should be implemented.
   1. Cluster data.
   2. Identify conclusions.
   3. Interpret clustered data.
   4. Communicate conclusion to other health team members.
   5. Identify when additional data are needed to further validate clustered data.
   Answer: _____

27. Which patient statements provide subjective data? **Select all that apply.**
   1. _____"I'm not sure that I am going to be able to manage at home by myself."
   2. _____"I can call a home-care agency if I feel I need help at home."
   3. _____"What should I do if I have uncontrollable pain at home?"
   4. _____"Will a home health aide help me with my care at home?"
   5. _____"I'm afraid because I live alone and I'm on my own."

28. Which nursing action reflects an activity associated with the analysis step of the nursing process? **Select all that apply.**
   1. _____Formulating a plan of care
   2. _____Identifying the patient's potential risks
   3. _____Categorizing data into meaningful relationships
   4. _____Designing ways to minimize a patient's stressors
   5. _____Making decisions about the effectiveness of patient care

29. A nurse is interviewing a patient. Which patient statements are examples of objective data? **Select all that apply.**
   1. _____"I am hungry."
   2. _____"I feel very warm."
   3. _____"I ate half my lunch."
   4. _____"I have a rash on my arm."
   5. _____"I have the urge to urinate."
   6. _____"I vomit every time I eat something."

30. Which statement indicates that the nurse is using inductive reasoning? **Select all that apply.**
   1. A patient is admitted with a diagnosis of dehydration and the nurse assesses the patient's skin for tenting.
   2. A nurse observes a patient falling out of bed on the right hip and immediately assesses the patient for pain in the right hip.
   3. A patient has an elevated white blood cell count and a fever. The nurse concludes that the patient may have an infection.
   4. A patient is scheduled for surgery and is crying, trembling, and has a rapid pulse. The nurse makes the inference that the patient is anxious.
   5. A nurse receives a call from the admission department that a patient with hypoglycemia is being admitted to the unit. The nurse plans to assess the patient for pale, cool, clammy skin and a low blood glucose level.
   Answer: _____

31. The following statements reflect steps in the nursing process. Place the statements in order as the nurse advances through the steps of the nursing process, beginning with assessment and ending with evaluation.
1. "The patient is encouraged to attempt to defecate after meals."
2. "The patient reports not having had a bowel movement for 8 days."
3. "The patient has constipation related to limited mobility and inadequate fluid intake."
4. "The patient will have a bowel movement within 2 days that is of normal consistency."
5. "The patient's stool is still hard and dry 2 days after initiating an increase in fluids and activity."

Answer: _____

32. A nurse is interviewing a patient at the change of shift. Which patient statements reflect subjective data? **Select all that apply.**
1. _____ "When I lift my head up off the bed I feel like vomiting."
2. _____ "I just went in the urinal and it needs to be emptied."
3. _____ "My pain feels like a 5 on a scale of 0 to 5."
4. _____ "The physician said I can go home today."
5. _____ "I ate only 50% of my breakfast."

33. A nurse identifies that the patient's report of decreased activity and intake of fluids may be the underlying cause of the patient's constipation. Place an X over the word that reflects the step of the nursing process that is functioning.

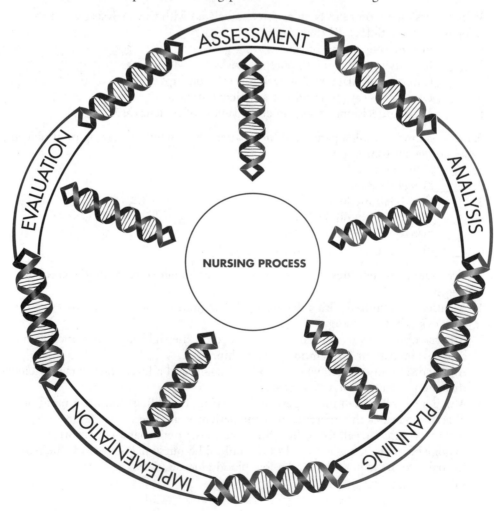

34. A patient is transferred from the emergency department to a medical-surgical unit at 6:30 p.m. The nurse arriving on duty at 8 p.m. reviews the patient's clinical record. Which information documented in the clinical record reflects the evaluation step of the nursing process?
1. Productive cough
2. Seek order for chest physiotherapy
3. No dizziness reported by the patient
4. Acetaminophen 650 mg administered at 5 p.m.

PATIENT'S CLINICAL RECORD

Nurse's Transfer Note From the Emergency Department
Patient admitted to the emergency department at 3 p.m. complaining of shortness of breath, which patient reported became worse over the last few days. Sputum culture and metabolic panel and complete blood count drawn and sent to laboratory. Oxygen ordered at 2 L via nasal cannula, acetaminophen 650 mg PO administered at 5 p.m. Patient transferred to 5 South with a diagnosis of R/O pneumonia at 6 p.m.

Vital Signs Sheet
Oxygen saturation: 85%
Temperature: 102.4°F, temporal
Pulse: 92 beats per minute, regular rate
Respirations: 28 breaths per minute
Blood pressure: 160/90 mm Hg

Nurse's Progress Note
7 p.m.: IV 0.45% sodium chloride running at 100 mL per hour. IV site is clean, dry, and intact. Patient has a productive cough, and respirations are 28 breaths per minute related to excessive respiratory secretions. Called primary health-care provider for an order for chest physiotherapy. Patient states feeling tired and nauseated. Patient had 4 ounces of soup and 3 ounces of water and refused rest of dinner. Patient assisted to the bathroom to void; no dizziness reported by the patient.

35. The nurse assesses a patient and collects a variety of data. Identify the human responses that are subjective data. **Select all that apply.**
1. _____Nausea
2. _____Jaundice
3. _____Dizziness
4. _____Diaphoresis
5. _____Hypotension

1. 1. During the implementation step of the nursing process, outcomes are not determined, but rather planned nursing care is delivered.
   2. **Evaluation occurs when actual outcomes are compared with expected outcomes that reflect goal achievement. If the goal is achieved, the patient's needs are met.**
   3. During the planning step of the nursing process, expected outcomes are determined, but their achievement is measured in another step of the nursing process.
   4. During the analysis step of the nursing process, outcomes are not determined; rather, the nurse identifies human responses to actual or potential health problems.

2. 1. The definitions of the words "observe" and "assess" are similar. Observe means to view something scientifically, and assess means to collect information. The word "plan" does not fit the analogy because the definitions of the words "plan" and "explore" are not similar. Explore means to examine. Plan means to design an intention.
   2. **The definitions of the words "observe" and "assess" are similar. Observe means to view something scientifically, and assess means to collect information. The word "analyze" fits the analogy. Explore means to examine. Analysis means to investigate.**
   3. The definitions of the words "observe" and "assess" are similar. Observe means to view something scientifically, and assess means to collect information. The word "evaluation" does not fit the analogy because the definitions of explore and evaluate are not similar. Explore means to examine. Evaluation within the concept of the nursing process means to come to a conclusion about a patient's response to a nursing intervention.
   4. The definitions of the words "observe" and "assess" are similar. Observe means to examine something scientifically, and assess means to collect information. The word "implement" does not fit the analogy because the definitions of explore and

implement are not similar. Explore means to examine. Implement means to carry out an action.

3. 1. **The nursing process is a dynamic five-step problem-solving process (assessment, analysis, planning, implementation, and evaluation) designed to diagnose and treat human responses to health problems.**
   2. The nursing process focuses on the needs of the patient, not the role of the nurse.
   3. Moving from the simple to the complex is a principle of teaching, not the nursing process. The nursing process is a complex interactive five-step problem-solving process designed to meet a patient's needs. It requires an understanding of systems and information-processing theory and the critical-thinking, problem-solving, decision-making, and diagnostic-reasoning processes.
   4. The nursing process is concerned with a person's human responses to actual or potential health problems, not the patient's medical problem.

4. 1. Although functioning as a teacher is an important role of the nurse, it is a limited role compared with another option. As a teacher, the nurse helps the patient gain new knowledge about health and health care to maintain or restore health.
   2. **When the nurse supports, protects, and defends a patient from a holistic perspective, the nurse functions as an advocate. Advocacy includes exploring, informing, mediating, and affirming in all areas to help a patient navigate the health-care system, maintain autonomy, and achieve the best possible health outcomes.**
   3. The word surrogate is not the word that best describes the role of the nurse providing holistic care. The nurse is placed in the surrogate role when a patient projects onto the nurse the image of another and then responds to the nurse with the feelings for the other person's image.
   4. Although functioning as a counselor is an important role of the nurse, it is a limited role compared with another option. As

counselor, the nurse helps the patient improve interpersonal relationships, recognize and deal with stressful psychosocial problems, and promote achievement of self-actualization.

5. 1. The word "data" (information) is not associated with the term "scientific principles" (established rules of action).
   2. The word "problem" (difficulty) is not associated with the term "scientific principles" (established rules of action).
   3. The word "rationale" (justification based on reasoning) is closely associated with the term "scientific principles" (established rules of action). Scientific principles are based on rationales.
   4. The word "evaluation" (determining the value or worth of something) is not associated with the term "scientific principles" (established rules of action).

6. 1. Defining characteristics do not contribute to the problem statement but support or indicate the presence of the nursing diagnosis. Defining characteristics are the major and minor signs and symptoms that support the presence of a nursing diagnosis.
   2. Outcome criteria are not a part of the nursing diagnosis. Outcome criteria (goals) are part of the planning step of the nursing process.
   3. The etiology (also known as related to or contributing factors) are the conditions, situations, or circumstances that cause the development of the human response identified in the problem statement of the nursing diagnosis. The etiology precipitates the human response just as a pebble dropped in a pond causes ripples on the surface of water.
   4. Goals are not part of the nursing diagnosis. Goals are the expected outcomes or what is anticipated that the patient will achieve in response to nursing intervention.

7. 1. This is not an example of the planning step of the nursing process. During the planning step the nurse identifies the nursing interventions that are most likely to be effective.
   2. This is not an example of the analysis step of the nursing process. During the analysis step data are critically explored and

interpreted, significance of data is determined, inferences are made and validated, signs and symptoms and clusters of signs and symptoms are compared with the defining characteristics of nursing diagnoses, contributing factors are identified, and nursing diagnoses are identified and organized in order of priority.
   3. This is not an example of the evaluation step of the nursing process. Evaluation occurs when actual outcomes are compared with expected outcomes that reflect goal achievement.
   4. This is an example of the implementation step of the nursing process. It is during the implementation step that planned nursing care is delivered.

8. 1. This action reflects the step of implementation. The nurse puts into action the plan to monitor the patient's vital signs after a cardiac event is suspected.
   2. This action reflects the planning step of the nursing process.
   3. This action reflects the assessment step of the nursing process. Assessment involves collecting data via observation, physical examination, and interviewing.
   4. This action reflects the evaluation step of the nursing process. The nurse assesses the patient's respiratory rate and effort after a nebulizer treatment to determine if the treatment was effective in reducing airway resistance, thereby improving the patient's respiratory rate and reducing respiratory effort.

9. 1. This goal is inappropriate because the word "lower" is not specific, measurable, or objective.
   2. This is not a goal. This is an action the nurse plans to implement to help a patient achieve a goal.
   3. This is a well-written goal. Goals must be patient centered, specific, measurable, and realistic and have a time frame in which the expected outcome is to be achieved. The words "adequate" and "dehydration" are based on generally accepted criteria against which to measure the patient's actual outcome. The word "maintain" connotes continuously, which is a time frame.

4. This is not a goal. This is an action the nurse plans to implement to help a patient achieve a goal.

10. 1. Setting time frames for goals to be achieved is part of the planning, not evaluation, step of the nursing process.

2. **Revising a plan of care takes place in the evaluation step of the nursing process. If during evaluation it is determined that the goal was not met, the reasons for failure have to be identified and the plan modified.**

3. Determining priorities is part of the planning, not evaluation, step of the nursing process. Priority setting is a decision-making process that ranks a patient's nursing needs and nursing interventions in order of importance.

4. Establishing outcomes is part of the planning, not evaluation, step of the nursing process.

11. 1. This does not occur during the implementation step of the nursing process. During the implementation step the nurse puts the plan of care into action. Nursing interventions include actions that are dependent (requiring a primary health-care provider's order), independent (autonomous actions within the nurse's scope of practice), and interdependent (interventions that require a primary health-care provider's order but that permit the nurse to use clinical judgment in their implementation).

2. This does not occur during the assessment step of the nursing process. During the assessment step the nurse uses various skills such as observation, interviewing, and physical examination to collect data from various sources.

3. **The identification of nursing actions designed to help a patient achieve a goal occurs during the planning step of the nursing process.**

4. This does not occur during the analysis step of the nursing process. The nurse identifies the patient's human responses to actual or potential health problems during the analysis step of the nursing process.

12. 1. **The defining characteristics are the major and minor cues that form a cluster that support or validate the presence of a nursing diagnosis. At least one major defining characteristic**

must be present for a nursing diagnosis to be considered appropriate for the patient.

2. Planned interventions do not support the nursing diagnosis. They are the nursing actions designed to help resolve the "related to" or "contributing to" factors and achieve expected patient outcomes that reflect goal achievement.

3. The diagnostic statement cannot support the nursing diagnosis because it is the first part of the nursing diagnosis. A nursing diagnosis is made up of two parts, the diagnostic statement (also known as the problem statement) and the "related to" factors (also known as factors that contribute to the problem or the etiology).

4. Related risk factors cannot support the nursing diagnosis because they are the second part of the nursing diagnosis. A nursing diagnosis is made up of two parts, the diagnostic statement (also known as the problem statement) and the "related to" factors (also known as factors that contribute to the problem or the etiology).

13. 1. Although trust may be established during the assessment phase of the nursing process, it is not the purpose of this step of the nursing process. The development of trust generally takes time.

2. **The primary purpose of the assessment step of the nursing process is to collect data (information) from various sources using a variety of approaches.**

3. When a five-step nursing process is followed, formulating goals occurs during the planning, not assessment, step of the nursing process.

4. Validating the medical diagnosis is not within a nurse's legal scope of practice.

14. 1. **Related factors (i.e., "contributing to" factors, etiology) contribute to the problem statement of the nursing diagnosis and directly impact on the planning step of the nursing process. Nursing interventions are selected to minimize or relieve the effects of the related factors. If nursing interventions are appropriate and effective, the human response identified in the problem statement part of the nursing diagnosis will resolve.**

2. The planning step of the nursing process includes setting a goal, identifying the outcomes that will reflect goal achievement, and planning nursing interventions. Although the wording of the goal is directly influenced by the diagnostic label (problem statement of the nursing diagnosis), the selection of nursing interventions is not.

3. Secondary factors generally have only a minor influence on the planning step of the nursing process.

4. The medical diagnosis does not influence the planning step of the nursing process. The nurse is concerned with human responses to actual or potential health problems, not the medical diagnosis.

15. 1. Nursing care is planned after nursing diagnoses and goals are identified, not immediately after data are collected.

2. Goals are designed after a nursing diagnosis is identified, not after data are collected.

3. Once data are collected, the nurse must first organize and cluster the data to determine significance and make inferences. After all this is accomplished, then the nurse can formulate a nursing diagnosis.

4. **After data are collected, they are clustered to determine their significance.**

16. 1. If a thorough assessment was completed initially, a reassessment should not be necessary.

2. To establish which of two nursing diagnoses is most appropriate is not dependent upon identifying the factors that *contributed to* (also known as *related to* or *etiology of*) the nursing diagnosis. These factors are identified after the problem statement is identified.

3. To establish which of two nursing diagnoses is more appropriate is not dependent upon analyzing the *secondary to* factors. *Secondary to* factors generally are medical conditions that precipitate the *related to* factors. The *secondary to* factors are identified after the *related to* factors of the problem are identified.

4. **The first thing the nurse should do to differentiate between two closely associated nursing diagnoses is to compare the data collected to the major and minor defining**

characteristics of each of the nursing diagnoses being considered.

17. 1. Although completing a nursing physical assessment includes an assessment of the risk for falls, it is only one component of the assessment.

2. Although completing a nursing physical admission assessment includes an assessment of the skin, it is only one component of the assessment.

3. **This is the primary purpose of a nursing physical assessment. Data must be collected and then analyzed to determine significance and grouped in meaningful clusters before a nursing diagnosis or plan of care can be made.**

4. Although completing a nursing physical assessment helps to initiate the nurse-patient relationship, it is not the primary purpose of completing a nursing admission assessment.

18. 1. **To evaluate the effectiveness of a nursing action the nurse must compare the actual patient outcome with the expected patient outcome. The expected outcomes are the measurable data that reflect goal achievement, and the actual outcomes are what really happened.**

2. The problem is associated with the first half (problem statement) of the nursing diagnosis, not the evaluation step of the nursing process.

3. Etiology is a term used to identify the factors that relate to or contribute to the problem statement of the nursing diagnosis, not the evaluation step of the nursing process.

4. Implementation is a step separate from evaluation in the nursing process. Nursing care must be performed before it can be evaluated.

19. 1. This is not an example of the implementation step of the nursing process. It is during the implementation step that planned nursing care is delivered.

2. This is not an example of the assessment step of the nursing process. Although data may be gathered during the assessment step, the manipulation of the data is conducted in a different step of the nursing process.

3. This is not an example of the evaluation step of the nursing process. Evaluation occurs when actual outcomes are compared with expected outcomes, which reflect attainment or nonattainment of the goal.

4. **During the analysis step of the nursing process, data are critically explored and interpreted, significance of data is determined, inferences are made and validated, cues and clusters of cues are compared with the defining characteristics of nursing diagnoses, contributing factors are identified, and nursing diagnoses are identified and organized in order of priority.**

20. 1. The words "identify" and "recognize" have the same definition. They both mean the same as that which is known. The word "plan" does not fit the analogy because the definitions of plan and do are different. The word "plan" means a method of proceeding. The word "do" means to carry into effect or to accomplish.

2. The words "identify" and "recognize" have the same definition. They both mean the same as that which is known. The word "analyze" does not fit the analogy because the definitions of analyze and do are different. The word "analyze" means to investigate the patient's human response to an actual or potential health problem. The word "do" means to carry into effect or to accomplish.

3. The words "identify" and "recognize" have the same definition. They both mean the same as that which is known. The word "evaluate" does not fit the analogy because the definitions of evaluate and do are different. The word "evaluate" means to determine the worth of something, whereas the word "do" means to carry into effect or to accomplish.

4. **This is the correct analogy. The words "identify" and "recognize" have the same definition. They both mean the same as that which is known. The words "do" and "implement" both have the same definition. They both mean to carry out some action.**

21. 1. Observation is the deliberate use of all the senses and involves more than just inspection and examination. It includes surveying, looking, scanning, scrutinizing, and appraising. Although the nurse makes inferences based on data collected by observation, this is not as effective as another data collection method to identify subjective data associated with a patient's anxiety.

2. Inspection involves the act of making observations of physical features and behavior. Although the nurse observes behaviors and makes inferences based on their perceived meaning, another data collection method is more effective in identifying subjective data associated with a patient's anxiety.

3. Auscultation is listening for sounds within the body. This collects objective, not subjective, data, which are measurable.

4. **Interviewing a patient is the most effective data collection method when collecting subjective data associated with a patient's anxiety. The patient is the primary source for subjective data about beliefs, values, feelings, perceptions, fears, and concerns.**

22. 1. Epigastric discomfort after eating (dyspepsia) may be sign of a gastrointestinal problem. Dyspepsia is unrelated to the patient's other clinical manifestations.

2. **The body continuously secretes saliva (approximately 1,000 mL/day) that usually is swallowed. If a patient is having difficulty swallowing, the patient may aspirate saliva, which can cause coughing.**

3. **The body continuously secretes saliva (approximately 1,000 mL/day) that usually is swallowed. When saliva accumulates and is not swallowed it dribbles out of the mouth (drooling). Drooling in addition to the patient's other clinical manifestations indicates that the patient may have impaired swallowing.**

4. **The body continuously secretes saliva (approximately 1,000 mL/day) that usually is swallowed. When saliva accumulates and is not swallowed it makes a bubbling or gurgling sound in the posterior oropharynx as air is inhaled and exhaled.**

5. A thin film of mucin, food debris, and dead epithelial cells on the teeth (plaque) is not related to the patient's other clinical

manifestations. Plaque is related to the development of dental caries.

23. 4. Objective and subjective data must be collected, verified, and communicated during the assessment step of the nursing process.
   2. Data are clustered and analyzed, and their significance is determined, leading to a conclusion about the patient's condition, during the analysis step of the nursing process.
   3. Identifying goals, projecting outcomes, setting priorities, and identifying interventions are all part of the planning step of the nursing process.
   5. Planned actions are initiated and completed during the implementation step of the nursing process.
   1. Identifying responses to care, comparing actual outcomes with expected outcomes, analyzing factors that affected outcomes, and modifying the plan of care if necessary are all part of the evaluation step of the nursing process.

24. 1. This statement is not a goal. This is an action the nurse plans to implement to help a patient achieve a goal.
   2. This goal is inappropriate because the word "fewer" is not specific, measurable, or objective.
   3. This is a correctly worded goal. Goals must be patient-centered, measurable, realistic, and include the time frame in which the expected goal is to be achieved. The word "independently" indicates that no help is needed, and the word "safely" indicates that no injury will occur. The time frame is "before discharge."
   4. This statement is not a goal. This is an action the nurse plans to implement to help a patient achieve a goal.
   5. This is a correctly worded goal. Goals must be patient-centered, measurable, realistic, and include the time frame in which the expected goal is to be achieved. The words "one or less event . . . daily" comprise a measurable statement and the words "within 6 weeks" establish a time frame.

25. 1. A radial pulse is objective information. Objective data are measurable and checkable.

2. The sound of wheezing is objective data because it can be heard by others. Air becomes turbulent when it moves through narrow passages that cause vibration of airway walls, resulting in high-pitched whistling sounds (wheezing).
3. A temperature of 99°F is objective information. Objective data are measurable and can be verified.
4. A patient's report about shortness of breath is an example of subjective, not objective, data. Subjective data are those responses, feelings, beliefs, preferences, and information that only the patient can confirm.
5. A patient's report about dizziness is an example of subjective, not objective, data. Subjective data are those responses, feelings, beliefs, preferences, and information that only the patient can confirm.

26. 1. The first step in the analysis phase of the nursing process is to group and cluster data that appear to have a relationship. The nurse uses indicative reasoning, moving from the specific to the general.
   5. The second step in analysis involves gathering additional data to corroborate, substantiate, support, and validate clustered data further.
   3. The third step in analysis involves interpreting the data. The nurse uses reasoning based on knowing commonalities and differences and a scientific foundation of knowledge and experiential background to determine if the data cluster is significant.
   2. The fourth step in analysis involves the nurse making a conclusion about the clustered and validated data.
   4. The fifth step in analysis involves communicating conclusions to other health team members such as a nursing diagnosis in a nursing plan of care.

27. 1. Knowing one's own abilities is subjective information because it is the patient's perception and can be verified only by the patient. Subjective data are those responses, feelings, beliefs, preferences, and information that only the patient can confirm.

2. This statement is neither subjective nor objective data. It is a statement indicating an understanding of how to seek home-care services after discharge.

3. This statement is neither subjective nor objective data. It is a question indicating that the patient wants more information about how to control pain when at home.

4. This statement is neither subjective nor objective data. It is a statement exploring who will provide assistance with care once the patient goes home.

5. **Fear is subjective information because it is the patient's perception and can be verified only by the patient. Subjective data are those responses, feelings, beliefs, preferences, and information that only the patient can confirm.**

28. 1. This occurs during the planning, not analysis, step of the nursing process.

2. **Potential risk factors are identified during the analysis step of the nursing process. Risk diagnoses are designed to address situations in which patients have a particular vulnerability to health problems.**

3. **Determining which data are significant or insignificant and then categorizing the meaningful data into clusters of data that are related are parts of the analysis step of the nursing process.**

4. This occurs during the planning, not analysis, step of the nursing process.

5. This occurs during the evaluation, not analysis, step of the nursing process.

29. 1. Hunger is an example of subjective, not objective, data. Subjective data are those responses, feelings, beliefs, preferences, and information that only the patient can confirm.

2. Feeling warm is an example of subjective, not objective, data. Subjective data are those responses, feelings, beliefs, preferences, and information that only the patient can confirm.

3. **The amount of food eaten by a patient can be objectively verified. The nurse measures and documents the percentage of a meal ingested by a patient to quantify the amount of food consumed.**

4. **A rash on a patient's arm can be objectively verified via inspection.**

5. Having the urge to void is an example of subjective, not objective, data. Subjective data are those responses, feelings, beliefs, preferences, and information that only the patient can confirm.

6. **Vomiting is a human response that is observable and the amount vomited can be measured. Vomiting is objective information.**

30. 1. This statement reflects the nurse using deductive reasoning. It moves from a general premise (the patient is dehydrated) to a specific deduction (the patient will probably have tenting of the skin, which is a sign of dehydration).

2. This statement reflects the nurse using deductive reasoning. It moves from a general premise (the patient may have fractured the head of the femur in the fall) to a specific deduction (the patient will probably have pain in the hip if it is fractured).

3. **This statement reflects the nurse using inductive reasoning. It moves from the specific to the general. A pattern of information (an elevated white blood cell count and elevated temperature) leads to a generalization (the patient may have an infection).**

4. **This statement reflects the nurse using inductive reasoning. It moves from the specific to the general. A pattern of information (crying, trembling, and a rapid pulse) leads to a generalization (the patient may be anxious).**

5. This statement reflects the nurse using deductive reasoning. It moves from a general premise (the patient is experiencing hypoglycemia) to a specific deduction (the patient will probably have pale, cool, clammy skin and a low blood glucose level).

31. 2. **This statement reflects data collection that occurs in the assessment phase of the nursing process, which is the first step.**

3. **This statement reflects etiological factors contributing to the nursing diagnosis problem statement, which is "constipation." This step analyzes the data collected in the assessment phase of the nursing process.**

4. This statement is a measurable goal. Identifying goals occurs after the nursing diagnosis is identified.

1. This statement indicates implementation of a planned action that is designed to address the problem statement.

5. Information about a patient's response to nursing care can be used to compare the patient's actual outcome with the expect outcome, which is the evaluation phase of the nursing process.

32. 1. Feeling like vomiting is something that only the patient can perceive. Subjective data are those responses, feelings, beliefs, preferences, and information that only the patient can confirm.

2. This statement reflects objective, not subjective, information. The urine is observable and measurable. Objective data can be verified.

3. A patient's perception about a level of pain is subjective information. Subjective data are those responses, feelings, beliefs, preferences, and information that only the patient can confirm.

4. This information reflects objective, not subjective, data. The statement can be verified.

5. This information reflects objective, not subjective, data. The statement can be verified.

33. Determining relationships of data and their significance are associated with the analysis phase of the nursing process.

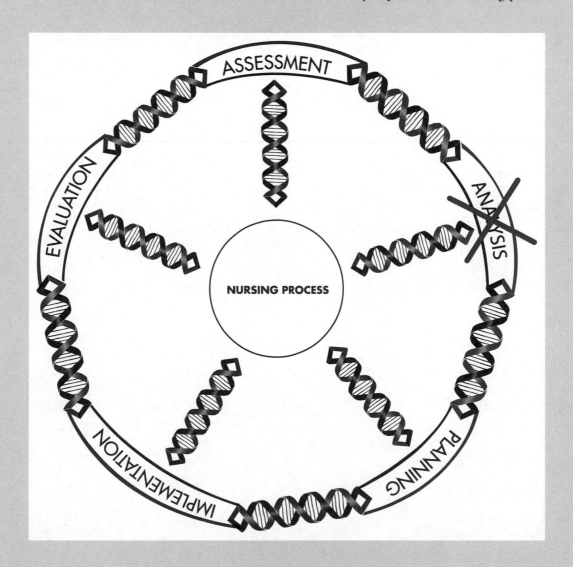

34. 1. A productive cough is information collected during the assessment phase of the nursing process.
2. Seeking an order for chest physiotherapy reflects the planning phase of the nursing process.
3. This statement reflects an evaluation of the patient's response to ambulation.
4. Administering an ordered medication reflects the implementation phase of the nursing process.

35. 1. Nausea is an unpleasant, wave-like sensation in the back of the throat, epigastrium, or abdomen that may lead to vomiting. It is considered subjective data because it cannot be measured by the nurse objectively. It is experienced only by the patient.
2. A yellow color of the skin, whites of the eyes, and mucous membranes (jaundice) because of deposition of bile pigments from excess bilirubin in the blood is objective, not subjective, information. Objective data are measurable and checkable.
3. This is subjective information because it is the patient's perception and can be verified only by the patient. Subjective data are those responses, feelings, beliefs, preferences, and information that only the patient can confirm.
4. Excessive sweating (diaphoresis) is objective, not subjective, information. Objective data are measurable and checkable.
5. Abnormally low systolic and diastolic blood pressure levels (hypotension) can be measured and verified and therefore are objective data.

Physical Assessment

KEYWORDS

The following words include nursing/medical terminology, concepts, principles, and information relevant to content specifically addressed in the chapter or associated with topics presented in it. English dictionaries, nursing textbooks, and medical dictionaries, such as *Taber's Cyclopedic Medical Dictionary,* are resources that can be used to expand your knowledge and understanding of these words and related information.

Afebrile

Asymptomatic

Autonomic nervous system

Barrel chest

Blood pressure:
  Auscultatory gap
  Korotkoff's sounds
  Pulse pressure
  Systolic/diastolic

Body weight

Borborygmi (bowel sounds)

Breathing:
  Costal (thoracic)
  Diaphragmatic (abdominal)
  Patterns:
    Biot
    Cheyne-Stokes
    Eupnea
    Kussmaul
  Rate:
    Apnea
    Bradypnea
    Tachypnea

Breath sounds:
  Adventitious:
    Crackles (rales)
    Gurgles (rhonchi)
    Pleural friction rub
    Stridor
    Wheeze
  Expected:
    Bronchial
    Bronchovesicular
    Vesicular

Capillary refill

Circadian rhythms, diurnal variations

Clubbing

Cognitive impairment:
  Confusion
  Delirium
  Dementia

Data:
  Objective, subjective
  Primary source of
  Secondary source of

Ecchymosis

Edema:
  Dependent
  Sacral

Erythema

Exacerbation

Fever (pyrexia), stages of:
  Onset (cold or chill phase)
  Course (plateau phase)
  Defervescence (fever abatement, flush phase)

General adaptation syndrome

Heart rate:
  Bradycardia
  Irregular rhythm (dysrhythmia)
  Pulse deficit
  Tachycardia

Hirsutism

Hyperemia

Hypertension

Hypotension

Hypovolemic shock

Jaundice

Lesions

Lethargy

Level of consciousness

Local adaptation syndrome

Malaise

Memory:
  Long term
  Short term

Mental status

Mobility:
  Balance
  Gait
  Posture
  Strength

Mood

Neuro-checks

Neurovascular assessment

Orientation to time, place, person

Orthostatic hypotension

Pain assessment scales:

   FLACC pain rating scale

   Numerical scales

   Wong-Baker FACES Rating Scale

Parasympathetic nervous system

Physical assessment:

   Auscultation

   Inspection

   Palpation

   Percussion

Pruritus

Pulse sites:

   Apical

   Brachial

Carotid

Femoral

Pedal

Popliteal

Posterior tibial

Temporal

Tibial

Remission

Shivering

Sympathetic nervous system

Temperature sites:

   Axillary

   Oral

   Rectal

   Tympanic

Tremor

Turgor

Urticaria

PHYSICAL ASSESSMENT: QUESTIONS

1. A nurse is assessing a patient's bilateral pulses for symmetry. Which pulse site should not be assessed on both sides of the body at the same time?
   1. Radial
   2. Carotid
   3. Femoral
   4. Brachial

2. A nurse is caring for a patient who is experiencing an increase in signs and symptoms associated with multiple sclerosis. Which term describes a recurrence of signs and symptoms associated with a chronic disease?
   1. Variance
   2. Remission
   3. Adaptation
   4. Exacerbation

3. When evaluating the vital signs of a group of patients the nurse takes into consideration the circadian rhythm of body temperature. At which time of day is body temperature usually at its lowest?
   1. 4 p.m. to 6 p.m.
   2. 4 a.m. to 6 a.m.
   3. 8 p.m. to 10 p.m.
   4. 8 a.m. to 10 a.m.

4. Which method of examination is being used when the nurse's hands are used to assess the temperature of a patient's skin?
   1. Palpation
   2. Inspection
   3. Percussion
   4. Observation

5. A nurse must assess for the presence of bowel sounds in a postoperative patient. Which technique should the nurse employ to obtain accurate results when auscultating the patient's abdomen?
   1. Listen for several minutes in each quadrant of the abdomen.
   2. Place a warmed stethoscope on the surface of the abdomen.
   3. Perform auscultation before palpation of the abdomen.
   4. Start at the left lower quadrant of the abdomen.

6. Which assessment requires the nurse to assess the patient further?
   1. 18-year-old woman with a pulse rate of 140 after riding 2 miles on an exercise bike
   2. 50-year-old man with a BP of 112/60 mm Hg on awakening in the morning
   3. 65-year-old man with a respiratory rate of 10
   4. 40-year-old woman with a pulse of 88

7. A nurse is monitoring the status of postoperative patients. Which vital sign will change **first** when a postoperative patient has internal bleeding?
   1. Body temperature
   2. Blood pressure
   3. Pulse pressure
   4. Heart rate

8. A patient has had a 101°F fever for the past 24 hours. How often should the nurse monitor this patient's temperature?
   1. Every 2 hours
   2. Every 4 hours
   3. Every 6 hours
   4. Every 8 hours

9. A nurse is unable to palpate a patient's brachial pulse. Which pulse should the nurse assess to determine adequate brachial blood flow in this patient?
   1. Radial
   2. Carotid
   3. Femoral
   4. Popliteal

10. Which of the following can cause urine to appear red?
    1. Beets
    2. Strawberries
    3. Red food dye
    4. Cherry gelatine

11. A nurse is assessing a patient's heart rate by palpating the carotid artery. Which action should the nurse implement when assessing a pulse at this site?
    1. Monitor for a full minute.
    2. Palpate just below the ear.
    3. Press gently when palpating the site.
    4. Massage the site before assessing for rate.

12. A nurse obtains the blood pressure of several adults. Which blood pressure result should cause the **most** concern?
    1. 102/70 mm Hg
    2. 140/90 mm Hg
    3. 125/85 mm Hg
    4. 118/75 mm Hg

13. A nurse is planning care for a patient who has intolerance to activity. Which is the **first** assessment that should be made by the nurse?
    1. Range of motion
    2. Pattern of vital signs
    3. Impact on functional health patterns
    4. Influence on the other family members

14. The nurse must take a patient's rectal temperature. Which should the nurse do?
    1. Take the temperature for 5 minutes.
    2. Wear gloves throughout the procedure.
    3. Place the patient in the right lateral position.
    4. Insert the thermometer 2 inches into the patient's anus.

15. Which usually is **unrelated** to a nursing physical assessment?
    1. Posture and gait
    2. Balance and strength
    3. Hygiene and grooming
    4. Blood and urine values

16. A nurse is performing a psychosocial assessment. Which assessment should be identified as a subtle indicator of depression?
    1. Unkempt appearance
    2. Anxious behavior
    3. Tense posture
    4. Crying

17. A nurse in the emergency department is caring for a patient who is diagnosed with hypothermia. The presence of which factor in the patient's history may have precipitated this condition?
    1. Heat stroke
    2. Inability to sweat
    3. Excessive exercise
    4. High alcohol intake

18. Which is common to the collection of specimens for culture and sensitivity tests regardless of their source?
    1. Preservative media must be used.
    2. Two specimens should be obtained.
    3. Surgical asepsis must be maintained.
    4. A morning specimen should be collected.

19. An adult patient's vital signs are: oral temperature 99°F, pulse 88 beats per minute with a regular rhythm, respirations 16 breaths per minute and deep, and blood pressure 180/110 mm Hg. Which sign should cause concern?
    1. Pulse
    2. Respirations
    3. Temperature
    4. Blood pressure

20. A patient is admitted to the emergency department with difficulty breathing. Which patient response identified by the nurse causes the **most** concern?
    1. Low pulse oximetry
    2. Wheezing on expiration
    3. Shortness of breath on exertion
    4. Using accessory muscles of respiration

21. When evaluating the vital signs of a group of patients the nurse takes into consideration the circadian rhythm of body temperature. At which time of day is body temperature usually at its highest?
    1. 12 a.m. to 2 a.m.
    2. 6 a.m. to 8 a.m.
    3. 4 p.m. to 6 p.m.
    4. 8 p.m. to 10 p.m.

22. Which physical examination method should a nurse use when assessing for borborygmi?
    1. Palpation
    2. Inspection
    3. Percussion
    4. Auscultation

23. Which nursing action is common to all instruments when taking a temperature?
    1. Ensure that the instrument is clean.
    2. Place a disposable sheath over the probe.
    3. Wash with cool soap and water after use.
    4. Check that it is below ninety six degrees before insertion.

24. A nurse concludes that a patient is experiencing pyrexia. Which assessment precipitated this conclusion?
    1. Mental confusion
    2. Increased appetite
    3. Rectal temperature of 101°F
    4. Heart rate of 50 beats per minute

25. A nurse in the emergency department is engaging in an initial assessment of a patient. Which assessment takes priority?
    1. Blood pressure
    2. Airway clearance
    3. Breathing pattern
    4. Circulatory status

26. A nurse plans to take a patient's radial pulse. Which method of examination should be used by the nurse?
    1. Palpation
    2. Inspection
    3. Percussion
    4. Auscultation

27. The nurse is obtaining a patient's blood pressure. Which information is **most** important for the nurse to document?
    1. Staff member who took the blood pressure
    2. Patient's tolerance to having the blood pressure taken
    3. Position of the patient if the patient is not in a sitting position
    4. Difference between the palpated and auscultated systolic readings

28. A nurse is teaching a cancer prevention community health class. Which recommended cancer screening guideline for asymptomatic people not at risk for cancer should the nurse include?
    1. Pap smear annually for females 13 years of age and older
    2. Mammogram annually for women 30 years of age and older
    3. Colonoscopy at 50 years of age and every 10 years thereafter
    4. Prostate-specific antigen yearly for men 30 years of age and older

29. A nurse is assessing a patient who states "I feel cold." Which mechanism that helps regulate body temperature will increase body heat?
    1. Vasodilation
    2. Evaporation
    3. Shivering
    4. Radiation

30. Edrophonium IV is administered to a patient suspected of having myasthenia gravis. Within 30 seconds after administration of the edrophonium, the patient experiences a cholinergic reaction with increased muscle weakness, bradycardia, diaphoresis, and hypotension. The primary health-care provider prescribes atropine sulfate 1 mg IV STAT. The vial of atropine sulfate indicates 0.5 mg/mL. Calculate how many milliliters of atropine sulfate the nurse should administer. **Record your answer using a whole number.**

Answer: _____ mL.

31. A nurse in the clinic must obtain the vital signs of each patient via an electronic thermometer before patients are assessed by the primary health-care provider. Which patient characteristics indicate that the nurse should take the patient's temperature via the rectal, rather than the oral, route? **Select all that apply.**
    1. _____Mouth breather
    2. _____History of vomiting
    3. _____Presence of confusion
    4. _____Intolerance of the semi-Fowler position
    5. _____Seven-year-old child level of intelligence

32. A patient with hypertension is given discharge instructions to take the blood pressure every day. A nurse is evaluating a family member taking the patient's blood pressure as part of the patient's discharge teaching plan. Which behaviors indicate that the family member needs additional teaching? **Select all that apply.**
    1. _____Positions the arm higher than the level of the heart
    2. _____Places the diaphragm of the stethoscope over the brachial artery
    3. _____Applies the center of the bladder of the cuff directly over an artery
    4. _____Releases the valve on the manometer so that the gauge drops 10 mm Hg per heartbeat
    5. _____Inserts the earpieces of the stethoscope into the ears so that they tilt slightly backward

33. A nurse is caring for a patient who sustained trauma in an automobile collision. The nurse makes the following assessments: Does not open the eyes when asked a question but opens eyes and withdraws from painful stimulus when turned and positioned; makes sounds but does not speak words. The nurse uses the Glasgow Coma Scale (GCS) to rate the patient's level of consciousness. Which point total on the Glasgow Coma Scale should the nurse document in the patient's clinical record indicating the patient's level of consciousness?
    1. 4
    2. 6
    3. 8
    4. 10

GLASGOW COMA SCALE

Eye Opening Points
Eyes open spontaneously 4
Eyes open in response to voice 3
Eyes open in response to pain 2
No eye opening response 1
Best Verbal Response Points
Oriented (e.g., to person, place, time) 5
Confused, speaks but is disoriented 4
Inappropriate, but comprehensible words 3
Incomprehensible sounds, but no words are spoken 2
None 1
Best Motor Response Points
Obeys command to move 6
Localizes painful stimulus 5
Withdraws from painful stimulus 4
Flexion, abnormal decorticate posturing 3
Extension, abnormal decerebrate posturing 2
No movement or posturing 1

Total Points ?

34. A patient has a serious vitamin K deficiency. For which clinical manifestations should the nurse assess this patient? **Select all that apply.**
   1. _____Bone pain
   2. _____Skin lesions
   3. _____Bleeding gums
   4. _____Ecchymotic area
   5. _____Muscle weakness

35. A patient has lost approximately 2 units of blood during a vaginal delivery. For which responses to this blood loss should the nurse assess this patient? **Select all that apply.**
   1. _____Increased urinary output
   2. _____Rapid, shallow breathing
   3. _____Hypertension
   4. _____Tachycardia
   5. _____Bradypnea

36. A nurse identifies that a patient with a fever has cool skin. Which additional signs confirm the onset (cold or chill phase) of a fever? **Select all that apply.**
   1. _____Goose bumps on the skin
   2. _____Decreased shivering
   3. _____Cyanotic nail beds
   4. _____Flushed skin
   5. _____Sweating

37. A nurse is interviewing a newly admitted patient. Which words used by the patient describe data associated with the defervescence phase (fever abatement, flush phase) of a fever? **Select all that apply.**
   1. _____Cold
   2. _____Achy
   3. _____Warm
   4. _____Sweaty
   5. _____Thirsty

38. A nurse is caring for a patient who had surgery for a hysterectomy 2 days ago. After reviewing the patient's medical record, which piece of data should cause the nurse the most concern?

1. Respirations: 10 breaths per minute
2. Vomited after eating 6 ounces of soup
3. IV infiltration in left hand
4. Temperature: 99.4°F

PATIENT'S CLINICAL RECORD

Primary Health-Care Provider's Orders
Hydromorphone 6 mg PO every 4 hours for severe incisional pain
Acetaminophen 325 mg PO every 4 hours prn for mild incisional pain or 650 mg PO every 4 hours prn for moderate incisional pain
Diet: Clear liquids, progress to regular as tolerated
Activity: OOB 3 times a day, ambulate in hallway
Vital signs every 4 hours

Nurse's Progress Notes
Patient progressed to full liquids; full liquids not well tolerated, vomited after eating 6 ounces of soup; ambulated in hallway 30 feet, tolerated well without signs of activity intolerance. Administered hydromorphone 6 mg at 4 p.m. for incisional pain reported at level 7 out of 10. Abdominal dressing dry and intact. IV 0.9% sodium chloride at 100 mL per hour infiltration in left hand, discontinued and moved to right hand. Warm soak applied 20 minutes to left hand as per protocol.

Vital Signs Sheet 6 p.m.
Temperature: 99.4°F, orally
Pulse: 68 beats per minute, regular
Respirations: 10 breaths per minute
Blood pressure: 110/68 mm Hg

---

39. A nurse concludes that a patient has inadequate nutrition. Which patient adaptations support this conclusion? **Select all that apply.**

1. _____Presence of surface papillae on the tongue
2. _____Reddish-pink mucous membranes
3. _____Cachectic appearance
4. _____Spoon-shaped nails
5. _____Shiny eyes

40. A nurse is performing a physical assessment on a newly admitted patient. The photograph reflects the condition of the patient's tongue. Which nursing intervention should the nurse anticipate will address the origin of this patient's problem?

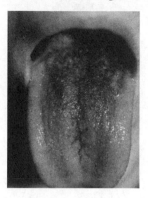

1. Administering prescribed B vitamins
2. Providing oral hygiene 4 times a day
3. Administering prescribed antifungal medication
4. Encouraging the intake of 3,000 mL of oral fluid daily

41. A patient has an elevated temperature and reports feeling cold. Which additional physical changes should the nurse expect during the onset phase (cold or chill phase) of a fever? **Select all that apply.**
1. _____Restlessness with confusion
2. _____Decreased respiratory rate
3. _____Profuse perspiration
4. _____Pale, cold skin
5. _____Shivering

42. At which day and time did the patient have a pulse rate of 75 beats per minute?

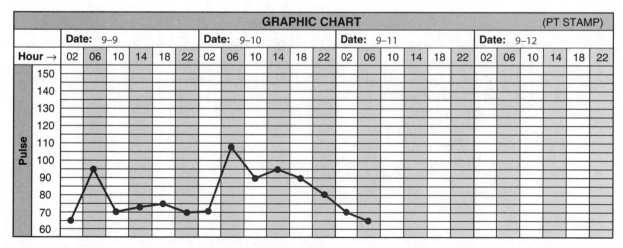

1. 9-9 at 0002
2. 9-9 at 1800
3. 9-11 at 0006
4. 9-10 at 1000

43. A nurse is assessing a postoperative patient for signs of hemorrhage. Which clinical manifestations are indicative of shock? **Select all that apply.**
1. _____Hyperemia
2. _____Hypotension
3. _____Irregular pulse
4. _____Fast respirations
5. _____Cold, clammy skin

44. Place an X over the site in the illustration that is used **most** often by nurses for assessing a patient's heart rate.

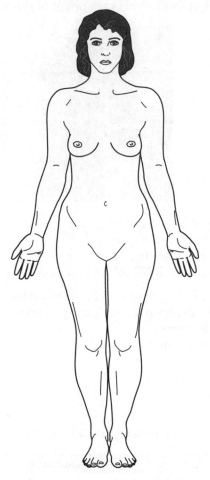

45. A nurse refers to the Glasgow Coma Scale when assessing a patient's level of consciousness. Place the following statements related to verbal response in the Glasgow Coma Scale in order from behaviors that support alertness to those that support unresponsiveness.
    1. No response
    2. Oriented, converses
    3. Disoriented, converses
    4. Uses inappropriate words
    5. Makes incomprehensible sounds
    Answer: _____

1. 1. There are no contraindications for palpating both radial arteries at the same time.
   2. **It is unsafe to palpate both carotid arteries at the same time. Slight compression of both carotid arteries can interfere with blood flow to the brain. In addition, excessive compression of the carotid arteries can stimulate the carotid sinuses, which causes a reflex drop in the heart rate.**
   3. There are no contraindications for palpating both femoral arteries at the same time.
   4. There are no contraindications for palpating both brachial arteries at the same time.

2. 1. The word "variance" is not a term that describes recurrence of signs and symptoms of a chronic illness. Variance occurs when there is a deviation from a critical pathway. This occurs when goals are not met or interventions are not performed according to the stipulated time period.
   2. The word "remission" is not a term that describes recurrence of signs and symptoms of a chronic illness. A remission is a period during a chronic illness of lessened severity or cessation of symptoms.
   3. The word "adaptation" is not a term that describes recurrence of signs and symptoms of a chronic illness. An adaptation is a physical or emotional response to an internal or external stimulus.
   4. **An exacerbation is the period during a chronic illness when signs and symptoms reappear after a remission or absence of symptoms.**

3. 1. Body temperature is rising between 4 p.m. and 6 p.m.
   2. **Diurnal variations (circadian rhythms) vary throughout the day with the lowest body temperature usually occurring between 4 a.m. and 6 a.m. The metabolic rate is at its lowest while the person is sleeping.**
   3. Body temperature is at its highest between 8 p.m. and 10 p.m.
   4. Body temperature is rising between 8 a.m. and 10 a.m.

4. 1. **Gross temperature assessments (e.g., cold, cool, warm, hot) can be obtained by palpation. Palpation is the examination of the body using the sense of touch. Sensory nerves in the fingers transmit messages through the spinal cord to the cerebral cortex, where they are interpreted by the nurse.**
   2. Inspection cannot assess skin temperature. Inspection uses the naked eye to perform a visual assessment of the body.
   3. Percussion cannot assess skin temperature. Percussion is the act of striking the body's surface to elicit sounds that provide information about the size and shape of internal organs or whether tissue is air filled, fluid filled, or solid.
   4. Observation cannot assess skin temperature. Observation uses the naked eye to perform a visual assessment of the body.

5. 1. This is unnecessary. Bowel sounds may be hyperactive (1 every 3 seconds) or hypoactive (1 every minute). After a sound is heard, the stethoscope is moved to the next site. For sounds to be considered absent there must be no sounds for 3 to 5 minutes.
   2. This is done for patient comfort, not to influence the accuracy of the assessment.
   3. **Bowel sounds are auscultated before palpation and percussion because these techniques stimulate the intestines and thus cause an increase in peristalsis and a false increase in bowel sounds.**
   4. This is not necessary. However, many people do begin the systematic four-quadrant assessment in the lower right quadrant over the ileocecal valve, where the digestive contents from the small intestine empty through a valve into the large intestine.

6. 1. This is an acceptable increase in heart rate with strenuous aerobic exercise.
   2. This is an acceptable blood pressure with the body at rest. The expected blood pressure in an adult is a systolic value of 90 to 119 mm Hg and a diastolic value of 60 to 79 mm Hg.
   3. **A respiratory rate of 10 is below the expected respiratory rate for an adult and should be assessed further. The**

expected respiratory rate for an adult is 12 to 20 breaths per minute.

4. This is within the expected range of 60 to 100 beats per minute.

7. 1. Although the body temperature decreases as shock progresses because of a decreased metabolic rate, it is not one of the first signs of shock.

2. Two other vital signs will alter before blood pressure as the heart attempts to compensate for decreased circulating blood volume.

3. Although during shock the pulse pressure will narrow, other vital signs will change first. Pulse pressure is the difference between the systolic and diastolic pressures.

4. **The initial stage of shock begins when baroreceptors in the aortic arch and the carotid sinuses detect a drop in the mean arterial pressure. The sympathetic nervous system responds by constricting peripheral vessels and increasing the heart and respiratory rates. During the compensatory stage of shock, the effects of epinephrine and norepinephrine continue with stimulation of alpha-adrenergic fibers causing vasoconstriction of vessels supplying the skin and abdominal viscera and beta-adrenergic fibers causing vasodilation of vessels supplying the heart, skeletal muscles, and respiratory system.**

8. 1. This is too frequent for routine monitoring of body temperature. Although the set point for body temperature changes rapidly, it takes several hours for the core body temperature to change.

2. **This is an appropriate interval of time for routine monitoring of body temperature. It is frequent enough to identify trends in changes in body temperature while limiting unnecessary assessments.**

3. Every 6 hours is too long an interval for monitoring a patient with a fever and is unsafe.

4. Every 8 hours is too long an interval for monitoring a patient with a fever and is unsafe.

9. 1. **The brachial artery splits (bifurcates) into the radial and ulnar arteries. When there is an adequate radial pulse, the brachial artery must be patent.**

2. This information will not provide information about brachial artery blood flow. The carotid arteries are in the neck, whereas the brachial arteries are in the arms. A carotid pulse site is located on the neck at the side of the larynx, between the trachea and the sternomastoid muscle.

3. This information will not provide information about brachial artery blood flow. The femoral arteries are in the legs, whereas the brachial arteries are in the arms. A femoral pulse site is in the groin in the femoral triangle. It is in the anterior, medial aspect of the thigh, just below the inguinal ligament, halfway between the anterior superior iliac spine and the symphysis pubis.

4. This information will not provide information about brachial artery blood flow. The popliteal arteries are in the legs, whereas the brachial arteries are in the arms. A popliteal pulse site is in the lateral aspect of the hollow area at the back of the knee (popliteal fossa).

10. 1. **Betacyanin, a pigment that gives beets their purplish red color, is excreted in the urine and feces of some people when it is nonmetabolized (a genetically determined trait). This bright red pigment turns the urine and feces red for several days after eating beets.**

2. Strawberries will not turn the urine red. However, they can cause an allergic reaction (reason is unknown), producing the cellular release of histamine and hives.

3. Red food dye does not turn the urine red. Red dye No. 3, found in foods such as maraschino cherries, is a suspected carcinogen.

4. Red food dye does not turn the urine red. However, red dye No. 3, found in foods such as gelatine desserts and maraschino cherries, is a suspected carcinogen.

11. 1. This is unnecessarily long, and even slight compression can interfere with blood flow to the brain.

2. This is not the site to access the carotid artery. A carotid pulse site is located on the neck at the side of the larynx, between the trachea and the sternomastoid muscle.

3. **The carotid artery should be palpated with a light touch to prevent interference to blood flow to the brain and stimulation of the carotid sinus**

that can cause a reflex drop in the heart rate.

4. This is contraindicated. Massage can stimulate the carotid sinus located at the level of the bifurcation of the carotid artery, and this results in a reflex drop in the heart rate.

12. 1. This blood pressure reading is within the acceptable ranges for an adult, which are a systolic value of 90 to 119 mm Hg and a diastolic value of 60 to 79 mm Hg.
2. **This blood pressure is within the parameters of stage I hypertension and is the blood pressure that should cause the most concern. A systolic reading of 140 to 159 mm Hg or a diastolic reading of 90 to 99 mm Hg indicates stage I hypertension.**
3. Although this blood pressure is within the parameters of pre-hypertension and should cause concern, it is not the highest blood pressure of the options offered. Pre-hypertension is indicated by a systolic reading in the range of 120 to 139 mm Hg or a diastolic reading in the range of 80 to 89 mm Hg.
4. This blood pressure reading is within the expected range for an adult, which is a systolic value of 90 to 119 mm Hg and a diastolic value of 60 to 79 mm Hg.

13. 1. Activity intolerance is related to the cardiovascular and respiratory systems, not the nervous and musculoskeletal systems.
2. **Activity intolerance is related to the inability to maintain adequate oxygenation to body cells, which is associated with respiratory and cardiovascular problems. Obtaining the vital signs (e.g., pulse, respirations, and blood pressure) will provide valuable information about these systems.**
3. Although the impact on functional health patterns might eventually be assessed, it is not the priority.
4. Although the influence on the other family members might eventually be assessed, it is not the priority.

14. 1. A plastic rectal thermometer must remain in place 2 to 4, not 5, minutes to obtain an accurate reading. An electronic thermometer usually will obtain a reading within several seconds.
2. **Gloves, personal protective pieces of equipment, are the best way the nurse**

is protected from contracting or transmitting a pathogen.

3. The left, not right, lateral position is the best position to place a patient when obtaining a rectal temperature because it utilizes the anatomical position of the anus and rectum for safe, easy insertion of the thermometer.
4. Inserting the thermometer 2 inches into the anus can cause damage to the mucous membranes. A lubricated thermometer should be inserted 1.5 inches into the anus to ensure a safe, accurate reading.

15. 1. Assessing posture and gait is within the scope of nursing practice because posture and gait reflect human responses.
2. Assessing balance and strength is within the scope of nursing practice because balance and strength reflect human responses.
3. Assessing hygiene and grooming is within the scope of nursing practice because hygiene and good grooming reflect human responses.
4. **Ordering and assessing urine and blood values are not in the independent practice of nursing. These assessments are dependent or interdependent functions of the nurse and are covered by specific orders or standing orders, respectively.**

16. 1. **When people are depressed they frequently do not have the physical or psychic energy to perform the activities of daily living and often exhibit an unkempt appearance. A dishevelled, untidy appearance is a covert, subtle indication of depression.**
2. Anxious behavior is overt, not covert and subtle.
3. Tense posture is overt, not covert and subtle.
4. Crying is overt, not covert and subtle.

17. 1. Hyperthermia, not hypothermia, is associated with this condition. Heat stroke (heat hyperpyrexia) is failure of the heat-regulating capacity of the body that results in extremely high body temperatures (105°F).
2. Hyperthermia, not hypothermia, can result from the lack of sweat. The inability to perspire does not allow the body to cool by the evaporation of sweat (vaporization).
3. Hyperthermia, not hypothermia, can result from excessive exercise. Exercise increases

heat production as carbohydrates and fats break down to provide energy. Body temperature temporarily can increase as high as 104°F.

4. **Excessive alcohol intake interferes with thermoregulation by providing a false sense of warmth, inhibiting shivering and causing vasodilation, which promotes heat loss. In addition, it impairs judgment, which increases the risk of making inappropriate self-care decisions.**

18. 1. This is not necessary for all specimens.
    2. Generally, if a specimen is collected using proper technique, one specimen is sufficient for testing for culture and sensitivity.
    3. **The results of culture and sensitivity tests are faulty and erroneous if the collection container or inappropriate collection technique introduces extraneous microorganisms that falsify and misrepresent results. Surgical asepsis (sterile technique) must be maintained.**
    4. This is not necessary for any culture and sensitivity specimen.

19. 1. This is within the expected adult pulse range of 60 to 100 beats per minute and the rhythm is regular; the patient should be assessed further and the information compared with the patient's baseline data.
    2. This is within the expected adult respiratory range of 14 to 20 breaths per minute.
    3. This is within the expected adult temperature range of 97.6°F to 99.6°F for an oral temperature.
    4. **The blood pressure is more than the expected systolic value of less than 120 mm Hg and a diastolic value less than 80 mm Hg and, of the options presented, should cause the most concern. A blood pressure with a systolic reading more than 160 or a diastolic reading more than 100 indicates stage II hypertension.**

20. 1. **Pulse oximetry is a noninvasive procedure to measure the oxygen saturation of the blood. The expected value is 95% or more. If a patient's pulse oximetry result is low, the patient is hypoxic and needs medical intervention.**

2. Although wheezing on expiration, which is associated with bronchial constriction, requires continuous monitoring, it is not as critical an assessment as a low pulse oximetry. Wheezing on exhalation that increases in severity or wheezing on both inhalation and exhalation becomes a priority in relation to the situation presented.
3. Shortness of breath is an expected response to exertion and is not a cause for concern.
4. Although using accessory muscles of respiration requires monitoring, it is not as critical an assessment as low pulse oximetry. Some people with chronic respiratory problems always use accessory muscles of respiration when breathing.

21. 1. The body temperature is on the decline during this time.
    2. The body temperature is just beginning to rise from its lowest level, which occurs between 4 a.m. and 6 a.m.
    3. Although the body temperature is rising, it has not reached its peak at this time.
    4. **Diurnal variations (circadian rhythms) vary throughout the day, with the highest body temperature usually occurring between 8 p.m. and midnight.**

22. 1. Palpation may stimulate intestinal motility, which increases bowel sounds, but it is not the assessment method used to hear bowel sounds. Palpation is the examination of the body using the sense of touch.
    2. Inspection cannot assess bowel sounds. Inspection uses the naked eye to perform a visual assessment of the body.
    3. Percussion may stimulate intestinal motility, which increases bowel sounds, but it is not the assessment method used to hear bowel sounds. Percussion is the act of striking the body's surface to elicit sounds that provide information about the size and shape of internal organs or whether tissue is air filled, fluid filled, or solid.
    4. **Auscultation is the process of listening to sounds produced in the body. It is performed directly by just listening with the ears or indirectly by using a stethoscope that amplifies the sounds and conveys them to the nurse's ears. Active intestinal peristalsis causes rumbling, gurgling, and tinkling abdominal sounds known as bowel sounds (borborygmi).**

23. 1. **This is an acceptable medical asepsis practice. All instruments, regardless of their type, must be clean before and after use.**
2. This is true only for electronic thermometers and sometimes used for plastic thermometers.
3. This is true only for plastic thermometers.
4. This is not true for all thermometers, such as chemical disposable thermometers, temperature-sensitive tape, and electronic thermometers. This is true for plastic thermometers.

24. 1. Mental confusion is a not a common human response to pyrexia.
2. Loss of appetite (anorexia), not an increased appetite, is a common human response to pyrexia.
3. **A rectal temperature of 101°F (38.3°C) or oral temperature of 100°F (37.8°C) is a common human response that indicates pyrexia (fever).**
4. An increased heart rate (tachycardia), not a decreased heart rate (bradycardia), is a common human response to pyrexia.

25. 1. Although important, blood pressure is related to circulation which is not the priority.
2. **Patient assessment must always be conducted in order of priority of needs. In an emergency, the ABCs of assessment are airway, breathing, and circulation. A clear airway is essential for life and therefore has priority.**
3. Although important, assessment of a breathing pattern is not the priority.
4. Although important, circulation is not the priority.

26. 1. **Palpation, the examination of the body using the sense of touch, is used to obtain the heart rate at a pulse site. When measuring a pulse, an artery is compressed slightly by the fingers so that the pulsating artery is held between the fingers and a bone or firm structure.**
2. A pulse is not measured by using the sense of sight. Inspection uses the naked eye to perform a visual assessment of the body.
3. Percussion cannot measure a pulse. Percussion is the act of striking the body's surface to elicit sounds that provide information about the size and shape of internal organs or whether tissue is air filled, fluid filled, or solid.

4. Auscultation is used to obtain an apical, not radial, pulse. Auscultation is the process of listening to sounds produced in the body. It is performed directly by just listening with the ears or indirectly by using a stethoscope that amplifies the sounds and conveys them to the nurse's ears.

27. 1. Although this should be done, it is not the most important information that should be documented.
2. This is necessary only if the patient did not tolerate the procedure.
3. **The patient's position when the blood pressure is measured may influence results. Generally, systolic and diastolic readings are lower in the horizontal than in the sitting position. There is a lower reading in the uppermost arm when a person is in a lateral recumbent position. A change from the horizontal to an upright position may result in a temporary decrease (5 to 10 mm Hg) in blood pressure; when this decrease exceeds 25 mm Hg systolic or 10 mm Hg diastolic, it is called orthostatic hypotension.**
4. This is unnecessary because they are approximately the same.

28. 1. The American Cancer Society recommends that women should not have a Pap test before age 21.
2. The American Cancer Society recommends that women receive yearly mammograms at 40 years of age.
3. **A colonoscopy should be performed at age 50 and every 10 years thereafter. This is the age when the risk for colon cancer increases.**
4. The American Cancer Society recommends that screening for cancer of the prostate be conducted on an individual basis. Individuals who are African American or have a family member with the disease before the age of 65 should discuss the need for screening with a primary health-care provider starting at age 45.

29. 1. Vasodilation brings warm blood to the peripheral circulation where it is lost through the skin via radiation; this produces heat loss.
2. Evaporation (vaporization) is the conversion of a liquid into a vapor. When perspiration on the skin evaporates, it promotes heat loss.

3. Shivering generates heat by causing muscle contraction, which increases the metabolic rate by 100% to 200%.

4. Radiation is the transfer of heat from the surface of one object to the surface of another without direct contact; this produces heat loss.

30. Answer: 2 mL. Solve the question by using ratio and proportion.

$$\frac{\text{Desired}}{\text{Have}} \quad \frac{1\,\text{mg}}{0.5\,\text{mg}} = \frac{x\,\text{mL}}{1\,\text{mL}}$$

$0.5x = 1\,\text{mL}$
$x = 1 \div 0.5$
$x = 2\,\text{mL}$

31. 1. Mouth breathing allows environmental air to enter the mouth, which may result in an inaccurately low reading. To take an oral temperature the instrument must remain under the tongue of a closed mouth until the reading is obtained. This can take as little as several seconds (electronic thermometers) or as long as 3 to 4 minutes (plastic thermometers).

2. A history of vomiting does not negate the use of an oral thermometer. If the patient should begin to vomit, the nurse can remove the thermometer.

3. Taking an oral temperature when a patient is confused is unsafe. A patient who is confused may bite down on an oral thermometer and cause injury to the mouth.

4. An oral thermometer can be used with a patient maintained in any position.

5. A 7-year-old child understands cause and effect and can follow directions regarding the use of an oral thermometer.

32. 1. A blood pressure should be taken with the arm supported at the level of the heart. If the arm is above the level of the heart, the blood pressure reading will be inaccurately decreased, and if the arm is below the level of the heart or not supported, the blood pressure reading will be inaccurately increased.

2. This is a correct action when obtaining a blood pressure reading. The brachial artery is close to the skin's surface, and the diaphragm of the stethoscope is used for low-pitched sounds of a blood pressure reading.

3. This ensures an accurate reading because it provides uniform and complete compression of the brachial artery.

4. This may result in an inaccurate reading. The valve on the manometer should be opened to allow the gauge to drop 2 to 3 mm Hg per heartbeat.

5. The earpieces of the stethoscope should be placed into the ears so that they tilt slightly forward, not backward. This ensures that the openings in the earpieces of the stethoscope are facing toward the ear canal for uninterrupted transmission of sounds.

33. 1. The number 4 does not reflect the patient's total points on the Glasgow Coma Scale.

2. The number 6 does not reflect the patient's total points on the Glasgow Coma Scale.

3. The number 8 reflects the patient's total points on the Glasgow Coma Scale as demonstrated in the scale below.

4. The number 10 does not reflect the patient's total points on the Glasgow Coma Scale.

GLASGOW COMA SCALE

Eye Opening Points
Eyes open spontaneously 4
Eyes open in response to voice 3
Eyes open in response to pain 2
No eye opening response 1
Best Verbal Response Points
Oriented (e.g., to person, place, time) 5
Confused, speaks but is disoriented 4
Inappropriate, but comprehensible words 3
Incomprehensible sounds but no words are spoken 2
None 1
Best Motor Response Points
Obeys command to move 6
Localizes painful stimulus 5
Withdraws from painful stimulus 4
Flexion, abnormal decorticate posturing 3
Extension, abnormal decerebrate posturing 2
No movement or posturing 1

Total Points 8
Major Head Injury ≤8
Moderate Head Injury 9–12
Minor Head Injury 13–15

34. 1. A deficiency in vitamin D, not vitamin K, causes bone pain associated with osteoporosis.
   2. Vitamin K deficiency is not associated with skin lesions. Ascorbic acid (vitamin C) deficiency causes small skin hemorrhages and delays wound healing. Riboflavin (vitamin B$_2$) deficiency causes lip lesions, seborrheic dermatitis, and scrotal and vulval skin changes.
   3. **A disruption in the clotting mechanism of the body can result in bleeding. Vitamin K plays an essential role in the production of the clotting factors II (prothrombin), VII, IX, and X.**
   4. **An ecchymotic area is caused by extravasation of blood into skin or mucous membranes. In this patient's situation, it is caused by a disruption in the clotting mechanism of the body as a result of a vitamin K deficiency.**
   5. A deficiency in thiamine (vitamin B$_1$), not vitamin K, causes muscle weakness.

35. 1. With a reduction in blood volume there will be less blood circulating through the kidneys, resulting in a decreased, not increased, urinary output.
   2. **With a decrease in circulating red blood cells, the respiratory rate will increase to meet oxygen needs.**
   3. With a reduction in blood volume, the blood pressure will be decreased, not increased.
   4. **Tachycardia occurs with hemorrhage as the body attempts to bring more oxygen to cells via the circulation.**
   5. **Rapid breathing, not bradypnea, occurs with hemorrhage as the respiratory rate increases to meet oxygen needs.**

36. 1. **Contraction of the *arrector pili* muscles (goose bumps), an attempt by the body to trap air around body hairs, is associated with the onset phase (cold or chill phase) of a fever. During this phase, the body responds to pyrogens by conserving heat to raise the body's temperature and reset the body's thermostat.**
   2. Decreased shivering is a response associated with the defervescence phase (fever abatement, flush phase) of a fever. During this stage the hypothalamus attempts to lower the body's temperature and heat loss responses occur. Shivering, which increases the body's temperature, occurs during the onset phase (cold or chill phase) of a fever.
   3. **Cyanosis of the nail beds occurs during the onset phase (cold or chill phase) of a fever. Vasoconstriction and shivering are the body's attempt to conserve heat.**
   4. Flushed skin occurs during the defervescence phase (fever abatement, flush phase) of a fever as the hypothalamus attempts to lower the body's temperature. Quick vasodilation occurs, which helps to cool the body.
   5. Profuse diaphoresis (sweating) occurs during the defervescence phase (fever abatement, flush phase) of a fever as the hypothalamus attempts to lower the body's temperature. During this phase, the fever abates and the body's temperature returns to the expected range.

37. 1. Feeling cold occurs during the onset phase (cold or chill phase) of a fever because of vasoconstriction, cool skin, and shivering.
   2. Feeling achy occurs during the course phase (plateau phase) of a fever. Generally this is the result of extra energy being exerted by the body fighting the infection, as well as a response to activation of the immune system.
   3. Feeling warm is associated with the defervescence phase (fever abatement, flush phase) of a fever because of sudden vasodilation.
   4. Feeling sweaty occurs during the defervescence phase (fever abatement, flush phase) of a fever because of the body's heat loss response.
   5. Feeling thirsty is associated with the course phase (plateau phase) of a fever because of mild to severe dehydration.

38. 1. **A respiratory rate of 10 or below is a concern. The patient is receiving hydromorphone, an opioid, which depresses the central nervous system. A respiratory rate is depressed when an opioid medication is excessive. The dose of hydromorphone may need to be reduced.**
   2. Although vomiting is a concern, it is not as important as data presented in another option. The patient is receiving 100 mL of fluid hourly; therefore, the patient is most likely well hydrated.
   3. Although an IV infiltration is a concern, it is not as important as data presented in

another option. The IV was discontinued and replaced in the other hand and a warm soak was applied.

4. Although an increase in temperature after surgery is a concern, an oral temperature of 99.4°F is within the normal range of 97.6°F to 99.6°F.

39. 1. The tongue usually is pink, moist, and smooth, with papillae and fissures present. A beefy red or magenta color, smooth appearance, and increase or decrease in size indicates nutritional problems.
2. This is the usual color of mucous membranes because of their rich vascular supply. Pale mucous membranes or the presence of lesions indicates nutritional problems.
3. **Cachexia is general ill health and malnutrition marked by weakness and excessive leanness (emaciation).**
4. **Fingernails that curve inward like spoons can be caused by iron deficiency, vitamin B$_{12}$ deficiency, or anemia.**
5. The eyes are always moist and shiny because lacrimal fluid continually washes the eyes. Pale or red conjunctivae, dryness, and soft or dull corneas are signs of nutritional problems.

40. 1. The patient is not exhibiting the signs of a vitamin B deficiency. B vitamins treat fissures and cracking at the corners of the mouth (cheilosis) caused by a deficiency of B vitamins.
2. Providing oral hygiene 4 times a day will not address the origin of this patient's problem.
3. **The photograph demonstrates a human response to a fungal infection in the oral cavity. When documenting this assessment the nurse should describe this patient's tongue as a "black, hairy**

tongue," which is characteristic of an oral fungal infection.
4. Encouraging an increase in the intake of oral fluids does not address the origin of this patient's problem.

41. 1. Restlessness with confusion may indicate the beginning of delirium associated with high fevers that alter cerebral functioning. Delirium is associated with the course phase (plateau phase) of a fever.
2. During the course phase (plateau phase) of a fever, the pulse and respiratory rates will increase because of an increase in the basal metabolic rate, in an attempt to pump oxygenated blood to the tissues.
3. Profuse diaphoresis (sweating) occurs during the defervescence phase (fever abatement, flush phase) of a fever.
4. **Pale, cold skin occurs during the onset phase (cold or chill phase) of a fever because of vasoconstriction, which is an attempt to conserve body heat.**
5. **Shivering occurs during the onset phase (cold or chill phase) of a fever. Fever is caused by the release of inflammatory mediators (pyrogens) that cause the hypothalamus to reset the set point of temperature. When this happens the body feels cold and shivering occurs. Shivering involves muscle contraction that produces heat, which increases the temperature to the new hypothalamic set point.**

42. 1. On 9-9 at 0002 the patient's pulse rate was 65 beats per minute.
2. **On 9-9 at 1800 the patient's pulse rate was 75 beats per minute.**
3. On 9-11 at 0006 the patient's pulse rate was 65 beats per minute.
4. On 9-10 at 1000 the patient's pulse rate was 90 beats per minute.

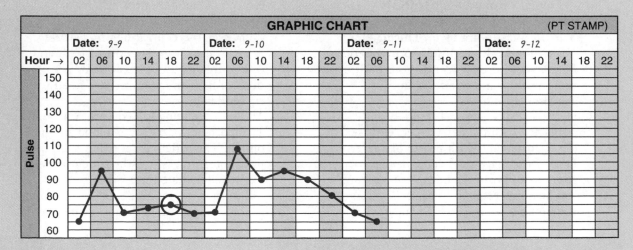

43. 1. During the compensatory stage of shock, blood is shunted away from, not toward, the periphery. Hyperemia is an increase in blood flow to an area where the overlying skin becomes reddened and warm.

2. The circulating blood volume is reduced by 25% to 35% during the compensatory stage of shock and by 35% to 50% during the progressive stage of shock as the peripheral vessels constrict to increase blood flow to vital organs. This shunting of blood causes hypotension.

3. With shock the heart rate increases (tachycardia); it is not irregular. The heart rate increases during the compensatory stage of shock to maintain adequate blood flow to body tissues.

4. During the compensatory stage of shock, the respiratory rate increases, not decreases, to maintain adequate oxygenation of body cells.

5. With hemorrhage there is a decrease in blood pressure as a result of hypovolemia, which in turn stimulates the sympathetic nervous system. The sympathetic nervous system stimulates vasoconstriction, which moves blood from the periphery of the body to vital organs. The decrease in circulation to the skin causes it to become cold and clammy.

44. The radial pulse is the most easily found and accessible site for routine monitoring of the pulse, and it provides accurate information when the heart rate is regular. The radial pulse site is where the radial artery runs along the radial bone, on the thumb side of the inner aspect of the wrist.

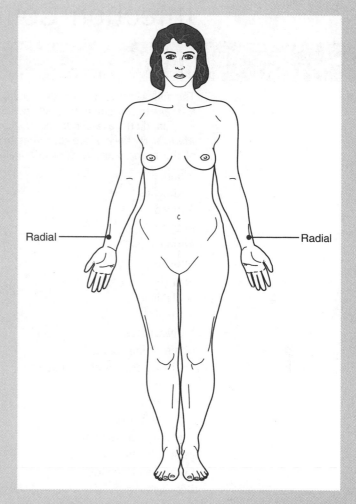

Radial ———   ——— Radial

45. 2. *Oriented and converses* is rated 5, the highest level of functioning of the 5 levels in the Verbal Response category of the Glasgow Coma Scale.

3. *Disoriented and converses* is rated 4 out of 5 levels of functioning and is after *oriented and converses* level 5 in the Verbal Response category of the Glasgow Coma Scale.

4. *Uses inappropriate words* is rated 3 out of 5 levels of functioning and is after *disoriented and converses* level 4 in the Verbal Response category of the Glasgow Coma Scale.

5. *Makes incomprehensible sounds* is rated 2 out of 5 levels of functioning and is after *uses inappropriate words* level 3 in the Verbal Response category of the Glasgow Coma Scale.

1. *No response* is rated 1, the lowest level of the 5 levels of functioning and is after *makes incomprehensible sounds* level 2 in the Verbal Response category of the Glasgow Coma Scale.

Infection Control

The following words include nursing/medical terminology, concepts, principles, and information relevant to content specifically addressed in the chapter or associated with topics presented in it. English dictionaries, nursing textbooks, and medical dictionaries, such as *Taber's Cyclopedic Medical Dictionary,* are resources that can be used to expand your knowledge and understanding of these words and related information.

Afebrile
Antibiotics
Antibody
Antigen
Antimicrobial
Antipyretic
Asepsis:
  Medical
  Surgical
Biohazardous
Chain of infection:
  Characteristics of the pathogen
  Portal of entry
  Reservoir
  Portal of exit
  Mode of transmission
Characteristics of the host
Culture and sensitivity
Débridement
Drainage, exudate:
  Purulent, pus
  Sanguineous
  Serosanguineous
  Serous
Erythema
Fever (febrile, pyrexia)
General adaptation syndrome (GAS)
Healing:
  Primary intention
  Secondary intention
Hyperthermia

Immune response
Immune system
Immunity
Immunization
Immunocompromised
Immunosuppression
Inflammatory response
Infection, types:
  Iatrogenic
  Health-care–associated infection (HAI)
    (formerly called nosocomial infection)
  Local
  Opportunistic
  Systemic
Leukocytosis
Local adaptation syndrome (LAS)
Microorganisms:
  Bacteria
  Fungi
  Viruses
Neutropenia
Ova and parasites
Pediculosis
Phagocytosis
Pyrogens
Standard precautions
Transmission-based precautions:
  Airborne precautions
  Contact precautions
  Droplet precautions
White blood cell count

INFECTION CONTROL: QUESTIONS

1. Which is the **primary** reason why the nurse should avoid glued-on artificial nails?
   1. They interfere with dexterity of the fingers.
   2. They could fall off in a patient's bed.
   3. They harbor microorganisms.
   4. They can scratch a patient.

2. A nurse working in a clinic is assessing patients of a variety of ages. People within which age group should the nurse particularly assess for subtle signs and symptoms of subclinical infections?
   1. Children of school age
   2. Older adults
   3. Adolescents
   4. Infants

3. Which condition places a patient at the **greatest** risk for developing an infection?
   1. Implantation of a prosthetic device
   2. Burns over more than 20% of the body
   3. Presence of an indwelling urinary catheter
   4. More than 2 puncture sites from laparoscopic surgery

4. Which does the nurse determine is a secondary line of defense against infection?
   1. Mucous membrane of the respiratory tract
   2. Urinary tract environment
   3. Integumentary system
   4. Immune response

5. A nurse is concerned about a patient's ability to withstand exposure to pathogens. Which blood component should the nurse monitor?
   1. Platelets
   2. Hemoglobin
   3. Neutrophils
   4. Erythrocytes

6. When brushing a patient's hair, the nurse identifies white oval particles attached to the hair behind the ears. For which should the nurse assess the patient?
   1. Pediculosis
   2. Hirsutism
   3. Dandruff
   4. Scabies

7. A nurse educator is evaluating whether a new staff nurse understands the relationship between a fever and an infection. Which statement by the new staff nurse indicates an understanding of this relationship?
   1. "Phagocytic cells release pyrogens that stimulate the hypothalamus."
   2. "Leukocyte migration precipitates the inflammatory response."
   3. "Erythema increases the flow of blood throughout the body."
   4. "Pain activates the sympathetic nervous system."

8. A nurse is caring for the following group of patients with infections. Which infection is classified as a hospital-acquired infection?
   1. Respiratory infection contracted from a visitor
   2. Vaginal canal infection in a postmenopausal woman
   3. Urinary tract infection in a patient who is sedentary
   4. Wound infection caused by unwashed hands of a caregiver

9. A nurse is caring for a patient with a high fever secondary to septicemia. The primary health-care provider orders a cooling blanket (hypothermia blanket). Through which mechanism does the hypothermia blanket achieve heat loss?
   1. Radiation
   2. Convection
   3. Conduction
   4. Evaporation

10. Which patient condition identified by a nurse is unrelated to infection?
    1. Catabolism
    2. Hyperglycemia
    3. Ketones in the urine
    4. Decreased metabolic activity

11. A nurse is caring for a group of hospitalized patients. Which should the nurse do **first** to prevent patient infections?
   1. Provide small bedside bags to dispose of used tissues.
   2. Encourage staff to avoid coughing near patients.
   3. Administer antibiotics as prescribed.
   4. Identify patients at risk.

12. A patient has a wound that is healing by secondary intention. Which solution to cleanse the wound and dressing should the nurse expect will be ordered to support wound healing?
   1. Normal saline and a gauze dressing.
   2. Normal saline and a wet-to-damp dressing.
   3. Povidone-iodine and a dry sterile dressing.
   4. Half peroxide and half normal saline and a wet-to-dry dressing.

13. A nurse is caring for a group of patients experiencing various medical conditions. The patient with which condition is at the **greatest** risk for a wound infection?
   1. Surgical creation of a colostomy
   2. First-degree burn on the back
   3. Puncture of the foot by a nail
   4. Paper cut on the finger

14. A school nurse is teaching a class of adolescents about the function of the integumentary system. Which fact about how the skin protects the body against infection is important to include in this discussion?
   1. Cells of the skin are constantly being replaced, thereby eliminating external pathogens.
   2. Epithelial cells are loosely compacted on skin, providing a barrier against pathogens.
   3. Moisture on the skin surface prevents colonization of pathogens.
   4. Alkalinity of the skin limits the growth of pathogens.

15. A patient's stool specimen is positive for *Clostridium difficile*. Which isolation precautions should the nurse institute for this patient?
   1. Droplet
   2. Contact
   3. Reverse
   4. Airborne

16. Which should the nurse do to interrupt the transmission link in the chain of infection?
   1. Wash the hands before providing care to a patient.
   2. Position a commode next to a patient's bed.
   3. Provide education about a balanced diet.
   4. Change a dressing when it is soiled.

17. Which patient statements indicate that further teaching by the nurse is necessary regarding how to ensure protection from food contamination? **Select all that apply.**
   1. _____"I should stuff a turkey an hour before putting it in the oven."
   2. _____"I love juicy rare hamburgers with onion and tomato."
   3. _____"I prefer chicken salad sandwiches with mayonnaise."
   4. _____"I know to spit out food that does not taste good."
   5. _____"I should defrost frozen food in the refrigerator."

18. A patient is admitted to the ambulatory surgery unit for an elective procedure. When performing a physical assessment the nurse identifies that the patient has *Pediculus capitis* (head lice). Place the nurse's interventions in the order in which they should be implemented.
1. Establish contact isolation.
2. Comb the hair with a fine-toothed comb.
3. Notify the provider of the patient's condition.
4. Obtain a prescription for a pediculicidal shampoo.
5. Wash the patient's hair with a pediculicidal shampoo.
Answer: _____

19. Which primary defenses protect the body from infection? **Select all that apply.**
1. _____Tears in the eyes
2. _____Healthy intact skin
3. _____Cilia of respiratory passages
4. _____Alkalinity of gastric secretions
5. _____Bile in the gastrointestinal system
6. _____Moist environment of the epidermis

20. A nurse is caring for patients with a variety of wounds. Which wounds will likely heal by primary intention? **Select all that apply.**
1. _____Cut in the skin from a kitchen knife
2. _____Excoriated perianal area
3. _____Abrasion of the skin
4. _____Surgical incision
5. _____Pressure ulcer

21. A nurse changes a patient's dressing when it is soiled. Place an X in the center of the step where this nursing action breaks the chain of infection.

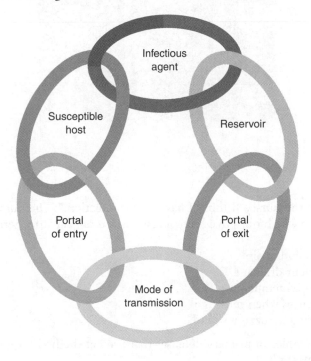

22. A patient has a wound infection. Which local human responses should the nurse expect to identify? **Select all that apply.**
    1. _____Neutropenia
    2. _____Malaise
    3. _____Edema
    4. _____Fever
    5. _____Pain

23. Which nursing actions protect patients as susceptible hosts in the chain of infection? **Select all that apply.**
    1. _____Wearing personal protective equipment
    2. _____Administering childhood immunizations
    3. _____Recapping a used needle before discarding
    4. _____Instituting prescribed immunoglobulin therapy
    5. _____Disposing of soiled gloves in a waste container

24. From which type of isolation precaution is this mask designed to protect the nurse?

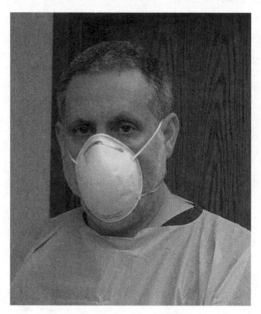

    1. Contact
    2. Airborne
    3. Standard
    4. Protective

25. A patient tells the nurse, "I think I have an ear infection." The nurse should assess this patient for which objective human responses to an ear infection? **Select all that apply.**
    1. _____Throbbing pain
    2. _____Purulent drainage
    3. _____Elevated temperature
    4. _____Dizziness when moving
    5. _____Hearing a buzzing sound

26. Which are examples of primary defenses that protect the body from infection? **Select all that apply.**
    1. _____Antibiotic therapy
    2. _____Lysozymes in saliva
    3. _____The low pH of the skin
    4. _____The alkaline environment of the vagina
    5. _____Production of mucus by cells in the genitourinary tract

27. A nurse is caring for a patient who has an order for shortening a Penrose drain 1 inch daily. The nurse washes the hands, removes the soiled dressing, sets a sterile field, dons sterile gloves, and cleans around the drain with sterile saline solution as ordered. Place the following steps in the order in which they should be implemented by the nurse.
    1. Complete dressing the wound.
    2. Pull the drain out 1 inch gently and steadily.
    3. Grip the Penrose drain with a pair of sterile forceps.
    4. Remove the pin and replace it at the surface of the wound.
    5. Cut off the excess drain using sterile scissors, ensuring that 2 inches remain outside the wound.

    Answer: _____

28. Which nursing actions protect patients from infection at the portal of entry portion of the chain of infection? **Select all that apply.**
    1. _____ Positioning an indwelling urine collection bag below the level of the patient's pelvis
    2. _____ Using sterile technique when administering an intramuscular injection
    3. _____ Enclosing a urine specimen in a biohazardous transport bag
    4. _____ Wearing clean gloves when handling a patient's excretions
    5. _____ Washing the hands after removal of soiled gloves
    6. _____ Maintaining a dressing over a surgical incision

29. The nurse is reviewing the clinical record of a newly admitted older adult male patient. Which piece of data should cause the **most** concern?
    1. WBC 30,000 mm^3
    2. Temperature 103°F
    3. Abdominal cramping
    4. Blood pressure 110/86 mm Hg

PATIENT'S CLINICAL RECORD

Laboratory Results
WBC: 30,000 mm^3
Hct: 52%
Hb: 13 g/dL

Emergency Department Nurse's Admission Note
Patient reports feeling overwhelming fatigue, anorexia, "high" fevers, burning on urination, "frequently urinating small amounts," and abdominal cramping. States that these signs and symptoms have progressively worsened over the last few days.

Vital Signs Sheet
Pulse: 100 beats per minute, regular
Temperature (oral): 103°F
Respirations: 24 breaths per minute
Blood pressure: 110/86 mm Hg

30. A nurse identifies that a patient has an inflammatory response. Which localized patient responses support this conclusion? **Select all that apply.**
    1. _____ Fever
    2. _____ Swelling
    3. _____ Erythema
    4. _____ Bradypnea
    5. _____ Tachycardia

31. A nurse must collect the following specimens. Which specimens do not require the use of surgical aseptic technique? **Select all that apply.**
    1. _____Stool for occult blood
    2. _____Stool for ova and parasites
    3. _____Oropharyngeal mucus for a culture
    4. _____Urine from a retention catheter for a urinalysis
    5. _____Exudate from a wound for culture and sensitivity

32. A nurse plans to remove a patient's wound dressing. The nurse identifies the patient, explains what is going to be done and why, washes the hands, collects equipment, provides for the patient's privacy, and places the patient in an appropriate and comfortable position. Place the following steps in the order in which they should be implemented when removing the soiled dressing.
    1. Don clean gloves.
    2. Pull the tape away from the skin gently.
    3. Assess the volume, color, and odor of exudate.
    4. Place the soiled dressing and gloves in a biohazardous waste receptacle.
    5. Remove the dressing by lifting the edge of the dressing upward and toward the center of the wound.
    6. Loosen the edges of the tape around the dressing starting from the outside and moving toward the center of the dressing.
    Answer: _____

33. Which patient information collected by the nurse reflects a systemic response to a wound infection? **Select all that apply.**
    1. _____Increased body temperature
    2. _____Increased heart rate
    3. _____Leukocytosis
    4. _____Exudate
    5. _____Edema
    6. _____Pain

34. A nurse is caring for a patient who has an order for a vacuum-assisted closure device using black foam to facilitate wound healing. The nurse verifies the order, explains to the patient what is to be done and why, gathers equipment, washes the hands, sets a sterile field, and dons sterile gloves. Place the following steps in the order in which they should be implemented.
    1. Trim the black foam to the size of the wound cavity.
    2. Pinch and cut a 2-cm round hole in the center of the transparent film.
    3. Connect the suction device tubing to the collection canister tubing and pump.
    4. Place the foam in the wound cavity without overlapping onto the surrounding skin.
    5. Place the suction device over the hole in the film and apply gentle pressure to secure in place.
    6. Apply the transparent film 1 to 2 inches beyond wound edges without stretching or wrinkling the film.
    Answer: _____

35. A primary health-care provider prescribes azithromycin "Z-Pak" for a patient with a diagnosis of chronic bronchitis. Which should the nurse teach the patient that is important to know about taking azithromycin? **Select all that apply.**
    1. _____"Take this medication with food."
    2. _____"You can discontinue the medication as soon as you feel better."
    3. _____"Take 500 mg on the first day and then 250 mg for 4 more days, for a total of 1.5 g."
    4. _____"The first dose should be taken after we notify you of the results of the culture and sensitivity."
    5. _____"Avoid taking an antacid containing aluminum or magnesium within 2 hours of taking this medication."

1. 1. Artificial nails do not interfere with finger dexterity if kept at a reasonable length (not longer than 1/4 inch beyond the end of the finger).
2. Although this is a concern, it is not the main reason they should be avoided.
3. **Studies have demonstrated that artificial nails, especially when cracked, broken, or split, provide crevices in which microorganisms can grow and multiply and therefore should be avoided by direct care providers.**
4. When artificial nails are cared for so that they remain intact and free of cracks or breaks, they should not scratch the skin.

2. 1. School-aged children generally respond to infections with acute signs and symptoms that are identified easier and earlier than in an age group in another option.
2. **Infections are more difficult to identify in the older adult because the signs and symptoms are not as acute and obvious as in other age groups, as a result of the decline in all body systems related to aging.**
3. Adolescents generally respond to infections with acute signs and symptoms that are identified more easily and earlier than in an age group in another option.
4. Infants generally respond to infections with acute signs and symptoms that are identified more easily and earlier than in an age group in another option.

3. 1. Although wound infections can occur when prosthetic devices are implanted, they are surgically implanted under sterile conditions to minimize this risk.
2. **Burns more than 20% of a person's total body surface generally are considered major burn injuries. When the skin is damaged by a burn, the underlying tissue is left unprotected and the individual is at risk for infection. The greater the extent and the deeper the depth of the burn, the higher is the risk for infection.**
3. Although urinary tract infections can occur with an indwelling urinary catheter, these catheters are closed systems in which sterile technique is maintained; this minimizes the risk for infection.

4. Laparoscopic surgery is performed using sterile technique to minimize the risk of infection.

4. 1. Protective mechanisms in the respiratory tract provide a primary, not secondary, line of defense against pathogenic microorganisms. Primary defenses are nonspecific immune defenses that are anatomical, mechanical, or chemical barriers. In the respiratory tract they include intact mucous membranes, mucus, bactericidal enzymes, cilia, sneezing, and coughing.
2. Protective mechanisms in the urinary tract environment provide a primary, not secondary, line of defense against pathogenic microorganisms. These defenses include intact mucous membranes, urine flowing out of the body, and urine acidity.
3. Skin provides a primary, not secondary, line of defense against pathogenic microorganisms. These defenses include intact skin, surface acidity, and the usual flora that is found on the skin.
4. **The immune response is a specific, secondary line of defense against pathogenic microorganisms. The production of antibodies to neutralize and eliminate pathogens and their toxins (immune response) is activated when phagocytes fail to destroy invading microorganisms completely. The primary, nonspecific defenses (e.g., anatomical, mechanical, chemical, and inflammatory) work in harmony with the secondary defense (immune response) to defend the body from pathogenic microorganisms.**

5. 1. Platelets are essential for blood clotting and are unrelated to an individual's ability to withstand exposure to pathogens.
2. Hemoglobin is the part of the red blood cell that carries oxygen from the lungs to the tissues and is unrelated to the assessment of an individual's ability to withstand exposure to pathogens.
3. **Neutrophils, the most numerous leukocytes (white blood cells), are a primary defense against infection because they ingest and destroy microorganisms (phagocytosis). When the leukocyte count is low, it indicates**

a compromised ability to fight infection.

4. Red blood cells (erythrocytes) do not reflect an individual's ability to withstand exposure to pathogens. Erythrocytes transport oxygen via hemoglobin molecules.

6. 1. **Pediculosis** *(Pediculus humanus capitis)* **is characterized by white oval particles attached to the hair. When identified, the nurse should assess the patient further for the presence of scratch marks on the scalp and by asking the patient if the head feels itchy. Also, the nurse must assess the extent of infestation and if any other areas of the body are infested with other types of lice** *(P. humanus corporis* **[body hair] and** *Phthirus pubis* **[pubic and axillary hair]). A patient with this infestation should be on contact isolation to prevent spread of the infestation to others.**

2. White oval particles attached to hair are not indicative of hirsutism. Hirsutism is the excessive growth of hair or hair growth in unusual places, particularly in female patients. In female patients usually it is caused by excessive androgen production or metabolic abnormalities.

3. White oval particles attached to hair are not indicative of dandruff. Dandruff is the excessive shedding of dry white scales as a result of the expected exfoliation of the epidermis of the scalp. Dandruff scales do not attach to the hair and are easily brushed away from the hair shaft.

4. White oval particles attached to hair are not indicative of scabies. Scabies is a communicable skin disease caused by an itch mite *(Sarcoptes scabiei)* and is characterized by skin lesions (e.g., small papules, pustules, excoriations, and burrows ending in a vesicle) with intense itching.

7. 1. **Microorganisms or endotoxins stimulate phagocytic cells, which release pyrogens that stimulate the hypothalamic thermoregulatory center, causing fever.**

2. Leukocyte migration does not precipitate the inflammatory response but is a phase of the inflammatory response. White blood cells reach a wound within a few hours after the injury to ingest bacteria and clean a wound of debris through the process of phagocytosis.

3. Erythema does not increase the flow of blood throughout the body. Increased blood flow to a localized area causes erythema.

4. Pain does not cause an increase in body temperature directly.

8. 1. A respiratory infection contracted from a visitor is not an example of an infection that directly resulted from a diagnostic or therapeutic procedure.

2. A vaginal infection in a postmenopausal woman is not an example of an infection that directly resulted from a diagnostic or therapeutic procedure.

3. A urinary tract infection in a patient who is sedentary is not an example of an infection that directly resulted from a diagnostic or therapeutic procedure.

4. **A hospital-acquired infection directly results from a diagnostic or therapeutic procedure. When a caregiver does not wash his/her hands, thereby transmitting a pathogen that causes a wound infection, the result is an iatrogenic infection.**

9. 1. Radiation is not related to heat loss via a cooling (hypothermia) blanket. Radiation is heat loss from one surface to another surface without direct contact.

2. Convection is not related to heat loss via a cooling (hypothermia) blanket. Convection is the loss of heat as a result of the motion of cool air flowing over a warm body. The heat is carried away by air currents that are cooler than the warm body.

3. **Conduction is the transfer of heat from a warm object (skin) to a cooler object (hypothermia blanket) during direct contact.**

4. Evaporation is unrelated to heat loss via a cooling (hypothermia) blanket. Evaporation is the conversion of a liquid to a vapor, which occurs when perspiration on the skin is vaporized. For each gram of water that evaporates from the skin, approximately 0.6 of a calorie of heat is lost.

10. 1. Catabolism, the destructive phase of metabolism with its resultant release of energy, is related to infection.

2. Serum glucose is increased (hyperglycemia) in the presence of an infection because of the release of glucocorticoids in the general adaptation syndrome.

3. The presence of ketones in the urine, a sign that the body is using fat as a source

of energy, is related to infection because of the associated increased need for calories for fighting the infection.

4. Metabolic activity increases, not decreases, with an infection as the body mounts a defense to fight invading pathogenic microorganisms.

11. 1. Although this is something the nurse may provide to contain soiled tissues, it is not the first action the nurse should implement to prevent infection.

2. Although this is something the nurse may do to limit airborne or droplet transmission of microorganisms, it is not the first action the nurse should implement to prevent infection.

3. Antibiotics generally are prescribed for patients who have infections. Antibiotics rarely are prescribed prophylactically to prevent the development of resistant strains of microorganisms.

4. **This is the most important first step in the prevention of infection. A patient who is at risk to transmit an infection or at risk to be physiologically unable to protect the self from infection may require the institution of special precautions (e.g., transmission-based precautions, protective isolation).**

12. 1. Although normal saline is appropriate for cleansing a wound, a moist, not dry, environment facilitates epithelialization and minimizes scar formation.

2. **Cleaning with normal saline will not damage fibroblasts. Wet-to-damp dressings allow epidermal cells to migrate more rapidly across the wound surface than dry dressings, thereby facilitating wound healing.**

3. Povidone-iodine is cytotoxic and should not be used on clean granulating wounds.

4. Hydrogen peroxide is cytotoxic and should not be used on clean granulating wounds. Removal of a dressing that has dried on a wound will pull recently granulated tissue off of the wound bed.

13. 1. Surgery is conducted using sterile technique. In addition, preoperative preparation of the bowel helps to reduce the presence of organisms that have the potential to cause infection.

2. There is no break in the skin in a first-degree burn; therefore, there is less of a risk for a wound infection than an example in another option.

3. **Of all the options, puncture of the foot by a nail has the greatest risk for a wound infection. A nail is a soiled object that has the potential of introducing pathogens into a deep wound that can trap them under the surface of the skin, a favorable environment for multiplication.**

4. Paper generally is not heavily soiled, and the wound edges are approximated. This is less of a risk than an example in another option.

14. 1. **Epithelial cells of the skin are regularly shed along with potentially dangerous microorganisms that adhere to the skin's outer layers, thereby reducing the risk of infection.**

2. Epithelial cells on the skin are closely, not loosely, compacted, providing a barrier against pathogens.

3. Moisture on the skin surface facilitates, not prevents, colonization of pathogens.

4. Acidity, not alkalinity, of the skin limits the growth of pathogens.

15. 1. Droplet precautions are used for patients who have an illness transmitted by particle droplets larger than 5 μm (micrometers) (e.g., mumps, rubella, pharyngeal diphtheria, *Mycoplasma* pneumonia, pertussis, streptococcal pharyngitis, and pneumonic plague).

2. Contact precautions are used for patients who have an illness transmitted by direct contact or with items contaminated by the patient, for example, gastrointestinal, respiratory, skin, or wound infections or colonization with drug-resistant bacteria including *Clostridium difficile, Escherichia coli, Shigella,* as well as other infections/infestations, such as hepatitis A, herpes simplex virus, impetigo, pediculosis, scabies, syncytial virus, and parainfluenza.

3. Reverse precautions, also known as neutropenic precautions or protective isolation, are used for patients who are immunocompromised; isolation practices are employed, and personal protective equipment is worn by the caregiver to protect the patient from the caregiver.

4. Airborne precautions are used for patients who have an illness transmitted by airborne droplet nuclei smaller than 5 μm (micrometers), for example, varicella, rubeola, and tuberculosis.

16. 1. This is an example of controlling the mode of transmission. Direct transmission of microorganisms from one person to another is interrupted when microorganisms are removed from the skin surface by hand washing. Hand washing is part of hand hygiene, which also includes nail care, skin lubrication, and wearing of minimal jewelry in a health-care environment. Hand hygiene should be performed before and after patient care and whenever contamination has occurred.
    2. The use of a commode is an example of controlling the reservoir and the portal of exit from the reservoir links in the chain of infection.
    3. Ingesting a balanced diet is an example of reducing the susceptibility of the host link in the chain of infection.
    4. Changing a soiled dressing is an example of controlling the reservoir and portal of exit from the reservoir links in the chain of infection.

17. 1. The practice of placing stuffing inside a turkey and letting it stand at room temperature is not advisable because it promotes the multiplication of microorganisms.
    2. Hamburger meat should be thoroughly cooked so that disease-producing microorganisms within the meat are destroyed.
    3. This statement does not indicate a lack of knowledge about the use or storage of mayonnaise.
    4. This statement does not indicate a lack of knowledge about what to do when it is determined that something does not taste right.
    5. This is the correct way to defrost frozen food. Food should not be defrosted in an environment between 45°F and 140°F because bacteria will rapidly grow in this temperature range.

18. 1. Medical aseptic techniques must be instituted to protect others from being exposed to the infestation.
    3. The primary health-care provider must be notified because the surgery must be cancelled and treatment instituted.
    4. Treatment with a pediculicidal shampoo requires a prescription; it is a dependent function of the nurse.

    5. The patient's hair should be washed as soon as possible with a medicated shampoo (e.g., permethrin, crotamiton).
    2. After the hair is washed with a pediculicidal shampoo, it should be combed with a fine-toothed comb to remove the nits (eggs).

19. 1. Tears flush the eyes of microorganisms and debris and are a primary defense that protects the body from infection.
    2. Healthy, intact skin prevents entry of many pathogens. In addition, the normal flora of the skin hinders growth of disease-causing microorganisms that settle on the skin.
    3. Cilia line the nasal passages, sinuses, trachea, and larger bronchi and are tiny hair-like cells that sweep microorganisms up from the lower airways. These microorganisms are then expelled from the body by coughing and sneezing.
    4. Acidity, not alkalinity, of gastric secretions is a primary defense mechanism that protects the body from infection.
    5. Bile helps emulsify fats; it does not protect the body from infection.
    6. A dry, not moist, epidermis is a primary defense mechanism that protects the body from infection.

20. 1. A cut in the skin caused by a sharp instrument with minimal tissue loss can heal by primary intention when the wound edges are lightly pulled together (approximated).
    2. Excoriation heals by secondary, not primary, intention. Excoriation is an injury to the surface of the skin. It can be caused by friction, scratching, and chemical or thermal burns.
    3. An abrasion heals by secondary, not primary, intention. With an abrasion, friction scrapes away the epithelial layer, exposing the underlying tissue.
    4. A surgical incision is caused by a scalpel, which is a sharp instrument. This type of wound can heal by primary intention when the wound edges are lightly pulled together (approximated) with sutures.
    5. A pressure ulcer heals by secondary, not primary, intention. Secondary intention healing occurs when wound edges are not approximated because of full-thickness tissue loss; the wound is left open until it fills with new tissue.

21.   Changing a soiled dressing breaks the chain of infection at the *Reservoir* (source) step. Soiled or wet dressings are a perfect environment for pathogens to proliferate.

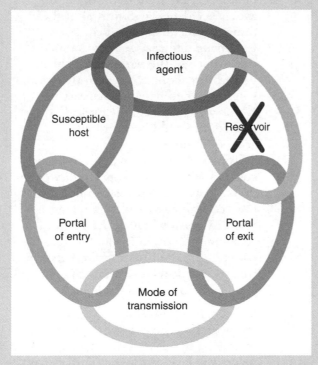

22.   1.   An increase in white blood cells (leukocytosis), not a decrease in white blood cells (neutropenia), occurs in response to both local and systemic infections.
      2.   Discomfort, uneasiness, or indisposition (malaise) is a systemic, not local, response to infection.
      3.   **Chemical mediators increase the permeability of small blood vessels, thereby causing fluid to move into the interstitial compartment, with resulting local edema.**
      4.   Fever is a systemic, not local, response to a wound infection. Microorganisms, or endotoxins, stimulate phagocytic cells that release pyrogens, which stimulate the hypothalamic thermoregulatory center to produce an increased temperature (fever, pyrexia).
      5.   **Pain is caused by localized edema that puts pressure on the surrounding nerves; this is associated with the local adaptation syndrome.**

23.   1.   This is an example of controlling the mode of transmission, not the susceptible host, link in the chain of infection.
      2.   **This is an example of an action designed to interrupt the susceptible**

host link in the chain of infection by increasing the resistance of the host to an infectious agent.
      3.   Discarding uncapped, used syringes in a sharps container disrupts the chain of infection at the reservoir link in the chain of infection. The nurse should never recap a used needle because of the risk of a needle-stick injury.
      4.   **Immunoglobulins are a group of related proteins able to act as antibodies. Immunoglobulin therapy helps defend a susceptible host against infection.**
      5.   This is an example of controlling the mode of transmission, not the susceptible host, link in the chain of infection.

24.   1.   An N95 respirator mask is not necessary when caring for a patient receiving contact precautions. Patients receiving contact precautions have infections that are transmitted by contact with wounds, dressings, contaminated supplies, or patients' secretions or excretions. A regular mask with an eye shield is necessary when providing care when splashing of blood, body fluids, or secretions is likely, such as when irrigating a wound.
      2.   **This mask is an N95 respirator mask, which should be worn when entering the room of a patient receiving airborne precautions. The National Institute for Occupational Safety and Health tests and certifies special fitted masks such as the N95 respirator mask for use when maintaining airborne precautions. Infections such as tuberculosis, severe acute respiratory syndrome (SARS), rubeola (measles), and varicella (chickenpox) are considered airborne infections whereby microorganisms are transmitted via air currents. Patients with these infections receive airborne precautions.**
      3.   An N95 respirator mask is not necessary when implementing standard precautions. Standard precautions are actions implemented by the nurse in the care of all persons regardless of their diagnosis.
      4.   An N95 respirator mask is not necessary when implementing protective precautions. Protective precautions (reverse isolation, neutropenic precautions) include actions designed to protect the immunocompromised patient from

infection. The nurse wears a mask so as not to introduce microorganisms into the air, thereby protecting the patient from the nurse. Additional actions include such actions as restricting fresh fruit, vegetables, and flowers. Depending on the degree of immunosuppression, the patient may be placed in a room with positive airflow, have water purity monitored, and have air conduits in the room checked for the presence of microorganisms.

25. 1. Throbbing pain is subjective, not objective, information because pain cannot be observed; it is felt and described only by the patient.
    2. Purulent drainage from the ear is objective information because it can be observed and measured.
    3. An elevated temperature is a cardinal sign of infection and is objective data because it is measured with a thermometer. A fever is a secondary defense against infection. An increase in core body temperature increases metabolism, impedes growth of pathogens, and activates specific immune responses to protect the body.
    4. Dizziness is subjective, not objective, information because it cannot be measured; dizziness is experienced and described only by the patient.
    5. Hearing a buzzing sound (tinnitus) is subjective, not objective, information because it cannot be observed; a buzzing sound is perceived and described only by the patient.

26. 1. Antibiotic therapy is the use of chemotherapeutic agents to control or eliminate bacterial infections. It is not a primary defense that protects the body from infection. The inappropriate use of antibiotics destroys the usual flora of the body and can predispose an individual to additional infections.
    2. Lysozymes in saliva help wash microorganisms from the teeth and gums.
    3. The low pH of the skin is caused by phospholipids that help prevent the development of bacterial infections.
    4. The acidic, not alkaline, environment of the vagina protects it from the growth of pathogens.
    5. Mucus produced by epithelial cells in the genitourinary tract adheres to

pathogens to facilitate their elimination through urination.

27. 3. Using sterile forceps maintains sterility of the drain.
    2. Gentle, steady pulling on the drain avoids accidental withdrawal of the drain farther than intended.
    4. Removing and reattaching the pin at the surface of the wound prevent the drain from sliding back into the wound where it could become inaccessible. If this were to occur, a surgical procedure would be required to access the drain.
    5. Cutting off the excess drain by using sterile scissors maintains sterility of the drain. Leaving 2 inches to the length of the drain allows an adequate length of drain to grasp when shortening or removing the drain in the future.
    1. Completing the dressing protects the wound and provides an environment conducive for wound healing.

28. 1. This is an action designed to interrupt the portal of entry link in the chain of infection. By keeping the collection bag below the level of the patient's pelvis, backflow is prevented, which reduces the risk of introducing pathogens into the bladder.
    2. Using sterile technique when administering medication parenterally helps to reduce the risk of introducing a pathogen into the body.
    3. Using a biohazardous transport bag is an example of controlling the reservoir and mode of transmission links in the chain of infection.
    4. Wearing clean gloves is an example of controlling the mode of transmission, not the portal of entry, link in the chain of infection.
    5. Hand washing is an example of controlling the mode of transmission, not the portal of entry, link in the chain of infection.
    6. A dressing over a surgical incision provides a barrier between the healing incision and the environment. The dressing protects the patient from potential invading microorganisms at the portal of entry portion of the chain of infection.

29. 1. A white blood cell count of 30,000 mm³ or higher is a critical

finding indicating a potential life-threatening health situation. The clinical indicators support a medical diagnosis of urosepsis—septicemia from bacteria entering the bloodstream from a urinary cause.

2. Although a temperature of 103°F is higher than the expected range of 96.8°F to 100.4°F, it is not as critical as data in another option.

3. Although abdominal cramping is an important piece of data, it is not as critical as data in another option.

4. A blood pressure of 110/86 mm Hg is low for an older adult man and probably is low because of dehydration associated with "high" fevers of a few days' duration. Although the blood pressure indicates a need for fluid replacement, it is not as critical as data in another option.

30. 1. A fever is a systemic, not local, response to inflammation.

2. **Chemical mediators released at the site of an injury increase capillary permeability, causing excessive interstitial fluid that results in swelling (edema).**

3. **Local trauma or infection stimulates the release of kinins, which increase capillary permeability and blood flow to the local area. The increase of blood flow to the area causes erythema (redness).**

4. Bradypnea is a regular but excessively slow rate of breathing (less than 12 breaths per minute) and is not a response associated with the local adaptation syndromes.

5. Tachycardia is an elevated heart rate more than 100 beats per minute and is unrelated to the local adaptation syndrome.

31. 1. **Stool for occult blood does not have to be sterile because test results for the presence of blood are not altered if the specimen is contaminated with exogenous organisms.**

2. **Stool for ova and parasites does not have to be sterile because test results for the presence of parasitic eggs and parasites are not altered if the specimen is contaminated with exogenous microorganisms.**

3. Sterile technique is used to collect a throat culture, to avoid contaminating the specimen with exogenous organisms that may alter the accuracy of test results.

4. The bladder is a sterile cavity, and the nurse must use sterile technique to collect urine from the port of a retention catheter (Foley) so as not to introduce any pathogens. In addition, it is important not to introduce exogenous organisms that may contaminate the specimen and alter the accuracy of test results.

5. Sterile technique is used to collect exudate from a wound to avoid contaminating the specimen with exogenous organisms that may alter the accuracy of test results.

32. 1. **Clean gloves protect the nurse from the patient's blood and body fluids.**

6. **Loosening the edges of the tape around the entire dressing prepares the tape to be removed by the nurse. Moving from the edge toward the center of the wound avoids pulling on the wound.**

2. **Pulling the tape away from the skin gently reduces discomfort and skin trauma during tape removal.**

5. **Gently lifting the dressing upward and toward the center of the wound avoids dragging the edges of the dressing into the center of the wound contaminating the wound.**

3. **Assessing the status of the wound provides data for evaluating the progress of wound healing.**

4. **Placing soiled dressings and contaminated gloves in a biohazardous waste receptacle breaks the chain of infection at the transmission link.**

33. 1. **Fever is a common systemic response to infection. Microorganisms or endotoxins stimulate phagocytic cells that release pyrogens, which stimulate the hypothalamic thermoregulatory center, resulting in fever.**

2. **An increased heart rate (tachycardia) occurs in response to the increase in the metabolic rate associated with an infection. In addition, blood volume increases as peripheral and visceral vasoconstriction enhances blood flow to the heart and lungs as the body prepares to fight the infection.**

3. **The number of white blood cells increases above the expected range (leukocytosis) to help fight the infection.**

4. Exudate is a local, not systemic, response to an injury or inflammation. Exudate is

cleared away through lymphatic drainage or exits from the body via a wound.

5. Edema is a local, not systemic, response to infection. Chemical mediators increase the permeability of small blood vessels, thereby causing fluid to enter the interstitial compartment, resulting in local edema.

6. Pain is a local, not systemic, response to inflammation because swelling of inflamed tissue exerts pressure on nerve endings.

34. 1. **The black foam is cut to the exact size of the cavity of the wound so that suction is applied to the full surface of the wound cavity.**

4. **Avoiding overlapping surrounding intact skin with the foam prevents skin from becoming macerated as the foam becomes wet during therapy.**

6. **The transparent film creates a seal so that negative pressure can be created by the device. Avoiding stretching the film during application prevents excess tension when negative pressure is established, which can cause tissue injury.**

2. **Creating a 2-cm hole in the transparent film provides a port over which the suction device is applied.**

5. **The suction device placed over the 2-cm hole in the transparent film once connected to the pump draws excess** exudate away from the wound and into the tubing.

3. **Connecting the suction device tubing to the collection canister and pump establishes negative pressure, which draws excess exudate from the wound. Suctioned exudate exits the wound via the suction device that is secured to the transparent film, is drawn into the tubing, and is collected in the collection canister.**

35. 1. Azithromycin should be taken 1 hour before or 2 hours after meals because food can decrease the amount of medication absorbed by as much as 50%.

2. The entire regimen should be completed, not discontinued once the patient feels better. Taking the entire regimen of an antibiotic eradicates the pathogens that have invaded the body. Stopping an antibiotic early promotes the development of resistant bacteria and a return of the infection.

3. **This is the dose and administration regimen for azithromycin "Z-Pak."**

4. The first dose can be administered once the specimen for culture and sensitivity is collected. The patient does not have to wait for the results of the culture and sensitivity test to initiate therapy. Waiting will only prolong the infection.

5. **Antacids may decrease the peak level of azithromycin and decrease its effectiveness.**

Safety

KEYWORDS

The following words include nursing/medical terminology, concepts, principles, and information relevant to content specifically addressed in the chapter or usually associated with topics presented in it. English dictionaries, nursing textbooks, and medical dictionaries, such as *Taber's Cyclopedic Medical Dictionary*, are resources that can be used to expand your knowledge and understanding of these words and related information.

Abdominal thrust (Heimlich maneuver)

Allergies:
  Food
  Latex
  Medication

Aspiration

Call bell

Cardiopulmonary resuscitation (CPR)

Child-proof devices

Dysphagia

Electrical:
  Grounding
  Hazards
  Surge

Falls

Fire safety:
  Fire extinguishers—A, B, C
  RACE model (**R**escue, **A**larm, **C**onfine, **E**xtinguish)

Functional alignment

Incident report

Knots:
  Clove hitch
  Half bow
  Slip

Restraints:
  Belt
  Elbow
  Jacket
  Mitt
  Mummy
  Poncho
  Vest

Side rails

SAFETY: QUESTIONS

1. A resident brings several electronic devices to a nursing home. One of the devices has a two-pronged plug. Which rationale should the nurse provide when explaining why an electrical device must have a three-pronged plug?
   1. Controls stray electrical currents
   2. Promotes efficient use of electricity
   3. Shuts off the appliance if there is an electrical surge
   4. Divides the electricity among the appliances in the room

2. A nurse is caring for a patient with Parkinson disease who is experiencing difficulty swallowing. Which potential problem associated with dysphagia has the **greatest** influence on the plan of care?
   1. Anorexia
   2. Aspiration
   3. Self-care deficit
   4. Inadequate intake

3. A nurse is caring for a confused patient. Which should the nurse do to prevent this patient from falling?
   1. Encourage the patient to use the corridor handrails.
   2. Place the patient in a room near the nurses' station.
   3. Reinforce how to use the call bell.
   4. Maintain close supervision.

4. A school nurse is teaching children about fire safety procedures. Which is the **first** thing they should be taught to do if their clothes catch on fire?
   1. Yell for help.
   2. Roll on the ground.
   3. Take their clothes off.
   4. Pour water on their clothes.

5. A primary health-care provider orders a vest restraint for a patient. Which should the nurse do **first** when applying this restraint?
   1. Perform an inspection of the patient's skin where the restraint is to be placed.
   2. Ensure that the back of the vest is positioned on the patient's back.
   3. Permit four fingers to slide between the patient and the restraint.
   4. Secure the restraint to the bed frame using a slipknot.

6. An unconscious patient begins vomiting. In which position should the nurse place the patient?
   1. Supine
   2. Side-lying
   3. Orthopneic
   4. Low-Fowler

7. A toaster is on fire in the pantry of a hospital unit. Which should the nurse do **first**?
   1. Activate the fire alarm.
   2. Unplug the toaster from the wall.
   3. Put out the fire with an extinguisher.
   4. Evacuate the patients from the room next to the kitchen.

8. The risk management coordinator is preparing a program on the factors that contribute to falls in a hospital setting. Which factor that **most** often contributes to falls should be included in this program?
   1. Wet floors
   2. Frequent seizures
   3. Advanced age of patients
   4. Misuse of equipment by nurses

9. A nurse is assessing a patient who is being admitted to the hospital. Which is the **most** important information that indicates whether the patient is at risk for physical injury?
   1. Weakness experienced during a prior admission
   2. Medication that increases intestinal motility
   3. Two recent falls that occurred at home
   4. The need for corrective eyeglasses

10. Which should the nurse do to **best** prevent a patient from falling?
    1. Provide a cane.
    2. Keep walkways clear of obstacles.
    3. Assist the patient with ambulation.
    4. Encourage the patient to use hallway handrails.

11. Which is the **last** step in making an occupied bed that the nurse should teach a nursing assistant?
    1. Elevating the head of the bed to a semi-Fowler position
    2. Ensuring that the patient is in a comfortable position
    3. Lowering the height of the bed toward the floor
    4. Raising both the side rails on the bed

12. A nurse is caring for a patient with a nasogastric tube for gastric decompression. Which nursing action takes priority?
    1. Discontinuing the wall suction when providing nursing care
    2. Positioning the patient in the semi-Fowler position
    3. Instilling the tube with 30 mL of air every 2 hours
    4. Caring for the nares at least every 8 hours

13. A patient states that when turning on an electric radio a strong electrical shock was felt. Which should the nurse do **first**?
    1. Arrange for the maintenance department to examine the radio.
    2. Disconnect the radio from the source of energy.
    3. Check the patient's skin for electrical burns.
    4. Take the patient's apical pulse.

14. A nurse educator is teaching a group of newly hired nursing assistants. Which hospitalized patient should they be taught is at the **greatest** risk for injury?
    1. School-aged child
    2. Comatose teenager
    3. Postmenopausal woman
    4. Confused middle-aged man

15. A nurse in the nursing education department of a community hospital is planning an inservice education class about injury prevention. Which factor that **most** commonly causes physical injuries in hospitalized patients should be included in the teaching plan?
    1. Malfunctioning equipment
    2. Failure to use restraints
    3. Visitors
    4. Falls

16. Which is the **priority** nursing intervention to prevent patient problems associated with latex allergies?
    1. Use nonlatex gloves.
    2. Identify persons at risk.
    3. Keep a latex-safe supply cart available.
    4. Administer an antihistamine prophylactically.

17. Which nursing intervention enhances an older adult's sensory perception and thereby helps prevent injury when walking from the bed to the bathroom?
    1. Providing adequate lighting
    2. Raising the pitch of the voice
    3. Holding onto the patient's arm
    4. Removing environmental hazards

18. A nurse is preparing a patient for a physical examination. Which is **most** important for the nurse to do in this situation?
    1. Identify the positions contraindicated for the patient during the examination.
    2. Explore the patient's attitude toward health-care providers.
    3. Inquire about other professionals caring for the patient.
    4. Ask when the patient last had a physical examination.

19. A patient has dysphagia. Which nursing action takes priority when feeding this patient?
    1. Ensuring that dentures are in place
    2. Medicating for pain before providing meals
    3. Providing verbal cueing to swallow each bite
    4. Checking the mouth for emptying between every bite

20. A 3-year-old child is admitted to the pediatric unit. Which should the nurse do to maintain the safety of this preschool-aged child?
    1. Teach the child how to use the call bell.
    2. Put the child in a crib with high side rails.
    3. Ensure the child is under continuous supervision.
    4. Have the child stay in the playroom most of the day.

21. Which time of day is of **most** concern for the nurse when trying to protect a patient with dementia from injury?
    1. Afternoon
    2. Morning
    3. Evening
    4. Night

22. A nurse is orienting a newly admitted patient to the hospital. Which is **most** important for the nurse to teach the patient how to do?
    1. Notify the nurse when help is needed.
    2. Get out of the bed to use the bathroom.
    3. Raise and lower the head and foot of the bed.
    4. Use the telephone system to call family members.

23. Profuse smoke is coming out of the heating unit in a patient's room. Which should the nurse do **first**?
    1. Open the window.
    2. Activate the fire alarm.
    3. Move the patient out of the room.
    4. Close the door to the patient's room.

24. A nurse must apply a hospital gown that does not have snaps on the shoulders to a patient receiving an intravenous infusion in the forearm. Which should the nurse do?
    1. Insert the IV bag and tubing through the sleeve from inside of the gown first.
    2. Disconnect the IV at the insertion site, apply the gown, and then reconnect the IV.
    3. Close the clamp on the IV tubing no more than 15 seconds while putting on the gown.
    4. Don the gown on the arm without the IV, drape the gown over the other shoulder, and adjust the closure behind the neck.

25. A nurse is planning care for a patient with a wrist restraint. How often should a restraint be removed, the area massaged, and the joints moved through their full range?
    1. Once a shift
    2. Once an hour
    3. Every 2 hours
    4. Every 4 hours

26. Which is the **first** action the home-care nurse should employ to prevent falls by an older adult living at home?
    1. Conduct a comprehensive risk assessment.
    2. Encourage the patient to remove throw rugs in the home.
    3. Suggest installation of adequate lighting throughout the home.
    4. Discuss with the patient the expected changes of aging that place one at risk.

27. A nurse is preparing a bed to receive a newly admitted patient. Which action is **most** important?
    1. Placing the patient's name on the end of the bed
    2. Ensuring that the bed wheels are locked
    3. Positioning the call bell in reach
    4. Raising one side rail

28. Which are appropriately worded goals for a patient who is at risk for falling? **Select all that apply.**
    1. _____ "The patient will be able to walk from a bed to a chair safely while hospitalized."
    2. _____ "The patient will be taught how to call for help to ambulate."
    3. _____ "The patient will be kept on bedrest when dizzy."
    4. _____ "The patient will be restrained when agitated."
    5. _____ "The patient will be free from trauma."

29. A nurse is caring for a patient who has an order for a mitt restraint. Place an X where the mitt restraint strap should be secured with a quick-release knot.

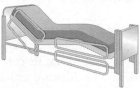

30. Which interventions should a nurse implement when assisting a patient to use a bedpan? **Select all that apply.**
1. _____Dust powder on the rim before placing the bedpan under the patient.
2. _____Ensure that the bed rails are raised once the patient is on the bedpan.
3. _____Position the rounded rim of the bedpan toward the front of the patient.
4. _____Encourage the patient to help as much as possible when using the bedpan.
5. _____Raise to the semi-Fowler position once the patient is placed on the bedpan.

31. A nurse identifies the presence of smoke exiting the door to the dirty utility room. Place the nurse's actions in order of priority using the RACE model.
1. Pull the fire alarm.
2. Close unit doors and windows.
3. Shut the door to the utility room.
4. Provide emotional support to agitated patients.
Answer: _____

32. Which clinical manifestation indicates that a further nursing assessment is necessary to determine if the patient is having difficulty swallowing? **Select all that apply.**
1. _____Debris in the buccal cavity
2. _____Abdominal cramping
3. _____Epigastric pain
4. _____Slurred speech
5. _____Constipation
6. _____Drooling

33. A male patient is admitted to ambulatory care for a bilateral herniorrhaphy. A nurse on the unit interviews the patient, obtains the patient's vital signs, and reviews the primary health-care provider's orders. Which should the nurse do **first**?
1. Contact the operating suite and inform them of the patient's latex allergy.
2. Ensure the patient's allergy band includes the patient's identified allergies.
3. Notify the primary health-care provider of the patient's elevated vital signs.
4. Share the information about the patient's anxiety with health team members.

PATIENT'S CLINICAL RECORD

Primary Health-Care Provider's Orders
Nothing by mouth
IVF: 0.9% sodium chloride at 125 mL/hour
Midazolam 5 mg, IM on call to preoperative suite

Vital Signs
Temperature: 99.2°F, orally
Pulse: 96 beats per minute
Respirations: 22 breaths per minute
Blood pressure: 124/82 mm Hg

Patient Interview
Patient states "I am a little nervous because I have never had surgery before." During preoperative testing patient indicated an allergy to oxycodone/acetaminophen but forgot to include allergies to latex and peanuts.

34. A nurse is planning care for a patient who requires bilateral arm restraints because the patient is delirious and attempting to pull out a urinary retention catheter. Which information is important to consider when planning care for this patient? **Select all that apply.**
    1. _____Use of restraints adequately prevents injuries.
    2. _____Reasons for use of restraints must be clearly documented.
    3. _____Most patients recognize that restraints contribute to their safety.
    4. _____Restraints need a primary health-care provider order before application.
    5. _____Laws permit the use of restraints when specific guidelines are followed.

35. A nurse is implementing the action demonstrated in the illustration. Which is the nurse doing?
    1. Transferring a patient into a wheelchair
    2. Teaching abdominal breathing to a patient
    3. Dislodging an object from a patient's airway
    4. Holding a patient up after the patient became dizzy when walking

36. An adult patient consistently tries to pull out a urinary retention catheter. As a last resort to maintain integrity of the catheter and patient safety, the nurse obtains an order for a restraint. Which types of restraints are most appropriate in this situation? **Select all that apply.**
    1. _____Mummy restraint
    2. _____Elbow restraint
    3. _____Jacket restraint
    4. _____Wrist restraint
    5. _____Mitt restraint

37. A nurse uses the *Get Up and Go* test to assess a patient for weakness, poor balance, and decreased flexibility. Place the following actions in the order in which they should be implemented when employing the *Get Up and Go* test.
    1. Ask the patient to walk 10 feet and then to return to the chair.
    2. Ask the patient to close the eyes.
    3. Ask the patient to open the eyes.
    4. Ask the patient to sit in a chair.
    5. Ask the patient to stand.
    Answer: _____

38. Which actions are important when the nurse uses a stretcher? **Select all that apply.**
    1. _____Lowering the bed below the level of the stretcher when transferring a patient from the stretcher to a bed
    2. _____Guiding the stretcher around a turn leading with the end with the patient's head
    3. _____Ensuring the patient's head is at the end with the swivel wheels
    4. _____Pulling the stretcher on the elevator with the patient's feet first
    5. _____Pushing the stretcher from the end with the patient's head

39. Which human responses to illness alert the nurse that a patient is at risk for aspiration during meals? **Select all that apply.**

1. _____Bulimia
2. _____Lethargy
3. _____Anorexia
4. _____Stomatitis
5. _____Dysphagia

40. A nurse is caring for a patient with a moderate problem with balance. Place an X over the cane that is most appropriate for this patient.

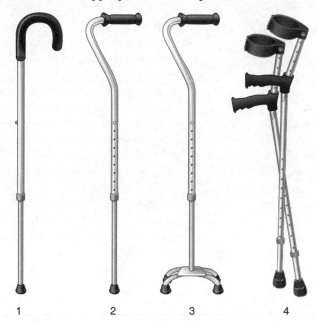

1   2   3   4

1. 1. **A three-pronged plug functions as a ground to dissipate stray electrical currents.**
   2. The purpose of a three-pronged plug is not to promote efficient use of electricity.
   3. A surge protector shuts off the appliance.
   4. A multiple outlet plug divides the electricity among appliances in the room.

2. 1. Although lack of an appetite (anorexia) can occur with dysphagia, it is not the most serious associated risk.
   2. **When a person has difficulty with swallowing (dysphagia), food or fluid can pass into the trachea and be inhaled into the lungs (aspiration), rather than swallowed down the esophagus. This can result in choking, partial or total airway obstruction, or aspiration pneumonia.**
   3. Dysphagia is unrelated to self-care deficit. Feeding self-care deficit occurs when a person is unable to cut food, open food packages, or bring food to the mouth.
   4. Inadequate intake of food and fluid can result with dysphagia because of fear of choking. However, it is not the most serious associated risk.

3. 1. A confused patient may not be able to follow directions or understand how to use corridor handrails.
   2. Moving the patient near the nurses' station may be impossible and impractical.
   3. A confused patient may not be able to follow directions or understand how to use a call bell.
   4. **Maintaining safety of the confused patient is best accomplished through close or direct supervision. Confused patients cannot be left on their own because they may not have the cognitive ability to understand cause and effect, and therefore their actions can result in harm.**

4. 1. This eventually may be done, but the child must do something immediately before waiting for help to arrive.
   2. **Rolling on the ground will smother the flames and put the fire out. Children should be taught to: "Stop, drop, and roll."**
   3. Taking off their clothes may be impossible. In addition, it will take time, and the clothing and skin will continue to burn.
   4. Finding and obtaining water will take too much time, and the clothing and skin will continue to burn. Something must be done immediately.

5. 1. **Even when applied correctly, restraints can cause pressure and friction. A baseline assessment of the skin under the restraint should be made. In addition, the presence of a dressing, pacemaker, subcutaneous infusion port, or subclavian catheter may influence the type of restraint to use.**
   2. Although the back of the vest should be positioned on the patient's back, it is not the first intervention.
   3. The jacket may be too loose if four fingers are used. The jacket should be applied so that two, not four, fingers can slide between the patient and the restraint.
   4. Securing the restraint to the bed frame using a slipknot should be done; however, it is the last, not the first, intervention associated with the application of a vest restraint.

6. 1. The supine position will promote aspiration and should be avoided in this situation.
   2. **The side-lying position prevents the tongue from falling to the back of the oropharynx, thus allowing the vomitus to flow out of the mouth by gravity and preventing aspiration.**
   3. The orthopneic position is an unsafe, impossible position in which to maintain an unconscious patient.
   4. The low-Fowler position will allow the tongue to fall to the back of the oropharynx, promoting aspiration. This position should be avoided in this situation.

7. 1. **Because no patient is in jeopardy, the nurse's initial action should be to activate the fire alarm. The sooner the alarm is set, the sooner professional firefighters will reach the scene of the fire.**
   2. Unplugging the toaster is unsafe because it places the nurse in jeopardy. The nurse

may be exposed to an electrical charge or become burned.

3. This is an inappropriate intervention because the nurse may not be capable of containing or fighting the fire. Not calling for professional firefighting help first places the nurse, staff, and patients in jeopardy.

4. Evacuating patients is premature at this time, but it may become necessary eventually.

8. 1. Although wet floors can contribute to falls, they are not the most common factor that contributes to falls in the hospital setting.

2. Although seizures can contribute to falls, most patients do not experience seizures.

3. **Older adults who are hospitalized frequently have multiple health problems, are frail, and lack stamina. All of these factors contribute to the inability to maintain balance and ambulate safely.**

4. Although this occasionally happens and is negligence, it is not the most common factor that contributes to falls in the hospital setting.

9. 1. Although this is important information, it is not the most important factor of the options offered in this question. In addition, the prior admission may have been too long ago to have any current relevance.

2. A patient with increased intestinal motility may experience diarrhea, which may place the patient at risk for a fluid and electrolyte imbalance, not a physical injury. Although a person with diarrhea may need to use the toilet more frequently, a bedside commode or bedpan can be used to reduce the risk of falls.

3. **This is significant information that must be considered because if falls occurred before, then they are likely to occur again. When a risk is identified, additional injury prevention precautions can be implemented.**

4. Although this is important information, it is not the most important factor of the options offered in this question.

10. 1. The patient may or may not need a cane. An unnecessary cane may actually increase the risk of a fall.

2. Although this should be done, it is not the best intervention of the options presented.

3. This widens the patient's base of support, which improves balance and decreases the risk of a fall.

4. Although this should be done, it is not the best intervention of the options presented.

11. 1. Elevating the head of the bed may not be necessary. This action should be based on the individual needs of the patient.

2. Assisting the patient to a comfortable position should be done while the bed is at an effective working height for the caregiver.

3. **It is safer if the bed is in the lowest position because a greater risk for injury to a patient occurs when the mattress of the bed is farther from the floor.**

4. Raising the side rails on the bed may not be necessary. This action should be based on the individual needs of the patient.

12. 1. Discontinuing the wall suction is unnecessary and can result in vomiting and aspiration.

2. **A nasogastric (NG) tube for gastric decompression passes down the esophagus, through the cardiac sphincter, and into the stomach. The cardiac sphincter remains slightly open because of the presence of the NG tube. The semi-Fowler position keeps gastric secretions in the stomach via gravity (preventing reflux and aspiration) and allows the gastric contents to be suctioned out by the NG tube.**

3. Instilling the NG tube with air is not done routinely every 2 hours. This may be done to identify the presence of the tube in the stomach or help re-establish patency of the tube when it is clogged.

4. Caring for the nares should be done more frequently than every 8 hours to prevent irritation and pressure.

13. 1. Having the radio examined may be done eventually; it is not the priority at this time.

2. Disconnecting the radio is contraindicated because it may place the nurse in jeopardy.

3. Inspecting the patient's skin is not the priority, and electrical burns may or may not be evident.

4. **An electric shock can interfere with the electrical conduction system within the heart and result in dysrhythmias. An**

electric shock can be transmitted through the body because body fluids (consisting of sodium chloride) are an excellent conductor of electricity.

14. 1. Although a school-aged child is at risk for injury in a hospital setting, age-related precautions are always instituted. More nurses generally are assigned to pediatric units and frequently family members are at the bedside.
   2. A patient in a coma is not at as high a risk for injury as a patient in another option. A patient in a coma demonstrates less response to painful stimuli, generally has an absence of muscle tone and reflexes in the extremities, and appears to be in a deep sleep.
   3. A woman after menopause is not at a high risk for injury.
   4. **A confused patient is at an increased risk for injury because of the inability to comprehend cause and effect and therefore lacks the ability to make safe decisions.**

15. 1. Malfunctioning equipment is not a common cause of injuries in a hospital.
   2. The use of restraints has declined dramatically, and now they are used only when patients may harm themselves or others.
   3. Visitors are not the main cause of injuries in a hospital.
   4. **Research demonstrates that most physical injuries experienced by hospitalized patients occur from falls. Failing to call for assistance, inadequate lighting, and the altered health status of patients all contribute to falls.**

16. 1. This may or may not be necessary depending on the needs of the patient.
   2. **Patient allergies must be identified (e.g., latex, food, and medication) before any care is provided, be documented in the patient's clinical record, and appear on an allergy-alert wristband. After a risk is identified, additional safety precautions can be implemented to prevent exposure to the offending allergen. Assessment is the first step of the nursing process.**
   3. Keeping a latex-safe supply cart available may be useless unless the supplies are used appropriately.
   4. Administering an antihistamine is unnecessary. A person with a latex allergy

should not be exposed to products with latex.

17. 1. **Adequate lighting provides for the safety of patients, staff, and visitors within a hospital. Inadequate lighting causes shadows, a dark environment, and the potential for misinterpreting stimuli (illusions) and is a contributing cause of accidents in the hospital setting. This intervention maximizes a patient's sense of sight.**
   2. When talking with older adults it is better to lower, not raise, the pitch of the voice. As people age they are more likely to have impaired hearing with higher-pitch sounds.
   3. Holding the patient's arm does not enhance a patient's sensory perception. Holding a patient's arm is not always necessary and therefore could be degrading or promote regression.
   4. Although this should be done, removing environmental hazards will not enhance a patient's sensory perception.

18. 1. **A physical examination requires a patient to assume a variety of positions such as supine, side-lying, sitting, and standing. The nurse should inquire about any positions that are uncomfortable or contraindicated because of past or current medical conditions to prevent complications.**
   2. Although the patient's attitude toward health-care providers may be obtained before a physical examination, it is not the priority.
   3. Inquiring about other professionals caring for the patient is not the priority before a physical examination. This might be done later to prevent fragmentation of care and ensure continuity of care.
   4. Although identifying when the last physical examination was performed may be done, it is not a priority before a physical examination.

19. 1. Although this should be done if a patient has dentures, it is not the priority.
   2. Although an analgesic may be administered, it can cause drowsiness that may increase the potential for aspiration in a patient with dysphagia.
   3. Although this should be done, the patient may be physically incapable of following this direction.
   4. **This is the safest way to ensure that a bolus of food is not left in the mouth**

where it can be aspirated and cause an airway obstruction.

20. 1. A preschool-aged child does not have the cognitive and emotional maturity to use a call bell.

    2. A preschool-aged child might attempt to climb over the side rails. A crib with high side rails is more appropriate for an infant.

    3. **Constant supervision ensures that an adult can monitor the preschool-aged child's activity and environment so that safety needs are met. Preschool-aged children are active, curious, and fearless and have immature musculoskeletal and neurological systems, narrow life experiences, and a limited ability to understand cause and effect. All of these factors place preschool-aged children at risk for injury unless supervised.**

    4. This is inappropriate because most preschoolers still take one or two naps daily, the child may be on bedrest, and periods of activity and rest should be alternated to conserve the child's energy.

21. 1. The sunlight and usual afternoon activities generally help keep patients with dementia more oriented and safe.

    2. The sunlight and the routine morning activities of hygiene, grooming, dressing, and eating generally help keep patients with dementia more oriented and safe.

    3. As the day progresses and the sun sets, the concern for safety increases because of altered cognition (sundowner syndrome). However, in the evening there are activities of daily living and available caregivers to distract the patient and provide for safety.

    4. **At night, patients with dementia often continue to experience confusion and agitation. At night there is less light, less activity, and fewer caregivers, so there are fewer orienting stimuli. Patients who are confused or agitated are at an increased risk for injury because they may not comprehend cause and effect and therefore lack the ability to make safe judgments.**

22. 1. **Explaining how to use a call bell meets safety and security needs. It reinforces that help is immediately available at a time when the patient may feel physically or emotionally vulnerable in an unfamiliar environment.**

2. Patients generally do not need teaching about how to get out of bed to go to the bathroom. This instruction depends on the individual needs of a patient.

3. How to manipulate the bed is part of orienting a patient to the hospital environment; however, it is not the most important point to emphasize with a patient.

4. Use of the telephone is part of orienting a patient to the hospital environment; however, it is not the most important point to emphasize with a patient.

23. 1. Opening a window is contraindicated because environmental air will feed the fire and cause it to increase in severity.

    2. Although activating the alarm will be done, it is not the priority at this point in time.

    3. **The patient's physical safety is the priority. The patient must be removed from direct danger before the alarm is activated and the fire contained.**

    4. Although closing the door will be done eventually, it is not the priority at this point in time.

24. 1. **This ensures that the IV bag and tubing are safely passed through the armhole of the gown before the patient puts the arm with the insertion site through the gown. This prevents tension on the tubing and insertion site, which limits the possibility of the catheter dislodging from the vein.**

    2. Disconnecting the IV tubing at the catheter insertion site is unnecessary. This increases the risk of contaminating the equipment and the potential for infection.

    3. Stopping the flow of the IV solution can result in blood coagulating at the end of the catheter in the vein, compromising the patency of the IV tubing.

    4. Draping the gown over the shoulder leaves the patient exposed unnecessarily. It interferes with privacy, and the patient may feel cold.

25. 1. Once a shift is too long a period; it promotes the development of injuries (e.g., contractures, pressure ulcers).

    2. Once an hour generally is too often and unnecessary.

    3. **Restraints should be removed every 2 hours. The extremities must be moved through their full range of**

motion to prevent muscle shortening and contractures. The area must be massaged to promote circulation and prevent pressure injuries.

4. Four hours is too long a period between activities and promotes the development of injuries.

26. 1. Assessment is the first step of the nursing process. The best way to prevent falls is by identifying those at risk and instituting multiple interventions that prevent falls.
2. This is inadequate. Removing throw rugs is just one strategy.
3. This is inadequate. Ensuring adequate lighting is just one strategy.
4. This is inadequate. Exploring the issues of aging with a patient is just one strategy.

27. 1. Placing patients' names on the end of their beds violates the patient's right to privacy. An identification wristband must be worn for patient identification.
2. **Locked bed wheels are an important safety precaution. The bed must be an immovable object because the patient may touch the bed for support, lean against it when getting in or out of bed, or move around when in bed. If bed wheels are unlocked during these maneuvers, the bed may move and the patient can fall.**
3. The call bell cord may become an obstacle when moving the patient into the bed. This should be done after the patient is in the bed.
4. The side rail may become an obstacle when moving the patient into the bed. This should be done after the patient is in the bed.

28. 1. **This is an appropriate goal. It is realistic, specific, measurable, and has a time frame. It is realistic to expect that all patients be safe. It is specific and measurable because safety from trauma can be compared with standards of care within the profession of nursing. It has a time frame because the words "while hospitalized" reflect the time frames of always, constantly, and continuously while directly under the care of a health team.**
2. Being taught how to call for help is a planned intervention, not a goal.
3. Maintaining a patient on bedrest is a planned intervention, not a goal.

4. This is a planned intervention, not a goal. In addition, it is inappropriate to restrain a person automatically for agitation. A restraint should be used as a last resort to prevent the patient from self-injury or injuring others.
5. **This is an appropriate goal. It is realistic, specific, and measurable and has a time frame. It is realistic to expect that all patients be safe. It is specific and measurable because safety from trauma can be compared with standards of care within the profession of nursing. It has a time frame because the words "free from" reflect the time frames of always, constantly, and continuously.**

29. **A restraint strap should always be tied with a quick-release knot to the frame of the bed. Tying a restraint strap to the side rail is contraindicated because when the side rail is lowered it may become too tight, causing an injury.**

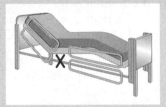

30. 1. The use of powder should be avoided because it is a respiratory irritant.
2. **Patient safety is a priority. A bedpan is not a stable base of support, and the effort of elimination may require movements that alter balance. Side rails provide a solid object to hold while balancing on the bedpan and supply a barrier to prevent falling out of bed.**
3. The rounded rim of a bedpan should be placed under the patient's buttocks, not toward the front of the patient.
4. **Encouraging the patient to help promotes the patient's independence and limits strain on the nurse.**
5. The semi-Fowler position is comfortable and provides a more normal position for defecation that helps prevent straining.

31. 1. **Pulling the fire alarm ensures that appropriate hospital personnel and the fire department are notified of the fire. Trained individuals will arrive to contain and extinguish the fire and help move patients if necessary. The RACE model should be followed in a**

fire emergency: rescue, alarm, confine, and extinguish).

3. Closing the door to the dirty utility room protects the patients and staff members in the immediate vicinity of the fire.

2. Closing unit doors and windows provides a barrier between the patients and the fire and limits drafts that could exacerbate the fire.

4. Patients should be supported emotionally during a crisis because anxiety can be contagious.

32. 1. Retention of food in the oral cavity indicates that the patient is not swallowing ingested food completely. Food collects in the buccal cavity because the area between the teeth and cheek forms a pocket that traps food.

2. Abdominal cramping is related to problems such as flatus, malabsorption, and increased intestinal motility, not difficulty swallowing.

3. Epigastric pain is related to problems such as gastritis, cholecystitis, and angina, not difficulty swallowing.

4. Slurred speech reflects an inability of the tongue and muscles of the face to form words. Dysfunction of the muscles of the face and tongue will interfere with the ability to chew and swallow food.

5. Constipation is not related to difficulty swallowing.

6. Drooling indicates that oral secretions are accumulating in the mouth. This may occur when a person has difficulty swallowing.

33. 1. This intervention should be performed immediately after the priority intervention. Patients with latex allergies require special precautions to be taken in the operating suite. The use of latex products can be life-threatening for the patient if appropriate precautions are not taken. All equipment, such as gloves and tubes, must be latex free to protect the patient from experiencing an allergy that can progress to anaphylaxis.

2. Protecting the patient is the priority, and a red allergy band is the first line of defense. In addition, the patient's allergies must be included on other designated places on the patient's medical record.

3. Although the patient's vital signs are on the high side of normal or slightly elevated, their elevations probably are related to the patient's anxiety. These elevations should be documented and reported but they are not the priority at this time. Normal ranges for vital signs include: temperature, 98.6°F to 99.8°F; pulse, 60 to 100 beats per minute; respirations, 12 to 20 breaths per minute; blood pressure: systolic pressure, 90 to 120 mm Hg, and diastolic pressure 60 to 80 mm Hg.

4. Although this should be done, this is not the priority at this time. Mild to moderate anxiety is a common response when anticipating surgery, especially when being experienced for the first time. The patient's anxiety should be documented and communicated to other members of the health team, but it is not the priority at this time. However, when a patient has a sense of impending doom, the surgeon should be notified immediately because the patient may not be in the right frame of mind for surgery; if surgery is performed, it can be a self-fulfilling prophesy.

34. 1. This statement is not true. Injuries and falls can occur if restraints are not applied appropriately. In addition, research indicates that patients incur less severe injuries if they are left unrestrained.

2. The reason for the use of restraints must adhere to standards of care and be documented on the patient's clinical record to create a legal document that protects the patient as well as health-care providers.

3. The opposite is true. Patients resist the use of restraints and usually are mentally or emotionally incompetent to understand their necessity or benefits.

4. Restraints can be applied by nurses in emergencies without a primary health-care provider order to protect patients from harming themselves or others. Restraints can be used for nonviolent patients who are at risk for harming themselves (level 1 restraint) or violent patients who are at risk for harming themselves or others (level 2 restraint). A primary health-care provider must assess the patient and document the need for the original application of the restraint and its

continued use within specified time frames. For example, for a level 1 restraint, a primary health-care provider's order must be obtained within 12 hours after its application and daily thereafter, whereas for a level 2 restraint, a primary health-care provider must evaluate the patient within 1 hour after its application and every 4 hours thereafter.

5. Federal and state laws provide specific guidelines regarding patients' rights and responsibilities of caregivers associated with the use of restraints. In addition, The Joint Commission has specific guidelines that require documentation of: previous restraint-free interventions that have failed to protect the patient; a description of the situation indicating a need for the restraint; the least restrictive restraint that has been selected; and assessments and orders by a primary health-care provider within specified time frames.

35. 1. A nurse stands in front of a patient when transferring the patient from a bed to a wheelchair.
2. Abdominal breathing is best taught when the nurse demonstrates placement of the hands on one's own abdomen. The nurse teaches the patient to contract and relax the diaphragm when inhaling and exhaling. With the patient's hands resting on his or her own abdomen, the abdomen will rise on inspiration and relax on exhalation when abdominal breathing is implemented correctly.
3. This is an illustration of the abdominal thrust maneuver (Heimlich maneuver) used to dislodge a foreign object from a person's airway. An abdominal thrust applies pressure up against the diaphragm that forces air out the lungs, exerting pressure behind the obstruction, thus dislodging the foreign object from the airway.
4. When a patient becomes dizzy and begins to fall, the nurse should not try to keep the patient in the standing position because this can cause injury to the patient and/or nurse. The nurse should project one hip forward and with a wide base of support guide the patient down along that leg until the patient reaches the floor. Once the patient is on the floor, the nurse protects the patient's head to prevent a head injury.

36. 1. A mummy restraint usually is used to immobilize an infant or very young child during a procedure.
2. A soft limb splint that extends from the mid-forearm to the mid-upper arm can be applied to inhibit flexion of the elbow, which can prevent the pulling out of tubes.
3. A jacket restraint usually is used to keep a person from falling out of bed while not immobilizing the extremities.
4. A wrist restraint encircles the wrist and has ties that are secured with a slipknot to the bed frame so that a patient is unable to reach tubes.
5. A mitt restraint covers the hand to prevent the fingers from grasping and pulling out tubes.

37. 4. The first step involves asking the patient to sit in a chair. This allows the nurse time to observe the patient's posture while sitting in a straight-backed chair before any other activity.
5. The second step involves asking the patient to stand. This allows the nurse to observe the patient's use of the leg muscles to stand or whether the patient has to push up and off the seat with the hands to stand. This helps to assess leg strength when moving to a standing position.
2. The third step involves asking the patient to close the eyes. This allows the nurse to observe if the patient sways to maintain balance when the eyes are closed.
3. The fourth step involves asking the patient open the eyes. This prepares the patient for the next step in the procedure.
1. The fifth step involves asking the patient to walk 10 feet, turn around, and return to the chair. This allows the nurse to observe the patient's gait, posture, stability, pace, and balance when ambulating.

38. 1. Keeping a bed lower than a stretcher when transferring a patient from the stretcher to a bed uses gravity, which places less stress and strain on both the patient and nurses.
2. It is too difficult and unsafe to maneuver a stretcher with the nonswivel wheels on the leading end of the stretcher. The end of

the stretcher with the patient's head does not have swivel wheels.

3. The swivel-wheeled end of the stretcher should be the leading end of the stretcher, and it is unsafe to lead with the patient's head. In addition, the end of the stretcher with the swivel wheels moves through greater arcs; this can cause dizziness. The swivel wheels of a stretcher should be at the end under the patient's feet, not the head.

4. This is unsafe and places the patient in physical jeopardy. The elevator doors may inadvertently close by the patient's head while the nurse is pulling the feet end of the stretcher into the elevator. The patient should be moved into an elevator head, not feet, first.

5. A stretcher should always be pushed, not pulled, so that the transporter stays at the patient's head for protection. The swivel wheels must be under the patient's feet on the leading end of the stretcher for safe maneuverability.

39. 1. The risk for aspiration in a patient with bulimia occurs after, not during, meals. Bulimia is characterized by episodes of binge eating followed by purging, depression, and self-deprecation.

2. **When a person is sleepy, sluggish, or stuporous (lethargic), there may be a reduced level of consciousness and diminished reflexes, including the gag and swallowing reflexes. This condition can result in aspiration of food or fluids that can compromise the person's airway and respiratory status.**

3. A lack of appetite (anorexia) is unrelated to aspiration. The less food or fluid that is placed in the mouth, the less the risk is for aspiration.

4. An inflammation of the mucous membranes of the mouth (stomatitis) may result in dysphagia and increase the risk of aspiration.

5. Dysphasia, difficulty swallowing, places a patient at risk for aspiration generally because of impaired innervation of the tongue and muscles used for swallowing.

40. 1. This is a single-ended cane with a half circle handle. It is used by patients who can navigate stairs and need minimal support.

2. This is a single-ended cane with a straight handle. It is used by patients who need minimal support but have hand weakness.

3. **This is a quad cane and is the most appropriate cane to meet this patient's needs. It has four prongs that provide a wide base of support and it has a straight handle. It is used by patients with moderate balance problems.**

4. This is a Lofstrand (forearm support) crutch, not a cane. It is used by patients who need to limit or eliminate weight-bearing on a lower extremity. The patient relies on the strength in the arms and shoulders when walking. The Lofstrand crutch supports the wrist, thus making walking safer.

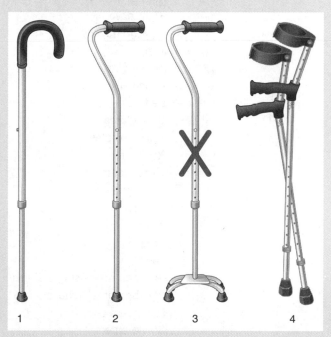

Medication Administration

KEYWORDS

The following words include nursing/medical terminology, concepts, principles, and information relevant to content specifically addressed in the chapter or associated with topics presented in it. English dictionaries, nursing textbooks, and medical dictionaries, such as *Taber's Cyclopedic Medical Dictionary,* are resources that can be used to expand your knowledge and understanding of these words and related information.

Air-lock (air-bubble) technique
Bevel
Bolus
Canthus, inner/outer
Diluent
Drug levels:
  Therapeutic
  Peak
  Toxic
  Trough
Filtered needle
Five Rights:
  Right patient
  Right medication
  Right route
  Right dose
  Right frequency
Gauge
Injection sites:
  Abdomen
  Deltoid
  Dorsogluteal
  "Love handles"
  Rectus femoris
  Vastus lateralis
  Ventrogluteal
Instillation
Interaction:
  Drug
  Food
Medication-dispensing systems
Medication prescriptions:
  prn orders
  Single orders
  Standing orders

STAT orders
Stop orders
Telephone orders
Metered-dose inhaler
Over-the-counter drugs (OTCs)
Parenteral
Reconstitution
Routes of administration:
  Buccal
  Ear (otic)
  Epidural
  Eye (ophthalmic)
  Intradermal
  Intramuscular
  Intrathecal
  Intravenous:
    Intravenous piggyback infusion (IVPB), intermittent infusion
    IV push
  Nasal cavity
  Rectal
  Subcutaneous
  Sublingual
  Topical
  Transdermal
  Urinary bladder
  Vaginal
Substance abuse
Systemic/local effects
Titrate
Troche
Tuberculin syringe
Unit-dose system
Z-track

MEDICATION ADMINISTRATION: QUESTIONS

1. A nurse instructs a patient to close the eyes after the administration of eye drops. Which rationale for this instruction should the nurse explain to the patient?
   1. Limits corneal irritation
   2. Squeezes excess medication from the eyes
   3. Disperses the medication over the eyeballs
   4. Prevents medication from entering the lacrimal duct

2. How often should "docusate sodium 100 mg PO bid" be given?
   1. Three times a day
   2. Two times a day
   3. Every other day
   4. At bedtime

3. A nurse is preparing to reconstitute a medication in a multiple-dose vial. Which is the **most** essential step in the preparation of this medication?
   1. Instilling an accurate amount of diluent into the vial
   2. Using a filtered needle when drawing up the medication from the vial
   3. Instilling air into the vial before withdrawing the reconstituted solution
   4. Wiping the rubber seal of the vial with alcohol before and after each needle insertion

4. Which characteristic is associated with a subcutaneous injection of 5,000 units of heparin?
   1. 3-mL syringe
   2. 22-gauge needle
   3. 1½-inch needle length
   4. 90-degree angle of insertion

5. A home-care nurse observes the spouse of a patient inserting a rectal suppository. Which behavior indicates that the nurse must provide further teaching about suppository administration?
   1. Lubricates the tip of the suppository
   2. Inserts the suppository while wearing a glove
   3. Inserts the suppository while the patient bears down
   4. Places the suppository a finger length into the rectum

6. A primary health-care provider prescribes a medication that must be administered via the intramuscular route. Which site should the nurse eliminate from consideration because it has the **highest** potential for injury when administering an intramuscular injection?
   1. Vastus lateralis
   2. Rectus femoris
   3. Ventrogluteal
   4. Dorsogluteal

7. Which information about a parenteral medication indicates that the nurse should use a filtered needle when preparing the medication?
   1. Has to be reconstituted
   2. Is supplied in an ampule
   3. Appears cloudy in the vial
   4. Is to be mixed with another medication

8. Which should the nurse use when administering a subcutaneous injection?
   1. 5-mL syringe
   2. 25-gauge needle
   3. Tuberculin syringe
   4. 1½-inch-long needle

9. When the nurse brings pills to a patient, the patient is unable to hold the paper cup with the medications. Which should the nurse do?
   1. Crush the pills and mix them with applesauce.
   2. Use the paper cup to introduce the pills into the patient's mouth.
   3. Have the primary health-care provider prescribe the liquid form of the drug.
   4. Put the pills into the patient's hand and have the patient self-administer the pills.

10. Which route is inappropriate for a topical medication?
    1. Intradermal
    2. Bladder
    3. Rectum
    4. Vagina

11. A nurse holds a bottle with the label next to the palm of the hand when pouring a liquid medication. Which is the rationale for this action?
    1. Prevent soiling of the label by spilled liquid.
    2. Conceal the label from the curiosity of others.
    3. Ensure accuracy of the measurement of the dose.
    4. Guarantee the label is read before pouring the liquid.

12. A primary health-care provider prescribes a medicated powder to be applied to a patient's lower leg. Which is **most** essential for the nurse to do when applying the medicated powder?
    1. Apply a thin layer in the direction of hair growth.
    2. Protect the patient's face with a towel.
    3. Dress the area with dry sterile gauze.
    4. Ensure that the skin surface is dry.

13. A nurse must administer a medication that is supplied in an ampule. Which should the nurse do **first** to access the ampule?
    1. Inject the same amount of air as the fluid to be removed.
    2. Wipe the constricted neck with an alcohol swab.
    3. Break the constricted neck using a barrier.
    4. Insert the needle into the rubber seal.

14. A nurse must administer a medication into the ear of an adult. Which should the nurse do to limit patient discomfort when administering ear drops?
    1. Warm the solution to body temperature.
    2. Place the patient in a comfortable position.
    3. Pull the pinna of the ear upward and backward.
    4. Instill the fluid in the center of the auditory canal.

15. A nurse instructs a patient to inhale deeply and hold each breath for a second when using a hand-held nebulizer. The patient asks, "Why do I have to hold my breath?" Which information should the nurse include in the response to the patient's question?
    1. "It prolongs treatment."
    2. "It limits hyperventilation."
    3. "It disperses the medication."
    4. "It prevents bronchial spasms."

16. Which abbreviation indicates that the primary health-care provider wants a medication administered before meals?
    1. pc
    2. OD
    3. PO
    4. ac

17. A home-care nurse is helping a patient with short-term memory loss with how to remember to take multiple drugs throughout the day. Which should the nurse do when teaching this patient?
    1. Suggest that the patient wear a watch with an alarm.
    2. Ask a family member to call the patient when medications are to be taken.
    3. Design a chart of the medications the patient takes each day during the week.
    4. Instruct the patient to put medications in a weekly organizational pill container.

18. Which action should be implemented by the nurse when a medication is delivered by the Z-track method?
    1. Use a special syringe designed for Z-track injections.
    2. Pull the skin laterally away from the injection site before inserting the needle.
    3. Administer the injection in the muscle on the anterolateral aspect of the thigh.
    4. Insert the needle in a separate spot for each dose on a Z-shaped grid on the abdomen.

19. A nurse must reconstitute a powdered medication. Which action should the nurse implement?
    1. Keep the needle below the initial fluid level as the rest of the fluid is injected.
    2. Instill the solvent that is consistent with the manufacturer's directions.
    3. Score the neck of the ampule before breaking it.
    4. Shake the vial to dissolve the powder.

20. A nurse is preparing to administer a tablet to a patient. When should the nurse remove the medication from its unit dose package?
    1. Outside the door to the patient's room
    2. At the patient's bedside
    3. In the medication room
    4. At the medication cart

21. Which nursing action is appropriate when administering an analgesic?
    1. Reassess drug effectiveness every eight hours.
    2. Follow the prescription exactly for the first twenty-four hours.
    3. Seek a new prescription after two doses that do not achieve a tolerable level of relief.
    4. Ask the primary health-care provider to prescribe another medication for breakthrough pain.

22. The primary health-care provider prescribes a troche. In which part of the body should the nurse administer the troche?
    1. Ear
    2. Eye
    3. Mouth
    4. Rectum

23. A nurse teaches a patient about taking a sublingual nitroglycerin tablet. Which part of the body identified by the patient indicates that the patient understands the teaching?
    1. "On my skin."
    2. "Inside my cheek."
    3. "Under my tongue."
    4. "In my eye on the lower lid."

24. A nurse plans to administer a bolus dose of a medication via a currently running intravenous infusion. Which should the nurse do **first**?
    1. Use a volume-control infusion set with microdrip tubing.
    2. Ensure that it is compatible with the IV solution being infused.
    3. Pinch the tubing above the infusion port while instilling the bolus.
    4. Instill it into a 50-mL bag of normal saline and infuse it via a secondary line.

25. A nurse is administering an intradermal injection. At which angle should the nurse insert the needle?
    1. 90-degree angle
    2. 45-degree angle
    3. 30-degree angle
    4. 15-degree angle

26. A nurse plans to administer a 3-mL intramuscular injection. Which muscle is the **least** desirable to use for the administration of this medication?
    1. Deltoid
    2. Dorsogluteal
    3. Ventrogluteal
    4. Vastus lateralis

27. A nurse is preparing to administer a subcutaneous injection of insulin. Which site should the nurse use to **best** promote its absorption?
    1. Upper lateral arms
    2. Anterior thighs
    3. Upper chest
    4. Abdomen

28. Which should a nurse use when placing a cream into a patient's vaginal canal?
    1. A finger
    2. A gauze pad
    3. An applicator
    4. An irrigation kit

29. A primary health-care provider prescribes a medication that must be administered transdermally. Which information about the route of administration does the nurse understand is related to a drug prescribed to be administered transdermally?
    1. Inhaled into the respiratory tract
    2. Dissolved under the tongue
    3. Absorbed through the skin
    4. Inserted into the rectum

30. Which should the nurse do to limit discomfort when administering an injection to an adult?
    1. Pull back on the plunger before injecting the medication.
    2. Apply ice to the area before the injection.
    3. Pinch the area while inserting the needle.
    4. Inject the medication slowly.

31. A nurse is preparing to draw up medication from a vial. Which action should the nurse implement **first**?
    1. Ensure that the needle is firmly attached to the syringe.
    2. Rub vigorously back and forth over the rubber cap with an alcohol swab.
    3. Inject air into the vial with the needle bevel below the surface of the medication.
    4. Draw up slightly more air than the volume of medication to be withdrawn from the vial.

32. A primary health-care provider prescribes 18 units of regular insulin and 26 units of NPH insulin to be given at 0730 a.m. in the same syringe. Indicate on the syringe, by shading in the appropriate area, how many total units of regular and NPH insulin are to be drawn into the syringe.

33. A primary health-care provider prescribes a topical medication to be administered to a patient with an area of excoriated skin. Place the following steps in the order in which they should be implemented.
    1. Don clean gloves.
    2. Evaluate the results of the lotion on the skin.
    3. Warm the tube of medication before application.
    4. Cleanse the skin gently with soap and water and pat dry.
    5. Don sterile gloves and apply a thin layer of lotion to the desired area.
    Answer: _____

34. The instructions with a medication states to use the Z-track method. Which actions should the nurse implement that are specific to this procedure? **Select all that apply.**
    1. _____Pinch the site throughout the procedure.
    2. _____Massage the site after the needle is removed.
    3. _____Add 0.3 to 0.5 mL of air after drawing up the correct dosage.
    4. _____Remove the needle immediately after the medication is injected.
    5. _____Change the needle after the medication is drawn into the syringe.

35. A health-care provider prescribes benztropine 1.5 mg PO STAT. Benztropine is available in 0.5 mg scored tablets. How many tablets should the nurse administer? **Record your answer using a whole number.**
    Answer: _____tablets.

36. Which routes are **unrelated** to the parenteral administration of medications? **Select all that apply.**
    1. _____Buccal
    2. _____Z-track
    3. _____Sublingual
    4. _____Intravenous
    5. _____Intradermal

37. Which interventions are uniquely related to the administration of an intradermal injection? **Select all that apply.**
    1. _____Using the air-bubble technique
    2. _____Circling the injection site with a pen
    3. _____Pinching the skin during needle insertion
    4. _____Inserting the needle with the bevel upward
    5. _____Massaging the area after the fluid is instilled

38. A primary health-care provider prescribes an intravenous antibiotic to be administered 4 times a day. The patient has a primary infusion of 0.9% sodium chloride infusing. The medication is compatible with the sodium chloride. Place an X over the port that should be used when administering this drug as an IVPB infusion.

39. A nurse is assessing a patient to determine if it is appropriate to administer a prescribed medication via the oral route. Which information indicates that the nurse should ask the primary health-care provider for a change in route? **Select all that apply.**
    1. _____Nausea
    2. _____Unconsciousness
    3. _____Gastric suctioning
    4. _____Emergency situation
    5. _____Difficulty swallowing

40. A primary health-care provider prescribes a medication via a transdermal patch. Place the following steps in the order in which they should be implemented when administering this medication.
1. Remove the previous patch.
2. Contain and dispose of the used patch.
3. Wear clean gloves throughout the procedure.
4. Write the date, time, and your initials on the patch.
5. Apply a new patch to a different section of the skin.
6. Wash and dry the skin after removal of the used patch.
Answer: _____

41. A primary health-care provider prescribes an oral medication for a patient. The nurse identifies that the patient is having some difficulty swallowing. What should the nurse plan to do? **Select all that apply.**
1. _____Crush tablets that are crushable and mix with a small amount of applesauce.
2. _____Have the patient hyperextend the neck slightly when swallowing.
3. _____Give water before, during, and after medication administration.
4. _____Stroke under the chin over the larynx.
5. _____Have the patient use a straw.

42. The primary health-care provider prescribes 500 mL of D_5W with 10 mEq of KCl to be administered over 10 hours. The intravenous tubing states that each mL delivers 60 gtts. At what rate per minute should the nurse adjust the flow rate of the intravenous solution? **Record your answer using a whole number.**
Answer: _____gtts/min

43. A primary health-care provider prescribes nose drops to be administered twice a day. Which should the nurse do when instilling the nose drops? **Select all that apply.**
1. _____Tell the patient not to sniff the medication once administered.
2. _____Place the patient in the supine position with the head tilted backward.
3. _____Pinch the nares of the nose together briefly after the drops are instilled.
4. _____Instruct the patient to blow the nose 5 minutes after the drops are instilled.
5. _____Insert the drop applicator ½ inch into the nose toward the base of the nasal cavity.

44. Which routes are associated with the administration of a suppository? **Select all that apply.**
1. _____Ear
2. _____Nose
3. _____Mouth
4. _____Vagina
5. _____Rectum

45. A primary health-care provider prescribes a monthly intramuscular injection of fluphenazine 37.5 mg. The medication is available as 25 mg/mL. How much solution of fluphenazine should the nurse administer? **Record your answer using one decimal place.**
Answer: _____mL.

46. A nurse is to administer an eye irrigation to a patient's right eye. Which should the nurse do? **Select all that apply.**
1. _____Direct the flow of solution from the inner to the outer canthus.
2. _____Irrigate with a bulb syringe held several inches above the eye.
3. _____Expose the conjunctival sac and hold open the upper lid.
4. _____Don sterile gloves before beginning the procedure.
5. _____Position the patient in a right lateral position.

47. A primary health-care provider prescribes medicated ear drops for a patient. Place the following steps in the order in which they should be implemented after cleaning the patient's ear.
   1. Release the pinna and gently press on the tragus several times.
   2. Pull up and back on the cartilaginous part of the pinna gently.
   3. Place the drops on the side of the ear canal without touching the canal with the dropper.
   4. Position the patient in the side-lying position with the affected ear facing toward the ceiling.
   5. Warm the refrigerated ear drops to room temperature by holding the container in the palm of a hand for several minutes.

   Answer: _____

48. A primary health-care provider prescribes a rectal suppository for an adult patient. Which actions should the nurse implement when administering the rectal suppository? **Select all that apply.**
   1. _____Lubricate the medication before insertion.
   2. _____Warm the medication equal to body temperature.
   3. _____Instruct the patient to take deep breaths through the mouth.
   4. _____Insert the medication just inside the rectum's external sphincter.
   5. _____Place the patient in the prone position to administer the medication.

49. A primary health-care provider orders an IV infusion of 1,000 mL 0.9% sodium chloride to be followed by 1,000 mL D$_5$W with 20 mEq of potassium chloride. The infusion is to be administered at 125 mL/hour. The drop factor of the IV tubing states 10 drops/mL. At how many drops per minute should the nurse set the IV infusion? **Record your answer using a whole number.**

   Answer: _____gtts/min

50. A primary health-care provider prescribes a liquid medication that has an unpleasant taste for a school-aged child. What should the nurse do to facilitate administration of this medication? **Select all that apply.**
   1. _____Mix it with the child's favorite food.
   2. _____Teach that the taste only lasts a short time.
   3. _____Give an ice pop just before giving the medication.
   4. _____Have a parent administer the medication if present.
   5. _____Offer the child the choice of a spoon, needleless syringe, or dropper.

51. A primary health-care provider prescribes acetaminophen 320 mg PO every 6 hours prn for pain for a 12-year-old child. The child has difficulty swallowing pills and the nurse obtains a liquid form of the drug. The bottle of acetaminophen states that there are 160 mg/5 mL. Put an X at the point on the graduated medicine cup that indicates how much solution of acetaminophen should be administered.

52. A nurse is interviewing a newly admitted patient in the process of completing a nursing admission history and physical. Which information should be included in a medication reconciliation form? **Select all that apply.**
    1. _____Vitamins
    2. _____Drug allergies
    3. _____Food supplements
    4. _____Over-the-counter herbs
    5. _____Prescribed medications

53. Which equipment and technique should the nurse use to administer most intramuscular injections? **Select all that apply.**
    1. _____Use a 1-inch needle.
    2. _____Use a 25-gauge needle.
    3. _____Insert the needle at a 45-degree angle.
    4. _____Aspirate before instilling the medication.
    5. _____Massage the insertion site after needle removal.

54. A primary health-care provider prescribes a vaginal suppository for a patient. The nurse obtains the suppository, pulls the curtain around the patient's bed, encourages the patient to void, provides perineal care, and then dons a new pair of clean gloves. Place the following steps in the order in which they should now progress to complete the administration of the vaginal suppository.
    1. Drape the patient exposing only the vaginal area.
    2. Position the patient in the dorsal recumbent position.
    3. Encourage the patient to remain in the supine position for 10 to 20 minutes.
    4. Lubricate the suppository and the nurse's index finger with a water-soluble jelly.
    5. Insert the suppository downward and backward using the full length of the index finger.
    Answer: _____

55. A primary health-care provider prescribes a liquid oral medication for a patient. Which actions should the nurse implement when administering this medication? **Select all that apply.**
    1. _____Vigorously shake the liquid before pouring a dose.
    2. _____Measure oral liquids in a calibrated medication cup at eye level.
    3. _____Pour liquids with the label facing away from the palm of the hand.
    4. _____Place an opened top of a container on a surface with the inside lid facing up.
    5. _____Use a needless syringe to measure an oral liquid less than 5 mL and transfer it to a medication cup.

56. A patient in the emergency department becomes agitated, and limit setting by the nurse is ineffective. The patient's behavior escalates, and the patient attempts to punch the nurse. The primary health-care provider prescribes a STAT dose of haloperidol 2.5 mg IM. The haloperidol available states that there is 5 mg/mL. Indicate on the syringe, by shading in the appropriate area, how much solution of haloperidol should be administered.

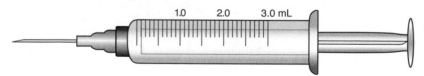

57. A primary health-care provider prescribes an oral medication for a patient with a nasogastric tube on low continuous suction. Which actions should the nurse implement when administering this medication? **Select all that apply**.
    1. _____Give each medication separately.
    2. _____Follow medication administration with 100 mL of free water.
    3. _____Crush crushable tablets into a fine powder and mix with 30 mL of warm water.
    4. _____Shut off nasogastric tube suctioning for 30 minutes after medication administration.
    5. _____Ensure nasogastric tube placement by instilling 30 mL of air while auscultating over the epigastric area for a "whooshing" sound.

58. An older adult is transported via ambulance to the emergency department of the hospital after being found unconscious on the living room floor by a family member. The patient regains consciousness and tells the nurse that everything went blank after standing up abruptly from a lounge chair. The patient is diagnosed with dehydration and is admitted for observation and rehydration therapy. The nurse performs a routine patient assessment 18 hours after initiation of the IV therapy. What should the nurse do **first** after reviewing the patient's clinical record and assessing the patient?
    1. Administer oxygen via a nasal cannula.
    2. Slow the rate of the intravenous fluid infusion.
    3. Elevate the head of the bed to the semi-Fowler position.
    4. Notify the primary health-care provider of the patient's status.

PATIENT'S CLINICAL RECORD

Vital Signs on Admission
Temperature: 99.6°F
Pulse: 96 beats per minute
Respirations: 22 breaths per minute, regular rhythm
Blood pressure: 100/60 mm Hg

Primary Health-Care Provider Orders
IVF: 0.9% sodium chloride at 125 mL/hour for 24 hours
Docusate sodium 100 mg PO once a day

Nurse's Physical Assessment of the Patient
Temperature: 99.8°F
Pulse: 112 beats per minute
Respirations: 26 breaths per minute, labored
Blood pressure: 150/98 mm Hg
Breath sounds: Fine rales at base of lungs

59. A primary health-care provider orders a unit of packed red blood cells for a patient with a low hemoglobin level. Which actions should be implemented by the nurse when administering this transfusion? **Select all that apply.**
    1. _____Adjust the flow rate to 20 drops per minute for the first 15 minutes.
    2. _____After 15 minutes with no reaction, assess the vital signs every 45 minutes.
    3. _____Administer 100 mL of 0.9% sodium chloride before administering the transfusion.
    4. _____Discontinue the blood transfusion if it extends beyond 4 hours after its initiation.
    5. _____Stay with the patient for 15 minutes after initiating the blood transfusion while taking vital signs every 5 minutes.

60. A primary health-care provider orders NPH and regular insulin to be administered to a patient with diabetes. Place the following illustrations in the order in which they should be implemented when mixing NPH and regular insulin in the same syringe.

Answer: _____

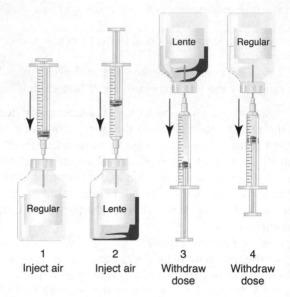

1	2	3	4
Inject air	Inject air	Withdraw dose	Withdraw dose

MEDICATION ADMINISTRATION: ANSWERS AND RATIONALES

1. 1. Instilling medication into the conjunctival sac prevents the trauma of drops falling on the cornea.
   2. Closing the eyes gently, rather than squeezing the lids shut, prevents the loss of medication from the conjunctival sac.
   3. Closing the eyes moves the medication over the conjunctiva and eyeball and helps ensure an even distribution of medication.
   4. Gentle pressure over the inner canthus for 1 minute after administration prevents medication from entering the lacrimal duct.

2. 1. The abbreviation for three times a day is tid (ter in die).
   2. The abbreviation bid (bis in die) represents twice a day.
   3. Bid does not mean every other day. Every other day must be written out. The abbreviation for every other day QOD (quaque altera die) should not be used.
   4. Bid does not mean at bedtime. Formerly the abbreviation for bedtime (hour of sleep) was hs (hora somni); however, The Joint Commission disallows the use of the abbreviation of hs because of the frequency of errors with its use.

3. 1. **The required amount of diluent must be followed exactly in a multiple-dose formulation to ensure accurate dosage preparation. The diluent for a single-dose formulation also must be exact so that the medication is diluted enough not to injure body tissues.**
   2. A filtered needle should be used when drawing up fluid from an ampule, not a vial. A filter prevents shards of glass from entering the syringe.
   3. Although this is an advisable practice, it is not as important as administering an accurate dose.
   4. The rubber seal must be wiped with alcohol before, not after, needle insertion.

4. 1. Most doses of heparin are less than 1 mL. Three milliliters of heparin is excessive and may result in bleeding.
   2. A 22-gauge needle is too large and can cause unnecessary trauma and bleeding at the insertion site. A 25- or 26-gauge needle is adequate.
   3. A 1½-inch length needle is unnecessarily long and may enter a muscle rather than subcutaneous tissue.
   4. **A ½-inch-length needle inserted at a 90-degree angle will ensure that the heparin is inserted into subcutaneous tissue.**

5. 1. Lubrication is required to limit tissue trauma and ease insertion.
   2. Standard precautions should be employed when there is exposure to patients' body fluids.
   3. **Bearing down increases intra-abdominal pressure, which impedes the insertion of the suppository. The patient should be instructed to relax and breathe deeply and slowly while the suppository is inserted.**
   4. In an adult, a suppository should be inserted 4 inches to ensure it is beyond the internal sphincter.

6. 1. The vastus lateralis site is not near large nerves or blood vessels, and the muscle does not lie over a joint. It is a preferred site for infants 7 months of age and younger.
   2. The rectus femoris site is not near major nerves, blood vessels, or bones. It is a preferred site for adults.
   3. The ventrogluteal site is not near large nerves or blood vessels. It is a preferred site in adults and children.
   4. **The dorsogluteal site has the highest risk for injury because of the close proximity of the sciatic nerve, blood vessels, and bone.**

7. 1. Reconstitution occurs within a closed vial and does not require a filtered needle.
   2. **The top of an ampule must be snapped off at its neck to access the fluid. A filtered needle prevents glass particles from being drawn into the syringe.**
   3. The majority of medications in vials are clear solutions. Cloudy fluid usually indicates contamination. Additional information from a drug guide or pharmacist is necessary to determine if the cloudiness is an expected characteristic of the drug or it indicates contamination.
   4. It is not necessary to use a filtered needle when mixing medications.

8. 1. A subcutaneous injection should not exceed 1 mL. A 3-mL, not a 5-mL, syringe is acceptable for a subcutaneous injection.
   2. A subcutaneous injection should use a 25- to 29-gauge needle, which minimizes tissue trauma. The diameter of a needle is referred to as its gauge, which ranges from 28 (small) to 14 (large).
   3. The volume of a tuberculin syringe is only 1 mL. For most subcutaneous injections, a syringe that can accommodate up to 3 mL is preferred to facilitate handling of the syringe.
   4. A 1½-inch length is appropriate for an intramuscular, not subcutaneous, injection.

9. 1. Mixing medication with applesauce is done if the patient has dysphagia.
   2. The patient needs assistance. Keeping medication in the cup, rather than touching it with the hands, maintains medical asepsis.
   3. It is not necessary to obtain an order for the liquid form of the medication. An order is required if a route other than oral is necessary.
   4. This action is unrealistic and unsafe. The patient has demonstrated the need for assistance.

10. 1. An intradermal injection is inserted below, not on top of, the epidermis.
    2. Medications in the form of solutions can be instilled into the bladder. They are designed to work locally and are considered topical medications.
    3. Medications in the form of a suppository can be inserted into the rectum and are considered topical medications. Most are designed to work locally, although some are absorbed systemically.
    4. Medications in the form of a suppository, tablet, cream, foam, or jelly can be instilled into the vagina. They are designed to work locally and are considered topical medications.

11. 1. Liquid medication may drip down the side of the bottle and soil the label, which may interfere with the ability to read the label accurately.
    2. Although patient confidentiality should always be maintained, this is not the reason for holding the label toward the palm of the hand.
    3. Accuracy of the dose is ensured by using a calibrated cup and measuring the liquid

at the base of the meniscus while positioning the cup at eye level.
    4. The label should be read before holding it against the palm of the hand.

12. 1. This action is done with lotions, creams, or ointments.
    2. It is unnecessary to protect the patient's face. When the powder is sprinkled gently on the site, the powder should not become aerosolized.
    3. A dressing is not a universal requirement. When necessary, a dressing is applied with a primary health-care provider's order.
    4. Moisture harbors microorganisms and when mixed with a powder will result in a paste-like substance. The site should be clean and dry before medication administration to ensure effective action of the drug.

13. 1. Injecting air is done with a vial, not an ampule.
    2. The rubber seal of a vial, not the neck of an ampule, should be wiped with alcohol.
    3. A barrier, such as a commercially manufactured ampule opener, gauze, or an alcohol swab, should be used to protect the hands from broken glass.
    4. Piercing a rubber seal is done with a vial, not an ampule.

14. 1. Instilling cold medication into the ear canal is uncomfortable and can cause vertigo and nausea. Holding the bottle of medication in the hand for several minutes warms the solution to body temperature.
    2. The side-lying position with the involved ear upward must be maintained for 2 to 3 minutes while the instilled medication disperses throughout the ear canal.
    3. These actions straighten the ear canal and facilitate the flow of medication toward the eardrum in an adult; it does not limit discomfort.
    4. This action is contraindicated because the force of the fluid may injure the eardrum. The drops should be directed along the side of the ear canal.

15. 1. There is no advantage in prolonging the treatment.
    2. Slow, deep breathing will limit hyperventilation.
    3. A pause at the height of inspiration will promote distribution and absorption of the medication before exhalation begins.

4. Slow inhalations and exhalations with pursed lips help prevent bronchial spasms.

16. 1. The abbreviation for after meals is pc (post cibum).
2. The abbreviation for right eye is OD. However, this abbreviation should be spelled out because there is confusion among the following abbreviations: right eye—OD (oculus dexter), left eye—OS (oculus sinister), and both eyes—OU (oculus utro).
3. The abbreviation for by mouth is PO (per os).
4. The abbreviation for before meals is ac (ante cibum).

17. 1. This suggestion is unrealistic. When the alarm goes off, the patient may not remember why it is ringing.
2. This suggestion is unrealistic and puts an excessive burden on family members.
3. A chart is unrealistic. The chart may be complex, confusing, and require repeated cognitive decisions throughout the day that may be beyond the patient's ability.
4. **Pill distribution can be set up once a week. After the medication is taken, the empty section reminds the patient that the medication was taken, which prevents excessive doses. This is a major issue for patients with short-term memory loss.**

18. 1. A special syringe is not needed for administering a medication via Z-track. The barrel of the syringe must be large enough to accommodate the volume of solution to be injected (usually 1 to 3 mL) and the needle long enough to enter a muscle (usually 1½ inches).
2. **This action creates a zigzag track through the various tissue layers. The track prevents backflow of medication up the needle track when simultaneously removing the needle and releasing the traction on the skin after the medication is injected.**
3. The use of the vastus lateralis muscle for a Z-track injection may cause discomfort for the patient. Z-track injections are tolerated more when the well-developed gluteal muscles are used.
4. The needle is inserted into the muscle once for a Z-track injection. The Z represents the zigzag pattern of the needle track that results when the skin traction and the needle are simultaneously removed.

19. 1. This will create excessive bubbles that can interfere with complete reconstitution or result in bubbles being drawn into the syringe. Both occurrences can result in an inaccurate dose.
2. **Compatibility is necessary so that a compound or precipitate that is harmful to a patient does not result.**
3. Reconstitution occurs in a vial (a closed system), not an ampule (an open system).
4. Shaking the vial will create excessive bubbles. The vial should be rotated between the hands to facilitate reconstitution.

20. 1. Opening the package outside the room exposes the medication to the environment, where it may become contaminated or grouped with other medications being administered to the patient, thus interfering with safe administration of one or more of the medications.
2. **The medication should be opened and administered immediately to the patient, thereby limiting the potential for contamination. Reading the label immediately before opening the package is an additional safety check. Immediate administration prevents accidental disarrangement of medications that may result in a medication error.**
3. Opening the package in the medication room exposes the medication to the environment because it requires the nurse to carry the medication through the unit to the patient's room. In addition, it can become confused with the medications for other patients.
4. Opening the package at the medication cart exposes the medication unnecessarily to the environment, and it can be inadvertently confused with the medications for other patients.

21. 1. The patient should be assessed every 1 to 2 hours to ensure effectiveness of the drug.
2. The prescription should be followed exactly if it is a safe dose; however, if the medication is not effective, 24 hours is too long a period not to intervene.
3. **Two doses provide enough time to evaluate the effectiveness of a medication for pain. Patients should not have to endure intolerable levels of pain.**
4. Requesting additional medication is unnecessary if the drug is the appropriate dose.

22. 1. Medications in the form of a solution are instilled into the ear.
    2. Ophthalmic medications in the form of a solution or an ointment are administered in the eye.
    3. A troche, a lozenge-like tablet, dissolves slowly in the mouth in the buccal cavity to provide a localized effect.
    4. Medications in the form of suppositories are inserted through the anus into the rectum.

23. 1. Topical medications are applied on the skin.
    2. A troche or lozenge given by the buccal route is placed between the cheek and gums.
    3. **A sublingual medication is placed under the tongue. It is absorbed quickly through the mucous membranes into the systemic circulation.**
    4. A medication placed in the lower conjunctival sac of the eye is administered for its local effect and is considered a topical medication.

24. 1. The volume of fluid of a bolus dose is too small to necessitate a volume-control infusion set.
    2. **An incompatible solution can increase, decrease, or neutralize the effects of the medication. In addition, an incompatibility may result in a compound or cause a precipitate that is harmful to the patient.**
    3. Pinching the tubing is not done first. Pinching is done immediately before and while instilling the medication to ensure that the medication flows toward the patient, rather than in the opposite direction up the tubing.
    4. This is done for a medication administered via an intermittent intravenous infusion over a 30- to 90-minute period rather than an intravenous bolus (IV push) dose that is administered over 1 to 5 minutes.

25. 1. A 90-degree angle is appropriate for an intramuscular, not an intradermal, injection.
    2. A 45-degree angle is appropriate for a subcutaneous, not an intradermal, injection.
    3. A 30-degree angle is too steep an angle for an intradermal injection, and a wheal will not form.
    4. **An intradermal injection is administered by inserting a needle at a 10- to 15-degree angle through the skin with the bevel of the needle facing upward toward the skin. The small volume of**

medication instilled just below the epidermis causes the formation of a wheal (localized area of swelling that appears like a small bubble).

26. 1. **The deltoid muscle, on the lateral aspect of the upper arm, is a small muscle that is incapable of absorbing a large medication volume. This site is more appropriate for 1 mL of solution.**
    2. The dorsogluteal site uses the gluteus maximus muscles in the buttocks, which can absorb larger medication volumes.
    3. The ventrogluteal site uses the gluteus medius and minimus muscles in the area of the hip, which can absorb larger medication volumes.
    4. The vastus lateralis muscles are located on the anterolateral aspect of the thighs, which can absorb larger medication volumes.

27. 1. Although insulin can be administered at the deltoid site, it is a small area that is not conducive to injection rotation within the site. The rate of absorption at this site is slower than at the preferred site for insulin administration.
    2. Although insulin can be administered in this site, tissues of the thighs and buttocks have the slowest absorption rate.
    3. The chest is not an acceptable site for the administration of insulin because of the lack of adequate subcutaneous tissue.
    4. **The abdomen is the preferred site for administration of insulin because it is a large area that promotes a systematic rotation of injections, and it has the fastest rate of absorption.**

28. 1. Either a gloved finger or an applicator is used to insert a vaginal suppository, not a cream.
    2. It is impossible to insert a cream into the vaginal canal with a gauze pad. If attempted, it will traumatize the mucous membranes of the vagina.
    3. **The consistency of a cream requires that an applicator be used to ensure that the medication is deposited along the full length of the vaginal canal.**
    4. The consistency of a cream is too thick to be inserted into the vagina with an irrigating kit.

29. 1. A medication that is aerosolized is inhaled.
    2. A tablet, such as nitroglycerin, is dissolved under the tongue.
    3. **A medicated patch or disk can be applied directly to the skin, where the**

medication is released and absorbed over time. This method ensures a continuous therapeutic drug level and reduces fluctuations in circulating drug levels.

4. Medications in the form of a suppository are inserted into the rectum.

30. 1. Testing for a blood return prevents injecting medication directly into the circulatory system, rather than limiting the discomfort of an injection.
2. Applying ice is contraindicated because it causes vasoconstriction, which limits absorption of the medication.
3. Pinching the skin aids in needle insertion when administering a subcutaneous injection. It does not limit the discomfort of an injection.
4. Injecting slowly allows the fluid to be dispersed gradually, which limits tissue trauma and discomfort.

31. 1. **This will ensure a tight seal and a closed system. If not firmly connected, the hub of the needle may disengage from the barrel of the syringe during preparation or administration of the medication when internal and external pressures are exerted on the needle and syringe.**
2. The top just needs to be swiped. Rubbing back and forth is a violation of surgical asepsis because it reintroduces microorganisms to the area being cleaned.
3. Injecting air below the surface of the solution should be avoided because it causes bubbles that may interfere with the drawing up of an accurate volume of solution.
4. Excess air in the closed system raises pressure in the vial that may cause bubbles when withdrawing the fluid and result in an inaccurate volume of solution.

32. **Answer: 44 units total.**
A total of 44 units of insulin should be drawn into the syringe. Eighteen units of regular insulin are drawn into the syringe first and then the 26 units of NPH insulin are drawn into the syringe. It is done in this order to ensure that the NPH insulin, which is longer acting, does not dilute the regular insulin in the vial, which is fast acting.

33. 1. Using clean gloves conforms to standard precautions; they protect the nurse from the patient's body fluids.
4. Cleansing the area removes debris and previously applied topical medication; doing so allows the skin to be accessible to the lotion. Patting the skin dry is less irritating to the skin than rubbing, and the dry surface facilitates adherence of the lotion.
3. Warming the medication promotes comfort for the patient when it is applied.
5. Sterile gloves maintain sterility of the procedure and prevent the nurse from contacting and absorbing the medication. Excessive lotion can irritate the skin.
2. Evaluating the results of the lotion on the skin ensures that therapeutic and nontherapeutic responses to the medication are identified. These responses must be documented and communicated to other members of the health-care team.

34. 1. When the Z-track method is used during an intramuscular injection, the skin and subcutaneous tissue are pulled laterally 1 to 1½ inches away from the injection site, not pinched.
2. Massage is contraindicated because it will force medication back up the needle track, which may result in tissue irritation or staining.
3. The injection of a small amount of air after the medication is administered instills air into the Z track, and this helps to keep the medication deeply seated in the muscle.
4. Removal of the needle should be delayed 10 seconds to allow the medication to begin to be dispersed and absorbed.
5. The Z-track method is used with viscid or caustic solutions. Changing the needle ensures that medication is not on the outside of the needle, which prevents tracking of the medication into subcutaneous tissue during needle insertion.

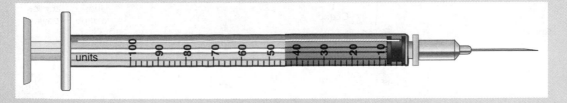

35. Solve the problem using the "Desire Over Have" formula.

$$\frac{\text{Desire}}{\text{Have}} \frac{1.5 \text{ mg}}{0.5 \text{ mg}} = \frac{x \text{ tablets}}{1 \text{ tablet}}$$

$0.5x = 1 \times 1.5$

$x = 1.5 \div 0.5$

$x = 3 \text{ tablets}$

36. 1. A parenteral route is outside the gastrointestinal tract. A medication administered by the buccal route dissolves between the cheeks and gums, where it acts on the oral mucous membranes or is swallowed with saliva. Most troches are used for their local effect. The mucosal route of administration includes the nasal mucosa, the buccal mucosa, sublingually, and the bronchioles.
   2. Z-track is a method of administering an intramuscular injection. The intramuscular route is a parenteral route.
   3. A parenteral route is outside the gastrointestinal tract. With the sublingual route medication dissolves under the tongue, where it is rapidly absorbed. The sublingual route is a mucosal route of administration.
   4. The intravenous route, a parenteral route, instills medication directly into the venous circulation.
   5. The intradermal route, a parenteral route, injects medication just under the epidermis.

37. 1. The air-bubble or air-lock technique can be used with intramuscular, not intradermal, injections. Its use is controversial, particularly with disposable plastic syringes.
   2. Circling the injection site with a pen indicates the area that must be evaluated; generally the site is assessed 72 hours after the intradermal injection.

3. Pinching or bunching up tissue is appropriate with subcutaneous, not intradermal, injections.
4. When medication is injected with the bevel up, a small wheal will form under the skin. This technique is used only with intradermal injections.
5. Massaging the site of an intradermal injection will disperse the medication beyond the intended injection site and is contraindicated.

38. This port is accessible to the short length of a secondary administration set tubing. The port is above the roller clamp on the primary tubing. When the bag of medication is hung higher than the primary solution bag, the back check valve on the primary tubing will shut off the flow of the primary infusion until the secondary infusion is almost complete. See figure below.

39. 1. Vomiting, not nausea, is a contraindication for oral medications.
   2. Nothing that requires swallowing should ever be placed into the mouth of an unconscious patient because of the risk for aspiration.
   3. Gastric suctioning can be interrupted for 20 to 30 minutes after medication has been instilled via a nasogastric tube.
   4. In an emergency a drug is best administered intravenously, rather than orally, because it is faster acting.
   5. Nursing interventions, such as positioning, mixing a crushed medication in applesauce, and dissolving a medication in a small amount of fluid, can be employed to facilitate the ingestion of medication.

40. 3. Wearing clean gloves protects the nurse from contact with the medication.
   1. Removing the previous patch reduces the risk of an overdose of the medication.

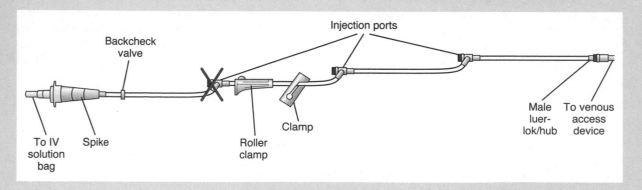

Backcheck valve / Injection ports / To IV solution bag / Spike / Roller clamp / Clamp / Male luer-lok/hub / To venous access device

2. Containing and disposing of the used patch protect others from contact with the active substance still on the patch.

6. Washing and drying the skin after removing a used patch eliminate lingering medication from the skin and minimize the risk of overdose.

5. Applying a patch to a different surface of the skin avoids irritation to a surface that is used excessively.

4. Writing the date, time, and your initials on the patch allows for accountability and helps minimize the risk of a medication error.

41. 1. **Reducing the size of a tablet and mixing it with a food the consistency of applesauce facilitate ingestion and minimize the risk of aspiration. The thickness of applesauce is easier to control in the mouth than water for a person who has difficulty swallowing.**

2. Hyperextending the neck when swallowing facilitates entry of the substance ingested into the trachea; this action is unsafe. Slightly flexing, not hyperextending, the neck helps to open the esophagus and bypass the trachea when swallowing.

3. **Giving fluid before, during, and after medication administration lubricates the oral cavity and facilitates movement of medication toward the esophagus and stomach.**

4. **Stroking under the chin over the larynx encourages laryngeal elevation, which facilitates swallowing.**

5. A straw deposits fluid in the back of the mouth and does not allow time for a coordinated approach to swallowing. The use of a straw increases the risk of aspiration.

42. **Solve the problem by using the following formula.**

$$\frac{\text{Total volume to be infused} \times \text{drop factor}}{\text{Total time in minutes}}$$

$$\frac{500 \text{ (total volume ordered)} \times 60 \text{ (drop factor of the IV tubing)}}{60 \text{ (minutes within an hour)} \times 10 \text{ (number of hours ordered)}}$$

$$\frac{500 \times 60 = 30,000}{60 \times 10 = 600}$$

$30,000 \div 600 = 50$ drops per minute (gtts/min)

43. 1. **Avoiding sniffing the nose drops after administration allows the medication to reach desired areas (ethmoid and sphenoid sinuses) via gravity.**

2. This position ensures that gravity will promote the flow of medication to the nasopharynx. Five minutes is the length of time the patient should remain in the supine position with the head tilted backward.

3. Pinching the nose is unnecessary and can frighten the patient, who already may be having difficulty breathing.

4. Blowing the nose should be avoided because it may remove medication from the nose.

5. Nose drops should be directed toward the midline of the ethmoid bone with the dropper held ½ inch above the nares. Holding the dropper ½ inch above the nares prevents contamination of the dropper.

44. 1. Medicated solutions are administered via drops in the ear.

2. Medicated solutions are dropped or sprayed in the nose.

3. Tablets, lozenges, and troches are administered in the mouth.

4. **Semisolid cone-shaped or oval suppositories that melt at body temperature can be inserted into the vagina.**

5. **Semisolid cone-shaped or oval suppositories that melt at body temperature can be inserted into the rectum.**

45. **Solve the problem using the "Desire Over Have" formula.**

$$\frac{\text{Desire}}{\text{Have}} \frac{37.5 \text{ mg}}{25 \text{ mg}} = \frac{x \text{ mL}}{1 \text{ mL}}$$

$25x = 37.5$
$x = 37.5 \div 25$
$x = 1.5$ mL

46. 1. **This action prevents secretions and fluid from entering and irritating the lacrimal ducts.**

2. A bulb syringe produces a flow of fluid that is forceful and difficult to control. An IV bag of solution is preferred to provide a flow of fluid by gravity that is gentle and controllable.

3. These actions provide access to the eye.
4. Medical, not surgical, asepsis is required for this procedure.
5. The patient should be placed in a sitting or back-lying position with the head tilted toward the affected eye.

47. 5. Warming the medication to room temperature minimizes discomfort when the medication enters the external ear canal.
4. The side-lying position helps to retain the drops in the external ear canal via gravity.
2. Gently pulling up and back on the pinna for an adult helps to straighten the ear canal, and this promotes the flow of drops toward the tympanic membrane.
3. Placing the drops on the side of the ear canal allows the fluid to flow down the wall of the external ear canal and avoid injury to the tympanic membrane.
1. Pressing gently on the tragus several times moves the medication along the external ear canal toward the tympanic membrane.

48. 1. Lubrication eases insertion by reducing friction, which limits tissue trauma and discomfort.
2. Warming the medication causes it to melt, making it impossible to insert. Most rectal suppositories are kept refrigerated until used.
3. Taking deep breaths relaxes the rectal sphincters.
4. Rectal suppositories should be inserted 3 inches into the rectal canal of an adult. This can be accomplished by using the full length of a lubricated, gloved index finger to place the suppository.
5. The patient should be placed in the left-lateral or left-Sims position to take advantage of the anatomical curve of the rectum and sigmoid colon.

49. Solve the problem by using the following formula.

$$\frac{\text{Total volume to be infused} \times \text{drop factor}}{\text{Total time in minutes}}$$

$$\frac{125 \text{ (ordered mL/hr)} \times 10 \text{ (drop factor of the IV tubing)}}{60 \text{ (number of minutes in 1 hour)}}$$

$125 \times 10 = 1{,}250$
$1{,}250 \div 60 = 20.8$

Because 0.8 is greater than 0.5, round the answer up to 21 drops/minute.

50. 1. Using a favorite food or liquid to mask the taste of a medication may promote a negative association with and subsequent refusal of the favorite food or liquid. This practice should be avoided.
2. Although this may be a true statement, it denies the child's dislike of the medication's unpleasant taste.
3. An ice pop just before administration may numb the taste buds and minimize the unpleasant taste of the medication.
4. A parent should not be asked to administer unpleasant tasting medication to avoid the child associating the parent with the unpleasant medication.
5. Offering the child a choice supports a sense of control. Involvement in decisions limits resistance.

51. Solve the problem using the "Desire Over Have" formula.

$$\frac{\text{Desire}}{\text{Have}} \frac{320 \text{ mg}}{160 \text{ mg}} = \frac{x \text{ mL}}{5 \text{ mL}}$$

$160x = 320 \times 5$
$160x = 1{,}600$
$x = 1{,}600 \div 160$
$x = 10 \text{ mL}$

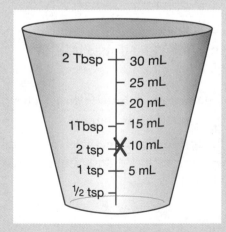

52. 1. Vitamins are a medication and should be included on a medication reconciliation form. An accurate list of all the drugs that a patient is taking (e.g., name, dose, route, and frequency) should be reconciled on admission and during transitions (e.g., transfer between units, shift reports, when new medication administration records are implemented, and at discharge). This list needs to be compared with new medications prescribed and education provided to the patient about each medication.
    2. Generally drug allergies are documented on a health history, not the drug reconciliation form.
    3. Food supplements are considered medications because they often contain ingredients that may interact with medicinal products.
    4. Over-the-counter herbs are considered medications because they contain ingredients that may unfavorably interact with medicinal products.
    5. Prescribed medications should be included on a medication reconciliation form.

53. 1. A 1½-inch needle is required to reach muscular tissue.
    2. A 22-gauge needle usually is used for an intramuscular injection; a 25-gauge needle usually is used for a subcutaneous injection.
    3. The needle should be inserted at a 90-degree angle; a 45-degree angle is used for a subcutaneous injection.
    4. Aspiration is done before instilling the medication to ensure that a blood return does not occur, which indicates that the needle is in a blood vessel.
    5. Massage promotes dispersion of the medication.

54. 2. Positioning the patient in the dorsal recumbent position provides access to the vaginal area and is a comfortable position for the patient during the procedure.
    1. Exposing only the vaginal area provides for privacy and supports dignity.

4. Lubricating the suppository and the nurse's gloved index finger facilitates insertion and limits tissue trauma.
5. Directing insertion downward and backward using the full length of the nurse's index finger follows the contour of the vaginal anatomy and ensures that the medication is inserted deep in the vaginal canal.
3. Encouraging the patient to remain in the supine position for 10 to 20 minutes after insertion allows time for the suppository to melt and to keep it in contact with vaginal tissue, which facilitates absorption.

55. 1. Not all liquids should be vigorously shaken. Only liquids that contain constituents that must be evenly distributed need to be vigorously shaken; the nurse should follow the manufacturer's directions.
    2. Measuring oral liquids in a calibrated medication cup at eye level ensures accuracy.
    3. Liquids should be poured with the label against the palm of the hand to allow a view of the label to facilitate the three checks of medication administration and prevent the liquid from dripping on and obscuring the label.
    4. Placing an opened top of a container on a surface with the inside lid facing up prevents contamination of the inside of the lid and subsequent contamination of the bottle when the lid is returned and closed.
    5. Using a needless syringe to measure an oral liquid volume less than 5 mL and transferring it to a medication cup are acceptable practices because they ensure accuracy.

56. Solve the problem using the "Desire Over Have" formula.

$$\frac{\text{Desire}}{\text{Have}} \quad \frac{2.5 \text{ mg}}{5 \text{ mg}} = \frac{x \text{ mL}}{1 \text{ mL}}$$

5x = 2.5
x = 2.5 ÷ 5
x = 0.5 mL

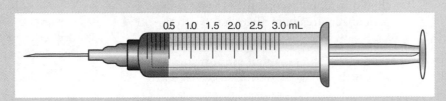

57. 1. If the tube used to administer a medication via a nasogastric tube becomes accidently disconnected during administration, the nurse can identify the approximate volume of the one medication that was lost when reporting the event to the primary health-care provider.

2. Oral medication via a nasogastric tube should be followed by 30 mL, not 100 mL, of tap water to ensure tube patency. Free water refers to larger volumes of water administered at routine intervals as per orders by a primary health-care provider.

3. Crushing crushable tablets into a fine powder and mixing it with 30 mL of warm water dissolve the medication and prevent clogging the enteral tube.

4. Shutting off nasogastric tube suctioning for 30 minutes after medication administration enhances medication absorption in the stomach.

5. This method is the most unreliable method of assessing placement of a nasogastric tube. Measuring the pH of gastric aspirate is more accurate. A low pH (1 to 5; acidic) indicates the tube probably is in the stomach; a high pH (more than 6; alkaline) indicates the tube probably is in the intestine or respiratory tract.

58. 1. Although this should be done to increase the amount of oxygen reaching body cells, it is not the priority.

2. The patient is exhibiting signs of fluid volume overload and pulmonary edema. The intravenous fluid infusion rate should be slowed to 15 to 30 mL per hour to decrease the amount of fluid entering the patient's intravenous compartment while maintaining the integrity of the intravenous access site until the rapid response team is notified and arrives.

3. Although elevating the head of the bed should be done because it will promote respirations and reduce the amount of blood returning from the lower extremities, it is not the priority.

4. Notifying the primary health-care provider should be done eventually. However, the patient requires immediate intervention.

59. 1. This is the recommended initial flow rate. It delivers a small amount of blood that allows the nurse to evaluate the patient's response to the blood. If the patient does not experience a reaction within the first 15 minutes, then the remainder of the packed red blood cells can be administered over 2 to 4 hours.

2. Vital signs should be taken every 15 to 30 minutes depending on the agency's policy; this supports early detection of a transfusion reaction or fluid overload, which enables early intervention.

3. Administering 100 mL of 0.9% sodium chloride before administering a blood transfusion is unnecessary; 0.9% sodium chloride solution is used to prime the tubing, and a small amount may be infused to assess patency of the venipuncture site.

4. Blood transfusions that extend to 4 hours are discontinued because bacterial growth may occur in the product.

5. The majority of severe transfusion reactions occur during the first 15 minutes of the procedure. Identifying a reaction early minimizes consequences. Clinical indicators of a transfusion reaction include back pain, chills, itching, or shortness of breath.

60. 2. First: The nurse should use an insulin syringe to draw up environmental air equal to the combined volume of both insulins. While keeping the NPH vial right-side up, the nurse should inject air equal to the prescribed amount of NPH into the air pocket at the top of the vial. This air prevents negative pressure inside the NPH vial when the NPH solution is withdrawn later in the procedure. Injecting air into the air pocket at the top of the vial avoids needle exposure to the NPH insulin and prevents bubbles that later can cause an inaccurate dose when the NPH insulin is withdrawn.

1. Second: The nurse should inject the remaining air into the air pocket of the regular insulin vial while the vial is right-side up. Keeping the needle in the air pocket avoids causing bubbles in the solution. Bubbles displace solution, increasing the risk of an incorrect dose. Also, the injected air prevents negative pressure inside the regular insulin vial later when withdrawing the regular insulin.

4. Third: The nurse should invert the regular insulin vial and draw up the prescribed amount of regular insulin. By drawing up the regular insulin first, it prevents contamination of the regular insulin vial with NPH insulin, which is slower acting.

3. Fourth: The nurse should reinsert the needle into the NPH vial, invert the vial, and withdraw the prescribed amount of NPH insulin. The mixed insulin is now ready to be administered.

Pharmacology

The following words include nursing/medical terminology, concepts, principles, and information relevant to content specifically addressed in the chapter or associated with topics presented in it. English dictionaries, nursing textbooks, and medical dictionaries, such as *Taber's Cyclopedic Medical Dictionary,* are resources that can be used to expand your knowledge and understanding of these words and related information.

Adverse effect
Allergic/allergy
Blood level
Controlled substance
Dependence
Drug effect:
  Adverse
  Anaphylaxis, anaphylactic
  Idiosyncratic
  Local
  Side
  Synergistic
  Systemic
  Therapeutic
  Topical
  Toxic, toxicity
Drug levels, terms related to:
  Duration
  Peak
  Onset
  Therapeutic range
  Trough
Drug names:
  Generic
  Trade
Food and Drug Administration (FDA)
Half-life
Hypersensitivity
Interaction
Prophylactic
Teratogenic
Tolerance/threshold
CLASSIFICATIONS OF DRUGS
  Analgesic
  Antacid
  Antianxiety agent
  Antiarrhythmic, antidysrhythmic
  Antibacterial
  Antibiotic
  Anticholinergic
  Anticoagulant
  Anticonvulsant/antiepileptic
  Antidepressant

Antidiabetic
Antidiarrheal
Antiemetic
Antifungal
Antihistamine
Antihypertensive
Anti-inflammatory
Antineoplastic
Antiparkinson
Antipsychotic
Antipyretic
Antiretroviral
Antitussive
Antiulcer
Bronchodilator
Cathartic
Diuretic
Emetic
Expectorant
Hypnotic
Laxative
Lipid-lowering agent
Mucolytic
Narcotic
Opioid
Skeletal muscle relaxant
Thyroid agent
Vasodilator
Vitamins and minerals
DRUG FORMS
  Caplet
  Capsule
  Elixir
  Emulsion
  Enteric-coated
  Extract
  Liniment
  Lotion
  Metered-dose inhaler (MDI)
  Ointment
  Paste
  Pill
  Powder

Solution	Tablet
Suppository	Tincture
Suspension	Transdermal
Syrup	Troche, lozenge

PHARMACOLOGY: QUESTIONS

1. Which effect on the body does the nurse understand is the reason for the need to discontinue a medication when the patient's liver function tests become elevated as a result of the medication?
   1. Side effect
   2. Toxic effect
   3. Adverse effect
   4. Synergistic effect

2. Which nursing action is important in relation to the administration of most antibiotics?
   1. Assessing for constipation
   2. Administering between meals
   3. Encouraging foods high in vitamin K
   4. Monitoring the volume of urinary output

3. A nurse is preparing to administer an injection of heparin. Which is the preferred site for this injection?
   1. Leg
   2. Arm
   3. Buttock
   4. Abdomen

4. Which concept associated with drug therapy and quality of sleep is important for a nurse to consider when planning nursing care?
   1. Aggressive pain management will reduce pain but increase insomnia.
   2. Abrupt discontinuation of hypnotic drugs can lead to withdrawal.
   3. Sedatives support restful sleep for people experiencing hypoxia.
   4. Barbiturates are the drugs of choice for insomnia.

5. A primary health-care provider prescribes a medication that is known to cause nephrotoxicity. Which element of pharmacokinetics does the nurse understand is critical when assessing this patient's response to this medication?
   1. Excretion
   2. Absorption
   3. Distribution
   4. Biotransformation

6. After administering a drug, the nurse monitors the patient for reactions. Which reaction has the **greatest** potential to be life-threatening?
   1. Toxicity
   2. Habituation
   3. Anaphylaxis
   4. Idiosyncratic

7. A nurse is assessing patients' responses to medications received. Which must the nurse know about these drugs to **best** evaluate whether the expected outcomes of the drug therapy have been achieved?
   1. Side effects
   2. Therapeutic effect
   3. Mechanism of action
   4. Chemical composition

8. A nurse is to administer a variety of analgesics. For which medication is it **most** important that the nurse know its daily dose limit?
1. Meperidine
2. Ibuprofen
3. Morphine
4. Codeine

9. A patient in pain requests the prescribed pain medication, which is an opioid. Which nursing assessment is essential before administering the opioid?
1. Blood pressure
2. Respirations
3. Temperature
4. Pulse

10. A primary health-care provider prescribes an antihypertensive medication to be administered twice a day. Which is essential for the nurse to assess before administering the antihypertensive agent?
1. Level of consciousness
2. Apical heart rate
3. Blood pressure
4. Respirations

11. Which is a common concern of the nurse when caring for patients taking drugs that depress the immune system?
1. Inability to follow the therapeutic regimen
2. Sensory perceptual alterations
3. Constipation
4. Infection

12. After the nurse administers an opioid, the patient becomes excitable. Which response should the nurse identify as being experienced by the patient?
1. Toxic
2. Allergic
3. Synergistic
4. Idiosyncratic

13. A patient experiences unrelenting neuropathic pain. Which classification of drug should the nurse anticipate will be prescribed for this patient?
1. Anticonvulsant
2. Antidepressant
3. Antihistamine
4. Anesthetic

14. A nurse is administering 10 a.m. medications to several patients on a hospital unit. The nurse anticipates that a patient with which condition is at the **greatest** risk for toxicity associated with most drugs?
1. Liver disease
2. Kidney insufficiency
3. Respiratory difficulty
4. Malabsorption syndrome

15. A nurse is discussing with a patient the variety of routes that medications can be administered. The nurse explains that medications are absorbed **most** efficiently through which route?
1. Orally
2. Rectally
3. Intravenously
4. Intramuscularly

16. A patient has been taking an antianxiety medication for a prolonged period of time. Which information is helpful to the nurse when attempting to determine if the patient has developed a physiological dependence on the drug?
    1. Degree of tolerance
    2. Strength of the dose
    3. Perceived need by the patient
    4. Time it takes to achieve the therapeutic effect

17. A patient has a prescription for an antiemetic as an adjunct to antineoplastic therapy. Which dosing schedule should the nurse anticipate that the primary health-care provider will prescribe?
    1. After the patient vomits
    2. Thirty minutes before meals
    3. When the patient reports nausea
    4. Four and eight hours after the initial dose

18. After the ingestion of a new medication the patient develops a rash, urticaria, and pruritus. Which should the nurse conclude that the patient is experiencing?
    1. Allergic response
    2. Idiosyncratic effect
    3. Anaphylactic reaction
    4. Synergistic interaction

19. A patient is taking hydrochlorothiazide (HCTZ) once a day. Which fruit should the nurse encourage the patient to eat because it contains the **highest** amount of potassium?
    1. Plum
    2. Orange
    3. Banana
    4. Tangerine

20. A nurse must administer a medication that is a digitalis derivative. Which nursing assessment is essential before administering this medication?
    1. Pulse rate
    2. Blood pressure
    3. Respiratory rate
    4. Level of consciousness

21. A nurse teaches a patient to use a metered-dose inhaler (MDI). The patient asks, "Why do I need this instead of just taking a pill?" Which should the nurse respond is the primary purpose of a metered-dose inhaler?
    1. "It provides you with a sense of control."
    2. "It directs the medication into your upper respiratory tract."
    3. "It delivers medication via positive pressure into your lungs."
    4. "It releases the medication in small particles that you can inhale deeply."

22. Patients with multiple health problems often go to a variety of medical specialists. Which response to medication occurs more frequently in patients who go to several medical specialists?
    1. Interactions
    2. Habituation
    3. Tolerance
    4. Allergies

23. A nurse is responsible for administering medications via various routes to a group of patients. Which route of administration is the **most** effective way to achieve and maintain a drug's therapeutic level?
    1. IV push
    2. Sublingual route
    3. Oral administration
    4. Large-volume infusion

24. A nurse is administering a variety of medications via the following routes. Which of these routes is the **fastest** acting?
    1. Buccal
    2. Transdermal
    3. Subcutaneous
    4. Intramuscular

25. A patient asks the nurse why a lipid-lowering drug was prescribed. Before formulating a response, which should the nurse consider is the reason why primary health-care providers generally prescribe a hyperlipidemic drug?
    1. After failure of diet therapy
    2. For those who are unable to exercise
    3. For patients older than 60 years of age
    4. After 2 consecutive months of elevated serum lipid levels

26. A nurse administers a prescribed antiemetic. A reduction in which clinical manifestation indicates that the patient is experiencing a therapeutic response?
    1. Fever
    2. Anxiety
    3. Vomiting
    4. Coughing

27. A nurse is contrasting prefilled, disposable unit-dose intramuscular drug cartridges versus multidose vials. Which does the nurse conclude is the **primary** purpose of unit-dose cartridges?
    1. Ensure that the appropriate-length needle is attached.
    2. Reduce the incidence of drug interactions.
    3. Limit preparation time in emergencies.
    4. Ensure purity of the drugs.

28. Which human response does the nurse understand is prevented by weaning a patient from a long-term prescribed corticosteroid rather than experiencing a sudden discontinuance of the corticosteroid?
    1. Shock
    2. Seizures
    3. Bleeding
    4. Hypothermia

29. The nurse is administering an antihypertensive medication to a patient. Which clinical manifestation should the nurse identify as an excessive response to the antihypertensive agent?
    1. Respirations of 24 breaths per minute
    2. Heart rate of 60 beats per minute
    3. Blood pressure of 80/60 mm Hg
    4. Oral temperature of 98°F

30. A patient has a prescription for sertraline, an antidepressant. Which is **most** important for the nurse to do?
    1. Monitor the patient for suicidal tendencies.
    2. Advise the patient to engage in psychotherapy.
    3. Teach the patient to limit alcohol intake to one drink per day.
    4. Encourage the patient to diet because weight gain is common with this drug.

31. A patient is receiving an antipyretic agent. Which patient assessment should be performed to determine if the medication has achieved a therapeutic response?
    1. Urine output
    2. Pain tolerance
    3. Respiratory rate
    4. Body temperature

32. Which is the **most** important action by the nurse before instituting patient-controlled analgesia (PCA) via a continuous intravenous route for the relief of pain?
    1. Identify the patient's pain tolerance.
    2. Assess the patient's respiratory status.
    3. Determine the patient's pain threshold.
    4. Monitor the patient's analgesic blood levels.

33. Identify the drug classifications that are correctly associated with their expected therapeutic outcomes. **Select all that apply.**
    1. _____Bronchodilators: relieve dyspnea
    2. _____Diuretics: increase urinary output
    3. _____Antitussives: prevent or relieve coughing
    4. _____Expectorants: decrease mucus production
    5. _____Antiemetics: prevent or treat nausea and vomiting

34. A primary health-care provider prescribes aluminum hydroxide/magnesium hydroxide tablets, an antacid agent, for a patient with symptoms of indigestion. Which are the important things the nurse should teach this patient to do? **Select all that apply.**
    1. _____Document the characteristics of gastric discomfort in a log.
    2. _____Notify the health team if coffee-ground vomitus occurs.
    3. _____Monitor for the presence of diarrhea.
    4. _____Take the drug an hour before meals.
    5. _____Swallow the tablets whole.

35. A nurse in the hospital is evaluating patient responses to medications. Which classifications of drugs commonly precipitate diarrhea? **Select all that apply.**
    1. _____Sedatives
    2. _____Narcotics
    3. _____Laxatives
    4. _____Antibiotics
    5. _____Antiemetics

36. A public health nurse is planning a health class about herbal remedies for a group of older adults at the community center. Which information about herbal remedies should the nurse include in the class? **Select all that apply.**
    1. _____Can cause serious herbal-to-drug interactions with prescribed medications
    2. _____Required to be labeled with information about their structure
    3. _____Approved by the Food and Drug Administration
    4. _____Natural because they are botanical in origin
    5. _____Safe because they are organic

37. A primary health-care provider tells a patient who is receiving an antibiotic that several blood specimens will be taken to evaluate the effectiveness of the antibiotic therapy. The patient asks the nurse, "Why do these tests have to be done?" Which information included in a response by the nurse answers this patient's question? **Select all that apply.**
    1. _____Maintain constant drug levels in the body.
    2. _____Determine the half-life of a drug in the body.
    3. _____Identify whether the dose of the drug is adequate.
    4. _____Establish where biotransformation occurs in the body.
    5. _____Monitor the rate of absorption of the drug in the body.

38. The primary health-care provider prescribes cefaclor 1.5 g IVPB 30 minutes before surgery to prevent infection. The medication is supplied in a 10-g vial that states that after reconstitution there will be 500 mg/mL. How much solution should the nurse administer? **Record your answer using a whole number.**
    Answer: _____mL.

39. A patient with a severe upper respiratory tract infection is being treated with a bronchodilator. Which patient responses indicate that the therapeutic effect has been achieved? **Select all that apply.**
1. _____Oxygen saturation of 95%
2. _____Presence of viscous secretions
3. _____Experiencing no difficulty breathing
4. _____Exhibiting a decrease in respiratory excursion
5. _____Decrease in bronchovesicular breath sounds on auscultation

40. A patient admits to taking magnesium hydroxide for its laxative effect several times a week. Which information should the nurse teach the patient about this medication? **Select all that apply.**
1. _____It can cause dependence and dehydration if taken for more than 2 weeks.
2. _____It can cause an accumulation of sodium and potassium ions in the body.
3. _____It should be discontinued if you experience watery diarrhea.
4. _____It should be accompanied by 2 to 3 glasses of fluid.
5. _____It should be taken at bedtime.

41. While the nurse is applying a transdermal patch, the patient asks the nurse, "Why can't I just take a pill?" Which should the nurse explain are the advantages of administering a medication via a transdermal patch? **Select all that apply.**
1. _____"It limits allergic responses."
2. _____"It prevents drug interactions."
3. _____"It delivers the drug over a period of time."
4. _____"It bypasses the harsh acidic digestive system."
5. _____"It provides a local rather than a systemic effect."

42. A patient has a prescription for diphenoxylate/atropine, an antidiarrheal agent. Which should the nurse teach the patient about this medication? **Select all that apply.**
1. _____Report the occurrence of decreased urination, muscle cramps, weakness, or fainting.
2. _____Inform the primary health-care provider if diarrhea persists for more than 2 days.
3. _____Be alert to the fact that the medication may cause hyperactivity.
4. _____Limit fluid intake to 2,000 mL/day.
5. _____Avoid crushing the tablets.

43. A primary health-care provider prescribes famotidine 20 mg PO bid to inhibit gastric acid secretion for a patient reporting epigastric discomfort. What should the nurse do when caring for this patient? **Select all that apply.**
1. _____Assess for constipation.
2. _____Evaluate the oral cavity for stomatitis.
3. _____Check for a decreased serum creatinine.
4. _____Monitor a complete blood count with differential.
5. _____Encourage the intake of the full course of therapy as prescribed.

44. A primary health-care provider prescribes zolpidem, an extended-release tablet, 12.5 mg PO at hour of sleep for a patient experiencing insomnia. What is important for the nurse to teach the patient about this medication? **Select all that apply.**
1. _____Avoid drinking alcohol.
2. _____Swallow the tablet whole.
3. _____Take it with food for best results.
4. _____Repeat the dose if not asleep in 3 hours.
5. _____Take it when you are able to stay in bed for at least 6 hours.

45. Place the elements of pharmacokinetics in order from the first step to the last step as a medication moves from its entry to its exit from the body.
1. Excretion
2. Absorption
3. Distribution
4. Biotransformation
Answer: _____

46. A patient at the outpatient clinic reports increasing joint pain caused by arthritis associated with the aging process. The primary health-care provider prescribes ibuprofen 600 mg PO qid for joint pain. What should the nurse teach the patient about this medication? **Select all that apply.**
1. _____Take it with a full glass of water.
2. _____Do not exceed 4,000 mg of this drug daily.
3. _____Double a dose if a previous dose is forgotten.
4. _____Report the intake of the drug if dental treatment or surgery is necessary.
5. _____Use an oatmeal bath for a mild skin rash because it is a common side effect.

47. A primary health-care provider prescribes nitrofurantoin 100 mg PO every 6 hours for a patient who reports signs and symptoms of a urinary tract infection. What should the nurse teach the patient to do when taking nitrofurantoin? **Select all that apply**.
1. _____Take this drug on an empty stomach.
2. _____Use a straw to take the medication and rinse the mouth afterward.
3. _____Note that urine will be reddish/orange in color but do not be alarmed.
4. _____Report diarrhea, abdominal cramping, fever, and bloody stools if they occur.
5. _____Inform the primary health-care provider if signs and symptoms do not resolve within a week of therapy.

48. An active older adult female patient reports episodes of urinary urgency and frequency, urge incontinence, and bladder spasms. The primary health-care provider diagnoses an overactive bladder and prescribes oxybutynin 2.5 mg PO tid. What should the nurse teach this patient? **Select all that apply.**
1. _____Catheterize yourself periodically after urinating to determine the presence of residual urine.
2. _____Sedation and weakness may occur when taking this medication.
3. _____Refrain from activities requiring alertness when drowsy.
4. _____Report an inability to pass urine if it should occur.
5. _____Avoid strenuous activity in a warm environment.

49. A nurse is caring for a patient who is receiving 2 types of analgesics. Which effects does the nurse understand occur when these medications are administered together? **Select all that apply.**
1. _____Curative
2. _____Palliative
3. _____Synergistic
4. _____Potentiation
5. _____Antagonistic

50. A primary health-care provider prescribes the corticosteroid budesonide 180 mcg, 2 inhalations, bid, along with a bronchodilator. What should the nurse teach the patient about these medications? **Select all that apply.**
1. _____"Let the health team know if you have a lactose intolerance."
2. _____"Take your budesonide first and the bronchodilator 5 minutes later."
3. _____"You can expect an improvement in your symptoms within 2 weeks of use."
4. _____"Use tap water to rinse and spit after each time you use your budesonide inhaler."
5. _____"If you experience an acute bronchospasm between doses, you can take an additional dose of budesonide."

51. Dextromethorphan 30 mg and guaifenesin 600 mg PO every 4 hours prn is prescribed for a patient with a cough and respiratory tract infection. What should the nurse teach the patient who is taking this medication? **Select all that apply.**
    1. _____ "Increase your fluid intake to a minimum of 2 quarts of fluid daily."
    2. _____ "Report if signs and symptoms do not improve after 2 weeks of therapy."
    3. _____ "Talk with the primary health-care provider before taking another over-the-counter cold remedy."
    4. _____ "Avoid diet and caffeine pills or stimulants prescribed for attention deficit hyperactivity disorder."
    5. _____ "Tell your primary health-care provider if severe dizziness, anxiety, confusion, or slow or shallow breathing occur.

52. Which information documented in the clinical record of an adult male patient should the nurse consider problematic?
    1. Calcium: 5.4 mEq/L
    2. Temperature: 97.8°F
    3. Docusate sodium: 1,000 mg, PO, daily
    4. Respirations: 14 breaths per minute, unlabored

PATIENT'S CLINICAL RECORD

Laboratory Results
Calcium: 5.4 mEq/L
Sodium: 137 mEq/L
Potassium: 4.2 mEq/L

Physical Assessment
Temperature (oral): 97.8°F
Pulse: 62 beats per minute
Respirations: 14 breaths per minute, unlabored
Blood pressure: 128/84 mm Hg

Medication Reconciliation Form
Aspirin 81 mg, PO, daily
Docusate sodium 1,000 mg, PO, daily
Alprazolam 2 mg, PO, qid

---

53. A primary health-care provider prescribes simvastatin 20 mg PO daily, a lipid lowering agent for a patient with an elevated cholesterol level. What should the nurse teach the patient receiving this medication? **Select all that apply.**
    1. _____ Exchange vegetable oils containing monounsaturated fatty acids with vegetable oils containing polyunsaturated fatty acids.
    2. _____ Report the presence of muscle aches, pains, stiffness, or weakness to the primary health-care provider immediately.
    3. _____ Consume 2 to 3 servings of fish high in omega-3 fatty acids weekly.
    4. _____ Monitor for is cola-colored urine or if output is reduced or absent.
    5. _____ Take the medication in the morning.

54. A primary health-care provider prescribes esomeprazole 20 mg PO daily for a patient reporting gastroesophageal reflux at night. What should the nurse teach the patient receiving this medication? **Select all that apply.**
    1. _____ Take the drug one hour after meals.
    2. _____ Do not to crush or chew the medication.
    3. _____ Taking antacids and esomeprazole concurrently is acceptable.
    4. _____ Avoid nonsteroidal anti-inflammatory drugs while on this medication.
    5. _____ Mix the capsule contents with applesauce if having difficulty swallowing.

55. A primary health-care provider prescribes acetylsalicylic acid (aspirin) for a patient experiencing body aches and fever associated with an upper respiratory tract infection. Which nontherapeutic responses related to acetylsalicylic acid should the nurse teach the patient to report to the primary health-care provider? **Select all that apply.**
    1. _____Rash
    2. _____Tinnitus
    3. _____Bleeding
    4. _____Dizziness
    5. _____Constipation

56. A nurse is caring for a patient receiving morphine for intractable pain associated with cancer. For what nontherapeutic effects should the nurse monitor the patient? **Select all that apply.**
    1. _____Sedation
    2. _____Confusion
    3. _____Tachypnea
    4. _____Constipation
    5. _____Hypertension

57. Which words are associated with the medication levothyroxine. **Select all that apply.**
    1. _____Trade
    2. _____Generic
    3. _____Curative
    4. _____Antidote
    5. _____Substitutive

58. A primary health-care provider prescribes a medication that must maintain effective blood concentrations of the drug to be effective. Which information is essential for the nurse to know about this medication to ensure its effectiveness? **Select all that apply.**
    1. _____Therapeutic range
    2. _____Trough level
    3. _____Peak level
    4. _____Half-life
    5. _____Onset

59. A primary health-care provider prescribes medication for a hospitalized older adult patient with a diagnosis of the flu, an oral candida infection, and a history of hypothyroidism and moderate dementia. Which prescriptions should the nurse discuss with the primary health-care provider before administering medications? **Select all that apply.**
    1. _____Nystatin 1 lozenge 200,000 units, via buccal cavity, four times a day for 14 days
    2. _____Acetaminophen 1,000 mg, PO, every 6 hours prn for headache
    3. _____Levothyroxine 100 mcg PO once a day
    4. _____Simvastatin 20 mg PO hour of sleep
    5. _____Docusate sodium 100 mg PO bid

60. Which type of insulin is reflected by the illustration regarding its length of action?
    1. Glargine
    2. Regular
    3. Lispro
    4. NPH

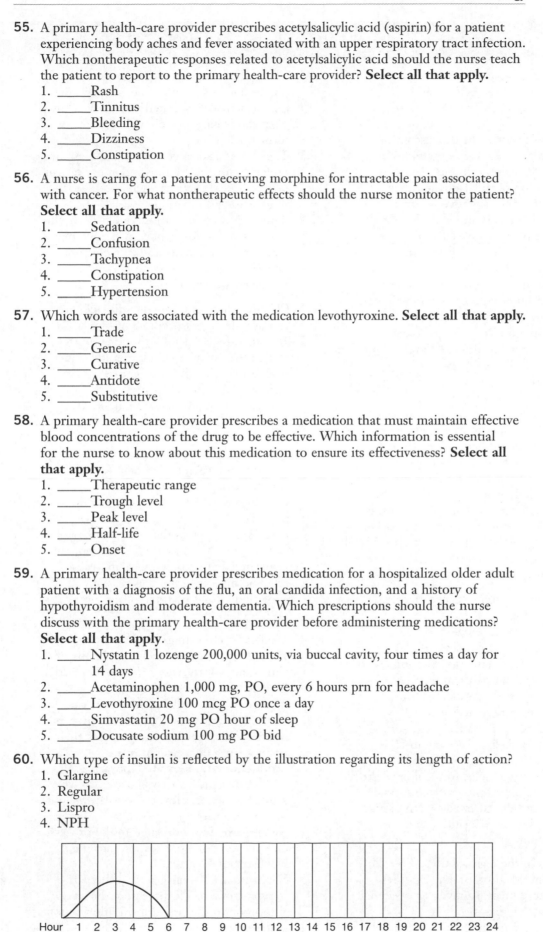

Hour 1 2 3 4 5 6 7 8 9 10 11 12 13 14 15 16 17 18 19 20 21 22 23 24

1. 1. A side effect is an unintended response that generally is predictable and well tolerated. It usually does not require discontinuation of the drug because the drug's benefit outweighs the discomfort. Dry mouth and nausea are examples of side effects that do not require discontinuation of the drug, and they usually respond to palliative interventions.

2. **Liver impairment is an example of a toxic effect that requires discontinuation of a medication. Toxic effects are dangerous and harmful responses to a medication that are often predictable. When a patient exhibits a toxic effect to a medication, the nurse should hold the medication and notify the primary health-care provider immediately. The only time holding a dose would not apply is if the drug dose must be tapered to discontinue the drug safely.**

3. An adverse effect is an unintended, usually unpredictable response to a medication that is more severe than a side effect. When an adverse effect occurs, the medication may or may not be discontinued, depending on its severity.

4. A synergistic effect does not apply in this situation. A synergistic effect occurs when the combined effect of two medications is greater than when the effects of each are just added together.

2. 1. Most antibiotics tend to cause diarrhea, not constipation.

2. **Food often interferes with the dissolution and absorption of antibiotics and delays their action. Also, food can combine with molecules of certain drugs and can change their molecular structure and ultimately inhibit or prevent their absorption.**

3. Yogurt, not foods high in vitamin K, is encouraged for a patient receiving antibiotics. Yogurt helps to recolonize the endogenous flora of the gastrointestinal tract that can be eradicated by antibiotics.

4. Antibiotics do not affect the volume of urinary output.

3. 1. The tissues in the legs are not preferred for the administration of heparin (Hep-Lock) because muscle activity associated with walking increases the risk of hematoma formation.

2. The tissues in the arms are not preferred for the administration of heparin because muscle activity associated with movement of the arms increases the risk of hematoma formation.

3. The tissues associated with walking are not preferred for the administration of heparin because muscle activity increases the risk of hematoma formation.

4. **The abdomen is a preferred site for the administration of heparin because it lacks major muscles and muscle activity. This site has the least risk for hematoma formation.**

4. 1. Effective pain management will facilitate rest and sleep, not promote insomnia.

2. **Barbiturate sedative-hypnotics depress the central nervous system and when withdrawn abruptly can cause withdrawal symptoms such as restlessness, tremors, weakness, and insomnia. Long-term use should be tapered by 25% to 30% weekly.**

3. Sedatives, central nervous system depressants, are not advocated for patients with hypoxia because they depress respirations, which may exacerbate the hypoxia.

4. Barbiturates depress the central nervous system, alter REM and NREM sleep, result in daytime drowsiness, and cause rebound insomnia. For this reason, antianxiety drugs or tranquilizers are preferred.

5. 1. **Medication elimination occurs primarily via urine produced by the nephrons of the kidneys (*excretion*). If a medication is toxic to nephrons, damage to nephrons can result. A drug that can cause damage to nephrons is known as nephrotoxic. A nurse must assess the patient for a decrease in urine production and identify laboratory results that indicate impairment of the kidneys, such as elevated creatinine and blood urea nitrogen levels.**

2. Nephrotoxicity is unrelated to the process of movement of a medication into the bloodstream (*absorption*).

3. Nephrotoxicity is unrelated to the transport of a medication from the site of absorption to the site of medication action (*distribution*).

4. Nephrotoxicity is unrelated to the process of biotransformation. Biotransformation is the conversion of a medication to a less active form (*detoxification*) in preparation for excretion.

6. 1. Medication toxicity results from excessive amounts of the drug in the body because of overdosage or impaired metabolism or excretion. Most drug toxicity that occurs immediately after administration is preventable through accurate prescribing and administering of the medication. Toxicity that occurs through the cumulative effect occurs over time and, if recognized early, is not life-threatening.
   2. Drug habituation is a mild form of psychological dependence that occurs over time and is not life-threatening.
   3. **Anaphylaxis, a severe allergic reaction, requires immediate intervention (e.g., epinephrine, IV fluids, corticosteroids, and antihistamines) because it can be fatal.**
   4. An idiosyncratic effect is an unexpected, individualized response to a drug. The response can be an underresponse or an overresponse, or it can cause unpredictable, unexplainable symptoms. Usually, it is not life-threatening.

7. 1. Side effects are unintended effects other than the therapeutic effect.
   2. **Therapeutic effects are the desired, intended effects of the drug. They are the reason for which the drug is prescribed.**
   3. Although it is important to know the mechanism of action of a drug (pharmacodynamics), this knowledge is not as important as knowing the physical, mental, behavioral, or emotional responses indicating that a drug is having the desired impact on the patient.
   4. Although it is important to know the chemical composition of a drug, this is not as significant as knowing the desired response to the medication.

8. 1. When administered to an adult under the supervision of a primary health-care provider, meperidine may exceed the recommended oral dosage of 1,200 mg/day or the IV dose of 15 to 35 mg/hr.
   2. **In adults, ibuprofen should not exceed 3,600 mg/day when used as an anti-inflammatory agent or 1,200 mg/day when used as an analgesic or**

antipyretic. Higher doses do not increase effectiveness and may cause major gastrointestinal and central nervous system adverse effects. Ibuprofen is an over-the-counter medication which increases the risk for an overdose as a result of self-medication by an uninformed consumer.
   3. Recommended daily doses for morphine vary based on weight of the patient and route of administration. Recommended dosages routinely are exceeded in pain management of patients with chronic, intractable (malignant) pain when prescribed by a primary health-care provider.
   4. When administered to an adult under the supervision of a primary health-care provider, codeine may exceed the recommended daily dosage of 120 mg.

9. 1. An opioid can cause the side effect of hypotension. However, assessment of blood pressure is not as essential as another vital sign.
   2. **An opioid depresses the respiratory center in the medulla, which results in a decrease in the rate and depth of respirations. When a patient's respiratory rate is less than 10 breaths per minute the drug should be withheld and the primary health-care provider notified.**
   3. The side effects and adverse reactions to opioids do not include alterations in temperature.
   4. An opioid analgesic can cause the side effect of bradycardia, so the pulse should be assessed before administration. However, assessment of heart rate is not as essential as another vital sign.

10. 1. This is unnecessary because antihypertensives do not alter the level of consciousness.
   2. The apical heart rate should be assessed before administering cardiac glycosides and antidysrhythmics, not antihypertensives.
   3. **Antihypertensives, such as beta-adrenergic blockers, calcium channel blockers, vasodilators, and angiotensin-converting enzyme (ACE) inhibitors, all act to reduce blood pressure; therefore, the blood pressure should be obtained before and monitored after administration.**

4. Respirations and breath sounds should be assessed before administering bronchodilators and expectorants, not antihypertensive agents.

11. 1. Although this is a concern for any patient who must follow a pharmacological regimen, it is not the most common risk associated with drugs that suppress the immune system.
    2. Medications that depress the immune system usually do not cause sensory problems. Although some antineoplastic drugs can cause peripheral neuropathy, this response is not as common as gastrointestinal, hematological, integumentary, and immune system adverse effects.
    3. Medications that depress the immune system are more likely to cause gastrointestinal disturbances such as anorexia, nausea, vomiting, and diarrhea, not constipation.
    4. **Medications that suppress the immune system, such as antineoplastics (destroy stem cells that are precursors to white blood cells), corticosteroids (suppress function and numbers of eosinophils and monocytes), and antibiotics (destroy body flora), lower the body's ability to fight microorganisms that can cause infection.**

12. 1. Toxicity is manifested by sedation, respiratory depression, and coma. The antidote naloxone may be necessary.
    2. Allergic responses frequently manifest as a rash, urticaria, and pruritus.
    3. A synergistic response associated with an opioid is reflected by a lowered level of consciousness and sedation.
    4. **Excitability is an unexpected, unexplainable response to an opioid. Opioids are central nervous system depressants that relieve pain and promote sedation, not cause excitability.**

13. 1. Anticonvulsants do not relieve pain. Anticonvulsants depress abnormal neuronal discharges in the central nervous system and limit or prevent seizures.
    2. **Antidepressants, particularly amitriptyline, potentiate the effects of opioids and have innate analgesic properties.**
    3. Antihistamines do not relieve pain. Antihistamines block the effects of histamine at the H_1 receptor.

4. Although anesthetics do block pain, they generally are not used to relieve neuropathic pain. General anesthetics depress the central nervous system sufficiently to allow pain-free invasive procedures (e.g., surgery), and local anesthetics produce brief episodes of decreased nerve transmission when general anesthesia is not warranted.

14. 1. **Drug-metabolizing enzymes in the liver detoxify drugs to a less active form (biotransformation). With liver dysfunction, biotransformation is impaired and drugs accumulate, ultimately reaching toxic levels.**
    2. Although decreased kidney function will adversely affect drug excretion, it does not pose the greatest risk for toxicity.
    3. Most drugs are degraded in the liver and excreted through the kidneys, not the lungs.
    4. Most drugs are degraded in the liver and excreted through the kidneys, not the intestines.

15. 1. Food, fluid, and gastric acidity can influence the dissolution and absorption of medications.
    2. The absorption of rectal medications is influenced by the presence of fecal material and is unpredictable.
    3. **Intravenous medications enter the bloodstream directly by way of a vein. Intravenous administration offers the quickest rate of absorption, and it is within the circulatory system for easy distribution.**
    4. The intramuscular route is not the most efficient route for absorption of medication.

16. 1. Tolerance is not a reliable indicator of dependence. Tolerance to a drug has occurred when increasing amounts of the drug must be administered to achieve the therapeutic effect.
    2. Strength of a dose is not a reliable indicator of dependence. Factors such as age, weight, gender, and drug tolerance also influence the strength of a dose.
    3. **Drug dependence, a form of drug abuse, occurs when a person has an emotional reliance on a drug because there is a craving for the effect or response that the drug produces.**
    4. The length of time a drug takes to achieve its therapeutic effect is unrelated to the

development of physiological dependence on the drug.

17. 1. This is too late. When an antiemetic is administered as an adjunctive to chemotherapy, vomiting should not occur.
2. This is inappropriate. When an antiemetic is given prophylactically for a chemotherapeutic regimen, it is administered in relation to when the chemotherapeutic agent is given, not meals.
3. This is too late. Prophylactic administration of an antiemetic will prevent nausea and vomiting.
4. **Antiemetics should be administered 30 minutes before initiation of chemotherapy and then 4 and 8 hours after the initial dose of the antiemetic.**

18. 1. **A drug allergy is an immunological response to a drug. In addition to integumentary responses, the patient may develop angioedema, rhinitis, lacrimal tearing, nausea, vomiting, wheezing, dyspnea, and diarrhea.**
2. An idiosyncratic effect is an unexpected, individualized response to a drug. The response can be an underresponse or an overresponse, or it may cause unpredictable, unexplainable signs or symptoms.
3. The early signs of anaphylaxis are shortness of breath, acute hypotension, and tachycardia.
4. When a drug interaction occurs where the action of one or both drugs is potentiated, it is called a synergistic effect.

19. 1. One medium-size plum contains approximately 114 mg of potassium.
2. One medium-size orange contains approximately 237 mg of potassium.
3. **One medium-size banana contains approximately 450 mg of potassium. Hydrochlorothiazide (HCTZ), by its action in the distal convoluted tubule, promotes the excretion of potassium. Potassium must be replenished because of its vital role in the sodium-potassium pump.**
4. One medium-size tangerine contains approximately 132 mg of potassium.

20. 1. **A medication that is a digitalis derivative such as digoxin decreases conduction through the sinoatrial (SA) and atrioventricular (AV) nodes and**
prolongs the refractory period of the AV node, resulting in a slowing of the heart rate (negative chronotropic effect). When the heart rate is less than preset parameters (e.g., 60 beats per minute) or higher than preset parameters (e.g., 100 beats per minute), the medication should be held and a serum digoxin level assessed for exceeding its therapeutic range of 0.5 to 2 ng/mL. It is important to remember that the heart rate may exceed a rate of 100 beats per minute with toxicity.
2. Dysrhythmias, not alterations in blood pressure, are cardiovascular signs of toxicity.
3. This assessment is unnecessary because a change in respiratory status is not a symptom of toxicity.
4. Toxicity may cause confusion and disorientation, not an altered level of consciousness.

21. 1. Although this may be a secondary benefit for some patients, it is not the reason for using a metered-dose inhaler (MDI).
2. The medication from an MDI is delivered to the lungs, which comprise the lower, not upper, respiratory tract.
3. Although an MDI delivers the medication via pressure to the patient's mouth, it is the act of the patient's inhalation that delivers the medication to its site of action.
4. **An MDI aerosolizes the medication so that the suspension of microscopic liquid droplets can be inhaled deep into the lung.**

22. 1. **A drug interaction occurs when one drug affects the action of another drug. The effect of one or both drugs increases, decreases, or is negated. The risk for drug interactions increases when multiple drugs are prescribed by several primary health-care providers with inadequate communication among the providers.**
2. Drug habituation is a mild form of psychological dependence.
3. Tolerance occurs when a patient develops a decreased response to a medication and therefore requires an increased dose to achieve the therapeutic response.
4. An allergic reaction results from an immunological response to a medication to which the patient has been sensitized.

23. 1. An IV push (bolus) is the administration of a drug directly into the systemic circulation. Usually, it is administered as a single dose in an emergency. It achieves the desired level quickly but does not maintain it.

2. The sublingual route is used intermittently and only when necessary. It is not used to maintain constant therapeutic drug levels.

3. Although the oral route is the safest, easiest, and most desirable way to administer medications, there are fluctuations in serum blood levels because the medication is administered intermittently one or more times throughout the day.

4. **With a large-volume infusion, a drug is added to an IV container (usually 250 mL, 500 mL, or 1,000 mL), and the resulting solution is administered over time. This approach maintains a constant serum drug level.**

24. 1. Medications administered via the buccal route dissolve between the teeth and gums, mix with saliva, and are swallowed. This route has a slow onset of action.

2. The transdermal route is noted for its ability to sustain the absorption of medication, not because it produces a rapid response. The absorption of medications administered via the transdermal route is influenced by the condition of the skin, the presence of interstitial fluid, and the adequacy of circulation to the area.

3. The subcutaneous route is faster-acting than some routes because it is a parenteral route but slower-acting than other parenteral routes because subcutaneous tissue does not have a large blood supply.

4. **Of the options offered, the intramuscular route is the fastest-acting route because muscles have a large vascular network that ensures rapid absorption into the bloodstream.**

25. 1. **Generally, conservative management of hyperlipidemia through dietary modifications and exercise is attempted before resorting to a medication. Lipid-lowering agents have side effects and adverse effects and may interact with other drugs.**

2. Exercise is only one factor that influences the patient's lipid status. Factors such as diet, cigarette smoking, stress, concurrent diseases, and family history are additional factors that must be considered when a pharmacological regimen is prescribed.

3. Lipid-lowering agents are prescribed for patients who are older than 60 years old only when necessary, not because they are older than 60 years old.

4. Only people with chronically elevated lipid levels receive antilipidemics because of their significant side effects. Lifestyle modifications are attempted first.

26. 1. Antipyretics, not antiemetics, reduce fever.
2. Anxiolytics, not antiemetics, reduce anxiety.
3. **Antiemetics block the emetogenic receptors to prevent or treat nausea or vomiting.**
4. Antitussives, not antiemetics, reduce the frequency and intensity of coughing.

27. 1. Although generally this is true, there are times the attached needle is inappropriate for a particular patient and the nurse must change the needle or transfer the medication into a standard syringe.

2. Drug interactions can still occur with prefilled, disposable cartridges because the drug within the cartridge may alter or be altered by the concurrent presence of another medication in the patient's body.

3. Although prefilled cartridges are convenient in an emergency, it is not the primary purpose of having prefilled cartridges.

4. **Single-dose cartridges prepared by a medication manufacturer or pharmacy ensure the purity of the drug. Multiple-dose vials can be contaminated by rubber debris and microorganisms.**

28. 1. **Exogenous glucocorticoids cause adrenal suppression. When exogenous corticosteroids are withdrawn abruptly, the adrenal glands are unable to produce adequate amounts of glucocorticoids, thus causing acute adrenal insufficiency and shock.**

2. Acute adrenal insufficiency may cause dizziness and syncope, not seizures.

3. Acute adrenal insufficiency is unrelated to hemorrhage.

4. Acute adrenal insufficiency may cause hyperthermia, not hypothermia.

29. 1. Antihypertensive agents do not directly affect respirations. Respirations may return to the expected range of 12 to

20 breaths per minute when cardiac output improves.

2. This heart rate is within the expected range of 60 to 100 beats per minute.

3. **The acceptable range for the systolic pressure is 90 to less than 120 mm Hg. This patient's systolic reading is outside the expected range, which is an excessive decrease when receiving an antihypertensive agent.**

4. Antihypertensive agents do not influence body temperature. Expected adult oral temperatures range between 97.5°F and 99.5°F.

30. 1. **When depression lifts during the early stages of antidepressant therapy, the individual has renewed energy that may support the implementation of suicidal ideation. Patient safety is the priority.**

2. Although this should be done, it is not the priority.

3. Alcohol should be avoided because it potentiates the central nervous system depressive effects of sertraline.

4. A person will more likely lose, not gain, weight when taking sertraline because its side effects include anorexia, nausea, and vomiting.

31. 1. Intake and output are monitored when a patient is taking a diuretic, not an antipyretic.

2. Pain tolerance is monitored when a patient is taking an analgesic, not an antipyretic.

3. Respirations are monitored when a patient is taking a central nervous system depressant or bronchodilator, not an antipyretic.

4. **Antipyretics lower fever by affecting thermoregulation in the central nervous system and/or inhibiting the action of prostaglandins peripherally.**

32. 1. Although this may be done, it is not the priority. Pain tolerance is the highest intensity of pain that the person is willing to endure.

2. **Analgesics depress the central nervous system; therefore, the respiratory status must be monitored before and routinely throughout administration for signs of respiratory depression.**

3. Although this may be done, it is not the priority. Pain threshold is the amount of pain stimulation a person requires before pain is felt.

4. Monitoring analgesic blood levels is unnecessary.

33. 1. **Bronchodilators relax smooth muscles of the bronchi and bronchioles, thus increasing the diameter of their lumens (bronchodilation) and resulting in a decrease in airway resistance.**

2. **Diuretics increase the urinary excretion of water and electrolytes such as sodium, potassium, calcium, and chloride.**

3. **Antitussives prevent or relieve coughing by depressing the cough center in the medulla.**

4. Expectorants increase, not decrease, the flow of respiratory secretions; they decrease the viscosity of secretions and promote the coughing up and removal of mucus from the lungs.

5. **Antiemetics, depending on the agent (e.g., antihistamines, anticholinergics, neuroleptic agents, prokinetic agents, serotonin antagonists, and substance P neurokinin-1 receptor antagonist), act in a variety of ways to prevent, limit, or treat nausea and vomiting.**

34. 1. **A log will help evaluate the patient's response to the aluminum and magnesium hydroxide regimen. Characteristics include location, duration, intensity, and description of the discomfort.**

2. **These are symptoms of gastric bleeding, and the primary health-care provider should be notified immediately. Enzymes act on blood to produce coffee-ground emesis and tarry stools.**

3. **The magnesium in the aluminum and magnesium hydroxide preparation can cause diarrhea in some people.**

4. This medication should be taken 1 to 3 hours after a meal and at bedtime to neutralize gastric acid.

5. This medication should be thoroughly chewed and taken with at least a half glass of water to prevent the tablet from entering the intestine undissolved.

35. 1. Sedatives, used to promote sleep, depress the central nervous system, which may cause constipation, not diarrhea.

2. Narcotics, opium derivatives used to relieve pain, depress the central nervous system, which may cause constipation, **not** diarrhea.

3. Diarrhea is an adverse reaction to a laxative. Laxatives are agents that increase evacuation of the bowel via various mechanisms. An excessive dose or taking a laxative when it is not necessary can cause diarrhea.
4. Antibiotics can alter the flora of the body, with resulting superinfections. Opportunistic fungal infections of the gastrointestinal system may cause a black, furred tongue, nausea, and diarrhea.
5. Antiemetics, used to prevent or alleviate nausea and vomiting, may cause constipation, not diarrhea.

36. 1. Some herbal supplements can cause dangerous herbal-to-drug interactions or nontherapeutic responses when taken concurrently with over-the-counter or prescribed medication.
2. The Dietary Supplement Health and Education Act of 1994 stipulated that herbs must be labeled with information about their effects on the structure and function of the body. Herbal substances officially are considered food supplements.
3. The Food and Drug Administration (FDA), a division of the U.S. Department of Health and Human Services, regulates the manufacture, sale, and effectiveness of prescription and nonprescription medications, not herbal remedies.
4. Herbs, considered by some to be "natural," are plants that are valued for their medicinal properties. As medicinal substances, they should be viewed by the consumer as drugs.
5. Just because herbs are organic does not ensure that they are safe. Many herbs even though organic can be toxic if ingested in unsafe amounts.

37. 1. Drug levels are maintained within a therapeutic range that is less than the peak level and more than the trough level. The peak serum level of a drug is the maximum concentration of a drug in the blood (occurs when the elimination rate equals the absorption rate). Trough levels indicate the serum level of a drug just before the next dose is to be administered. The results of these two values determine the dose and time a drug should be administered to maintain a serum level of a drug within its therapeutic range.

2. Although a drug's half-life, the usual amount of time needed by the body to reduce the concentration of the drug by one half, is helpful in determining how frequently a drug should be given initially, it does not reflect an individual patient's response to the drug.
3. Based on peak and trough levels of a drug, the dosage is adjusted to ensure that the concentration of the drug in the blood remains in the therapeutic range over a 24-hour period.
4. Biotransformation, the process of inactivating and breaking down a drug, takes place primarily in the liver. Peak and trough levels may indirectly reflect the rate of biotransformation, not the place where it occurs.
5. This is not the purpose of peak and trough levels, although peak and trough levels indirectly measure both the absorption and the inactivation and elimination of a drug from the body.

38. Answer: 3 mL. Use ratio and proportion to convert grams to milligrams first and then perform a calculation to determine the dose.

$$\frac{\text{Desired} \quad 1.5\,\text{g}}{\text{Have} \quad 1\,\text{g}} = \frac{\text{x mg}}{1{,}000\,\text{mg}}$$

1x = 1.5 × 1,000
x = 1,500 mg; therefore, 1,500 mg is equal to 1.5 g

$$\frac{\text{Desired}}{\text{Have}} \quad \frac{1{,}500\,\text{mg}}{500\,\text{mg}} = \frac{\text{x mL}}{1\,\text{mL}}$$

500x = 1,500
x = 1,500 ÷ 500
x = 3 mL

39. 1. Oxygen saturation measures the ratio of oxyhemoglobin to the total concentration of hemoglobin in the blood. It indicates how much a person is being oxygenated. An oxygen saturation level of 95% or higher indicates an acceptable range.
2. Mucolytic agents, not bronchodilators, liquefy thick, sticky (viscous) secretions.
3. Bronchodilators expand the airways of the respiratory tract, and this promotes air exchange and easier respirations.
4. The ability of the chest to expand (respiratory excursion) increases, not decreases.

5. Bronchovesicular breath sounds will increase, not decrease, after the administration of a bronchodilator. Bronchovesicular sounds are expected blowing sounds heard over the mainstem bronchi. They are blowing sounds that are moderate in pitch and intensity and equal in length on inspiration and expiration.

40. 1. **Prolonged laxative use weakens the bowel's natural responses to fecal distention and results in chronic constipation. The osmotic action of magnesium salts in magnesium hydroxide draws water into the intestine, which can cause dehydration and electrolyte imbalances.**
2. Magnesium hydroxide causes sodium and potassium to be lost from, rather than accumulate in, the body. The magnesium in magnesium hydroxide may be absorbed and result in hypermagnesemia.
3. **Watery diarrhea is a sign of an overdose of magnesium hydroxide. The drug should be discontinued because watery diarrhea can lead to a serious imbalance in fluid and electrolytes.**
4. Each dose should be followed by 8 ounces of water to promote a faster effect and help replenish lost fluid. Daily fluid intake should be 2,000 to 3,000 mL.
5. This will interrupt sleep. Magnesium hydroxide causes bowel elimination 3 to 6 hours after its administration.

41. 1. The composition of the drug and the patient's response to the drug, not the route by which it is administered, determine if an allergic response occurs.
2. The composition of a drug and its molecular reaction with another drug that is concurrently present determine if a drug interaction will occur.
3. A transdermal patch placed on the skin gradually releases a predictable amount of medication that is absorbed into the bloodstream for a prescribed period of time. This approach maintains therapeutic blood levels and reduces fluctuations in circulating drug levels.
4. A drug administered via a transdermal patch cannot be inactivated by gastric acidity. Drugs taken orally can cause gastric irritation, which can be avoided if the drugs are administered via a transdermal patch.
5. Transdermal patches are used for their systemic, not local, effects.

42. 1. **These are clinical indicators of dehydration and should be reported to the primary health-care provider because rehydration therapy may be necessary.**
2. Diphenoxylate/atropine depresses intestinal motility and effectively controls diarrhea within 24 to 36 hours. If diarrhea persists beyond 48 hours, the primary health-care provider should be notified.
3. Diphenoxylate/atropine may depress the central nervous system, which causes drowsiness and sedation, not hyperactivity.
4. When a patient is experiencing diarrhea, fluid should be encouraged, not restricted, to prevent dehydration and electrolyte imbalances.
5. The tablets for this medication are not enteric coated and do not have extended-release properties; therefore, they may be crushed if necessary.

43. 1. **Constipation and diarrhea are both side effects of famotidine for which the nurse should assess the patient.**
2. Although administered by mouth, famotidine is not known to cause stomatitis.
3. An increase, not decrease, in serum creatinine is a side effect associated with famotidine. Seventy percent of famotidine is excreted unchanged via the kidneys, and the drug may cause kidney damage.
4. **The nurse should monitor a patient's CBC with differential periodically during famotidine therapy to identify hematological adverse reactions. Serious hematological adverse reactions include agranulocytosis, aplastic anemia, anemia, neutropenia, and thrombocytopenia.**
5. **Completing the full course of therapy and not discontinuing the medication when feeling better support the achievement of the maximum therapeutic effect.**

44. 1. **Mixing alcohol and zolpidem can intensify the effects of both and can precipitate dangerous side effects such as dizziness, shallow breathing, and impaired motor control, judgment, and thinking; it can even cause loss of consciousness or coma.**
2. **Controlled-release (CR) medications should never be chewed, crushed, divided, or dissolved. A damaged tablet**

alters the process by which the medication is released. Too much medication may be released into the system at once, causing an excessive dose. Zolpidem is a dual-layer tablet: 10.5 mg is released immediately and another 2.5 mg later. The first layer dissolves rapidly to help a person get to sleep, and the second layer dissolves gradually to help a person stay asleep.

3. Zolpidem is better absorbed and therefore more effective when taken when the stomach is empty.

4. Zolpidem is a central nervous system depressant that has a habit-forming potential if taken in higher doses than prescribed. Excessive doses can lead to tolerance and abuse. Also, a second dose so close to a previous dose can dramatically increase the risk of adverse reactions associated with the central nervous system such as irregular heart rate, impaired breathing, and memory loss.

5. **Zolpidem is a central nervous system depressant that has a duration of action of approximately 7 to 8 hours. If the person is active before the medication is metabolized, drowsiness, dizziness, light-headedness, and impaired balance may occur, increasing the risk for injury.**

45. 2. **The process of movement of a medication into the bloodstream (*absorption*) is the first element of pharmacokinetics as medication moves from its entry to its exit from the body.**

3. The transport of a medication from the site of absorption to the site of medication action (*distribution*) is the second element of pharmacokinetics as medication moves from its entry to its exit from the body.

4. Conversion of a medication to a less active form (*biotransformation*) in preparation for excretion is the third element of pharmacokinetics as medication moves from its entry to its exit from the body.

1. Elimination of a medication by the body (*excretion*) is the fourth element of pharmacokinetics as medication moves from its entry to its exit from the body.

46. 1. Taking ibuprofen with a full glass of water and maintaining adequate fluid intake help to prevent renal adverse reactions.

2. The patient should not exceed 2,400 mg of ibuprofen daily because this is the total number of milligrams prescribed by the primary health-care provider. However, information from the manufacturer states that patients should not exceed a total daily dose of 3,200 mg, to avoid stomach or intestinal damage.

3. The patient should avoid taking a double dose. However, if a forgotten dose is remembered, it can be taken as long as it not too close to the next scheduled dose.

4. **Research demonstrates that bleeding time is increased when taking ibuprofen; therefore, ibuprofen should be discontinued if dental treatment or surgery is scheduled.**

5. If a skin rash occurs the patient should discontinue taking ibuprofen immediately. A rash may indicate toxic epidermal necrolysis or Stevens-Johnson syndrome, which can be life-threatening.

47. 1. Nitrofurantoin should be administered with food, not on an empty stomach, to minimize gastric irritation.

2. **This helps to prevent staining of the teeth associated with nitrofurantoin.**

3. The urine is brown or rust colored, not reddish/orange, with nitrofurantoin. Reddish/orange urine is associated with the drug phenazopyridine, a urinary tract analgesic that contains a type of azo dye.

4. **The patient should monitor for these signs and symptoms because they are indicative of pseudomembranous colitis, a serious adverse reaction to nitrofurantoin.**

5. A week is too long to wait to report lack of improvement in signs and symptoms of the urinary tract infection. The patient should be instructed to notify the primary health-care provider if signs and symptoms do not resolve within several days.

48. 1. This is a dependent function of the nurse and requires an order by the primary health-care provider.

2. **Sedation and weakness may result from the anticholinergic effects of oxybutynin, especially in older adults.**

3. **Drowsiness is a side effect of oxybutynin because of its anticholinergic effects. The patient should avoid activities such as driving**

when the level of alertness is diminished.

4. **Urinary retention requires immediate medical attention to avoid permanent bladder damage resulting from overstretching of the bladder and kidney damage caused by a backup of urine into the kidneys. Oxybutynin exerts an antispasmodic effect on smooth muscle by inhibiting the action of acetylcholine and also relaxes the bladder's detrusor muscle. These actions can lead to urinary retention in some people.**

5. Oxybutynin decreases the ability to perspire because of its anticholinergic effect, which may cause fever and heat stroke if a person engages in strenuous activity in a warm environment.

49. 1. Analgesics do not have a curative action.
2. **Analgesics decrease the intensity of pain (palliative treatment). Palliative treatments minimize signs and symptoms or promote comfort; palliative treatments do not produce a cure.**
3. **When 2 analgesics are administered together they exert a synergistic effect. A synergistic effect occurs when the combined effect of two medications is greater than when the effects of each are added together.**
4. **When 2 analgesics are given together they potentiate the action of each other. Potentiation occurs when drugs administered together increase the action of one or both drugs.**
5. Two analgesics will increase, not decrease (antagonize), the action of each other.

50. 1. **Budesonide, an inhaled corticosteroid, contains a small amount of milk sugar (lactose) that may cause an allergic reaction in a patient with lactose intolerance.**
2. **The bronchodilator reduces airway resistance, and then the budesonide can be aspirated deeper into the lungs for maximal effect.**
3. Improvement in asthma control can occur within 24 hours of starting treatment; however, 1 to 2 weeks of treatment may be necessary to achieve a maximum benefit from an inhaled corticosteroid.
4. **Rinsing the mouth with water and avoiding swallowing after use of**

budesonide will help to reduce the risk of an oral fungal (candida) infection.
5. Budesonide, a corticosteroid, is not indicated for the immediate relief of bronchospasms. A short-acting beta$_2$-agonist medication is indicated in the event of a sudden asthma attack or in the presence of breathing problems.

51. 1. **Increased fluid intake will help to decrease the viscosity of respiratory secretions and moisten the throat. At least 2,000 mL or more of fluid is suggested when taking dextromethorphan and guaifenesin.**
2. One week, not 2 weeks, is long enough to wait before informing the primary health-care provider of a lack of improvement in signs and symptoms. Another intervention may be required.
3. **Dextromethorphan, a cough suppressant, and guaifenesin, an expectorant, are contained in other over-the-counter cough remedies. Taking multiple drugs with the same or similar properties can cause an overdose of these elements.**
4. **Although taking a stimulant concurrently with dextromethorphan and guaifenesin can increase the risk of unpleasant side effects, it is not within the nurse's role to discontinue a medication.**
5. **These are serious side effects of dextromethorphan and guaifenesin; these medications should be discontinued with medical supervision.**

52. 1. A calcium level of 5.4 mEq/L is within the expected range of 4.5 to 5.5 mEq/L and is not a cause for concern.
2. A temperature of 97.8°F is within the expected range of 97.5°F to 99.5°F for an adult and is not a cause for concern.
3. **One thousand milligrams of docusate sodium daily exceeds the recommended daily dose of 50 to 500 mg and is a cause for concern.**
4. A respiratory rate of 14 breaths per minute is within the expected range of 12 to 20 breaths per minute for an adult and is not a cause for concern.

53. 1. The opposite should be encouraged. Vegetable oils with polyunsaturated fatty acids should be exchanged for vegetable oils with monounsaturated fatty acids.

2. These human responses may indicate a serious adverse reaction to simvastatin and must be evaluated. In addition to reducing the liver's production of cholesterol, simvastatin affects several enzymes in muscle cells that are responsible for muscle growth; this may be the cause of muscle symptoms. However, these symptoms may indicate the presence of rhabdomyolysis. Rhabdomyolysis is a condition that breaks down skeletal muscle fibers and myocyte cell membranes which leads to muscle necrosis. Because rhabdomyolysis can be fatal, muscle symptoms must be seriously evaluated.

3. Research demonstrates that omega-3 fatty acids help limit triglycerides, inflammation, hypertension, and cardiovascular and autoimmune diseases.

4. Cola-colored urine indicates the presence of myoglobin, which is a skeletal muscle protein involved in metabolism. When skeletal muscles are damaged, they release myoglobin into the bloodstream. The blood is then filtered by the kidneys, thus causing urine to be cola or tea colored. Reduced urine output or absence of urine may indicate kidney damage caused by rhabdomyolysis necessitating immediate medical attention.

5. Simvastatin should be taken at bedtime or during the evening meal, not in the morning. Research demonstrates that the body makes cholesterol at night and that cholesterol levels are lower when simvastatin is taken in the evening rather than in the morning.

54. 1. Food activates the proton pump mechanism, which releases gastric acid in the stomach. When esomeprazole, a proton pump inhibitor, is taken 30 minutes to 1 hour before a meal, it allows time for esomeprazole to be absorbed into the bloodstream, which then prevents the final transport of hydrogen ions into the gastric lumen.

2. This prevents damage to the delayed-release pellets within the esomeprazole capsule.

3. Antacids may be used when taking esomeprazole.

4. NSAIDs may cause an increase in gastrointestinal irritation and should be avoided.

5. Opening the capsule can be done as long as the pellets are not crushed or chewed.

55. 1. One type of rash is a hypersensitivity (allergic) reaction to a chemical element in a drug. Hypersensitivity reactions can be mild if localized, but if the exposure is systemic, the reaction is on a larger scale and may even be life-threatening.

2. Tinnitus is caused by damage to the eighth cranial nerve, which is a toxic effect of acetylsalicylic acid.

3. Acetylsalicylic acid has antiplatelet agglutination properties that cause an increase in clotting time.

4. Dizziness is indicative of hypotension, which is not a common nontherapeutic response to acetylsalicylic acid.

5. Diarrhea, rather than constipation, is more likely to occur with the intake of acetylsalicylic acid. Aspirin inhibits the COX-1 enzyme and causes a thinning of the stomach lining that increases the prospect of gastrointestinal irritation from digestive juices and contributes to diarrhea, heartburn, abdominal pain, bloating, and bleeding.

56. 1. Morphine, an opioid analgesic, is a central nervous system depressant. A central nervous system depressant reduces the activity and slows down the normal functions of the brain, thus leading to a decreased level of alertness.

2. Morphine, an opioid analgesic, is a central nervous system depressant. A central nervous system depressant has a sedating effect on brain function that can lead to confusion.

3. Morphine, an opioid analgesic, is a central nervous system depressant. A central nervous system depressant decreases the respiratory center of the brain, thus causing bradypnea, not tachypnea.

4. Morphine, an opioid analgesic, is a central nervous system depressant. A central nervous system depressant decreases gastrointestinal motility and contributes to constipation.

5. Morphine, an opioid analgesic, is a central nervous system depressant. A central

nervous system depressant relaxes the neurovascular system and contributes to hypotension, not hypertension.

57. 1. Synthroid is a proprietary brand (trade) name for levothyroxine. Trade names of drugs are patented by drug companies. They begin with a capital letter and usually are short and easy to recall.
2. **Levothyroxine is the generic (non-proprietary, official) name for the synthetic thyroid hormone that is chemically identical to thyroxine (T4). It is used to treat thyroid hormone deficiency.**
3. Levothyroxine does not have a curative action. It is a synthetic hormone used to treat a thyroid deficiency.
4. Levothyroxine does not have an antidotal action. An antidote is used to reverse the toxic effect of another medication. An example of a medication that is an antidote is naloxone; it limits central nervous system depression resulting from opioids.
5. **Levothyroxine is a supportive (substitutive) medication because it maintains health by providing an essential hormone that is deficient in the body.**

58. 1. **Knowing a drug's therapeutic range is essential. It indicates the lowest blood concentration level that is effective and the highest blood concentration level that is effective without causing toxicity.**
2. **A trough level reflects the lowest plasma concentration of a drug in the patient's body. The nurse must determine if a trough level is within the drug's therapeutic range. A trough plasma level is determined by a blood test that assesses the level of the drug in the patient's body just before the administration of a prescribed dose of the medication.**
3. **A peak level reflects the highest plasma concentration of a drug in the patient's body. The nurse must determine if a peak level is high enough to be within the therapeutic range yet not too high to be toxic. A peak plasma level is determined by a blood test that assesses the level of the drug in the patient's body 30 minutes to 1 hour after administration of the medication.**

4. Knowing the time needed by the body to metabolize or inactivate one-half the amount of a medication (half-life) will not help the nurse determine if an effective blood concentration level of the drug is being maintained.
5. Knowing the length of time it takes the body to respond to a medication (onset) will not help the nurse determine if an effective blood concentration level of the drug is being maintained.

59. 1. **The prescription for the nystatin lozenge should be discussed with the primary health-care provider. It is unlikely that a patient with moderate dementia will be able to follow directions to keep a lozenge in the mouth for the length of time necessary for it to dissolve without swallowing. Also, it places the patient at risk for aspiration.**
2. **The prescription for acetaminophen should be discussed with the primary health-care provider. Acetaminophen 1,000 mg administered every 6 hours will deliver 4,000 mg of acetaminophen, which exceeds the recommended maximum daily intake of 3,000. Excessive doses can cause liver damage.**
3. It is not necessary to discuss the prescription for levothyroxine 100 mcg. It is within the appropriate range of dosage for this medication and it will not interact with any of the other prescribed medications.
4. It is not necessary to discuss the prescription for simvastatin with the primary health-care provider. There are no concerns associated with administering simvastatin concurrently with the other prescribed medications and the dose is within the acceptable dosage range for an adult.
5. It is not necessary to discuss the prescription for docusate sodium with the primary health-care provider. There are no concerns associated with administering docusate sodium concurrently with the other prescribed medications and the dose is within the acceptable dosage range for an adult.

60. 1. Glargine is a long-acting insulin with an onset of 1 to 2 hours. It has no pronounced peak and it has a duration of 24 hours or more.

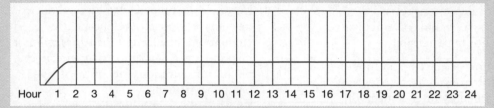

2. The graphic illustrates that regular insulin is short acting, with an onset of ½ to 1 hour. It has a peak of 2 to 3 hours and a duration of 3 to 6 hours.

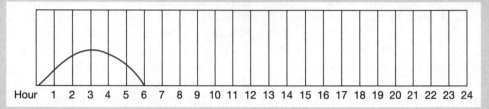

3. Lispro is a rapid-acting insulin with an onset of 15 minutes, a peak of 60 to 90 minutes, and a duration of 3 to 4 hours.

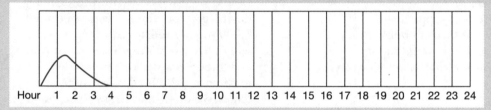

4. NPH is an intermediate-acting insulin with an onset of 2 to 4 hours, a peak of 4 to 10 hours, and a duration of 10 to 16 hours.

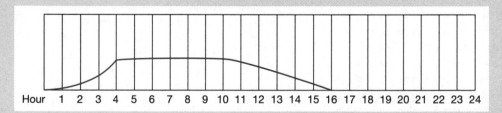

5

Basic Human Needs and Related Nursing Care

Hygiene

KEYWORDS

The following words include nursing/medical terminology, concepts, principles, and information relevant to content specifically addressed in the chapter or associated with topics presented in it. English dictionaries, nursing textbooks, and medical dictionaries, such as *Taber's Cyclopedic Medical Dictionary,* are resources that can be used to expand your knowledge and understanding of these words and related information.

Activities of daily living
Asepsis
Back massage
Baths:
  Bag bath (towel bath)
  Bed bath (partial, complete)
  Shower (standup, shower chair)
  Sitz bath
  Tub bath
Canthus, outer and inner
Cerumen
Circumcised, uncircumcised
Cuticles
Dental caries
Dentures
Distal
Effleurage
Flossing
Halitosis
Heat loss, mechanisms of:
  Conduction
  Convection

Evaporation
Radiation
Hirsutism
Integumentary
Labia, majora and minora
Mucous membrane
Oral hygiene
Orange stick
Pediculosis
Perianal area
Perineal care
Peripheral neuropathy
Plaque
Proximal
Sebaceous glands
Skin, dermis and epidermis
Smegma
Sordes
Toe pleat

HYGIENE: QUESTIONS

1. A nurse is bathing a patient who has a fever. Why should the nurse use tepid bath water for this procedure?
   1. Increases heat loss
   2. Removes surface debris
   3. Reduces surface tension of skin
   4. Stimulates peripheral circulation

2. A nurse must make the decision to give a patient a full or partial bed bath. Which criterion is **most** important for the basis of this decision?
   1. Primary health-care provider's order for the patient's activity
   2. Immediate need of the patient
   3. Time of patient's last bath
   4. Patient preference

3. A patient has had a nasogastric tube to decompress the stomach for 3 days and is scheduled for intestinal surgery in the morning. For which of the following is the patient at the **greatest** risk?
   1. Physical injury
   2. Ineffective social interaction
   3. Decreased nutritional intake
   4. Altered oral mucous membranes

4. A patient is incontinent of urine and stool. For which patient response should the nurse be **most** concerned?
   1. Impaired skin integrity
   2. Altered sexuality
   3. Dehydration
   4. Confusion

5. A nurse is giving a patient a bed bath. Which nursing action is **most** important?
   1. Lower the 2 side rails on the working side of the bed.
   2. Ensure that the bath water is at least 110°F.
   3. Fold the washcloth like a mitt on the hand.
   4. Raise the bed to the highest position.

6. A nurse plans to give a patient a back rub. Which is the product the nurse should use for this intervention?
   1. Baby powder
   2. Rubbing alcohol
   3. Moisturizing lotion
   4. Antimicrobial cream

7. A nurse changes the linen of a bed while the patient sits in a chair. Of the options presented, which is the **most** important nursing action when changing bed linens?
   1. Ensuring the hem of the bottom sheet is facing the mattress
   2. Arranging the linen in the order in which it is to be used
   3. Shifting the mattress up to the headboard of the bed
   4. Checking the soiled bed linens for personal items

8. A nurse is responsible for providing hair care for a patient. Which should the nurse do to distribute oil evenly along hair shafts?
   1. Brush from the scalp toward the hair ends
   2. Lift opened fingers through the hair
   3. Apply a conditioner to wet hair
   4. Use a fine-toothed comb

9. Which condition identified by the nurse places a patient at the **greatest** risk for impaired self-care when toileting?
   1. Amputation of a foot
   2. Early dementia
   3. Fractured hip
   4. Pregnancy

10. A patient asks the nurse, "Why do I have to use mouthwash if I brush my teeth?" Which rationale should the nurse include when responding to this question?
    1. Minimizes the formation of cavities
    2. Helps reduce offensive mouth odors
    3. Softens debris that accumulates in the mouth
    4. Destroys pathogens that are found in the oral cavity

11. A nurse is planning to shampoo the hair of a patient who has an order for bedrest. Which should the nurse do **first**?
    1. Wet hair thoroughly before applying shampoo.
    2. Encourage the use of dry shampoo.
    3. Brush the hair to remove tangles.
    4. Tape eye shields over both eyes.

12. A patient has just had perineal surgery. Which type of bath should the nurse expect to be ordered for this patient?
    1. Sponge bath
    2. Sitz bath
    3. Tub bath
    4. Bed bath

13. A nurse plans to assist a patient who has impaired vision with a bed bath. Which is the **most** appropriate nursing intervention to facilitate bathing for this patient?
    1. Providing the patient with a liquid bath gel rather than a bar of soap
    2. Giving the patient an adapted toothbrush to use when brushing the teeth
    3. Checking the patient's ability to give self-care through a crack in the curtain
    4. Ensuring the patient can locate bathing supplies placed on the over-bed table

14. A nurse plans to meet the hygiene needs of a hospitalized patient who is experiencing hemiparesis because of a brain attack (cerebrovascular accident). Which is an appropriate nursing intervention?
    1. Assisting with the bath as needed
    2. Giving total assistance with a complete bath
    3. Providing minimal supervision during the bath
    4. Encouraging a family member to bathe the patient

15. A nurse is making an occupied bed. Which nursing action is **most** important?
    1. Securing top linens under the foot of the mattress and mitering the corners
    2. Ensuring that the patient's head is supported and is in functional alignment
    3. Fan-folding soiled linens as close to the patient's body as possible
    4. Positioning the bed in the horizontal position

16. A nurse must bathe the feet of a patient with diabetes. Which should the nurse do before bathing this patient's feet?
    1. File the nails straight across with an emery board.
    2. Teach that daily foot care is essential to healthy feet.
    3. Ensure a provider's order for hygienic foot care is obtained.
    4. Assess for additional risk factors that may contribute to localized problems.

17. Which should be the nurse's **first** intervention after removing a bedpan from under a debilitated patient who has just had a bowel movement?
    1. Document results.
    2. Provide perineal care.
    3. Reposition the patient.
    4. Cover the patient with the top linens.

18. Which common problem with the hair should the nurse anticipate when patients are on complete bedrest?
    1. Dry hair
    2. Oily hair
    3. Split hair
    4. Matted hair

19. A nurse is helping a patient who has right hemiparesis to get dressed. Which action should the nurse implement?
    1. Put the gown's right sleeve on first.
    2. Keep the patient in an open-backed gown.
    3. Encourage the patient to dress independently.
    4. Leave the right sleeve off while adjusting the tie at the neck.

20. A patient is incontinent of loose stools and is cognitively impaired. Which action should the nurse implement to help the patient prevent skin breakdown?
    1. Wash the buttocks with strong soap and water.
    2. Bathe immediately after a bowel movement.
    3. Place the call bell in easy reach.
    4. Put a pad under the buttocks.

21. A nurse covers the patient with a cotton blanket during a bath. Which of the following mechanisms of heat loss is prevented by the nurse's action?
    1. Vasodilation
    2. Conduction
    3. Convection
    4. Diffusion

22. Which is the **first** assessment that should be performed by the nurse before planning to meet the hygiene needs of a patient?
    1. Recognize the patient's developmental stage.
    2. Collect the patient's toiletries needed for the bath.
    3. Identify the patient's ability to assist in hygiene activities.
    4. Determine the patient's preferences about hygiene practices.

23. A nurse gives a bed-bound patient a bed bath. Which is the **primary** reason why the nurse provides hygiene care to this patient?
    1. Support a sense of well-being by increasing self-esteem.
    2. Promote circulation by stimulating peripheral nerve endings.
    3. Remove excess oil, perspiration, and bacteria by mechanical cleansing.
    4. Exercise muscles by contraction and relaxation of muscles when bathing.

24. Which human response, identified by the nurse, **best** supports the concern that a patient has a reduced capacity to provide for activities of daily living?
    1. Presence of joint contractures
    2. Inability to wash body parts
    3. Postoperative lethargy
    4. Visual disorders

25. When giving a patient a bed bath, a nurse washes the patient's extremities from distal to proximal. Which is the rationale for this nursing action?
    1. Decreases the chance of infection
    2. Facilitates removal of dry skin
    3. Stimulates venous return
    4. Minimizes skin tears

26. During oral care the nurse identifies a patch of dried food and debris adhered to the hard palate of the patient's mouth. Which word should the nurse use when documenting this condition?
    1. Sordes
    2. Plaque
    3. Glossitis
    4. Stomatitis

27. A nurse is teaching a patient about how many times a day it is necessary to brush the teeth to achieve effective dental hygiene. According to the American Dental Association, how many times a day should the nurse teach the patient to brush the teeth?
    1. 6
    2. 4
    3. 3
    4. 2

28. A nurse is providing hygiene to a patient with peripheral neuropathy. Which action should the nurse implement?
    1. Seek an order for foot care.
    2. File the toenails straight across the nail.
    3. Wash the feet with lukewarm water and dry well.
    4. Apply moisturizing lotion to the feet, especially between the toes.

29. Which nursing intervention **most** requires the nurse to consider the concept of personal space?
    1. Providing a bed bath
    2. Obtaining the vital signs
    3. Performing a health history
    4. Ambulating the patient down the hall

30. Which nursing actions are common to both a bed bath and a tub bath? **Select all that apply.**
    1. _____Obtaining an order from the primary health-care provider
    2. _____Helping the patient wash parts that cannot be reached
    3. _____Exposing just the part of the body being washed
    4. _____Providing for privacy throughout the bath
    5. _____Ensuring that the call bell is in reach

31. A nurse plans to provide a patient with a partial bath. Place the steps in the order in which the nurse should proceed.
    1. Back
    2. Face
    3. Axilla
    4. Both hands
    5. Genital area
    6. Change water
    Answer: _____

32. Which should the nurse implement when caring for a patient who wears eyeglasses? **Select all that apply.**
    1. _____Encourage use of artificial tears while hospitalized.
    2. _____Store eyeglasses in a safe place when not being worn.
    3. _____Dry the lenses with a paper towel after they are washed.
    4. _____Limit the time that eyeglasses are worn in an effort to rest the eyes.
    5. _____Use warm water to clean the lenses of eyeglasses at least once a day.

33. When providing morning care for a patient, the nurse identifies crusty debris around the patient's eyes. Which actions should the nurse implement when cleaning the patient's eyes? **Select all that apply.**
    1. _____Wear sterile gloves.
    2. _____Use a tear-free baby soap.
    3. _____Position the patient on the same side as the eye to be cleaned.
    4. _____Wash the eyes with cotton balls from the inner to outer canthus.
    5. _____Use a separate cotton ball for each stroke when washing the eyes.

34. A nurse must make an unoccupied bed. Which nursing actions are essential? **Select all that apply.**
    1. _____Position the call bell in reach.
    2. _____Place a pull sheet on top of the draw sheet.
    3. _____Ensure that the bottom sheet is free of wrinkles.
    4. _____Ensure that there is a toe pleat at the foot of the bed.
    5. _____Complete one side of the bed before completing the other side.

35. A nurse plans to administer a foot bath to a patient who is sitting in a chair and has no contraindications for this intervention. Place the following steps in the order in which they should be implemented.

    Answer: _____

    1. Soak each foot individually for 5 to 20 minutes subject to the patient's tolerance, condition of the skin, and absence of a history of diabetes or peripheral vascular disease.
    2. Don clean gloves and assist the patient to position one foot in the water, verifying with the patient that the water temperature is comfortable.
    3. Position a waterproof pad on the floor on which to place a basin half-filled with warm water approximately 105°F to 110°F.
    4. Wash each foot with rinse-free soap and clean under the nails with an orange stick.
    5. Apply lotion to each foot, avoiding between the toes.
    6. Dry each foot gently, especially between the toes.

36. A nurse teaches a patient effective oral hygiene practices. Which patient behaviors indicate that the teaching about preventing and removing dental plaque was understood? **Select all that apply.**
    1. _____Uses an abrasive toothpaste
    2. _____Brushes the teeth with a toothbrush
    3. _____Gargles with anti-plaque mouthwash
    4. _____Flosses the teeth with unwaxed floss
    5. _____Has teeth cleaned regularly by a dental hygienist

37. A nurse is providing for the hygiene and grooming needs of an obese patient who easily becomes short of breath when moving about. Which nursing interventions are important? **Select all that apply.**
    1. _____Administering oxygen during provision of care
    2. _____Maintaining the bed in a high-Fowler position
    3. _____Assessing the patient's response to the activity
    4. _____Bathing areas that the patient cannot reach
    5. _____Providing rest periods every ten minutes

38. A nurse plans to shave a male patient's facial hair. Which actions should the nurse implement? **Select all that apply.**
    1. _____Shave in the direction of hair growth.
    2. _____Hold the razor perpendicular to the skin.
    3. _____Use long, downward strokes with the razor.
    4. _____Ensure that the patient is not receiving an anticoagulant.
    5. _____Use a hot, wet washcloth to wrap the face before shaving.

39. A nurse is caring for a patient who was newly admitted to a rehabilitation facility. The nurse reviews the patient's clinical record and chooses which of the following bathing plans to meet the patient's hygiene needs?
    1. Complete bath with partial assistance
    2. Towel bath with total assistance
    3. Shower with partial assistance
    4. Tub bath with total assistance

PATIENT'S CLINICAL RECORD

History
A 74-year-old woman admitted for rehabilitation after a total hip replacement 6 days ago due to chronic pain from osteoarthritis. Postoperative status was uneventful; suture line intact and free of signs or symptoms of complications. Ingesting a regular diet; fluid and electrolytes in balance. Vital signs stable, although the respiratory rate is slightly elevated and labored due to a history of emphysema.

Nursing Admission Assessment
Resting in the semi-Fowler position with an abduction pillow in place. Oriented to person but not time and place. Patient keeps saying, "This does not look like my home. I want to go home." Surgical site is dry and intact, wound edges approximated, and is free of any signs or symptoms of complications. Patient is pulling on the linen and appears agitated and is attempting to turn from side to side. Incontinent of urine.

Vital Signs
Temperature: 99.4°F, temporal
Pulse: 98 beats per minute, regular
Respirations: 28 breaths per minute, pursed-lip breathing
Blood pressure: 150/90 mm Hg

40. A nurse is caring for a patient with an excessively dry mouth. Which nursing actions are important when providing mouth care for this patient? **Select all that apply.**
    1. _____Wearing clean gloves
    2. _____Providing oral care every 2 hours
    3. _____Rinsing frequently with mouthwash
    4. _____Cleansing 4 times a day with a water pick
    5. _____Swabbing with a sponge-tipped applicator of lemon and glycerin

41. A nurse is providing perineal care to a male patient. Which should the nurse do? **Select all that apply.**
    1. _____Wash the genital area with hot, sudsy water.
    2. _____Wash the scrotum before washing the glans penis.
    3. _____Wash the shaft of the penis while moving toward the urinary meatus.
    4. _____Wash the penis with one hand while holding it firmly with the other hand.
    5. _____Wash the glans with a circular motion starting at the tip and then proceeding down the shaft.

42. A school nurse teaches an adolescent who has dry skin and acne about skin care. Which statements by the adolescent indicate that the information is understood? **Select all that apply.**
    1. _____"I will scrub my face every day with a strong soap."
    2. _____"I will carefully break pustules after washing my face."
    3. _____"I will apply a water-based emollient after washing my face."
    4. _____"I will bathe my face with cool water when I shower in the morning."
    5. _____"I will use mild soap to gently cleanse my face thoroughly twice a day."

43. A nurse is observing a nursing assistant in a home care setting administering a bed bath. Which issues apparent in the photograph indicate that the nursing assistant has violated the standards of care for a bed bath? **Select all that apply.**

1. _____The pillows behind the patient's body should be removed before the bath.
2. _____The nursing assistant's uniform is in contact with the patient's linens.
3. _____The nursing assistant should be making eye contact with the patient.
4. _____The patient's left leg should be covered with the bath blanket.
5. _____The nursing assistant is not wearing clean gloves.

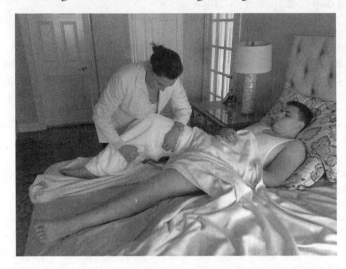

44. Which statements made by an older adult indicate to the nurse that additional teaching about skin care is necessary? **Select all that apply.**

1. _____"I limit my baths to twice a week."
2. _____"I humidify my home in the winter."
3. _____"I apply moisturizing lotion to my body daily."
4. _____"I use a bubble-bath product when I take a bath."
5. _____"I love to relax in a hot bath before going to bed."

45. Which actions should the nurse implement when providing fingernail care during a patient's bath? **Select all that apply.**

1. _____Push cuticles back with the rounded end of a metal nail file.
2. _____File nails straight across, rounding corners slightly.
3. _____Apply a moisturizing lotion around cuticles.
4. _____Clean under nails with an orange stick.
5. _____Soak hands in hot water first.

1. 1. **Heat is transferred from the warm surface of the skin to the water that is in direct contact with the body, and evaporation of the water promotes cooling. Tepid water is slightly below body temperature, and a person with a fever has an elevated body temperature (febrile).**
   2. Friction, not the temperature of the bath water, helps to remove surface debris.
   3. Soap, not the temperature of bath water, reduces the surface tension of water, not the surface tension of skin.
   4. Peripheral circulation is increased by warm water and by rubbing the skin with a washcloth.

2. 1. Full or partial bed baths can be administered regardless of the activity order written by the primary health-care provider because it is an independent function of the nurse.
   2. **A total patient assessment with an analysis of the data identifies the needs of the patient and the appropriate intervention to meet those needs.**
   3. Time has no relevance in relation to identifying what type of bed bath to administer to a patient.
   4. Although patient preference is a consideration, patient teaching should convince a patient what should be done to meet physical needs.

3. 1. This patient is not at risk for physical injury. A person at risk for physical injury is in jeopardy for harm because of a perceptual or physiological deficit, a lack of awareness of hazards, or maturational age.
   2. This patient is not at risk for ineffective social interaction. A person at risk for ineffective social interaction is in jeopardy of experiencing negative, insufficient, or unsatisfactory interactions with others.
   3. Inadequate nutritional intake generally is not a concern. Most postoperative patients usually progress from a clear liquid to a regular diet in 2 to 3 days once bowel function returns. This is too short a time frame to be concerned about decreased nutritional intake.
   4. **Not drinking anything by mouth and having a tube through the nose and posterior pharynx can result in drying**

of the oral mucous membranes and a coated, furrowed tongue.

4. 1. **Fecal material contains enzymes that erode the skin, and urine is an acidic fluid that macerates the skin. As a result, altered skin integrity is a serious concern.**
   2. Although incontinence may contribute to low self-esteem, which may impact a person's sexual patterns, it is not the priority.
   3. Incontinence is unrelated to dehydration.
   4. Although confusion may contribute to a patient experiencing incontinence, confusion is not a reaction to incontinence.

5. 1. Although lowering the two side rails on the working side of the bed might be done to promote safe body mechanics of the nurse, it is not a necessity.
   2. **The temperature of bath water should be between 110°F and 115°F to promote comfort, dilate blood vessels, and prevent chilling. A lower temperature can cause chilling, and a higher temperature can cause skin trauma.**
   3. Although a mitt retains water and heat and prevents loose ends from irritating the skin, it is not as essential as other factors that relate to patient safety.
   4. Although the height of the bed should be adjusted to promote the nurse's body mechanics, it is not as essential as other factors that relate to patient safety.

6. 1. Baby powder mixed with secretions of the skin forms a paste-like substance that supports antimicrobial growth and irritates the skin, promoting skin breakdown. Also, baby powder should be avoided because it is a respiratory irritant.
   2. Rubbing alcohol causes drying of the skin and should not be used.
   3. **Moisturizing lotion lubricates the skin and reduces friction between the nurse's hands and the patient's back. Lotion facilitates smooth movement of the hands across the patient's skin, which is relaxing and prevents trauma to the skin. The use of a moisturizing lotion for a back rub does not require a primary health-care provider's order.**

4. An antimicrobial cream is inappropriate for a back rub. It can dry the skin and eliminate the integument's natural flora. Use of an antimicrobial cream requires a primary health-care provider's order.

7. 1. Although it is important to provide a smooth surface by placing the seam of a hem facing the mattress, it is not the priority.
2. Arranging linen in the order in which it is to be used is an efficient approach that permits each sheet to be accessible when needed; however, it is not a priority.
3. Although shifting the mattress up to the headboard of the bed is important to ensure that the patient is well supported when the head of the bed is elevated or the knee gatch employed, it is not the priority.
4. **A nurse must take reasonable precautions to ensure that a patient's personal belongings, especially eyeglasses, dentures, and prosthetic devices, are kept safe. Checking for personal belongings before placing soiled linen into a linen hamper is a reasonable, prudent nursing action.**

8. 1. **Brushing the hair from the scalp to the ends of the hair massages the scalp and distributes oils secreted by the scalp down along the length of the hair shaft.**
2. Lifting opened fingers through the hair to distribute oil evenly along hair shafts is inadequate hair care. It might be done at the completion of hair care to style the hair.
3. Although a conditioner will make hair more supple, it will not facilitate distribution of oil along the hair shaft.
4. A fine-toothed comb has pointed ends and should not be used for daily grooming because it can injure the scalp, damage the hair shaft, and split the ends of hair.

9. 1. A patient with an amputation of a foot can still transfer to a bedside commode or ambulate with crutches to a bathroom.
2. When a person has early dementia, frequent reminders to perform self-toileting activities or declarative directions about toileting usually are adequate.
3. **Discomfort resulting from the proximity of the fracture to the pelvic area and the limitations placed on the positioning of, or weight-bearing on, the affected leg impact a patient's ability to use a bedpan or transfer to a commode.**

4. Although the enlarging uterus exerts pressure on the bladder, causing urinary frequency and alteration of the person's center of gravity, self-toileting usually is not impaired.

10. 1. Dental caries are caused by plaque. Therefore, brushing and flossing, not the use of mouthwash, are the most efficient ways to prevent dental caries.
2. **An offensive odor to the breath (halitosis) can be caused by inadequate oral hygiene, periodontal disease, or systemic disease. Rinsing the mouth with mouthwash will flush the oral cavity of debris and microorganisms, which will reduce halitosis if it is caused by a localized problem.**
3. Mouthwash flushes debris away from the teeth; it does not soften debris.
4. Only bactericidal mouthwashes can limit the amount of bacterial flora in the mouth; prolonged or excessive use can result in oral fungal infections.

11. 1. Although wetting the hair thoroughly before applying shampoo is done, it is not the first intervention.
2. Dry powder shampoos can irritate the scalp and dry the hair.
3. **It is easier and causes less trauma to the hair to brush out tangles when the hair is dry rather than wet.**
4. Taping eye shields over both eyes is unnecessary. Appropriate positioning will let the water flow by gravity away from the face, and a washcloth can be placed over the eyes.

12. 1. A sponge bath is given to reduce a patient's fever through heat loss via conduction and vaporization. Giving a sponge bath is an independent function of the nurse and does not require a primary health-care provider's order.
2. **A sitz bath immerses a patient from the mid-thighs to the iliac crests, or umbilicus, in a special tub, or the patient sits in a basin that fits onto the toilet seat, so the legs and feet remain out of the water. The moist heat to the genital area increases local circulation, cleans the skin, reduces soreness, and promotes relaxation, voiding, drainage, and healing. A sitz bath requires a primary health-care provider's order because it is a method of applying local heat to the perineal area.**

3. Tubs generally are used for therapeutic baths when medications are added to the water to soothe irritated skin.

4. A bed bath is indicated for patients with restricted mobility or decreased energy. Giving a bed bath is an independent function of the nurse and does not require a primary health-care provider's order.

13. 1. Manipulating a bottle of bath gel may be more difficult than using a bar of soap for a patient who is vision impaired.

2. Adapted toothbrushes are intended for people who have neuromuscular problems that interfere with grasping and manipulating a toothbrush, not for people with impaired vision.

3. Monitoring a patient through a crack in the bedside curtain is a violation of patient privacy. Patients have a right to know when they are being assessed.

4. **Identifying the placement of supplies on the over-bed table facilitates the use of equipment by a person with impaired vision and encourages self-care.**

14. 1. **Hemiparesis is a weakness on one side of the body that can interfere with the performance of activities of daily living. Encouraging the patient to do as much as possible will support self-esteem, and assisting when necessary will ensure that hygiene needs are met.**

2. Providing total assistance is unnecessary and may lower the patient's self-esteem, precipitate regression, or promote dependence.

3. Minimal supervision may result in the completion of an inadequate bath.

4. It is not the responsibility of the family to meet the physical needs of a hospitalized relative.

15. 1. These actions will promote plantar flexion and should not be done without a toe pleat.

2. **Maintaining functional alignment of a patient's head when making an occupied bed promotes comfort and minimizes stress to the respiratory passages and vital anatomy in the neck.**

3. Although fan-folding soiled linens as close to the patient's body as possible is done, it is not the priority.

4. Although positioning the bed in the horizontal position may be done to facilitate tight sheets with minimal

wrinkles, it is not the priority. In addition, there are many patients who cannot assume this position.

16. 1. A podiatrist should file or cut the toenails of a patient with diabetes. The toenails usually are thickened and hardened, and an accidental injury can take a long time to heal, become infected, and, if gangrene occurs, can even lead to an amputation.

2. Although patient teaching about daily foot care is important, it is not the priority.

3. A primary health-care provider's order is unnecessary. Foot care in relation to hygiene is within the scope of independent nursing practice.

4. **A thorough assessment of the patient is the first step of the nursing process. People with diabetes frequently have thick, hardened toenails, peripheral neuropathy, impaired arterial and venous circulation in the feet, and foot or leg ulcers.**

17. 1. Documenting results is done after the patient's immediate needs are met.

2. **When rolling a debilitated patient off a bedpan the perianal area is exposed, which permits the nurse to provide immediate perineal hygiene. A bed-bound, debilitated patient is incapable of providing self-hygiene after having a bowel movement on a bedpan.**

3. Repositioning the patient is not the priority after removing a debilitated patient from a bedpan.

4. The top linens should not have been removed during this procedure because they provide privacy and maintain dignity.

18. 1. Bedrest does not cause dry hair. Malnutrition, aging, and excessive shampooing cause dry hair.

2. Bedrest does not cause oily hair. Infrequent shampooing causes oily hair.

3. Bedrest does not cause hair to split. Excessive brushing, blow drying, and coloring cause hair to split.

4. **Bedrest causes matted, tangled hair because of friction and pressure related to the movement of the head on a pillow.**

19. 1. **Putting the right sleeve of the gown on the weak extremity first puts less stress on affected muscles; the stronger side can stretch more easily to dress.**

2. Although dressing the patient in an open-backed gown is helpful, the nurse still needs to put the gown on without stressing the joints, tendons, muscles, and nerves of the weak arm.

3. Encouraging the patient to dress independently may be frustrating and tiring and may cause further damage to the weak arm.

4. Leaving the right sleeve off while adjusting the tie at the neck is unnecessary. The patient should be dressed appropriately.

20. 1. Strong soap may further irritate the skin.

2. Loose stool contains digestive enzymes that are irritating to the skin and should be cleaned from the skin as soon as possible after soiling.

3. The patient is cognitively impaired and may be unaware of needs or how to use a call bell.

4. Placing a pad under the buttocks will not keep stool off the skin.

21. 1. Vasodilation increases blood flow to the surface of the skin, which promotes, not prevents, heat loss.

2. Conduction is the transfer of heat between two objects in physical contact.

3. Convection is the transfer of heat by movement of air along a surface. Using a bath blanket limits the amount of air flowing across the patient, which prevents heat loss.

4. Diffusion is the movement of molecules from a solution of higher concentration to a solution of lower concentration.

22. 1. The patient's developmental level will influence how the nurse will proceed, but it is not the first assessment.

2. Collecting the patient's toiletries is done after several other considerations and just before actually beginning the bath.

3. Although identifying the patient's ability to assist in hygiene activities is significant in relation to the extent of self-care that may be expected, it is not the first assessment.

4. Hygiene is a personal matter determined by individual beliefs, values, and practices. Hygiene practices are influenced by culture, religion, environment, age, health, and personal preferences. When personal preferences are supported, the patient has a sense of control and usually is more accepting of care.

23. 1. Although a bath is refreshing and relaxing and may support self-esteem, this is not the primary reason for bathing.

2. Although friction from rubbing the skin increases surface temperature, which increases circulation to the area, this is not the primary purpose of a bed bath.

3. The removal of accumulated oil, perspiration, dead cells, and bacteria from the skin limits the environment conducive to the growth of bacteria and skin breakdown. Intact, healthy skin is one of the body's first lines of defense.

4. Although range-of-motion exercises may be performed while bathing a patient, this is not the purpose of the bath.

24. 1. Although a person may have contractures, a person may still be able to provide self-care.

2. Being unable to wash body parts is a human response indicating that a patient is unable to provide for one's own activities of daily living, such as meeting hygiene and grooming needs.

3. People who are lethargic or listless generally are still able to provide for their own basic self-care needs. However, they may require frequent rest periods or more time to complete the task.

4. People who are legally blind are still able to provide for their own self-care needs.

25. 1. Friction, regardless of the direction of the washing strokes, in conjunction with soap and water, mechanically removes secretions, dirt, and microorganisms that decrease the potential for infection.

2. Friction, regardless of the direction of the washing strokes, mechanically removes dry, dead skin cells.

3. The pressure exerted on the skin surface by long, smooth strokes moving from distal to proximal areas also presses on the veins, which promotes venous return.

4. Long, smooth washing strokes that avoid a shearing force minimize skin tears.

26. **1. The accumulation of matter, such as food, epithelial elements, dried secretions, and microorganisms (sordes) eventually can lead to dental caries and periodontal disease and therefore must be removed during oral hygiene.**

2. Plaque is an invisible film composed of secretions, epithelial cells, leukocytes, and bacteria that adheres to the enamel surface of teeth.

3. Glossitis is an inflammation of the tongue.

4. Stomatitis is an inflammation of the oral mucosa.

27. 1. Brushing the teeth 6 times a day is more than the number of times a day recommended by the American Dental Association. Brushing the teeth 6 times a day is unnecessary for effective dental hygiene. It may cause gum recession which can lead to dentine hypersensitivity or cause damage to the neck of the teeth.

2. Brushing the teeth 4 times a day is more than the number of times a day recommended by the American Dental Association. It is important to know that excessive brushing with a soft brush using minimal pressure will not wear away enamel in the absence of an acidic environment. However, brushing the teeth 4 or more times a day may cause problems such as gum recession, which can lead to dentine hypersensitivity or cause damage to the neck of the teeth.

3. Brushing the teeth 3 times a day is more than the number of times a day recommended by the American Dental Association. However, some reputable Web sites recommend brushing the teeth after each meal. Some sites recommend brushing the teeth upon awakening to facilitate removal of bacteria from the mouth.

4. **The American Dental Association recommends brushing the teeth for 2 minutes 2 times a day and it should be done at least 30 minutes after consuming acidic food or drinks.**

28. 1. A primary health-care provider's order is unnecessary because providing foot care is within the scope of nursing practice.

2. When the patient has peripheral neuropathy, cutting or filing toenails should be provided by a podiatrist.

3. **Lukewarm water is comfortable and limits the potential for burns. Drying the feet limits moisture that promotes bacterial growth.**

4. Lotion between the toes in the dark warm environment of shoes promotes the growth of bacteria and the development of an infection.

29. 1. **Touching a patient during a bed bath invades the person's intimate space (physical contact to 1½ feet) because of the need to expose and touch personal body parts.**

2. Although the nurse enters a patient's intimate space when obtaining vital signs, it does not involve touching the intimate parts of a patient's body and is therefore less intrusive than other procedures.

3. This can be accomplished by remaining in a person's personal space (1½ to 4 feet) or social space (4 to 12 feet).

4. Although touching a patient while ambulating invades the person's intimate space, it does not involve touching the intimate parts of a patient's body and is therefore less intrusive than other procedures.

30. 1. Providing a bed bath is within the scope of nursing practice, so a primary health-care provider's order is unnecessary. An order is necessary for a tub bath or shower because it requires an activity order and is therefore a dependent function of the nurse.

2. **Patients should provide self-care within their abilities. When they have limitations, such as an inability to reach a body area, an activity intolerance, a decreased level of consciousness, or dementia, it is the nurse's responsibility to assist the patient regardless of the type of bath.**

3. It is impossible to expose just the body parts being washed during a tub bath or shower. During a tub bath or shower the entire body is exposed.

4. **Bathing is a private matter and an invasion of personal space. The nurse provides privacy by pulling a curtain, closing a door, and keeping the patient covered as much as possible. These interventions maintain the patient's dignity.**

5. There is no need for a call bell when a patient is taking a tub bath or a shower because it is unsafe to leave a patient alone.

31. 2. **The bath should follow a cephalocaudal progression and be based on the principle of from "clean to dirty." The face is washed first before soap is place in the bath water.**

3. The axillae are less soiled than the hands but are more soiled than the face.
4. The hands are more soiled than the axilla.
6. The water is changed after washing the soiled hands so as not to contaminate other areas of the body.
1. The back is less soiled than the genital area.
5. The genital area is considered the most soiled and should be washed last.

32. 1. Encouraging the use of artificial tears is unnecessary. Not everyone who wears eyeglasses has dry eyes. Also, this intervention requires a health-care provider's order.
2. Storing eyeglasses in a safe place when not being worn protects them from loss or damage.
3. A paper towel is coarse and may scratch the lenses of eyeglasses. A soft nonabrasive cloth or chamois should be used.
4. Patient preference determines how long eyeglasses can be worn.
5. Eyeglasses should be cleaned at least once a day because dirty lenses impair vision. Warm, not hot, water is used to prevent distortion of the lens or frame, particularly if it is made of a plastic compound.

33. 1. Medical, not surgical, asepsis is necessary. Clean gloves are adequate.
2. Soap is never used around the eyes. The eyes should be washed only with water.
3. Tilting the head or turning the patient toward the same side as the eye to be washed facilitates the flow of water from the inner to the outer canthus. This limits secretions from entering the lacrimal ducts.
4. Washing the eyes from the inner canthus to the outer canthus moves debris away from the lacrimal duct.
5. Using a new cotton ball for each stroke prevents reintroducing debris removed during the initial stroke.

34. 1. The call bell does not have to be positioned until there is a patient occupying the bed.
2. A pull sheet is not included in the procedure for an unoccupied bed. In addition, this creates too many layers of linens that may wrinkle under a patient. The draw sheet can be used as a pull sheet.

3. Wrinkles create ridges that exert additional pressure on the skin, promoting discomfort, skin irritation, and the development of pressure ulcers.
4. A toe pleat is essential because it allows room for movement of the feet and helps to prevent plantar flexion as a result of top sheets that are too tight.
5. Although this action is advisable to conserve the nurse's time and energy, it is not a priority.

35. 3. The first step involves positioning a waterproof pad on the floor on which to place the foot basin. Warm water promotes circulation. Avoiding hot water protects the patient from sustaining a burn injury.
2. The second step involves donning clean gloves to protect the nurse from the patient's body fluids. The heel of a foot is a common place for skin cracks and skin breakdown. Ensuring that the water temperature is comfortable helps to prevent a burn injury.
1. The third step involves soaking a foot for the appropriate length of time considering the patient's condition. A foot bath for a patient with diabetes or peripheral vascular disease may dry the skin, placing the patient at risk for cracks in the skin, and should be conducted over 5 minutes or less.
4. The fourth step involves washing each foot with rinse-free soap because this avoids the drying effect of soap residue. Cleaning under the nails with an orange stick removes debris and minimize the risk of injury that could occur when using a sharp instrument.
6. The fifth step involves drying each foot, especially between the toes, because moisture can cause maceration and support the growth of fungal infections.
5. The sixth step involves applying lotion to each foot while avoiding between the toes. Lotion hydrates the skin and keeps skin supple, reducing the risk of cracks in the skin. Lotion between the toes should be avoided because it can cause skin maceration and support the growth of fungal infections.

36. 1. Abrasive toothpaste (dentifrice) can harm the enamel of teeth. Nonabrasive toothpaste and a soft toothbrush should be used.

2. Brushing the teeth involves several techniques: brushing back and forth strokes across the biting surface of teeth; brushing from the gum line to the crown of each tooth; and, with the bristles at a 45-degree angle at the gum line, vibrating the bristles while moving from under the gingival margin to the crown of each tooth.

3. Mouthwash with anti-plaque properties can help prevent plaque buildup.

4. Unwaxed floss is thin, slides between the teeth easily, and is more effective than waxed floss.

5. A dental hygienist is a licensed oral health-care professional educated to provide such services as dental education, dental radiographs, oral prophylaxis, and plaque removal.

37. 1. Administration of oxygen is a dependent function of the nurse and requires a primary health-care provider's order unless it is needed in an emergency situation. The situation in this question is not an emergency.

2. When an obese patient is in the high-Fowler position the abdominal organs press against the diaphragm, which limits respiratory excursion. The semi-Fowler position is preferred.

3. Evaluation of a patient's response to care allows the nurse to alter care to meet the patient's individual needs.

4. Bathing body parts that the patient cannot reach ensures that the patient receives adequate hygiene care.

5. A rest period every 10 minutes may be inadequate or may unnecessarily prolong the bath. This is not individualized to the patient's needs.

38. 1. Shaving in the direction of hair growth limits skin irritation and prevents ingrown hairs.

2. A safety razor should be held at a 45-, not 90-, degree angle to the skin.

3. Short firm but gentle strokes should be used when shaving a patient.

4. Ensuring that the patient is not receiving an anticoagulant is essential. A patient receiving an anticoagulant should use an electric razor to avoid the risk of blood loss associated with an accidental cut using a safety razor.

5. A hot washcloth may cause a burn injury. A warm, not hot, washcloth applied to the face for several minutes before shaving helps to soften the beard.

39. 1. The patient is too confused to provide self-care even with partial assistance.

2. A towel bath is the most appropriate bathing plan for this patient. It is quick and easy to administer and is the intervention that is least taxing physically considering the patient's recent surgery, confusion, and respiratory status.

3. The patient is too confused and physically dependent to participate in a shower even with partial assistance.

4. It is too soon after surgery to submerse the patient's body in a tub bath. Generally a tub bath is contraindicated until a surgical wound is fully healed.

40. 1. Wearing clean gloves protects the nurse from the blood and body fluids of the patient. This interrupts the chain of infection.

2. Mouth breathing, oxygen use, unconsciousness, and debilitation, among other conditions, can lead to dry oral mucous membranes. The nurse should provide oral hygiene with saline rinses frequently to keep the oral mucosa moist.

3. Mouthwash contains astringents that can injure sensitive, delicate dry mucous membranes.

4. Oral hygiene four times a day is inadequate for a patient with a dry mouth, and a water pick is contraindicated because the force of the water can injure delicate dry mucous membranes.

5. Lemon and glycerin swabs are counterproductive because their use can lead to further dryness of the mucosa and an alteration in tooth enamel.

41. 1. Warm, not hot, water is used to clean the perineal area because the skin and mucous membranes of the genital area are sensitive, and hot water may cause harm.

2. The glans penis, foreskin, and shaft of the penis are cleaned before the scrotum. The scrotum is considered more soiled than the penis because of its proximity to the rectum.

3. When cleaning the shaft of the penis, bathing should start at the glans penis and then proceed down the shaft toward the scrotum.

4. **Stabilizing the penis and holding it firmly facilitates the bathing procedure and usually prevents an erection.**

5. **Washing from the tip of the penis in a circular motion and then down the shaft of the penis follows the principle of "clean to dirty," the meatus being the cleanest.**

42. 1. Strong soap may irritate fragile skin, and washing every other day is inadequate to cleanse the skin.

    2. Breaking pustules should be avoided because it can spread infection and cause skin damage and scarring. Acne with pustules requires the intervention of a dermatologist because topical or oral medications maybe necessary to treat the acne.

    3. **A water-based emollient for dry skin is less likely to block sebaceous gland ducts and hair follicles than an oil-based emollient, which will aggravate the condition.**

    4. Washing once a day is inadequate to cleanse the skin. Warm, not cool, water is necessary to remove the oily accumulation on the face.

    5. **Washing the face with mild soap and water twice a day will remove dirt and oil, which helps prevent secondary infection. Washing the face more than twice a day can irritate the skin and make acne worse.**

43. 1. The pillows can remain under the patient's head throughout the bath as long as this position is not contraindicated by the patient's condition. A patient does not have to remain in the supine position to receive a bed bath.

    2. **When a nursing care provider's uniform touches a patient's linens the uniform is considered contaminated. Microorganisms from the patient can be carried on the uniform to other patients. This is a violation of medical asepsis.**

    3. The nursing assistant should not be making eye contact with the patient. The nursing assistant should be concentrating on looking at the action being implemented.

4. Body parts should be covered when not being bathed to prevent heat loss and chilling. The left leg should be covered to promote comfort, prevent heat loss, and provide for privacy.

5. **Clean gloves should be worn to provide a barrier between the nursing assistant's hands and the patient's body fluids. This is an important medical aseptic practice associated with standard precautions.**

44. 1. Limiting baths to twice a week is an acceptable practice. Excessive exposure to warm water and soap exacerbates dry skin associated with aging.

    2. A humidified environment limits the amount of insensible loss of moisture through the skin, which helps the skin retain fluid and remain supple.

    3. Applying moisturizing lotion to the body daily is an acceptable practice. Older adults experience less sebum produced by sebaceous glands, causing dry and scaly skin. Moisturizing lotion helps to keep skin supple and less dry.

    4. **Bubble-bath preparations cause irritation and dryness of the skin because they remove essential skin surface oils. Showers are preferable to baths because baths require submersion in warm water, which is detrimental to skin hydration and resiliency.**

    5. Hot bath water removes essential skin surface oils, causing skin to be dry and scaly, and should be avoided. A short shower with warm water should be encouraged instead.

45. 1. Cuticles should be pushed back with a washcloth or an orange stick.

    2. **Filing nails straight across helps to avoid ingrown nails. Rounding corners slightly reduces sharp edges that may scratch the skin.**

    3. **Applying a moisturizing lotion around cuticles helps to soften cuticles.**

    4. **An orange stick is an implement that is shaped to facilitate removal of debris from under the nails without causing tissue injury. Removal of dirt and debris decreases the risk of infection.**

    5. Hot water can cause tissue injury and should be avoided. Warm, not hot, water should be used.

Mobility

KEYWORDS

The following words include nursing/medical terminology, concepts, principles, and information relevant to content specifically addressed in the chapter or associated with topics presented in it. English dictionaries, nursing textbooks, and medical dictionaries, such as *Taber's Cyclopedic Medical Dictionary,* are resources that can be used to expand your knowledge and understanding of these words and related information.

Ambulation
Atrophy
Blanchable erythema
Body mechanics
Bony prominence
Contracture
Exercises:
  Aerobic
  Anaerobic
  Isometric
  Isotonic
Flaccidity
Footdrop
Functional alignment
Gait
Hemiparesis
Hemiplegia
Joints:
  Ball and socket
  Condyloid
  Hinge
  Pivot
  Saddle
Mechanical lift, Hoyer lift
Paraplegia
Paresis
Popliteal
Positioning devices:
  Bed cradle
  Hand roll
  Hand-wrist splint
  Heel and elbow protectors
  Pillow
  Side rail
  Trapeze bar
  Trochanter roll
  Turning and pull sheet
Positions:
  Contour
  Dorsal recumbent
  Fowler (low-, semi-, high-)
  Knee-chest
  Lateral

Lithotomy
Orthopneic
Prone
Sims
Supine
Trendelenburg
Posture
Pressure relief, reduction devices:
  Mattresses:
    Air mattress
    Dense foam and gel
    Egg-crate mattress
  Cushions:
    Air
    Gel
    Heel and elbow protectors
    Sheepskin
Pressure ulcer, stages I, II, III, IV
Quadriplegia
Range-of-motion exercises:
  Active
  Active-assistive
  Passive
Range-of-motion movements:
  Abduction
  Adduction
  Circumduction
  Eversion
  Extension
  Flexion:
    Dorsal flexion
    Lateral flexion
    Plantar flexion
    Radial flexion
    Ulnar flexion
  Hyperextension
  Inversion
  Opposition of thumb
  Pronation
  Rotation:
    External
    Internal
  Supination

Reactive hyperemia	Mitt
Restraints:	Poncho
Belt	Vest
Chest	Wrist
Elbow	Shearing force
Four-point	

MOBILITY: QUESTIONS

1. A nurse turns a patient's ankle so that the sole of the foot moves medially toward the midline. Which word should the nurse use when documenting exactly what was done during range-of-motion exercises?
   1. Inversion
   2. Adduction
   3. Plantar flexion
   4. Internal rotation

2. A nurse is transferring a patient from a bed to a wheelchair. Which should the nurse do to quickly assess this patient's tolerance to the change in position?
   1. Obtain a blood pressure.
   2. Monitor for bradycardia.
   3. Determine if the patient feels dizzy.
   4. Allow the patient time to adjust to the change in position.

3. A nurse is transferring a patient from the bed to a wheelchair using a mechanical lift. Which is a basic nursing intervention associated with this procedure?
   1. Lock the base lever in the open position when moving the mechanical lift.
   2. Raise the mechanical lift so that the patient is six inches off the mattress.
   3. Keep the wheels of the mechanical lift locked throughout the procedure.
   4. Ensure the patient's feet are guarded when sitting on the mechanical lift.

4. A patient has hemiplegia as a result of a brain attack (cerebrovascular accident). Which complication of immobility is a concern to the nurse?
   1. Dehydration
   2. Contractures
   3. Incontinence
   4. Hypertension

5. Which stage pressure ulcer requires the nurse to measure the extent of undermining?
   1. Stage 0
   2. Stage I
   3. Stage II
   4. Stage III

6. A patient has a cast from the hand to above the elbow because of a fractured ulna and radius. After the cast is removed, the nurse teaches the patient active range-of-motion exercises. Which patient action indicates that further teaching is necessary?
   1. Moves the elbow to the point of resistance
   2. Keeps the elbow flexed at 90° after the procedure
   3. Assesses the elbow's response after this procedure
   4. Puts the elbow through its full range at least 3 times

7. Which word is **most** closely associated with nursing care strategies to maintain functional alignment when patients are bed bound?
   1. Endurance
   2. Strength
   3. Support
   4. Balance

8. A patient with impaired mobility is to be discharged within a week from the hospital. Which is an example of a discharge goal for this patient?
   1. The patient will understand range-of-motion exercises before their initiation.
   2. The patient will be taught range-of-motion exercises after they are ordered.
   3. The patient will transfer independently to a chair by discharge.
   4. The patient will be kept clean and dry at all times.

9. A nurse is performing passive range-of-motion exercises for a patient who is in the supine position. Which motion occurs when the nurse bends the patient's ankle so that the toes are pointed toward the ceiling?
   1. Adduction
   2. Supination
   3. Dorsal flexion
   4. Plantar extension

10. A nurse is caring for a patient with impaired mobility. Which position contributes **most** to the formation of a hip flexion contracture?
   1. Low-Fowler
   2. Orthopneic
   3. Supine
   4. Sims

11. A patient is diagnosed with a stage IV pressure ulcer with eschar. Which medical treatment should the nurse anticipate the primary health-care provider will order for this patient?
   1. Heat lamp treatment three times a day
   2. Application of a topical antibiotic
   3. Cleansing irrigations twice daily
   4. Débridement of the wound

12. A nurse raises a patient's arm forward and upward over the head during range-of-motion exercises. Which word should the nurse use when documenting exactly what was done during this range-of-motion exercise?
   1. Flexion
   2. Supination
   3. Opposition
   4. Hyperextension

13. A patient with a history of thrombophlebitis should not have pressure exerted on the popliteal space. In which position should the nurse **avoid** placing this patient?
   1. Prone
   2. Supine
   3. Contour
   4. Trendelenburg

14. A nurse is caring for a variety of patients, each experiencing one of the following problems. Which health problem places a patient at the **greatest** risk for complications associated with immobility?
   1. Incontinence
   2. Quadriplegia
   3. Hemiparesis
   4. Confusion

15. A nurse in a community center is conversing with a group of older adults who voiced fears about falling. Which is the **most** common consequence associated with older adults' fear of falling that the nurse should discuss with them?
1. Impaired skin integrity
2. Occurrence of panic attacks
3. Self-imposed social isolation
4. Decreased physical conditioning

16. A nurse is evaluating an ambulating patient's balance. Which factor about the patient is **most** important for the nurse to assess?
1. Posture
2. Strength
3. Energy level
4. Respiratory rate

17. A patient with an order for bedrest has diaphoresis. Which should the nurse use to **best** limit the negative effects of perspiration on dependent skin surfaces of this patient?
1. Ventilated heel protectors
2. Air-filled rings
3. Air mattress
4. Sheepskin

18. A nurse is teaching a class to nursing assistants about how to care for patients who are immobile. Which should the nurse include about why immobilized people develop contractures?
1. Muscles that flex, adduct, and internally rotate are stronger than weaker opposing muscles.
2. Muscular contractures occur because of excessive muscle flaccidity.
3. Muscle mass and strength decline at a progressive rate weekly.
4. Muscle catabolism exceeds muscle anabolism.

19. A nurse turns the palm of a patient's hand downward when performing range-of-motion exercises. Which word should the nurse use when documenting exactly what was done?
1. Pronation
2. Lateral flexion
3. Circumduction
4. External rotation

20. Which nursing action is **most** effective in relation to the concept *Immobility can lead to occlusion of blood vessels in areas where bony prominences rest on a mattress?*
1. Encouraging the patient to breathe deeply 10 times per hour
2. Performing range-of-motion exercises twice a day
3. Placing a sheepskin pad under the sacrum
4. Repositioning the patient every 2 hours

21. A nurse plans to use a trochanter roll when repositioning a patient. Where should the nurse place the trochanter roll?
1. Under the small of the back
2. Behind the knees when supine
3. Alongside the ilium to mid-thigh
4. In the palm of the hand with the fingers flexed

22. Which is the earliest nursing assessment that indicates permanent damage to tissues because of compression of soft tissue between a bony prominence and a mattress?
1. Nonblanchable erythema
2. Circumoral cyanosis
3. Tissue necrosis
4. Skin abrasion

23. An emaciated patient is at risk for developing a pressure ulcer. In which position should the nurse avoid placing the patient?
    1. Thirty-degree lateral position
    2. Side-lying position
    3. Supine position
    4. Prone position

24. A nurse is making an occupied bed. Which should the nurse do to prevent plantar flexion?
    1. Tuck in the top linens on just the sides of the bed.
    2. Place a toe pleat in the top linens over the feet.
    3. Let the top linens hang off the end of the bed.
    4. Use trochanter rolls to position the feet.

25. A nurse identifies that a patient's pressure ulcer has just partial-thickness skin loss involving the epidermis and dermis. Which stage pressure ulcer should the nurse document based on this assessment?
    1. Stage I
    2. Stage II
    3. Stage III
    4. Stage IV

26. Which nursing action should be implemented when assisting a patient to move from a bed to a wheelchair?
    1. Lowering the bed to 2 inches below the height of the patient's wheelchair
    2. Applying pressure under the patient's axillae areas when standing up
    3. Letting the patient help as much as possible when permitted
    4. Keeping the patient's feet within 6 inches of each other

27. A nurse places a patient in the orthopneic position. Which is the **primary** reason for the use of this position?
    1. Facilitates breathing
    2. Supports hip extension
    3. Prevents pressure ulcers
    4. Promotes urinary elimination

28. An immobilized bed-bound patient is placed on a 2-hour turning and positioning program. Which should the nurse explain to the patient is the **primary** reason why this program is important?
    1. Supports comfort
    2. Promotes elimination
    3. Maintains skin integrity
    4. Facilitates respiratory function

29. Which do nurses sometimes do that increase their risk for injury when moving patients?
    1. Use longer, rather than shorter, muscles when moving patients
    2. Place their feet wide apart when transferring patients
    3. Pull rather than push when turning patients
    4. Rotate their backs when moving patients

30. Nurses should monitor for which systemic responses in immobilized patients? **Select all that apply.**
    1. _____Pressure ulcer
    2. _____Dependent edema
    3. _____Hypostatic pneumonia
    4. _____Plantar flexion contracture
    5. _____Increased cardiac workload

31. A nurse moves a patient's leg through the range of motion demonstrated in the figure. Which word should the nurse use when documenting exactly what was done during the range-of-motion exercise?
    1. Eversion
    2. Circumduction
    3. Plantar flexion
    4. External rotation

32. A nurse is placing a patient in the left lateral position. Which actions should the nurse implement when positioning this patient? **Select all that apply.**
    1. _____Maintain the left knee flexed at ninety degrees.
    2. _____Rest the right leg on top of the left leg.
    3. _____Place the ankles in plantar flexion.
    4. _____Align the shoulders with the hips.
    5. _____Protract the left shoulder.

33. A nurse places a patient with a sacral pressure ulcer in the left Sims position. How should the nurse position the patient's right arm? **Select all that apply.**
    1. _____On a pillow
    2. _____Behind the back
    3. _____With the palm up
    4. _____In internal rotation
    5. _____With the elbow flexed

34. A nurse concludes that a patient has the potential for impaired mobility. Which assessments reflect risk factors that support this conclusion? **Select all that apply.**
    1. _____Joint pain
    2. _____Exertional fatigue
    3. _____Sedentary lifestyle
    4. _____Limited range of motion
    5. _____Increased respiratory rate

35. A nurse enters the room of the patient in the photograph. The patient has right-sided weakness and is attempting to transfer out of bed without the nurse's knowledge. What should the nurse do **first**?
    1. Lower the height of the bed to its lowest position to the floor.
    2. Reposition the patient back to the semi-Fowler position.
    3. Move the wheelchair parallel to the foot of the bed.
    4. Put on the patient's slippers.

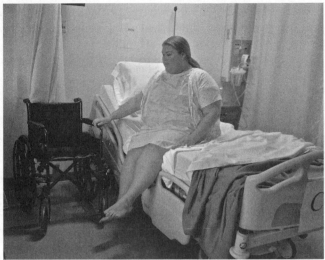

36. A nurse plans to teach a patient with hemiparesis to use a cane. Which should the nurse teach the patient to do? **Select all that apply.**
    1. _____Move forward 1 step with the weak leg first followed by the strong leg and cane.
    2. _____Adjust the cane height 12 inches lower than the waist.
    3. _____Hold the cane in the strong hand when walking.
    4. _____Look at the feet when walking with the cane.
    5. _____Avoid learning over onto the cane.

37. A nurse is planning to help move a patient up in bed. Which actions can the nurse implement to reduce the risk of self-strain when performing this action? **Select all that apply.**
    1. _____Move the patient up against gravity.
    2. _____Use the large muscles of the legs.
    3. _____Bend the body from the waist.
    4. _____Keep the knees slightly bent.
    5. _____Raise the bed to waist level.

38. A primary health-care provider orders crutches for a person who has a left lower leg injury. The nurse is teaching the person how to move from a standing to a sitting position in a chair. Place the following steps in the order in which they should be implemented.
    1. While standing, back up so that the unaffected leg is against the edge of the center of the chair seat.
    2. Hold the hand bars of both crutches with the left hand.
    3. Lean forward slightly and flex the knees and hips.
    4. Grasp the arm of the chair with the right hand.
    5. Lower the body into the chair.
    Answer: _____

39. A patient sits for excessive lengths of time in a wheelchair. Which sites should the nurse assess for skin breakdown in this patient? **Select all that apply.**
    1. _____Ischial tuberosities
    2. _____Bilateral scapulae
    3. _____Trochanters
    4. _____Malleolus
    5. _____Sacrum

40. A patient with limited mobility has an order to be out of bed to a chair for 1 hour daily. The nurse plans to transfer the patient using a mechanical lift. Which actions should the nurse implement? **Select all that apply.**
    1. _____Apply gentle pressure against the patient's knees while lowering the patient into the chair.
    2. _____Ensure that there is an order to use this device to transfer the patient out of bed.
    3. _____Hook the longer straps on the end of the sling closest to the patient's feet.
    4. _____Place a sheepskin inside the sling so that it is under the patient.
    5. _____Lead with the patient's feet when exiting the bed.

41. A primary health-care provider orders a standard walker for a patient who has left-sided weakness and requires some assistance with balance, but can bear weight on both legs. Which should the nurse teach the patient about how to use the walker safely? **Select all that apply.**
    1. _____Advance the strong leg last by itself.
    2. _____Lift the walker and move it forward twelve inches.
    3. _____Advance the walker and the weak leg ahead together first.
    4. _____Adjust the height of the walker so that it is equal with the hip joint.
    5. _____Roll the walker a comfortable distance ahead before stepping forward.

42. A nurse is to transfer a patient from a bed to a chair. After washing the hands, providing privacy, and explaining the transfer to the patient, the nurse ensures that the wheels on the bed are locked and moves the bed to the lowest position. Place the following steps in the order in which they should be implemented.
    1. Verify if the patient feels dizzy.
    2. Assess the patient's vital signs and strength while in the supine position.
    3. Assist the patient to a sitting position on the side of the bed with the feet on the floor.
    4. Elevate the head of the bed to the high-Fowler position and put footwear on the patient's feet.
    5. Support the patient sitting on the side of the bed for several minutes before transferring to a chair.
    Answer: _____

43. Which actions employed by the nurse indicate acceptable body mechanics to avoid self-injury? **Select all that apply.**
    1. _____Keep back, neck, pelvis, and feet aligned.
    2. _____Position oneself close to the patient.
    3. _____Keep knees and hips slightly flexed.
    4. _____Arrange for adequate help.
    5. _____Keep feet close together.

44. A nurse is assessing a patient's risk for thrombus formation associated with impaired mobility. Which factors constitute Virchow's triad? **Select all that apply.**
    1. _____Compression of small vessels in the legs
    2. _____Orthostatic hypotension
    3. _____Coagulation activation
    4. _____Hypostatic pneumonia
    5. _____Venous stasis

45. A nurse is caring for a male patient who is at risk for a pressure ulcer. After reviewing the patient's clinical record, which area of the body should the nurse identify is **most** at risk for a pressure ulcer?
    1. Greater trochanters
    2. Ischial tuberosities
    3. Medial malleolus
    4. Spinal processes

PATIENT'S CLINICAL RECORD

Primary Health-Care Provider Orders
Oxygen via simple face mask, humidified, 8 L flow rate

Levofloxacin 500 mg, PO, daily for 14 days

Prednisone 30 mg, PO, daily for 2 days; 20 mg, PO, daily for 2 days; 10 mg, PO, daily for
   2 days; and 5 mg, PO, daily for 2 days

Position for comfort

OOB to bathroom

Fluid intake, at least 3,000 mL daily, soft diet

Nurse's Progress Note
Patient sitting in an upright position leaning on a pillow on the over-bed table, oxygen face mask in place and set at a flow rate of 8 L, patient has a productive cough, expectorating clear-colored mucous. Respirations are 34 and labored, with mild retractions and flaring of nares. Assisted with activities of daily living, shortness of breath on activity.

Patient Interview
Patient states that he was fine until he caught his 5-year-old granddaughter's cold. He developed a fever, nasal stuffiness, and a "heavy cough" that got progressively worse. The primary health-care provider admitted him to the hospital with the diagnosis of pneumonia and an oxygen saturation rate of 88%. He said that since he is in the hospital he "feels much better." He stated that he is able to breathe best leaning over the over-bed table, that his cough is improved, and his fever is resolving.

1. 1. **Inversion, a gliding movement of the foot, occurs by turning the sole of the foot medially toward the midline of the body.**
2. Adduction occurs when an arm or leg moves toward and/or beyond the midline of the body.
3. Plantar flexion occurs when the joint of the ankle is in extension by pointing the toes of the foot downward and away from the anterior portion of the lower leg.
4. Internal rotation of a leg occurs by turning the foot and leg inward so that the toes point toward the other leg.

2. 1. Although a blood pressure reading may indicate the presence of hypotension, the blood pressure should be obtained before and after a transfer to allow a comparison to conclude that the hypotension is orthostatic hypotension.
2. If the patient is experiencing orthostatic hypotension, the heart rate will increase, not decrease.
3. **Feeling dizzy is a subjective response to orthostatic hypotension. Obtaining feedback from the patient provides a quick evaluation of the patient's tolerance of the transfer.**
4. Allowing the patient time to adjust to the change in position is not an assessment. This is a safe intervention for a patient who is experiencing orthostatic hypotension.

3. 1. The width of the base depends on the configuration of the bed, objects in the room, and the ultimate destination. The base usually is locked open when lifting or lowering the patient and locked closed when moving the lift.
2. Raising the mechanical lift so that the patient is six inches off the mattress is unsafe. The lift should raise the patient high enough to clear the surface of the bed.
3. The wheels must be unlocked to move the lift from under the bed to its ultimate destination.
4. **The legs dangle from the sling and therefore may drag across the linens or hit other objects if not protected.**

4. 1. Dehydration is not a response to immobility.
2. **Contractures result from permanent shortening of muscles, tendons, and ligaments. Routine range-of-motion exercises and maintaining the body in functional alignment can prevent contractures.**
3. The decreased tone of the urinary bladder and the inability to assume the usual voiding position in bed promote urinary retention, rather than urinary incontinence.
4. With immobility, the increased heart rate reduces the diastolic pressure. In addition, there is a decrease in blood pressure related to postural changes from lying to sitting or standing (orthostatic hypotension). This situation is manageable with a priority on maintaining patient safety.

5. 1. There is no stage 0 in the classification system for staging pressure ulcers.
2. The skin is still intact and there is no undermining in a stage I pressure ulcer.
3. Tissue damage is superficial and there is no undermining in a stage II pressure ulcer.
4. **In a stage III pressure ulcer there is full-thickness skin loss involving damage to subcutaneous tissue that may extend to the fascia and there may or may not be undermining, which is tissue destruction underneath intact skin along wound margins.**

6. 1. Moving the elbow to the point of resistance is desirable. Performing range of motion beyond resistance may injure muscles and joints and should be avoided.
2. **Keeping the elbow flexed after the procedure is undesirable because it contributes to a flexion contracture. Slight flexion to maintain functional alignment is preferred because it minimizes stress and strain on muscles, tendons, ligaments, and joints.**
3. Responses to range-of-motion exercises must be evaluated and compared with the assessment performed before the procedure.
4. Sequential flexion and extension of a hinge joint are efficient in facilitating full range of motion of the joint.

7. 1. Endurance relates to aerobic exercise that improves the body's capacity to consume oxygen for producing energy at the cellular level.
   2. Strength relates to isometric and isotonic exercises, which contract muscles and promote their development.
   3. **The line of gravity passes through the center of gravity when the body is correctly aligned; this results in the least amount of stress on the muscles, joints, and soft tissues. Bed-bound patients often need assistive devices such as pillows, sandbags, bed cradles, wedges, rolls, and splints to support and maintain the vertebral column and extremities in functional alignment.**
   4. Balance relates to body mechanics and is achieved through a wide base of support and a lowered center of gravity.

8. 1. This goal is not measurable as stated. Understanding is not measurable unless parameters are identified.
   2. This statement is a nursing intervention, not a patient goal.
   3. **This is a patient-centered goal that is specific and measurable and has a time frame.**
   4. This statement is a nursing goal, not a patient goal.

9. 1. Adduction occurs when an arm or leg moves toward and/or beyond the midline of the body.
   2. Supination occurs when the hand and forearm rotate so that the palm of the hand is facing upward.
   3. **Dorsal flexion (dorsiflexion) of the joint of the ankle occurs when the toes of the foot point upward and backward toward the anterior portion of the lower leg.**
   4. There is no range of motion called plantar extension. Plantar flexion occurs when the joint of the ankle is in extension by pointing the toes of the foot downward and away from the anterior portion of the lower leg.

10. 1. In the low-Fowler position the hips are slightly flexed.
   2. **While in the high-Fowler position the patient is then positioned leaning forward with arms resting on an over-bed table (orthopneic position). In the orthopneic position, the hips are**
   extensively flexed, creating an angle less than 90 degrees.
   3. In the supine position the hips are extended (180 degrees), not flexed.
   4. In the Sims position, the hip and knee of the upper leg are just slightly flexed.

11. 1. Heat lamp treatments will further dry out the wound and can cause burns.
   2. Topical antibiotics are used only when the ulcer is infected, not to treat eschar.
   3. Cleansing irrigations are ineffective in removing the thick, fibrin-containing cells of eschar covering the surface of the wound.
   4. **Thick, leather-like, necrotic devitalized tissue (eschar) must be removed surgically or enzymatically before wound healing can occur.**

12. 1. **The shoulder, a ball-and-socket joint, flexes by raising the arm from a position by the side of the body forward and upward to a position beside the head.**
   2. Supination occurs when the hand and forearm rotate so that the palm of the hand is facing upward.
   3. Opposition is the touching of the thumb of the hand to each fingertip of the same hand.
   4. Hyperextension of the arm occurs by moving an arm from a resting position at the side of the body to a position behind the body.

13. 1. In the prone position there is pressure in front of, not behind, the knees.
   2. In the supine position the hips and legs are extended, which does not exert pressure on the popliteal spaces.
   3. **In the contour position the head of the bed and the knee gatch are slightly elevated. The elevated knee gatch puts pressure on the popliteal spaces.**
   4. In the Trendelenburg position the hips and knees are extended, which does not exert pressure on the popliteal spaces.

14. 1. Patients who are incontinent are not necessarily immobile.
   2. **Quadriplegia, paralysis of all four extremities, places the patient at greatest risk for pressure ulcers because the patient has no ability to shift body weight off of bony prominences or change position without total assistance.**

3. Hemiparesis, muscle weakness on one side of the body, does not prevent a person from shifting or changing position to relieve pressure on the skin.
4. Confused patients can move independently when uncomfortable or when encouraged and assisted to move by the nurse.

15. 1. A person who chooses not to ambulate still has the ability to assume many different sitting or lying-down positions.
2. The occurrence of panic attacks is not the most common consequence. Anxiety and ultimately panic that is precipitated by a situation can be prevented by avoiding the situation.
3. A person who chooses not to ambulate because of a fear of falling still can socialize.
4. **Most falls occur when ambulating. Fear of falling results in the conscious choice not to place oneself in a position where a fall can occur. Disuse and muscle wasting cause a reduction of muscle strength at the rate of 5% to 10% per week so that within 2 months of immobility more than 50% of a muscle's strength can be lost. In addition, there is a decreased cardiac reserve. These responses result in decreased physical conditioning.**

16. 1. **Assessing posture will identify whether the patient's center of gravity is in the midline from the middle of the forehead to a midpoint between the feet and therefore balanced within the patient's base of support.**
2. Strength has more to do with the exertion of power, not balance.
3. Energy has more to do with endurance, not balance.
4. Assessing the respiratory rate before activity establishes a baseline against which to compare the respiratory rate after activity to determine tolerance for activity, not balance.

17. 1. Ventilated heel protectors protect only the heels, not the other dependent areas of the body.
2. Air-filled rings usually are made of plastic, which tends to promote sweating. Air rings rarely are used because they are designed for just the sacral area and often they increase, not decrease, pressure.
3. Air mattresses usually are made of plastic, which tends to promote sweating.

4. **The soft tuffs of sheepskin allow air to circulate, thereby promoting the evaporation of moisture that can precipitate skin breakdown.**

18. 1. **The state of balance between muscles that serve to contract in opposite directions is impaired with immobility. The fibers of the stronger muscles contract for longer periods than do those of the weaker, opposing muscles. This results in a change in the loose connective tissue to a denser connective tissue and to fibrotic changes that limit range of motion.**
2. Contractures occur because of muscle spasticity and shortening, not muscle flaccidity.
3. Disuse and muscle wasting cause a reduction in muscle strength at the rate of 5% to 10% a week so that within 2 months more than 50% of a muscle's strength can be lost. This results in muscle atrophy, not contractures.
4. Muscle catabolism exceeding muscle anabolism is unrelated to contractures. In unused muscles, catabolism exceeds anabolism and the muscles decrease in size (disuse atrophy).

19. 1. **Pronation of the hand occurs by rotating the hand and arm so that the palm of the hand is facing down toward the floor.**
2. Lateral flexion of the hand occurs with both abduction (radial flexion) and adduction (ulnar flexion). With the hand supinated, radial flexion occurs by bending the wrist laterally toward the thumb and ulnar flexion occurs by bending the wrist laterally toward the fifth finger.
3. Circumduction, associated with a ball-and-socket joint, occurs when an extended extremity moves forward, up, back, and down in a full circle.
4. External rotation is associated with ball-and-socket joints. External rotation of a shoulder occurs when the upper arm is held parallel to the floor, the elbow is at a 90-degree angle, the fingers are pointing toward the floor, and the person moves the arm upward so that the fingers point toward the ceiling. External rotation of the hip occurs when a leg in extension is turned so that the foot points outward from the midline of the body.

20. 1. Deep breathing prevents atelectasis and hypostatic pneumonia, not pressure ulcers, which this question is about.
    2. Range-of-motion exercises help prevent contractures, not pressure ulcers.
    3. Although sheepskin reduces friction and limits pressure, its main purpose is to allow air to circulate under the patient to minimize moisture and maceration of skin.
    4. **Turning a patient relieves pressure on the capillary beds of the dependent areas of the body, particularly the skin overlying bony prominences, which reestablishes blood flow to the area. When pressure on a capillary exceeds 15 to 32 mm Hg its lumen is occluded, depriving oxygen to local body cells.**

21. 1. Placing a trochanter roll under the small of the back is unsafe. A trochanter roll placed in the small of the back is uncomfortable and produces an excessive lumbar curvature.
    2. Placing a trochanter roll behind the knees when supine is contraindicated because it places unnecessary pressure on the popliteal area.
    3. **A trochanter roll is a rolled wedge, pillow, or sandbag placed by the lateral aspect of the leg between the iliac crest and knee to prevent external hip rotation.**
    4. The diameter of a trochanter roll is too wide to maintain the hand in functional alignment.

22. 1. **Nonblanchable erythema refers to redness of intact skin that persists when finger pressure is applied. This is the classic sign of a stage I pressure ulcer.**
    2. Circumoral cyanosis is associated with hypoxia, not pressure ulcers.
    3. With necrosis, death of cells has occurred. Necrosis occurs in stage III and stage IV pressure ulcers.
    4. With an abrasion, the superficial layers of the skin are scraped away. This stage II, not stage I, pressure ulcer appears reddened and may exhibit localized serous weeping or bleeding.

23. 1. The 30-degree lateral position is the preferred position to prevent pressure ulcers because it limits body weight directly over bony prominences, versus other positions.

2. **In the side-lying position the majority of the body weight is borne by the greater trochanter. The bone is close to the surface of the skin, with minimal overlying protective tissue.**
    3. In the supine position the occiput, scapulae, spine, elbows, sacrum, and heels are at risk for pressure; however, the body weight is distributed more evenly than in some other positions.
    4. In the prone position the ears, cheeks, acromion process, anterior-superior spinous process, knees, toes, male genitalia, and female breasts are at risk for pressure; however, the body weight is distributed more evenly than in some other positions.

24. 1. Top sheets tucked in along the sides of the bed still exert pressure on the upper surface of the feet, which may promote plantar flexion. The sides of top sheets, mitered at the foot of the bed, hang feely off the side of the bed.
    2. **Making a vertical or horizontal toe pleat in the linen at the foot of the bed over the patient's feet leaves room for the feet to move freely and avoids exerting pressure on the upper surface of the feet, thus minimizing plantar flexion.**
    3. The weight of the top sheets still exerts pressure on the upper surface of the feet, promoting plantar flexion.
    4. Trochanter rolls prevent external hip rotation, not plantar flexion.

25. 1. In a stage I pressure ulcer the skin is still intact and manifests clinically as reactive hyperemia.
    2. **In a stage II pressure ulcer the partial-thickness skin loss manifests clinically as an abrasion, blister, or shallow crater.**
    3. In a stage III pressure ulcer there is full-thickness skin loss involving the subcutaneous tissue that may extend to the underlying fascia. The ulcer manifests clinically as a deep crater with or without undermining.
    4. In a stage IV pressure ulcer there is full-thickness skin loss with extensive destruction, tissue necrosis, or damage to muscle, bone, or supporting structures.

26. 1. The bed should be higher, not lower, than the wheelchair so that gravity can facilitate the transfer.

2. Applying pressure under the patient's axillae areas when standing up should be avoided because it can injure local nerves and blood vessels.

3. **Encouraging the patient to be as self-sufficient as possible ensures that the transfer is conducted at the patient's pace, promotes self-esteem, and decreases the physical effort expended by the nurse.**

4. Keeping the patient's feet within 6 inches of each other will provide a narrow base of support and is unsafe.

27. 1. **Sitting in the high-Fowler position and leaning forward (orthopneic position) allow the abdominal organs to drop by gravity, which promotes contraction of the diaphragm. The arms resting on an over-bed table increase thoracic excursion. This position promotes breathing.**

2. The hips will be in extreme flexion, not extension.

3. Pressure ulcers can still occur on the ischial tuberosities.

4. Standing (for men) and sitting on a toilet/commode (for women) are superior to any position for promoting urinary elimination.

28. 1. Although turning the patient to a new position every 2 hours provides variety and increased comfort, these are not the primary reasons for this intervention.

2. Although turning frequently promotes elimination, the upright positions, such as high-Fowler and sitting, have a greater influence on elimination because of the effect of gravity.

3. **Compression of soft tissue greater than 15 to 32 mm Hg interferes with capillary circulation and compromises tissue oxygenation in the compressed area. Turning the patient relieves the compression of tissue in dependent areas, particularly those tissues overlying bony prominences.**

4. Although turning and positioning promote respiratory functioning, other interventions, such as sitting, deep breathing, coughing, and incentive spirometry, have a greater influence on respiratory status.

29. 1. Nurses should use the longer, stronger muscles of the thighs and buttocks when moving patients to protect their weaker back and arm muscles.

2. Nurses should have a wide base of support when moving patients to provide better stability.

3. Nurses should use a pulling motion to turn patients because the muscles that flex, rather than extend, the arm are stronger, and pulling, rather than pushing, creates less friction and therefore less effort.

4. **Twisting (rotation) of the thoracolumbar spine and flexion of the back place the line of gravity outside the base of support, which can cause muscle strain and disabling injuries. Misaligning the back when moving patients occurs most often when not facing the direction of the move.**

30. 1. Prolonged pressure on skin over a bony prominence interferes with capillary blood flow to the skin, which ultimately can result in the localized response of a pressure ulcer.

2. **Decreased calf muscle activity and pressure of the bed on the legs allow blood to accumulate in the distal veins. The resulting increased hydrostatic pressure moves fluid out of the intravascular compartment and into the interstitial compartment, causing edema.**

3. **Static respiratory secretions provide an excellent media for bacterial growth that can result in hypostatic pneumonia, which is a systemic response to immobility.**

4. Plantar flexion contracture (footdrop) is a localized response to prolonged extension of the ankle.

5. **An increased cardiac workload results from a decrease in vessel resistance and redistribution of blood in the body with blood pooling in the lower extremities. These are systemic responses to immobility.**

31. 1. Eversion, a gliding movement of the foot, occurs by turning the sole of the foot away from the midline of the body.

2. Circumduction is a range of motion that is performed with a ball-and-socket joint. It occurs when an extended extremity moves forward, up, back, and down in a full circle.

3. Plantar flexion occurs when the joint of the ankle is in extension by pointing the toes of the foot downward and away from the anterior portion of the lower leg.

4. External rotation occurs when the entire leg is rolled outward from the body so that the toes point away from the opposite leg.

32. 1. This excessive flexion can result in contractures of the hip and knee. The left leg should be slightly flexed or extended.
2. The right leg should be supported on a pillow in front of the left leg.
3. The ankles should be maintained at 90 degrees.
4. **Maintaining alignment of the shoulders and hips avoids stress and strain on the bones, muscles, and joints.**
5. **In the left lateral (side-lying) position, the left arm is positioned in front of the body with the shoulder pulled forward (protracted). This reduces pressure on the joint in the shoulder and acromial process.**

33. 1. In the left Sims position the patient's right arm and leg are supported on pillows to prevent internal rotation of the shoulder and hip.
2. The right arm is positioned in front of, not behind, the back.
3. The right hand is positioned in pronation, not supination.
4. The right arm is positioned to maintain the shoulder in functional alignment, not internal rotation.
5. **The right elbow should be slightly flexed at the elbow; this supports comfort and functional alignment.**

34. 1. **Joint pain may prevent the patient from moving about, leading to contractures resulting in impaired mobility.**
2. Exertional fatigue is associated with activity intolerance. People who are fatigued are still able to move.
3. People who are sedentary are still able to move.
4. **Limited range of motion is associated with contracture formation and impaired mobility.**
5. An increased respiratory rate is a response to activity, not impaired mobility.

35. 1. The patient may fall if the bed is lowered while the patient is sitting on the side of the bed. Although lowering the height of the bed closer to the floor should be done, it is not the first thing that the nurse should do in this scenario.

2. **The patient should be repositioned back in bed. The height of the bed from the floor is in the highest position and must be lowered before the patient can be transferred out of bed. It is unsafe to lower the height of the bed while the patient is sitting on the side of the bed.**
3. Repositioning the wheelchair is not the first thing that the nurse should do. Also, the wheelchair should be positioned at the head of the left side of the bed. A patient with right-sided weakness should exit the bed leading with the strong left arm and leg.
4. Putting on the patient's slippers is not the first thing the nurse should do in this scenario. Once the patient is returned to bed then slippers can be placed on the patient's feet and then the patient can be transferred.

36. 1. The unaffected leg should be advanced first because the weight of the body is supported by the leg with the greatest strength.
2. With the tip of the cane placed 6 inches lateral to the foot, the handle should be at the level of the patient's greater trochanter to ensure that the elbow will be flexed 15 to 30 degrees when using the cane.
3. **A cane is a hand-gripped assistive device; therefore, the hand opposite the hemiparesis should hold the cane. Exercises can strengthen the flexor and extensor muscles of the arms and the muscles that dorsiflex the wrist.**
4. This will cause flexion of the neck, hips, or waist that will move the center of gravity outside the base of support. Body alignment is essential for balance, stability, and safe ambulation.
5. **Leaning over onto the cane should be avoided. The patient should distribute weight between the feet and cane while standing in an upright posture. This is the most stable position when using a cane.**

37. 1. Muscle strain is reduced when moving patients with gravity, not with the added effort needed to move patients against gravity.
2. **To exert an upward lift the gluteal and leg muscles should be used, rather than the sacrospinal muscles of the back.**

The gluteal and leg muscles are larger than the sacrospinal muscles and therefore fatigue less quickly, and their use protects the intervertebral disks.

3. Bending from the waist increases the strain on the sacrospinal muscles and intervertebral disks.

4. The muscles of the legs are most efficient when the knees and hips are slightly bent. This reduces strain on the muscles being used.

5. Positioning the bed at waist height avoids the need to reach and stretch, which may strain a caregiver's muscles, bones, joints, tendons, or ligaments.

38. 1. Being as close as possible to the chair allows a person to use the chair for support when sitting. Also, it supports sitting deeper into the seat of the chair, which is safer than sitting on the edge of the seat.

2. Holding the hand bars of both crutches with the left hand frees the right hand for the next step in the procedure.

4. Grasping the arm of the chair with the right hand allows the person to support body weight partially on the right arm and the right leg.

3. Leaning forward slightly and flexing the knees and hips partially lowers the body and prepares it for the next step in the procedure.

5. Lowering the body into the chair protects the body from injury.

39. 1. When in the sitting position, the hips and knees are flexed at 90 degrees and the body's weight is borne by the pelvis, particularly the ischial tuberosities, which are bony protuberances of the lower portion of the ischium. Using a wheelchair results in prolonged sitting unless interventions are implemented to promote local circulation.

2. Pressure to the scapulae occurs when in a sitting position as well as when in the supine and Fowler positions.

3. Pressure to a trochanter occurs in a side-lying, not the sitting, position.

4. Pressure to the lateral malleolus of an ankle occurs in a side-lying, not a sitting, position.

5. Pressure to the sacrum occurs when in a sitting position, as well as when in the supine and Fowler positions.

40. 1. Applying gentle pressure against the patient's knees while lowering the patient into the chair facilitates an upright sitting position in a chair.

2. Moving patients with a mechanical lift is within the scope of nursing practice, and a primary health-care provider's order is unnecessary.

3. The longer straps/chains go in the holes for the seat support, which keep the legs and pelvis below the upper body. Appropriate placement of the upper and lower straps/chains creates a bucket seat in which a patient is moved safely.

4. Placing a sheepskin inside the sling so that it is under the patient may result in the patient's sliding down and out of the sling during the transfer. Nylon, net, or canvas slings are available.

5. It does not matter whether the feet or the head exit the bed first as long as functional alignment and safety are maintained.

41. 1. Advancing the unaffected leg last by itself allows weight to be borne by the affected leg while both arms are supported on the walker.

2. Six, not 12, inches is the proper distance to advance a walker. Twelve inches will require the patient to reach too far forward, moving beyond a stable center of gravity.

3. Advancing the walker and the affected leg together ensures that weight is borne by the unaffected leg.

4. Adjusting the height of the walker so that it is equal with the hip joint is too low and will require the patient to stoop to reach the hand bar. The hand bar should be at a height just below the patient's waist, allowing the elbows to be slightly flexed. A walker that is the correct height allows a patient to assume a more functional posture.

5. A standard walker does not have wheels. Directing a person to advance a walker a comfortable distance is unsafe. The word "comfortable" is subjective and unclear. Walkers should be advanced 6 inches at a time to ensure that a person's weight does not extend beyond the center of gravity.

42. 2. Assessing vital signs is the first step in the procedure because results provide baseline data against which to compare outcomes when evaluating activity tolerance.

4. Elevating the head of the bed is the second step in the procedure. It minimizes the effort required by the patient to move to a sitting position in the bed as well as minimizes lifting by the nurse. Footwear protects the patient's feet from physical injury and contamination from pathogens that may be on the floor.

3. Assisting the patient to a sitting position on the side of the bed with the feet on the floor facilitates pivoting of the trunk of the body perpendicular to the length of the bed. This prepares the body eventually to assume a wide base of support with the greatest mass between the feet.

1. Verifying if the patient feels dizzy evaluates tolerance to the activity and is the fourth step in the transfer procedure. Dizziness indicates orthostatic hypotension. If this occurs the nurse should support the patient in the sitting position for a few minutes. If dizziness does not resolve, then return the patient to a semi-Fowler position to provide for the safety of the patient.

5. Supporting the patient in the sitting position for several minutes before transferring to a chair is the fifth step in the transfer procedure. This reduces the possibility of orthostatic hypotension and allows more time for an evaluation of the patient's response to the change in position.

43. 1. Alignment reduces the risk of lumbar vertebrae and muscle group injury resulting from torqueing (twisting).

2. Positioning oneself close to the patient keeps the patient closer to your center of gravity. Increased stability reduces strain on back muscles.

3. Keeping knees and hips slightly flexed facilitates using the large muscles of the legs rather than the back to move the patient.

4. Multiple caregivers share the load of moving a patient safely.

5. Feet should be positioned wide apart, not close together, to provide a wide base of support, which increases stability.

44. 1. Compression of small vessels in the legs is one of the three factors that make up Virchow's triad. Immobility leads to vessel compression which can cause injury to small vessels.

2. Orthostatic hypotension is not one of the three factors that make up Virchow's triad. Orthostatic hypotension occurs when prolonged inactivity deactivates the baroreceptors associated with constriction and distention of blood vessels. When changing position there is a decrease in venous return, followed by a decrease in cardiac output and a decline in blood pressure. It may take several seconds to several minutes for the blood pressure to respond to the change in position.

3. Coagulation activation is one of the three factors that make up Virchow's triad. As a result of venous pooling there is a decreased clearance of coagulation factors, resulting in activation of clotting (i.e., the blood clots faster).

4. Hypostatic pneumonia is not one of the three factors that make up Virchow's triad. Hypostatic pneumonia is an inflammation of the lung as a result of stasis of respiratory secretions.

5. Venous stasis is one of the three factors that make up Virchow's triad. Inactive skeletal muscles of the legs do not adequately compress the peripheral vessels in the legs and therefore do not assist with the return of blood back to the heart; this results in stasis of blood in the lower extremities.

45. 1. Greater trochanters are at risk when a patient is in the side-lying position.

2. Ischial tuberosities are at greatest risk when a patient is in the orthopneic or mid- to high-Fowler positions because the greatest weight of the body is exerted against the genital, perianal, and sacral areas of the body.

3. A lateral malleolus is at risk when a patient is in a side-lying position.

4. Spinal processes are at risk when a patient is in the supine or a Fowler position.

Nutrition

KEYWORDS

The following words include nursing/medical terminology, concepts, principles, and information relevant to content specifically addressed in the chapter or associated with topics presented in it. English dictionaries, nursing textbooks, and medical dictionaries, such as *Taber's Cyclopedic Medical Dictionary,* are resources that can be used to expand your knowledge and understanding of these words and related information.

Amino acids:
  Essential
  Nonessential
Basal metabolic rate
Calorie, kilocalorie
Calorie count
Cellular metabolism:
  Anabolism
  Catabolism
Fiber:
  Insoluble
  Soluble
Food consistency:
  Chopped
  Liquid
  Pureed
  Regular
  Soft
Ideal body weight
Laboratory values:
  Blood urea nitrogen
  Serum albumin
  Total cholesterol
  Transferrin level
  Triglycerides
Malnutrition
MyPlate
Nausea
Nutrients:
  Carbohydrates
  Fats
  Minerals:
    Fluoride
    Iodine
    Iron
    Potassium
    Sodium
  Protein:
    Complete
    Incomplete
  Water

Obesity
Recommended dietary allowances
Stomatitis
Therapeutic diets:
  Clear liquid
  Full liquid
  2 g sodium
  Low residue
  Mechanical soft
  Protein restricted
Tube feedings:
  Continuous
  Gastrostomy
  Intermittent
  Jejunostomy
  Nasogastric
Underweight
Vegetarian:
  Flexitarian
  Lactovegetarian
  Vegan
  Ovolactovegetarian
Vitamins:
  Fat soluble:
    A
    D
    E
    K
  Water soluble:
    C (ascorbic acid)
    B_1 (thiamine)
    B_2 (riboflavin)
    B_3 (niacin)
    B_6 (pyridoxine)
    B_{12} (cobalamin)
    Biotin
    Folic acid
    Pantothenic acid
Vomiting

NUTRITION: QUESTIONS

1. A patient is admitted to the hospital with a history of liver dysfunction associated with hepatitis. With which metabolic problem does the nurse anticipate that this patient may have a problem?
   1. Emulsifying fats
   2. Digesting carbohydrates
   3. Manufacturing red blood cells
   4. Reabsorbing water in the intestines

2. A nurse is assessing a patient who is admitted to the hospital with withdrawal from alcohol. Which effect of alcohol on the body will influence the patient's plan of care?
   1. Interferes with the absorption of glucose
   2. Accelerates the absorption of medications
   3. Decreases the absorption of many important nutrients
   4. Lengthens passage time of stool through the intestinal tract

3. An obese resident of a nursing home who is receiving a 1,500-calorie weight reduction diet has not lost weight in the past 2 weeks. Which should the nurse do **first**?
   1. Inform the primary health-care provider of the patient's lack of progress.
   2. Instruct the patient to limit intake to 1,000 calories per day.
   3. Schedule a multidisciplinary team conference.
   4. Keep a log of the oral intake for 3 days.

4. A patient of Latino heritage is prescribed a low-fat diet. The patient tells the nurse, "I am going to have a hard time giving up my favorite family recipes." Which food should the nurse recommend that is low in fat and generally is included in the Latino culture?
   1. Salsa
   2. Pasta
   3. Steamed fish
   4. Refried beans

5. A patient is diagnosed with a vitamin A deficiency. Which type of pie should the nurse encourage the patient to ingest?
   1. Blueberry
   2. Pumpkin
   3. Cherry
   4. Pecan

6. A patient is anorexic because of stomatitis related to chemotherapy. Which should the nurse be **most** concerned about when planning care for this patient?
   1. Aspiration
   2. Dehydration
   3. Malnutrition
   4. Constipation

7. A nurse is counseling a patient with the diagnosis of osteoporosis. In addition to calcium, which vitamin supplement should the nurse anticipate that the primary health-care provider will prescribe for this patient?
   1. B
   2. K
   3. D
   4. E

8. An older adult is admitted to the hospital for multiple health problems. Assessment reveals that the patient has no teeth and is having difficulty eating. Which diet should the nurse encourage the primary health-care provider to order for this patient?
   1. Liquid supplements
   2. Mechanical soft
   3. Pureed
   4. Soft

9. A nurse is caring for patients with a variety of nutrition-related problems. Which problem eventually may require a patient to have a nasogastric feeding tube inserted?
   1. Malabsorption syndrome
   2. Difficulty swallowing
   3. Nausea and vomiting
   4. Stomatitis

10. A nurse is caring for a patient who is confused and disoriented. Which type of food containing chicken is **most** appropriate for this patient?
    1. Soup
    2. Salad
    3. Fingers
    4. Casserole

11. An older adult tends to bruise easily and the primary health-care provider recommends that the patient eat foods high in vitamin K. In addition to teaching the patient about food sources of vitamin K, the nurse should include nutrients that must be ingested for vitamin K to be absorbed. Which foods that increase the absorption of vitamin K should be included in the teaching plan?
    1. Carbohydrates
    2. Starches
    3. Proteins
    4. Fats

12. A school nurse is preparing a health class about vitamins. Which information about vitamins that is based on a scientific principle should the nurse include?
    1. Eating a variety of foods prevents the need for supplements.
    2. Megadoses of vitamins have proved to be most effective in preventing illness.
    3. Taking a prescribed vitamin supplement is the best way to ensure adequate intake.
    4. Vitamins that are more expensive are more pure than those that are less expensive.

13. A patient without any identified current health problems is having a yearly physical examination. The laboratory results indicate the presence of ketosis. Which rationale explains the presence of ketosis in this otherwise healthy adult?
    1. Inadequate intake of carbohydrates
    2. Increased intake of protein
    3. Excessive intake of starch
    4. Decreased intake of fiber

14. Which vitamin should a nurse teach a patient does not require fat in the diet to be absorbed?
    1. Vitamin C
    2. Vitamin A
    3. Vitamin E
    4. Vitamin D

15. An occupational nurse is facilitating a weight reduction group discussion. Which should the nurse explain is the **most** common contributing factor of obesity?
    1. Sedentary lifestyle
    2. Low metabolic rate
    3. Hormonal imbalance
    4. Excessive caloric intake

16. A nurse is evaluating the effectiveness of a nutritional program for a patient with anemia. Which clinical finding is a short-term indicator of an improved nutritional status?
    1. Weight gain of two pounds daily
    2. Increasing transferrin level
    3. Decreasing serum albumin
    4. Appropriate skin turgor

17. A patient is diagnosed with iron deficiency anemia. Which major cause of iron deficiency will influence a focused assessment by the nurse?
    1. Metabolic problems
    2. Inadequate diets
    3. Malabsorption
    4. Hemorrhage

18. A primary health-care provider identifies that a patient may have a fluoride deficiency. Which physical characteristic supports this conclusion?
    1. Stomatitis
    2. Dental caries
    3. Bleeding gums
    4. Mottling of the teeth

19. A nurse identifies that a vegetarian understands the importance of eating kidney beans when the patient indicates that they are essential because they contain which nutrient?
    1. Carbohydrates
    2. Minerals
    3. Protein
    4. Fat

20. Which is the **most** common independent nursing intervention to help a hospitalized debilitated older adult maintain body weight?
    1. Making mealtime a social activity
    2. Taking a thorough nutritional history
    3. Providing assistance with the intake of meals
    4. Encouraging dietary supplements between meals

21. An adult female patient with which total cholesterol level requires health teaching about a low-cholesterol diet?
    1. 210 mg/dL
    2. 190 mg/dL
    3. 150 mg/dL
    4. 100 mg/dL

22. A nurse is caring for a patient who is expending energy that is greater than the patient's caloric intake. Which human response will occur?
    1. Fever
    2. Anorexia
    3. Malnutrition
    4. Hypertension

23. A nurse is reviewing the laboratory findings of a patient to assess the patient's nutritional status. Which laboratory result from among the following tests is an indicator of inadequate protein intake?
1. High hemoglobin
2. Low serum albumin
3. Low specific gravity
4. High blood urea nitrogen

24. A patient of Asian heritage is recommended to follow a low-fat diet to lose weight. Which food low in fat generally is consumed by members of an Asian population?
1. Egg rolls
2. Spareribs
3. Crispy noodles
4. Hot and sour soup

25. A nurse is teaching a patient about the importance of balancing protein, carbohydrates, and fats in the diet. The nurse identifies that the teaching about carbohydrates is understood when the patient states that carbohydrates are known for providing which of the following?
1. Electrolytes
2. Vitamins
3. Minerals
4. Energy

26. A patient has been blind in one eye for several years because of the complications associated with diabetes mellitus. The patient is admitted to the hospital with a detached retina and resulting loss of sight in the other eye. Which should the nurse do to assist this patient with meals?
1. Explain to the patient where items are located on the plate according to the hours of a clock.
2. Encourage eating one food at a time according to the preference of the patient.
3. Order finger foods that are permitted on the patient's diet.
4. Feed the patient the ordered meals.

27. Which is **unrelated** to the balance of calcium in the body?
1. Osteoporosis
2. Vitamin D
3. Tetany
4. Iron

28. A nurse is caring for a patient receiving bolus enteral feedings several times daily. Which nursing intervention is **most** important to help prevent diarrhea?
1. Flush the tube after every feeding.
2. Check the residual before each feeding.
3. Elevate the head of the bed 30 degrees continuously.
4. Discard the refrigerated opened cans of formula after 24 hours.

29. A nurse teaches a patient about the prescribed low-fat diet. Which foods selected by the patient indicate that the teaching was understood? **Select all that apply.**
1. _____Eggs
2. _____Liver
3. _____Cheese
4. _____Turkey
5. _____Scallops
6. _____Flounder

30. A patient has a high serum cholesterol level. Which foods should the nurse teach the patient to **avoid? Select all that apply.**
    1. _____Liver
    2. _____Shrimp
    3. _____Skim milk
    4. _____Turkey burger
    5. _____Sliced bologna

31. A primary health-care provider prescribes folic acid 0.8 mg PO once daily for a patient with anemia. Unit-dose tablets of 0.4 mg/tablet are available. How many tablets should the nurse administer? **Record your answer using a whole number.**
    Answer: _____ tablets

32. A patient has a decreased hemoglobin level because of a low intake of dietary iron. Which foods should the nurse teach the patient are excellent sources of iron? **Select all that apply.**
    1. _____Eggs
    2. _____Fruit
    3. _____Meat
    4. _____Bread
    5. _____Spinach

33. A primary health-care provider orders a low-residue diet for a patient with an inflammatory bowel disease. Which foods should the nurse teach the patient to include in the diet? **Select all that apply.**
    1. _____Scrambled eggs
    2. _____Iceberg lettuce
    3. _____Orange juice
    4. _____Green beans
    5. _____Rye bread

34. A patient is admitted to the hospital with a diagnosis of alcoholism. The primary health-care provider prescribes thiamine hydrochloride (vitamin B_1) 50 mg IM three times a day. The drug is supplied 100 mg/mL. Indicate on the syringe the line to which the nurse should fill the syringe to administer the prescribed dose.

35. A patient has multiple fractures from a skiing accident. To **best** facilitate bone growth the nurse should encourage the patient to eat more foods high in calcium. Which foods selected by the patient indicate an understanding of foods that are high in calcium? **Select all that apply.**
    1. _____Orange juice
    2. _____Peanut butter
    3. _____Cottage cheese
    4. _____Baked flounder
    5. _____Low-fat yogurt
    6. _____Cooked spinach

36. A nurse is obtaining a health history from a patient. Which information reflects healthy behaviors? **Select all that apply.**
    1. _____Increasing fruits and vegetables to 50% of food intake
    2. _____Substituting fish for meat in the diet
    3. _____Wanting to lose 20 pounds
    4. _____Consuming 4 eggs a week
    5. _____Eating foods low in fat

37. A nurse is caring for a postoperative patient. The nurse reviews the patient's concurrent health problems, checks the medications prescribed by the primary health-care provider, and performs a focused assessment. Which should the nurse do at 12 p.m.?

1. Administer 5 units of regular insulin subcutaneously to the patient.
2. Notify the primary health-care provider of the patient's status.
3. Give the oral solution of 15 mg of oxycodone.
4. Provide an additional dose of ipratropium.

Concurrent Health Problems
Diabetes mellitus for 10 years
Obstructive lung disease (COPD) for 6 years

Prescribed Medications
Ipratropium 17 mcg aerosol inhaler, 2 inhalations four times a day
Oxycodone oral solution 15 mg PO every 6 hours whenever necessary
NPH insulin 20 units subcutaneously 8 a.m.
Regular insulin 8 units subcutaneously 8 a.m.
Regular insulin coverage subcutaneously before meals and at hour of sleep
   <150 mg/dL to 0 units
   151–200 mg/dL to 3 units
   201–250 mg/dL to 5 units
   251–300 mg/dL to 7 units
   301–350 mg/dL to 9 units
   >351: Call provider

Physical Assessment
11:50 a.m.: Breath sounds indicate slight wheezing over right sternal border
Respirations: 22 breaths per minute, unlabored
Serum glucose finger stick: 235 mg/dL
Incisional pain of 3 on pain scale of 0 to 10

---

38. A primary health-care provider orders a clear liquid diet for a patient. Which foods should the nurse teach the patient to **avoid** when following this diet? **Select all that apply.**

1. _____Strawberry gelatin
2. _____Decaffeinated tea
3. _____Strong coffee
4. _____Pureed soup
5. _____Ice cream

39. A nurse teaches a postoperative patient about foods high in protein that will promote wound healing. Which food selection by the patient indicates that the teaching was effective? **Select all that apply.**

1. _____Milk
2. _____Meat
3. _____Bread
4. _____Cheese
5. _____Vegetables

40. A nurse must obtain the serum glucose level of a patient with diabetes mellitus. The nurse completes all the initial preparations for the procedure including verifying the order, identifying the patient, and washing the hands. Place the following steps in the order in which they should be performed.

1. Don clean gloves.
2. Wipe away the first drop with sterile gauze.
3. Hold the patient's finger in a dependent position.
4. Drop the second drop of blood on the reagent strip.
5. Puncture the side of the end of a finger with a sterile lancet.
6. Wipe the intended puncture side with an approved antiseptic.

Answer: _____

41. A patient is scheduled for surgery and the nurse is teaching the patient about the importance of vitamin C in wound healing. Which sources of vitamin C should the nurse include in the teaching plan? **Select all that apply.**

1. _____Potatoes
2. _____Papayas
3. _____Yogurt
4. _____Beans
5. _____Milk

42. A nurse is administering enteral nutrition via the method depicted in the photograph. Identify the steps that should be implemented when administering enteral nutrition via this method. **Select all that apply.**

1. _____Administer water after the feeding.
2. _____Administer the bolus over 60 minutes.
3. _____Elevate the head of the bed 15 degrees.
4. _____Ensure that the formula is at room temperature.
5. _____Add formula continuously to the syringe just before it empties.

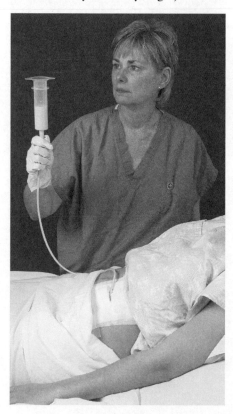

43. A young adult woman tells the nurse that she has been taking St. John's wort for several weeks for depression. Which should the nurse teach the patient that is important to know about taking St. John's wort? **Select all that apply.**
    1. _____St. John's wort should not be taken without an evaluation by a primary health-care provider.
    2. _____Use an additional method of birth control if taking an oral contraceptive.
    3. _____Discontinue it if there is no improvement in symptoms within 3 months.
    4. _____Discontinue it 2 weeks before surgery with general anesthesia.
    5. _____Apply sunscreen to skin exposed to the sun.

44. An older adult states that he is experiencing all the signs and symptoms of an enlarged prostate and is interested in taking the herbal supplement saw palmetto. Which is important for the nurse to teach the patient about treatment with saw palmetto? **Select all that apply.**
    1. _____It should not be taken until after a workup by a urologist.
    2. _____Taking saw palmetto is generally safe as a dietary supplement.
    3. _____Saw palmetto interferes with the measurement of prostate-specific antigen.
    4. _____Some patients report an improvement in erectile dysfunction after taking saw palmetto.
    5. _____The most recent research by reputable institutions indicates that saw palmetto is more effective than a placebo in reducing the symptoms of an enlarged prostate.

45. A nurse is providing for the nutritional needs of several patients. Which problems increase patients' caloric requirements? **Select all that apply.**
    1. _____Burns
    2. _____Nausea
    3. _____Dysphagia
    4. _____Pneumonia
    5. _____Depression

1. **1. Bile is produced and concentrated in the liver and stored in the gallbladder. As fat enters the duodenum, it precipitates the release of cholecystokinin, which stimulates the gallbladder to release bile. Bile, an emulsifier, enlarges the surface area of fat particles so that enzymes can digest the fat.**
   2. The liver is not involved with carbohydrate digestion. Ptyalin (secreted by the parotid glands), amylase (secreted by the pancreas), and sucrase, lactase, and maltase (secreted by the walls of the small intestine) digest carbohydrates.
   3. The liver is not involved with red blood cell production. People who are deficient in iron and protein have difficulty with red blood cell production.
   4. The large intestine, not the liver, is involved with reabsorbing water. The majority of the water in chyme is reabsorbed in the first half of the colon, leaving the remainder (approximately 100 mL) to form and eliminate feces.

2. **1.** Alcohol interferes with the absorption of thiamine, which is essential to oxidize, not absorb, glucose.
   2. The damaging effects of alcohol decrease, not increase, the efficiency of the process of absorption of medications in the stomach and intestines. However, alcohol can potentiate the action of drugs, such as central nervous system depressants.
   3. Alcohol interferes with vitamin intake, absorption, metabolism, and excretion. It specifically interferes with the absorption of vitamins A, D, K, thiamine, folic acid, pyridoxine, and B$_{12}$.
   4. Alcohol increases intestinal motility so that it decreases, not increases, the length of time it takes intestinal contents to pass through the body.

3. **1.** Informing the primary health-care provider of the patient's status is premature. The nurse is abdicating the responsibility to help the patient.
   2. A change in diet requires a primary health-care provider's order. Generally, calories should not be restricted below 1,200 cal/day for women or 1,500 cal/day for men so that they receive adequate amounts of essential nutrients.
   3. Conducting a multidisciplinary team conference may eventually be done, but it is premature at this time.
   4. When the expected outcome of an intervention is not attained, the situation must be reassessed to determine the problem and the plan changed appropriately. A record of a dietary intake provides objective information about the amounts and types of food consumed. This information provides data about nutrient deficiencies or excesses, eating patterns, behaviors associated with eating, and potential problems and needs.

4. **1. Salsa predominantly contains tomatoes, onions, and peppers, all which are low in fat.**
   2. Pasta contains predominantly carbohydrates, not fat. In addition, in the Latino culture, rice and beans are preferred over pasta. Pasta is associated with the Italian culture.
   3. Although steamed fish is low in fat, foods in the Latino culture generally are stewed or fried. Vegetables, legumes, and meat usually are preferred over fish.
   4. Refried beans are a fried food that should be avoided on a low-fat diet. Frying involves cooking food with a saturated or unsaturated fat solution, which is composed mostly of fatty acids. Fatty acids combine with glycerol to form triglycerides.

5. **1.** One piece of blueberry pie contains only 14 mcg RE of vitamin A.
   2. Pumpkin is an excellent source of vitamin A. One piece (one-sixth of a 9-inch diameter pie) contains 3,750 mcg RE (retinol equivalents) of vitamin A.
   3. One piece of cherry pie contains only 70 mcg RE of vitamin A.
   4. One piece of pecan pie contains only 115 mcg RE of vitamin A.

6. **1.** Although in some patients stomatitis may cause difficulty with swallowing (dysphagia), which may contribute to aspiration, a bland diet soft in consistency will help to minimize dysphagia.

2. Ingesting adequate amounts of fluid generally is not a problem as long as acidic fluids are avoided because they irritate the lesions of the mucous membranes.

3. **Stomatitis, inflammation of the mucous membranes of the oral cavity, can be painful. Patients with stomatitis frequently avoid eating to limit discomfort, which can lead to inadequate nutritional intake and malnutrition.**

4. Although a loss of appetite may contribute to constipation, an increase in fluid intake and activity can help prevent constipation.

7. 1. The B-complex vitamins are related to protein synthesis and cross-linking of collagen fibers, which are essential for integrity of the integumentary system, not strong bones.

2. Vitamin K promotes blood clotting by increasing the synthesis of prothrombin by the liver; it does not promote strong bones.

3. **Vitamin D (also regarded as a hormone) promotes bone mineralization by producing transport proteins that bind calcium and phosphorus, which increases intestinal absorption, stimulates the kidneys to return calcium to the bloodstream, and stimulates bone cells to use calcium and phosphorus to build and maintain bone tissue.**

4. Vitamin E prevents the oxidation of unsaturated fatty acids and thereby prevents cell damage; it does not promote strong bones.

8. 1. A person with few or no teeth, should be able to meet all daily nutrient requirements without liquid supplements.

2. **A mechanical soft diet is modified only in texture. It includes moist foods that require minimal chewing and eliminates most raw fruits and vegetables and foods containing seeds, nuts, and dried fruit.**

3. A person with few or no teeth, can handle a diet with a more solid consistency than pureed foods. A pureed diet is a soft diet processed to a semisolid consistency.

4. A person with few or no teeth, can handle a diet with a more solid consistency than a soft diet. A soft diet is moderately low in fiber and lightly seasoned. A soft diet usually is ordered for patients who are unable to tolerate a regular diet after

surgery as a transition between liquids and a regular diet.

9. 1. A nasogastric feeding (enteral feeding) enters the stomach and is not an appropriate therapy for a patient with malabsorption syndrome. The formula would still have to be absorbed by the gastrointestinal tract.

2. **If a patient with difficulty swallowing (dysphagia) does not respond to a dysphagia diet (mechanical soft, soft, blended or pureed liquids), there may be a need for the insertion of a gastrostomy tube. Gastrostomy feedings can be administered to meet nutritional needs and minimize the risk of aspiration.**

3. Nasogastric feedings are contraindicated in the presence of vomiting because of the potential for aspiration. The cause of the nausea and vomiting should be identified and treated.

4. Nasogastric feedings are a drastic measure for stomatitis. Stomatitis, an inflammation of the mouth, usually is a temporary problem that responds to pharmacological therapy and frequent, appropriate oral hygiene.

10. 1. A confused patient may not know how to manipulate a spoon to eat soup. This may result in spilling and frustration.

2. Eating chicken salad requires the use of a utensil that may be beyond the patient's cognitive ability.

3. **Chicken fingers are a single food item that usually is familiar to most people in the United States. A single familiar food is an easier symbol to decode cognitively than food mixed together in one dish. Food that the patient can eat with the fingers, rather than a utensil, promotes independence.**

4. Eating a casserole requires the use of a utensil that may be beyond the patient's ability. In addition, food mixed together is more confusing than food that is presented individually for patients who are confused or disoriented.

11. 1. Carbohydrates are not necessary for the absorption of vitamin K.

2. Starches are not necessary for the absorption of vitamin K.

3. Proteins are not necessary for the absorption of vitamin K.

4. Vitamin K is one of the fat-soluble vitamins (A, D, E, and K) that require the presence of fat to be absorbed. Vitamin K plays an essential role in the production of the clotting factors II (prothrombin), VII, IX, and X.

12. 1. **A balanced diet with choices in moderation from a variety of foods will provide the recommended daily allowances of essential nutrients without the need for supplements.**
    2. Megadoses of vitamins no longer operate as nutritional agents, and excesses are detrimental to the body, particularly to the liver and brain.
    3. Vitamins by themselves will not ensure an adequate intake. Their action contributes to chemical reactions (i.e., they act as catalysts), and they must have their substrate materials to work on, which are carbohydrates, protein, and fats and their metabolites.
    4. It may or may not be true that expensive vitamins are more pure than inexpensive vitamins.

13. 1. **When the amount of carbohydrates ingested does not meet the energy requirements of an individual, the body will break down stored fat to meet its energy needs. Ketone bodies are produced during the oxidation of fatty acids.**
    2. An increased intake of protein helps meet energy demands because when the energy from carbohydrates is depleted, the body converts protein and fatty acids to glucose (gluconeogenesis).
    3. Starch is the major source of carbohydrates in the diet and it yields simple sugars on digestion. Adequate serum glucose levels provide for energy needs, thus negating the need to break down body fat, resulting in ketosis.
    4. Fiber is unrelated to ketosis.

14. 1. **Vitamin C (ascorbic acid) is a water-soluble vitamin. The presence of fat or bile salts is unnecessary for its absorption.**
    2. Vitamin A is a fat-soluble vitamin that requires fat and bile salts to be absorbed.
    3. Vitamin E is a fat-soluble vitamin that requires fat and bile salts to be absorbed.
    4. Vitamin D is a fat-soluble vitamin that requires fat and bile salts to be absorbed.

15. 1. A sedentary lifestyle is only one theory associated with the cause of obesity.
    2. A low metabolic rate is only one theory associated with the cause of obesity.
    3. A hormonal imbalance is only one theory associated with the cause of obesity.
    4. **An excessive caloric intake is the basis of all weight gain regardless of the etiology. Excess ingested nutrients are stored in adipose tissue (fat) and muscle, which increases body weight. Obesity is body weight 20% or greater than ideal body weight. Glucose is stored as glycogen in the liver and muscle with surplus amounts being converted to fat. Glycerol and fatty acids are stored as triglycerides in adipose tissue. Excess amino acids are used for glucose formation or are stored as fat.**

16. 1. A rapid weight gain indicates fluid retention, not an improved nutritional status. One liter of fluid weighs 2.2 pounds.
    2. **Transferrin is a glycoprotein formed in the liver. Serum transferrin is a marker for iron metabolism and protein status. Because its half-life is 8 days compared with albumin, which is 20 days, serum transferrin levels will provide earlier objective information concerning a person's increasing or decreasing nutritional status. Serum transferrin ranges between 215 and 380 mg/dL in adults depending on gender.**
    3. A decreasing serum albumin level indicates a deteriorating, not improving, nutritional status. A serum albumin level should range between 3.5 and 5.0 g/dL. Mild depletion values range between 2.8 and 3.4 g/dL. Moderate depletion values range between 2.1 and 2.7 g/dL. In severe depletion, values are less than 2.1 g/dL.
    4. Appropriate skin turgor, fullness, and elasticity that allow the skin to spring back to its previous state after being pinched reflect an adequate fluid, not nutritional, balance.

17. 1. Although the inability to form hemoglobin in the absence of other necessary factors, such as vitamin B_{12} (pernicious anemia), can result in iron deficiency, it is not the major cause of iron deficiency.
    2. **The most common nutrient deficiency in the United States is that of iron, which results from an inadequate**

supply of dietary iron. The major condition indicating iron deficiency is anemia because iron is a key component of red blood cells.

3. Malabsorption of iron is not the major cause of iron deficiency. However, the malabsorption of iron can be caused by a lack of gastric hydrochloric acid, which is necessary to help liberate iron for absorption, and the presence of phosphate or phytate, inhibitors of iron absorption.

4. Although hemorrhage can precipitate iron deficiency, it is not the major etiological factor.

18. 1. Stomatitis, inflammation of the mucous membranes of the mouth, is most often caused by infectious sources (e.g., herpes simplex virus, *Candida albicans*, and hemolytic streptococci) or chemotherapy, not fluoride deficiency.

2. **Fluoride strengthens the ability of the tooth structure to withstand the erosive effects of bacterial acids on the teeth. The recommended daily intake of fluoride for adults is 1.5 to 4.0 mg.**

3. Bleeding gums is caused by inflammation of the gums (gingivitis), not fluoride deficiency.

4. Mottling of the teeth is related to a fluoride excess, not a fluoride deficiency. Yellow, brown, or black discoloration of teeth may indicate other problems, such as staining, a partial or total nonviable nerve, or tetracycline administration during the prenatal period or early childhood.

19. 1. Although kidney beans are an excellent source of carbohydrates, a vegetarian diet has many other foods that can be selected to provide this nutrient.

2. Although kidney beans are an excellent source of minerals, especially sodium, potassium, and phosphorus, a vegetarian diet has many other foods that can be selected to provide this nutrient.

3. **Kidney beans are high in protein. One cup of kidney beans contains 15 g of protein. Complete proteins come from animal sources, such as meat, poultry, and fish, but they are not included on a vegetarian diet. Kidney beans combined with a grain are a substitute for a complete protein.**

4. One cup of kidney beans contains only 1 g of fat.

20. 1. Although making mealtime a social activity is desirable, it may be impractical or impossible in an acute care facility. Patient rooms may be private or semiprivate, which limits exposure to other patients, and patients often are too sick to socialize.

2. Although obtaining a nutritional history is done, the information will not necessarily improve intake.

3. **Sick older adults often are debilitated, lack energy, and do not feel well. Assistance with meals conserves the patient's energy and demonstrates a caring concern, which may increase the intake of food.**

4. Dietary supplements require a primary health-care provider's order. Providing dietary supplements is a dependent function of the nurse.

21. 1. **A total cholesterol level of 210 mg/dL in a woman is 10 mg more than the acceptable limit of 200 mg/dL. Patients should be taught the foods to avoid that are high in cholesterol to prevent excessive cholesterol levels.**

2. 190 mg/dL is an acceptable level of cholesterol for an adult woman.

3. 150 mg/dL is an acceptable level of cholesterol for an adult woman.

4. 100 mg/dL is an acceptable level of cholesterol for an adult woman.

22. 1. During the states of malnutrition and starvation, the basal metabolic rate (BMR) decreases because the lean body mass decreases. Fever is associated with an increased, not decreased, BMR.

2. When energy expended is greater than the caloric intake, an individual will experience hunger, not anorexia. Hunger is a dull or acute pain felt around the epigastric area caused by a lack of food. Anorexia is the loss or lack of appetite.

3. **When energy expenditure exceeds caloric intake, eventually body fat and muscle mass break down to supply the fuel needed for metabolism. Malnutrition results when the body's cells have a deficiency or excess of one or more nutrients.**

4. When a person is malnourished, eventually the serum protein will be low, which may result in decreased colloid osmotic pressure and then movement of fluid from the intravascular compartment into the

peritoneal cavity. When the circulating blood volume decreases, the blood pressure decreases, not increases.

23. 1. Hemoglobin concentration of the blood correlates closely with the red blood cell count. Elevated hemoglobin suggests hemoconcentration from increased numbers of red blood cells (polycythemia) or dehydration.
   2. **Serum proteins, particularly albumin, reflect a person's skeletal muscle and visceral protein status. An expected serum albumin level ranges between 3.5 and 5.0 g/dL. Mild depletion ranges between 2.8 and 3.4 g/dL. Moderate depletion ranges between 2.1 and 2.7 g/dL. Severe depletion is less than 2.1 g/dL.**
   3. Specific gravity is a urine test that measures the kidney's ability to concentrate urine. A low specific gravity reflects dilute urine that suggests a high urine volume, diabetes insipidus, kidney infection, or severe renal damage with disturbances in concentrating and diluting abilities.
   4. Blood urea nitrogen (BUN) measures the nitrogen fraction of urea, a product of protein metabolism. An elevated BUN suggests renal disease, reduced renal perfusion, urinary tract obstruction, and increased protein metabolism.

24. 1. Egg rolls are a fried food. Frying involves cooking food in a solution consisting of saturated or unsaturated fat, which is composed mostly of fatty acids. Fatty acids combine with glycerol to form triglycerides.
   2. Spareribs are high in saturated fat and cooked with sauces that are high in saturated or unsaturated fat.
   3. Crispy noodles are a fried food that should be avoided. Frying involves cooking food with a saturated or unsaturated fat solution, which is composed mostly of fatty acids.
   4. **Hot and sour soup contains less fat than the other food choices listed.**

25. 1. An electrolyte is a chemical substance that, in solution, dissociates into electrically charged particles. Electrolytes maintain the chemical balance between cations and anions in the body, which is essential for acid-base balance.
   2. Vitamins are organic compounds that do not provide energy but are needed for the metabolism of energy.

3. Minerals are inorganic elements or compounds essential for regulating body functions. The major minerals of the body are calcium, phosphorus, sodium, potassium, magnesium, chloride, and sulfur.
   4. **Carbohydrates, a group of organic compounds, such as saccharides, starch, cellulose, and gum, are the main fuel sources for energy. Athletes competing in endurance events often adhere to a diet that increases carbohydrates to 70% of the diet for the last 3 days before a race (carbohydrate loading) to maximize muscle glycogen storage.**

26. 1. **The clock system, which identifies where certain foods are on a plate in relation to where numbers are located on a clock, allows the patient to be independent when eating. Independence with activities of daily living supports self-esteem.**
   2. Eating one food at a time is unnecessary and may decrease the patient's appetite.
   3. Ordering finger foods is unnecessary and limits the patient's food choices.
   4. Feeding the patient does not promote independence and may precipitate feelings of low self-esteem.

27. 1. Osteoporosis is a disease characterized by a decrease in total bone mass and deterioration of bone tissue that leads to bone fragility and the risk of fractures. Adequate calcium is necessary for building and strengthening bones and preventing osteoporosis.
   2. Vitamin D promotes bone mineralization by producing transport proteins that bind calcium and phosphorus. This increases intestinal absorption, stimulates the kidneys to return calcium to the bloodstream, and stimulates bone cells to use calcium and phosphorus to build and maintain bone tissue.
   3. A decrease in calcium in the blood (hypocalcemia) can eventually lead to tetany, which is characterized by muscle spasms, paresthesias, and convulsions.
   4. **Iron is unrelated to calcium balance. Iron is essential for hemoglobin formation.**

28. 1. Flushing the tube after every feeding moves the formula into the stomach and helps maintain tube patency; it does not reduce the risk of diarrhea.

2. Checking residual volume informs the nurse about the absorption of the last feeding. This step prevents the addition of more feeding than the patient can digest; it does not prevent diarrhea. Generally feedings are withheld when a certain residual volume is identified. Protocols may include withholding the next feeding when a residual of half the volume of the last feeding is removed just before the next feeding, or the primary health-care provider may give specific instructions if there is a residual volume.

3. Elevating the head of the bed 30 degrees at all times helps to keep the formula in the stomach via the principle of gravity and helps to prevent aspiration; it does not prevent diarrhea.

4. **Contaminated formula can cause diarrhea. Opened cans of formula support bacterial growth and must be discarded after 24 hours even when refrigerated.**

29. 1. Eggs should be avoided on a low-fat diet. One egg contains 1.7 g of saturated fat.

2. Liver should be avoided on a low-fat diet. Three ounces of liver contain 2.5 g of saturated fat.

3. Cheese should be avoided on a low-fat diet. Depending on the cheese, 1 ounce contains 4.4 to 6.2 g of saturated fat.

4. **Turkey is permitted on a low-fat diet. Three ounces of turkey contain 0.9 g of saturated fat. A low-fat food should contain less than 1.0 g of saturated fat per serving.**

5. **Scallops are permitted on a low-fat diet. Three ounces of scallops contain 0.1 g of saturated fat.**

6. **Flounder is permitted on a low-fat diet. Three ounces of flounder contain 0.3 g of saturated fat.**

30. 1. **Liver is high in cholesterol. Three ounces of beef, calf, and chicken liver contain 331, 477, and 537 mg of cholesterol, respectively.**

2. **Shrimp are high in cholesterol. Three ounces of shrimp contain 166 mg of cholesterol.**

3. One cup of skim milk contains only 18 mg of cholesterol.

4. Three ounces of turkey contain only 59 mg of cholesterol.

5. Two slices of bologna contain only 31 mg of cholesterol.

31. Answer: 2 tablets.
Solve the problem by using ratio and proportion.

$$\frac{\text{Desired } 0.8 \text{ mg}}{\text{Have } 0.4 \text{ mg}} = \frac{\text{x tab}}{1 \text{ tab}}$$

0.4 x = 0.8
x = 0.8 ÷ 0.4
x = 2 tablets

32. 1. One egg contains only 1.0 mg of iron.

2. One serving of fruit contains less than 1.0 mg of iron.

3. **Meat, especially liver, is an excellent source of iron. Three ounces of meat contain 1.6 to 5.3 mg of iron depending on the type of meat and whether it is a regular or lean cut.**

4. One slice of bread contains 0.7 to 1.4 mg of iron depending on the type of bread.

5. **Spinach is an excellent source of iron. A half cup of boiled spinach contains 3.2 mg of iron.**

33. 1. **All eggs, except fried, are permitted on a low-residue (low-fiber) diet. A low-residue diet is easily digested and absorbed and limits bulk in the intestines after digestion.**

2. **Lettuce is permitted on a low-residue diet. One cup of shredded iceberg lettuce contains 0.8 g of fiber.**

3. Orange juice contains pulp, a soluble fiber, which is not permitted on a low-residue diet.

4. Green beans contain polysaccharides that provide structure to plants and result in a residual after digestion that is not permitted on a low-residue diet. One cup of green beans contains 4.19 g of dietary fiber.

5. Whole-grain breads, breads with seeds or nuts, and breads made with bran consist of insoluble fibers that are not permitted on a low-residue diet. Two slices of whole-wheat bread contain 4 g of fiber.

34. Solve the problem by using ratio and proportion.

$$\frac{\text{Desired } 50 \text{ mg}}{\text{Have } 100 \text{ mg}} = \frac{\text{x mL}}{1 \text{ mL}}$$

100 x = 50
x = 50 ÷ 100
x = 0.5 mL

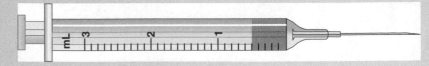

35. 1. One cup of orange juice contains only 27 mg of calcium.
2. One tablespoon of peanut butter contains only 5 mg of calcium.
3. Cottage cheese is an excellent source of calcium, which is essential for bone growth. One cup of cottage cheese contains 155 mg of calcium. The NIH Consensus Conference—Optimal Calcium Intake recommends an average intake of 1,000 to 1,500 mg of calcium daily for an adult depending on various factors.
4. Three ounces of baked flounder contain only 13 mg of calcium.
5. Low-fat yogurt is an excellent source of calcium, which is essential for bone growth. One cup of low-fat yogurt contains 345 mg of calcium.
6. Cooked spinach is an excellent source of calcium, which is essential for bone growth. One cup of cooked spinach contains 276 mg of calcium.

36. 1. The Center for Nutrition Policy and Promotion advocates in the MyPlate diet that fruits should be 25% of one's diet and vegetables should be 25% of one's diet.
2. Fish, such as flounder and haddock, contain extremely low levels of saturated fat compared with meat, which is much higher in saturated fat.
3. Wanting to lose 20 pounds reflects cognition, not behavior. Desiring something may or may not progress to action.
4. Although eggs are high in cholesterol, they are low in saturated fats, and they can be eaten in moderation (e.g., 4 to 6 eggs or less a week). Recent studies indicate that even 1 egg a day is not associated with an increased risk of coronary heart disease or stroke.
5. Eating foods low in fat is a healthy behavior because it is an action that promotes a healthy lifestyle. Implementing health-promotion behaviors is based on the perceived benefits of the actions.

37. 1. The patient's serum glucose level is 235. The primary health-care provider wrote a prescription for regular insulin coverage. When the serum glucose level is between 201 and 250 the patient is to receive 5 units of regular insulin subcutaneously.

2. It is unnecessary to notify the primary health-care provider of the patient's status.
3. The patient's pain is at level 3 on a scale of 0 to 10. The nurse can delay the administration of oxycodone, a potent analgesic, until the patient is experiencing a higher level of pain.
4. The patient's respiratory status is stable. There is no prescription to administer an additional dose of ipatropium. The administration of medication is a dependent function of the nurse.

38. 1. Gelatin is a clear liquid that is a solid when refrigerated and a liquid at room temperature. It is permitted in either form on a clear liquid diet.
2. Caffeinated or decaffeinated tea is permitted on a clear liquid diet.
3. Weak or strong and caffeinated or decaffeinated coffee is permitted on a clear liquid diet.
4. Pureed soups are permitted on a full-liquid, not clear liquid, diet. Pureed soups have a high-solute load, including fats and proteins, which stimulates the digestive process.
5. Milk and milk products are not included on a clear liquid diet. Ice cream contains a high-solute load, including fat and proteins, which stimulates the digestive process.

39. 1. One cup of milk contains only 8 g of protein.
2. Food from animal sources (e.g., meat, poultry, fish, and eggs) provides complete proteins and therefore is the best source of protein. Three ounces of meat or poultry contain 19 to 25 g of protein depending on the type of meat or poultry.
3. Although a serving of a grain product contains approximately 2 g of protein, it primarily provides carbohydrates and fiber.
4. Cheese is a product that is produced from an animal source. It provides a complete protein and promotes wound healing. Cheese, depending on the type, consists of 18 to 30 g of protein per 3 ounces.
5. The majority of vegetables provide only 1 to 3 g of protein.

40. 1. Wearing clean gloves protects the nurse from the patient's blood. This is not a sterile procedure.

3. Holding the finger in a dependent position allows more blood to enter the distal portion of the finger. Avoid squeezing the finger because it increases the likelihood of an inaccurate low reading.

6. Wiping the site with an approved antiseptic will remove some surface microorganisms that could enter the skin when punctured. The antiseptic used should not interfere with the reagent on the strip and it should dry on the skin before the puncture occurs. The use of alcohol is controversial because it dries the skin, and if it interacts with the reagent it will give a false low reading.

5. The side of a finger has fewer nerve endings than the pad of a fingertip and, therefore, during and after the procedure the discomfort will be less. Some advocate using just the two last digits of a hand because they are not used as much as the other fingers.

2. The first drop of blood should be wiped away with sterile gauze because the first drop contains more serous fluid, which can alter test results. Sterile gauze limits microorganisms from entering the puncture site.

4. The finger should hover over the reagent strip, and the drop of blood should make minimal contact with the reagent strip. This provides a full drop of blood for testing. A smeared blood sample will provide an inadequate amount of blood resulting in an inaccurate reading.

41. 1. Potatoes are an excellent source of vitamin C (ascorbic acid). One medium potato contains approximately 42 mg of vitamin C.

2. Papayas are an excellent source of vitamin C. One cup of papayas contains 87 mg of vitamin C.

3. Eight ounces of yogurt contain only 1 mg of vitamin C.

4. Dried beans (legumes) contain no vitamin C. One cup of green beans contains only 12 mg of vitamin C.

5. One cup of milk contains only 2 mg of vitamin C.

42. 1. This is a photograph of a formula being administered via a gastrostomy tube. Thirty to 60 mL of water should be added to the catheter-tip syringe when the syringe is nearly empty of formula. This will clear the tube of formula at the end of the feeding and will prevent occlusion of the tube.

2. This is a photograph of a formula being administered via a gastrostomy tube. Bolus feedings administered over a 60-minute period generally are controlled by a feeding pump, not administered by gravity, as indicated in the photograph.

3. This is a photograph of a formula being administered via a gastrostomy tube. The head of the bed should be elevated 30 to 45 degrees during the feeding and for 1 hour after the feeding to minimize the risk of gastroesophageal reflux and aspiration.

4. This is a photograph of a formula being administered via a gastrostomy tube. A formula at room temperature is less likely to cause gastric discomfort.

5. This is a photograph of a formula being administered via a gastrostomy tube. Formula is added continuously to the catheter-tip syringe just before it empties until the entire feeding is administered. Just before the final amount of formula exits the syringe, 30 to 60 mL of water is added to the syringe to clear the tubing of formula.

43. 1. A primary health-care provider should assess the patient's level of depression. St. John's wort is not recommended for moderate to severe depression. Other medications may be of greater benefit.

2. St. John's wort may decrease the effectiveness of oral contraceptives.

3. A lifting of depression may be identified as early as 2 to 3 weeks after initiation of St. John's wort. If no improvement is identified in 4 to 6 weeks, discontinue the medication.

4. St. John's wort must be discontinued before surgery because patients exposed to general anesthesia may experience cardiovascular collapse.

5. A heightened reaction to the sun (photosensitization) is a response that can occur with exposure to sunlight when taking St. John's wort.

44. 1. It is advisable to be evaluated by an urologist because the symptoms that the patient is experiencing may be caused by a serious medical condition

other than benign enlargement of the prostate.

2. Side effects are not common and generally are mild. Side effects include dizziness, headache, nausea, vomiting, constipation, and diarrhea. Primary health-care providers generally permit a patient to take saw palmetto if the patient is insistent because it has so few side effects.

3. There is no evidence that saw palmetto interferes with the measurement of prostate-specific antigen (PSA), a protein associated with prostate cancer. However, a primary health-care provider may order a PSA test and implement a rectal examination for baseline data before initiating treatment with saw palmetto.

4. Some men do report an enhanced ability to maintain an erection. It is believed that saw palmetto relaxes smooth muscle, allowing blood to flow smoothly and supporting an erection.

5. Research supported by the National Institute of Diabetes and Digestive and Kidney Diseases, the National Center for Complementary and Alternative Medicine, and the National Institutes of Health Office of Dietary Supplements indicates that saw palmetto has no greater effect on the signs and symptoms of benign prostatic hypertrophy than treatment with a placebo.

45. 1. Burns interrupt the integrity of the skin and as a result a primary defense against infection is disrupted. The body's metabolic rate increases dramatically in an attempt to repair the skin and protect the body from infection. Nutrients are required to provide the building blocks for skin cells, white blood cells, and immunoglobulins.

2. Nausea does not precipitate a need for an increase in caloric intake above average requirements. However, frequent small dry feedings and medications to limit nausea may be used.

3. Difficulty swallowing (dysphagia) does not precipitate a need for an increase in caloric intake above average requirements. However, the texture of foods and the rate of feeding may have to be adjusted.

4. An individual with pneumonia requires an increase in caloric requirements because of an increased resting energy expenditure and hypermetabolic state. With an infection, more energy is needed to regulate an elevated body temperature and extra protein is needed to produce antibodies and white blood cells.

5. Depression does not precipitate a need for an increase in caloric intake above average requirements. If a depressed patient becomes withdrawn and sedentary, caloric requirements may decrease.

Oxygenation

OXYGENATION: KEYWORDS

The following words include English vocabulary, nursing/medical terminology, concepts, principles, and information relevant to content specifically addressed in the chapter or associated with topics presented in it. English dictionaries, nursing textbooks, and medical dictionaries, such as *Taber's Cyclopedic Medical Dictionary,* are resources that can be used to expand your knowledge and understanding of these words and related information.

Abdominal thrust
Accessory muscles of respiration
Activity intolerance
Aerosol therapy
Airway clearance
Airway obstruction
Airway resistance
Alveoli
Arterial blood gases
Aspiration
Atelectasis
Auscultation
Breathing, types of:
  Abdominal
  Apnea
  Bradypnea
  Deep
  Diaphragmatic
  Eupnea
  Pursed-lip
  Tachypnea
  Thoracic
Breath sounds:
  Adventitious:
  Crackles (rales)
  Gurgles (rhonchi)
  Pleural friction rub
  Stridor
  Wheezes
  Normal:
    Bronchial
    Bronchovesicular
    Vesicular
Bronchial spasm
Bronchoscopy
Capillary refill
Cardiac output
Cardiac workload
Cardiopulmonary resuscitation
Cardiovascular
Chest physiotherapy
Chest percussion

Chest vibration
Postural drainage vibration
Chest radiograph (x-ray)
Chest tube
Choking
Cilia
Circumoral cyanosis
Cough:
  Nonproductive
  Productive
Cyanosis
Diffusion
Dyspnea
Dysrhythmias
Electrocardiogram
Endotracheal tube
Excursion
Exhale, exhalation
Expectorate
Expiration
Extubation
Fatigue
Heimlich maneuver
Hemoglobin saturation
Hemoptysis
Hemorrhage
Humidify
Hypercapnia
Hypertension/hypotension
Hyperventilation/hypoventilation
Hypostatic pneumonia
Hypovolemic shock
Hypoxia, hypoxemia
Incentive spirometer
Inhale, inspiration
Intrathoracic pressure
Intubation
Iron deficiency anemia
Laryngeal spasm
Metered-dose inhaler (MDI)
Mucous membranes
Mucus

Nares

Nebulizer

Oropharynx

Orthopnea

Orthostatic hypotension

Oxygen delivery systems:

  Face mask

  Nasal cannula

  Nonrebreather mask

  Venturi mask

Oxygen liter-flow gauge

Oxygen saturation

Oxygen therapy

Pallor

Palpable

Patency, patent

Peripheral pulses

Pneumothorax

Positive-pressure ventilation

Postural hypotension

Pulmonary embolus

Pulmonary function tests

Pulse oximetry

Secretions:

  Tenacious

  Viscous

Sedentary

Sputum

Sternum

Suctioning:

  Nasal

  Oropharyngeal

  Tracheal

Thoracentesis

Thoracic

Thoracotomy

Thrombophlebitis

Tidal volume

Tissue perfusion

Tracheostomy

Valsalva maneuver

Vasoconstriction

Vasodilation

Ventilation

Vital capacity

Xiphoid process

OXYGENATION: QUESTIONS

1. A nurse teaches a patient how to use an incentive spirometer. Which projected patient outcome will support the conclusion that the use of the incentive spirometer was effective?
   1. Supplemental oxygen use will be reduced.
   2. Inspiratory volume will be increased.
   3. Sputum will be expectorated.
   4. Coughing will be stimulated.

2. A primary health-care provider orders chest physiotherapy with percussion and vibration for a newly admitted patient. Which information obtained by the nurse during the health history should alert the nurse to question the provider's order?
   1. Emphysema
   2. Osteoporosis
   3. Cystic fibrosis
   4. Chronic bronchitis

3. Which nursing assessment **best** indicates a patient's ability to tolerate activity?
   1. Vital signs that take three minutes to return to preactivity level
   2. Absence of adventitious breath sounds on auscultation
   3. Flexibility of muscles and joints
   4. Reports of weakness

4. Which should the nurse do if an adult is choking on food?
   1. Apply sharp upward thrusts over the patient's xiphoid process.
   2. Determine if the patient can make any verbal sounds.
   3. Hit the middle of the patient's back firmly.
   4. Sweep the patient's mouth with a finger.

5. A patient has thick tenacious respiratory secretions. Which should the nurse do to liquefy the patient's respiratory secretions?
   1. Change the patient's position every two hours.
   2. Get a prescription for an antitussive agent.
   3. Encourage the patient to drink more fluid.
   4. Teach effective deep breathing.

6. Which action is effective in meeting the needs of a patient experiencing laryngospasm after extubation?
   1. Ensuring hyperextension of the head
   2. Providing positive-pressure ventilation
   3. Instituting cardiopulmonary resuscitation
   4. Administering oxygen by using a face mask

7. A patient's hemoglobin saturation via pulse oximetry indicates inadequate oxygenation. Which should the nurse do **first**?
   1. Notify the primary health-care provider.
   2. Encourage breathing deeply.
   3. Raise the head of the bed.
   4. Administer oxygen.

8. A nurse is reviewing the laboratory results of a patient with the preliminary diagnosis of anemia. An abnormal response of which diagnostic test reflects iron deficiency anemia?
   1. Hemoglobin
   2. Platelet count
   3. Serum albumin
   4. Blood urea nitrogen

9. A patient is admitted with the diagnosis of lower extremity arterial disease (LEAD). Which is a specific desirable outcome for a patient with this diagnosis?
   1. Respirations within the expected range
   2. Oriented to the environment
   3. Palpable peripheral pulses
   4. Prolonged capillary refill

10. A primary health-care provider orders bedrest for a patient. Which should the nurse explain to the patient is the **primary** purpose of bedrest?
    1. Conserve energy.
    2. Maintain strength.
    3. Enhance protein synthesis.
    4. Reduce intestinal peristalsis.

11. A nurse is planning to teach one patient pursed-lip breathing and another patient diaphragmatic breathing. Which technique associated with diaphragmatic breathing is different from pursed-lip breathing that the nurse should include in the teaching plan?
    1. Inhale through the mouth.
    2. Exhale through pursed lips.
    3. Raise both shoulders while breathing deeply.
    4. Tighten the abdominal muscles while exhaling.

12. A meal tray arrives for a patient who is receiving 24% oxygen via a Venturi mask. Which should the nurse do to meet this patient's needs?
    1. Request an order to use a nasal cannula during meals.
    2. Discontinue the oxygen when the patient is eating meals.
    3. Obtain an order to change the mask to a nonrebreather mask during meals.
    4. Arrange for liquid supplements that can be administered via a straw through a valve in the mask.

13. A nurse evaluates that the patient understood teaching about the purpose of pursed-lip breathing when the patient includes which information when explaining its purpose to a relative?
    1. Precipitates coughing
    2. Helps maintain open airways
    3. Decreases intrathoracic pressure
    4. Facilitates expectoration of mucus

14. An unconscious patient who had oral surgery is admitted to the postanesthesia care unit. In which position should the nurse place the patient?
    1. Prone
    2. Supine
    3. Fowler
    4. Lateral

15. A primary health-care provider orders chest physiotherapy with percussion and vibration for a patient. After the primary health-care provider leaves, the patient says, "I still don't understand the purpose of this therapy." Which statement should be included in the nurse's response?
    1. "It eliminates the need to cough."
    2. "It limits the production of bronchial mucus."
    3. "It helps clear the airways of excessive secretions."
    4. "It promotes the flow of secretions to the base of the lungs."

16. A nurse raises the head of the bed for a patient who has difficulty breathing. Which science includes the principle that explains how this intervention facilitates respiration?
    1. Physics
    2. Biology
    3. Anatomy
    4. Chemistry

17. Which clinical manifestation is of **most** concern when the nurse assesses a patient who has impaired mobility?
    1. Shallow respirations
    2. Increased oxygen saturation
    3. Decreased chest wall expansion
    4. Gurgling sounds when breathing

18. A nurse teaches a patient to make a series of short, forceful exhalations (huffing) just before actually coughing. Which information should the nurse include when explaining the purpose of this action?
    1. Conserves energy
    2. Liquefies respiratory secretions
    3. Limits pain precipitated by coughing
    4. Raises sputum to a level where it can be expectorated

19. Which are effective leg exercises the nurse should encourage a patient to perform to prevent circulatory complications during the postoperative period?
    1. Flexing the knees
    2. Isometric exercises
    3. Dorsiflexion exercises
    4. Passive range of motion

20. Which outcome **best** reflects achievement of the goal, "The patient will expectorate lung secretions with no signs of respiratory complications"?
    1. Absence of adventitious breath sounds
    2. Deep breathing and coughing nonproductively
    3. Drinking 3,000 mL of fluid in the last 24 hours
    4. Expectorating sputum three times between 3 p.m. and 11 p.m.

21. Which should the nurse do **first** when caring for a nonverbal patient who is restless, agitated, and irritable?
    1. Administer oxygen.
    2. Suction the oropharynx.
    3. Reduce environmental stimuli.
    4. Determine patency of the airway.

22. Which action should the nurse implement to increase both the respiratory and the circulatory functions of a patient in a coma?
    1. Encourage the patient to cough.
    2. Massage the patient's bony areas.
    3. Assist the patient with breathing exercises.
    4. Change the patient's position every two hours.

23. A patient sucking on a hard candy inhales while laughing and develops a total airway obstruction. Which is the nurse attempting to do when implementing an abdominal thrust?
    1. Produce a burp
    2. Pump the heart
    3. Push air out of the lungs
    4. Put pressure on the stomach

24. A nurse in the postanesthesia care unit is monitoring several patients who received general anesthesia. Which patient response causes the **most** concern?
    1. Pain
    2. Stridor
    3. Lethargy
    4. Diaphoresis

25. A primary health-care provider orders oxygen for a patient to be delivered at a high flow rate. Which additional nursing action is necessary when implementing a high-liter flow as opposed to a low-liter flow?
    1. Attaching a flow meter to the wall outlet
    2. Providing oral hygiene whenever necessary
    3. Using an oil-based lubricant when caring for the nares
    4. Humidifying oxygen before it is delivered to the patient

26. A nurse is teaching a patient how to use an incentive spirometer. Which position should the nurse assist the patient to assume during this procedure?
    1. Sitting
    2. Side-lying
    3. Orthopneic
    4. Low-Fowler

27. Which is the **most** important action by the nurse after a patient has a thoracotomy?
    1. Ensure the patient's intake is at least 3,000 mL of fluid per 24 hours.
    2. Provide the patient with adequate medication for pain relief.
    3. Maintain the integrity of the patient's chest tube.
    4. Reposition the patient every 2 hours.

28. A nurse is assessing a postoperative patient. Which complication has occurred when the patient experiences purulent sputum, dyspnea, and chest pain?
    1. Hypostatic pneumonia
    2. Hypovolemic shock
    3. Thrombophlebitis
    4. Pneumothorax

29. An obese patient has limited mobility after an open reduction and internal fixation of a fractured hip. For which human response related to increased blood coagulability should the nurse monitor this patient?
    1. Muscle deterioration
    2. Pain in the calf
    3. Hypotension
    4. Bradypnea

30. For which clinical manifestation should the nurse monitor the patient when concerned about a potential for respiratory distress?
    1. Productive cough
    2. Sore throat
    3. Orthopnea
    4. Eupnea

31. A nurse identifies that a patient's hands are edematous when attempting to apply a pulse oximetry probe. Which action should the nurse implement?
    1. Attach the probe to one of the patient's toes.
    2. Connect the probe to one of the patient's earlobes.
    3. Wash the patient's hand before attaching the probe to the finger.
    4. Encourage the patient to perform active range-of-motion exercises of the hand.

32. A primary health-care provider's order reads, "6 L oxygen via face mask." The patient, who has been extremely confused since being in the unfamiliar environment of the hospital, becomes agitated and repeatedly pulls off the mask. Which should the nurse do?
    1. Tighten the strap around the head.
    2. Reapply the mask every time the patient pulls it off.
    3. Provide an explanation of why the oxygen is necessary.
    4. Request that the order for oxygen be changed to a nasal cannula.

33. A nurse is caring for a male patient. Which laboratory results place this patient at risk for an impaired ability to tolerate activity? **Select all that apply.**
    1. _____Hct of 45%
    2. _____Hb of 10 g/dL
    3. _____O_2 saturation of 90%
    4. _____RBC count of $3.8 \times 10^6/mm^3$
    5. _____WBC count of $7.5 \times 10^6/mm^3$

34. A nurse teaches a preoperative patient how to use an incentive spirometer. Place the steps of the use of an incentive spirometer in the order in which they should be performed.
    1. Inhale slowly.
    2. Hold the incentive spirometer level.
    3. Remove the mouthpiece and exhale normally.
    4. Keep the visual indicator at the inspiratory goal for several seconds.
    5. Maintain a firm seal with the lips around the mouthpiece during inhalation.
    Answer: _____

35. A primary health-care provider orders a loading dose of theophylline 6 mg/kg IV over 30 minutes. The patient weighs 150 pounds. How many milligrams of theophylline should the nurse administer? **Record your answer using a whole number.**
    Answer: _____mg

36. A nurse in the operative suite is preparing an older adult for surgery. Which physiological factors place the older adult at **greater** risk of life-threatening complications associated with surgery for which the nurse should be aware? **Select all that apply.**
    1. _____Skin elasticity
    2. _____Bladder emptying
    3. _____Tolerance for pain
    4. _____Respiratory excursion
    5. _____Cardiovascular capacity

37. Which instructions should the nurse give a patient who is using the device in the illustration?

    1. Breathe out normally, seal your mouth around the mouthpiece, breathe in slowly and deeply as possible, hold your breath at least three seconds, and remove the mouthpiece and exhale.
    2. Hold the device, seal your mouth around the mouthpiece, and breathe in and out slowly and deeply.
    3. Seal your mouth around the mouthpiece and breathe in and out normally.
    4. Take a deep breath and forcefully exhale through the mouthpiece.

38. A nurse is caring for a patient who has a chest tube after thoracic surgery. Which actions should the nurse implement when caring for this patient? **Select all that apply.**
    1. _____Encourage the patient to cough and deep breathe at regular intervals.
    2. _____Clamp the tube when providing for activities of daily living.
    3. _____Position the collection device at the same level as the chest.
    4. _____Maintain an airtight dressing over the puncture wound.
    5. _____Empty chest tube drainage every shift.
    6. _____Avoid using pins to secure tubing.

39. A nurse is concerned about the risk for thrombophlebitis when caring for a patient with impaired mobility. For which clinical manifestations associated with thrombophlebitis should the nurse monitor the patient? **Select all that apply.**
    1. _____Postural hypotension
    2. _____Difficulty breathing
    3. _____Blanchable erythema
    4. _____Dependent edema
    5. _____Acute chest pain

40. Which is the nurse preparing to do with the equipment depicted in the photograph?

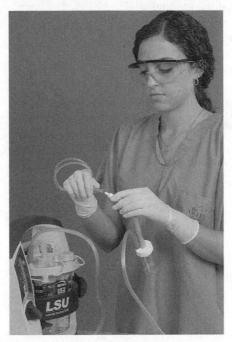

1. Perform gastric lavage.
2. Obtain a sputum specimen.
3. Institute gastric decompression.
4. Administer a nebulizer treatment.

41. A nurse is caring for a patient receiving oxygen via a nasal cannula. Which actions should the nurse implement? **Select all that apply.**
1. _____Adjust the flow meter to the ordered oxygen flow rate.
2. _____Reassess nares, cheeks, and ears for signs of pressure every 2 hours.
3. _____Loop the tubing over the patient's ears and adjust it firmly under the chin.
4. _____Ensure hygiene includes applying an oil-based lubricant to the patient's nares.
5. _____Alternate the position of the prongs curving upward versus downward every 2 hours.

42. A nurse is assessing a patient with a respiratory problem. Which clinical manifestations are **most** reflective of an early response to hypoxia? **Select all that apply.**
1. _____Dysrhythmias
2. _____Restlessness
3. _____Irritability
4. _____Cyanosis
5. _____Apnea

43. Which piece of information documented in the clinical record of a male adult should the nurse consider problematic?
1. Simvastatin 20 mg, PO, in the evening
2. Pulse 100 beats per minute
3. Oxygen saturation 85%
4. WBC 8,000/mm^3

PATIENT'S CLINICAL RECORD

Laboratory Results
WBC 8,000/mm^3
Hb 17 g/dL
Hct 50%

Physical Assessment
BP: 132/70 mm Hg
Pulse: 100 beats per minute
Respirations: 22 breaths per minute
Temperature: 99°F, oral
Oxygen saturation: 85%

Medication Reconciliation Form
Levothyroxine 100 mcg, PO, daily
Simvastatin 10 mg, PO, hs
Montelukast 10 mg, PO, hs

44. A primary health-care provider orders oxygen via a simple face mask at a flow rate of six liters for a patient. The nurse explains the procedure to the patient and maintains standard precautions. Place the following steps in the order in which they should be implemented.
1. Place the mask on the patient's face from the bridge of the nose to under the chin.
2. Secure the elastic bands around the back of the patient's head.
3. Attach the prefilled humidifier to the flow meter.
4. Attach the flow meter to the wall oxygen source.
5. Attach the face mask tubing to the humidifier.
6. Turn the oxygen flow meter on to six liters.
Answer: _____

45. A primary health-care provider prescribes zafirlukast 40 mg daily to be divided into two doses, one in the morning and one in the evening. How many tablets should the nurse administer for each dose? **Record your answer using a whole number.**
Answer: _____tablets

1. 1. Patients who use an incentive spirometer may or may not be receiving oxygen.
   2. **An incentive spirometer provides a visual goal for and measurement of inspiration. It encourages the patient to execute and maintain a sustained inspiration. A sustained inspiration opens airways, increases the inspiratory volume, and reduces the risk of atelectasis.**
   3. Although sputum may be expectorated after the use of an incentive spirometer, this is not the primary reason for its use.
   4. Although the deep breathing associated with the use of an incentive spirometer may stimulate coughing, this is not the primary reason for its use.

2. 1. These are appropriate interventions for a patient with emphysema. Emphysema is a chronic obstructive pulmonary disease characterized by an abnormal increase in the size of air spaces distal to the terminal bronchioles with destructive changes in their walls.
   2. **Implementing the primary health-care provider's order may compromise patient safety because percussion and vibration in the presence of osteoporosis may cause fractures. Osteoporosis is an abnormal loss of bone mass and strength.**
   3. These are appropriate interventions for a patient with cystic fibrosis. Cystic fibrosis causes widespread dysfunction of the exocrine glands. It is characterized by thick, tenacious secretions in the respiratory system that block the bronchioles, creating breathing difficulties.
   4. These are appropriate interventions for a patient with chronic bronchitis. Bronchitis is an inflammation of the mucous membranes of the bronchial airways.

3. 1. **Vital signs reflect cardiopulmonary functioning of the body. Vital signs obtained before and after activity provide data that can be compared to determine the body's response to the energy demands of ambulation. When the vital signs return to the preactivity level within 3 minutes it indicates that the patient has tolerated the activity.**
   2. The absence of abnormal breath sounds (adventitious sounds) indicates the nonexistence of a respiratory problem. Adventitious breath sounds (e.g., wheezes, rhonchi, rales, pleural friction rub, and stridor) indicate narrowed airways, presence of excessive respiratory secretions, pleural inflammation, or diminished ventilation and are not the best signs to use when assessing a person's tolerance to activity.
   3. Flexibility relates to mobility, not one's physiological capacity to endure activities that require energy.
   4. A report of weakness indicates that the patient has not tolerated the activity.

4. 1. Thrusts to the xiphoid process may cause a fracture that may result in a pneumothorax.
   2. **When a person is choking on food, the first intervention is to determine if the person can speak because the next intervention will depend on if it is a partial or total airway obstruction. Ask the patient "Are you choking?" With a partial airway obstruction, the person will be able to make sounds because some air can pass from the lungs through the vocal cords. In this situation, the person's own efforts (gagging and coughing) should be allowed to clear the airway. With a total airway obstruction, the person will not be able to make a sound because the airway is blocked and the nurse should immediately initiate the abdominal thrust maneuver (Heimlich maneuver).**
   3. Hitting the middle of the patient's back firmly should never be done with an adult because if it is a partial obstruction it interferes with the person's own efforts to clear the airway or can cause the bolus of food to lodge farther down the trachea. If it is a total obstruction, slapping the back will be useless and delay the initiation of the abdominal thrust maneuver.
   4. Sweeping the patient's mouth with a finger can force the bolus of food farther down the trachea and is contraindicated.

5. 1. Changing positions will mobilize, not liquefy, respiratory secretions.
   2. Mucolytics, not antitussives, liquefy respiratory secretions. Antitussives prevent or relieve coughing.

3. A fluid intake of 2,500 to 3,000 mL is recommended to maintain the moisture of the respiratory mucous membranes. Adequate fluid keeps respiratory secretions thin so that they can be moved by ciliary action or coughed up and spat out (expectorated).

4. Deep breathing mobilizes, not liquefies, respiratory secretions.

6. 1. Although tilting the head backward (hyperextension of the head) elongates the pharynx, reducing airway resistance, this will do nothing to correct the obstruction at the glottis (opening through the vocal cords). Also, the tongue will block the airway unless there is forward pressure applied on the lower angle of the jaw (jaw thrust maneuver).

2. **Positive pressure will push the vocal cords backward toward the wall of the larynx, opening the glottis (space between the vocal cords), which allows ventilation of the lung.**

3. Instituting cardiopulmonary resuscitation is unnecessary. The patient is having a respiratory, not a cardiac, problem.

4. Administering oxygen by using a face mask is useless because the glottis is obstructed and the oxygenated air will not enter the lung.

7. 1. Notifying the primary health-care provider is premature. The patient's needs must be met first.

2. Although encouraging deep breathing might be done eventually, it is not the priority at this time. This may or may not help. Inadequate oxygenation can be caused by a variety of problems other than shallow breathing.

3. **A nurse can implement this immediate, independent action. Nurses are permitted to treat human responses. Raising the head of the bed facilitates the dropping of the abdominal organs by gravity away from the diaphragm, which permits the greatest lung expansion.**

4. Obtaining and setting up the equipment take time that can be used for other more appropriate interventions first.

8. 1. **Iron is necessary for hemoglobin synthesis. Therefore, reduced intake of dietary iron results in iron deficiency anemia. Hemoglobin is the main component of red blood cells and** transports oxygen and carbon dioxide through the bloodstream.

2. Platelets are unrelated to iron deficiency anemia. Platelets (thrombocytes) are nonnucleated, round or oval, flattened, disk-shaped, formed elements in the blood that are necessary for blood clotting.

3. Albumin is unrelated to iron deficiency anemia. Albumin is a protein in the blood that helps to maintain blood volume and blood pressure.

4. Blood urea nitrogen (BUN) is unrelated to iron deficiency anemia. BUN is a test that measures the nitrogen portion of urea present in the blood. It is an index of glomerular function in the production and excretion of urea.

9. 1. Respirations within the expected range are unrelated to lower extremity arterial disease (LEAD).

2. LEAD usually involves inadequate circulation in the lower extremities, not the brain.

3. **Palpable peripheral pulses are an appropriate expected outcome for a patient with arterial vascular disease, which is a decrease in nutrition and respiration at the peripheral cellular level because of a decrease in capillary blood supply. A physiological response associated with LEAD is diminished or absent arterial pulses.**

4. A prolonged capillary refill indicates a continued problem with peripheral tissue perfusion. After compression, blanched tissue should return to its original color within 2 seconds (blanch test).

10. 1. **Bedrest reduces cardiopulmonary demands, muscle contraction, and other bodily functions. All of this reduces the basal metabolic rate, which conserves energy.**

2. Activity, not bedrest, maintains strength.

3. Protein synthesis is enhanced by the intake of amino acids, not bedrest.

4. Although bedrest may limit peristalsis, it is not the most common reason bedrest is ordered.

11. 1. Inhalation is through the nose for both diaphragmatic and pursed-lip breathing.

2. Exhalation through pursed lips is performed only with pursed-lip breathing.

3. Raising both shoulders while breathing deeply is not part of diaphragmatic or pursed-lip breathing. The use of these

accessory muscles of respiration is a compensatory mechanism that helps to increase thoracic excursion when inhaling.

4. **With diaphragmatic breathing the contraction of abdominal muscles at the end of expiration helps to reduce the amount of air left in the lungs (residual volume).**

12. 1. **A Venturi mask interferes with eating because it covers the nose and mouth. Using a nasal cannula during meals will help meet both the nutritional and oxygen needs of the patient. A nasal cannula delivers oxygen via prongs placed in the patient's nares, leaving the mouth unobstructed, which promotes talking and eating. Specific oxygen delivery systems require an order and are a dependent function of the nurse, except in emergency situations.**
    2. Discontinuing oxygen when the patient is eating is unsafe because it can compromise the patient's respiratory status while the oxygen is disconnected.
    3. A Venturi mask and a nonrebreather mask are both masks that cover the mouth, which interferes with eating.
    4. Liquid supplements are unnecessary. The patient should eat the diet ordered by the primary health-care provider.

13. 1. Deep breathing and huff coughing, not pursed-lip breathing, stimulate effective coughing.
    2. **Pursed-lip breathing involves deep inspiration and prolonged expiration against slightly closed lips. The pursed lips create a resistance to the air flowing out of the lungs, which prolongs exhalation and maintains positive airway pressure, thereby maintaining an open airway and preventing airway collapse.**
    3. Pursed-lip breathing increases, not decreases, intrathoracic pressure.
    4. The huff cough stimulates the natural cough reflex and is effective for clearing the central airways of sputum. Saying the word huff with short, forceful exhalations keeps the glottis open, mobilizes sputum, and stimulates a cough.

14. 1. Although the prone position allows for drainage from the mouth, it is contraindicated because lying on the side of the face compresses oral tissues, impedes

assessment, complicates oral suctioning, and may compromise the airway.
    2. The supine position is unsafe. In an unconscious patient, the gag and swallowing reflexes may be impaired, which increases the risk for aspiration as the tongue falls to the back of the oropharynx, occluding the airway.
    3. The Fowler position is unsafe. An unconscious patient is unable to maintain an upright position.
    4. **The lateral position facilitates the flow of secretions out of the mouth by gravity, keeps the tongue to the side of the mouth, maintaining the airway, and permits effective assessment of the oropharynx and respiratory status.**

15. 1. Chest physiotherapy promotes, not eliminates, the need for coughing.
    2. Chest physiotherapy promotes the expectoration of, not limits the production of, bronchial mucus.
    3. **The forceful striking of the skin over the lung (percussion, clapping) and fine, vigorous, shaking pressure with the hands on the chest wall during exhalation (vibration) mobilize secretions so that they can be coughed up and expectorated.**
    4. Chest physiotherapy mobilizes secretions, thus facilitating expectoration and interfering with the flow of secretions to the base of the lungs.

16. 1. **Raising the head of the bed drops the abdominal organs away from the diaphragm via the principle of gravity, facilitating breathing. Gravity, the tendency of weight to be pulled toward the center of the earth, is a physics principle.**
    2. Raising the head of the bed is not related to biology. Biology is the study of living organisms.
    3. Raising the head of the bed is not related to anatomy. Anatomy is the study of the form and structure of living organisms.
    4. Raising the head of the bed is not related to chemistry. Chemistry is the study of elements, compounds, and atomic relations of matter.

17. 1. Although shallow respirations are a concern, they are not as serious as a clinical manifestation in another option.
    2. Oxygen saturation may be decreased, not increased, with immobility.

3. Although decreased chest wall expansion is a concern, it is not as serious as a clinical manifestation in another option.

4. **Respirations that sound gurgling (gurgles, rhonchi) indicate air passing through narrowed air passages because of secretions, swelling, or a tumor. A partial or total obstruction of the airway can occur, which is life-threatening.**

18. 1. Regardless of the type of cough, coughing uses, not conserves, energy. However, after the airway is cleared of sputum, the patient's oxygen demands will be met more effectively.

2. An increased fluid intake, not coughing, liquefies respiratory secretions.

3. Limiting pain precipitated by coughing is not the purpose of huff coughing. Coughing usually is not painful unless the thoracic muscles are strained or the patient has had abdominal or pelvic surgery.

4. **The huff cough stimulates the natural cough reflex and is effective for clearing the central airways of sputum. Saying the word huff with short, forceful exhalations keeps the glottis open and raises sputum to a level where it can be coughed up and expectorated.**

19. 1. Flexing the knees exerts pressure on the veins in the popliteal space; this reduces venous return, which increases, not decreases, the risk of postoperative circulatory complications.

2. Isometric exercises strengthen muscles; they do not prevent postoperative circulatory complications. Isometric exercises change the muscle tension but do not change the muscle length or move joints.

3. **Alternating dorsiflexion and plantar flexion (calf pumping) contracts and relaxes the calf muscles, including the gastrocnemius muscles. This muscle contraction promotes venous return, preventing venous stasis that contributes to the development of postoperative thrombophlebitis.**

4. Passive range-of-motion exercises are done by another person moving a patient's joints through their complete range of movement. This does not prevent postoperative circulatory complications

because the power is supplied by a person other than the patient. To facilitate circulation a patient has to contract and relax muscles actively.

20. 1. Adventitious breath sounds are abnormal breath sounds that occur when pleural linings are inflamed or when air passes through narrowed airways or through airways filled with fluid. The absence of abnormal sounds is desirable.

2. To expectorate secretions, coughing must be productive, not nonproductive. A nonproductive cough is dry, which means that no respiratory secretions are raised and spat out (expectorated) because of coughing.

3. Drinking fluid is an intervention that will liquefy respiratory secretions, thus facilitating their expectoration. However, just drinking fluid will not ensure that the secretions will be expectorated.

4. Although spitting out sputum reflects achievement of the goal in relation to expectorating lung secretions, it does not address the absence of respiratory complications, which is the ultimate goal of decreasing stasis of respiratory secretions.

21. 1. Administering oxygen may or may not be necessary. The need for oxygen administration will depend on the results of other interventions that should be done first.

2. Suctioning the oropharynx is premature. Mucus or sputum may not be the cause of the problem.

3. Reducing environmental stimuli will serve no purpose at this time and is not the priority.

4. **Early signs of hypoxia are restlessness, agitation, and irritability resulting from reduced oxygen to brain cells. A partial or completely obstructed airway prevents the passage of gases into and out of the lungs. The ABCs (Airway, Breathing, Circulation) of emergency care identify airway as the priority.**

22. 1. A patient in a coma is unable to respond to an instruction to cough.

2. Massage increases circulation only in the localized area being massaged. In addition, massage should be performed around, not over, boney prominences.

3. A patient in a coma is unable to respond to an instruction to perform breathing exercises.

4. **Changing the patient's position every 2 hours helps respirations by preventing fluid from collecting in the lung, which can cause infection; it helps circulation because activity increases circulation, and it relieves local pressure.**

23. 1. Producing a burp in this situation is ineffective. Whatever is causing the obstruction is not caught in the esophagus, which leads to the stomach, but in the respiratory system.

2. Pressing on the heart (compression) is used in cardiopulmonary resuscitation (CPR).

3. **When trapped air behind an obstruction is forced out in response to an abdominal thrust, the forced air may push out what is causing the obstruction.**

4. Applying pressure against the stomach is ineffective in this situation. Whatever is causing the obstruction is not lodged in the esophagus, which leads to the stomach, but in the respiratory system.

24. 1. Pain is an expected response to the trauma of surgery and usually can be managed effectively.

2. **Stridor is an obvious audible shrill, harsh sound caused by laryngeal obstruction. The larynx can become edematous because of the trauma of intubation associated with general anesthesia. Obstruction of the larynx is life-threatening because it prevents the exchange of gases between the lungs and the atmosphere.**

3. Lethargy, which is drowsiness or sluggishness, is an expected response to anesthesia and opioid medications because these medications depress the central nervous system.

4. Although diaphoresis is a cause for concern, it is not as immediately life-threatening as an adaptation in another option. Diaphoresis can be related to a warm environment, impaired thermoregulation, the general adaptation syndrome, or shock.

25. 1. All oxygen systems should have a flow meter to control and maintain the flow of oxygen.

2. All oxygen is drying to the oral mucosa. Therefore, oral hygiene should be provided frequently to moisten the mucous membranes.

3. The use of an oil-based lubricant is unsafe because it is a volatile, flammable material in the presence of oxygen. A water-based lubricant should be used.

4. **A low-liter flow system administers a volume of oxygen designed to supplement the inspired room air to provide airflow equal to the person's minute ventilation (total volume of gas in liters exhaled from the lung per minute). A high-liter flow system administers a volume of oxygen designed to exceed the volume of air required for the person's minute ventilation. The low-liter flow system is less drying than the high-liter flow system, and humidification is unnecessary. A humidifier is a mechanical device that adds water vapor to air in a particle size that can carry moisture to the small airways.**

26. 1. **An upright sitting position in a bed or chair facilitates maximum thoracic excursion because it permits the diaphragm to contract without pressure being exerted against it by abdominal viscera.**

2. The side-lying position is not ideal for the use of an incentive spirometer because it limits thoracic expansion. The side-lying position allows abdominal viscera to exert pressure against the diaphragm during inspiration, and the lung on the lower side of the body is compressed by the weight of the body.

3. Although the orthopneic position allows for thoracic expansion, leaning forward with the arms on an over-bed table does not free the hands for holding the spirometer.

4. The low-Fowler position does not maximize the effects of gravity. In the high-Fowler position gravity moves abdominal viscera away from the diaphragm and thus facilitates the contraction of the diaphragm, both of which promote thoracic expansion.

27. 1. Ensuring a fluid intake of at least 3,000 mL is unnecessary. A fluid intake of approximately 2,000 mL is adequate.

2. Although this is extremely important, it is not the priority.

3. A tension pneumothorax may occur if the integrity of the chest drainage system becomes compromised (e.g., open to atmospheric pressure, clogged drainage tube, or mechanical dysfunction). Maintaining respiratory functioning is the priority.

4. Although repositioning is done to promote drainage of secretions from lung segments and aeration of lung tissue, it is not the priority.

28. 1. **Postoperative patients often experience hypoventilation, immobility, and ineffective coughing that may lead to stasis of respiratory secretions and the multiplication of microorganisms, causing hypostatic pneumonia. Dyspnea results from decreased lung compliance, chest pain results from coughing and the increased work of breathing, and purulent sputum results from the presence of pathogens in sputum.**

2. Hypovolemic shock is characterized by tachycardia, tachypnea, and hypotension.

3. Thrombophlebitis is characterized by localized pain, swelling, warmth, and erythema. If a thrombus breaks loose and travels through the venous circulation to the lung (pulmonary embolus), it will cause dyspnea and chest pain, not purulent sputum.

4. Pneumothorax is characterized by a sudden onset of sharp pain on inspiration, dyspnea, tachycardia, and hypotension.

29. 1. Although muscle deterioration (atrophy) can occur with immobility, it is unrelated to hypercoagulability. Muscle atrophy is the decrease in the size of a muscle resulting from disuse.

2. **Immobility promotes venous vasodilation, venous stasis, and hypercoagulability of the blood, which can precipitate the formation of a clot in a vein of the leg (venous thrombus) and inflammation of the vein (phlebitis).**

3. Hypotension, an abnormally low systolic blood pressure (less than 100 mm Hg), is not related to hypercoagulability precipitated by immobility.

4. Bradypnea, abnormally slow breathing (less than 10 breaths per minute), is unrelated to hypercoagulability caused by immobility.

30. 1. A productive cough indicates that the person is managing respiratory secretions adequately and keeping the airway patent.

2. A sore throat indicates posterior oropharyngeal irritation or inflammation. This may or may not progress to respiratory distress.

3. **Orthopnea, the ability to breathe easily only in an upright (standing or sitting) position, is a classic sign of respiratory distress. The upright position permits maximum thoracic expansion because the abdominal organs do not press against the diaphragm and inspiration is aided by the principle of gravity.**

4. Eupnea is respirations that are quiet, rhythmic, and effortless within the expected rate per minute for age.

31. 1. The use of a toe for pulse oximetry can result in inaccurate results because of concurrent problems, such as vasoconstriction, hypothermia, impaired peripheral circulation, and movement of the foot.

2. **An earlobe is an excellent site to monitor pulse oximetry. It is least affected by decreased blood flow, has greater accuracy at lower saturations, and rarely is edematous. This site is used for intermittent, not continuous, monitoring.**

3. Soap and water will not resolve edema. In addition, attaching a pulse oximeter clip sensor to an edematous finger is contraindicated because interstitial fluid interferes with obtaining an accurate oxygen saturation level.

4. The cause of the edema must be identified first because range-of-motion exercises may be contraindicated.

32. 1. Tightening the strap around the head is unsafe because it can compress the capillaries under the strap, which may interfere with tissue perfusion and result in pressure ulcers.

2. Reapplying the mask every time the patient pulls it off may increase the patient's agitation and it is impractical.

3. Providing an explanation of why the oxygen is necessary will probably be ineffective because an agitated patient often does not understand cause and effect.

4. **Agitated, confused patients generally tolerate a nasal cannula better than a**

face mask. A nasal cannula (nasal prongs) is less intrusive than a mask. Masks are oppressive and may cause a patient to feel claustrophobic.

33. 1. A hematocrit of 45% is within the expected range for hematocrit for men (42% to 52%) and women (36% to 48%).

2. A hemoglobin of 10 g/dL is less than the expected range for hemoglobin for men (14.0 to 17.4 g/dL) and women (12.0 to 16.0 g/dL).

3. An oxygen saturation of 90% is below the expected level of 95% or more. Adequate oxygen levels are necessary to meet the metabolic demands of activity that requires muscle contraction.

4. A red blood cell count of $3.8 \times 10^6/mm^3$ is below the expected range of 4.71 to $5.14 \times 10^6/mm^3$ for red blood cells for men. Hemoglobin, which carries oxygen, is a component of red blood cells.

5. A white blood cell (WBC) count of $7.5 \times 10^6/mm^3$ is within the expected range of 4.5 to $11 \times 10^6/mm^3$ for WBCs. WBCs are not related to a patient's oxygenation status; they are related to protecting the patient from infection.

34. 2. Holding the incentive spirometer level prevents factors, such as friction and gravity, from altering the correct function of the device.

5. A firm seal around the mouthpiece is necessary during inhalation, but the mouthpiece should be removed during exhalation.

1. Inspiration should be accomplished through a slow, deep breath. A rapid, forceful inhalation can collapse the airway and is contraindicated.

4. When the visual indicator reaches the preset goal during inhalation the inhalation should be maintained for 2 to 6 seconds to ensure ventilation of the alveoli.

3. Each exhalation should be an unforced, normal exhalation. A seal does not need to be maintained around the mouthpiece.

35.   Answer: 408 mg
      To solve this problem, first convert150 pounds to its equivalent in kilograms by using the formula for ratio and proportion.

$$\frac{Desire}{Have} \frac{150 \text{ lb}}{2.2 \text{ lb}} = \frac{x \text{ kg}}{1 \text{ kg}}$$

2.2 x = 150
x = 150 ÷ 2.2
x = 68.18 kg
Round down to 68 because 0.18 is less than 0.5.
150 lb is equivalent to 68 kg.
Next calculate the number of milligrams to be administered by multiplying the patient's weight in kilograms by the ordered dose per kilogram: 68 kg × 6 mg = 408 mg.

36. 1. In older adults, atrophy and thinning of both the epithelial and subcutaneous layers of tissue occur, collagenous attachments become less effective, sebaceous gland activity decreases, and interstitial fluid decreases. These changes lead to decreased skin elasticity and the potential to take longer for an incision to heal; however, these are not life-threatening complications associated with surgery and the aging process.

2. In older adults, bladder muscles weaken, bladder capacity decreases, the micturition reflex is delayed, emptying of the bladder becomes more difficult, and residual volume increases; however, these are not life-threatening complications associated with surgery and age-related changes.

3. In older adults there is an increased threshold for sensations of pain, touch, and temperature because of age-related changes in the nerves and nerve conduction; this is not a life-threatening complication associated with surgery and the aging process.

4. Age-related changes in older adults include calcification of costal cartilage (making the trachea and rib cage more rigid), an increase in the anteroposterior chest diameter, and weakening of thoracic muscles. These changes decrease respiratory excursion, which can result in multiple life-threatening postoperative complications such as atelectasis and hypostatic pneumonia.

5. In older adults there is a decrease in functioning capacity of the heart and vascular system. Atherosclerosis of the aorta, coronary arteries, and carotid arteries could decrease cardiac output, impair circulation to vital organs and distal extremities, and increase the

workload of the heart at times of stress. These age-related changes are associated with life-threatening dysrhythmias, thrombophlebitis, and pulmonary emboli.

37. 1. These are the instructions for using an incentive spirometer. An incentive spirometer is designed to have a person deep breathe and expand the lungs to help prevent respiratory complications of immobility.
    2. These are instructions for using a nebulizer. A nebulizer is a medication delivery system that delivers aerosol spray which is inhaled via a mouthpiece. Breathing deeply and slowly facilitates contact of the medication with the respiratory tract mucosa.
    3. These are instructions for assessing tidal volume. Tidal volume is the volume of air inhaled and exhaled with each normal breath; a tidal volume is approximately 500 mL.
    4. **These are the instructions for using a peak expiratory flow meter (PEFM), which is the device in the photograph. A peak expiratory flow meter measures the peak expiratory flow rate (PEFR). A peak expiratory flow rate is the volume of air that can be forcefully exhaled after taking a deep breath.**

38. 1. **Coughing and deep breathing should be encouraged because this helps to expand the lungs.**
    2. Clamping the tube when providing for activities of daily living is contraindicated because clamping a chest tube may cause a tension pneumothorax.
    3. The chest drainage system should be kept below the level of the insertion site to promote the flow of drainage from the pleural space and prevent the flow of drainage back into the pleural space.
    4. **An airtight dressing seals the pleural space from the environment. If left open to the environment, atmospheric pressure causes air to enter the pleural space, which results in a tension pneumothorax.**
    5. Emptying chest tube drainage every shift is unnecessary. Chest drainage systems are closed, self-contained systems that have a chamber for drainage. At routine intervals (as per hospital policy) the date, time, and nurse's initials mark the level of drainage on the drainage collection chamber.

6. Avoiding using pins to secure tubing averts the risk of puncturing the tubing, which will cause an air leak.

39. 1. Postural hypotension is unrelated to thrombophlebitis caused by immobility. Postural hypotension (orthostatic hypotension) is a decrease in blood pressure related to positional or postural changes from the lying down to sitting or standing positions.
    2. **Dyspnea is a clinical manifestation of a pulmonary embolus, a life-threatening condition. A thrombus that breaks loose from a vein wall and travels through the circulation (embolus) eventually will obstruct a pulmonary artery or one of its branches (pulmonary embolus).**
    3. Blanchable erythema is unrelated to thrombophlebitis caused by immobility. Blanchable erythema (reactive hyperemia) is a reddened area caused by localized vasodilation in response to lack of blood flow to the underlying tissue. The reddened area will turn pale with fingertip pressure.
    4. Dependent edema is unrelated to thrombophlebitis caused by immobility. Although fluid will collect in the interstitial compartment (edema) around a thrombophlebitis, it is localized, not dependent, edema. Dependent edema is the collection of fluid in the interstitial tissues below the level of the heart; it occurs bilaterally and usually is caused by cardiopulmonary problems.
    5. **Immobility promotes venous stasis, which in conjunction with hypercoagulability and injury to vessel walls predisposes patients to thrombophlebitis. These three factors are known as Virchow's triad. A thrombus can break loose from the vein wall and travel through the circulation (embolus), where eventually it obstructs a pulmonary artery or one of its branches and causes sudden, acute chest pain, dyspnea, coughing, and frothy sputum.**

40. 1. This is not the equipment used for the purpose of gastric lavage.
    2. **The nurse is preparing to collect a sputum specimen via suctioning. The nurse is attaching a catheter to a sputum trap that attaches to the suction tubing.**

3. This is not the equipment used for gastric decompression.

4. This is not the equipment used to administer a nebulizer treatment.

41. **1. Adjusting the flow meter to the ordered oxygen flow rate ensures that the patient is receiving the prescribed dose of oxygen.**

2. Reassessing the patient's skin for signs of pressure every 2 hours ensures that tissue irritation or capillary compression does not occur from the nasal prongs or tubing. The tubing should be snug enough to keep the nasal prongs from becoming displaced but loose enough not to compress or irritate tissue.

3. Looping the tubing over the patient's ears and adjusting it firmly under the chin provide the correct placement of the tubing; however, the tubing should be secured gently, not firmly, under the chin.

4. The use of an oil-based lubricant, a volatile, flammable material, should be avoided in the presence of oxygen. A water-based lubricant should be used.

5. Placing the nasal prongs curving upward does not follow the natural curve of the nasal passage, which can cause tissue injury. The nasal prongs should always be curving downward to follow the natural curve of the nares.

42. 1. A dysrhythmia, a heart rate with an irregular rhythm, can occur with hypoxia but it is a late response.

2. Hypoxia is insufficient oxygen anywhere in the body. An early sign of hypoxia is restlessness, which is caused by impaired cerebral perfusion of oxygen.

3. Irritability is an early sign of hypoxia caused by impaired cerebral perfusion of oxygen.

4. Cyanosis, a bluish discoloration of the skin and mucous membranes caused by reduced oxygen in the blood, is a late sign of hypoxia.

5. Apnea, a complete absence of respirations, is the cause of, not a response to, hypoxia.

43. 1. Simvastatin 10 mg once a day is within the expected dose range of 5 to 40 mg daily and is not a cause for concern. Simvastatin, a lipid-lowering agent, should be taken in the evening because the body produces the most cholesterol overnight.

2. A pulse rate of 100 beats per minute is within the expected range of 60 to 100 beats per minute and is not a cause for concern.

3. An oxygen saturation level of 85% is a cause for concern. An oxygen saturation level of 95% to 100% is considered expected. An oxygen saturation level less than 90% is considered low and is associated with hypoxemia.

4. A WBC count of 8,000/mm^3 is within the expected range of 5,000 to 10,000/mm^3 and is not a cause for concern.

44. **4. The first step is to attach the flow meter to the wall oxygen source. The flow meter controls the amount of oxygen delivered.**

3. The second step is to attach the prefilled humidifier to the flow meter. Humidification reduces drying of the respiratory system mucous membranes and is essential when oxygen delivery is 4 L or higher.

5. The third step is attaching the mask's tubing to the humidifier. This prepares the equipment for use.

6. The fourth step is turning on the oxygen flow rate to 6 L. This primes the tubing and mask with oxygen so that there is no delay once the mask is applied to the patient's face.

1. The fifth step is placing the mask on the patient's face. Applying it from the bridge of the patient's nose to under the chin limits oxygen from leaking around the edges of the mask.

2. The sixth step is securing the elastic bands around the back of the patient's head. This helps to hold the mask in position.

45.   Answer: 2 tablets. First determine the number of milligrams prescribed for each dose. Divide the daily dose (40 mg) by the number of times the medication should be administered (2 times, once in the morning and once in the evening): 40 ÷ 2 = 20 mg per dose. The package insert for zafirlukast states that each tablet is 10 mg. Solve the problem using the formula for ratio and proportion.

$$\frac{\text{Desire } 20 \text{ mg}}{\text{Have } 10 \text{ mg}} = \frac{\text{x tablet}}{1 \text{ tablet}}$$

10 x = 20 mg

x = 20 ÷ 10

x = 2 tablets

Urinary Elimination

KEYWORDS

The following words include English vocabulary, nursing/medical terminology, concepts, principles, and information relevant to content specifically addressed in the chapter or associated with topics presented in it. English dictionaries, nursing textbooks, and medical dictionaries, such as *Taber's Cyclopedic Medical Dictionary,* are resources that can be used to expand your knowledge and understanding of these words and related information.

Acidic urine
Anuria
Bacteriuria
Bladder cues
Bladder irritability
Bladder training
Catheter port
Commode chair
Credé maneuver
Cystoscopy
Detrusor muscles
Dysuria
Enuresis
Excretion
Foreskin
Fracture bedpan
Frequency
Glomerular filtration rate
Graduate
Hematuria
Hesitancy
Incontinence, types:
   Functional
   Overflow
   Reflex
   Stress
   Total
   Urge
Incontinent
Kegel exercises
Ketones
Micturition
Nocturia
Oliguria
Perineal care

Polyuria
Prostate
Pyuria
Reagent strips
Renal calculi
Renal perfusion
Residual urine
Retention
Specific gravity
Suprapubic distention
Trigone
Turbidity
Urea
Ureter
Urethra
Urgency
Urinary catheters:
   Condom (Texas)
   Indwelling (retention, Foley)
   Straight
   Suprapubic
Urinary diuresis
Urinary diversion
Urinary drainage system
Urinary meatus
Urinary obstruction
Urinary output
Urinary tract infection
Urine clarity
Urine specimens:
   Clean catch
   From a catheter port
   Urinalysis
   24-hour urine collection
Void

URINARY ELIMINATION: QUESTIONS

1. A nurse identifies that the patient has overflow incontinence. Which factor contributes to this clinical manifestation?
   1. Coughing
   2. Mobility deficits
   3. Prostate enlargement
   4. Urinary tract infection

2. A nurse must measure the intake and output (I&O) of a patient who has a urinary retention catheter. Which equipment is **most** appropriate to use to measure urine output from a urinary retention catheter accurately?
   1. Urinal
   2. Graduate
   3. Large syringe
   4. Urine collection bag

3. A patient's urine is cloudy, is amber, and has an unpleasant odor. Which problem may this information indicate that requires the nurse to make a focused assessment?
   1. Urinary retention
   2. Urinary tract infection
   3. Ketone bodies in the urine
   4. High urinary calcium level

4. A nurse is caring for a debilitated female patient with nocturia. Which nursing intervention is the **priority** when planning to meet this patient's needs?
   1. Encouraging the use of bladder training exercises
   2. Providing assistance with toileting every 4 hours
   3. Positioning a bedside commode near the bed
   4. Teaching the avoidance of fluids after 5 p.m.

5. A primary health-care provider orders a urine specimen for culture and sensitivity via a straight catheter for a patient. Which should the nurse do when collecting this urine specimen?
   1. Use a sterile specimen container.
   2. Collect urine from the catheter port.
   3. Inflate the balloon with sterile water.
   4. Have the patient void before collecting the specimen.

6. A nurse reviews the results of a patient's urinalysis. Which constituent found in urine indicates the presence of an abnormality?
   1. Electrolytes
   2. Protein
   3. Water
   4. Urea

7. A patient is reporting burning on urination. Which question should the nurse ask to **best** obtain information about the patient's dysuria?
   1. "Can you tell me about the problems you have been having with urination?"
   2. "How would you describe your experience with incontinence?"
   3. "What are your usual bowel habits?"
   4. "What color is your urine?"

8. A nurse is caring for a group of patients with a variety of urinary problems. Which patient's physical response should cause the **most** concern?
   1. Anuria
   2. Dysuria
   3. Diuresis
   4. Enuresis

9. A nurse is performing a physical assessment on a newly admitted patient. Which problem identified by the nurse is often associated with urinary incontinence?
   1. Chronic pain
   2. Reduced fluid intake
   3. Disturbed self-esteem
   4. Insufficient knowledge

10. A nurse is caring for two patients. One patient has reflex incontinence and the other has total incontinence. Which characteristic is common to both reflex incontinence and total incontinence?
    1. Urination following an increase in intra-abdominal pressure
    2. Loss of urine without awareness of bladder fullness
    3. Retention of urine with overflow incontinence
    4. Strong, sudden desire to void

11. Which clinical manifestation can a nurse expect when a postoperative patient experiences stress associated with surgery?
    1. Decreased urinary output
    2. Low specific gravity
    3. Reflex incontinence
    4. Urinary hesitancy

12. Which assessment is not related to monitoring both urine and stool?
    1. Constituents
    2. Urgency
    3. Shape
    4. Color

13. A nurse is assessing the urinary status of a patient. Which sign indicates that additional nursing assessments are necessary?
    1. Aromatic odor
    2. Pale yellow urine
    3. Output of 50 mL hourly
    4. Specific gravity of 1.035

14. A patient tells the nurse, "I have to urinate as soon as I get the urge to go." For which contributing factor to urinary urgency should the nurse implement a focused assessment?
    1. Anesthesia
    2. Dehydration
    3. Full bladder
    4. Urinary tract infection

15. Which is an effective nursing intervention to prevent urinary tract infections?
    1. Teach female patients to wipe from the back to the front after urinating.
    2. Advise patients to report burning on urination to health-care providers.
    3. Instruct patients to use bath powder to absorb perineal perspiration.
    4. Encourage patients to drink several quarts of fluid daily.

16. A patient has urinary incontinence. Which is the **best** nursing intervention for this patient?
    1. Providing skin care immediately after soiling
    2. Using a deodorant soap when providing skin care
    3. Drying the area well after providing perineal care
    4. Dusting the perineal area with a light film of cornstarch

17. A confused patient is incontinent of urine and stool and smears the stool on the bed linens and bed rails. Which should be the initial patient goal?
    1. The patient will be clean and dry continuously.
    2. The patient will become continent within a week.
    3. The patient will stop soiling the environment immediately.
    4. The patient will call for the bedpan whenever the urge to eliminate occurs.

18. A patient has a urinary retention catheter. Which is **most** important when the nurse cares for this patient?
   1. Applying an antimicrobial agent to the urinary meatus 2 times a day
   2. Ensuring that the catheter remains connected to the collection bag
   3. Wearing sterile gloves when accessing the specimen port
   4. Increasing fluid intake to 3,000 mL a day

19. Which information about a patient is communicated when a nurse documents that the patient has polyuria?
   1. Excreting excessive amounts of urine
   2. Experiencing pain on urination
   3. Retaining urine in the bladder
   4. Passing blood in the urine

20. A patient is experiencing bladder irritability. Which fluid should the nurse teach the patient to include in the diet?
   1. Beer
   2. Coffee
   3. Orange juice
   4. Cranberry juice

21. Which clinical manifestation identified by the nurse commonly is associated with excessive production of antidiuretic hormone (ADH)?
   1. Diuresis
   2. Oliguria
   3. Retention
   4. Incontinence

22. A nurse must obtain a urine specimen from a patient. Which nursing intervention is the **greatest** help to most people who need to void for a urine test?
   1. Exerting manual pressure on the abdomen
   2. Encouraging a backward rocking motion
   3. Running water in the sink
   4. Providing for privacy

23. A patient is admitted to the emergency department because of hypertension and oliguria. For which additional clinical manifestation associated with this cluster of information should the nurse assess the patient?
   1. Thirst
   2. Retention
   3. Weight gain
   4. Urinary hesitancy

24. A nurse must obtain a clean-catch urine specimen from one patient and a urine specimen via a straight catheterization from another. Which intervention is not performed for both when obtaining these specimens?
   1. Cleanse around the urinary meatus with antiseptic swabs.
   2. Send the specimen to the laboratory immediately.
   3. Use a sterile cup for the collected urine.
   4. Wear sterile gloves.

25. A primary health-care provider discusses the need for a cystoscopy with a patient. Which is **most** important for the nurse to do when caring for this patient before the procedure?
   1. Monitor the patient's I&O.
   2. Assess the patient's urine routinely.
   3. Encourage the patient to increase the intake of oral fluids.
   4. Have the patient sign an informed consent form before the procedure.

26. An older adult with an indwelling urinary catheter is receiving 75 mL of 0.9% sodium chloride hourly. The patient has had several hospital admissions in the last year for dehydration. The nurse is concerned about the patient's renal function. What is the **best** intervention by the nurse to assess this patient's renal functioning?
    1. Inspect the patient's dependent areas for signs of edema.
    2. Calculate the patient's intake and output every shift.
    3. Monitor the patient's urine output hourly.
    4. Obtain the patient's weight daily.

27. A nurse is inserting an indwelling urinary catheter into a male patient. The nurse feels firm resistance while inserting the urinary catheter through the penis. What should the nurse do?
    1. Lower the penis until it is parallel to the length of the body.
    2. Inflate the balloon of the catheter with 10 mL of normal saline.
    3. Interrupt the procedure and notify the primary health-care provider.
    4. Use a twisting motion and firmly advance the catheter 2 inches farther into the penis.

28. When a nurse assesses a patient, which clinical manifestations support the presence of urinary retention? **Select all that apply.**
    1. _____Nocturia
    2. _____Hematuria
    3. _____Bladder contractions
    4. _____Suprapubic distention
    5. _____Frequent small voidings

29. A nurse plans to clamp a patient's urinary drainage system to obtain a urine specimen for a urine culture and sensitivity. Indicate with an X, on the figure below, where the nurse should clamp the catheter drainage system.

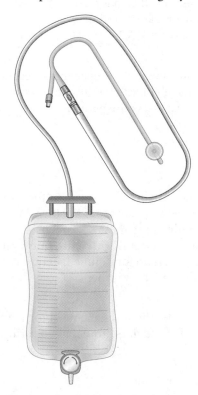

30. A nurse is caring for a patient with a condom catheter. Which nursing actions are important? **Select all that apply.**
1. _____Providing perineal care every shift
2. _____Avoiding kinks in the collection tubing
3. _____Ensuring that the adhesive band is snug, not tight
4. _____Retracting the foreskin before the catheter is applied
5. _____Leaving one inch between the glans penis and drainage tubing

31. A primary health-care provider orders 250 mL 0.9% sodium chloride to be administered over 30 minutes to challenge a patient's kidneys to produce urine. The nurse obtains an electronic infusion device to administer the solution. At what rate should the nurse program the infusion device? **Record your answer using a whole number.**
Answer: _____mL/hour

32. A nurse is caring for a female patient on bedrest who has a urinary retention catheter. Which should the nurse do? **Select all that apply.**
1. _____Position the tubing through the side rail of the bed.
2. _____Ensure the tubing is positioned over the leg.
3. _____Label the tubing with the date of insertion.
4. _____Irrigate the tubing to ensure its patency.
5. _____Secure the tubing to the patient's leg.

33. A primary health-care provider orders a bladder ultrasound scan be performed after a patient voids to determine the amount of residual urine. The nurse explains the test to the patient. Place the following steps in the order that they should be performed by the nurse.
1. Clean the patient's abdomen to remove the gel and clean the scan head with isopropyl alcohol.
2. Put 5 mL of conducting gel on the patient's symphysis pubis and place the scan head on the gel.
3. Aim the scan head toward the patient's coccyx and press the scan head button.
4. Drape the patient exposing only the lower abdomen and suprapubic area.
5. Obtain the bladder volume and repeat the measurement several times.
6. Place the patient in the supine position.
Answer: _____

34. Which should a nurse teach the patient to avoid to prevent urinary diuresis? **Select all that apply.**
1. _____Narcotics
2. _____Caffeine
3. _____Activity
4. _____Alcohol
5. _____Protein

35. A primary health-care provider prescribes furosemide 40 mg to be added to 50 mL of D_5W to infuse at a rate of 3 mg/minute. Furosemide for IV infusion is 10 mg/mL. The nurse uses a secondary infusion set that has a drop factor of 10. How many drops per minute should the nurse administer?
Answer: _____drops/minute

36. Which nursing actions should be implemented by a nurse to facilitate bladder continence for a male patient who is cognitively impaired? **Select all that apply.**
1. _____Offer toileting reminders every 2 hours.
2. _____Apply a condom catheter in the morning.
3. _____Provide clothing that is easy to manipulate.
4. _____Encourage avoidance of fluids between meals.
5. _____Explain the need to call for help with toileting every 4 hours.

37. When planning nursing care, which factors in the patient's history place the patient at risk for stress incontinence? **Select all that apply.**
    1. _____Lumbar spinal cord injury
    2. _____Urinary obstruction
    3. _____Six vaginal births
    4. _____Menopause
    5. _____Confusion

38. A patient returns from the surgical unit after a transurethral resection of the prostate gland. The nurse reviews the primary health-care provider's orders, obtains the patient's vital signs, and performs a focused patient assessment. Which is the **best** intervention by the nurse?
    1. Discontinue the continuous compression devices to the lower extremities.
    2. Notify the surgeon of the status of the patient's urinary drainage.
    3. Obtain the patient's temperature using a rectal thermometer.
    4. Increase the flow rate of the continuous bladder irrigation.

PATIENT'S CLINICAL RECORD

Primary Health-Care Provider's Orders
Regular diet
Vital signs every 4 hours
IV morphine via PCA pump: basal rate 1.5 mg/hour; PCA dose 1 mg; lockout interval 12 minutes; maximum dose over 4 hours, 26 mg
IVF: 0.9% sodium chloride 125 mL/hour
Docusate sodium 100 mg PO once daily
Out of bed to chair in p.m., ambulate twice a day
Continuous compression devices to lower extremities when in bed
Continuous bladder irrigation 0.9% sodium chloride to run at rate to keep output pink

Patient's Vital Signs
Temperature: 100.2°F, oral
Pulse: 88 beats per minute
Respirations: 20 breaths per minute
Blood pressure: 136/80 mm Hg

Focused Physical Assessment
IVF: 0.9% sodium chloride at 125 mL/hour, insertion site right forearm with no signs of infiltration or infection. Continuous compression devices in place. Pedal pulses palpable, toes pink and warm to touch. Patient reporting abdominal pain of 2 on scale of 0 to 10 with occasional severe abdominal cramps. CBI in progress at 150 mL per hour. Urinary drainage is light red with numerous clots.

39. A patient who had prostate surgery has a continuous bladder irrigation (CBI) in place. The nurse maintains the CBI at 200 mL/hour of GU irrigant as ordered. The urine drainage bag was emptied several times during the course of the shift for a total of 3,200 mL. How many milliliters should the nurse calculate was urine at the end of the 12-hour shift? **Record your answer using a whole number.**
    Answer: _____mL

40. A nurse must obtain a urine specimen for a culture and sensitivity test from a patient who has an indwelling urinary catheter. Place the following steps in the order in which they should be performed.
1. Wash your hands and don clean gloves.
2. Remove the clamp from the drainage tubing.
3. Drain the urine in the tubing into the drainage bag.
4. Clamp the drainage tubing below the specimen port for 15 to 30 minutes.
5. Swab the specimen port with an antiseptic and aspirate urine via a sterile syringe.
6. Transfer the urine to a sterile specimen cup and discard the syringe into a sharps container.

Answer: _____

1. 1. Coughing, which raises the intra-abdominal pressure, is related to stress incontinence, not overflow incontinence.
   2. Mobility deficits, such as spinal cord injuries, are related to reflex incontinence, not overflow incontinence.
   3. **An enlarged prostate compresses the urethra and interferes with the outflow of urine, resulting in urinary retention. With urinary retention, the pressure within the bladder builds until the external urethral sphincter temporarily opens to allow a small volume (25 to 60 mL) of urine to escape (overflow incontinence).**
   4. Urinary tract infections are related to urge incontinence, not overflow incontinence.

2. 1. Although urinals have volume markings on the side, usually they occur in 100-mL increments that do not promote accurate measurements.
   2. **A graduate is a collection container with volume markings usually at 25-mL increments that promote accurate measurements of urine volume.**
   3. Using a large syringe is impractical. A large syringe is used to obtain a sterile specimen from a retention catheter (Foley catheter).
   4. A urine collection bag is flexible and balloons outward as urine collects. In addition, the volume markings are at 100-mL increments that do not promote accurate measurements.

3. 1. These clinical manifestations do not reflect urinary retention. Urinary retention is evidenced by suprapubic distention and lack of voiding or small, frequent voidings (overflow incontinence).
   2. **The urine appears concentrated (amber) and cloudy because of the presence of bacteria, white blood cells, and red blood cells. The unpleasant odor is caused by pus in the urine (pyuria).**
   3. These clinical manifestations do not reflect ketone bodies in the urine. A reagent strip dipped in urine will measure the presence of ketone bodies.
   4. These clinical manifestations do not reflect excessive calcium in the urine. Urine calcium levels are measured by assessing a 24-hour urine specimen.

4. 1. Although encouraging the use of bladder training exercises should be done, it is not the priority.
   2. Toileting the patient every 4 hours may be too often or not often enough for the patient. Care should be individualized for the patient.
   3. **The use of a commode requires less energy than using a bedpan and is safer than walking to the bathroom. Sitting on a commode uses gravity to empty the bladder fully and thus prevents urinary stasis.**
   4. Fluids may be decreased during the last 2 hours before bedtime, but they should not be avoided completely after 5 p.m. Some fluid intake is necessary for adequate renal perfusion.

5. 1. **A culture attempts to identify the microorganisms present in the urine, and a sensitivity study identifies the antibiotics that are effective against the isolated microorganisms. A sterile specimen container is used to prevent contamination of the specimen by microorganisms outside the body (exogenous).**
   2. The urine from a straight catheter (single-lumen tube) flows directly into the specimen container. Collecting a urine specimen from a catheter port is necessary when the patient has a urinary retention catheter.
   3. A straight catheter has a single lumen for draining urine from the bladder. A straight catheter does not remain in the bladder and therefore does not have a second lumen for water to be inserted into a balloon.
   4. Having the patient void before collecting the specimen may result in no urine left in the bladder for the straight catheter to collect. A minimum of 3 mL of urine is necessary for a specimen for urine culture and sensitivity.

6. 1. Electrolytes are usual constituents of urine, and they fluctuate to help maintain fluid and electrolyte and acid-base balance.
   2. **The presence of protein in the urine indicates that the glomeruli have become too permeable, which occurs with kidney disease. Most plasma proteins are too large to move out of**

the glomeruli, and the small proteins that enter the filtrate are reabsorbed by pinocytosis.

3. Urine usually is composed of 95% water.
4. Urea is an expected constituent of urine. It is formed by liver cells when excess amino acids are broken down (deaminated) to be used for energy production.

7. 1. This open-ended question encourages the patient to talk about the problem from a personal perspective. Follow-up questions can be more specific.
2. Dysuria is not necessarily related to incontinence.
3. Dysuria is a problem associated with urine, not fecal, elimination.
4. Although an abnormal color of urine may indicate a potential urinary tract infection, which is associated with dysuria, the question is too narrow because it focuses on only one issue.

8. 1. The inability to produce urine (anuria) is a life-threatening situation. If the cause is not corrected, the patient will need dialysis to correct fluid and electrolyte imbalances and rid the body of the waste products of metabolism.
2. Although dysuria is a concern because it may indicate a urinary tract infection, it is not as serious as a response in another option.
3. The secretion and excretion of large amounts of urine (diuresis) are a concern, but they are not as serious as a response in another option.
4. Involuntary discharge of urine after an age when bladder control should be established (enuresis) is a concern, but it is not as serious as a response in another option.

9. 1. Urinary incontinence usually is not related to chronic pain. Chronic pain is the state in which an individual experiences pain that is persistent or intermittent and lasts for longer than 6 months.
2. Reduced fluid intake is unrelated to urinary incontinence. A reduced fluid intake places an individual at risk of experiencing vascular, interstitial, or intracellular dehydration.
3. Disturbed self-esteem is the state in which an individual experiences, or is at risk of experiencing, negative self-evaluation about self or capabilities. Incontinence may be viewed by a patient as regressing to child-like behavior and has a negative impact on feelings about the self.
4. Urinary incontinence may be unpreventable and uncontrollable. Sufficient knowledge may not prevent or promote continence. Inadequate knowledge is the state in which an individual experiences a deficiency in cognitive information or psychomotor skills, concerning a condition or treatment plan.

10. 1. Urination following an increase in intra-abdominal pressure is related to stress incontinence, which is an immediate involuntary loss of urine during an increase in intra-abdominal pressure.
2. Involuntary voiding and a lack of awareness of bladder distention are related directly to both reflex incontinence and total incontinence. Reflex incontinence is the predictable, involuntary loss of urine with no sensation of urgency, the need to void, or bladder fullness. Total incontinence is the continuous unpredictable loss of urine without distention or awareness of bladder fullness.
3. Retention of urine with overflow incontinence is related to urinary retention, which is the chronic inability to void followed by involuntary voiding (overflow incontinence).
4. A strong, sudden desire to void is related to urge incontinence, which is an involuntary loss of urine associated with a strong, sudden desire to void.

11. 1. During surgery, because of the effects of the general adaptation syndrome, the posterior pituitary secretes antidiuretic hormone that promotes water reabsorption in the kidney tubules. Also, the anterior pituitary secretes adrenocorticotropic hormone (ACTH) that stimulates the adrenal cortex to secrete aldosterone, which reabsorbs sodium and thus water.
2. A low specific gravity reflects dilute urine. With the stress response, the urine will be concentrated and the specific gravity will be elevated.
3. The stress response is unrelated to reflex incontinence. Reflex incontinence is a predictable, involuntary loss of urine with no sensation of urgency, the need to void, or bladder fullness.

4. The stress response is unrelated to urinary hesitancy. Hesitancy is the involuntary delay in initiating urination.

12. 1. Both urine and stool have usual constituents. Urine has organic constituents (e.g., urea, uric acid, and creatinine) and inorganic constituents (e.g., ammonia, sodium, chloride, potassium, and calcium). Feces have waste residues of digestion (e.g., bile, intestinal secretions, and bacteria) and inorganic constituents (e.g., calcium and phosphorus).
    2. A person can feel an overwhelming need to void as well as defecate.
    3. **Only stool can be assessed regarding shape. Stool usually is tubular in shape. Urine is a liquid that assumes the shape of the container in which it is collected.**
    4. Both urine and stool can be assessed for color. Stool usually is brown and urine usually is yellow, straw-colored, or amber depending on its concentration.

13. 1. An aromatic odor is the usual odor of urine.
    2. Urine usually is pale yellow, straw-colored, or amber depending on its concentration.
    3. Adequate renal perfusion and kidney function are reflected by an hourly urine output of 30 mL or more of urine.
    4. **Specific gravity is the measure of the concentration of dissolved solids in the urine. The expected range is 1.001 to 1.029. A specific gravity of 1.035 indicates concentrated urine.**

14. 1. Anesthesia is a central nervous system depressant that tends to cause urinary retention, not urgency.
    2. Dehydration causes a decrease in renal perfusion resulting in a diminished capacity to form urine (oliguria), not urgency.
    3. The urinary bladder does not have to be full to precipitate the urge to void. The urge to void can be felt when 150 to 200 mL of urine collects and stimulates the trigone of the urinary bladder.
    4. **Feeling the need to void immediately (urgency) occurs most often when the urinary bladder is irritated. In the adult, the usual bladder capacity is 400 to 600 mL of urine, although the desire to urinate can be sensed when it contains as little as 150 to 200 mL. As the volume increases, the bladder**

wall stretches, sending sensory messages to the sacral spinal cord, and parasympathetic impulses stimulate the detrusor muscle to contract rhythmically. Bladder contractions precipitate nerve impulses that travel up the spinal cord to the pons and cerebral cortex, where the person experiences a conscious need to void.

15. 1. The opposite should be done to prevent microorganisms from the intestines (e.g., *Escherichia coli*) from being drawn from the anus toward the urinary meatus. Wiping from front to back follows the principle of clean to dirty.
    2. This will not prevent a urinary tract infection. Burning on urination (dysuria) is a response to acedic urine flowing over inflamed mucous membranes and is a sign of a urinary tract infection.
    3. Bath powder should be avoided because it has been implicated as a precipitating cause of gynecological cancer.
    4. **Drinking a minimum of 2,000 mL of fluid a day produces adequately dilute urine, washes out solutes, and flushes microorganisms from the distal urethra and urinary meatus.**

16. 1. **As soon as possible after an incontinence episode the patient should receive thorough perineal care with soap and water and the area dried well. This action removes urea from the skin, which can contribute to skin breakdown.**
    2. Plain soap, not deodorant soap, is all that is necessary when providing perineal care after urinary or bowel incontinence.
    3. Although drying the area well after providing perineal care is done, it is not the best intervention of the options offered.
    4. Dusting the perineal area with cornstarch should be avoided. Cornstarch can accumulate in folds of the skin and when damp can become like sandpaper, causing friction upon movement and then skin breakdown.

17. 1. **A patient's basic physical needs should be given first priority. As soon as a patient is incontinent of either urine or stool, the patient should receive perineal care. Remaining "continuously" clean and dry meets the criterion of a time frame when writing a goal.**

2. The patient may not have the physical, mental, or emotional ability to achieve the goal of becoming continent.
3. The patient may not have the physical, mental, or emotional ability to achieve the goal of continence and stop soiling the environment.
4. The patient may not have the physical or cognitive ability to achieve the goal of calling for a bedpan.

18. 1. Research demonstrates that cleansing the urinary meatus with soap and water daily is adequate to prevent an infection. An antimicrobial ointment provides no additional benefit. Also, it requires a prescription.
2. **Maintaining the connection of the catheter to the collection bag prevents the introduction of microorganisms that can cause infection. A urinary retention catheter is a closed system that should remain closed.**
3. Clean, not sterile, gloves should be worn. Surgical asepsis (use of a sterile syringe and alcohol swab) is necessary when accessing the specimen port on a urinary retention catheter.
4. Although increasing fluid intake will increase urinary output, thereby flushing the bladder of microorganisms, it is not as important as another option.

19. 1. **Polyuria is an excessive output of urine. This is associated with problems such as diabetes mellitus, diabetes insipidus, the acute (diuresis) phase after a burn injury, and reduced levels of antidiuretic hormone.**
2. Pain on urination is the description of dysuria.
3. Retaining urine in the bladder is the description of urinary retention.
4. Passing blood in the urine is the description of hematuria.

20. 1. Beer contains alcohol, which is irritating to the bladder.
2. Coffee contains caffeine, which is irritating to the bladder.
3. Orange juice, a citrus fruit, is irritating to the bladder. Citrus fruits are acidic.
4. **Cranberries have no constituents that irritate the bladder. In addition, they produce a more acidic environment that is less conducive to the growth of microorganisms and prevents bacteria from adhering to the mucous**

membranes of the urinary tract, thus promoting bacterial excretion.

21. 1. Diuresis occurs when there is inadequate antidiuretic hormone.
2. **Antidiuretic hormone increases the reabsorption of water by the kidney tubules, thus decreasing the amount of urine formed. Oliguria is diminished urinary output relative to intake (less than 400 mL in 24 hours).**
3. With urinary retention, urine is formed, but it accumulates in the bladder and is not excreted.
4. Antidiuretic hormone is unrelated to incontinence.

22. 1. Manual bladder compression (Credé maneuver) is performed when a patient has bladder flaccidity.
2. This rocking motion is used to promote a bowel movement, not voiding.
3. Although running water in the sink may be helpful, it is not as effective as an intervention in another option.
4. **Tending to bodily functions is a personal, private activity in the North American culture. Providing privacy supports patient dignity and generally promotes voiding.**

23. 1. Thirst is associated with dehydration, not hypertension and oliguria.
2. Urinary retention is unrelated to hypertension and oliguria. Urinary retention is the inability to empty the bladder. It is caused by urethral obstruction, lesions involving the nerve pathways to and from the bladder or involving reflex centers in the brain or spinal cord, and medications. Urine is retained in the bladder when high urethral pressure inhibits complete emptying of the bladder or until increased abdominal pressure causes urine to be lost involuntarily.
3. **Oliguria is the inability to produce more than 400 to 500 mL of urine daily. Expected daily urinary output is 1,000 to 3,000 mL depending on the volume of fluid intake. If urine is not being produced in the presence of an average daily intake of 2,500 mL of fluid, then fluid will be retained and reflected in a gain in weight. One liter of fluid weighs 2.2 pounds. Excess fluid contributes to an increase in circulating blood volume, causing hypertension.**

4. Urinary hesitancy is an involuntary delay in initiating urination and is unrelated to hypertension and oliguria. It often is related to an enlarged prostate gland.

24. 1. Both tests require the area around the urinary meatus to be swiped several times with an antiseptic solution. This limits the presence of microorganisms that can contaminate the urine specimen, thus preventing inaccurate test results.
2. Both urine specimens should be sent to the laboratory immediately to prevent deterioration of the specimen that could result in inaccurate results. Casts in the urine will break down if urine is not tested for an extended period of time.
3. A sterile cup maintains the sterility of the specimen, a requirement of both tests.
4. **Sterile gloves must be worn when obtaining a urine specimen via a catheter. The nurse's hands touch the patient and catheter tubing, which must remain sterile. Clean, rather than sterile, gloves are worn when obtaining a clean-catch urine specimen. Urine flowing out of the patient is collected mid-stream into a sterile specimen cup.**

25. 1. Although monitoring the patient's intake and output (I&O) may be done, it is not the priority when a cystoscopy is scheduled.
2. Although this should be done, it is not the priority before the procedure. The amount and color of urine are assessed after the procedure. Pink urine after a cystoscopy is common because of slight bleeding from irritation of the mucous membranes of the urinary tract.
3. Although encouraging the intake of oral fluid before and after the procedure should be done, it is not the most important thing a nurse should do when a cystoscopy is scheduled. Keeping the patient well hydrated ensures that adequate intravascular fluid will pass through the kidneys, facilitating the production and passage of urine.
4. **During a cystoscopy a fiberoptic instrument is inserted through the urethra and into the bladder. It is an invasive procedure that requires the patient's written permission. The primary health-care provider's discussion with the patient includes the purpose of the procedure, its risks and benefits, and alternatives.**

26. 1. Dependent edema is more of a reflection of cardiac output. Edema associated with renal disease usually is generalized rather than localized in dependent areas.
2. A shift generally is 8 to 12 hours long. A period of 8 to 12 hours is too long a time to wait to collect information.
3. **The kidneys should produce more than 30 mL/hour. The patient has an indwelling urinary catheter that facilitates the assessment of urine output hourly. Patients without an indwelling urinary catheter should void a minimum of 240 mL of urine in 8 hours.**
4. Daily weights effectively monitor a patient's fluid balance because 1 L of retained fluid weighs 2.2 pounds. However, a 24-hour period is too long a time to wait to collect information.

27. 1. Lowering the penis until it is parallel to the length of the body will increase the trauma to the mucous membranes of the urinary tract because placing the penis parallel to the length of the body will create a 90-degree angle in the urethra where the shaft of the penis meets the abdominal wall. The penis should be held perpendicular to the patient's body during catheter insertion.
2. Inflating the balloon of the catheter in this situation will traumatize the urethra and inflict pain. The balloon is inflated once urine flows and the catheter is advanced another 1 to 2 inches to ensure that it is completely inside the urinary bladder and not the urethra.
3. **Resistance indicates that there may be a blockage in the urethra (e.g., enlarged prostate, tumor). The procedure should be discontinued when firm resistance is felt, to prevent trauma to the urinary system. The event should be documented in the patient's clinical record and the primary health-care provider notified.**
4. Using force or a twisting motion while advancing the catheter is contraindicated because it can traumatize the structures and mucous membranes of the urinary tract.

28. 1. Excessive urination at night is called nocturia. A person with urinary retention will have small, frequent voidings or dribbling (overflow incontinence) rather

than a complete discharge of urine from the bladder.

2. Hematuria is the presence of red blood cells in the urine. It is associated with bladder inflammation, infection, or trauma, not urinary retention.
3. Urinary retention may produce an atonic bladder rather than bladder contractions.
4. **The bladder lies in the pelvic cavity behind the symphysis pubis. When it fills with urine (600 mL), it extends above the symphysis pubis, and when greatly distended (2,000 to 3,000 mL), it can reach to the umbilicus.**
5. With urinary retention the bladder fills with urine, causing distention. Eventually the external urethral sphincter temporarily opens to allow a small volume of urine to pass out of the bladder (overflow incontinence, retention with overflow).

29. **The tubing from the collection bag that is attached to the catheter inserted into the bladder should be clamped 2 to 3 inches below the collection port. This location allows urine to collect above the port. The catheter inserted into the bladder should not be clamped to prevent trauma to the catheter lumen or the lumen leading to the inflated balloon.**

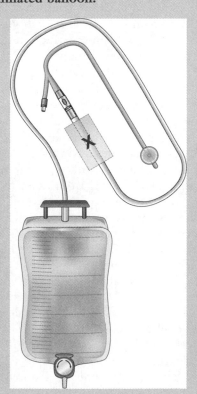

30. 1. Providing perineal care every shift is unnecessary. Perineal hygiene should be performed at least once a day, after a bowel movement, and whenever the catheter is changed or replaced.
2. **Avoiding kinks is essential so that urine flows unimpeded to the urine collection bag.**
3. **The anchoring device (e.g., adhesive band, elastic strip, or inflatable ring) must be snug enough to prevent the condom from falling off but not so tight that it interferes with blood circulation to the penis.**
4. If the foreskin is left in the retracted position it can constrict the penis, resulting in edema and tissue injury.
5. **Placing the condom over and beyond the glans penis and leaving one inch between the glans penis and drainage tubing prevents pressure against the glans penis that could cause excoriation and skin trauma.**

31. **Answer: 500 mL/hour. The electronic infusion device should be programmed for 500 mL/hour. An electronic infusion device uses milliliters (mL) per hour as the programmable infusion rate. The volume ordered (250 mL) is to be infused over 30 minutes. Therefore, the nurse must double the infusion volume to 500 mL to maintain a rate that will infuse the 250 mL in 30 minutes.**

32. 1. If retention catheter tubing is left on or through a side rail the catheter may inadvertently be pulled out when the side rail is moved. In addition, the collection bag must be kept below the level of the bladder to promote the flow of urine from the bladder by gravity and prevent a flow of urine back into the bladder from the catheter.
2. **Ensuring the tubing is positioned over the leg prevents pressure of the leg on the drainage tube that can interrupt the flow of urine from the bladder.**
3. Labeling the tubing with the date of insertion should be documented on the patient's clinical record, not the tubing.
4. Irrigating the tubing is contraindicated because it may introduce microorganisms into the bladder that can cause an infection. Irrigation of a urinary retention catheter requires an order and is a dependent function of the nurse.

5. Securing the tubing to the patient's leg prevents tension on the urinary meatus.

33. 6. The supine position permits access to the patient's lower abdomen and suprapubic area.

4. Draping the patient and exposing just the lower abdomen and suprapubic area provide for patient privacy.

2. The use of conducting gel or an ultrasound gel pad improves transmission of the ultrasound image.

3. The scan head should be placed approximately 1.5 inches (4 cm) above the pubic bone midline below the umbilicus (symphysis pubis) while aiming the scan head toward the coccyx. This permits visualization of the urinary bladder. In women the bladder lies in front of and below the uterus. In men the bladder can be partly obstructed by the pubic bone and the scan head may require a slightly oblique angle to visualize the bladder.

5. Several measurements should be obtained to ensure accuracy of the results.

1. Removing the gel and washing the patient's abdomen promote hygiene and comfort. Cleaning the scan head removes the gel on the end of the probe.

34. 1. Narcotics are central nervous system depressants that can cause urinary retention, not diuresis.

2. Drinks with caffeine (e.g., coffee, tea, and some carbonated beverages) promote the secretion and excretion of increased amounts of urine. This may be related to the inhibition of phosphodiesterases and/or antagonism of adenosine receptors. Antagonism of adenosine receptors inhibits proximal tubular reabsorption resulting in an increased urine output.

3. Although activity increases renal perfusion, which may increase urinary output, the increased fluid lost during activity usually is through insensible losses (e.g., perspiration, moisture in exhaled breaths).

4. Alcohol limits the production of vasopressin, a hormone that tells the kidneys to reabsorb water. Urine output increases as fluid is not reabsorbed in the kidneys.

5. Avoiding protein does not prevent diuresis. The presence of protein in the urine indicates that the glomeruli have become too permeable, which occurs in kidney disease. Most plasma proteins are too large to move out of the glomeruli and the small proteins that enter the filtrate are reabsorbed by pinocytosis.

35. Answer: 40 drops per minute. Four mL of furosemide must be added to the diluent, yielding a total volume of 54 mL to be infused. First determine how many milliliters contain 3 mg. Use ratio and proportion.

$$\frac{\text{Desire}}{\text{Have}} \ \frac{3 \text{ mg}}{40 \text{ mg}} = \frac{x \text{ mL}}{54 \text{ mL}}$$

40 x = 162
x = 162 ÷ 40
x = 4.05 mL

Round 4.05 down to 4 because 0.05 is less than 0.5. Each 4 mL of solution contains 3 mg of furosemide.

Now determine how many drops 4 mL contains when the drop rate of the secondary infusion set is 10.

4 mL (mL to be administered in 1 minute) × 10 (drop factor of the infusion set) = 40 drops per minute.

36. 1. A cognitively impaired person may not be able to receive, interpret, or respond to cues for voiding. Reminding the person to void every 2 hours empties the bladder, which may limit episodes of incontinence.

2. Applying a condom catheter in the morning is unnecessary and intrusive. Also, it may create a safety issue because the patient's mobility may be impaired by the tubing and urine drainage bag.

3. Cognitively impaired individuals may have problems handling clothing, particularly when attempting to respond to the urge to void. Clothing that is easy to manipulate, such as articles with elastic waistbands and zippers, will facilitate undressing and dressing to void.

4. Restriction of fluid intake is an inappropriate way to manage urinary incontinence. The body needs fluids throughout the day to maintain renal perfusion, kidney function, and fluid balance.

5. Toileting every 4 hours is too long a period of time to wait between

opportunities to void and usually will result in an episode of incontinence. Also, a cognitively impaired individual may not understand cause and effect or be able to follow directions.

37. 1. A person with a spinal cord injury will experience reflex incontinence, not stress incontinence.
    2. A person with a urinary tract obstruction will experience urinary retention, not stress incontinence.
    3. **Stress incontinence is an immediate involuntary loss of urine during an increase in intra-abdominal pressure. It is associated with weak pelvic muscles and structural supports resulting from multiple pregnancies, age-related degenerative changes, and overdistention between voiding.**
    4. After menopause women experience a weakening of the muscles surrounding the urinary and reproductive systems.
    5. Confused people may experience total, not stress, incontinence because they do not recognize bladder cues.

38. 1. Discontinuing the continuous compression devices to the lower extremities is unsafe and may result in the patient experiencing deep vein thrombosis and pulmonary embolus. Maintaining this device is a dependent function of the nurse.
    2. Notifying the surgeon is unnecessary at this time. If the status of the patient's urinary drainage intensifies then the surgeon should be notified.
    3. Obtaining a rectal temperature from a patient who has had a prostatectomy is contraindicated. The rectal probe could traumatize the surgical area.
    4. **The surgeon's orders indicate that the continuous bladder irrigation should be maintained at a flow rate that keeps the urinary drainage pink; this also implies the absence of clots.**

39.   **Answer: 800 mL. To calculate the amount of urine output of a patient receiving CBI, the total amount of the instilled irrigant must be subtracted from the total output. The patient received 200 mL of GU irrigant per hour for 12 hours. To determine the total amount of GU irrigant received, multiply 200 × 12 (2,400). Subtract 2,400 mL from 3,200 mL (total amount of urinary drainage) to determine the amount of urine contained in the total output. 3,200 mL minus 2,400 mL equals 800 mL.**

40. 3. Draining the urine ensures that previously produced urine is not collected for a current specimen.
    4. Clamping the drainage tubing allows urine to collect above the specimen port.
    1. Washing the hands limits the amount of microorganisms on the hands. Clean gloves protect the nurse from the patient's body fluids. Both practices are part of standard precautions.
    5. The use of an antiseptic swab removes microorganisms on the specimen port and sterile equipment maintains the sterility of the closed urinary drainage system.
    6. The sterility of the specimen must be maintained to prevent contamination of the specimen, which can result in inaccurate results. Discarding used equipment in a sharps container prevents accidental injury to self or others.
    2. Removing the clamp from the drainage tubing reestablishes the flow of urine from the patient to the drainage bag. If it is left clamped, urine will not drain, causing bladder distention, and may precipitate a stasis-induced urinary tract infection.

Fluids and Electrolytes

KEYWORDS

The following words include nursing/medical terminology, concepts, principles, and information relevant to content specifically addressed in the chapter or associated with topics presented in it. English dictionaries, nursing textbooks, and medical dictionaries, such as *Taber's Cyclopedic Medical Dictionary,* are resources that can be used to expand your knowledge and understanding of these words and related information.

Acid
Active transport
Aldosterone
Anion
Antidiuretic hormone
Anuria
Base
Catheter
Cation
Colloid osmotic/oncotic pressure
Dehydration
Diaphoresis
Diffusion
Diluent
Diuretic
Edema:
  Dependent
  Peripheral
  Pitting
  Sacral
Electrolytes:
  Calcium
  Magnesium
  Phosphorus
  Potassium
  Sodium
Fluid compartments:
  Extracellular
  Interstitial
  Intracellular
  Intravascular
  Third-compartment spacing
Fluid restriction

Fluid volume:
  Deficient
  Excess
Hydrostatic pressure
Hypercalcemia/hypocalcemia
Hyperkalemia/hypokalemia
Hypermagnesemia/hypomagnesemia
Hyperosmolar/hypo-osmolar
Hypertension/hypotension
Hypertonic/hypotonic
Hypervolemic/hypovolemic
Icteric
Infiltration
Infusion port
Insensible fluid loss
Ion
Irrigant
Isotonic
Macrodrip/microdrip
Milliequivalent
Osmolality
Osmolarity
Osmosis
Primary infusion line
Residual urine
Secondary infusion line
Sensible/insensible fluid loss
Skin turgor
Solute
Specific gravity
Tenting
Thirst
Vaporization

FLUIDS AND ELECTROLYTES: QUESTIONS

1. A nurse is caring for a critically ill patient with a urinary retention catheter. Which hourly urine output should **first** alert the nurse that the primary health-care provider should be notified?
   1. 20 mL
   2. 30 mL
   3. 60 mL
   4. 120 mL

2. A nurse is caring for a patient who has dependent edema. Which pressure has caused the excess fluid in the interstitial compartment?
   1. Oncotic pressure
   2. Diffusion pressure
   3. Hydrostatic pressure
   4. Intraventricular pressure

3. A nurse evaluates a patient's fluid balance by monitoring the patient's intake and output. Which must the nurse understand about the ratio of the patient's fluid intake to output?
   1. Intake should be slightly more than the output.
   2. Intake should be higher than the fluid output.
   3. Intake should be lower than the urine output.
   4. Intake should be equal to the urine output.

4. Hydrochlorothiazide (HCTZ), a diuretic, is prescribed for a patient who is retaining fluid. The nurse should encourage the patient to ingest nutrients that contain which electrolyte?
   1. Magnesium
   2. Potassium
   3. Calcium
   4. Sodium

5. Which should a nurse do to encourage a confused patient to drink more fluid?
   1. Serve fluid at a tepid temperature.
   2. Explain the reason for the desired intake.
   3. Offer the patient something to drink every hour.
   4. Leave a pitcher of water at the patient's bedside.

6. A nurse suspects that an older adult may have a fluid and electrolyte imbalance. Which assessment **best** reflects fluid and electrolyte balance in an older adult?
   1. Intake and output results
   2. Serum laboratory values
   3. Condition of the skin
   4. Presence of tenting

7. A patient has continuous bladder irrigation. Which should the nurse do with the irrigant on the I&O sheet when calculating the fluid balance for this patient?
   1. Add it to the oral intake column.
   2. Deduct it from the total urine output.
   3. Subtract it from the intravenous flow sheet as output.
   4. Document the intake hourly in the urine output column.

8. A nurse is caring for two patients; one has oliguria and the other has polyuria. Which is the **priority** problem that is a concern for the nurse regarding both of these patients?
   1. Diarrhea
   2. Cachexia
   3. Fluid volume deficit
   4. Impaired skin integrity

9. A primary health-care provider orders a patient's IV fluids to be discontinued. Which is an essential nursing intervention when discontinuing the patient's intravenous infusion?
   1. Withdraw the intravenous catheter along the same angle of its insertion.
   2. Use an alcohol swab to scrub the insertion site.
   3. Flush the line with normal saline.
   4. Don sterile gloves.

10. A patient is admitted to the hospital for a fever of unknown origin. The nursing assessment reveals profuse diaphoresis, dry, sticky mucous membranes, weakness, disorientation, and a decreasing level of consciousness. Which electrolyte imbalance does this data support?
    1. Hyperkalemia
    2. Hypercalcemia
    3. Hypernatremia
    4. Hypermagnesemia

11. A patient exhibits an increasing blood pressure and 2-lb weight gain over 2 days. Which additional clinical manifestation can be clustered with these data?
    1. Decrease in heart rate
    2. Increase in skin turgor
    3. Increase in pulse volume
    4. Decrease in pulse pressure

12. An assessment of which of the following is **most** important when a nurse is caring for an adult patient experiencing vomiting?
    1. Oral mucous membranes
    2. Electrolyte values
    3. Bowel function
    4. Body weight

13. A primary health-care provider orders an intravenous infusion containing potassium for a patient. Which is the **most** important nursing intervention before administering this solution to the patient?
    1. Assess the skin turgor.
    2. Obtain the blood pressure.
    3. Measure the depth of edema.
    4. Determine the presence of urinary output.

14. Which is the **best** choice for an appetizer when teaching a patient about a 2-g sodium diet?
    1. Pigs in a blanket
    2. Stuffed mushrooms
    3. Cheese and crackers
    4. Fresh vegetable sticks

15. A nurse is documenting a patient's I&O. Which should be recorded at approximately half its volume?
    1. Ice chips given by mouth
    2. A continuous bladder irrigation
    3. Solution used to maintain patency of a tube
    4. A tube feeding of half formula and half water

16. Several patients are taking supplemental calcium daily. The nurse teaches them to maintain their fluid intake at a minimum of 2,500 mL. The nurse explains that this intervention is designed to prevent which complication?
    1. Mobilization of calcium from bone
    2. Irritation of the bladder mucosa
    3. Occurrence of muscle cramps
    4. Formation of kidney stones

17. A patient receiving an enteral feeding develops diarrhea. Which characteristic of the tube feeding formula does the nurse conclude precipitated the diarrhea?
    1. Icteric
    2. Isotonic
    3. Hypotonic
    4. Hypertonic

18. A nurse identifies that an older adult patient may have a problem with excess fluid volume. Which characteristics of the patient's skin support this conclusion?
    1. Dry and scaly
    2. Taut and shiny
    3. Red and irritated
    4. Thin and inelastic

19. When a patient is under extreme stress, there is an increased production of antidiuretic hormone (ADH) and aldosterone. The nurse plans to monitor the patient routinely because an increase in these hormones will cause a decrease in which of the following?
    1. Blood pressure
    2. Urinary output
    3. Body temperature
    4. Sweat gland secretions

20. A nurse checks a meal tray for a patient on a clear liquid diet. Which item is acceptable on this diet?
    1. Ginger ale
    2. Lemon sherbet
    3. Vanilla ice cream
    4. Cream of chicken soup

21. A nurse is caring for a patient who has a reduced fluid intake. The nurse assesses the patient for which response to this reduced fluid intake?
    1. Urinary retention
    2. Frequent urination
    3. Incontinence of urine
    4. Decreased urine output

22. A nurse is monitoring a patient who is receiving intravenous fluid. Which clinical findings indicate that the patient has a fluid overload?
    1. Chills, fever, and generalized discomfort
    2. Blood in the tubing close to the insertion site
    3. Dyspnea, headache, and increased blood pressure
    4. Pallor, swelling, and discomfort at the insertion site

23. With which complication of the administration of intravenous fluids should the nurse slow the rate of flow of the infusion rather than stop the infusion and remove the catheter?
    1. Infiltration
    2. Extravasation
    3. Inflamed vein
    4. Fluid overload

24. When a nurse evaluates the effectiveness of patient teaching, which food selections by a patient indicate understanding regarding an abundant source of calcium? **Select all that apply.**
    1. _____Bread
    2. _____Yogurt
    3. _____Spinach
    4. _____Green beans
    5. _____Peanut butter

25. A nurse is caring for a postoperative patient over an 8-hour period. The patient vomits 300 mL of greenish-yellow fluid. The patient's intravenous fluids are infusing at 125 mL per hour. The patient received 2 intermittent infusions of antibiotics each in 50 mL of solution and they were infused at a different site than the IV fluid infusion. The patient was given 8 ounces of ice chips which were retained. The patient urinated twice—250 mL and 400 mL. Which is the patient's total fluid intake at the end of the 8-hour period? **Record your answer using a whole number.**
Answer: _____ mL

26. A patient's diet is progressed from clear liquid to full liquid. Which can the nurse include on the full-liquid diet that is not included on the clear-liquid diet? **Select all that apply.**
1. _____ Vanilla ice cream
2. _____ Cream of Wheat
3. _____ Cranberry juice
4. _____ Ginger ale
5. _____ Gelatin
6. _____ Milk

27. A nurse is caring for a patient in the emergency department. The patient's ECG tracing is indicated below. For which additional responses should the nurse assess the patient that can be clustered with the results of this ECG tracing? **Select all that apply.**
1. _____ Bradycardia
2. _____ Flaccid paralysis
3. _____ Increased bowel sounds
4. _____ Ventricular dysrhythmias
5. _____ Decreased deep tendon reflexes

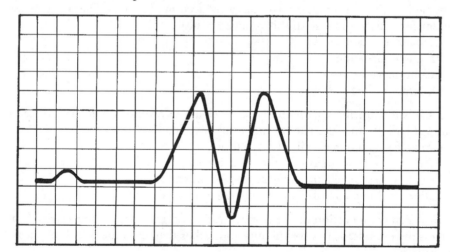

28. A nurse is assessing several patients for fluid and electrolyte imbalances. Which responses are common to both excess fluid volume and deficient fluid volume? **Select all that apply.**
1. _____ Increased pulse amplitude
2. _____ Decreased blood pressure
3. _____ Difficulty breathing
4. _____ Mental confusion
5. _____ Muscle weakness

29. The illustration reflects a patient's upper extremity while the nurse is obtaining the patient's blood pressure. Which should the nurse do **next** after releasing the pressure in the sphygmomanometer cuff?

1. Notify the primary health-care provider of the patient's response.
2. Assess the patient's radial pulse in the affected arm.
3. Retake the patient's blood pressure.
4. Tap over the patient's facial nerve.

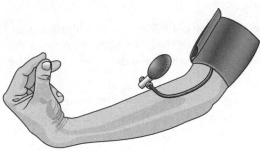

30. A nurse is monitoring a patient who is receiving fluids intravenously. Which clinical manifestations at the insertion site indicate that the IV has infiltrated? **Select all that apply.**

1. _____Redness
2. _____Swelling
3. _____Firmness
4. _____Coolness
5. _____Inflammation

31. An older adult is diagnosed with congestive heart failure and pulmonary edema, and the primary health-care provider prescribed furosemide 40 mg PO twice a day. The patient has slight dysphagia as a result of a brain attack a year ago. The nurse obtains an oral solution of furosemide that states that there is 8 mg/mL. How many milliliters should the nurse administer? **Record your answer using a whole number.**

Answer: _____mL

32. A patient receiving a diuretic is encouraged to increase the intake of potassium. Which foods selected by the patient indicate that the teaching is understood? **Select all that apply.**

1. _____Pears
2. _____Cabbage
3. _____Cantaloupe
4. _____Fresh salmon
5. _____Chicken liver

33. A nurse must discontinue a patient's intravenous infusion. The nurse shuts off the infusion, washes the hands, and dons clean gloves. Place the following steps in the order in which they should be performed.

1. Apply counter-traction to the skin while loosening the tape at the venipuncture site.
2. Apply firm pressure to the site with sterile gauze for two to three minutes.
3. Apply a sterile dressing with tape over the venipuncture site.
4. Withdraw the needle/catheter along the line of insertion.
5. Examine the end of the needle/catheter.

Answer: _____

34. A nurse is assessing a patient's fluid status. Which assessments indicate that the patient has a deficient fluid volume? **Select all that apply.**
1. _____Negative balance of intake and output
2. _____Decreased body temperature
3. _____Increased blood pressure
4. _____Shortness of breath
5. _____Flat neck veins
6. _____Weight loss

35. A patient is to receive 250 mL of 0.9% sodium chloride over 30 minutes. The nurse obtains an electronic infusion devise. At which hourly rate should the nurse set the infusion device? **Record your answer using a whole number.**
Answer: _____mL

36. A 2-g sodium diet is ordered for a patient with hypertension. Which foods should the nurse teach the patient to avoid? **Select all that apply.**
1. _____American cheese
2. _____Canned tuna fish
3. _____Shredded wheat
4. _____Potatoes
5. _____Cashews

37. A nurse assesses a patient for electrolyte imbalances. Which clinical manifestations indicate that the patient may have a potassium deficiency? **Select all that apply.**
1. _____Ventricular dysrhythmias
2. _____Increased blood pressure
3. _____Muscle weakness
4. _____Chest pain
5. _____Dry hair

38. A primary health-care provider orders 1,000 mL 0.9% sodium chloride to be infused over 6 hours. A gravity flow infusion set states that the drop factor is 15. At which rate should the nurse set the IV flow rate? **Record your answer using a whole number.**
Answer: _____drops/minute

39. Which characteristics associated with touching an intravenous insertion site support the conclusion that the insertion site may be inflamed? **Select all that apply.**
1. _____Warmth
2. _____Softness
3. _____Firmness
4. _____Coolness
5. _____Discomfort

40. A patient in the hospital emergency department tells the nurse, "I feel lousy and I've had diarrhea for several days. I have nausea and I don't feel like eating or drinking." The nurse obtains the patient's vital signs, performs a focused physical assessment, and reviews the results of laboratory studies. Which should the nurse conclude is the patient's human response based on this information?
1. Hypokalemia
2. Hypervolemia
3. Metabolic acidosis
4. Respiratory alkalosis

PATIENT'S CLINICAL RECORD

Vital Signs
Temperature: 101.2°F, oral
Pulse: 92 beats per minute, regular, thready
Respirations: 26 breaths per minute, deep
Blood pressure: 100/60 mm Hg

Focused Physical Assessment
Weight loss of 4 pounds in 3 days
Tenting of the skin

Laboratory Values
Urine specific gravity: 1.036
Serum potassium: 5.3 mEq/L
Arterial blood gases:
pH: 7.30
$Paco_2$: 24 mEq/L
HCO_3: 18 mEq/L

1. 1. The primary health-care provider should be notified long before the hourly urine output reaches 20 mL.
   2. **The circulating blood volume perfuses the kidneys, producing a glomerular filtrate of which varying amounts are either reabsorbed or excreted to maintain fluid balance. When a person's hourly urine output is only 30 mL, it indicates a deficient circulating fluid volume, inadequate renal perfusion, and/or kidney disease. The primary health-care provider should be notified.**
   3. An hourly urine output of 60 mL is close to the expected range of 1,400 mL to 1,500 mL/24 hours or 30 mL to 50 mL/hour.
   4. The primary health-care provider does not have to be notified about this. An hourly urine output of 120 mL indicates that there is adequate kidney perfusion.

2. 1. **Oncotic (colloid osmotic) pressure is the force exerted by colloids (e.g., proteins) that pull or keep fluid within the intravascular compartment. Oncotic pressure is the major force opposing hydrostatic pressure in the capillaries.**
   2. Diffusion is a continual intermingling of molecules with movement of molecules from a solution of higher concentration to a solution of lower concentration.
   3. Hydrostatic pressure is the pressure exerted by a fluid within a compartment, such as blood within the vessels. Hydrostatic pressure moves fluid from an area of greater pressure to an area of lesser pressure. Hydrostatic pressure within vessels of the body moves fluid from the intravascular compartment into the interstitial compartment. Interstitial fluid is extracellular fluid that surrounds cells.
   4. Intraventricular pressure is the pressure that exists in the left and right ventricles of the heart. These pressures do not move fluid from the intravascular compartment to the interstitial compartment.

3. 1. **The volume and composition of body fluids are kept in a delicate balance (total intake is slightly more than total output) by a harmonious interaction of** the kidneys and the endocrine, respiratory, cardiovascular, integumentary, and gastrointestinal systems.
   2. If the total intake is higher than the total output, the patient will develop an excess fluid volume.
   3. If the total intake is lower than the urine output, the patient will develop a deficient fluid volume.
   4. If intake and urine output are equal, the patient will develop a deficient fluid volume because of fluid loss through routes other than the kidneys. In addition to urine output, the body has insensible fluid loss through the skin, in feces, and as water vapor in expired air.

4. 1. Although loop and thiazide diuretics enhance magnesium excretion, which may produce mild hypomagnesemia, it does not require magnesium supplementation.
   2. **Most diuretics affect the renal mechanisms for tubular secretion and reabsorption of electrolytes, particularly potassium. Because of potassium's narrow therapeutic window of 3.5 to 5.0 mEq/L and its role in the sodium-potassium pump and muscle contraction, depleted potassium must be supplemented by increasing the dietary intake of foods high in potassium and/or the administration of potassium drug therapy.**
   3. Serum calcium levels vary depending on the diuretic. Thiazide diuretics, such as HCTZ, decrease calcium excretion, which may produce hypercalcemia. Loop diuretics increase calcium excretion, which may produce hypocalcemia.
   4. Although sodium deficit (hyponatremia) may occur with diuretics, usually it is mild and does not require sodium supplementation.

5. 1. Fluids should be administered at the temperature usually associated with the fluid, for example, cool temperatures for juice, soda, and milk and warm temperatures for tea, coffee, and soup. Hot liquids should be avoided for safety reasons.
   2. This explanation probably will be ineffective because a confused person has difficulty understanding cause and effect.

3. **Frequent smaller volumes of fluid (50 to 100 mL/hr) are better tolerated physiologically and psychologically than infrequent larger volumes of fluid.**
4. A confused patient, having difficulty understanding cause and effect, may ignore a pitcher of water.

6. 1. Monitoring intake and output results assesses only fluid balance.
2. **Laboratory studies provide objective measurements of indicators of fluid, electrolyte, and acid-base balance. Common diagnostic tests include serum blood studies of electrolytes (e.g., sodium, potassium, chloride, and calcium), osmolarity, hemoglobin, hematocrit, and arterial blood gases.**
3. Assessment of the skin in the context of this question assesses only fluid balance. In addition, the changes in the integumentary system as a person ages complicate assessment of the skin for fluid balance disturbances in the older adult. Skin changes include loss of dermal and subcutaneous mass (thin and wrinkled), decreased secretion from sebaceous and sweat glands (dry skin), and less organized collagen and elastic fibers (wrinkles, decreased elasticity).
4. Presence of tenting assesses only fluid balance. Tenting occurs when the skin of a dehydrated person remains in a peak or tent position after the superficial layers of the skin are pinched together. Caution is advised when assessing an older person because some degree of tenting may occur even when hydrated because of the decrease in skin elasticity and tissue fluid associated with aging. The skin over the sternum is the area that should be tested for tenting.

7. 1. The irrigant of a continuous bladder irrigation is instilled into the urinary bladder, not the mouth.
2. **When continuous bladder irrigation is in use, drainage from the urinary bladder will consist of both urine and the instilled irrigant. To determine the patient's urinary output, the amount of the irrigant instilled must be deducted from the total urinary output.**
3. The IV flow sheet should not contain any information regarding I&O other than the amount and type of fluid that is instilled into the circulatory system.

4. Intake anywhere in the body should be recorded in the appropriate intake column, not in the urinary output column.

8. 1. Frequent, loose, liquid stools, not oliguria or polyuria, are associated with diarrhea.
2. Oliguria and polyuria are related to fluid balance and kidney functioning, not nutrition. Cachexia is a profound state of malnutrition.
3. **The production of excessive amounts of urine by the kidneys (polyuria) without an increase in fluid intake can precipitate a fluid volume deficit. Oliguria, the production of excessively small amounts of urine by the kidney, is reflected as a negative balance in the intake and output. A negative balance of intake and output is a characteristic of fluid volume deficit.**
4. Oliguria and polyuria are related to fluid balance and kidney functioning, not skin integrity. However, because oliguria may be related to fluid retention and subsequent edema and polyuria may ultimately cause dehydration and dry skin, the patient may eventually be at risk for impaired skin integrity.

9. 1. **Removing an intravenous catheter by withdrawing it along the same path of its insertion minimizes injury to the vein and trauma to the surrounding tissue. This action limits seepage of blood and promotes healing of the puncture wound.**
2. Scrubbing the area with an alcohol wipe is unnecessary. The area should be compressed with a sterile gauze pad. Pressure helps stop the bleeding and prevents the formation of a hematoma. A sterile gauze pad provides for surgical asepsis, which prevents infection.
3. Flushing the line with normal saline is unnecessary.
4. Clean, not sterile, gloves should be worn by the nurse to prevent exposure to the patient's body fluids.

10. 1. Although muscle weakness and lethargy are associated with hyperkalemia, the patient's other responses are not.
2. Although weakness and lethargy are associated with hypercalcemia, the patient's other responses are not.

3. With profuse diaphoresis, the water loss exceeds the sodium loss, resulting in hypernatremia. Excess serum sodium precipitates changes in the musculoskeletal (weakness), neurological (disorientation and decreased level of consciousness), and integumentary (dry, sticky mucous membranes) systems.

4. Although muscle weakness, lethargy, and drowsiness are associated with hypermagnesemia, the patient's other responses are not.

11. 1. With an excess fluid volume the heart rate will increase, not decrease, in an attempt to maintain adequate cardiac output.

2. In the early stages of an excess fluid volume, a change in skin turgor may not be evident. One liter of fluid is equal to approximately 2.2 pounds.

3. **With an excess fluid volume the amount of circulating blood volume increases, resulting in full, bounding peripheral pulses.**

4. The pulse pressure is the difference between the systolic and diastolic pressures of a blood pressure measurement, and the acceptable range is 30 to 50 mm Hg. With an excess fluid volume, the pulse pressure increases, not decreases.

12. 1. Although the mouth is assessed and oral care is provided, it is performed for comfort, not because there is a life-threatening problem.

2. **Vomiting results in a loss of chloride (greatest amount), sodium (next greatest amount), and potassium (least amount, but of greatest importance because it can cause dysrhythmias and cardiac arrest).**

3. Although assessing bowel function will be done, it is not the priority.

4. Although obtaining a body weight will be done to assess fluid volume deficit (2.2 pounds equals approximately 1 L of fluid), it is not as critical as another assessment.

13. 1. Assessing skin turgor is unnecessary for the administration of potassium. This is part of the assessment of a patient's hydration status, particularly when the patient is at risk for dehydration.

2. Although all the vital signs should be measured when a patient is receiving any

fluids or electrolytes, monitoring the heart rate and rhythm is a more significant assessment than the blood pressure in relation to the administration of potassium. Both a serum potassium decrease (hypokalemia) and increase (hyperkalemia) cause cardiac dysrhythmias.

3. Measuring the depth of edema is unnecessary for the administration of potassium. This is part of the assessment when a patient has a fluid volume excess in dependent tissues in which the hydrostatic capillary pressure is high.

4. **Serum potassium has a narrow therapeutic window (3.5 to 5.0 mEq/L). When kidney function is impaired, potassium can accumulate in the body and exceed the therapeutic level of 5.0 mEq/L, which can cause cardiac dysrhythmias and arrest.**

14. 1. One-tenth of a pound of frankfurters contains approximately 168 mg of sodium and should be avoided on a 2-g sodium diet.

2. Although mushrooms are low in sodium, when stuffed with seasoned bread crumbs (⅓ cup contains approximately 370 mg of sodium) they should be avoided on a 2-g sodium diet.

3. One ounce of cheese contains approximately 106 to 400 mg of sodium depending on the cheese. Two crackers contain approximately 44 to 165 mg depending on the product. These foods should be avoided on a 2-g sodium diet.

4. **As a food group, fresh vegetables have low sodium content. The sodium content of vegetables includes 1 cup of broccoli, 17 mg; 1 cup of cauliflower, 20 mg; 1 carrot, 25 mg; 1 pepper, 2 mg; 1 radish, 1 mg; 1 cup of mushrooms, 3 mg; and 6 slices of cucumber, 1 mg.**

15. 1. **Ice chips are particles of frozen water that take up more volume when they are frozen than when they melt. When ice chips change from a solid to a liquid, the resulting fluid is approximately half the volume of the ice chips.**

2. The total amount of the irrigant instilled into the urinary bladder is accounted for as intake. The total volume that was instilled is then deducted from the total

urinary output to determine the patient's urinary output.

3. Whatever volume of solution is instilled into a catheter, the full volume used is recorded when the nurse documents the intervention.

4. When a tube feeding solution consists of half formula and half water, the final combined volume of the formula and water is recorded on the appropriate intake column of the I&O record.

16. 1. Calcium supplementation and weight bearing, not an increased fluid intake, prevent bone demineralization.

2. Neither hypocalcemia nor hypercalcemia irritates the bladder mucosa.

3. Excessive supplementation of calcium causes hypercalcemia. Muscle tremors and cramps are associated with hypocalcemia, not hypercalcemia.

4. **A high fluid intake increases the volume of urine produced. The resulting frequent urination of dilute urine prevents the formation of renal calculi, which may occur because of the increased precipitation of calcium salts associated with calcium supplementation.**

17. 1. Icteric is unrelated to enteral feedings and fluid shifts. Icteric is defined as pertaining to, or resembling, jaundice.

2. Isotonic solutions have the same concentration of solutes as the blood. With isotonic solutions there is no net transfer of water across two compartments separated by a semipermeable membrane.

3. Hypotonic solutions have a lesser concentration of solutes than does the blood. A hypotonic enteral feeding will result in fluid being absorbed from the gastrointestinal tract into the intravascular and intracellular compartments.

4. **Hypertonic solutions have a greater concentration of solutes than does the blood. The high osmolarity of a hypertonic enteral feeding exerts an osmotic force that pulls fluid into the gastrointestinal tract, resulting in intestinal cramping and diarrhea.**

18. 1. Dry skin and scaly skin are signs of aging and dehydration, not excessive fluid volume.

2. **With excessive fluid volume, the increased hydrostatic pressure moves fluid from the intravascular**

compartment into the interstitial compartment. As fluid collects in the interstitial compartment (edema), the skin appears taut and shiny.

3. Red skin and irritated skin are signs of the local inflammatory response, not of excessive fluid volume.

4. Thin skin and inelastic skin are characteristics of skin in the older adult because of a loss of subcutaneous fat and a reduced thickness and vascularity of the dermis, not of excessive fluid volume.

19. 1. The blood pressure will increase, not decrease, when the circulating fluid volume increases in response to these hormones.

2. **Both hormones are involved with water reabsorption, which conserves fluid and results in a decreased urinary output. With decreased kidney perfusion, the juxtaglomerular cells of the kidneys release angiotensin II, which stimulates the release of aldosterone from the adrenal cortex. Aldosterone promotes the excretion of potassium and reabsorption of sodium, which results in the passive reabsorption of water. As the concentration of the blood (osmolality) increases, the anterior pituitary releases antidiuretic hormone (ADH). ADH causes the collecting ducts in the kidneys to become more permeable to water, thus promoting its reabsorption into the blood.**

3. ADH and aldosterone do not regulate body temperature.

4. ADH and aldosterone influence the kidneys to maintain fluid balance. They do not affect insensible fluid loss through the skin, lungs, or intestinal tract.

20. 1. **Ginger ale is an easily ingested and digested liquid that is permitted on a clear liquid diet. It relieves thirst, prevents dehydration, and minimizes stimulation of the gastrointestinal tract.**

2. Sherbet contains milk, which is not permitted on a clear liquid diet.

3. When ice cream melts, it is not a clear liquid, and therefore is not permitted on a clear liquid diet. Milk contains protein and lactose, which stimulates the digestive process; this is undesirable when a patient is receiving a clear liquid diet.

4. Cream of chicken soup contains milk and small particles of chicken, both of which are contraindicated on a clear liquid diet.

21. 1. The accumulation of urine in the bladder with an inability to empty the bladder (urinary retention) is unrelated to a decreased fluid intake.
2. Frequent urination occurs with increased, not decreased, fluid intake.
3. Involuntary urination (incontinence) is not associated with a reduced fluid intake.
4. When the serum osmolarity increases because of insufficient fluid intake, antidiuretic hormone increases the permeability of the collecting tubules in the kidneys, which increases the reabsorption of water and decreases urine output.

22. 1. These physiological responses indicate the presence of an infection, not excess fluid volume.
2. Blood in the tubing is unrelated to fluid overload; it occurs when the IV bag is held lower than the IV insertion site and is an undesirable occurrence.
3. IV fluid flows directly into the circulatory system via a vein. Excess intravascular volume (hypervolemia) causes hypertension, pulmonary edema, and headache.
4. These physiological responses indicate an IV infiltration, not excess fluid volume.

23. 1. The infusion should be stopped and the catheter removed when a patient's IV infiltrates. When an IV catheter is displaced outside of a vein and IV fluid accidently leaks into the interstitial compartment, it is called an infiltration. If the solution is just slowed, additional fluid will collect in the interstitial compartment and cause tissue damage.
2. The infusion should be stopped and the catheter removed when extravasation occurs. Extravasation occurs when an IV catheter is displaced outside of a vein and a vesicant solution accidently leaks into the interstitial compartment. Vesicant solutions are extremely irritating solutions that cause tissues to blister, slough, and become necrotic.
3. The infusion should be stopped and the catheter removed when a patient's vein becomes inflamed because of the presence of the catheter. Inflammation of a vein (phlebitis) can progress to an infection or

promote the development of a thrombus at the site.
4. When intravenous fluids are infused too rapidly or an excess amount of fluid is infused, the patient can experience an overload of fluid in the intravascular compartment. The nurse should slow the rate of infusion to keep the venous access viable and notify the primary health-care provider for directions.

24. 1. Grain products are not high in calcium. One slice of bread contains approximately 20 to 49 mg of calcium depending on the type of grain.
2. Yogurt is an excellent dietary source of calcium. Eight ounces of yogurt contain 415 mg of calcium.
3. Spinach is an excellent dietary source of calcium. One cup of cooked fresh spinach contains 245 mg of calcium.
4. Green beans are not high in calcium. One cup of green beans contains approximately 60 mg of calcium.
5. Peanut butter is not high in calcium. One tablespoon of peanut butter contains approximately 5 mg of calcium.

25. **Answer: 1,220 mL. The patient's IV fluids infused at 125 mL/8 hours; therefore, 125 × 8 = 1,000 mL of IV fluids. The patient received 2 intermittent infusions of 50 mL each; therefore, 50 × 2 = 100 mL of antibiotic solution. The patient consumed 8 ounces of ice chips. When ice chips melt they are half the volume of the original amount of ice chips; therefore, 8 ounces × 30 mL (amount of mL per ounce) = 240 (the total volume of ice chips before they melted). Then 240 ÷ 2 = 120 mL to determine the amount of fluid in ice chips that the patient consumed. Finally, to determine the total intake for 8 hours, add 1,000 + 100 + 120 = 1,220 mL.**

26. 1. Vanilla ice cream is a liquid at room temperature and is permitted on a full-liquid diet, not a clear-liquid diet.
2. Cooked, refined cereals, such as Cream of Wheat, cream of rice, oatmeal, grits, and farina are permitted on a full-liquid diet, not a clear-liquid diet.
3. Cranberry juice is a clear liquid.
4. Ginger ale is a clear liquid.
5. Gelatin is a clear liquid that is a solid when refrigerated and a liquid at room

temperature. It is permitted in either form on a clear liquid diet.

6. **Milk contains a high solute load, including fat and proteins, which precipitates the digestive process. Milk is permitted on a full-liquid diet, not a clear-liquid diet.**

27. 1. **The ECG tracing indicates hyperkalemia (tall, thin T wave; prolonged PR interval, ST-segment depression; widened QRS; and loss of P wave). Bradycardia is associated with hyperkalemia. Potassium, an electrolyte, is part of the sodium-potassium pump that is involved in muscle contraction. The heart is a muscle.**

2. **The ECG tracing indicates hyperkalemia (tall, thin T wave; prolonged PR interval, ST-segment depression; widened QRS; and loss of P wave). Flaccid paralysis (muscles that lack tone and strength) is associated with hyperkalemia. Potassium, an electrolyte, is part of the sodium-potassium pump that is involved in muscle contraction.**

3. **The ECG tracing indicates hyperkalemia (tall, thin T wave; prolonged PR interval, ST-segment depression; widened QRS; and loss of P wave). Increased bowel sounds are associated with hyperkalemia because of hyperactivity of gastrointestinal smooth muscle.**

4. Ventricular dysrhythmias are associated with hypokalemia, not hyperkalemia. The ECG tracing indicates hyperkalemia.

5. Decreased deep tendon reflexes are associated with hypokalemia, not hyperkalemia. The ECG tracing indicates hyperkalemia.

28. 1. The pulse amplitude is increased with fluid volume excess because of hypervolemia. The pulse amplitude is decreased with fluid volume deficit because of a decrease in the circulating blood volume (hypovolemia).

2. A decrease in blood pressure is associated with fluid volume deficit, not excess, because of the decreased circulating blood volume.

3. Dyspnea is associated with fluid volume excess, not deficit, because fluid overload causes pulmonary congestion.

4. **Brain cells require a delicate balance of fluids and electrolytes. Too much fluid and too little fluid affect the appropriate balance of electrolytes, particularly sodium and potassium. Fluid and electrolyte imbalances cause cerebral changes such as headache, confusion, combative behavior, unconsciousness, and coma.**

5. **Muscle weakness is a musculoskeletal response to both increased fluid volume and decreased fluid volume because the fluid imbalances alter cellular and body metabolism.**

29. 1. Notifying the primary health-care provider is premature. The nurse should obtain additional information.

2. Obtaining the radial pulse is not necessary. Trousseau sign is a result of neuromuscular irritability, not a circulatory impairment.

3. It is not necessary to retake the patient's blood pressure. Information already has been obtained from performing this procedure.

4. **When a carpopedal spasm results from compression of a patient's arm by a sphygmomanometer cuff (Trousseau**

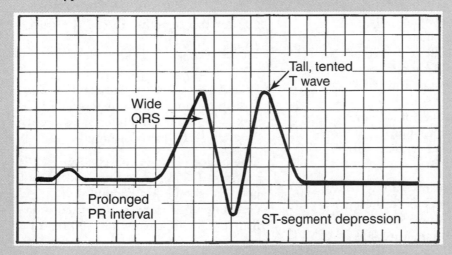

sign), it indicates that the patient may have hypocalcemia. Tapping over the patient's facial nerve will precipitate spasmodic spasms of the facial muscles (Chvostek sign) if the patient has hypocalcemia. This intervention provides more data to support the conclusion that the patient is hypocalcemic.

30. 1. When the insertion site of an IV is reddened, swollen, warm to the touch, and painful, the patient has phlebitis, not an infiltration of an IV.
    2. **When an IV line moves out of a vein and into subcutaneous tissue, the IV fluid will begin to collect in the interstitial compartment, causing swelling.**
    3. When IV fluid flows into the tissue surrounding a vein (infiltration), the area will feel soft and spongy, not hard.
    4. **The intravenous fluid that is infusing is at room temperature, which is cooler than body temperature. Therefore, IV fluid collecting at the site of an infiltration will cause the site to feel cool to the touch.**
    5. When the area at the insertion site of an IV appears inflamed, the patient has phlebitis, not an infiltration of an IV.

31.   **Answer: 5 mL. Solve the problem by using the formula for ratio and proportion.**

$$\frac{\text{Desire}}{\text{Have}} \frac{40\ mg}{8\ mg} = \frac{x\ mL}{1\ mL}$$

8 x = 40
x = 40 ÷ 8
x = 5 mL

32. 1. A half cup of pears contains only 100 mg or less of potassium.
    2. A half cup of cabbage contains only 100 mg or less of potassium.
    3. **Cantaloupe is an excellent source of potassium. One cup of cantaloupe contains 427 mg of potassium.**
    4. **Salmon is an excellent source of potassium. Three ounces of salmon contain 305 mg of potassium.**
    5. One cooked chicken liver contains only 28 mg of potassium.

33. 1. **Counter-traction prevents pulling the skin and moving the needle/catheter, which can result in trauma and discomfort at the venipuncture site.**

4. **Withdrawing the needle/catheter along the line of insertion prevents injury to the vein.**
2. **Pressure prevents bleeding and the development of a hematoma at the venipuncture site. Sterile gauze maintains sterility of the procedure and prevents the transfer of microorganisms to the patient.**
5. **Examining the end of the needle/ catheter ensures that it is intact and no portion remains in the patient.**
3. **A sterile dressing prevents exposure of the venipuncture site to the environment, limiting the risk of infection. The use of tape maintains pressure to prevent bleeding.**

34. 1. **A patient has a negative balance of I&O when the output exceeds the intake. This is a characteristic of a deficient fluid volume.**
    2. An elevated, not decreased, temperature is characteristic of a deficient fluid volume.
    3. A low, not increased, blood pressure is characteristic of a deficient fluid volume.
    4. Shortness of breath is a characteristic of excess, not deficient, fluid volume because of pulmonary congestion.
    5. **Flat neck veins are associated with a deficient fluid volume as a result of the decreased circulating blood volume.**
    6. **Weight loss occurs with a deficient fluid volume; 1 liter of fluid weighs 2.2 pounds.**

35.   **Answer: 14 drops/minute. Use the following formula to solve the problem.**

$$\text{Drops per minute} = \frac{\text{total mL to be infused} \times \text{drop factor}}{\text{total time in minutes}}$$

$$\frac{1,000\ (mL \times 10\ (\text{drop factor})}{60\ (\text{minutes in an hour}) \times 12\ (\text{hours to be infused}}$$

$$\frac{10,000}{720} = 13.8$$

Round 13.8 up to 14 because 0.8 of a drop cannot be administered and 0.8 is more than 0.5. The nurse should administer 14 drops/minute.

36. 1. **One ounce of American cheese contains 406 mg of sodium and should be avoided on a 2-g sodium diet.**
    2. **One and a half ounces of canned tuna fish contain approximately 400 mg of**

sodium and should be avoided on a 2-g sodium diet.

3. Two-thirds of a cup of shredded wheat cereal contains 3 mg of sodium and is permitted on a 2-g sodium diet.

4. One baked potato contains approximately 16 mg of sodium and is permitted on a 2-g sodium diet.

5. One ounce of roasted cashews, with no added salt, contains about 4 mg of sodium and is permitted on a 2-g sodium diet.

37. 1. **Potassium is essential to the sodium-potassium pump that regulates muscle contraction. The heart is a major muscle. Hypokalemia can precipitate a weak, irregular pulse and ventricular dysrhythmias.**

2. Hypertension is associated with hypervolemia, not a potassium deficiency.

3. **Potassium is an essential component in the sodium-potassium pump, cellular metabolism, and muscle contraction. Responses associated with hypokalemia include muscle weakness, fatigue, lethargy, leg cramps, and depressed deep-tendon reflexes.**

4. Chest pain is associated with a myocardial infarction (heart attack) and pulmonary embolus, not a potassium deficiency.

5. Dry hair is associated with malnutrition and hypothyroidism, not hypokalemia.

38.   Answer: 42 drops/minute. Solve the problem by using the following formula.

Drops per minute =

$$\frac{\text{total mL to be infused} \times \text{drop factor}}{\text{total time in minutes}}$$

$$\frac{1,000 \times 15}{60 \times 6}$$

$$\frac{15,000}{360} = 41.6 \text{ drops/min}$$

Round 41.6 up to 42 because 0.6 of a drop cannot be administered.

39. 1. Vasodilation related to inflamation increases blood flow to the affected area, which causes the site to feel warm and look red (erythema).

2. The site of an inflammation will feel firm, not soft.

3. **Edema related to inflamation causes the affected area to feel firm.**

4. Vasodilation related to inflamation increases blood flow to the affected area, which causes it to feel warm, not cool.

5. **Inflammation of a vein (phlebitis) causes a movement of fluid from the intravascular compartment into the interstitial compartment. Pressure of fluid on nerve endings causes local discomfort.**

40. 1. The patient has hyperkalemia. The potassium is more than the acceptable range of 3.5 to 5.0 mEq/L.

2. The patient has hypovolemia, not hypervolemia, because of dehydration. The pulse is rapid and thready, and the urine specific gravity is increased. An abrupt weight loss indicates fluid loss (2.2 pounds is equal to 1 L of fluid), and the patient is exhibiting decreased intracellular and interstitial fluid, as evidenced by tenting of the skin. Also, the blood pressure is on the low extreme of the acceptable range of 90 to 119 mm Hg for systolic and 60 to 79 mm Hg for diastolic.

3. **Intestinal secretions distal to the pyloric sphincter contain large amounts of bicarbonate, which is lost through diarrhea. The arterial blood gases indicate uncompensated metabolic acidosis: the pH is less than the acceptable range of 7.35 to 7.45; the HCO_3 is less than the acceptable range of 21 to 28 mEq/L; and the $Paco_2$ is within the acceptable range of 23 to 30 mEq/L.**

4. With respiratory alkalosis the pH will be more than 7.45, the $Paco_2$ will be less than 35 mm Hg, and the HCO_3 will be within the acceptable range of 21 to 28 mEq/L. Respiratory alkalosis usually is caused by hyperventilation precipitated by conditions such as anxiety, mechanical ventilation, early sepsis, and high fever.

Gastrointestinal System

KEYWORDS

The following words include English vocabulary, nursing/medical terminology, concepts, principles, and information relevant to content specifically addressed in the chapter or associated with topics presented in it. English dictionaries, nursing textbooks, and medical dictionaries, such as *Taber's Cyclopedic Medical Dictionary,* are resources that can be used to expand your knowledge and understanding of these words and related information.

Abdomen
Abdominal distention
Anus
Borborygmi
Bowel:
  Flora
  Habits
  Sounds
  Training
Cathartic
Colon
Colorectal
Constipation
Defecate
Diarrhea
Distention
Endoscopic
Enema:
  Cleansing
  Hypertonic
  Hypotonic
  Isotonic
  Large volume
  Oil retention
  Return flow (formerly Harris drip/flush)
  Saline
  Soapsuds
  Tap water
Evacuate, evacuation
Fecal diversion:
  Colostomy
  Ileostomy

Fecal impaction
Feces
Flatus, flatulence
Fracture bedpan
Gastrocolic reflex
Hemoccult test, guaiac
Hemorrhoids
Hypermotility/hypomotility
Irrigation
Laxative
Mucosal
Nasogastric tube
Occult blood
Ova and parasites
Paralytic ileus
Perianal
Perineal
Peristalsis
Pinworms
Prolapse
Rectal tube
Rectum
Sigmoidoscopy
Sitz bath
Spastic colon
Sphincter
Steatorrhea
Stoma
Stool
Suppository
Tarry stool (melena)

GASTROINTESTINAL SYSTEM: QUESTIONS

1. Which statement by a patient with an ileostomy alerts the nurse to the need for further education?
   1. "I don't expect to have much of a problem with fecal odor."
   2. "I will have to take special precautions to protect my skin around the stoma."
   3. "I'm going to irrigate my stoma so I have a bowel movement every morning."
   4. "I should avoid gas-forming foods like beans to limit funny noises from the stoma."

2. A primary health-care provider orders a return-flow enema (Harris flush/drip) for an adult patient with flatulence. When preparing to administer this enema the nurse compares the steps of a return-flow enema with cleansing enemas. Which nursing intervention is unique to a return-flow enema?
1. Lubricate the last 2 inches of the rectal tube.
2. Insert the rectal tube about 4 inches into the anus.
3. Raise the solution container about 12 inches above the anus.
4. Lower the solution container after instilling about 150 mL of solution.

3. A nurse discourages a patient from straining excessively when attempting to have a bowel movement. Which undesirable physiological response is the primary reason why straining on defecation should be avoided?
1. Dysrhythmia
2. Incontinence
3. Fecal impaction
4. Rectal hemorrhoid

4. A school nurse is planning a health class about bodily functions. Which information should be included regarding the purpose of mucus in the gastrointestinal tract?
1. Activates digestive enzymes
2. Protects the gastric mucosa
3. Enhances gastric acidity
4. Emulsifies fats

5. A nurse is caring for a patient who is experiencing diarrhea. About which physiological response to diarrhea should the nurse be **most** concerned?
1. Dehydration
2. Malnutrition
3. Excoriated skin
4. Urinary incontinence

6. A nurse identifies that a patient's colostomy stoma is pale. Which should the nurse do?
1. Notify the surgeon.
2. Listen for bowel sounds.
3. Wash the area with warm water.
4. Gently massage around the stoma.

7. A nurse is caring for a group of patients. Which patient factor should the nurse identify as placing a patient at risk for bowel incontinence?
1. Being ninety years old
2. Taking a sedative for sleep
3. Disoriented to time, place, and person
4. Receiving multiple antibiotic medications

8. A patient is admitted with lower gastrointestinal tract bleeding. Which characteristic of the stool supports this diagnosis?
1. Tarry stool
2. Orange stool
3. Green mucoid stool
4. Bright red–tinged stool

9. A nurse determines that the teaching about a guaiac test of stool is understood when the patient states that it identifies the presence of which of the following?
1. Ova and parasites
2. Hidden blood
3. Bacteria
4. Bile

10. A nurse must collect a specimen for the presence of pinworms. Which action is essential to ensure accuracy of the specimen?
    1. Press the sticky side of nonfrosted cellophane tape across the anus before the patient goes to bed at night.
    2. Pass a rectal swab beyond the internal anal sphincter and rotate gently to collect a specimen.
    3. Perform the procedure the first thing in the morning before the first bowel movement.
    4. Wash the rectal area gently with soap and water before collecting the specimen.

11. Which patient statement supports the nurse's conclusion that a patient understands the need to reestablish bowel flora after a week of diarrhea?
    1. "I must wean myself off of the antibiotics one day after my temperature is normal."
    2. "I should eat a container of yogurt every day for a few days."
    3. "I have to add rice to my diet in one meal each day."
    4. "I ought to drink eight glasses of water a day."

12. A nurse is teaching a patient with a history of constipation about the excessive use of laxatives. Which effect of laxatives should the nurse include as the **primary** reason why their use should be avoided?
    1. Weakens the natural response to defecation
    2. Results in distention of the intestines
    3. Causes abdominal discomfort
    4. Precipitates incontinence

13. A nurse identifies that a patient has tarry stools. Which problem should the nurse conclude that the patient is experiencing?
    1. Upper gastrointestinal bleeding
    2. Pancreatic dysfunction
    3. Lactulose intolerance
    4. Inadequate bile salts

14. A nurse is teaching a patient with a cardiac condition to avoid the Valsalva maneuver. Which should the nurse teach the patient to do?
    1. Eat rice several times a week.
    2. Take a cathartic on a regular basis.
    3. Attempt to have a bowel movement every day.
    4. Exhale while contracting the abdominal muscles.

15. A nurse is teaching a patient how to irrigate a colostomy. The patient asks why it is necessary to use the cone attachment to the irrigation catheter. What information should the nurse include in a response to this question?
    1. Stops enema solution from flowing out of the bowel during the procedure
    2. Prevents prolapse of the bowel during evacuation of the solution
    3. Dilates the stoma so that the enema tube can be inserted
    4. Facilitates the elimination of drainage from the colon

16. Which outcome is **most** appropriate for a patient with perceived constipation?
    1. Have a bowel movement without the use of a laxative.
    2. Verbalize the rationale for the use of laxatives.
    3. Drink eight glasses of water per day.
    4. Defecate every day.

17. Which action is important for the nurse to teach patients about the intake of bran to facilitate defecation?
    1. Eat 3 tablespoons of bran each morning.
    2. Drink at least 8 glasses of fluids each day.
    3. Have a bowel movement right after ingesting the bran.
    4. Take a cathartic that will supplement the action of bran.

18. A primary health-care provider orders a tap-water enema for a patient. The patient asks about the purpose of the enema. Which specific information about the purpose of a tap-water enema should be included in the nurse's response?
    1. "It reduces abdominal gas."
    2. "It drains the urinary bladder."
    3. "It empties the bowel of stool."
    4. "It limits nausea and vomiting."

19. Which word is specific regarding how a soapsuds enema works on the mucosa of the bowel?
    1. Dilating
    2. Irritating
    3. Softening
    4. Lubricating

20. A nurse is caring for a patient with an intestinal stoma. Which intervention is **most** important?
    1. Cleansing the stoma with cool water
    2. Spraying an air-freshening deodorant in the room
    3. Selecting a bag with an appropriate-size stomal opening
    4. Wearing sterile nonlatex gloves when caring for the stoma

21. Which should the nurse do when administering a small-volume hypertonic enema to an adult?
    1. Insert the rectal tube 1 to 1.5 inches into the anal canal.
    2. Position the enema bottle 12 inches above the level of the patient's anus.
    3. Direct the rectal tube toward the vertebrae as it is inserted into the rectum.
    4. Maintain the compression of the enema container until after withdrawing the tube.

22. Which should the nurse do before collecting a stool sample for occult blood?
    1. Plan to collect the first specimen of the day.
    2. Secure a sterile specimen container.
    3. Wash the patient's perianal area.
    4. Ask the patient to void.

23. A nurse performs a physical assessment of a newly admitted patient who is incontinent of stool. For which characteristic related to bowel incontinence should the nurse assess the patient?
    1. Frequent, soft stools
    2. Involuntary passage of stool
    3. Impaired anal sphincter control
    4. Greenish-yellow color to the stool

24. A nurse is collecting a bowel elimination history from a newly admitted patient with a medical diagnosis of possible bowel obstruction. Which question takes **priority**?
    1. "Do you use anything to help you move your bowels?"
    2. "When was the last time you moved your bowels?"
    3. "What color are your usual bowel movements?"
    4. "How often do you have a bowel movement?"

25. While providing a health history the patient tells the nurse, "I have gastroesophageal reflux disease." Which **most** serious consequence associated with this disorder should the nurse anticipate this patient may develop?
    1. Diarrhea
    2. Heartburn
    3. Gastric fullness
    4. Esophageal erosion

26. A nurse is implementing an ordered bowel preparation for a patient who is scheduled for a colonoscopy. Which is the **most** serious consequence that is prevented by an effective bowel preparation?
    1. Psychological stress
    2. Wasted expense
    3. Misdiagnosis
    4. Discomfort

27. A nurse is assessing a patient who has a distended abdomen resulting from flatulence. The patient has an order for a regular diet and an activity order for out of bed. Which can the nurse do to promote passage of the intestinal gas?
    1. Instruct the patient to increase the amount of fluid intake.
    2. Suggest that the patient avoid cruciferous foods.
    3. Obtain a prescription for a laxative.
    4. Encourage the patient to ambulate.

28. A nurse should use a fracture bedpan for patients with which conditions? **Select all that apply.**
    1. _____Peripheral vascular disease
    2. _____Spinal cord injury
    3. _____Fractured hip
    4. _____Dementia
    5. _____Obesity

29. A nurse is performing a physical assessment of a patient concerning the gastrointestinal system. Place the following interventions in the order in which they should be performed.
    1. Palpate the abdomen.
    2. Inspect the anus and perianal area.
    3. Percuss the abdomen for the quality of sounds.
    4. Auscultate the entire abdomen for bowel sounds.
    5. Observe the contour and symmetry of the abdomen.
    Answer: _____

30. A patient is experiencing constipation. Which independent nursing actions facilitate defecation of a hard stool? **Select all that apply.**
    1. _____Applying a lubricant to the anus
    2. _____Providing a sitz bath after defecation
    3. _____Instilling warm mineral oil into the rectum
    4. _____Placing a warm wet washcloth against the perianal area
    5. _____Encouraging the patient to rock forward and back while defecating

31. A patient with flatulence is concerned about the production of unpleasant odors. Which should the nurse encourage the patient to avoid? **Select all that apply.**
    1. _____Asparagus
    2. _____Alcohol
    3. _____Raisins
    4. _____Onions
    5. _____Eggs

32. A primary health-care provider prescribes docusate sodium in liquid form for a patient who is constipated but has difficulty swallowing tablets. The prescription is for 200 mg daily to be divided into two doses, one in the a.m. and one at hour of sleep. The package insert states that there is 50 mg/5 mL. How much solution of docusate sodium should the nurse administer per dose? **Record your answer using a whole number.**
    Answer: _____mL

33. A nurse is assisting a patient with a regular bedpan. Which nursing actions are essential? **Select all that apply.**
    1. _____Position the patient slightly off the back edge of the bedpan.
    2. _____Fold the top linen out of the way when putting the patient on the bedpan.
    3. _____Remain outside the curtains of the bed until the patient is done using the bedpan.
    4. _____Elevate the head of the bed to the Fowler position after the patient is on the bedpan.
    5. _____Raise the side rails on both sides of the bed after the patient is positioned on the bedpan.

34. A nurse is providing dietary teaching to a patient with diverticulitis who has an order for a low-fiber diet. Which food selected by the patient indicates that the dietary teaching was understood? **Select all that apply.**
    1. _____White rice
    2. _____Split peas
    3. _____Soft tofu
    4. _____Oatmeal
    5. _____Pasta

35. A patient is attending the health clinic for treatment of hemorrhoids. The nurse reviews the patient's history, interviews the patient, and performs a focused assessment. Which factors does the nurse conclude may have influenced the development of the hemorrhoids? **Select all that apply.**
    1. _____Stands for long periods of time at work
    2. _____Drinks a glass of wine with dinner
    3. _____Has had multiple pregnancies
    4. _____Tends to have constipation
    5. _____Is obese

PATIENT'S CLINICAL RECORD

Patient History
Married for 18 years
Has 5 children between the ages of 7 and 17: 3 single births and a set of twins
Works as a cashier 4 days a week

Patient Interview
Patient states that she drinks a glass of wine with dinner. When the hemorrhoids became increasingly painful and a continuous problem she decided to do something about them. States she sometimes takes a stool softener when she is constipated.

Focused Assessment
Patient is 60 pounds more than ideal body weight for height. Three external hemorrhoids are bright red, swollen, and oozing blood. Patient states, "My rectal area is itchy and painful."

36. A nurse is caring for a group of patients with a variety of gastrointestinal problems. Which of the following can cause both diarrhea and constipation? **Select all that apply.**
    1. _____Inability to perceive bowel cues
    2. _____Cancer of the large intestines
    3. _____Side effects of medications
    4. _____High-solute tube feedings
    5. _____Increased metabolic rate

37. Which statements by a patient with diverticulosis alert the nurse that the patient needs additional health teaching? **Select all that apply.**
1. _____ "I should avoid eating high-fiber cereal."
2. _____ "I sit on the toilet for 10 minutes after breakfast every day."
3. _____ "I am going to drink 8 glasses of water a day when I get home."
4. _____ "I should hold my breath and bear down when having a bowel movement."
5. _____ "I like to massage my lower abdomen when I'm trying to have a bowel movement."

38. A nurse is caring for a patient with a colostomy, and the patient's stool has a pasty consistency. Place an X over the area of the intestine where the nurse can expect a colostomy to produce stool with a pasty consistency.

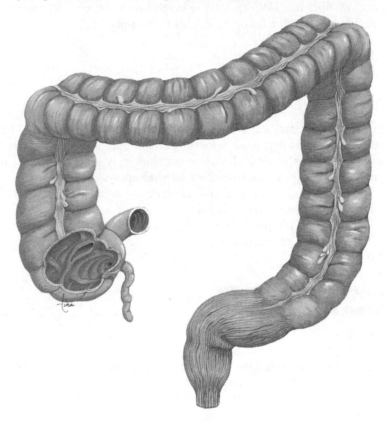

39. A patient had a colonoscopy with several polyps excised for biopsies. The nurse teaches the patient routine post-procedure expectations. Which physical responses should the nurse instruct the patient to report to the primary health-care provider? **Select all that apply.**
1. _____ Intermittent passage of gas from the anus
2. _____ Continuous abdominal cramping
3. _____ Extensive abdominal bloating
4. _____ Minimal rectal bleeding
5. _____ Mild fatigue

40. A nurse is to administer an oil-retention enema, a tap-water enema, and a return-flow enema to three different patients. Which nursing interventions should be performed with all three enemas? **Select all that apply.**
1. _____ Use between 500 and 1,000 mL of solution.
2. _____ Place the patient in the left side-lying position.
3. _____ Use water-soluble jelly to lubricate the tip of the rectal probe.
4. _____ Pull the curtain around the patient's bed and drape the patient.
5. _____ Hold the enema solution a minimum of 12 inches above the anus.

1. 1. The odor from drainage is minimal because fewer bacteria are present in the ileum compared with the large intestine. An ileostomy is an opening into the ileum (distal small intestine from the jejunum to the cecum).

2. Cleansing the skin, skin barriers, and a well-fitted appliance are precautions to protect the skin around an ileostomy stoma. The drainage from an ileostomy contains enzymes that can damage the skin.

3. **This statement is inaccurate in relation to an ileostomy and indicates that the patient needs more teaching. An ileostomy produces liquid fecal drainage, not formed stool that requires irrigation.**

4. An ileostomy stoma does not have a sphincter that can control the flow of flatus or drainage, resulting in noise.

2. 1. All rectal tubes should be lubricated to facilitate entry of the tube into the anus and rectum and prevent mucosal trauma.

2. The anal canal is 1 to 2 inches (2.5 to 5 cm) long. Inserting the rectal tube 3 to 4 inches (7 to 10 cm) ensures that the tip of the tube is beyond the internal and external anal sphincters. This action is appropriate for all types of enemas.

3. The solution container should be raised no higher than 12 inches for all enemas; this allows the solution to instill slowly, which limits discomfort and intestinal spasms.

4. **Lowering the container of solution creates a siphon effect that pulls the instilled fluid back out through the rectal tube into the solution container. The return flow promotes the evacuation of gas from the intestines. This technique is used only with a return-flow enema. When performing a cleansing enema, the tubing is removed after all the solution is instilled.**

3. 1. **Straining on defecation requires the person to hold the breath while bearing down (Valsalva maneuver). This maneuver increases the intrathoracic and intracranial pressures, which can precipitate dysrhythmias, brain attack (stroke), and respiratory difficulties; all of these can be life-threatening.**

2. The loss of the voluntary ability to control the passage of fecal or gaseous discharges through the anus (bowel incontinence) is caused by impaired functioning of the anal sphincters or their nerve supply, not straining on defecation.

3. Fecal impaction is caused by the accumulation and prolonged retention of fecal material in the large intestine, not straining on defecation.

4. Although straining on defecation can contribute to the formation of hemorrhoids, this is not the primary reason straining on defecation is discouraged. Hemorrhoids, although painful, are not life-threatening.

4. 1. The presence of fluid or food activates digestive enzymes, not mucus.

2. **Mucus secreted by mucous membranes and glands is a viscous, slippery fluid containing mucin, white blood cells, water, inorganic salts, and exfoliated cells. Mucin, a mucopolysaccharide, is a lubricant that protects body surfaces from friction and erosion.**

3. Mucus does not enhance gastric acidity. Gastric acidity enhances digestion.

4. The low surface tension of bile salts contributes to the emulsification of fats in the intestine.

5. 1. **Usually digestive juices of 3.5 to 5.0 L are secreted and reabsorbed by the body daily. With diarrhea, the transit time through the intestine is decreased, interfering with the reabsorption of water, resulting in frequent, loose, watery stools and dehydration.**

2. Although malnutrition may be related to diarrhea, particularly if it is prolonged, it is neither life-threatening nor the priority in comparison with another option.

3. Although the skin may become excoriated in the presence of diarrhea because the enzymes in fecal material can erode the skin, it is neither life-threatening nor the priority in comparison with another option.

4. Diarrhea is unrelated to urinary incontinence.

6. 1. **A pale stoma indicates that the circulation to the stoma is compromised, and viability of tissue is**

questionable without immediate intervention. The primary health-care provider should be notified immediately.

2. Although assessing bowel sounds might be done, it is not the priority. Active bowel sounds indicate peristalsis and the presence of flatus in the small intestines, which can occur even if there is an impending problem in the large intestine.

3. Washing the area with warm water is inappropriate. This will not improve circulation to the stoma and will waste valuable time.

4. Massaging around the stoma is inappropriate. This will not improve circulation and may injure surrounding tissue.

7. 1. Constipation, not bowel incontinence, is more common in older adults than in other age groups. Constipation in older adults is caused by decreased bowel motility, inadequate hydration, lack of fiber, sedentary lifestyle, abuse of laxatives, and side effects of medications.

2. Sedatives depress the central nervous system, which may precipitate constipation, not bowel incontinence.

3. **When a person is disoriented to time, place, and person, the individual may not have the cognitive ability to perceive and interpret intestinal distention and rectal pressure cues to defecate, resulting in bowel incontinence.**

4. Antibiotic medications are known for causing diarrhea, not bowel incontinence.

8. 1. Tarry stools indicate upper gastrointestinal bleeding.

2. Orange stools indicate the presence of infection.

3. Green mucoid stools indicate the presence of infection.

4. **Bright red–tinged stools are the cardinal sign of lower gastrointestinal bleeding. When bleeding occurs close to the anus, enzymes have not digested the blood, so the blood has not turned black.**

9. 1. Ova and parasites are identified through microscopic examination of feces, not the guaiac test.

2. Testing the feces for occult blood is called the guaiac test. This test uses a chemical reagent to detect the presence of the enzyme peroxidase in the hemoglobin molecule. Occult blood is obscure (hidden) and may not be visible to the naked eye.

3. Bacteria are identified in feces through a stool culture, not the guaiac test.

4. Bile is an expected constituent of fecal material and is not detected with the guaiac test.

10. 1. Specimen collection is done immediately after awakening from sleep, not before sleep.

2. Passing a rectal swab beyond the internal anal sphincter and rotating it gently are unnecessary and can injure the anal and rectal mucosa.

3. **Performing the procedure the first thing in the morning before the first bowel movement ensures that there will be eggs available for collection at the perianal area. The adult pinworm (*Enterobius vermicularis*) exits the anus at night to lay eggs. The cellophane tape (Scotch tape) test is performed first thing in the morning before a bowel movement or bathing so that these eggs are not disrupted or removed before obtaining a specimen for testing.**

4. Washing the rectal area before collecting the specimen will remove any eggs that are present in the perianal area, which will interfere with accurate test results.

11. 1. Weaning off the antibiotic 1 day after the temperature is normal will not reestablish bowel flora. Discontinuing antibiotics before the full course of therapy is completed can result in a return of the original infection or precipitate the development of a superinfection.

2. **Yogurt is merely milk that is curdled by the addition of bacteria, specifically *Lactobacillus bulgaricus* and *Streptococcus thermophilus*. Eating yogurt helps to restore the bacterial balance of the resident flora of the intestine.**

3. Although rice helps to limit diarrhea, it will not reestablish bowel flora.

4. Although water is essential for all body processes, and to replace fluid lost in the diarrhea, it does not reestablish bowel flora.

12. 1. Laxatives cause a rapid transit time of intestinal contents. When they are used excessively, the bowel's natural

responses to intestinal distention and rectal pressure weaken, resulting in chronic constipation.

2. Laxatives increase peristalsis, which helps evacuate the bowel, preventing, not promoting, abdominal distention from flatus or intestinal contents.

3. Although excessive laxative use can cause cramping, it is temporary and does not have long-term implications, as does the problem in another option.

4. The loss of the voluntary ability to control the passage of fecal or gaseous discharges through the anus (bowel incontinence) is caused by impaired functioning of the anal sphincters or their nerve supply, not excessive laxative use.

13. 1. **When blood from bleeding in the upper gastrointestinal tract is exposed to the digestive process, the fecal material becomes black (tarry). In addition, ingestion of exogenous iron, red meat, and dark green vegetables can make the stool look black.**

2. Pancreatic dysfunction results in impaired digestion of fats (by lipase), protein (by trypsin and chymotrypsin), and carbohydrates (by amylase). Pancreatic dysfunction results in pale, foul-smelling, bulky stools, not tarry stools.

3. A reduction or lack of the secretion of lactase from the wall of the small intestine results in the inability of the body to break down lactose to glucose and galactose. Lactose intolerance causes diarrhea, gaseous distention, and intestinal cramping, not tarry stools.

4. Inadequate bile salts result in less bile entering the intestinal tract. The brown color of stool is caused by the presence of stercobilin and urobilin, which are derived from a pigment in bile (bilirubin). The stool will appear clay colored with inadequate bile salts.

14. 1. Rice thickens stool, which promotes the development of constipation. Constipation may result in straining on defecation, which employs the Valsalva maneuver.

2. Prescribing a cathartic is a dependent, not an independent, function of the nurse. Regular use of a cathartic is contraindicated because it leads to dependence.

3. Attempting to have a bowel movement every day may result in straining, which

employs the use of the Valsalva maneuver. Also, the patient may not need to have a daily bowel movement.

4. **Exhaling requires the glottis to be open, which prevents the Valsalva maneuver. The Valsalva maneuver is bearing down while holding the breath by closing the glottis, which increases intrathoracic pressure. The Valsalva maneuver briefly interferes with blood flow to the heart. When the glottis opens during exhalation, the pressure is released and a surge of blood flows to the heart, which may precipitate a dysrhythmia in a person with a cardiac condition.**

15. 1. **The cone advances into the stoma until it effectively fills the opening, which prevents a reflux of solution while the irrigating solution is being instilled. In addition, it helps prevent accidental perforation of the bowel with the rectal catheter.**

2. A cone will not prevent the prolapse of the bowel. If a prolapse should occur, the surgeon should be notified immediately.

3. Using a cone to dilate the stoma so that the enema tube can be inserted is not the purpose of the cone. The catheter is threaded through the center of the cone.

4. The cone is removed before the bowel evacuates its contents.

16. 1. **Having a bowel movement without the use of a laxative is the most appropriate goal for a patient with perceived constipation. People with perceived constipation believe that they should have a daily bowel movement and use laxatives, suppositories, and/or enemas to achieve this objective.**

2. Although knowledge is essential, behavioral outcomes determine if a goal is achieved.

3. Drinking eight glasses of water per day is an intervention, not a goal. Although desirable for everyone, it does not specifically relate to perceived constipation.

4. The need to have a bowel movement every day is unnecessary, unrealistic, and a myth. Patterns of bowel elimination vary considerably depending on a multitude of factors.

17. 1. Eating 3 tablespoons of bran each morning is too stimulating for the intestines initially. Bran use should begin with 1 tablespoon and gradually increase as tolerated because it can cause flatus and distention.
2. **Bran is an insoluble fiber that increases bulk in the intestines. Eight glasses of water daily keep the body well hydrated and the stool soft. Intestinal elimination is dependent on the relationships among fiber, water, and activity.**
3. Having a bowel movement right after ingesting the bran is too soon to expect a physiological response to the bran.
4. Taking a cathartic is counterproductive. Cathartic use will weaken the bowel's natural responses to intestinal distention and rectal pressure, resulting in chronic constipation.

18. 1. A return-flow enema (Harris flush, Harris drip) helps eliminate intestinal gas.
2. A urinary retention catheter (Foley), not a tap-water enema, drains the urinary bladder of urine.
3. **A tap-water enema instills fluid into the large intestine; the pressure of this volume stimulates peristalsis, causing the colon to evacuate stool.**
4. A tap-water enema will not affect nausea and vomiting; taking nothing by mouth or medication can be used to limit nausea and vomiting.

19. 1. High-volume (not soapsuds) enemas, such as tap-water or saline enemas, work by distending (dilating) the lumen of the intestine.
2. **Although a soapsuds enema works by increasing the volume in the colon, its unique attribute is that soap is irritating to the intestinal mucosa. Irritation of the mucosa precipitates peristalsis, which facilitates the evacuation of fecal material.**
3. An oil-retention enema, a small-volume enema, introduces oil into the rectum and sigmoid colon; this softens the feces and lubricates the rectum and anal canal, facilitating defecation.
4. An oil-retention, not soapsuds, enema lubricates the rectum and anal canal, facilitating the passage of feces.

20. 1. Although a stoma can be cleaned with water as long as it is not at the extremes of hot or cold, it is not the priority.

2. Although this might be done, it is not the priority.
3. **The opening of the appliance must be large enough to encircle the stoma to within ½ to ⅙ inch to protect the surrounding tissue from the enzymes present in the intestinal discharge without impinging on the stoma. Pressure against the stoma can damage delicate mucosal tissue or impede circulation to the stoma, both of which can impair the viability of the stoma.**
4. Clean, not sterile, gloves should be worn when caring for a stoma. Medical, not surgical, asepsis should be practiced. Latex or nonlatex gloves can be worn as long as the patient or nurse does not have a latex allergy.

21. 1. Inserting a rectal tube 1 to 1.5 inches into the anal canal will not permit safe administration of the enema solution. The rectal tube must be inserted 3 to 4 inches to ensure that the catheter is beyond both the external and internal anal sphincters.
2. A small-volume enema bottle is held directly outside the anus because the solution container is attached to the prelubricated nozzle. The container of a large-volume enema should not exceed a height of 12 inches above the anus.
3. Directing the rectal tube toward the vertebrae as it is inserted into the rectum will injure the intestinal mucosa. The catheter should be directed toward the umbilicus, not the vertebrae.
4. **Maintaining compression of the enema container until after withdrawing the tube prevents suctioning back of the fluid that has just been instilled. Releasing compression on the bottle causes a vacuum at the tip of the nozzle that can injure mucous membranes.**

22. 1. Collecting the first specimen of the day is unnecessary.
2. Using a sterile specimen container is unnecessary. Medical, not surgical, asepsis should be followed.
3. Washing the perineal area is unnecessary. However, the nurse may assist the patient to perform perineal hygiene after the stool specimen is obtained.
4. **Emptying the urinary bladder before attempting to have a bowel movement prevents accidental contamination of the specimen by urine.**

23. 1. Frequent, soft stools are associated with diarrhea. Diarrhea is loose, liquid stools and/or increased frequency (three times a day or more) of stools.

2. **An involuntary passage of stool is a major clinical finding associated with bowel incontinence, which is the state in which an individual experiences a change in usual bowel habits characterized by involuntary passage of stool.**

3. Impaired anal sphincter control is not a characteristic a nurse can evaluate when performing a physical assessment.

4. A greenish-yellow color to the stool is unrelated to bowel incontinence. A green or orange color to the stool indicates intestinal infection.

24. 1. Although asking if anything is used to help move the bowels may be done, it is not the priority at this time.

2. **A cardinal sign of a bowel obstruction is the lack of a bowel movement (obstipation).**

3. Although asking about the color of bowel movements will be done, this information relates more to malabsorption, biliary problems, and gastrointestinal bleeding.

4. Although asking how often one has a bowel movement will be done to obtain baseline information about intestinal elimination, it is not specific to the presenting problem.

25. 1. Diarrhea is not associated with gastroesophageal reflux disease (GERD).

2. Pain occurring behind the sternum (heartburn) and sore throat are the predominant symptom of GERD. Although these responses are a concern, they can be treated.

3. Although feeling full, distended, or bloated can occur with GERD, it is not life-threatening and the patient can be taught interventions to limit its occurrence.

4. **With GERD a backflow of the contents of the stomach into the esophagus occurs. Gastric juices are acedic (pH less than 3.5), which can cause erosion of the mucous membranes of the esophagus, necessitating surgery. Cellular changes in the lining of the esophageal mucosa (Barrett's esophagus) are a risk factor for developing esophageal cancer.**

26. 1. Although psychological stress is a serious consequence, it is not life-threatening.

2. Although a cancelled or repeated colonoscopy may incur a wasted expense, this consequence is not life-threatening. A test may be cancelled or performed a second time if the patient has an ineffective bowel preparation.

3. **Fecal material in the intestines can interfere with the visualization, collection, and analysis of data obtained through a colonoscopy, resulting in diagnostic errors.**

4. Although discomfort may occur, it is not the most serious outcome of an inappropriate preparation for a colonoscopy.

27. 1. Increasing the amount of fluid intake will not facilitate the evacuation of intestinal gas.

2. Limiting the intake of cruciferous foods will prevent the development of intestinal gas, not promote its evacuation.

3. A laxative is an excessive intervention for a patient with flatulence.

4. **Ambulation increases metabolic activity, which increases intestinal peristalsis. Increased intestinal peristalsis moves intestinal gas toward the anus, where it can be expelled.**

28. 1. A regular bedpan is appropriate for a patient with peripheral vascular disease.

2. **A fracture bedpan has a low back that promotes functional alignment of the patient's lower back while on the bedpan.**

3. **A fracture bedpan has a low back that promotes functional alignment of the patient's lower back and hips while on the bedpan. A regular bedpan will raise the hips and place stress on the site of the fracture.**

4. A regular bedpan is appropriate for a patient with dementia.

5. A regular bedpan is appropriate for a patient who is obese.

29. 5. **Inspection should occur first because it is the least invasive assessment. The abdomen should be assessed before turning the patient, which slightly rearranges the internal organs.**

2. **The anus and perianal area should be inspected after a less invasive assessment and before other**

assessment techniques that can alter the results of inspection.

4. Auscultation should occur after less invasive assessment techniques and before other more invasive assessment techniques that can alter the results of auscultation.

3. Percussion should occur after less invasive techniques but before a more invasive assessment technique that can alter the results of percussion.

1. Palpation should occur after less invasive assessment techniques are completed.

30. 1. A lubricant reduces friction, which facilitates the passage of a hard, dry stool through the anus. Nurses are legally permitted to diagnose and treat human responses. Constipation is a human response, and applying a water-soluble lubricant to the anus is an independent function of the nurse.

2. A sitz bath requires a primary health-care provider's order and is a dependent, not independent, function of the nurse. A sitz bath will not promote the passage of a hard, dry stool, but it may promote hygiene and comfort after the bowel movement.

3. An oil-retention enema softens the feces and lubricates the rectum and anus. However, it requires a primary health-care provider's order and is a dependent, not independent, function of the nurse.

4. A warm wet washcloth placed against the perianal area may facilitate defecation by relaxing the surrounding muscles and the external sphincter.

5. Rocking forward and back when attempting to defecate increases both tension against the abdomen and intra-abdominal pressure; these facilitate the passage of stool from the rectum and anus.

31. 1. Asparagus contains a sulferous compound called mercaptan. Mercaptan, when broken down in the digestive system, releases by-products that cause the urine to smell. In addition, the patient should be taught about other odor-producing foods, such as fish, garlic, green peppers, mustard, radishes, and spicy foods.

2. Alcohol may cause gas, but it does not produce an odor.

3. Raisins may cause gas, but they do not produce an odor.

4. Onions contain mercaptan, which when broken down in the digestive system will produce odorous gas.

5. Eggs contain mercaptan, which when broken down in the digestive system will produce odorous gas.

32. Answer: 10 mL. First determine the amount of mg per dose of medication prescribed. 200 (total mg of medication daily) ÷ 2 (number of doses in the day) = 100 mg (amount of mg of medication per dose). Next, solve the problem by using the formula for ratio and proportion.

$$\frac{\text{Desired}}{\text{Have}} \frac{100 \text{ mg}}{50 \text{ mg}} = \frac{x \text{ mL}}{5 \text{ mL}}$$

$50x = 500$
$x = 500 \div 50$
$x = 10 \text{ mL}$

33. 1. Positioning a patient slightly off the back edge of a regular bedpan is unsafe and uncomfortable. The patient should be positioned so that the buttocks rest on, not slightly off of, the smooth, rounded rim of a regular bedpan.

2. Folding the top linen out of the way when putting the patient on the bedpan is unnecessary. The top linen can be draped over the patient in such a way as to promote placement of the bedpan while maintaining the privacy and dignity of the patient.

3. Remaining outside the curtains of the patient's bed while the patient is on the bedpan allows the nurse to be in close proximity to the patient. The nurse is available to assist the patient if needed and it provides a sense of security for the patient.

4. Elevating the head of the bed so that the patient is in the high-Fowler position assumes the familiar, usual position for having a bowel movement. A vertical position utilizes gravity and hip flexion raises intra-abdominal pressure, both of which maximize evacuation of feces.

5. Raising both side rails provides support on which the patient can rest the upper extremities and maintains patient safety.

34. 1. One cup of white rice contains just 0.6 g (grams) of fiber. Low-fiber foods limit the amount of material (residue) left in the intestines after the digestive process; this lessens the bulk of stool,

which is less irritating to the intestinal mucosa.

2. One cup of cooked split peas contains 16.3 g of fiber and should be avoided on a low-fiber diet.

3. One cup of soft tofu contains just 0.5 g of fiber.

4. One cup of oatmeal contains 4 g of fiber and should be avoided on a low-fiber diet.

5. Refined white flour products (e.g., pasta) contain just 1.6 g or less of fiber per one cup serving.

35. 1. **Prolonged standing or sitting increases pressure on the hemorrhoidal veins that can cause them to become dilated, enlarged, and inflamed.**

2. One drink a day with or without food will not precipitate hemorrhoids. However, liver disease associated with prolonged abuse of alcohol can cause hemorrhoids.

3. **Pregnancy increases intra-abdominal pressure causing elevated systemic and portal venous pressure, which is transmitted to the anorectal veins. The added pressure of multiple births and having twins aggravates the problem. Eventually the distended veins separate from the smooth muscle surrounding them, and prolapse of the hemorrhoidal vessels occurs.**

4. **Repeated straining on defecation increases intra-abdominal pressure, eventually causing the anorectal veins to distend and become inflamed, resulting in hemorrhoids. Repeated straining causes them to enlarge.**

5. **Increased intra-abdominal pressure associated with obesity causes elevated systemic and portal venous pressure, which is transmitted to the anorectal veins. Eventually the veins distend and become inflamed, resulting in hemorrhoids.**

36. 1. An inability to perceive bowel cues for defecation results in a lack of response that further weakens the defecation reflex, ultimately causing constipation, not diarrhea.

2. Cancer of the large intestine can cause constipation, diarrhea, and/or alternating constipation and diarrhea. The mass in the intestinal lumen may partially obstruct the lumen. The leakage of stool around the tumor results in a condition that appears to be diarrhea. The mass in the lumen can totally obstruct the passage of stool, resulting in a condition that appears to be constipation.

3. **Medications, depending on their physiological action, side effects, and toxic effects, can cause either constipation or diarrhea.**

4. A high-solute tube feeding has a greater osmotic pressure than surrounding interstitial tissue; it draws fluid into the gastrointestinal tract, which may result in diarrhea, not constipation.

5. An increased metabolic rate will increase peristalsis and possibly result in diarrhea, not constipation.

37. 1. **High-fiber foods are encouraged because they prevent constipation. Constipation increases intraluminal intestinal pressure, which promotes intestinal mucosal outpouching. Foods low in fiber are ordered when a patient has an acute inflammation of a diverticulum (diverticulitis) until the inflammation resolves.**

2. Sitting on the toilet for 10 minutes after breakfast every day is an accepted practice. Bowel elimination should follow a familiar routine, and attempting to defecate after breakfast takes advantage of the gastrocolic reflex.

3. Drinking 8 glasses of water a day is desirable for effective bowel function. An adequate intake of fluid ensures that after water is reabsorbed through the large intestines for essential body processes there is enough water left in the intestine to create a soft, formed stool.

4. **The Valsalva maneuver increases intraluminal intestinal pressure, which promotes intestinal mucosal outpouching and should be avoided.**

5. Massaging the lower abdomen when trying to have a bowel movement is an accepted practice. Light stroking of the skin (effleurage) reduces abdominal muscle tension, which may facilitate defecation.

38. **An X anywhere along the highlighted area is the correct answer. Stool in the ascending colon is the most liquid, but as it travels through the transverse colon, fluid is reabsorbed and stool becomes pasty in consistency. In the descending colon, stool becomes more dry, solid, and formed.**

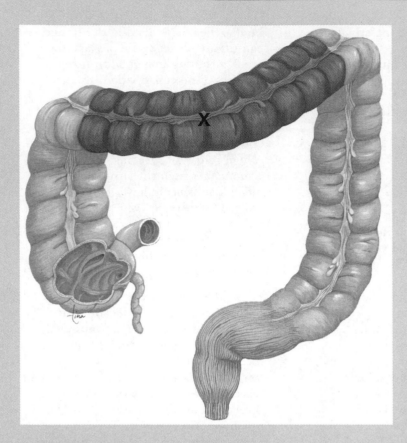

39. 1. This is an expected response after a colonoscopy. Carbon dioxide is inserted into the intestine (CO_2 insufflation) to distend the lumen, which permits visualization of internal intestinal structures. This gas will be passed through the anus for 24 to 48 hours after the procedure. Ambulation facilitates the passage of this gas.

2. **Some abdominal cramping may occur from irritability of the intestine. However, it should not be severe or continuous. Severe abdominal cramping may indicate perforation of the intestinal wall.**

3. **Some abdominal bloating is expected after a colonoscopy. However, it should not be extensive. Abdominal bloating and distention that is excessive or continues beyond 24 hours after the test may indicate perforation of the intestinal wall.**

4. Minimal rectal bleeding is expected after a colonoscopy when polyps are removed. When tissue is excised, the intestinal mucosa is traumatized and the site will leak blood and body fluids. The patient should be informed that an amount equal to several tablespoons of blood may exit the anus the day after the test.

5. Mild fatigue is expected after a colonoscopy. Fatigue results from the sedatives and conscious sedation used as well as the carbon dioxide that was inserted into the intestine during the procedure.

40. 1. The amount of solution used depends on the type of enema ordered. A tap-water enema uses 500 to 1,000 mL of tap water to distend the intestine and promote defecation. An oil-retention enema has 200 to 250 mL of an oil-based solution to soften feces and promote defecation. A return-flow enema begins with approximately 300 to 500 mL of tap water in the enema container. A small volume of the solution (e.g., 150 to 200 mL) is instilled and the enema container is immediately lowered below the anus to withdraw fluid and gas into the collection container. The purpose of a return-flow enema is to reduce abdominal distention caused by intestinal gas.

2. **The left side-lying position allows the fluid to flow via the principle of gravity as the fluid follows the normal curve of the anus, rectum, and sigmoid colon.**

3. **Lubrication of the tip of the catheter or probe limits trauma to the mucous membranes of the intestine.**

4. Enemas require that the patient's perianal area be exposed. Pulling the curtain around the patient's bed and draping the patient provide for patient privacy and dignity.

5. Oil-retention enemas and hypertonic enemas are administered in small volumes (e.g., 4.5 to 7.8 mL) via a soft-sided container. The container is squeezed and rolled slowly from the distal to the proximal end until empty. With tap-water and soapsuds enemas the solution is instilled holding the enema container 8 to 12 inches above the anus.

Pain, Comfort, Rest, and Sleep

KEYWORDS

The following words include nursing/medical terminology, concepts, principles, and information relevant to content specifically addressed in the chapter or associated with topics presented in it. English dictionaries, nursing textbooks, and medical dictionaries, such as *Taber's Cyclopedic Medical Dictionary,* are resources that can be used to expand your knowledge and understanding of these words and related information.

Addiction

Back rub

Bedtime routines

Biofeedback

Breakthrough pain

Circadian rhythm

Cold therapy

Continuous positive airway pressure (CPAP)

Contralateral stimulation

Distraction techniques

Enuresis

Epidural analgesia

Fatigue

Gate control theory

Grimacing

Guarding behaviors

Guided imagery

Heat therapy

Intensive care unit psychosis

Intrathecal analgesia

Massage

Meditation

Nocturia

Nonopioid

Opioid

Pain, characteristics:
  Aggravating factors
  Duration
  Intensity
  Onset
  Quality
  Relieving factors

Pain scale

Pain threshold

Pain tolerance

Pain, types:
  Acute
  Chronic

Episodic

Intermittent

Intractable

Malignant

Neuropathic

Phantom

Radiating

Remittent

Visceral

Patient-controlled analgesia (PCA)

Physical dependence

Placebo

Progressive muscle relaxation

Psychological dependence

Rest

Self-hypnosis

Self-splinting

Sleep:
  Non–rapid-eye-movement (NREM) sleep
  Rapid-eye-movement (REM) sleep

Sleep disorders:
  Bruxism
  Hypersomnia
  Insomnia
  Narcolepsy
  Night terrors
  Parasomnia
  Restless legs
  Sleep apnea
  Sleep deprivation
  Somnambulism
  Sleepiness

Sleep rituals

Snoring

Sundowning

Transcutaneous electrical nerve stimulation

PAIN, COMFORT, REST, AND SLEEP: QUESTIONS

1. A nurse is caring for a patient who is experiencing pain. For which common psychological response to pain should the nurse assess the patient?
   1. Experiencing fear related to loss of independence
   2. Withdrawing from social interactions with others
   3. Asking for pain medication to relieve the pain
   4. Verbalizing the presence of nausea

2. Which is the appropriate patient outcome for an adult who has disturbed sleep because of nocturia?
   1. Report fewer early morning awakenings because of a wet bed.
   2. Demonstrate a reduction in nighttime bathroom visits.
   3. Resume sleeping immediately after voiding.
   4. Use an incontinence device at night.

3. A patient who had a total abdominal hysterectomy two days ago reports abdominal pain at level 5 on a 0-to-10 pain scale. After assessing the pain further, which should the nurse do **first**?
   1. Reposition the patient.
   2. Offer a relaxing back rub.
   3. Use distraction techniques.
   4. Administer the prescribed analgesic.

4. A nurse is caring for a patient who is diagnosed with narcolepsy. Which is the **most** serious consequence of this disorder?
   1. Inability to provide self-care
   2. Impaired thought processes
   3. Potential for injury
   4. Excessive fatigue

5. A patient is experiencing discomfort associated with gastroesophageal reflux. In which position should the nurse teach the patient to sleep?
   1. Right lateral
   2. Semi-Fowler
   3. Prone
   4. Sims

6. A patient is experiencing anxiety. Which aspect of sleep should the nurse expect **primarily** will be affected as a result of the anxiety?
   1. Onset
   2. Depth
   3. Stage II
   4. Duration

7. A patient requests pain medication for severe pain. Which should the nurse do **first** when responding to this patient's request?
   1. Use distraction to minimize the patient's perception of pain.
   2. Place the patient in the most comfortable position possible.
   3. Administer pain medication to the patient quickly.
   4. Assess the various aspects of the patient's pain.

8. A nurse is planning a teaching program for a patient with a diagnosis of obstructive sleep apnea. Which should the nurse plan to discuss with this patient?
   1. Using the ordered device that supports airway patency
   2. Placing two pillows under the head when sleeping
   3. Requesting a sedative to promote sleep
   4. Sleeping in the supine position

9. Which is the **most** important nursing intervention that supports a patient's ability to sleep in the hospital setting?
   1. Providing an extra blanket
   2. Limiting unnecessary noise on the unit
   3. Shutting off lights in the patient's room
   4. Pulling curtains around the patient's bed at night

10. A patient has a history of severe chronic pain. Which is the **most** important intervention associated with providing nursing care to this patient?
    1. Asking what is an acceptable level of pain
    2. Providing interventions that do not precipitate pain
    3. Focusing on pain management intervention before pain is excessive
    4. Determining the level of function that can be performed without pain

11. Which concept should the nurse consider when assessing a patient's pain?
    1. The expression of pain is not always congruent with the pain experienced.
    2. Pain medication can significantly increase a patient's pain tolerance.
    3. The majority of cultures value the concept of suffering in silence.
    4. Most people experience approximately the same pain tolerance.

12. Which **most** common cause of sleep deprivation in the hospital should the nurse consider when planning care?
    1. Fragmented sleep
    2. Early awakening
    3. Restless legs
    4. Sleep apnea

13. A nurse is performing an admitting interview. Which patient statement about pain should cause the **most** concern for the nurse?
    1. "I try to pretend that it is not part of me, but it takes a lot of effort."
    2. "My pain medication works, but I'm afraid of becoming addicted."
    3. "At home I take something for the pain before it gets too bad."
    4. "They say my pain may get worse, and I can't stand it now."

14. A patient has been in the intensive care unit (ICU) for 3 days. For which common adaptation indicating ICU psychosis associated with sleep deprivation should the nurse assess the patient?
    1. Hypoxia
    2. Delirium
    3. Lethargy
    4. Dementia

15. Which concept associated with sleep should the nurse consider to plan nursing care for a hospitalized patient?
    1. People require eight hours of uninterrupted sleep to meet energy needs.
    2. Frequency of nighttime awakenings decreases with age.
    3. Fear can contribute to the need to stay awake.
    4. Bedrest decreases the need for sleep.

16. A nurse is assessing a patient in pain. Which word might the nurse use when documenting the pattern of a patient's pain?
    1. Tenderness
    2. Moderate
    3. Episodic
    4. Phantom

17. A nurse is obtaining a health history from a newly admitted patient. Which patient statement about alcohol intake is based on a common physiological response?
    1. "After I go drinking, I have to urinate during the night."
    2. "When I drink, I get hungry in the middle of the night."
    3. "Falling asleep is hard, but once asleep I sleep great."
    4. "If I drink too much, I oversleep in the morning."

18. A nurse is assessing a patient experiencing acute pain. Which characteristic is more common with acute pain than with chronic pain?
    1. Self-focusing
    2. Sleep disturbances
    3. Guarding behaviors
    4. Variations in vital signs

19. At which time does a nurse medicate a patient for pain for it to be considered preemptive analgesia?
    1. Before a patient goes to sleep
    2. At equally distant times around the clock
    3. As soon as a patient reports the occurrence of pain
    4. Before doing a dressing change that has been painful in the past

20. A patient is diagnosed with chronic fatigue syndrome. Which is **most** important for the nurse to explore in relation to the patient's status?
    1. Ability to provide self-care
    2. Physical mobility
    3. Social isolation
    4. Gas exchange

21. Which is **most** important for nurses to understand when caring for patients in pain?
    1. Patients who are in pain will request pain medication.
    2. Patients usually are able to describe the characteristics of their pain.
    3. Patients need to know that the nurse believes what they say about their pain.
    4. Patients will demonstrate vital signs that are congruent with the intensity of their pain.

22. A patient is experiencing lack of sleep because of pain. Which is the **most** appropriate goal for this patient?
    1. The patient will be provided with a back massage every evening before bedtime.
    2. The patient will report feeling rested after awakening in the morning.
    3. The patient will request less pain medication during the night.
    4. The patient will experience four hours of uninterrupted sleep.

23. A nurse is helping a patient who is experiencing mild pain to get ready for bed. Which nursing action is **most** effective to help limit pain?
    1. Assisting with relaxing imagery
    2. Obtaining a prescription for an opioid
    3. Encouraging the patient to take a warm shower
    4. Recommending that the patient be more active during the day

24. During which time frame do people tend to be the sleepiest?
    1. 12 noon and 2 p.m.
    2. 6 a.m. and 8 a.m.
    3. 2 a.m. and 4 a.m.
    4. 6 p.m. and 8 p.m.

25. Which patient statement indicates that the patient is experiencing bruxism?
    1. "I walk around in my sleep almost every night, but I don't remember it."
    2. "I annoy the whole family with the loud snoring noises I make at night."
    3. "I occasionally urinate in bed when I am sleeping, and it's embarrassing."
    4. "I am told by my wife that I make a lot of noise grinding my teeth when I sleep."

26. A nurse is caring for patients receiving a variety of interventions for pain management. Which pain relief method has the shortest duration of action?
    1. Patient-controlled analgesia
    2. Intramuscular sedatives
    3. Intravenous narcotics
    4. Regional anesthesia

27. A nurse is teaching a community health education class about rest and sleep. Which concept related to sleep should the nurse include?
    1. Total time in bed gradually decreases as one ages.
    2. Sleep needs remain consistent throughout the life span.
    3. Alcohol intake interferes with one's ability to fall asleep.
    4. Bedtime routines are associated with an expectation of sleep.

28. A nurse is teaching a patient various techniques to promote sleep. Which internal stimulus that **most** commonly interferes with sleep should the nurse include in the teaching?
    1. Ringing in the ears
    2. Bladder fullness
    3. Hunger
    4. Thirst

29. A nurse is giving a back rub. Which stroke is **most** effective in inducing relaxation at the end of the procedure?
    1. Percussion
    2. Effleurage
    3. Kneading
    4. Circular

30. A patient states, "The pain moves from my chest down my left arm." Which characteristic of pain is associated with this statement?
    1. Pattern
    2. Duration
    3. Location
    4. Constancy

31. A nurse is providing health teaching for a patient with the diagnosis of obstructive sleep apnea. Which aspect of sleep should the nurse explain is **most** often affected?
    1. Amount
    2. Quality
    3. Depth
    4. Onset

32. A patient is being admitted to the hospital and the nurse is performing a complete assessment. Which is the **most** therapeutic question the nurse can ask about the quality of the patient's sleep?
    1. "How would you describe your sleep?"
    2. "Do you consider your sleep to be restless or restful?"
    3. "Is the number of hours you sleep at night good for you?"
    4. "Does your bed partner complain about your sleep behaviors?"

33. A nurse strains a back muscle when moving a patient up in bed. Which can the nurse do at home that utilizes the gate-control theory of pain relief to minimize the discomfort?
    1. Use guided imagery.
    2. Perform progressive muscle relaxation.
    3. Apply a cold compress to the site for 20 minutes.
    4. Take a nonsteroidal anti-inflammatory medication every 6 hours.

34. A patient is having difficulty sleeping and may be experiencing shortened non–rapid-eye-movement (NREM) sleep. Which patient assessments support this conclusion? **Select all that apply.**
    1. _____Decreased pain tolerance
    2. _____Inability to concentrate
    3. _____Excessive sleepiness
    4. _____Irritability
    5. _____Confusion

35. A primary health-care provider prescribes oxycodone oral solution 15 mg every 6 hours. The drug is supplied in a 500-mL bottle that indicates 5 mg/5 mL. How much oral solution should the nurse administer? **Record your answer using a whole number.**

Answer: _____ mL

36. A 12-year-old boy is experiencing nocturnal enuresis. Which strategies should the nurse explore with the boy and his parents? **Select all that apply.**
1. _____Limiting fluid intake after dinner
2. _____Voiding immediately before going to bed
3. _____Eliminating caffeinated beverages from the diet
4. _____Thinking about waking up dry when going to bed at night
5. _____Having the boy change his own bed linens when he wets the bed

37. A nurse is using the FLACC behavioral scale to assess an 8-month-old child's level of pain. The nurse identified that the patient's legs were drawn up to the abdomen and the patient was whimpering. The patient was squirming and shifting back and forth and had a constant frown and the chin was quivering. The infant was reassured when cuddled by the nurse. On a scale of 0 to 10, which is the child's level of pain?
1. 3
2. 5
3. 7
4. 9

FLACC Behavioral Scale

Categories	Scoring		
	0	**1**	**2**
Face	No particular expression or smile	Occasional grimace or frown, withdrawn, disinterested	Frequent to constant frown, clenched jaw, quivering chin
Legs	Normal position or relaxed	Uneasy, restless, tense	Kicking, or legs drawn up
Activity	Lying quietly, normal position, moves easily	Squirming, shifting back and forth, tense	Arched, rigid, or jerking
Cry	No cry (awake or asleep)	Moans or whimpers, occasional complaint	Crying steadily, screams or sobs, frequent complaints
Consolability	Content, relaxed	Reassured by occasional touching, hugging, or being talked to, distractible	Difficult to console or comfort

Each of the 5 categories—(F) Face; (L) Legs; (A) Activity; (C) Cry; (C) Consolability—is scored from 0-2, which results in a total score between 0 and 10.

38. Which concepts associated with rest and sleep must the nurse consider when planning nursing care? **Select all that apply.**
1. _____Energy demands increase with age.
2. _____Metabolic rate increases during rest.
3. _____Sleep requirements increase during stress.
4. _____Catabolic hormones increase during sleep.
5. _____Lack of awareness of the environment increases with sleep.

39. A nurse is caring for a patient who is having difficulty sleeping. Which patient responses indicate to the nurse that the patient is not obtaining adequate rapid-eye-movement (REM) sleep? **Select all that apply.**
1. _____Hyporesponsiveness
2. _____Immunosuppression
3. _____Irritability
4. _____Confusion
5. _____Vertigo

40. An older female adult explains to the nurse that she has insomnia. The nurse interviews the patient and her husband and reviews the patient's medication reconciliation form. Which factors does the nurse conclude are associated with the patient's insomnia? **Select all that apply.**
1. _____Metformin
2. _____Older adult
3. _____Female gender
4. _____Alcohol intake
5. _____Diphenhydramine
6. _____Catnaps during the day

Interview with Patient
Patient reports having difficulty falling asleep, waking frequently during the night, and having difficulty falling back to sleep. Patient states, "I never feel rested in the morning."

Interview with Patient's Husband
My wife's problem with sleeping has been going on for several months. She is so tired during the day that she takes several 10 minute catnaps during the day. I encourage her to have a drink of whiskey to knock her out when she goes to bed.

Medication Reconciliation Form
Diphenhydramine 50 mg PO at hour of sleep
Metformin 100 mg PO twice a day

---

41. Which are **most** important for a nurse to consider when a patient reports the presence of pain? **Select all that apply.**
1. _____The extent of pain is directly related to the amount of tissue damage.
2. _____Fatigue increases the intensity of pain experienced by the patient.
3. _____Behavioral adaptations are congruent with statements about pain.
4. _____Giving opioids to a patient in pain will lead to an addiction.
5. _____The person feeling the pain is the authority on the pain.

42. Which statements by a patient indicate a precipitating factor associated with pain? **Select all that apply.**
1. _____"I usually feel a little dizzy and think I'm going to vomit when I have pain."
2. _____"My pain usually comes and goes throughout the night."
3. _____"I usually have pain after I get dressed in the morning."
4. _____"My pain feels like a knife cutting right through me."
5. _____"My incision hurts when I cough."

43. A nurse administers a back rub to a patient after first providing for privacy and maintaining standard precautions. Place the following steps in the order in which they should be implemented.
1. Apply warmed lotion to your hands.
2. Position the patient in the side-lying position.
3. Assess the skin for color, turgor, and skin breakdown.
4. Arrange the gown and top linens so that the patient's back is exposed.
5. Use a variety of strokes to massage the muscles of the back and sacral area.
    Answer: _____

44. When assessing patients who have difficulty sleeping, the nurse assesses for which common physiological responses to insomnia? **Select all that apply.**
   1. _____Vertigo
   2. _____Fatigue
   3. _____Irritability
   4. _____Headache
   5. _____Frustration

45. A nurse is assessing a patient experiencing chronic pain. Which characteristics are more common with chronic pain than with acute pain? **Select all that apply.**
   1. _____Gradual onset
   2. _____Long duration
   3. _____Anticipated end
   4. _____Psychologically depleting
   5. _____Responds to conventional interventions

1. 1. **Psychological or affective responses to pain relate to feelings and emotional distress. Fear of being dependent on others and loss of self-control are psychological responses to pain.**
   2. Withdrawing from social interactions with others is a behavioral response to pain.
   3. Requesting pain medication is a behavioral response to pain.
   4. Nausea is a physiological response to pain.

2. 1. Reporting fewer early morning awakenings because of a wet bed relates to enuresis, which is recurrent involuntary urination that occurs during sleep.
   2. **Demonstrating a reduction in night-time bathroom visits is an appropriate outcome for nocturia, which is voluntary urination during the night.**
   3. Resuming sleeping immediately after voiding relates to insomnia, which is difficulty initiating or maintaining sleep.
   4. Using an incontinence device at night is an intervention, not an outcome.

3. 1. Repositioning is effective for mild, not severe, pain.
   2. A back massage is ineffective for acute, severe pain; however, it may relax the patient and increase the effectiveness of analgesic medication.
   3. Guided imagery is more effective for mild pain, not acute, severe pain.
   4. **Major abdominal surgery involves extensive manipulation of internal organs and a large abdominal incision that require adequate pharmacological intervention to provide relief from pain.**

4. 1. Although the overwhelming daytime sleepiness associated with narcolepsy may interfere with the ability to perform some self-care activities, this is not the major problem related to narcolepsy.
   2. Narcolepsy does not involve disturbed thought processes, which is the state in which an individual experiences a disruption in mental activities, such as conscious thought, reality orientation, problem solving, and judgment.
   3. **Narcolepsy is excessive sleepiness in the daytime that can cause a person to fall asleep uncontrollably at inappropriate times (sleep attack) and**

result in physical harm to self or others.
   4. Although a person with narcolepsy may verbalize a lack of energy, this is not the primary concern associated with narcolepsy.

5. 1. The right-lateral position is a horizontal position that increases the pressure of the abdominal organs against the stomach and increases gastric reflux.
   2. **Gastric secretions increase during rapid-eye-movement (REM) sleep. The semi-Fowler position limits gastroesophageal reflux because gravity allows the abdominal organs to drop, which reduces pressure on the stomach and results in less stomach contents flowing upward into the esophagus.**
   3. The prone position is a horizontal position that increases the pressure of the abdominal organs against the stomach and increases gastric reflux. The abdomen rests on the mattress and the body exerts direct pressure on the stomach.
   4. The Sims position is a horizontal position halfway between lateral and prone. Direct pressure exerted on the stomach, particularly in the left Sims position, promotes gastric reflux.

6. 1. **Anxiety increases norepinephrine blood levels through stimulation of the sympathetic nervous system, which results in prolonged sleep onset.**
   2. Patients with anxiety still reach the depth of stage IV non–rapid-eye-movement (NREM) sleep.
   3. Stage IV, not stage II, of NREM sleep is affected.
   4. The duration of sleep is affected indirectly, not directly, because of the prolonged onset of sleep.

7. 1. Distraction is not effective for severe pain.
   2. There is not enough information to indicate that this intervention may be effective. In addition, the position the patient considers most comfortable may be contraindicated based on the provider's orders or safety issues.
   3. Administering pain medication to the patient quickly is a hasty, impulsive response that may or may not be necessary.

4. All the factors that affect the pain experience should be assessed, including location, intensity, quality, duration, pattern, aggravating and alleviating factors, and physical, behavioral, and attitudinal responses. Assessment must precede intervention.

8. 1. Encouraging sleeping in the supine position increases the episodes of sleep apnea because the structures of the mouth and oropharynx (i.e., tonsils, adenoids, mucous membranes, uvula, soft palate, and tongue) drop by gravity and ultimately obstruct the airway.
   2. Sedatives do not limit episodes of sleep apnea.
   3. Positioning two pillows under the head flexes the neck, which narrows the upper airway and thus contributes to episodes of sleep apnea. Pillows under the upper shoulders and head or small blocks under the head of the bed may assist in keeping the upper airway open.
   4. A continuous positive airway pressure (CPAP) device worn when sleeping keeps the upper airway patent by maintaining an open pathway that facilitates gas exchange.

9. 1. Although meeting the basic physiological need to feel warm is appropriate, a hospital's environment generally is warm, so a top sheet and spread are adequate.
   2. Noise is a serious deterrent to sleep in a hospital. The nurse should limit environmental noise (e.g., distributing fluids, providing treatments, rolling drug and linen carts) and staff communication noise.
   3. Shutting off lights in the patient's room is unsafe. Dim the lights or put a night-light on to provide enough illumination for safe ambulation to the bathroom.
   4. Although pulling curtains around the bed at night provides privacy, it does not limit the environmental factors that usually interfere with sleeping in a hospital.

10. 1. Although the nurse will ask this question to determine the patient's level of pain tolerance, it is not the priority.
    2. Although the nurse will attempt to provide interventions that do not precipitate pain, there may be significant interventions that must be performed that may precipitate pain.

3. Administration of analgesics around the clock (ATC administration) at regularly scheduled intervals or by long-acting controlled-release transdermal patches maintains therapeutic blood levels of analgesics, which limit pain at levels of comfort acceptable to patients.
4. Although the nurse and patient will determine the level of function that can be performed without pain, there may be unavoidable activities that may precipitate pain.

11. 1. An obvious response to pain is not always apparent because psychosociocultural factors may dictate behavior. Fear of the treatment for pain, lack of validation, acceptance of pain as punishment for previous behavior, and the need to be strong, courageous, or uncomplaining are factors that influence behavioral responses to pain.
    2. The opposite may be true. As a person experiences relief from pain, the person may be unwilling to endure previously acceptable levels of pain.
    3. This is not a true statement. Although a generalization, many members of Jewish, Italian, Greek, and Chinese ethnic groups, for example, are able to express pain.
    4. Pain tolerance varies widely among people and is influenced by experiential, psychological, and sociocultural factors.

12. 1. Sleep deprivation occurs with frequent interruptions of sleep because the sleeper returns to stage I rather than to the stage that was interrupted. There is a greater loss of stage III and IV non–rapid-eye-movement (NREM) sleep, which is essential for restorative sleep.
    2. Although early awakenings often do occur in hospital settings, it is not the most common cause of sleep deprivation in the hospital.
    3. Restless legs syndrome, an intrinsic sleep disorder, is not the most common cause of sleep deprivation in the hospital.
    4. Only 1% to 4% of the population has sleep apnea.

13. 1. This is not the statement of greatest concern. Nonpharmacological measures to relieve pain, such as imagery and self-hypnosis, use the mind-body (psyche-soma) connection to reduce pain.

The nurse should encourage the use of these measures and validate the energy expended.

2. The concern of addiction is not the priority among these statements. The nurse can respond to this common concern through education and judicious medication administration.

3. This is desirable because it keeps pain under control before it becomes excessive.

4. **The level of pain tolerance is exceeded. The present pain must be relieved and the patient assured that future pain also will be controlled.**

14. 1. Hypoxia is associated with obstructive sleep apnea because episodes of upper airway obstruction occur 50 to 600 times a night.

2. **Melatonin regulates the circadian phases of sleep. Environmental triggers called synchronizers adjust the sleep-wake cycle to a 24-hour solar day. Intensive care units have bright lights and increased sensory input that cause disorientation to day and night and interrupt sleep. Interrupted sleep results in lability of mood, irritability, excitability, suspiciousness, confusion, and delirium.**

3. Lethargy and fatigue are early signs of sleep deprivation, not ICU psychosis.

4. Sleep deprivation may cause impaired memory, confusion, illusions, and visual or auditory hallucinations, not dementia.

15. 1. Although uninterrupted sleep is advantageous for restorative sleep, the number of hours required depends on the individual.

2. In older adults, the length of stage IV sleep is markedly decreased; they awaken more frequently, and it takes them longer to go back to sleep.

3. **Fear of loss of control, the unknown, and potential death results in the struggle to stay awake, which interferes with the ability to relax sufficiently to fall asleep.**

4. Bedrest does not decrease the need for sleep. The body still needs stage IV restorative sleep. Often the physiological problems requiring the bedrest increase the need for sleep.

16. 1. Tenderness is a sensory word that describes pain and is related to the quality of pain.

2. The description of pain as being moderate is related to intensity of pain.

3. **The word *episode* refers to an incident, occurrence, or time period; therefore, the word episode refers to a pattern of pain and is concerned with time of onset, duration, recurrence, and remissions.**

4. Phantom pain is related to location of pain. Phantom pain is a painful sensation perceived in a body part that is missing.

17. 1. **Alcoholic beverages are fluids that have a mild diuretic effect. Frequent nighttime awakening to empty a full bladder is called nocturia.**

2. Drinking may cause nausea and vomiting rather than hunger.

3. Alcohol hastens, not delays, the onset of sleep.

4. Alcohol disrupts sleep and causes early morning awakening.

18. 1. Self-focusing is associated with chronic, not acute, pain because of chronic pain's unrelenting, prolonged nature it interferes with pursuing a normal life. As a result, there may be changes in family dynamics, sexual functioning, financial status, and self-esteem that result in introspection and depression.

2. Pain is an internal stimulus that can interrupt sleep. Because chronic pain is unrelenting and prolonged, over time, interrupted sleep results in sleep deprivation.

3. Guarding behaviors occur in both acute and chronic pain. However, because of the unrelenting and prolonged nature of chronic pain, behavioral responses, such as guarding, stooped posture, and altered gait, may become permanent adaptations.

4. **Acute pain stimulates the sympathetic nervous system, which responds by increasing pulse, respirations, and blood pressure. Chronic pain stimulates the parasympathetic nervous system, which results in lowered pulse and blood pressure.**

19. 1. Hour of sleep (h.s., *hora somni*) medications usually are sedatives that promote rest and sleep; they are not analgesics.

2. Medications administered around the clock (ATC) at regularly scheduled intervals usually maintain therapeutic drug levels regardless of other factors influencing the patient.

3. Medication administered when necessary at the patient's request will have a primary health-care prescription that states prn (*pro re nata*).

4. The word *preemptive* means preventive, anticipatory, and defensive. Therefore, preemptive analgesia is administered before an activity or intervention that may precipitate pain in an attempt to limit the anticipated pain.

20. 1. **Chronic fatigue syndrome is a condition characterized by the onset of disabling fatigue. The fatigue is so overwhelming and consuming that it interferes with the activities of daily living.**

2. Chronic fatigue syndrome does not impair mobility. Impaired physical mobility is the state in which an individual experiences limitation of physical movement but is not immobile.

3. The fatigue of chronic fatigue syndrome may be unrelated to social isolation, which is a state in which an individual experiences or perceives a desire for increased involvement with others but is unable to make that contact.

4. Although fatigue is related to impaired gas exchange, the fatigue caused by hypoxia is unrelated to chronic fatigue syndrome, which is a very different condition.

21. 1. Psychosociocultural factors influence patients' lack of request for medication when experiencing pain. Patients may not request medication because they fear the possibility of addiction, consider the pain as punishment for previous behavior, or need to be strong, courageous, or uncomplaining.

2. Patients, particularly children and those who are cognitively impaired, often have problems describing the characteristics of pain because of difficulty interpreting painful stimuli or having never experienced the sensation before.

3. **Pain is a personal experience, and the nurse must validate its presence and severity as perceived by the patient. This conveys acceptance and respect and promotes the development of trust.**

4. Acute pain increases vital signs because of sympathetic nervous system stimulation, but chronic pain will not.

22. 1. This is a planned nursing intervention, not a goal.

2. **Sleep is a sensory experience that restores cerebral and physical functioning. Evaluations related to sleep are based on patient reports because effectiveness of sleep is a subjective assessment.**

3. This is a goal that relates to relieving pain; it is not related to lack of sleep, which is the main issue in the question.

4. Four hours of sleep is not enough for most adults. Most adults require 6 to 8 hours of sleep.

23. 1. **Imagery, the internal experience of memories, dreams, fantasies, or visions, uses positive images to distract, which reduces stress, limits mild pain, and promotes relaxation and sleep.**

2. The use of opioids should be a last resort. Nursing interventions or nonopioid medications usually are effective in limiting mild pain.

3. Bathing preferences are highly individual, and the patient may not prefer a shower. In addition, a shower is stimulating and may be counterproductive.

4. Although daytime activity does promote sleep at night, patients with pain may be reluctant to be active.

24. 1. At this time of day, most people are engaged in stimulating activities and generally are not sleepy.

2. By this time of the sleep cycle, most people have had sufficient sleep and are beginning to awaken.

3. **Research demonstrates that most people experience sleep-vulnerable periods between 2 a.m. and 6 a.m. and between 2 p.m. and 5 p.m.**

4. At this time of day, most people are engaged in stimulating activities, such as preparing and eating dinner.

25. 1. Somnambulism, sleepwalking, is a parasomnia that occurs during stages III and IV of non–rapid-eye-movement (NREM) sleep.

2. Snoring relates to obstructive sleep apnea, which is a periodic cessation of airflow during inspiration that results in arousal from sleep.

3. Nocturnal enuresis, bedwetting, is a parasomnia that occurs when moving from stages III to IV of NREM sleep.

4. **Bruxism, clenching and grinding of the teeth, is a parasomnia that occurs during stage II NREM sleep. Usually,**

it does not interfere with sleep for the affected individual but rather the sleeper's partner.

26. 1. Patient-controlled analgesia delivers an intermittent dose of an opioid on demand within safe limitations. Pain relief can be maintained for hours to days.
2. Intramuscular injections of analgesics usually are effective for 3 to 6 hours.
3. **Intravenous analgesics act within 1 to 2 minutes but drug inactivation (biotransformation) also is fast, so there is a short duration of action.**
4. With regional anesthesia (e.g., nerve block, Bier block, spinal, epidural), an anesthetic agent is instilled around nerves to block the transmission of nerve impulses, thus reducing pain for many hours.

27. 1. The healthy older adult spends more time in bed, spends less time asleep, awakens more often, stays awake longer, and naps more often. Rapid-eye-movement (REM) sleep and stage IV non–rapid-eye-movement (NREM) sleep are reduced, resulting in less restorative sleep. Naps lead to desynchronization of the sleep-wake cycle.
2. The need for sleep varies and depends on factors such as age, activity level, and health.
3. Alcohol hastens the onset of sleep. Alcohol is associated with early awakening.
4. **An expectation of an outcome of behavior usually becomes a self-fulfilling prophecy. Bedtime rituals include activities that promote comfort and relaxation (e.g., music, reading, and praying) and hygienic practices that meet basic physiological needs (e.g., bathing, brushing the teeth, and toileting).**

28. 1. Although tinnitus can interfere with sleep, it is not the most common problem.
2. **Bladder fullness causes pressure in the pelvic area that interrupts sleep. Awakening to void during the night is a common occurrence, particularly in older adult men.**
3. Although hunger can interfere with sleep, it is not the most common problem. A light evening snack or glass of milk prevents hunger.
4. Although thirst can interfere with sleep, it is not the most common problem. Thirst

is prevented by drinking water as part of the bedtime routine.

29. 1. Percussion involves gentle tapping of the skin. Percussion is stimulating and usually is performed during the middle of a back massage.
2. **Effleurage involves long, smooth strokes sliding over the skin. When performed slowly with light pressure at the end of a back rub it has a relaxing, sedative effect.**
3. Kneading (pétrissage) involves squeezing the skin, subcutaneous tissue, and muscle with a lifting motion. Kneading is stimulating and usually is performed during the middle of a back rub.
4. Circular strokes usually are performed in the area around the buttocks, lower back, and scapulae. They are stimulating and are performed during the beginning of a back rub.

30. 1. The pattern of pain refers to time of onset, duration, recurrence, and remissions.
2. Duration refers to how long the pain lasts, which is an aspect of the pattern of pain.
3. **This is referred pain, which is pain felt in a part of the body that is at a distance from the tissues causing the pain. Referred pain is related to location of pain.**
4. Constancy refers to whether the pain is continuous or if there are periods of relief from pain, both of which relate to the pattern of pain.

31. 1. The amount of time spent sleeping usually is not affected.
2. **Sleep apnea is the periodic cessation of breathing during sleep. Episodes occur during rapid-eye-movement (REM) sleep (interfering with dreaming) and non–rapid-eye- movement (NREM) sleep (interfering with restorative sleep), both of which reduce the quality of sleep.**
3. Patients still reach the depth of stage IV NREM sleep.
4. Sleep apnea does not influence the onset of sleep.

32. 1. **This open-ended question requires patients to explore the topic of sleep as it relates specifically to their own experiences.**
2. This direct question gathers information about only one aspect of sleep.

3. This direct question precipitates just a yes or no response.
4. This direct question precipitates just a yes or no response about only one aspect of sleep.

33. 1. The gate-control theory of pain relief is not activated through guided imagery. Guided imagery uses positive thoughts and emotions to promote relaxation and limit discomfort.
2. The gate-control theory of pain relief is not activated through progressive muscle relaxation. The performance of progressive muscle relaxation requires the mind to focus on an issue other than the pain. It interferes with the perception and interpretation of pain because the mind can process only a certain amount of information at a time.
3. **Thermal therapy (e.g., application of heat or cold) stimulates the large A-delta fibers that close the gate that allows the transmission of pain impulses to the central nervous system.**
4. Nonsteroidal anti-inflammatory medication, such as ibuprofen, inhibits prostaglandin synthesis. Nonsteroidal anti-inflammatory medications do not activate the gate-control theory of pain relief.

34. 1. **An increased sensitivity to pain is associated with disturbed non–rapid-eye-movement (NREM) sleep. During NREM sleep the body is engaged in restoring physiological properties of the body.**
2. An inability to concentrate is associated with disturbed rapid-eye-movement (REM) sleep. REM sleep is involved with cognitive and emotional restoration processes.
3. **During NREM sleep the parasympathetic nervous system dominates and the vital signs and metabolic rate are low; also, growth hormone is consistently secreted, which provides for anabolism. Shortened NREM sleep decreases these restorative processes, resulting in fatigue, lethargy, and excessive sleepiness.**
4. Irritability and excitability are associated with disturbed REM, not NREM, sleep.
5. REM, not NREM, sleep is essential for maintaining mental and emotional

equilibrium and, when interrupted, results in confusion, irritability, excitability, suspiciousness, delusions, and hallucinations.

35. **Answer: 15 mL. Solve the problem by using the formula for ratio and proportion.**

$$\frac{\text{Desired}}{\text{Have}} \frac{15 \text{ mg}}{5 \text{ mg}} = \frac{x \text{ mL}}{5 \text{ mL}}$$

5 x = 75
x = 75 ÷ 5
x = 15 mL

36. 1. **Limiting fluid intake after dinner reduces the amount of urine production while asleep.**
2. **Voiding empties the bladder and makes room for urine produced during the night.**
3. **Caffeine irritates the mucous membranes of the urinary system and stimulates the need to void.**
4. Positive imagery supports self-esteem and may become a self-fulfilling prophesy.
5. This intervention may be perceived by the boy as parental disapproval or punishment. Linens and clothing should be changed with a nonjudgmental, nonchalant demeanor to support the boy's self-esteem.

37. 1. A score of 3 is too low for the behaviors exhibited by the infant.
2. A score of 5 is too low for the behaviors exhibited by the infant.
3. **According to the FLACC behavioral scale to assess pain, the child's level of pain is 7. A constant frown with a quivering chin receives a score of 2. Legs drawn up to the abdomen receives a score of 2. Squirming and shifting back and forth receives a score of 1. Moaning and whimpering receives a score 1. Reassured by hugging receives a score of 1.**
4. A score of 9 is too high for the behaviors exhibited by the infant.

38. 1. Energy requirements decrease with age as metabolic processes slow and older adults become more sedentary.
2. The metabolic rate decreases by 5% to 25% during rest.
3. **Stress precipitates the sympathetic nervous system, increasing cortisone, norepinephrine, and epinephrine, which increase the metabolic rate.**

Physical and psychic energy expended is restored through rest and sleep.

4. Catabolic hormones (cortisol and epinephrine) increase with activity, not during sleep. Catabolism is the breaking down of muscle and lean body mass to produce glucose to meet energy needs (gluconeogenesis).

5. Individuals experience varied levels of consciousness when asleep. There is a progressive lack of awareness of the environment as one passes from stages 1 through 4.

39. 1. Hyporesponsiveness, withdrawal, apathy, flat facial expression, and excessive sleepiness are physiological responses associated with a lack of non–rapid-eye-movement (NREM) sleep.

2. A depressed immune system is a physiological response to a lack of NREM sleep.

3. **Rapid-eye-movement (REM) sleep is essential for maintaining mental and emotional equilibrium and, when interrupted, results in irritability and excitability.**

4. **REM sleep is essential for maintaining mental and emotional equilibrium and, when interrupted, results in confusion and suspiciousness.**

5. Shortened NREM sleep can result in vertigo, which is a physiological response to sleep deprivation.

40. 1. Metformin is an antidiabetic medication that decreases hepatic glucose production, decreases intestinal absorption of glucose, and increases sensitivity of cells to insulin. Side effects are abdominal bloating, diarrhea, nausea, and vomiting, not insomnia.

2. **Sleep patterns tend to change as one ages. Older people become sleepy earlier and wake up earlier (alteration in circadian rhythms), wake up more frequently (lower levels of growth hormone and melatonin), and experience less deep sleep (more rapid sleep cycles).**

3. Hormonal shifts in women occur throughout life: monthly related to ovulation, during pregnancy, and during and after menopause. Hormonal changes can precipitate nausea, anxiety, weight gain, generalized discomfort, restless legs syndrome, acid reflux, and frequent urination. All of these physiological responses can precipitate insomnia.

4. **Alcohol is a sedative that can help one fall asleep but it prevents deeper stages of sleep and causes one to awaken frequently during the night and earlier in the morning.**

5. The medication diphenhydramine antagonizes the effects of histamine at H_1 receptor sites. It causes drowsiness and often is taken before retiring at night to treat insomnia.

6. Catnaps, if they do not exceed 10 to 30 minutes, can be rejuvenating. Longer catnaps can interfere with sleep at night, thus aggravating insomnia.

41. 1. This statement may or may not be true.

2. **Fatigue decreases a person's coping abilities which increases the intensity of pain.**

3. This statement may or may not be true. There may be behavioral signs of pain, such as guarding, grimaces, and clenching the teeth, at the same time that there are no verbal statements indicating the presence of pain. In some cultures it is unacceptable to complain about pain or tolerance of pain signifies strength and courage.

4. This is not a true statement. The judicious use of opioids does not necessarily result in addiction.

5. **Pain is a personal experience. Margo McCaffery, a pain researcher, has indicated that pain is whatever the person in pain says it is and exists whenever the person in pain says it exists.**

42. 1. These are physiological responses, not precipitating factors, associated with the pain experience.

2. This statement reflects the pattern (e.g., onset, duration, and intervals) of the pain experience.

3. **Anything that induces or aggravates pain is considered a precipitating factor of pain. For example, precipitating factors may be physical (e.g., exertion associated with activities of daily living, Valsalva maneuver), environmental (e.g., extremes in temperature, noise), or emotional (anxiety, fear).**

4. This statement reflects the quality of the pain. Descriptive adjectives, such as

knife-like, burning, or cramping explain how the pain feels.

5. Anything that induces or aggravates pain is considered a precipitating factor of pain. Coughing raises intra-abdominal pressure, which can aggravate the pain of a surgical incision. Patients are taught to support the operative site with the hands or a pillow when coughing to limit the extent of pain.

43. 2. The first step is to position the patient in the side-lying position because this provides for a comfortable, supported position during the procedure.
4. The second step is to arrange the gown and linens so that the patient's back is exposed because this provides access to the patient's back.
3. The third step is to assess the skin to ensure that there are no indications of a problem that is a contraindication for having a back rub.
1. The fourth step is to warm the lotion in your hands because warm lotion is more comfortable and supports muscle relaxation.
5. A variety of strokes (e.g., effleurage, pétrissage, tamponage, small circular movements, and feathering) relieves muscle tension, promotes physical and emotional relaxation, and increases circulation to the area.

44. 1. Shortened non–rapid-eye-movement (NREM) sleep can result in vertigo, which is a physiological response to sleep deprivation.
2. Interrupted NREM sleep can result in fatigue, which is a physiological response to sleep deprivation.

3. Irritability is a psychological response to sleep deprivation. As the difficulty of initiating or maintaining sleep continues, the person becomes progressively more upset about the lack of the amount and quality of sleep, further precipitating insomnia.
4. Shortened NREM sleep can result in headache, which is a physiological response to sleep deprivation.
5. Frustration is a psychological response to sleep deprivation.

45. 1. Chronic pain has a gradual progressive onset because it usually is related to a long-term problem (e.g., diabetic neuropathy). Acute pain has a rapid onset because it usually is related to abrupt trauma to the body (e.g., surgical incision, damage from an automobile collision).
2. Chronic pain is categorized as pain longer than 6 months' duration. Acute pain is categorized as pain shorter than 6 months' duration.
3. An anticipated end is associated with acute pain. Chronic pain is associated with conditions that usually are lifelong with no anticipated end in sight.
4. Chronic pain is psychologically depleting because it drains both physical and emotional resources; this is related to the unrelenting nature of the pain and that it usually continues for life.
5. Chronic pain usually does not respond to conventional interventions such as back rub, imagery, distraction, and analgesics. Complementary and alternative modalities such as acupuncture, biofeedback, hypnosis, yoga, and therapeutic touch may provide some relief.

Perioperative Nursing

KEYWORDS

The following words include nursing/medical terminology, concepts, principles, and information relevant to content specifically addressed in the chapter or associated with topics presented in it. English dictionaries, nursing textbooks, and medical dictionaries, such as *Taber's Cyclopedic Medical Dictionary,* are resources that can be used to expand your knowledge and understanding of these words and related information.

Abdominal binder
Anesthesia, types:
  Epidural
  Conscious sedation
  General
  Local
  Nerve block
  Regional
  Spinal
Antiembolism stockings:
  Elastic
  Sequential compression devices
Bowel preparation
Collagen production
Deep breathing and coughing
Drains, types:
  Penrose
  Portable wound drainage
   systems:
    Hemovac
    Jackson-Pratt
Dressings, types:
  Alginates (exudate absorbers)
  Dry sterile dressing
  Hydrocolloids
  Impregnated
  Transparent
  Wet-to-damp/moist
Granulation
Hypostatic pneumonia
Informed consent
Laparoscopic
Latex allergy
Leg exercises
Medication reconciliation
Nasogastric decompression
Negative pressure
NPO status
Pain management
Patient-controlled analgesia (PCA)

Perioperative:
  Preoperative
  Intraoperative
  Postoperative
Postanesthesia care unit (PACU)
Postoperative complications:
  Aspiration
  Deep vein thrombosis
  Dehiscence
  Evisceration
  Malignant hyperthermia
  Pneumonia
  Postoperative ileus
  Pulmonary embolus, emboli
  Wound infection
Preoperative checklist
Residual limb
Skin preparation
Surgery, purposes of:
  Ablative
  Constructive
  Diagnostic
  Palliative
  Reconstructive
  Transplant
Surgery types:
  Ambulatory surgery
  Elective surgery
  Urgent surgery
  Emergency surgery
  Minor surgery
  Major surgery
Surgical asepsis
Verification process:
  Patient identification
Wound drainage:
  Purulent
  Sanguineous
  Serosanguineous
  Serous

PERIOPERATIVE NURSING: QUESTIONS

1. There are discharge criteria for patients in the postanesthesia care unit (PACU) regardless of the type of anesthesia used and additional criteria for specific types of anesthesia. Which is the criterion specific for the patient who has received spinal anesthesia?
   1. Oxygen saturation reaches the presurgical baseline.
   2. Motor and sensory function returns.
   3. Nausea and vomiting are minimal.
   4. Headache is reported as tolerable.

2. A patient is admitted to the postanesthesia care unit. Which nursing action is **most** important during the patient's stay in this unit?
   1. Monitoring urinary output
   2. Assessing level of consciousness
   3. Ensuring patency of drainage tubes
   4. Suctioning mucus from respiratory passages

3. A postoperative patient is transferred back to the surgical unit with an abdominal dressing and a Penrose drain. Which is the **most** important nursing action associated with caring for a patient with a Penrose drain?
   1. Removing the excess external portion until drainage stops
   2. Changing the soiled dressing carefully
   3. Maintaining the negative pressure
   4. Pinning the drain to the dressing

4. A patient has abdominal surgery. Which should the nurse do to **best** assess for a sign of postoperative ileus in this patient after surgery?
   1. Identify the time of the first bowel movement.
   2. Monitor the tolerance of a clear liquid diet.
   3. Palpate for abdominal distention.
   4. Auscultate for bowel sounds.

5. Four days after abdominal surgery, while being transferred from a bed to a chair, a patient says to a nurse, "My incision feels funny all of a sudden." Which should the nurse do **first**?
   1. Take the vital signs.
   2. Apply an abdominal binder immediately.
   3. Place the patient in the low-Fowler position.
   4. Encourage slow deep breathing by the patient.

6. Which factor places a patient at the **greatest** risk for postoperative nausea and vomiting after receiving general anesthesia?
   1. Obesity
   2. Inactivity
   3. Hypervolemia
   4. Unconsciousness

7. On the second postoperative day after an above-the-knee amputation, the patient's elastic dressing accidentally comes off. Which should the nurse do **first**?
   1. Wrap the residual limb with an elastic compression bandage.
   2. Apply a saline dressing to the residual limb.
   3. Notify the primary health-care provider.
   4. Place two pillows under the limb.

8. A nurse is caring for a postoperative patient. Which action is effective in preventing postoperative urinary tract infections?
1. Eating foods with roughage
2. Taking sitz baths twice a day
3. Drinking an adequate amount of fluid
4. Increasing the intake of citrus fruit juices

9. A patient received conscious sedation during a colonoscopy. Which should the nurse expect regarding the patient's experience with this procedure?
1. Patient will be unresponsive and pain free.
2. Patient will be at risk for malignant hyperthermia.
3. Patient will be sleepy but able to follow verbal commands.
4. Patient will be positioned in the supine position to prevent headache.

10. Which patient having emergency surgery should the nurse anticipate to be at the **greatest** risk for postoperative mortality?
1. Individual who has alcoholism
2. Person who has epilepsy
3. Middle-aged adult
4. Infant

11. A nurse is caring for a patient who had an abdominal hysterectomy. Which intervention **best** prevents postoperative thrombophlebitis?
1. Utilization of compression stockings at night
2. Deep breathing and coughing exercises daily
3. Leg exercises 10 times per hour when awake
4. Elevation of the legs on 2 pillows

12. A patient has abdominal surgery for removal of the gallbladder. Which should the nurse be **most** concerned about if exhibited by the patient?
1. Constipation
2. Urinary retention
3. Shallow breathing
4. Inability to provide self-care

13. A patient arrives in the postanesthesia care unit. Which is the **most** important information that the nurse needs to know?
1. Anxiety level before surgery
2. Type and extent of the surgery
3. Type of intravenous fluids administered
4. Special requests that were verbalized by the patient

14. A nurse compares the advantages and disadvantages of a central venous catheter inserted into a peripheral vein and a central venous catheter inserted into a subclavian vein. Which of the following reasons does the nurse conclude is the reason why a peripheral catheter is more desirable?
1. Because it will not be in the superior vena cava
2. Because it will not cause a tension pneumothorax
3. Because it will not prevent the development of an infection
4. Because it will not allow large volumes of fluid to be administered

15. How many days after surgery should the nurse anticipate that a postoperative patient will begin to exhibit signs and symptoms of a wound infection if it should occur?
1. Fifth day
2. Third day
3. Ninth day
4. Seventh day

16. A nurse is assessing a patient who had spinal anesthesia. For which common response should the nurse assess the patient?
    1. Headache
    2. Neuropathy
    3. Lower back discomfort
    4. Increased blood pressure

17. A hospitalized patient who has been receiving medications via a variety of routes for several days is scheduled for surgery at 10 a.m. Which should the nurse plan to do on the day of surgery?
    1. Use an alternative route for the oral medications.
    2. Withhold all the previously prescribed medications.
    3. Withhold the oral medications and administer the other drugs.
    4. Obtain directions from the primary health-care provider regarding the medications.

18. Which is the **most** common dietary order the nurse can anticipate after a patient who had abdominal surgery exhibits a return of intestinal peristalsis?
    1. Clear liquids
    2. Full liquids
    3. Low fiber
    4. Regular

19. Which patient responses **best** support the decision to discharge the patient from the postanesthesia care unit?
    1. Sao$_2$ of 95%, vital signs stable for 30 minutes, active gag reflex
    2. Tolerable pain, ability to move extremities, dry intact dressing
    3. Urinary output of 30 mL/hr, awake, turning from side to side
    4. Afebrile, adventitious breath sounds, ability to cough

20. A postoperative patient experiences tachycardia, sudden chest pain, and low blood pressure. Which complication associated with the postoperative period should the nurse conclude that the patient **most** likely experienced?
    1. Pulmonary embolus
    2. Hemorrhage
    3. Heart attack
    4. Pneumonia

21. A nurse is assessing a postoperative patient. Which patient response identified by the nurse indicates altered renal perfusion?
    1. Oliguria
    2. Cachexia
    3. Yellow sclera
    4. Suprapubic distention

22. A nurse is evaluating the effectiveness of nursing interventions for meeting the nutrient needs of patients during the first 2 days after abdominal surgery. Which outcome is **most** important?
    1. Nausea and vomiting have not occurred.
    2. Fluid and electrolytes are balanced.
    3. Wound healing is progressing.
    4. Oral intake is reestablished.

23. Which is the next **most** important assessment made by the nurse after ensuring a postoperative patient has a patent airway?
    1. Condition of drains
    2. Level of consciousness
    3. Stability of the vital signs
    4. Location of the surgical dressing

24. In which position should the nurse in the operating room place the patient who is to undergo perineal surgery?
    1. Sims
    2. Supine
    3. Lithotomy
    4. Trendelenburg

25. A nurse is caring for two patients. One of the patients has a Jackson-Pratt drain and the other patient has a Hemovac drain. Which does the nurse understand is the difference between these two drains?
    1. The size of the collection container
    2. How the pressure within the collection container is reestablished
    3. The type of pressure that promotes drainage to the collection container
    4. Where the collection container should be placed in relation to the insertion site

26. A nurse is caring for several patients who received general anesthesia. Which concurrent health problem poses the **greatest** risk for the development of a postoperative complication?
    1. Gastroesophageal reflux disease
    2. Reduced reflexes
    3. Hypothyroidism
    4. Emphysema

27. A nurse is caring for a patient who had abdominal surgery. Which type of incisional drainage should the nurse expect 4 hours after surgery?
    1. Serous wound drainage
    2. Purulent wound drainage
    3. Sanguineous wound drainage
    4. Serosanguineous wound drainage

28. A patient spikes a fever during the first postoperative day after major abdominal surgery. The nurse suspects that the fever indicates an infection. Which site does the nurse conclude **most** likely is the source of the infection?
    1. Intestines
    2. Bladder
    3. Wound
    4. Lungs

29. A nurse is to apply a transparent wound barrier over a patient's incision. Which nursing action is appropriate?
    1. Stretch the transparent dressing snugly over the entire wound.
    2. Clean the skin with normal saline before applying the dressing.
    3. Cover the transparent wound barrier with a gauze dressing and secure with paper tape.
    4. Ensure the reinforcing tape extends several inches beyond the edges of the transparent wound barrier.

30. A nurse in the operating room is to position a patient for surgery. Which factor is **most** important for the nurse to consider?
    1. Allow for skeletal deformities.
    2. Prevent pressure on bony prominences.
    3. Provide for adequate thoracic expansion.
    4. Avoid stretching of neuromuscular tissue.

31. When should the nurse initiate planned interventions regarding a patient's perioperative management?
    1. When the consent form is signed
    2. When the decision for surgery is made
    3. When the patient is admitted for surgery
    4. When the patient is transferred to the operating room

32. One hour after the reduction of a compound fracture of the ulna and radius and application of a cast the nurse observes a centimeter circle of drainage on the patient's cast. Which should the nurse do **first**?
1. Inform the surgeon immediately.
2. Reinforce the cast with a gauze dressing.
3. Monitor the area frequently for expansion.
4. Circle the spot with a pen and date, time, and initial the area.

33. A nurse is caring for a patient with a nasogastric tube attached to suction. What is the **most** important nursing action in relation to the nasogastric tube?
1. Using sterile technique when irrigating the tube
2. Recording intake and output every 2 hours
3. Providing oral hygiene every 4 hours
4. Setting suction at the ordered level

34. A nurse is considering the commonalities and differences of equipment used for gastric decompression. Which is the major advantage to using a double-lumen tube?
1. Minimizes the risk of bowel obstruction
2. Ensures drainage of the intestines
3. Prevents gastric mucosal damage
4. Promotes gastric rest

35. A nurse is performing preoperative teaching a week before surgery. The patient is taking 650 mg of aspirin twice a day for arthritis. Which should the nurse instruct the patient to do?
1. Continue to take the aspirin indefinitely.
2. Stop taking the aspirin 5 days before surgery.
3. Hold the dose of aspirin on the morning of surgery.
4. Reduce the dose of aspirin to 81 mg a day until after surgery.

36. A patient has negative pressure wound therapy (vacuum-assisted closure [VAC]) after the amputation of a toe. The tubing is connected to intermittent negative pressure. What should the nurse do when the film over the wound collapses when negative pressure is exerted?
1. Notify the primary health-care provider.
2. Decrease the extent of negative pressure.
3. Apply a new transparent film over the wound.
4. Continue to observe the functioning of the device.

37. A primary health-care provider orders antiembolism stockings for a patient. Place the following steps in the order in which they should be implemented when applying these stockings.
1. Assess the patient for contraindications to the use of antiembolism stockings.
2. Apply the antiembolism stockings before getting the patient out of bed in the morning.
3. Ensure that the applied stockings are 1 to 2 inches below the popliteal fold (bend) in the back of the knee.
4. Explain that antiembolism stockings are ordered by the primary health-care provider and what is to be done and why.
5. Measure the smallest circumference of the ankle, the largest circumference of the calf, and the length from the heel to 1 to 2 inches below the popliteal fold (bend) in the back of the knee.
6. Turn the stocking inside out so that the foot portion is inside the stocking leg, stretch each side of the stocking and ease it over the toes, center the heel, and pull the stocking over the heel and up the leg.

Answer: _____

38. A nurse is caring for a patient recovering from abdominal surgery. Which nursing actions are effective in facilitating ventilation? **Select all that apply.**

1. _____Encouraging fluid intake
2. _____Preventing abdominal distention
3. _____Positioning in the side-lying position
4. _____Implementing passive range-of-motion exercises
5. _____Ensuring that an incentive spirometer is used every hour when awake

39. A nurse is caring for a patient in the ambulatory surgery unit who just had a laparoscopic cholecystectomy. The patient reports the presence of pain that is commonly associated with the migration of CO_2 used to inflate the abdominal cavity to improve visualization during surgery. Shade in the location of this referred pain on the illustration.

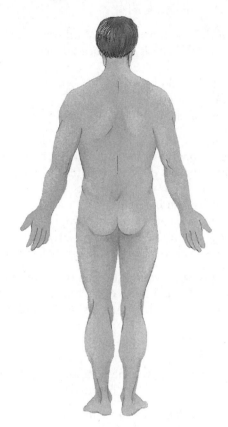

40. A patient has a tonsillectomy. Which are appropriate for the nurse to encourage this patient to have during the first 24 hours after surgery? **Select all that apply.**

1. _____Warm pudding
2. _____Milk shakes
3. _____Apple juice
4. _____Ice pops
5. _____Gelatin

41. A nurse in the postanesthesia care unit at 3 p.m. receives report from the nurse who is completing the day shift. The following information about a 65-year-old man who was admitted to the unit at 1:30 p.m. after repair of a double inguinal hernia is reported. Which information does not meet the standard criteria for discharge from the unit?

1. Stability of vital signs
2. Level of consciousness
3. Absence of bowel sounds
4. Presence of a urinary catheter

Vital Signs
Temperature: 99°F, temporal
Pulse: 98 beats per minute
Respirations: 30 breaths per minute
Blood pressure: 170/90 mm Hg

Physical Assessment
Abdominal dressing dry and intact; IV 0.9% sodium chloride at 125 mL per hour, site in left hand dry and intact, free of complications. Removed oral airway at 2 p.m.; gag reflex present; coughing, deep breathing and moving all extremities on command. Urinary catheter draining more than 50 mL per hour; bowel sounds absent.

Oxygen Status
Oxygen saturation 97% with nasal cannula at 2 L; breathing freely on own

42. A nurse is caring for a postoperative patient. The patient asks the nurse why vitamin C was prescribed by the primary health-care provider. Which information should the nurse include in a response to this question? **Select all that apply.**
1. _____Facilitates healing
2. _____Improves digestive processes
3. _____Supports collagen production
4. _____Encourages growth of red blood cells
5. _____Minimizes formation of deep vein thrombosis

43. A nurse assesses the patient on admission to the postanesthesia care unit and collects the following data: receiving oxygen via a simple face mask; oxygen saturation 92%; opens eyes and responds to commands to move all four extremities; deep breathes and coughs; and vital signs are temperature—97.8°F, pulse—82 beats per minute, respirations—18 breaths per minute, and blood pressure—140/88 mm Hg which is consistent with his previous blood pressures. Calculate the patient's Aldrete score.
1. 10
2. 9
3. 8
4. 7

Aldrete Score			On Admission to PCAU	5 Min	15 Min	30 Min	45 Min	60 Min	At Discharge
Able to move 4 extremities voluntarily or on command	= 2	Activity							
Able to move 2 extremities voluntarily or on command	= 1								
Able to move 0 extremities voluntarily or on command	= 0								
Able to deep breathe and cough freely	= 2	Respiration							
Dyspnea or limited breathing	= 1								
Apneic	= 0								
BP ± 20% of Pre-anesthetic level	= 2	Circulation							
BP ± 20%–50% of Pre-anesthetic level	= 1								
BP ± 50% of Pre-anesthetic level	= 0								
Fully awake	= 2	Consciousness							
Arousable on calling	= 1								
Not responding	= 0								
Able to maintain O_2 saturation >92% on room air	= 2	O_2 saturation							
Needs O_2 inhalation to maintain O_2 saturation >90%	= 1								
O_2 saturation <90% even with O_2 supplement	= 0								
		TOTAL							

44. A patient has a right abdominal incision. Which should the nurse teach the patient to do when getting out of bed? **Select all that apply.**
   1. _____Exit from the left side of the bed.
   2. _____Ask the nurse to apply an abdominal binder.
   3. _____Hold a pillow against the abdomen with both hands.
   4. _____Use the left arm to push up to a sitting position on the side of the bed.
   5. _____Sit on the side of the bed for a few minutes before moving to a standing position.

45. A nurse must initiate placement of a continuous passive motion machine after the patient had a total knee replacement. Place the following steps in the order in which they should be implemented.
   1. Position the extremity on the platform so the knee is centered over the break in the platform.
   2. Set the degree of flexion, speed, and time on and off the machine as ordered.
   3. Ensure that the extremity is aligned with the patient's hips and torso.
   4. Assess the patient's skin and provide skin care after the procedure.
   5. Position sheepskin on the platform especially at the gluteal fold.
   6. Position the controller within easy reach of the patient.
   Answer: _____

46. A nurse is teaching a postoperative patient the nutrients that are the best for supporting collagen production that promotes wound healing. Which foods selected by the patient indicate that the teaching was effective? **Select all that apply.**
   1. _____Yellow bell peppers
   2. _____Whole grain bread
   3. _____Cantaloupe
   4. _____Oranges
   5. _____Kiwi

47. A nurse is caring for a patient with the following type of portable wound drainage device. Identify the appropriate nursing actions associated with caring for a patient with this type of drainage system. **Select all that apply.**

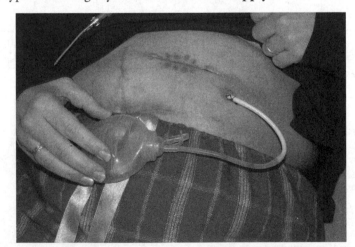

   1. _____Empty the container and then compress the collection container, close the port, and release hand compression.
   2. _____Wear sterile gloves when emptying the collection container.
   3. _____Keep the collection container below the insertion site.
   4. _____Shorten the length of the tubing by one inch daily.
   5. _____Empty the collection container when full.
   6. _____Attach tubing to clothing.

48. A nurse is caring for a postoperative patient who had abdominal surgery. The patient states, "The wound just felt like it gave way." The nurse identifies that the patient had a dehiscence with slight evisceration. Identify the actions that the nurse should implement. **Select all that apply.**
1. _____Instruct the patient to avoid coughing or bearing down.
2. _____Notify the primary health-care provider immediately.
3. _____Position the patient in the supine position.
4. _____Cover the incision with a sterile dressing.
5. _____Prepare the patient for surgery.

49. Which interventions help prevent thrombophlebitis during the postoperative period? **Select all that apply.**
1. _____Applying lower extremity sequential compression devices when in bed
2. _____Wearing antiembolism stockings when out of bed
3. _____Walking in the hall several times a day
4. _____Using an incentive spirometer
5. _____Coughing and deep breathing
6. _____Keeping the legs uncrossed

50. The primary health-care provider prescribes morphine sulfate 12 mg subcutaneously STAT for a postoperative patient. The morphine sulfate vial states that there are 10 mg per mL. Indicate on the syringe the line to which it should be filled to administer the prescribed dose.

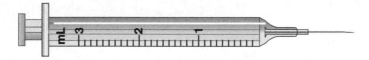

1. 1. The respiratory status of all postoperative patients should be stable and adequate regardless of the type of anesthesia used.

2. **The ability to move and feel sensations in all four extremities is especially important after receiving spinal anesthesia (subarachnoid block) because it indicates that nerve damage has not occurred because of the lumbar puncture necessary for the introduction of the anesthetic agent into the subarachnoid space.**

3. Nausea and vomiting are associated with general, not spinal, anesthesia.

4. This is unrealistic. Although a headache may be associated with spinal anesthesia (subarachnoid block), it may manifest after discharge from the postanesthesia care unit and persist for several days until the cerebrospinal fluid pressure returns to an acceptable level.

2. 1. Although monitoring urinary output is done to ensure that the minimal hourly urine output is 30 mL, it is not the priority.

2. Although assessing level of consciousness is part of the routine assessment of a patient recovering from anesthesia, particularly conscious sedation and general anesthesia, it is not the priority.

3. Although tubes and equipment are always monitored and maintained, the patency of drainage tubes is not the priority.

4. **Maintaining a patent airway is always the priority to prevent respiratory distress and hypoxia. This follows the ABCs (airway, breathing, circulation) of patient care.**

3. 1. Although this is done, it is not the priority action associated with a Penrose drain. A Penrose drain, a small pliable, flat tube, extends beyond the insertion site by approximately 2 inches. This prevents it from being lost inside the wound and allows its placement between gauze dressings to absorb drainage. As a Penrose drain is shortened, it is withdrawn approximately 1 inch and cut to maintain the same 2-inch length outside the body.

2. **Changing a soiled dressing carefully is necessary to prevent inadvertent removal of the Penrose drain because it** is placed between several layers of gauze to absorb drainage.

3. A Penrose drain functions by gravity, not negative pressure.

4. Pinning a Penrose drain to the dressing is contraindicated, to avoid removing the drain inadvertently during a dressing change.

4. 1. A bowel movement will occur long after the first signs of intestinal motility are evident.

2. Administration of fluids before intestinal motility has returned is unsafe and contraindicated. A clear liquid diet is not administered until there are definitive signs of intestinal motility.

3. Although palpating the abdomen for distention is done, it is not the best assessment for paralytic ileus. Abdominal distention can be caused by problems other than paralytic ileus, such as hemorrhage, peritonitis, and urinary retention.

4. **Bowel sounds are high-pitched gurgling sounds that vary in frequency, intensity, and pitch; they are caused by the propulsion of intestinal contents through the lower alimentary tract. These sounds are the first indication that intestinal motility is returning.**

5. 1. Vital signs should be assessed eventually, but it is not the priority.

2. An abdominal binder may be used in high-risk patients to prevent, not treat, dehiscence and evisceration.

3. **The low-Fowler position, a back-lying position, permits inspection of the operative site and promotes retention of abdominal viscera by gravity if dehiscence has occurred. Also, slight flexion of the hips reduces tension on the abdominal musculature.**

4. Deep breathing is contraindicated because it increases intra-abdominal pressure, which could cause evisceration.

6. 1. **Obese people have excess adipose tissue that exerts pressure on the abdominal cavity, which raises intra-abdominal pressure. Increased intra-abdominal pressure exerts pressure on the gastrointestinal tract, increasing the risk of nausea and vomiting.**

2. Although inactivity delays recovery of intestinal motility after surgery, a diligent activity and ambulation schedule should prevent postoperative ileus and its related nausea and vomiting.
3. Intestinal hypomotility, not hypervolemia, is related to postoperative nausea and vomiting. Hypervolemia is an increase in intravascular blood volume.
4. Unconsciousness is not directly related to postoperative nausea and vomiting.

7. **1. Gentle compression is desirable because it prevents bleeding and promotes molding and shrinkage of the residual limb.**
2. A saline dressing is unsafe because soaking promotes the breakdown of connective tissue fibers (maceration), which impedes wound healing by primary intention.
3. Notifying the primary health-care provider should be done eventually, but caring for the patient is the immediate priority.
4. Elevating the limb is unsafe because it promotes hip flexion contractures.

8. 1. Dietary roughage prevents constipation, not urinary tract infections.
2. A sitz bath can promote the development of a urinary tract infection if medical aseptic techniques are not followed.
3. Adequate (2,000 to 3,000 mL/day) fluid intake daily promotes a dilute urine and more frequent emptying of the bladder, both of which limit the development of a urinary tract infection. The stasis of concentrated urine promotes microbial growth.
4. The ingestion of citrus juice causes an alkaline urine, which provides a favorable environment for the multiplication of microorganisms and the development of a urinary tract infection.

9. 1. Unresponsiveness and being pain free occur with general anesthesia, not conscious sedation.
2. Life-threatening malignant hyperthermia is a rare, autosomal dominant–inherited syndrome that is precipitated by anesthetic inhalation agents and neuromuscular blocking medications used to induce general anesthesia, not conscious sedation.
3. Conscious sedation involves the use of intravenous opioids and sedatives to decrease the level of consciousness to a degree where the person can still maintain an airway, can respond to

verbal commands, and cannot remember the procedure.
4. Patients who have received spinal anesthesia (subarachnoid block), not conscious sedation, are placed in the supine position to limit leakage of cerebrospinal fluid from the needle insertion site. Bedrest in the supine position, hydration, and pressure against the infusion site limit headache associated with spinal anesthesia.

10. **1. Chronic alcoholism disrupts the structure and function of the liver. A decrease in the synthesis of bile salts prevents the absorption of vitamin K, which is essential for the production of clotting factors II, VII, IX, and X. Therefore, these patients are at risk for hemorrhage. In addition, malnutrition results in decreased protein synthesis, anemia, and vitamin deficiencies, all of which interfere with fluid and electrolyte balance and wound healing. Finally, the patient will have to be medically managed to minimize the responses to alcohol withdrawal.**
2. Although patients with epilepsy have their own unique problems that must be considered, they are not at the greatest risk for postoperative mortality as a group in another option.
3. Middle-aged adults are not at the greatest risk for postoperative mortality as a group in another option.
4. Although infants have a greater surgical risk than children and young to middle-aged adults because they have a lower total blood volume, a larger percentage of body fluid, and difficulty maintaining body temperature as a result of an immature shivering reflex, they are not at the greatest risk for postoperative mortality as a group in another option.

11. 1. Although compression stockings at night are helpful, they will promote venous return for a limited amount of time (approximately 8 hours). The patient will be at risk for the remaining time in the day (approximately 16 hours).
2. Deep breathing and coughing exercises help to prevent atelectasis and pneumonia, not thrombophlebitis; these exercises should be performed hourly when awake.
3. Leg exercises are an active intervention by the patient that contracts the

muscles of the legs. This rhythmically compresses the veins, which promotes venous return and prevents venous stasis.

4. Elevating the legs on two pillows is undesirable because pressure on the popliteal space constricts the vessels, which impedes venous return, promotes venous stasis, and injures tissues. Vessel injury, venous stasis, hypercoagulability, and dehydration all contribute to thrombophlebitis.

12. 1. Although constipation as a result of anesthesia is a concern, it is not life-threatening.
    2. Although urinary retention as a result of anesthesia is a concern, it is not life-threatening.
    3. **After abdominal surgery patients frequently have shallow respirations because when the diaphragm contracts with a deep breath it increases intra-abdominal pressure, which causes pain at the operative site. Shallow breathing may result in atelectasis and/or hypostatic pneumonia.**
    4. Although a person may experience an impaired ability to provide self-care during recovery from surgery, it is not life-threatening.

13. 1. The patient's level of anxiety may be communicated; however, in the immediate postoperative period the physiological needs of the patient are the priority.
    2. **The type and extent of the surgery are significant pieces of information because there are unique stressors and expected responses to various types of surgery that may direct the plan of care for the patient.**
    3. Although the type and amount of IV fluids ordered are important and should be communicated, this is only one aspect of the patient's care.
    4. Although reasonable requests are honored, the status of the patient or the environment may prohibit them.

14. 1. Both entry sites place the catheter in the superior vena cava.
    2. **A tension pneumothorax is not a concern with a peripherally inserted central venous catheter. Pneumothorax is a complication of a central venous catheter inserted into a subclavian vein**

because of the close proximity of its insertion site to the apex of the lung.
    3. Both entry sites carry a risk of infection because the first line of defense, the skin, has been pierced.
    4. Both entry sites allow for the administration of large volumes of fluid because the distal ends of their catheters are both in the superior vena cava.

15. 1. A wound infection is less likely to occur 5 days after surgery because the proliferative or reconstructive phase of wound healing begins approximately 3 days after tissue damage. By the fifth postoperative day, the wound has filled with highly vascular fibroblastic connective tissue that protects the body from microorganisms.
    2. **Microorganisms introduced into a surgical site take 72 hours to multiply and present local adaptations of pain, swelling, erythema, warmth, and purulent discharge and systemic adaptations of fever and tachycardia.**
    3. A wound infection is less likely to occur at the ninth day because by the second postoperative week there is progressive collagen accumulation and the formation of the basic structure of the scar, which protect the body from microorganisms.
    4. A wound infection is less likely to occur at the seventh day because by the seventh postoperative day the surface epithelium has an appropriate thickness and the subepithelial layers are bridged, which protect the body from microorganisms.

16. 1. **Leakage of cerebrospinal fluid from the needle insertion site reduces cerebrospinal fluid pressure, which causes a headache.**
    2. Neuropathy, resulting from inflammation or degeneration of the peripheral nerves, is not a response to spinal anesthesia.
    3. Although the needle insertion site may feel uncomfortable in some people, it is not a common problem after spinal anesthesia.
    4. Anesthetic agents cause a decrease, not increase, in blood pressure.

17. 1. Changing the route of a prescribed oral medication is beyond the scope of the legal practice of nursing.
    2. Withholding medications without a significant reason is unsafe. These medications may be essential to maintain the patient's physical or emotional status.

3. It is unsafe to withhold medications without an important reason. The withheld medications may be essential to maintain the patient's physical or emotional equilibrium.

4. **This intervention meets the patient's needs and adheres to the laws that govern the practice of nursing. A change in the route of medication delivery requires a prescription because medication administration is a dependent function of the nurse.**

18. 1. **The molecules in clear liquids are less complex and easier to ingest, tolerate, and digest than those in a full-liquid diet or food.**

2. A full-liquid diet is not the most common diet ordered postoperatively, although a full-liquid diet frequently precedes solid food.

3. A low-fiber diet is ordered for specific problems, such as intestinal inflammation or infection. When able to be tolerated postoperatively, dietary fiber promotes intestinal motility and prevents constipation.

4. A regular diet is not the most common diet ordered postoperatively, although most initial postoperative diets eventually progress to a regular diet.

19. 1. **These clinical findings are essential for discharge from the postanesthesia care unit because they reflect the body's vital functions, such as airway, breathing, and circulation.**

2. A dry dressing may be unrealistic. Some drainage from a surgical incision is expected in the immediate postoperative period. The other listed clinical findings are desirable.

3. A postoperative patient may not be able to turn from side to side, but the patient should be able to move all extremities. The other listed clinical findings are desirable for discharge.

4. The lack of a fever is not a criterion for discharge from the postanesthesia care unit because a low-grade fever is an expected response to the stress of surgery. Adventitious breath sounds are abnormal breath sounds (e.g., wheeze, crackles, and rhonchi) and indicate a respiratory problem. The ability to cough is desirable.

20. 1. **These are the classic clinical manifestations of a pulmonary embolus. Chest pain results from local tissue hypoxia, tachycardia from systemic hypoxia, and hypotension from decreased cardiac output. A pulmonary embolus is caused by an embolus lodging in a vessel in the pulmonary circulation, occluding blood supply to the capillary side of the alveolar-capillary membrane.**

2. Although tachycardia and hypotension occur with hemorrhage, chest pain does not.

3. Although tachycardia and chest pain occur with a myocardial infarction (heart attack), the blood pressure probably will increase, not decrease. If cardiogenic shock occurs, the blood pressure decreases eventually.

4. Pneumonia, inflammation of the lung with consolidation and exudation, is associated with tachycardia and chest discomfort. However, it does not have a sudden onset and the blood pressure will increase, not decrease.

21. 1. **Oliguria is diminished urine secretion in relation to fluid intake, which is indicated by a negative balance in the intake and output record or an hourly urine output of less than 30 mL. Oliguria is caused by decreased renal perfusion or kidney disease.**

2. Cachexia is not an adaptation related to altered renal perfusion. Cachexia is malnutrition and emaciation associated with serious diseases such as cancer.

3. Yellow sclera indicates jaundice. Jaundice is the accumulation of bile pigments in tissue, which is associated with liver or biliary problems, not altered renal perfusion.

4. Suprapubic distention indicates urinary retention, which is an inability of the bladder to empty, not a problem with renal perfusion. If it occurs, usually it becomes evident 6 to 8 hours after surgery.

22. 1. This is an unrealistic expectation considering all the stressors that can contribute to these problems. Essential nutrient needs can be met despite the presence of nausea and vomiting.

2. **Fluid is the most basic nutrient of the body, and it contains compounds such**

as electrolytes. Electrolytes help maintain fluid balance, contribute to acid-base balance, and facilitate enzyme and neuromuscular reactions. The narrow safe limits of the volumes and composition of fluid compartments are essential for the life-sustaining processes of nutrition, metabolism, and excretion.
3. Wound healing takes time, and it is difficult to evaluate during the inflammatory phase, which lasts 1 to 4 days.
4. Oral intake should not be reestablished until intestinal motility returns, which may take several days.

23. 1. Although the condition of drains ultimately will be assessed, the physiological status of the patient is the priority.
2. Although the patient's level of consciousness eventually will be assessed, it is not the priority at this time.
3. Assessment in acute situations always follows the ABCs: airway, breathing, and circulation. Respirations and pulse reflect the cardiopulmonary status of the patient.
4. Both the location and status of the dressing should be assessed but not until more critical assessments are completed.

24. 1. The Sims position is not used during the intraoperative period for perineal surgery.
2. The supine position is the most common position for abdominal, not perineal, surgery.
3. The lithotomy position, back-lying with the hips and knees flexed and the legs supported in stirrups, provides optimal visualization of and access to the area related to perineal surgery.
4. A patient's legs are adducted when in the Trendelenburg position, which does not permit visualization of or access to the perineal area.

25. **1. A Hemovac is designed to accommodate 100, 400, or 800 mL of drainage depending on the system used, whereas a Jackson-Pratt system accommodates volumes less than 100 mL of drainage.**
2. Both create a vacuum by closing the drainage port while compressing the device.

3. Both work by gentle negative pressure that draws fluid from the tissues to the collection chamber.
4. Both collection chambers should be placed below the site of insertion to allow gravity to work in conjunction with the negative pressure within the self-contained systems.

26. 1. Gastroesophageal reflex disease is not a problem with general anesthesia because of interventions such as NPO status before surgery, use of a cuffed endotracheal tube, and positioning.
2. Although reduced reflexes are significant to know when monitoring a patient throughout the surgical experience, they do not place a patient at the greatest risk.
3. Although a decreased metabolism is taken into consideration when monitoring reflexes during the induction, maintenance, and reversal phases of anesthesia, hypothyroidism does not place a patient at the greatest risk.
4. Respiratory problems complicate the administration of inhalation anesthesia. Emphysema is characterized by destruction of alveoli, loss of elastic recoil, and narrowing of bronchioles, which result in alveolar hyperinflation and increased airflow resistance.

27. 1. Serous exudate is a clear, watery fluid consisting mainly of serum. It is the exudate expected before final wound healing.
2. Purulent exudate is a thick drainage known as pus, which consists of leukocytes, liquefied dead tissue debris, and bacteria. This is unexpected and indicates the presence of a wound infection. Wound infections generally become apparent 2 to 11 days postoperatively.
3. Sanguineous (hemorrhagic) exudate consists of large amounts of red blood cells and is associated with open wounds or hemorrhage.
4. Serosanguineous exudate, a combination of serous and sanguineous drainage, consists of plasma and red blood cells and is pale red and watery. This is the initial drainage expected after surgery.

28. 1. The absence of intestinal motility (paralytic ileus), not infection, is the intestinal response that can occur during the first 24 to 36 hours after surgery.

Abdominal distention and absent bowel sounds, not a fever, indicate this problem.

2. A urinary catheter usually is inserted before major abdominal surgery. A bladder infection will not be apparent during the first 24 hours after catheterization because microorganisms take at least 72 hours to multiply sufficiently to manifest symptoms.

3. Microorganisms introduced into the incision at the time of surgery take at least 72 hours to multiply sufficiently to manifest symptoms.

4. **When postoperative pneumonia (an inflammation of the lung with consolidation and exudation) occurs, patient symptoms are evident usually any time within 36 hours after surgery.**

29. 1. This action restricts mobility and may exert undue pressure on the surface of the wound. The dressing should be laid gently over the wound and the edges pressed against the skin to ensure adherence.

2. **This action removes exudate and ensures adhesion of the dressing. Transparent adhesive films are nonabsorbent semipermeable, which allows oxygen exchange, dressings that are impermeable to water and bacteria.**

3. These actions defeat one of the purposes of a transparent dressing, which is the ability to visualize the wound.

4. A transparent dressing is self-contained, and reinforcing tape usually is not necessary.

30. 1. Although allowing for skeletal deformities is always taken into consideration when positioning a patient during the intraoperative period, it is not the priority.

2. It is impossible to prevent all pressure on bony prominences during the intraoperative period. Specific positions are necessary to allow exposure and access to the operative area. Positioning devices and padding are used to minimize trauma.

3. **Facilitating respirations always is the priority because permanent brain damage can result from cerebral hypoxia in as little as 4 to 6 minutes.**

4. Although stretching of neuromuscular tissue should be avoided during the intraoperative period, it is not the priority.

31. 1. Significant nursing care must be provided before this point in time. The operative consent form is signed during the preoperative phase of the perioperative experience.

2. **The surgical experience begins as soon as the decision for surgery is made. Perioperative nursing responsibilities begin immediately and continue throughout the preoperative, intraoperative, and postoperative phases.**

3. A nurse is negligent if nursing care begins at this point in the surgical experience.

4. The nurse is negligent if nursing care begins only at this point in the surgical experience. This is the intraoperative phase of the perioperative experience.

32. 1. Informing the surgeon is premature, because some drainage occurs with a compound fracture.

2. Reinforcing the cast with a gauze dressing is undesirable, because it impedes the ability to assess the site in the future.

3. The determination of expansion is a subjective assessment without objective parameters and is undesirable as a form of measurement.

4. **Circling the spot with a pen and indicating the date, time, and initials is appropriate. This determines objectively the time and extent of the bleeding and the person who performed the assessment. The extent of progression of the bleeding can be established objectively using the original circle as a standard.**

33. 1. Medical, not surgical, asepsis is necessary.

2. It is unnecessary to monitor the intake and output (I&O) this frequently. The I&O must be recorded at routine intervals as per hospital policy, usually every 8 and 24 hours.

3. Oral hygiene should be provided more frequently than every 4 hours. Because there is no food or fluid to stimulate salivary gland secretion and the tube in the nose may interfere with breathing, precipitating mouth breathing, the mouth becomes dry.

4. **The level of suctioning is part of the primary health-care provider's order for nasogastric decompression. Low suction pressure is between 80 and 100 mm Hg, and high suction pressure is between 100 and 120 mm Hg. Suctioning must be maintained continuously with a double-lumen**

tube (e.g., Salem sump) to prevent reflux of gastric secretions into the vent lumen, which will obstruct its functioning and result in mucosal damage. A single-lumen tube requires low intermittent suction to prevent the tube from adhering to the stomach mucosa.

34. 1. A double-lumen tube will not minimize the risk of a bowel obstruction.
    2. All nasogastric tubes attached to suction remove drainage from the stomach, not the intestine. Nasointestinal tubes attached to suction remove fluid from the intestine.
    3. A double-lumen tube has two lumens: one allows stomach secretions to be removed by suction (first lumen) and the other allows air to be drawn into the stomach (second lumen). The second lumen (blue pigtail) is open to environmental (atmospheric) air, which is drawn into the stomach to equalize the outside pressure with the pressure inside the stomach. This prevents the catheter tip from attaching to the gastric mucosa when the drainage lumen is attached to suction, limiting mucosal damage.
    4. All nasogastric tubes attached to suction empty the stomach contents in an effort to promote gastric and intestinal rest. Gastric glands produce up to 4 to 5 liters of fluid a day that stimulate the intestine unless removed.

35. 1. Continuing the aspirin is unsafe. Acetylsalicylic acid (aspirin) is a salicylate that inhibits thromboxane which binds platelet molecules together. Continuing the aspirin can interfere with platelet aggregation and may result in hemorrhage.
    2. Acetylsalicylic acid (aspirin) is a salicylate that inhibits thromboxane which binds platelet molecules together. It has a half-life of 15 to 30 hours. It should be discontinued at least 5 days before surgery. Some providers advocate discontinuing aspirin 7 days before surgery.
    3. It is unsafe to continue to take aspirin until the evening of surgery. On the day of surgery there will still be chemical properties of aspirin in the patient's body that inhibit platelet aggregation which may result in hemorrhage.

    4. The dose of 81 mg of aspirin will still interfere with platelet aggregation which may result in hemorrhage on the day of surgery. Also, changing the dose of a medication is not within the legal practice of nursing.

36. 1. It is not necessary to notify the primary health-care provider because this is an expected response when negative pressure is applied to the device.
    2. It is not necessary to change the setting of the negative pressure. Changing the setting of the negative pressure requires an order; it is a dependent function of the nurse. The pressure can be continuous or intermittent and set between 5 and 123 mm Hg.
    3. Changing the transparent film is not necessary because the device is intact. The film is expected to collapse when negative pressure is exerted.
    4. The device is functioning appropriately. The transparent film will collapse or wrinkle as negative pressure is applied to the wound. This indicates that there are no leaks in the dressing and the negative pressure is functioning.

37. **4. Patients have a right to know what is going to be done and why.**
    1. Antiembolism stockings should not be applied to a patient with such conditions as excessive peripheral edema or lower extremity arterial disease because doing so may make these conditions worse.
    5. Antiembolism stockings must fit the size of the patient for compression to be effective. If the stockings are too loose they will not provide adequate compression to facilitate venous return, and if they are too tight they will have a tourniquet effect.
    2. The supine position facilitates venous return via gravity, thereby limiting trapping of blood pooled in the lower extremities. When the legs are dependent, they can develop dependent edema. Antiembolism stockings should be applied before the patient gets out of bed in the morning before dependent edema has a chance to occur. Antiembolism stockings are elastic garments worn around the leg; they exert pressure against the legs,

thus reducing the diameter of the veins. When the diameter of veins are reduced the volume and velocity of blood flow increases, preventing venous stasis. Venous stasis promotes the formation of a thrombus.

6. Turning the stocking inside out and stretching each side make it easier to get the elastic over the toes and heel. Centering the heel keeps the stocking straight, providing for even compression.

3. Avoiding placement of antiembolism stockings over the popliteal fold prevents damage to nerves and blood vessels in the popliteal area.

38. 1. Increasing fluid intake will make respiratory secretions less viscous and easier to expectorate, thereby facilitating ventilation.

2. Abdominal distention raises the pressure within the abdominal cavity, which exerts pressure against the diaphragm, impeding its contraction and limiting thoracic excursion.

3. When in a side-lying position, aeration of the dependent side of the lung is limited because of pooling of secretions and the weight of the body compressing the dependent part of the body.

4. Passive range-of-motion exercises do not facilitate respirations; they help prevent contractures.

5. An incentive spirometer will help increase depth of inspirations, preventing stasis of secretions in the respiratory tract, which in turn will facilitate ventilation.

39. The carbon dioxide that is used to insufflate the abdominal cavity during a laparoscopic cholecystectomy that is not released or absorbed by the body can be trapped in the subdiaphragmatic recesses. This can irritate the diaphragm, causing referred pain to the right shoulder and scapular area. In addition, the retained carbon dioxide can irritate the phrenic nerve, causing dyspnea. Positioning the patient in the left Sims position will help move the gas away from the diaphragm. The nurse should encourage the patient to walk and breathe deeply periodically once fully recovered from anesthesia.

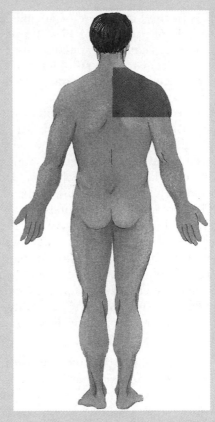

40. 1. Warm liquids and food are contraindicated during the first several days after a tonsillectomy because they cause vasodilation, which may increase bleeding from the vascular mucous membranes of the oropharynx.

2. Milk and milk products are avoided during recovery from oral surgery because some health-care professionals believe milk increases the consistency of phlegm.

3. Apple juice is a clear liquid that when cool will promote vasoconstriction and limit bleeding from the operative site.

4. An ice pop is a frozen clear liquid that promotes vasoconstriction and limits bleeding from the operative site. However, flavors that have a red color are contraindicated because they complicate assessing for bleeding.

5. Cool gelatin desserts promote vasoconstriction limiting bleeding from the operative site. Flavors that have a red color are contraindicated because they complicate assessing for bleeding.

41. 1. The patient's vital signs are not stable. Respirations at a rate of 30 are too rapid. A pulse rate of 98 is within the expected range of 70 to 100; however,

it is in the high range of normal, and the blood pressure of 170/90 mm Hg is higher than the expected range of 150/90 mm Hg for an older adult. The patient should be monitored further.

2. The patient's level of consciousness meets the criteria for discharge from the postanesthesia care unit. The patient is easily aroused as indicated by "coughing and deep breathing on command and able to move all extremities on command."

3. The absence of bowel sounds is an expected response to surgery and the use of anesthesia. The presence of bowel sounds is not a criterion for discharge from the postanesthesia care unit.

4. Urinary retention catheters are frequently in place postoperatively. The ability to void is not a criterion for discharge from a postanesthesia care unit.

42. 1. **Vitamin C (ascorbic acid) promotes collagen production, an essential component of the proliferative phase of wound healing. In addition, vitamin C enhances capillary formation, decreases capillary fragility, increases the tensile strength of the wound, and provides a defense against infection because of its role in the immune response.**

2. Vitamin C does not improve digestion.

3. **Vitamin C promotes collagen production, an essential component of the proliferative phase of wound healing. In addition, vitamin C enhances capillary formation, decreases capillary fragility, increases the tensile strength of the wound, and provides a defense against infection because of its role in the immune response.**

4. Vitamin B_{12} (cobalamin), folic acid, and iron promote red blood cell production, not vitamin C.

5. Vitamin C promotes the strength of capillaries, not large veins. Ambulation, leg exercises, and hydration prevent deep vein thrombosis.

43. 1. Ten is not the patient's Aldrete score.
2. **Nine is the correct Aldrete score for this patient. The patient received 2 points for moving all four extremities on command, 2 points for breathing deeply and coughing freely, 2 points for a blood pressure consistent with pre-anesthetic levels, 1 point for being**

aroused on calling, and 2 points for oxygen saturation of 92%.

3. Eight is not the patient's Aldrete score.
4. Seven is not the patient's Aldrete score.

44. 1. **When exiting from the left side of the bed, the left lateral side of the abdomen will be compressed against the bed by body weight. The left, not right, side of the abdomen will absorb the majority of the muscular strain exerted by the transfer.**

2. Although an abdominal binder might be applied for patients at high risk for dehiscence, abdominal binders are not used routinely because they increase intra-abdominal pressure; this exerts a force against the diaphragm that impedes maximum respiratory excursion.

3. Holding a pillow against the abdomen with both hands is unsafe. At least one upper extremity should be used to help raise the body to a sitting position and promote balance during the transfer out of bed.

4. Using the left arm to assist in lifting the body to a sitting position on the side of the bed places less strain on abdominal muscles in the area of the incision.

5. Sitting on the side of the bed for a few minutes before moving to a standing position allows the blood pressure to adjust to the change in position, thus avoiding orthostatic hypotension.

45. 5. Positioning sheepskin on the platform especially at the gluteal fold, provides a soft base on which to position the extremity. The site of the gluteal fold is the site that is most at risk for excess pressure.

1. Positioning the extremity on the platform so that the knee is centered over the break in the platform ensures that flexion occurs at the site of the knee joint when the device is in motion.

3. Ensuring that the extremity is aligned with the hips and torso prevents stress and strain on the muscles, bones, joints, ligaments, and tendons of the body.

2. Setting the degree of flexion, speed, and time on and off the machine as ordered ensures that the plan of care is implemented as ordered.

6. Positioning the controller within easy reach of the patient allows the patient to turn off the device if unable to tolerate the procedure.

4. Assessing the skin once the extremity is removed from the device ensures that a skin problem is immediately identified. Providing skin care keeps skin clean, dry, and moisturized, which helps to keep skin supple and intact.

46. 1. Selecting yellow bell peppers indicates learning. A half a cup of yellow bell peppers contains approximately 170 mg of vitamin C. Vitamin C promotes collagen production, which is essential in the proliferative and maturation phases of wound healing.
    2. Selecting whole grain bread does not indicate learning. Whole grains contain trace amounts or no vitamin C necessary for collagen production. Whole grains are noted primarily for containing vitamin E and potassium.
    3. Selecting cantaloupe indicates learning. A cup of cantaloupe contains approximately 68 mg of vitamin C. Vitamin C promotes collagen production, which is essential in the proliferative and maturation phases of wound healing.
    4. Selecting an orange indicates learning. One medium orange contains approximately 69 mg of vitamin C. Vitamin C promotes collagen production, which is essential in the proliferative and maturation phases of wound healing.
    5. Selecting kiwi indicates learning. One kiwi contains approximately 72 mg of vitamin C. Vitamin C promotes collagen production, which is essential in the proliferative and maturation phases of wound healing.

47. 1. Compressing the collection container, closing the port, and releasing hand compression after emptying the container establish negative pressure within the collection container.
    2. Clean, not sterile, gloves should be worn when emptying a Jackson-Pratt drain. Although the nurse should maintain sterile technique when emptying a Jackson-Pratt drain, it can be accomplished without wearing sterile gloves. Clean gloves are worn by the nurse to protect the nurse from the patient's blood or body fluids.
    3. Keeping the collection container below the insertion site augments the negative pressure of the system.
    4. A primary health-care provider may order a Penrose drain to be shortened daily, not the tubing of a Jackson-Pratt drain.
    5. The collection container should be emptied when half full, not when full. This action prevents weight of the bulb pulling on the tubing and helps maintain negative pressure. The amount of negative pressure decreases as drainage in the collection container increases.
    6. Attaching tubing to clothing prevents tension on the tubing.

48. 1. Coughing or bearing down will increase tension on the suture line, potentially extending the dehiscence and evisceration, and should be avoided.
    2. The patient needs emergency surgical care and the primary health-care provider should be notified immediately.
    3. The patient should be placed in the low-Fowler, not the supine, position with the knees slightly flexed to reduce stress on the suture line.
    4. Covering the wound with a sterile dressing protects the open wound from contamination.
    5. The patient should be prepared for surgery because the surgeon will most likely return the patient to the operating room for surgical repair of the incision.

49. 1. Sequential compression devices apply pressure progressively from the ankles to the thighs, promoting venous return. Volume and velocity of blood flow in the superficial and deep veins in the legs increase, preventing venous stasis. Venous stasis promotes the development of a thrombus.
    2. Antiembolism stockings are elastic garments worn around the leg; they exert pressure against the legs reducing the diameter of the veins. When the diameter of veins is reduced the volume and velocity of blood flow increases, preventing venous stasis. Venous stasis promotes the formation of a thrombus.

3. Walking contracts the muscles of the lower extremities and increases cardiac output. Both increase the volume and velocity of blood flow through the veins of the lower extremities, preventing venous stasis and thrombus formation.

4. Using an incentive spirometer prevents atelectasis, not thrombophlebitis.

5. Coughing and deep breathing prevent atelectasis, not thrombophlebitis.

6. Keeping the legs uncrossed eliminates pressure against the calves or behind the knee (popliteal space) depending on where the legs are crossed. Pressure to these areas impairs venous return, which promotes venous stasis and thrombus formation.

50. Solve the problem using the formula for ratio and proportion.

$$\frac{\text{Desire } 12 \text{ mg}}{\text{Have } 10 \text{ mg}} = \frac{x \text{ mL}}{1 \text{ mL}}$$

$$10 x = 12$$
$$x = 12 \div 10$$
$$x = 1.2 \text{ mL}$$

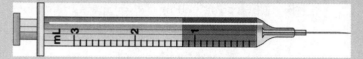

Alternate Item Formats

6

National Council Licensure Examinations (NCLEX) include multiple-choice questions and alternate item format questions. A typical multiple-choice question (one answer) presents a statement or situation and requires the test taker to identify the correct answer from among four presented options. Alternate item formats use the benefits of computer technology to assess knowledge via various methods. Alternate item formats include questions that require test takers to do the following: identify multiple answers (multiple-response items); identify a location on a presented image (hot spot items); perform a mathematical calculation (fill-in-the-blank calculation items); respond to a question in relation to an image such as a picture, table, photograph, or illustration (graphic items); identify priorities (drag and drop/ordered response items); and answer a question in relation to a patient situation that presents data such as information from a patient's clinical record (exhibit items). All item types may include multimedia such as illustrations, charts, tables, audio, or video technology to present information in the question. Alternate item formats are able to measure entry-level nursing competence in ways that are different from the typical multiple-choice format. It is believed that some nursing content is more readily and authentically evaluated using alternate item formats. This chapter includes 60 questions that use formats other than multiple-choice questions. For specific test-taking techniques for answering alternate item questions, see *Test-Taking Techniques for Beginning Nursing Students*. This is an F. A. Davis textbook written by Nugent and Vitale.

ALTERNATE ITEM FORMATS: QUESTIONS

Multiple-Response Items

A multiple-response item presents a statement or situation that asks a question that has more than one answer among presented options. The test taker is required to select all options that correctly answer the question.

1. A patient comes to the emergency department with a lacerated thumb. For which clinical manifestations associated with the local adaptation syndrome (LAS) should the nurse assess the patient? **Select all that apply.**
   1. _____Pain
   2. _____Heat
   3. _____Erythema
   4. _____Increased heart rate
   5. _____Decreased blood pressure
   6. _____Elevated blood glucose level

2. A nurse is assisting a postoperative patient to ambulate. Which postoperative complications will ambulation help prevent? **Select all that apply.**
   1. _____Hypovolemia
   2. _____Constipation
   3. _____Atelectasis
   4. _____Dehiscence
   5. _____Infection

3. A patient is learning self-care in relation to a 2-g sodium diet. Which foods selected by the patient indicate to the nurse that further teaching is necessary? **Select all that apply.**
   1. _____Apple juice
   2. _____Feta cheese
   3. _____Corned beef
   4. _____Canned soup
   5. _____Broccoli spears

4. A nurse is monitoring a patient's IV infusion. Which data are necessary to determine that the IV is "on time"? **Select all that apply.**
   1. _____Drip rate per minute
   2. _____Time the bag was hung
   3. _____Solution indicated on the IV bag
   4. _____Volume of solution in the IV bag
   5. _____Milliliters per hour ordered by the primary health-care provider

5. A patient who was in an automobile collision is brought to the emergency department by ambulance. The patient is exhibiting signs and symptoms of multiple trauma. For which common responses to hemorrhage should the nurse assess the patient? **Select all that apply.**
   1. _____Bradypnea
   2. _____Tachycardia
   3. _____Flushed skin
   4. _____Bounding pulse
   5. _____Delayed capillary refill

6. A nurse is caring for several postoperative patients who require common therapeutic interventions that involve the principle of gravity. Identify interventions that are associated with the principle of gravity. **Select all that apply.**
   1. _____Foley catheter
   2. _____Penrose drain
   3. _____Tap-water enema
   4. _____Gastric decompression
   5. _____Portable wound drainage system

7. A nurse is supervising a nursing team consisting of two nurses and two nursing assistants. Which tasks can the nurse delegate to the nursing assistants? **Select all that apply.**
   1. _____Helping a patient who is constipated choose foods from a diet menu
   2. _____Teaching a patient how to walk with a walker
   3. _____Applying antifungal cream to unbroken skin
   4. _____Weighing a patient using a bed scale
   5. _____Emptying a urine collection bag

8. Which actions are based on principles of surgical asepsis? **Select all that apply.**
   1. _____Washing hands
   2. _____Keeping a sterile field dry
   3. _____Holding sterile objects above the waist
   4. _____Wearing personal protective equipment when providing care
   5. _____Considering the outer half inch of the sterile field as contaminated

9. A newly admitted patient's respiratory status is assessed by a nurse who identifies the presence of gurgles and a productive cough. For which additional clinical manifestations associated with this data cluster should the nurse assess the patient? **Select all that apply.**
   1. _____Dyspnea
   2. _____Purulent sputum
   3. _____Decreased blood pressure
   4. _____Decreased pulse oximetry level
   5. _____Bronchovesicular breath sounds

10. A nurse is caring for a patient who is receiving continuous enteral feedings through an enteral tube via the nose. Which nursing interventions support comfort? **Select all that apply.**

1. _____Check tube patency frequently.
2. _____Administer oral hygiene every 2 hours.
3. _____Apply lubricant after cleaning the nares.
4. _____Ensure that the tube is secured to the nose.
5. _____Instill 30 mL of water into the tube every 4 to 6 hours.

11. A patient is receiving a diuretic that contributes to the loss of potassium, and the nurse provides dietary teaching. Which foods selected by the patient indicate an understanding of excellent sources of potassium? **Select all that apply.**

1. _____Cooked spinach
2. _____Baked potato
3. _____Green beans
4. _____Bran flakes
5. _____Lean meat

12. A nurse is caring for a patient who has the following medication prescribed by the primary health-care provider: albuterol sulfate inhalation aerosol 90 mcg, 2 puffs via a metered dose inhaler with a spacer, every 12 hours. Which actions should the nurse teach the patient to implement when using this inhaler? **Select all that apply.**

1. _____Seal the lips around the mouthpiece of the spacer.
2. _____Exhale fully through the nose before taking a dose.
3. _____Breathe in deeply and quickly after activating the canister.
4. _____Rinse the mouth with water and spit it out after the procedure.
5. _____Remove the cap, shake it well, and spray it into the air three times when using a metered dose inhaler for the first time.

13. A nurse is providing dietary teaching for a patient with the diagnosis of osteoporosis. Which foods selected by the patient indicate that the teaching was understood? **Select all that apply.**

1. _____Cheese
2. _____Lettuce
3. _____Peppers
4. _____Oranges
5. _____Sardines

14. Which nursing actions are important when applying antiembolism stockings? **Select all that apply.**

1. _____Eliminating the wrinkles in the stockings
2. _____Ensuring the toe window is properly positioned
3. _____Applying the stockings after the patient is out of bed
4. _____Flexing the knee as the stocking is pulled over the knee
5. _____Removing the stocking once a day for at least thirty minutes

Hot-Spot Items

A hot-spot item asks a question in relation to an illustration. The test taker must identify a location on the illustration that answers the question.

1. A patient with a primary health-care provider's order for bedrest consistently lies in the right lateral position. Place an X over the bony prominence the nurse should assess because it has the **greatest** risk for the development of a pressure ulcer?

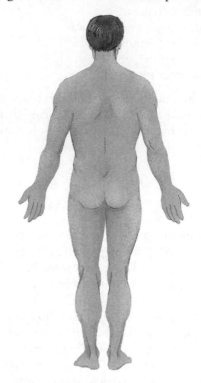

2. A nurse is caring for a patient who had the creation of a colostomy. Place an X over the large intestine that produces the most liquid stool, thereby placing the patient at risk for skin breakdown.

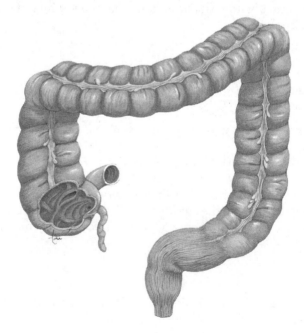

3. A nurse is to administer an intermittent tube feeding via a nasogastric tube. A nurse obtains gastric contents via the nasogastric tube and then assesses the patient's abdomen with a stethoscope when returning the gastric contents. Mark an X where the nurse should place the stethoscope when double-checking placement of the nasogastric tube.

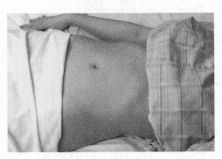

4. A primary health-care provider prescribes heparin 5,000 units subcutaneously twice a day. Place an X over the site that is most commonly used by the nurse to administer this medication.

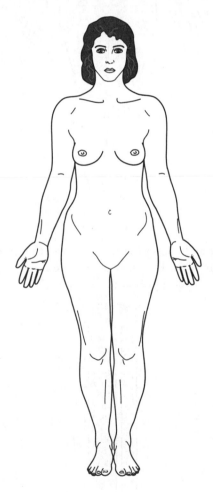

5. Two nurses are performing CPR on a postoperative patient. One nurse performs sternal compressions, and the other delivers breaths and monitors the patient. Place an X over the preferred site to obtain this patient's pulse.

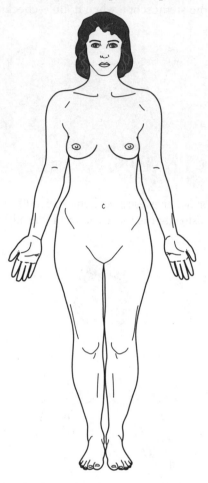

6. After assessing a patient and taking the temperature, the nurse determines that the patient is experiencing pyrexia. Put an X within the range of temperatures on the thermometer scale that reflects pyrexia.

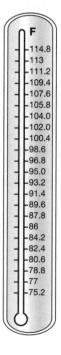

7. A primary health-care provider prescribes diphenhydramine 25 mg PO four times a day to minimize allergy symptoms. Diphenhydramine is supplied as a syrup 12.5 mg/5 mL. Put an X at the point on a graduated medicine cup that indicates the dose of diphenhydramine the nurse must dispense.

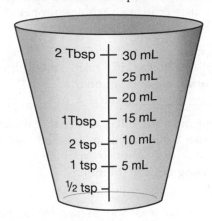

8. A nurse is caring for a patient who is receiving airborne precautions because of tuberculosis. Place an X within the chain of infection when the nurse wears a particulate filter mask (N95 respirator).

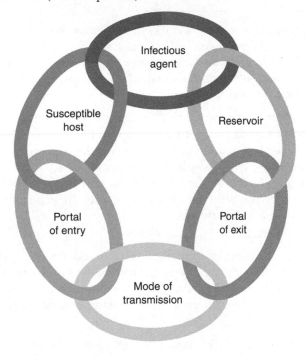

Fill-in-the-Blank Calculation Items

A fill-in-the-blank item asks a question that requires the test taker to perform a calculation. Fill-in-the-blank items are associated with pharmacological and parenteral therapies and other situations requiring a calculation.

1. A primary health-care provider prescribes an antidysrhythmic medication of 2 g in 1,000 mL D_5W at 4 mg/min. At what rate should the nurse set the infusion pump? **Record your answer using a whole number.**
   Answer: _____ mL/hr

2. A primary health-care provider prescribes an antibiotic of 400,000 units IVPB every 6 hours. The medication vial contains 1 million units with the following directions: add 4.6 mL of diluent to yield a concentrated solution of 200,000 units/mL. How much solution of the antibiotic should the nurse prepare to be added to IVBP solution? **Record your answer using a whole number.**
Answer: _____ mL

3. A primary health-care provider prescribes digoxin 0.25 mg PO once daily. Tablets are available that contain 0.125 mg. How many tablets should the nurse administer? **Record your answer using a whole number.**
Answer: _____ tablets

4. A primary health-care provider prescribes diphenhydramine elixir 25 mg PO twice a day for 3 days. The bottle of diphenhydramine states that there are 12.5 mg/mL. When preparing the first dose, how much solution should the nurse administer? **Record your answer using a whole number.**
Answer: _____ mL

5. A primary health-care provider prescribes human recombinant erythropoietin 100 units/kg/dose subcutaneously three times a day for a patient who weighs 110 pounds. The medication states that there are 2,000 units/mL. How much solution should the nurse administer? **Record your answer using one decimal place.**
Answer: _____ mL

6. A primary health-care provider prescribes ondansetron 6 mg to be administered via oral suspension to a 12-year-old child 30 minutes before chemotherapy and then every 8 hours for two more doses. The medication states that there are 4 mg/5 mL. How much oral solution should the nurse administer per dose? **Record your answer using one decimal place.**
Answer: _____ mL

7. A patient initially received ramipril 1.25 mg daily. The dose was increased to 2.5 mg once a day for several days, and finally the primary health-care provider increases the dose to 5 mg every day. The patient says to the nurse, "I still have a lot of 1.25-mg tablets left. Can I use these up with the new dose the doctor prescribed?" How many 1.25 mg tablets should the nurse instruct the patient to take? **Record your answer using a whole number.**
Answer: _____ tablets

8. A primary health-care provider prescribes warfarin sodium 10 mg PO once a day on the even days of the month and 15 mg on the odd days of the month. The 10-mg tablets supplied are scored. How many tablets should the nurse administer on the fifth day of the month? **Record your answer using one decimal place.**
Answer: _____ tablets

9. A primary health-care provider orders an IV infusion of 1,000 mL of D_5W with 20 mEq of potassium chloride to be administered at 125 mL/hr. The infusion set has a drop factor of 15. At how many drops per minute should the nurse set the IV infusion? **Record your answer using a whole number.**
Answer: _____ drops/min

10. A patient has a prescription for regular insulin. The prescription states: administer regular insulin before meals and at bedtime based on the patient's glucose monitoring results.
Blood glucose 71 to 150: no insulin
151 to 200: 3 units
201 to 250: 5 units
251 to 300: 7 units
301 to 350: 9 units
351 to 400: 11 units and call the primary health-care provider

The patient's blood glucose at 11:30 a.m. is 230. How many units of regular insulin should the nurse administer? **Record your answer using a whole number.**

Answer: _____ units

11. A nurse is calculating a patient's intake and output for an 8-hour period of time. The patient has 1,000 mL of 0.9% sodium chloride infusing intravenously at 75 mL/hour. The patient received 2 intermittent doses of an intravenous antibiotic in 50 mL of solution each. The intravenous antibiotic solutions were administered over 20 minutes each via a secondary intravenous line that was hung higher than the primary infusion of sodium chloride. For breakfast the patient had 4 ounces of coffee and 6 ounces of orange juice. For lunch the patient ingested 240 mL of beef broth. Later the patient experienced nausea and vomited 300 mL of greenish fluid. The patient consumed 8 ounces of ice chips. What was the patient's total fluid intake? **Record your answer using a whole number.**

Answer: _____mL

12. A patient who is taking a prescribed liquid oral medication at home calls the clinic for instructions. The dose prescribed is 30 mL but a measuring device is not supplied with the medication. How many tablespoons of the liquid medication should the nurse instruct the patient to take? **Record your answer using a whole number.**

Answer: _____tablespoons

13. A patient with the diagnosis of anorexia nervosa is admitted to the hospital. A nurse is calculating the total calories that the patient ingested for lunch. The patient ate 10 grams of carbohydrates, 4 grams of protein, and 3 grams of fat. How many calories did the patient consume with lunch? **Record your answer using a whole number.**

Answer: _____calories

14. A primary health-care provider prescribes a medication for a patient that should be administered based on body weight. The prescription states to administer 0.5 mg per kilogram of body weight once a day. The patient weighs 160 pounds. How many milligrams of medication should be administered per dose? **Record your answer using one decimal place.**

Answer: _____mg

Graphic Items (Items Using a Graphic, Chart, Table, or Illustration)

An item using a chart, table, or graphic image requires the test taker to refer to the illustration presented to arrive at the correct answer. It tests the ability to identify, calculate, analyze, or interpret data from a chart, table, or graphic image to arrive at the correct answer.

1. A nurse is reviewing a patient's temperatures over the course of hospitalization. What was the patient's temperature on June 7th at 4 p.m.?
   1. 97.8°F
   2. 99.2°F
   3. 101.2°F
   4. 102.6°F

Room No. 104 Hosp. No. 427396

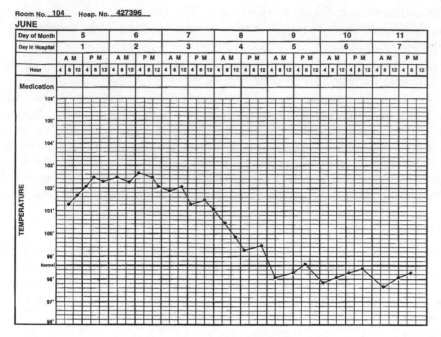

2. A nurse is caring for a patient who has an order for intake and output. Referring to the intake and output flow sheet, what was the patient's total output for the hours between 7 a.m. and 3 p.m.?

1. 355
2. 720
3. 1,300
4. 1,405

DAILY INTAKE AND OUTPUT RECORD

DATE JUNE 5

	INTAKE							OUTPUT			
	I.V. FLUIDS						ORAL	URINE	EMESIS	N.G. TUBE	HEMOVAC
Time	Bottle	Amount	Solution	Medication and Dosage	*ABS.	⊤ LIB					
8	1	1000	NS	20 mEq KCl				650			
8:30							360				
10:00							120				
11:30							240	150			
12:00									160		
1:40									90		60
2:15								250			
3:00						525	475				45
7-3 TOTAL		8-HR TOTAL									
3-11 TOTAL		8-HR TOTAL									
11-7 TOTAL		8-HR TOTAL									
24 HOUR TOTAL											

INTAKE GRAND TOTAL [ ]   OUTPUT GRAND TOTAL [ ]

*ABS. = amount absorbed   ⊤ LIB = left in bag

3. A nurse is making rounds at the beginning of a shift and enters the room of the patient depicted in the photograph. What should the nurse do? **Select all that apply.**
   1. _____Move the straps of the mask to above the patient's ears.
   2. _____Put a second pillow under the patient's head.
   3. _____Obtain the patient's oxygen saturation level.
   4. _____Elevate the head of the patient's bed.
   5. _____Place a hospital gown on the patient.

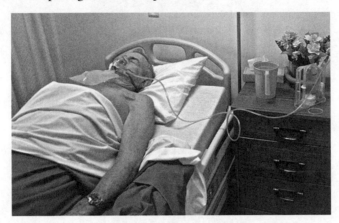

4. A patient is admitted to the emergency department for treatment after stepping on a rusty nail at a job site. The primary health-care provider prescribes tetanus immune globulin 250 units IM STAT. Which illustration indicates the angle at which this injection should be administered by the nurse?
   1. A
   2. B
   3. C
   4. D

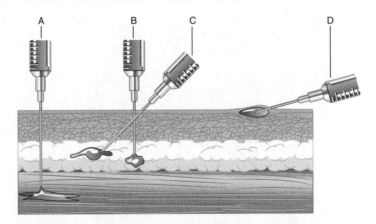

5. A patient is admitted to an extended-care facility after initially recovering from a brain attack resulting in right-sided hemiplegia. The nurse begins passive range-of-motion exercises on the patient's right upper and lower extremities. Which movement is indicated in the illustration?
   1. Inversion
   2. Adduction
   3. Supination
   4. Opposition

6. Which illustration indicates the type of thermometer that the nurse should use to obtain a temperature of an alert and active 2-year-old child?
1. A
2. B
3. C
4. D

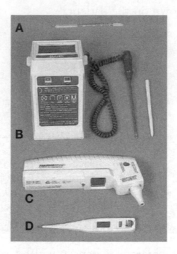

7. Review the illustration, and identify which site the nurse is landmarking for the administration of an intramuscular injection.
1. Dorsogluteal
2. Ventrogluteal
3. Rectus femoris
4. Vastus lateralis

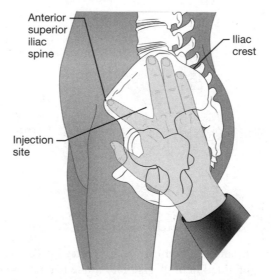

8. What instructions should the nurse give a patient who is using the device in the illustration?
1. Breathe out slowly and completely, seal your mouth around the mouthpiece, press down on the canister, slowly inhale, and hold your breath for ten seconds.
2. Hold the device, seal your mouth around the mouthpiece, and breathe in and out slowly and deeply.
3. Seal your mouth around the mouthpiece and breathe in and out normally.
4. Take a deep breath and forcefully exhale through the mouthpiece.

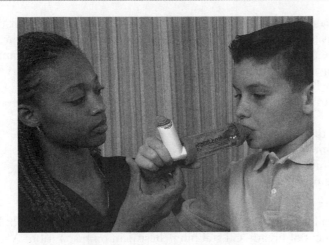

Drag and Drop/Ordered Response Items

A drag and drop/ordered response item presents a situation followed by a list of statements. The test taker is asked to place the statements in order of priority.

1. At the beginning of a 7 a.m. to 7 p.m. shift, a nurse receives a report, which is completed by 7:20 a.m. Place in order of priority the tasks that should be performed by the nurse.
   1. Give a prn pain medication to a patient in pain.
   2. Change a patient's dressing that must be done two times a day.
   3. Obtain the vital signs of a patient reporting shortness of breath.
   4. Administer the ordered 8 a.m. medications to the patients on the unit.
   Answer: _____

2. When assessing a patient's abdomen, nurses should follow a logical sequence. Place these assessments in the order in which they should be performed.
   1. Percuss the suprapubic area to determine bladder distention.
   2. Auscultate the four quadrants of the abdomen for bowel sounds.
   3. Observe the abdomen for contour and visible signs of peristalsis.
   4. Palpate the abdomen to determine the presence of tenderness and fluid.
   Answer: _____

3. A nurse must always be prepared for, and ready to respond to, a fire that may occur on a hospital unit. Place the following activities in the order in which they should be implemented.
   1. Know the location and use of alarms and extinguishers.
   2. Rescue patients in danger when a fire is identified.
   3. Pull the fire alarm to notify others about the fire.
   4. Close doors and windows on the unit.
   5. Be alert for the signs of a fire.
   Answer: _____

4. A nurse plans to reposition an unconscious patient from the supine position to the right side-lying position. Initially, the nurse explains the care to the patient, closes the door for privacy, and performs hand hygiene before touching the patient. Place the following nursing actions in the order they should be performed.
   1. Move the right shoulder and arm forward and downward.
   2. Place the patient's arms across the chest and the left foot over the right foot.
   3. Place pillows behind the patient's back and under the head, left arm, and left leg.
   4. Roll the patient toward the right side using one hand behind the patient's shoulder and the other behind the patient's hip.
   Answer: _____

5. A primary health-care provider orders a soapsuds enema for an adult patient. The nurse explains the procedure to the patient and arranges for the bathroom to be available. The nurse then performs hand washing, collects the equipment, and begins to prepare the enema equipment. Arrange the following interventions in the order in which they should be performed.
   1. Add soap to the container, and gently rock the enema bag to disperse the soap.
   2. Lubricate the catheter tip with water-soluble jelly.
   3. Fill the container with 1,000 mL of 110°F water.
   4. Flush the tubing with water.
   5. Clamp the tubing.
   Answer: _____

6. A patient who had a total abdominal hysterectomy 2 days ago is ambulating and reports shortness of breath and stabbing chest pain on inspiration. A nursing assessment reveals a pulse of 110 beats per minute and respirations of 35 breaths per minute. Place the nursing interventions in priority order.
   1. Administer oxygen.
   2. Assess breath sounds.
   3. Notify the primary health-care provider.
   4. Return the patient to bed by wheelchair.
   5. Place the patient in the high-Fowler position.
   Answer: _____

7. A nurse receives the following information about patients at the change-of-shift report. The nurse plans to assess the following patients in priority order depending on the importance of their needs. List the patients in order based on which patient should be assessed first, progressing to the patient who should be assessed last.
   1. A patient who reported feeling nauseated
   2. A patient who just was informed of having cancer
   3. A patient who is receiving a titrated medication via an infusion pump
   4. A patient whose vital signs include an irregular pulse and labored respirations
   5. A patient who received an analgesic by mouth for pain immediately before report
   Answer: _____

8. An older adult experienced a number of events during the last year while living in an assisted living residence. Place the following events in order progressing from the first-level need to the last-level need according to Maslow's Hierarchy of Needs theory.
   1. Learning how to use a computer
   2. Falling while walking in a hallway
   3. Having an episode of shortness of breath
   4. Being the honoree at a family birthday party
   5. Winning an art contest at the assisted living residence
   Answer: _____

Exhibit Items

An exhibit item asks a question that requires the test taker to analyze and interpret data, which are organized into sections such as information commonly found in a patient's clinical record, physical assessment results, and results of patient/family member interviews. The test taker must review all of this information to arrive at a conclusion to answer the question.

1. An older adult with multiple health problems is admitted to the hospital after a fainting episode. An electrocardiogram reveals a dysrhythmia, and the patient is scheduled for a cardiac catheterization. Twelve hours after admission a nurse reads the collected information about the patient and performs a physical assessment. Which response does the nurse conclude that the patient is exhibiting?
   1. Systemic infection
   2. Anaphylactic shock
   3. Fluid volume excess
   4. Orthostatic hypotension

PATIENT'S CLINICAL RECORD

Health History
Health problems: atherosclerosis, heart failure
Daily medications: digoxin, furosemide

Vital Signs on Admission
Temperature: 100.2°F, oral
Pulse: 94 beats/min, irregular
Respirations: 24 breaths/min
Blood pressure: 150/92 mm Hg

Physical Assessment
Subjective
   Headache
   Extreme fatigue
   Short of breath
Objective
   1+ pitting edema of ankles
   Crackles in base of lungs
   Vital signs
      Pulse—100 beats/min
      Respirations—26 breaths/min
      Blood pressure—170/96 mm Hg

---

2. A 75-year-old man who had been having transient ischemic attacks (TIAs) is admitted to the hospital after experiencing a brain attack (cerebrovascular accident [CVA]). The patient is semicomatose and has right hemiplegia. The nurse reviews the patient's clinical record. Which complication is this patient at the **greatest** risk of developing?
   1. Diarrhea
   2. Hemorrhage
   3. Pressure ulcers
   4. Excessive serum glucose

PATIENT'S CLINICAL RECORD

Physical Assessment
Right hemiplegia
Muscle flaccidity
Urinary and fecal incontinence
Responsive only to painful stimuli

Health History
Atherosclerosis, iron deficiency anemia

Laboratory Tests
RBC: 3.5 million/mcL
WBC: 9,000 mcL
Hb: 10.0 g/dL
Ferritin: 14 ng/mL
Fasting blood glucose: 85 mg/dL

3. A nurse is monitoring a patient who had major abdominal surgery. At 11 a.m. the patient reports difficulty breathing. The nurse reviews the patient's previous vital signs, performs a focused physical assessment, and obtains current vital signs. Which complication should the nurse conclude that the patient may be experiencing?
   1. Pulmonary embolus
   2. Respiratory infection
   3. Subcutaneous emphysema
   4. Postoperative hemorrhage

PATIENT'S CLINICAL RECORD

Vital Signs
10:30 a.m.: P—72 beats/min, R—16 breaths/min, BP—120/72 mm Hg
10:45 a.m.: P—70 beats/min, R—20 breaths/min, BP—118/74 mm Hg

Physical Assessment
Diaphoresis
Blood-tinged sputum
Right-sided chest pain
Dyspnea, decreased breath sounds on right side
Abdomen flat and nontender, abdominal dressing dry and intact

Current Vital Signs—11 a.m.
Temperature 100.2°F, temporal
Pulse: 92 beats/min, regular
Respirations: 28 breaths/min, shallow, labored
Blood pressure: 160/92 mm Hg

4. A nurse is caring for a patient who had abdominal surgery at 8 a.m., 12 hours ago. An abdominal dressing, two Jackson-Pratts, an IV of 1,000 mL of 0.95% NaCl with 20 mEq of KCl at 125 mL/hr, a PCA pump with an analgesic, and a urinary catheter are present. The nurse reviews the clinical record and performs a physical assessment. Which response does the nurse conclude that the patient is experiencing?
   1. Pain
   2. Hemorrhage
   3. Urinary retention
   4. Excess fluid volume

PATIENT'S CLINICAL RECORD

Vital Signs
4 p.m.: P—76 beats/min, R—18 breaths/min, BP—116/72 mm Hg
6 p.m.: P—80 beats/min, R—20 breaths/min, BP—120/76 mm Hg

I&O: 8 a.m. to 8 p.m.
Intake: IVF—1,500 mL
Output: urine—1,050 mL; wound drainage systems—210 mL

Physical Assessment at 8 p.m.
Dressing dry and intact
Pain of 8 on a scale of 0 to 10
IVF intact and infusing at 125 mL/hr
Retention catheter draining clear amber urine, no suprapubic distention
Vital signs: Pulse: 86 beats/min, Respirations: 24 breaths/min, Blood pressure:
    136/80 mm Hg

5. An older adult who is dehydrated is to receive rehydration therapy. The nurse collects a health history, obtains the vital signs, and performs a physical assessment. Which complication is this patient at the **greatest** risk for developing?
1. Infection
2. Aspiration
3. Malnutrition
4. Constipation

PATIENT'S CLINICAL RECORD

Health History
Brain attack 6 months ago
Flu and pneumonia vaccines in past 4 months

Vital Signs
Temperature: 99.6°F, oral
Pulse: 88 beats/min, regular rhythm
Respirations: 22 breaths/min, shallow
Blood pressure: 109/68 mm Hg

Physical Assessment
Lethargic
Dysphagia
Dysarthria
Diminished gag reflex
Skin dry, exhibiting "tenting"
Borborygmi auscultated in all four quadrants

6. An older adult is admitted to the hospital after several days of nausea, vomiting, and diarrhea. The nurse performs an assessment and reviews the patient's clinical record. Which does the nurse conclude that the patient is experiencing based on the data collected?
1. Hypokalemia
2. Hypocalcemia
3. Hypernatremia
4. Hypermagnesemia

PATIENT'S CLINICAL RECORD

Physical Assessment
Patient reports muscle weakness and leg cramps
Decreased bowel sounds
Weak irregular pulses
Weight loss of 8 pounds over the past few days

Laboratory Tests
Serum potassium: 3.1 mEq/L
Serum sodium: 138 mEq/L
Serum magnesium: 2.2 mEq/L
Serum calcium: 9 mg/dL

Medications
Furosemide 40 mg, PO once daily
Simvastatin 20 mg, PO at hour of sleep

7. A patient returns to the surgical unit from the postanesthesia care unit after surgical resection of the colon and removal of numerous regional lymph nodes. Two hours later, after a change-of-shift report, the oncoming nurse reviews the patient's vital signs flow sheet, performs a physical assessment, and interviews the patient. Which patient complication does the nurse identify after considering all the information?
   1. Pain
   2. Atelectasis
   3. Hemorrhage
   4. Constipation

PATIENT'S CLINICAL RECORD

Vital Signs
3 p.m.: P—86 beats/min, R—20 breaths/min, BP—116/70 mm Hg
4 p.m.: P—102 beats/min, R—26 breaths/min, BP—100/60 mm Hg

Physical Assessment—5 p.m.
Vital signs: P—126 beats/min, R—28 breaths/min, BP—86/60 mm Hg
Urinary retention catheter draining clear amber urine, 50 mL in collection bag
Intravenous solution infusing at 125 mL/hr
Absence of bowel sounds, no bowel movement
Two portable wound drainage devices in abdomen; one has 250 mL of sanguineous
   drainage, and the other has 300 mL of sanguineous drainage
Abdominal dressing is dry and intact
Vesicular, bronchovesicular, and bronchial breath sounds heard on auscultation of the lungs
Appears restless (e.g., moving around in bed, clenching and unclenching fists)

Patient Interview
Reports pain as 4 on a 0 to 10 numerical pain scale
Reports feeling anxious

8. A patient who sustained trauma to the right lower extremity in an automobile collision is placed in traction and scheduled for surgery in the morning. The nurse on the orthopedic unit obtains the patient's vital signs, interviews the patient, and reviews the patient's laboratory results. Which data should cause the nurse the **most** concern?

1. Sadness over death of his wife
2. Avoidance of prostate surgery
3. Pulse and respiratory rates
4. Smoking history

PATIENT'S CLINICAL RECORD

Vital Signs
Temperature: 97.8°F, temporal
Pulse: 96 beats/min, regular rhythm
Respirations: 24 breaths/min
Blood pressure: 150/88 mm Hg

Patient Interview
The patient is a 70-year-old retired man whose wife of 42 years died 4 months ago. He stated, "I miss her terribly and I'm so sad." He has 3 married sons and 8 grandchildren. He looks forward to playing with his grandchildren every day. He stated, "I am relatively healthy but I smoke 2 packs of cigarettes a day, am 40 pounds overweight, and drink a glass of wine every night." He has urinary hesitancy and a slow stream from an enlarged prostate but refused surgery. When asked about his current situation he stated, "I am not happy about having surgery for my leg but I really don't have a choice."

Laboratory Results
Hb: 16 g/dL
Hct: 45%
WBC: 8,000 mcL

Multiple-Response Items

1. 1. Pain is caused by irritation of nerve tissue by chemical substances and the pressure of fluid congestion in the area of local trauma.
    2. Heat is caused by an increased blood flow in response to release of histamine at the site of local trauma.
    3. Erythema is caused by an increased blood flow in response to release of histamine and an increased capillary permeability in response to kinins at the site of local trauma or infection.
    4. An increased heart rate is unrelated to the local adaptation syndrome (LAS). An increased heart rate is associated with activation of the sympathetic nervous system related to the general adaptation syndrome (GAS).
    5. A decreased blood pressure is unrelated to the LAS. An increased, not decreased, blood pressure is associated with activation of the sympathetic nervous system related to the GAS.
    6. An elevated blood glucose level is unrelated to the LAS. An elevated blood glucose level occurs in response to secretion of glucocorticoids in the GAS.

2. 1. Ambulation will not prevent blood loss that results in hypovolemia. Providing adequate hydration and assessing for hemorrhage help prevent hypovolemia.
    2. **Ambulation promotes intestinal peristalsis that may result in a bowel movement.**
    3. **Ambulation promotes deep breathing that helps alveoli to expand, preventing the collapse of alveoli (atelectasis).**
    4. Ambulation will not help prevent dehiscence. Supporting the incisional site during coughing, deep breathing, and activity helps prevent dehiscence.
    5. Ambulation will not help prevent infection. The use of sterile technique and hand washing help prevent infection.

3. 1. Apple juice contains approximately 7 mg of sodium per cup and is permitted on a 2-g sodium diet.
    2. **A quarter cup of crumbled feta cheese contains approximately 418 mg of sodium and should be avoided on a 2-g sodium diet.**
    3. **Corned beef contains approximately 800 mg of sodium per 3 ounces and should not be included on a 2-g sodium diet.**
    4. **Most canned soups contain between 800 and 1,000 mg of sodium per cup and are contraindicated on a 2-g sodium diet. Even soups stipulated as low sodium or heart healthy may contain significant amounts of sodium.**
    5. One broccoli spear contains approximately 20 mg of sodium and is permitted on a 2-g sodium diet.

4. 1. It is not necessary to know the drip rate per minute when determining whether an IV is "on time."
    2. **The time that the IV bag was hung is essential for the nurse to know when determining whether an IV is "on time." The nurse must identify how many minutes/hours the IV has been running and then multiply this number by the milliliters of solution ordered by the primary health-care provider per minute/hour. This volume is then deducted from the original volume in the IV bag. The actual volume in the bag should be compared with the volume that should be in the bag. If the volumes match, the IV is "on time"; if there is more fluid than should be in the bag, then the IV is "behind schedule"; and if there is less fluid than should be in the bag, then the IV is "ahead of schedule."**
    3. The solution indicated on the IV bag is necessary to know to ensure that it is identical to the solution ordered by the primary health-care provider, not to determine whether an IV is "on time."
    4. **The volume of solution in the IV bag is essential for the nurse to know to determine whether an IV is "on time." The nurse must identify how many minutes/hours the IV has been running and then multiply this number by the milliliters of solution ordered by the primary health-care provider per minute/hour. This volume is then deducted from the original volume in the IV bag. The actual volume that is in the bag should be compared with**

the volume that should be in the bag. If the volumes match, the IV is "on time"; if there is more fluid than should be in the bag, then the IV is "behind schedule"; and if there is less fluid than should be in the bag, then the IV is "ahead of schedule."

5. The number of milliliters per hour ordered by the primary health-care provider is essential for the nurse to know to determine whether an IV is "on time." The nurse must identify how many minutes/hours the IV has been running and then multiply this number by the milliliters of solution ordered by the primary health-care provider per minute/hour. This volume is then deducted from the original volume in the IV bag. The actual volume that is in the bag should be compared with the volume that should be in the bag. If the volumes match, the IV is "on time"; if there is more fluid than should be in the bag, then the IV is "behind schedule"; and if there is less fluid than should be in the bag, then the IV is "ahead of schedule."

5. 1. Tachypnea, not bradypnea, occurs in response to sympathetic nervous system stimulation as the body attempts to deliver more oxygen to body tissues.
   2. **Tachycardia occurs in response to sympathetic nervous system stimulation as the body attempts to deliver more oxygen to body tissues.**
   3. The skin becomes pale and cold, not flushed, in response to hemorrhage as peripheral vasoconstriction occurs in an attempt to shunt blood to vital organs of the body.
   4. A bounding pulse is reflective of fluid overload (hypervolemia), not hypovolemia associated with hemorrhage. A weak, thready pulse is related to hypovolemia.
   5. Delayed capillary refill occurs in response to peripheral vasoconstriction in an attempt to shunt blood to vital organs.

6. 1. Gravity is the force that pulls mass toward the center of the earth. Urine flows by gravity out of the bladder through a tube (indwelling catheter, Foley catheter) into a collection bag placed below the level of the bladder.

2. A Penrose drain is a flexible collapsible tube with a potential diameter of approximately 1 inch that drains fluid from inside a surgical site to a dressing via gravity.
3. Enema fluid flows from a container through a rectal tube into the large intestine via gravity. The force of the flow is regulated by raising or lowering the height of the enema bag in relation to the anus. Raising the bag increases the force; lowering the bag decreases the force.
4. A nasogastric tube removes fluid from the stomach via negative pressure, not gravity.
5. A portable wound drainage system is a closed system that uses negative pressure, not gravity, to drain secretions from an incisional site.

7. 1. Helping a patient who is constipated choose foods from a diet menu is outside the scope of practice of a nursing assistant. It requires knowledge about foods, fiber, and teaching principles.
   2. Patient teaching is an independent role of the nurse, not a nursing assistant. Teaching a patient how to walk with a walker requires an understanding of anatomy and principles of physics and teaching.
   3. Applying an antifungal cream includes assessment of the area and correct application requiring the knowledge and skill of a nurse. Antifungal cream is a topical medication that requires a primary health-care provider's prescription, and applying it is a dependent function of the nurse.
   4. **Weighing a patient using a bed scale is within the scope of practice of nursing assistants. Nursing assistants can collect vital statistics such as a patient's weight, temperature, pulse, respiration, and intake and output. However, it is the responsibility of the nurse to interpret the results.**
   5. **Emptying a urine collection bag is within the scope of practice of nursing assistants. Nursing assistants have been taught to implement medical aseptic principles and standard precautions. Once the nursing assistant documents the output on the I&O flow sheet, it is the responsibility of the nurse to interpret the results.**

8. 1. Hand washing is based on principles of medical, not surgical, asepsis.

 2. **Keeping a sterile field dry requires actions based on the principles of surgical asepsis. Moisture contaminates a sterile field by facilitating the movement of microorganisms from the unsterile surface below the field to the sterile field by capillary action.**

 3. **Holding sterile objects above the waist is based on a principle of surgical asepsis. Sterile items, including sterile gloved hands, should be held above the waist; when held below the waist, they are considered contaminated because they may be out of the visual field of the nurse.**

 4. Wearing personal protective equipment protects the caregiver and is a principle of medical, not surgical, asepsis.

 5. A 1-inch, not ½-inch, border of a sterile field is considered contaminated. This is based on a principle of surgical, not medical, asepsis.

9. 1. **The presence of gurgles and a cough indicate respiratory impairment. Difficult or uncomfortable breathing (dyspnea) is a clinical manifestation associated with impaired respiratory function.**

 2. **The presence of gurgles and a cough indicate respiratory tract impairment. These clinical manifestations along with purulent sputum may indicate the presence of a respiratory tract infection. A respiratory tract infection can be confirmed with a chest radiograph and sputum culture.**

 3. The presence of gurgles and a cough indicate impaired respiratory function. The blood pressure does not decrease with impaired respiratory function. However, it may increase with respiratory distress because of the influence of the sympathetic nervous system. A decreased blood pressure is associated with a decreased circulating blood volume, which is often caused by dehydration or hemorrhage.

 4. **A pulse oximeter is a device that measures a patient's arterial blood oxygen saturation (Sao_2) via a sensor attached to the patient (e.g., finger, earlobe). A value that is less than 95% indicates respiratory impairment.**

 5. Bronchovesicular breath sounds are expected sounds associated with an uncompromised respiratory function.

10. 1. Checking tube patency does not contribute to comfort. Checking tube patency ensures that the patient is receiving the ordered volume of formula.

 2. **Administering oral hygiene every 2 hours helps prevent drying of the oral mucosa, may relieve thirst, and supports oral comfort.**

 3. **Applying lubricant after cleaning the nares helps prevent drying of the respiratory mucosa of the nares, which supports comfort.**

 4. **Ensuring that the tube is secured to the nose helps reduce friction and trauma to the nares by the tube, which supports comfort.**

 5. Flushing the tubing helps maintain tube patency; it does not contribute to comfort. In addition, flushing the tubing is based on the primary health-care provider's order or a hospital policy.

11. 1. **Spinach is an excellent source of potassium. One cup of cooked spinach contains approximately 838 mg of potassium.**

 2. **A baked potato is an excellent source of potassium. A baked potato, depending on its size, contains approximately 844 to 955 mg of potassium.**

 3. A half cup of green beans provides less than 100 mg of potassium.

 4. Bran flakes do not contain potassium.

 5. Depending on the type of meat, 3 ounces of meat contain only 57 to 323 mg of potassium, and this is not the best choice of the options offered.

12. 1. **Sealing the lips around the mouthpiece prevents medication from escaping from around the mouth and mouthpiece and allows delivery of an accurate dose.**

 2. The patient should exhale through the mouth. Back pressure occurs when exhaling through the nose because the nostrils are smaller than the mouth. When using an inhaler, it is important to empty the lungs of as much air as possible to make a larger surface area available to come into contact with the subsequent inhaled medication.

3. Breathing in deeply is a correct action because it delivers medication deep into the lungs. However, inhalation should be slow, not quick. Inhaling slowly allows for even contact of the medication with the lining of the respiratory tract.

4. Medication in a metered-dose inhaler may cause irritation of the oral mucosa or a fungal infection of the oral cavity. A swish and spit procedure with water reduces the exposure of the oral mucosa to the medication and reduces the risk of irritation to or a fungal infection of the oral cavity.

5. Removing the cap, shaking it well, and spraying it into the air, repeating this three times before using it for the first time, primes the inhaler and ensures that the user is getting the correct dose. Also, this should be done when the inhaler has not been used for 14 or more days or when it has been dropped.

13. 1. Cheese, a dairy product, is an excellent dietary source of calcium. One ounce of cheese contains 150 to 406 mg of calcium depending on the type of cheese. Calcium is essential to maintain bone structure in addition to several neuromuscular, cardiac, and coagulation functions.

2. Lettuce is not high in calcium. One cup of shredded leaf lettuce contains approximately 38 mg of calcium.

3. Peppers are not high in calcium. One pepper contains approximately 4 mg of calcium.

4. Oranges are not high in calcium. One orange contains approximately 52 mg of calcium.

5. Sardines are high in calcium because they contain soft, edible bones. Three ounces of sardines (about seven fish) contain approximately 320 mg of calcium.

14. 1. Wrinkles create ridges causing unnecessary pressure that can lead to tissue injury.

2. The toe window should be positioned over the toes or sole of the feet depending on the manufacturer. This ensures that the stocking is aligned correctly and the distal portion of the foot can be accessed to perform the blanch test to assess peripheral circulation.

3. The stockings should be applied before, not after, the patient gets out of bed. Standing permits the development of dependent edema because of the force of gravity. Putting antiembolism stockings on while still in bed helps prevent dependent edema. If stockings are applied after getting out of bed, they will compress edematous tissues and cause tissue injury.

4. Flexion of the knee impedes, while extension of the knee promotes, application of an antiembolism stocking. Most antiembolism stockings are knee high rather than thigh high.

5. Removing the stocking once a day for at least 30 minutes is inadequate. Antiembolism stockings should be removed every 8 hours for 30 minutes. This permits inspection and physical hygiene.

Hot-Spot Items

1. This site is at risk because it is dependent when lying in a right lateral position; the majority of body mass overlies the greater trochanter. The area over the greater trochanter has limited subcutaneous tissue, and when exposed to pressure more than 32 mm Hg, the capillaries are compressed, and blood does not bring oxygen and nutrients to the tissues.

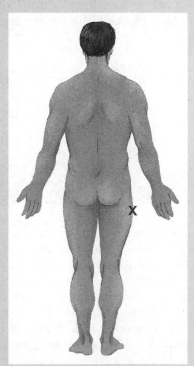

2.   An X anywhere along the highlighted area is the correct answer. This site is the ascending colon, which contains the most liquid stool because it is at the beginning of the large intestine. As stool moves through the large intestine, fluid is reabsorbed, and stool becomes more dry and formed.

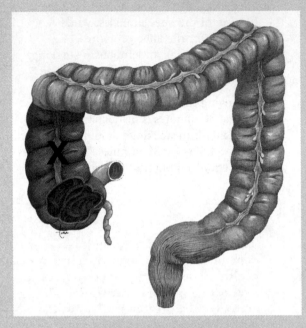

3.   Auscultating over the left upper quadrant slightly to the left of the midsternal line will detect whooshing, gurgling, or bubbling sounds in the stomach as gastric content or air is instilled through the nasogastric tube.

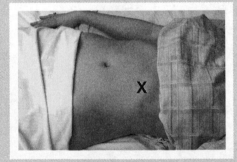

4.   An X anywhere within the shaded area of the illustration is a correct answer. The abdomen, level with or below the level of the umbilicus, is the preferred site for a subcutaneous injection of 5,000 units of heparin. The nurse must avoid the area 2 inches around the umbilicus. The abdomen generally provides a layer of fat located below the dermis and above the muscle for heparin to be administered deep into the subcutaneous tissue. Also, it allows for faster absorption than subcutaneous sites on thighs and buttocks. A large area of subcutaneous tissue, which generally is found over the abdomen, is preferred because heparin may cause a hematoma and pain if accidentally administered intramuscularly.

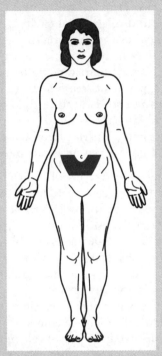

5.   An X over either the right or left carotid artery is a correct answer. The nurse performing sternal contractions is next to the patient's chest and abdomen. The nurse delivering breaths and monitoring the patient is next to the patient's head. The preferred site to assess the pulse is the carotid artery on the side in which the nurse delivering breaths is positioned because the nurse is next to the patient's head.

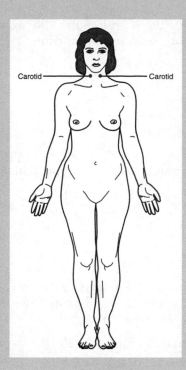

6.   A temperature in the range of 100.4°F
to 105.8°F is called pyrexia or fever. An
X placed anywhere within this range is
a correct answer.

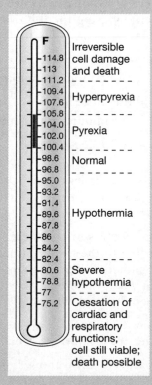

7.   Solve for x using ratio and proportion.

$$\frac{\text{Desired}}{\text{Have}} \quad \frac{25 \text{ mg}}{12.5 \text{ mg}} = \frac{\text{x mL}}{5 \text{ mL}}$$

12.5 x = 125

x = 10 mg

The 10-mL line is the second line up
from the bottom on the right side of
the medicine cup.

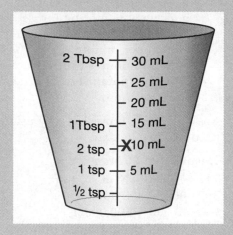

8.   When a nurse wears a particulate filter
mask (N95 respirator), the nurse is
protected from exposure to the
patient's respiratory pathogen,
Mycobacterium tuberculosis.

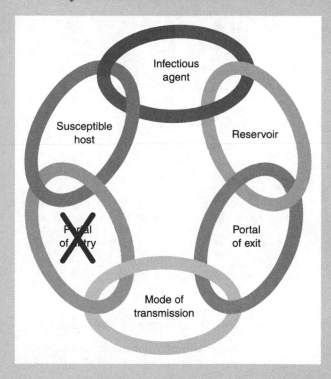

Fill-in-the-Blank Calculation Items

1.   Answer: 120 mL. The nurse has to
calculate how many milliliters to
administer per minute to deliver
4 mg/min. Solve for x using ratio and
proportion after converting 2 g to its
equivalent of 2,000 milligrams.

$$\frac{\text{Desired}}{\text{Have}} \quad \frac{4 \text{ mg}}{2,000 \text{ mg}} = \frac{\text{x mL}}{1,000 \text{ mL}}$$

2,000 x = 4,000

x = 4,000 ÷ 2,000

x = 2 mL (2 mL contains 4 mg)

The hourly volume to be infused is calculated by multiplying the milliliters per minute (2) by the number of minutes (60). Therefore, the infusion pump should be set at 120 mL per hour.

2. Answer: 2 mL. Solve for x by using ratio and proportion.

$$\frac{\text{Desired } 400,000 \text{ mg}}{\text{Have } 200,000 \text{ mg}} = \frac{x \text{ mL}}{1 \text{ mL}}$$
200,000 x = 400,000
x = 400,000 ÷ 200,000
x = 2 mL of the antibiotic solution

3. Answer: 2 tablets. Solve for x by using ratio and proportion.

$$\frac{\text{Desired } 0.25 \text{ mg}}{\text{Have } 0.125 \text{ mg}} = \frac{x \text{ tab}}{1 \text{ tab}}$$
0.125 x = 0.25
x = 0.25 ÷ 0.125
x = 2 tablets

4. Answer: 10 mL. Solve for x by using ratio and proportion.

$$\frac{\text{Desired } 25 \text{ mg}}{\text{Have } 12.5 \text{ mg}} = \frac{x \text{ mL}}{1 \text{ mL}}$$
12.5 x = 125
x = 125 ÷ 12.5
x = 10 mL

5. Answer: 2.5 mL. Use ratio and proportion to convert 110 pounds to kilograms.

$$\frac{\text{Desired } 110 \text{ pounds}}{\text{Have } 2.2 \text{ pounds}} = \frac{x \text{ kg}}{1 \text{ kg}}$$
2.2 x = 110
x = 110 ÷ 2.2
x = 50 (50 kg is equal to 110 pounds)

Now calculate the number of units of medication required using ratio and proportion.

$$\frac{\text{Desired } 50 \text{ kg}}{\text{Have } 1 \text{ kg}} = \frac{x \text{ units}}{100 \text{ units}}$$
1 x = 50 × 100
x = 5,000 units

Now calculate the amount of solution needed to administer the prescribed dose of 5,000 units by using ratio and proportion.

$$\frac{\text{Desired } 5,000 \text{ units}}{\text{Have } 2,000 \text{ units}} = \frac{x \text{ mL}}{1 \text{ mL}}$$
2,000 x = 5,000
x = 5,000 ÷ 2,000
x = 2.5 mL

6. Answer: 7.5 mL. Solve the problem by using ratio and proportion.

$$\frac{\text{Desired } 6 \text{ mg}}{\text{Have } 4 \text{ mg}} = \frac{x \text{ mL}}{5 \text{ mL}}$$
4 x = 30 mL
x = 30 ÷ 4
x = 7.5 mL

7. Answer: 4 tablets. Solve the problem by using ratio and proportion.

$$\frac{\text{Desired } 5 \text{ mg}}{\text{Have } 1.25 \text{ mg}} = \frac{x \text{ tab}}{1 \text{ tab}}$$
1.25 x = 5
x = 5 ÷ 1.25
x = 4 tablets

8. Answer: 1.5 tablets. Solve the problem by using ratio and proportion. Five is an odd-numbered day.

$$\frac{\text{Desired } 15 \text{ mg}}{\text{Have } 10 \text{ mg}} = \frac{x \text{ tab}}{1 \text{ tab}}$$
10 x = 15
x = 15 ÷ 10
x = 1.5 tablets

9. Answer: 31 drops/min. Solve the problem by using the following formula.

$$\frac{\text{Total volume to be infused} \times \text{drop factor}}{\text{Total time in minutes}}$$

$$\frac{125 \text{ (volume to be infused)} \times 15 \text{ (drop factor)}}{1 \text{ hour} \times 60 \text{ minutes}}$$

$$\frac{1,875}{60} = 31.25 \text{ drops/min}$$

Because 0.25 is less than half a drop, round the answer down to 31 drops/min.

10. Answer: 5 units of regular insulin. According to the prescription, the nurse should give 5 units of regular insulin when the blood glucose level is between 201 and 250 mg/dL.

11. Answer: 1,310 mL. Compute the amount of IV solution received.

The patient's intravenous fluid was prescribed at 75 mL/hour. Over an 8-hour period the patient should have received 600 mL of sodium chloride. Every 20 minutes 25 mL of the solution of the primary infusion should have infused. However, the primary infusion was interrupted for 40 minutes while the intermittent antibiotic infusions were administered. Therefore, for 40 minutes the patient received 100 mL of antibiotic solution rather than 50 mL of the primary solution of sodium chloride.

Add the amount of intravenous solution the patient received.

7 hours at 75/hour of the primary sodium chloride infusion = 525 mL.

100 mL of antibiotic solution (two doses of 50 mL each) over 40 minutes = 100 mL.

25 mL of the primary sodium chloride infusion over 20 minutes = 25 mL.

525 + 100 + 25 = 650 mL of intravenous solution (total amount of intravenous solution).

Now compute the patient's amount of oral intake. One ounce is equal to 30 mL.

4 ounces of coffee = 120 mL.

6 ounces of orange juice = 180 mL.

Beef broth = 240 mL.

8 ounces of ice chips = 120 mL. Ice chips are calculated as half their volume when melted.

Add the amount of oral fluid the patient received.

120 + 180 + 240 + 120 = 660 mL.

To determine the total fluid intake for the patient over 8 hours, add the total intravenous intake (650 mL) and the total oral fluid intake (660 mL): 650 mL + 660 mL = 1,310 mL.

12. Answer: 2 tablespoons. There are 15 mL of solution in 1 tablespoon; this is a memorized equivalent. Therefore, 2 tablespoons contain 30 mL of solution. Also, you can solve this problem by using ratio and proportion.

$$\frac{Desired}{Have} \frac{30 \text{ mL}}{15 \text{ mL}} = \frac{x \text{ tablespoons}}{1 \text{ tablespoon}}$$

15 x = 30

x = 30 ÷ 15

x = 2 tablespoons

13. Answer: 83 calories. There are 4 calories per gram of carbohydrate; therefore, 10 × 4 = 40 calories of carbohydrate. There are 4 calories per gram of protein; therefore, 4 × 4 = 16 calories of protein. There are 9 calories per gram of fat; therefore, 3 × 9 = 27 calories. Total the number of calories: 40 + 16 + 27 = 83 calories.

14. Answer: 36.4 mg. First determine how many kilograms are equal to 160 pounds by using a formula for ratio and proportion.

$$\frac{Desired}{Have} \frac{160 \text{ pounds}}{2.2 \text{ pounds}} = \frac{x \text{ kilograms}}{1 \text{ kilogram}}$$

2.2 x = 160

x = 160 ÷ 2.2

x = 72.72 kilograms is equal to 160 pounds.

Next multiply 72.72 kilograms by the ordered dose of 0.5 mg to determine the total dose to be administered. 72.72 × 0.5 = 36.36 mg. Round the dose up to 36.4 because the 6 following the 3 is more than 5. Therefore, the dose is 36.4 mg.

Graphic Items (Items Using a Graphic, Chart, Table, or Illustration)

1. 1. A temperature of 97.8°F occurred on the sixth day of hospitalization (June 10) at 4 a.m.
   2. A temperature of 99.2°F occurred on the fourth day of hospitalization (June 8) at 4 p.m.
   3. Find the box in the top left that indicates "Day of Month." Read toward the right across the row until you see the box with the 7 (indicating the seventh day of the month, also called the third day in hospital, as indicated in the box below it). Look two rows down below the box with the 7 until you see the box with p.m. Now look below the p.m. box for the box with the 4. Guide your eye down the column until you find a dot on a line. From the dot on the line, guide your eye left across the row until you reach the numbers running along the left end of the graph. The nearest dark line below the row with the dot that indicates a full degree of temperature is 101. The dot in the 4 p.m. column is one light-colored line above the 101 line indicating two-tenths of a degree of temperature. Therefore, the dot in the 4 p.m. column indicates a temperature of 101.2°F.
   4. A temperature of 102.6°F occurred on the second day of hospitalization (June 6) at 4 p.m.

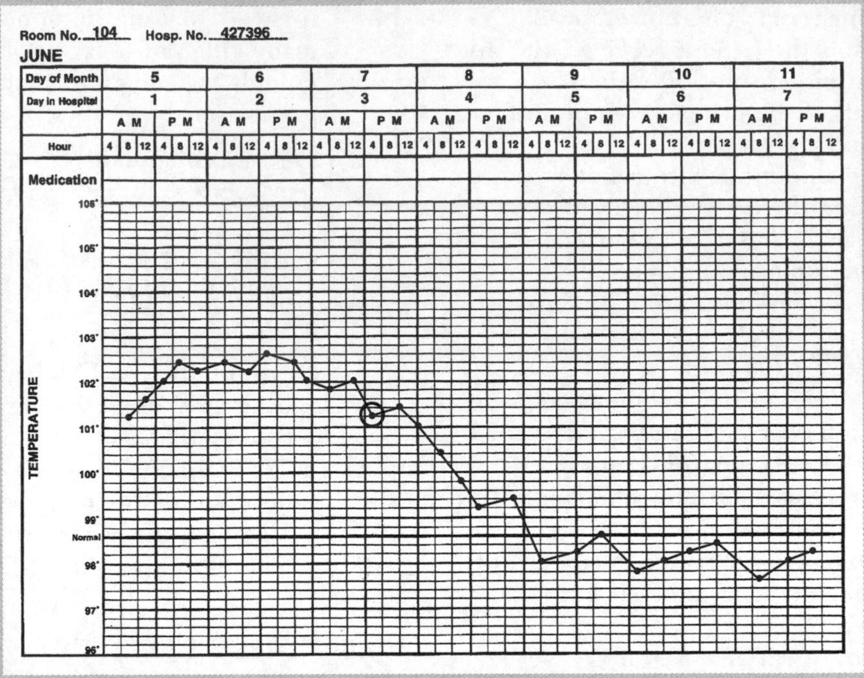

2. 1. This is an incorrect calculation.
   2. This is an incorrect calculation.
   3. This is an incorrect calculation.
   4. The total output between the hours of 7 a.m. and 3 p.m. is 1,405 mL. The nurse must first calculate the urine, emesis, and Hemovac totals and insert the amounts in the "7 to 3 Total" row under the appropriate column. Then the nurse must add the totals of the three columns (1,050 + 250 + 105 = 1,405) to arrive at the overall total output for the hours between 7 a.m. and 3 p.m.

DAILY INTAKE AND OUTPUT RECORD

DATE JUNE 5

INTAKE								OUTPUT			
I.V. FLUIDS							ORAL	URINE	EMESIS	N.G. TUBE	HEMOVAC
Time	Bottle	Amount	Solution	Medication and Dosage	* ABS.	∓ LIB					
8	1	1000	NS	20 mEq KCl	↓			650			
8:30							360				
10:00							120				
11:30							240	150			
12:00									160		
1:40									90		60
2:15								250			
3:00					525	475					45
7-3 TOTAL		8-HR TOTAL			525	475	720	1050	250		105
3-11 TOTAL		8-HR TOTAL									
11-7 TOTAL		8-HR TOTAL									
24 HOUR TOTAL											

INTAKE GRAND TOTAL ☐ OUTPUT GRAND TOTAL ☐

* ABS. = amount absorbed ∓ LIB = Left in bag

3. 1. Moving the straps of the mask to above the ears should be done to ensure that the mask is correctly positioned over the patient's nose and mouth.
   2. Two pillows under the head will flex the neck causing stress and strain on the anatomical structures of the neck which should be avoided. One pillow is sufficient to ensure functional alignment of the head and neck in relation to the torso.
   3. Monitoring a patient's oxygen saturation level is an objective assessment of a patient's respiratory status. This is an important assessment to make at the beginning of a shift and routinely throughout the shift of a patient with an oxygenation problem.
   4. A patient who has a medical condition impairing respiratory function requiring oxygen therapy should be positioned in the mid-Fowler or high-Fowler position. These Fowler positions cause abdominal structures to move down and away from the diaphragm via gravity facilitating respiratory exertion.
   5. A gown should be applied to provide for patient comfort and privacy.

4. 1. This illustration indicates a medication being administered into a muscle. The standard practice for an intramuscular injection is to use a 1.5-inch needle that is administered at 90 degrees into muscle tissue.
   2. This illustration indicates a medication being administered with a ⅝-inch needle inserted at 90 degrees into subcutaneous tissue. A ½-inch needle inserted at 90 degrees into subcutaneous tissue is also an acceptable technique. Both are considered standard practice.
   3. This illustration indicates a medication being administered with a ⅝-inch needle inserted at 45 degrees into the subcutaneous tissue and is considered standard practice.
   4. This illustration indicates an intradermal injection whereby solution is injected just beneath the skin surface.

5. 1. Inversion is when the foot is turned inward medially.
   2. Adduction is when a body part (e.g., leg, arm) is moved toward the midline.

3. Supination is when the forearm and hand are turned facing upward.
4. Opposition is when the thumb is moved so that it touches the tip of each finger.

6. 1. A plastic thermometer that requires insertion into the mouth or rectum is inappropriate for a 2-year-old child. A 2-year-old child does not have the cognitive ability to follow instructions or the behavioral ability to remain still during the 3 minutes required to obtain an accurate temperature.
   2. An electronic thermometer that requires the insertion of a probe into the mouth for the temperature to register is inappropriate for a 2-year-old child. A 2-year-old child does not have the cognitive ability to follow instructions or the behavioral ability to remain still during the 15 to 30 seconds required to obtain an accurate temperature.
   3. An electronic infrared tympanic membrane thermometer is most appropriate from among the options presented for a 2-year-old child because it takes only 2 to 5 seconds to register a temperature. Its ease of use and rapid measurement make it an effective choice for taking the temperature of an alert and active 2-year-old child.
   4. A plastic digital thermometer requires the insertion of a probe into the mouth or rectum for 10 or more seconds for an accurate result and is inappropriate for a 2-year-old child. A 2-year-old child does not have the cognitive ability to follow instructions or the behavioral ability to remain still during the 10 or more seconds required to obtain an accurate temperature.

7. 1. This is not an illustration landmarking the dorsogluteal site. To landmark the dorsogluteal site, the nurse palpates the posterior superior iliac spine and then draws a line to the greater trochanter. The dorsogluteal site is superior to halfway along this line.
   2. This is an illustration landmarking the ventrogluteal site. Place the heel of the hand on the greater trochanter with the fingers toward the patient's head. Use the right hand for the patient's left hip and the left hand for patient's right

hip. Place the index finger on the patient's anterior superior iliac spine, and stretch the middle finger dorsally (toward the buttocks), palpating the iliac crest and then pressing below it. The triangle formed by the third finger, the index finger, and the edge of the crest of the ilium is the ventrogluteal site.

3. This is not an illustration of the rectus femoris site. The rectus femoris is on the anterior aspect of the thigh.

4. This is not an illustration landmarking the vastus lateralis site. To landmark the vastus lateralis, the nurse identifies the middle third of the vastus lateralis muscle that is on the anterior lateral aspect of the thigh. It is within a rectangular area between a handbreadth above the knee and a handbreadth below the greater trochanter of the femur.

8. 1. These are the instructions for using a metered-dose inhaler, which is the device in the photograph. A prefilled pressurized canister delivers a measured dose of medication, which is inhaled by the patient. The patient must coordinate pushing the canister and inhaling the medication. This photograph exhibits a metered-dose inhaler with an extender (spacer). Rather than delivering a dose via a mouthpiece directly into the patient's mouth, a dose is pumped into the extender's chamber, where it is then inhaled by the patient. An extender can increase the volume of medication that moves deep into the lungs.

2. These are the instructions for using a nebulizer. A nebulizer is a medication delivery system that produces an aerosol spray that is inhaled via a mouthpiece. Breathing deeply and slowly facilitates contact of the medication with the respiratory tract mucosa.

3. These are instructions for assessing tidal volume. Tidal volume is the volume of air inhaled and exhaled with each normal breath, which is approximately 500 mL.

4. These are the instructions for using a peak expiratory flow meter (PEFM), which measures the peak expiratory flow rate (PEFR). A PEFR is the volume of air that can be forcefully exhaled after a deep inspiration.

Drag and Drop/Ordered Response Items

1. **3.** The basics of assessment should follow the ABCs (airway, breathing, and circulation). Shortness of breath reflects a potential respiratory or cardiac problem, and a further assessment is the priority.

    1. Relieving pain is a basic physiological and safety/security need. Relief from pain is not as high a priority as maintaining a patient's respiratory status but is more important than routine tasks.

    4. Administering medications is a dependent function of the nurse. It is accepted practice that medications ordered for 8 a.m. can be dispensed up to 1 hour before or 1 hour after the ordered time.

    2. A task ordered twice a day gives the nurse a range in the time frame in which it must be performed. Among the tasks presented, this task can be performed last because the others have greater priority.

2. **3.** Inspection uses purposeful observation in a systematic manner. It does not require touching the patient; therefore, it will not precipitate a response that will influence future assessments.

    2. Auscultation involves listening to sounds produced within the body. It requires the gentle placement of a warmed stethoscope progressively over all four quadrants of the abdomen; it will minimally influence future assessments.

    4. Palpation is the use of touch to assess temperature, turgor, texture, dampness, vibration, shape, and presence of fluid. Areas of tenderness are palpated last in the palpation process. Light palpation may cause responses that influence future assessments, but it is less invasive than another assessment listed.

    1. Percussion is striking a part of the body with short, sharp blows of the fingers. The sound obtained helps to determine the size, position, and density of the underlying body parts. It should be performed last in the assessment process because it is the most disruptive.

3. 1. Knowing where fire alarms/
    extinguishers are located saves time in
    the event of a fire.
5. By identifying a fire early, it may be
    extinguished quickly before it becomes
    a danger to patients.
2. Once the presence of a fire is
    identified, patients in danger must be
    rescued to prevent patient injury.
3. The fire alarm should be activated once
    patients in the immediate vicinity of
    the fire are removed from danger.
4. After patients in danger are moved
    to safety and the fire alarm is activated,
    the nurse should close all doors and
    windows on the unit to contain
    the fire.

4. 2. Crossing the arms facilitates turning
    and protects the patient's arms.
    Crossing the left leg over the right leg
    uses the patient's weight to facilitate
    movement.
4. Turning the patient with the hands
    spread apart and at strategic points of
    the patient's anatomy permits the body
    to turn along its vertical axis,
    minimizing strain on the patient's
    vertebral column.
1. Moving the right shoulder and arm
    forward and downward minimizes
    pressure on the ball-and-socket joint
    and rotator cuff of the shoulder.
3. Pillows under the head and extremities
    keep them in functional alignment. A
    pillow behind the back maintains the
    patient on the side and keeps the
    vertebral column in functional
    alignment.

5. 5. Clamping the tubing allows the water
    to collect in the container once it is
    added.
3. Soapsuds enema for an adult should be
    500 to 1,000 mL of water at 105°F to
    110°F. The volume is sufficient to
    distend the intestinal lumen, and the
    temperature is slightly more than body
    temperature to provide for comfort.
4. This action expels air from the tubing
    and prevents air from entering the
    intestine.
1. Soap is added after the container is
    filled to prevent the formation of
    bubbles and after the tubing is flushed
    to ensure that the soap is diluted in the
    total volume of solution (3 to 5 mL of

soap per 1,000 mL of water). Gently
rocking the enema bag prevents bubble
formation while dispersing the soap
evenly throughout the fluid.
2. The catheter is lubricated to limit
    trauma as the catheter is inserted into
    the patient's anus and rectum.

6. 4. The patient most likely experienced a
    pulmonary embolus. Using a wheelchair
    limits muscle activity. Activity can
    contribute to more emboli and increase
    the demand on the heart and lungs.
5. The high-Fowler position facilitates
    thoracic expansion and respirations,
    which are necessary to promote
    pulmonary functioning.
1. Administering oxygen is essential to
    provide more oxygen for gas exchange,
    which will increase oxygen to body
    cells.
2. After initial interventions the nurse can
    take the time to auscultate breath
    sounds to collect information that may
    be helpful to the primary health-care
    provider when making a medical
    diagnosis.
3. The primary health-care provider
    should be notified after immediate
    interventions are performed to assess
    and facilitate respirations.

7. 4. This patient should be assessed first.
    These vital signs are outside the
    expected range; therefore, this patient
    should be assessed first because these
    adaptations may indicate a life-
    threatening situation.
2. This patient should be assessed second.
    The diagnosis of cancer may have
    precipitated a crisis for this patient.
    Psychosocial needs of patients are as
    important as physiological needs.
1. This patient should be assessed third.
    Although nausea should be assessed, it
    is not life-threatening. Other patients
    are a greater priority.
3. This patient should be assessed fourth.
    Infusion pumps deliver fluid volumes
    safely. Other patient situations are a
    greater priority.
5. This patient should be assessed last.
    An analgesic by mouth takes
    approximately 30 minutes to be
    effective. This patient's response to the
    medication can be evaluated after other
    patients' needs are met.

8. **3.** Having an episode of shortness of breath is related to physiologic needs, the first step of Maslow's Hierarchy of Needs theory.
   2. Experiencing a fall is related to safety and security needs, the second step of Maslow's Hierarchy of Needs theory.
   4. Being the honoree at a family birthday party is related to loving and belonging needs, the third step of Maslow's Hierarchy of Needs theory.
   5. Winning an art contest at the assisted living residence is related to self-esteem needs, the fourth step of Maslow's Hierarchy of Needs theory.
   1. Learning how to use a computer is related to self-actualization needs, the fifth step of Maslow's Hierarchy of Needs theory.

Exhibit Items

1.   Answer: 3. Fluid volume excess

PATIENT'S CLINICAL RECORD

Health History
Health problems:
  Atherosclerosis
  Heart failure
Daily medications:
  Digoxin
  Furosemide

Vital Signs on Admission
Temperature: 100.2°F, oral
Pulse: 94 beats/min, irregular
Respirations: 24 breaths/min
Blood pressure: 150/92 mm Hg

Physical Assessment
Subjective:
  Headache
  Extreme fatigue
  Short of breath
Objective:
  1+ pitting edema of ankles
  Crackles in base of lungs
  Vital signs:
    Pulse—100 beats/min
    Respirations—26 breaths/min
    Blood pressure—170/96 mm Hg

---

1. Although the patient is manifesting increases in temperature, pulse, respirations, and blood pressure, which are associated with a systemic infection, the patient is not experiencing the other classic responses to a systemic infection which include chills, diaphoresis, malaise, and change in mental status.
2. Anaphylactic shock, caused by exposure to an allergen, is manifested by anxiety, tachypnea, throat tightness, stridor, diaphoresis, flushing, and urticaria. Except for tachypnea, none of the other responses are exhibited by the patient.
3. Fluid volume excess in this situation is caused by the inefficient pumping action of the heart. A decreased cardiac output results in decreased renal perfusion that stimulates a renin/angiotensin response; this precipitates vasoconstriction and the increased release of aldosterone, which causes sodium and fluid retention, resulting in a fluid volume excess. The patient has a history of heart failure and has been receiving digoxin, which slows and strengthens the heart rate and acts as a mild diuretic, and furosemide, which is a loop diuretic. Objective data: the vital signs have increased, particularly the blood pressure, which indicates an increase of fluid in the intravascular compartment, and the pulse and respirations, which indicate an attempt to increase the amount of oxygen being delivered to body cells. Pitting edema results because of the movement of excess fluid from the intravascular to the interstitial compartment. Crackles in the lungs indicate pulmonary edema associated with fluid moving from the capillaries in the lung into the alveoli. Subjective data: these symptoms all support a fluid volume excess as the body responds to the excess accumulated fluid.
4. Orthostatic hypotension, caused by inefficient vasomotor responses in the circulatory system, is manifested by lightheadedness, vertigo, weakness, and diaphoresis when transferring from lying to sitting or from sitting to standing. The patient is not experiencing these physiological responses.

2.   **Answer: 3. Pressure ulcers**

PATIENT'S CLINICAL RECORD

Physical Assessment
Right hemiplegia
Muscle flaccidity
Urinary and fecal incontinence
Responsive only to painful stimuli

Health History
Atherosclerosis
Iron deficiency anemia

Laboratory Tests
RBC: 3.5 million/mcL
WBC: 9,000 mcL
Hb: 10.0 g/dL
Ferritin: 14 ng/mL
Fasting blood glucose: 85 mg/dL

1. The patient is unable to control the passage of stool (fecal incontinence) and does not have diarrhea. Diarrhea is the passage of three or more liquid or unformed stools a day.
2. No data indicate the presence of hemorrhage. The CVA may be related to the development of a thrombus or embolus associated with the history of atherosclerosis and TIAs.
3. The patient is anemic. Older men should have an RBC count of 3.7 to 6.0 million/mcL; Hb level of 11.0 to 17.0 g/dL; and serum ferritin value of 18 to 270 ng/mL. The patient is underweight and has less subcutaneous fat because of aging. Urine and feces are irritating to the skin because of their acidity and enzyme content, respectively. The presence of inadequate nutrition, the inability to move the right side of the body, the potential presence of urine and feces on the skin, and the characteristics of skin in the aged all create a risk for pressure ulcers.
4. The patient's serum glucose is within the acceptable range for an older adult (70 to 120 mg/dL).

3.   **Answer: 1. Pulmonary embolus**

PATIENT'S CLINICAL RECORD

Vital Signs Flow Sheet
10:30 a.m.: P—72 beats/min, R—16 breaths/min, BP—120/72 mm Hg
10:45 a.m.: P—70 beats/min, R—20 breaths/min, BP—118/74 mm Hg

Physical Assessment
Diaphoresis
Blood-tinged sputum
Right-sided chest pain
Dyspnea, decreased breath sounds on the right side
Abdomen flat and nontender, abdominal dressing dry and intact

Vital Signs—11 a.m.
Temperature: 100.2°F, temporal
Pulse: 92 beats/min, regular
Respirations: 28 breaths/min, shallow, and labored
Blood pressure: 160/92 mm Hg

1. When an embolus obstructs an artery in the lung, it interrupts gas exchange at the cellular level. This precipitates unilateral chest pain, blood-tinged sputum (hemoptasis), and respirations that become rapid, shallow, and labored (dyspnea). Decreased breath sounds occur over the affected alveoli as a result of the lack of gas exchange. Diaphoresis and an increase in vital signs occur as a result of the release of epinephrine.
2. Although the patient is in respiratory distress, the patient responses do not support the presence of a respiratory infection. With a respiratory infection the sputum would be yellow or green rather than blood tinged unless the infection was severe and prolonged, which is unlikely because of preoperative testing. Also, the temperature would be elevated. A temperature of 100.2°F is common after the stress of surgery.
3. The patient is not exhibiting manifestations of subcutaneous

emphysema. Tenderness and crackling occur when suspect tissue is palpated. Subcutaneous emphysema is the presence of air in the subcutaneous tissue; this may occur with an open pneumothorax or around the side of a thoracotomy tube.

4. The patient is not experiencing hemorrhage. The dressing is dry and intact, and the abdomen is flat and nontender. Also, the blood pressure increased rather than decreased. If the patient were hemorrhaging, the blood pressure would decrease as a result of hypovolemia.

4. Answer: 1. Pain

PATIENT'S CLINICAL RECORD

Vital Signs
4 p.m.: P—76 beats/min, R—18 breaths/min, BP—116/72 mm Hg
6 p.m.: P—80 beats/min, R—20 breaths/min, BP—120/76 mm Hg

I&O: 8 a.m. to 8 p.m.
Intake: IVF—1,500 mL
Output: urine—1,050 mL; wound drainage systems—210 mL

Physical Assessment at 8 p.m.
Dressing dry and intact
Pain of 8 on a scale of 0 to 10
IVF intact and infusing at 125 mL/hr
Retention catheter draining clear amber urine, no suprapubic distention
Vital Signs:
  Pulse: 86 beats/min
  Respirations: 24 breaths/min
  Blood pressure: 136/80 mm Hg

---

1. The patient is in pain, as evidenced by a rating of 8 on a pain scale of 0 to 10. The increase in the pulse, respirations, and blood pressure reflects the response to the stress-related catecholamines.
2. The patient is not hemorrhaging. If the patient were hemorrhaging, the blood pressure should have decreased, not increased, the portable wound drainage systems would contain more than 210 mL, and the dressing may have evidence of blood.
3. The patient is not experiencing urinary retention. The urinary retention catheter

is draining clear amber urine, the suprapubic area is not distended, and the I&O are approximately equal, taking into consideration the fluid lost during surgery.

4. If the patient were experiencing excess fluid volume, the blood pressure would be much higher, and the fluid intake would exceed the output on the I&O record.

5. Answer: 2. Aspiration

PATIENT'S CLINICAL RECORD

Health History
Brain attack 6 months ago
Flu and pneumonia vaccines in past 4 months

Vital Signs
Temperature: 99.6°F, oral
Pulse: 88 beats/min, regular rhythm
Respirations: 22 breaths/min, shallow
Blood pressure: 109/68 mm Hg

Physical Assessment
Lethargic
Dysphagia
Dysarthria
Diminished gag reflex
Skin dry, exhibiting "tenting"
Borborygmi auscultated in all four quadrants

---

1. Although older adults have a diminished immune system, the patient is not at high risk for an infection because of medical aseptic practices in the hospital and the fact that the patient has received appropriate immunizations.
2. The patient is exhibiting imperfect articulation of speech (dysarthria), difficulty swallowing (dysphagia), a diminished gag reflex, and lethargy, which all are associated with brain attack (stroke, cerebrovascular accident). These clinical manifestations place the patient at high risk for aspiration. Airway is the priority as per the ABCs (airway, breathing, and circulation) of patient assessment.
3. With a mechanical soft diet and supervision during meals, the patient should ingest adequate nutrients to prevent malnutrition.

4. Although constipation may occur in the patient because of lethargy and decreased peristalsis associated with aging, the complication of constipation is not as likely as a complication in another option. The patient has borborygmi in all four quadrants of the abdomen, indicating the presence of intestinal peristalsis. Also, if constipation occurs, it can be diminished with stool softeners.

6. **Answer: 1. Hypokalemia**

PATIENT'S CLINICAL RECORD

Physical Assessment
Patient reports muscle weakness and leg cramps
Decreased bowel sounds
Weak irregular pulses
Weight loss of 8 pounds over the past few days

Laboratory Tests
Serum potassium: 3.1 mEq/L
Serum sodium: 138 mEq/L
Serum magnesium: 2.2 mEq/L
Serum calcium: 9 mg/dL

Medications
Furosemide 40 mg, PO once daily
Simvastatin 20 mg, PO at hour of sleep

1. **Muscle weakness, leg cramps, decreased bowel sounds, and a weak, irregular pulse are all clinical manifestations of hypokalemia. The serum potassium level of 3.1 mEq/L is below the expected range of 3.5 to 5.0 mEq/L. Furosemide is a diuretic that prevents the reabsorption of water and electrolytes from the tubules of the kidney into the bloodstream. When fluid is lost in response to furosemide, potassium is also eliminated, increasing the risk for hypokalemia. In addition, potassium is lost via vomiting and diarrhea. Weight loss occurs with dehydration.**
2. The patient is not experiencing hypocalcemia. The serum calcium level of 9 mg/dL is within the expected range of 8.5 to 10.5 mg/dL. The patient is not exhibiting the following clinical manifestations of hypocalcemia: depressed deep tendon reflexes, bone pain, polyuria, lethargy, and a positive Chvostek or Trousseau sign.

3. The patient is not experiencing hypernatremia. The serum sodium level of 138 mEq/dL is within the expected range of 135 to 145 mEq/L. Although the patient has nausea, vomiting, and muscle weakness, which are associated with hypernatremia, the patient is not exhibiting the following clinical manifestations of hypernatremia: thirst; dry, sticky mucous membranes; red, dry, swollen tongue; confusion; and agitation.
4. The patient is not experiencing hypermagnesemia. The serum magnesium level of 2.2 mEq/L is within the normal range of 1.5 to 2.5 mEq/L. The patient is not exhibiting the following clinical manifestations of hypermagnesemia: peripheral vasodilation, flushing, paralysis, hypotension, bradycardia, lethargy, and respiratory depression.

7. **Answer: 3. Hemorrhage**

PATIENT'S CLINICAL RECORD

Vital Signs
3 p.m.: P—86 beats/min, R—20 breaths/min, BP—116/70 mm Hg
4 p.m.: P—102 beats/min, R—26 breaths/min, BP—100/60 mm Hg

Physical Assessment—5 p.m.
Vital signs: P—126 beats/min, R—28 breaths/min, BP—86/60 mm Hg
Urinary retention catheter draining clear amber urine, 50 mL in collection bag
Intravenous solution infusing at 125 mL/hr
Absence of bowel sounds, no bowel movement
Two portable wound drainage devices in abdomen; one has 250 mL of sanguineous drainage, and the other has 300 mL of sanguineous drainage
Abdominal dressing is dry and intact
Vesicular, bronchovesicular, and bronchial breath sounds heard on auscultation of the lungs
Appears restless (e.g., moving around in bed, clenching and unclenching fists)

Patient Interview
Reports pain as 4 on a 0 to 10 numerical pain scale
Reports feeling anxious

1. A 4 on a pain scale of 0 to 10 usually indicates that the patient can tolerate the pain and perform essential activities.

2. Atelectasis is an incomplete expansion of the lung. Although restlessness and anxiety may accompany atelectasis, other clinical findings should include dyspnea, diminished breath sounds over the affected area, crackles, and cyanosis. Vesicular, bronchovesicular, and bronchial breath sounds heard on auscultation of the lungs are expected breath sounds and indicate effective pulmonary functioning.

3. **Hemorrhage is an excessive loss of blood. It is evidenced by sympathetic nervous system–precipitated responses such as tachycardia (heart rate more than 100 beats/min), tachypnea (respiratory rate more than 20 breaths/min), presence of behavioral signs of restlessness, and reports of feeling anxious. The decrease in the systolic and diastolic blood pressures reflects the decrease in the circulating blood volume. The inadequate urinary output in relation to the fluid intake reflects a decrease in kidney perfusion and the kidney's attempt to conserve fluid because of the decreased circulating blood volume. The collection of 550 mL of blood in the portable wound drainage systems is excessive. The patient is experiencing internal hemorrhage.**

4. Constipation is infrequent bowel movements (fewer than 2 per week) or hard, dry feces. After abdominal surgery, particularly surgery involving the intestine, peristalsis will be interrupted temporarily because of the effects of anesthesia and the manipulation of the intestines. The absence of bowel sounds and a bowel movement is not significant at this time.

8. Answer: 4. Smoking history

1. The patient's sadness over the death of his wife is within the realm of expected grieving because the death occurred only 4 months ago. The fact that he looks forward to playing with his grandchildren every day indicates that he is looking toward the future.

2. Although the patient's avoidance of prostate surgery may be a concern in the future, it is not the priority at this time.

PATIENT'S CLINICAL RECORD

Vital Signs
Temperature: 97.8°F, temporal
Pulse: 96 beats/min, regular rhythm
Respirations: 24 breaths/min
Blood pressure: 150/88 mm Hg

Patient Interview
The patient is a 70-year-old retired man whose wife of 42 years died 4 months ago. He stated, "I miss her terribly and it makes me so sad." He has 3 married sons and 8 grandchildren. He looks forward to playing with his grandchildren every day. He stated, "I am relatively healthy but I smoke 2 packs of cigarettes a day, am 40 pounds overweight, and drink a glass of wine every night." He has urinary hesitancy and a slow stream from an enlarged prostate but refused surgery. When asked about his current situation he stated, "I am not happy about having surgery for my leg but I really don't have a choice."

Laboratory Results
Hb: 16 g/dL
Hct: 45%
WBC: 8,000 mcL

3. A pulse of 96 beats per minute and respirations of 24 breaths per minute most likely are in response to anxiety associated with the scheduled surgery. Although the patient is unhappy with the need for surgery and the nurse should explore the patient's feelings, they are not as much a concern as another option.

4. **Based on Maslow's hierarchy of needs the patient's smoking history poses a serious physiological concern about his respiratory status. The reduced respiratory compensatory reserve associated with aging, the 2 pack a day smoking history, and the fact that general anesthesia will be administered during surgery to repair his right leg place him at risk for impaired oxygenation.**

Comprehensive Final Book Exam

This 100-item examination provides an opportunity to take a test that integrates content from among the topics included in Chapters 2 through 5. It includes alternate item formats that reflect the questions presented in Chapter 6. The answer(s) and rationales are provided to enhance your knowledge concerning the information being tested in each question. A Critical-Thinking Strategy (the RACE model), which is described in Chapter 1, is applied to every question to illustrate a methodical approach to analyze questions, eliminate options, and arrive at the correct answer.

COMPREHENSIVE FINAL BOOK EXAM

1. Which early responses indicate to the nurse that the patient is experiencing hypoxia? **Select all that apply.**
   1. _____Increased heart rate
   2. _____Difficulty breathing
   3. _____Restlessness
   4. _____Bradypnea
   5. _____Irritability

2. A patient has a history of chronic pain because of arthritis but dislikes taking large doses of analgesics. Which concept unique to unrelieved chronic pain should the nurse consider when caring for this patient?
   1. Generally, pain is better tolerated as the duration of exposure increases.
   2. Pain minimally interferes with activities of daily living.
   3. Usually, pain is related to the current pathology.
   4. Pain rarely affects the immune response.

3. A nurse is assessing several patients who had surgery the previous day. Which sudden patient response should the nurse identify as a potential life-threatening event?
   1. Slightly elevated temperature
   2. Separation of wound edges
   3. Edema of the legs
   4. Chest pain

4. A patient states, "I like to have a bowel movement every morning." Which additional information collected by the nurse supports a concern with perceived constipation?
   1. Hard, dry stools defecated daily
   2. Laxatives used excessively
   3. Abdominal distention
   4. Straining at stool

5. A nurse must administer a sedative to a patient before surgery. Which should the nurse do **first**?
   1. Verify that the preoperative checklist is completed.
   2. Check that the surgical consent is signed.
   3. Ensure an intravenous line is in place.
   4. Assess vital signs.

6. A primary health-care provider prescribes 500 mg of an antibiotic to be administered IVPB every 6 hours for a patient with a systemic infection. The vial dispensed by the hospital pharmacist contains 1 g of the prescribed antibiotic in powder form. The instructions on the vial state: "Instill 9.6 mL to yield 10 mL." How many milliliters of the antibiotic should the nurse add to the IVPB bag? **Record your answer using a whole number.**

   Answer: _____ mL

7. Which mechanism is designed to facilitate tracking a patient's progress as a cost-containment strategy in managed care?
   1. Primary nursing
   2. Critical pathways
   3. Functional method
   4. Quality management

8. A nurse is assisting a patient who has cognitive deficits with a bed bath. Which is important for the nurse to do?
   1. Explain in detail everything that will be done during the bath before beginning.
   2. Arrange the basin within the center of the patient's visual field.
   3. Encourage attention to each task of bathing.
   4. Check the patient every few minutes.

9. When interviewing the wife of a patient, which statements about her husband support the presence of obstructive sleep apnea? **Select all that apply.**
   1. _____ "He snores and gasps all night long and wakes me up."
   2. _____ "He falls asleep sometimes when he drives, so now I do all the driving."
   3. _____ "He kicks and thrashes so much that the bed linen is upside down by morning."
   4. _____ "He has nightmares that are so scary that he wakes me up because he is afraid."
   5. _____ "He has these episodes and never wakes up but I do and then I can't get back to sleep."

10. A primary health-care provider orders a clear liquid diet for a patient who had abdominal surgery 3 days ago. Which does the nurse conclude is the reason why a clear liquid diet was ordered for this patient?
    1. Relieves abdominal distention
    2. Stimulates digestive enzymes
    3. Prevents postoperative ileus
    4. Digests easily

11. For which common problem associated with prolonged diarrhea should the nurse assess a patient with this problem?
    1. Skin breakdown
    2. Self-care deficit
    3. Sexual dysfunction
    4. Disturbed body image

12. A nurse causes harm to a hospitalized patient because of improper use of medical equipment. Which is this tort specifically called?
    1. Battery
    2. Assault
    3. Negligence
    4. Malpractice

13. A patient with type 2 diabetes is experiencing blurred vision, generalized weakness, and fatigue. A nurse receives a report from the nurse on the previous shift and obtains additional information from the patient's clinical record. Which should the nurse conclude that the patient is experiencing?
1. Fluid retention
2. Kidney impairment
3. Hyperglycemic event
4. Hypertensive episode

PATIENT'S CLINICAL RECORD

Laboratory Results
BUN: 18 mg/dL
Creatinine: 1.2 mg/dL
Hemoglobin A_{1c}: 8%
Serum glucose: 350 mg/dL

I&O Record (past 24 hours)
Intake: 2,400 mL
Output: 4,200 mL

Nursing Progress Note
10 a.m.—patient reports "being thirsty and urinating a lot" and has lost 20 pounds over the past 2 months; has poor skin turgor and dry mucous membranes.

14. Nurses on a unit are personally and professionally mature and motivated. Which classic leadership style should the nurse manager employ when working with this group?
1. Directive
2. Autocratic
3. Democratic
4. Laissez-faire

15. A nurse transfers a patient from a bed to a wheelchair. Which is an important nursing intervention after placing the patient in the wheelchair?
1. Ensure the patient's popliteal areas are not touching the seat edge.
2. Attach the patient's transfer belt to clips on the wheelchair.
3. Support the patient's back with a pillow.
4. Put the patient's feet flat on the floor.

16. A nurse identifies a patient's perception of health. Which can the nurse do as a result of obtaining this information?
1. Identify the patient's needs based on Maslow's Hierarchy of Human Needs.
2. Provide meaningful assistance to help the patient regain a state of health.
3. Help the patient prevent the occurrence of human responses to disease.
4. Choose a place for the patient along the health-illness continuum.

17. An older adult asks the nurse, "I want to make sure I get enough vitamin A to keep my eyes healthy. Which fruits can I eat because I am not fond of vegetables?" Which fruits should the nurse explain are excellent sources of vitamin A? **Select all that apply.**
1. _____Cantaloupe
2. _____Apricots
3. _____Peaches
4. _____Raisins
5. _____Prunes

18. When caring for patients under stress, which is an important concept that nurses must consider when making assessments about nonverbal behavior?
   1. It is controlled by the conscious mind.
   2. It carries less weight than what the patient says.
   3. It does not have the same meaning for everyone.
   4. It is a poor reflection of what the patient is feeling.

19. Which action should the nurse use to landmark the left dorsogluteal site for an intramuscular injection that is to be administered to a patient?
   1. Locate the lower edge of the acromion and the midpoint of the lateral aspect of the arm.
   2. Identify the line from the posterior superior iliac spine to the greater trochanter.
   3. Place the heel of the hand on the greater trochanter.
   4. Palpate the anterior lateral aspect of the thigh.

20. Which level need in Maslow's Hierarchy of Needs is supported when the nurse places the patient's get-well cards where the patient can see them?
   1. Love and belonging
   2. Safety and security
   3. Self-actualization
   4. Physiological

21. A patient has a diagnosis of osteoporosis. Which nutrients should the nurse encourage this patient to eat? **Select all that apply.**
   1. _____Rice
   2. _____Milk
   3. _____Yogurt
   4. _____Sardines
   5. _____Almonds
   6. _____Tomatoes

22. A nurse must obtain a urine specimen from a patient with a urinary retention catheter (Foley) and drains urine in the tubing down into the collection bag. Which should the nurse do **next**?
   1. Cleanse the exit tube at the bottom of the drainage bag with an alcohol swab.
   2. Use a clamp to constrict the tubing immediately distal to the collection port.
   3. Position the patient in a semi-Fowler position.
   4. Don a pair of clean gloves.

23. Which nursing action is appropriate in relation to the concept, "Bacteria and enzymes in stool are irritating to the skin"?
   1. Wearing a pair of sterile gloves when collecting a patient's stool for culture and sensitivity
   2. Applying a moisture barrier to the perianal area of incontinent patients
   3. Encouraging a patient to drink a cup of cranberry juice daily
   4. Toileting a confused patient before each meal

24. A nurse decides to give a partial bath to a patient instead of a complete bath. How was the nurse working when this decision was made?
   1. Dependently
   2. Independently
   3. Collaboratively
   4. Interdependently

25. A primary health-care provider orders a 2-g sodium diet for a patient. Which fluids should the nurse teach are high in sodium? **Select all that apply.**
   1. _____Cocoa
   2. _____Seltzer
   3. _____Lemonade
   4. _____Low-fat milk
   5. _____Tomato juice

26. For which **most** serious complication of intubation associated with the administration of general anesthesia should the nurse assess a postoperative patient?
    1. Stomatitis
    2. Atelectasis
    3. Sore throat
    4. Laryngeal spasm

27. A patient in pain tells the nurse, "It feels like something is on fire." Which characteristic of pain is associated with this statement?
    1. Intensity
    2. Location
    3. Quality
    4. Pattern

28. A nurse places a patient who had abdominal surgery in the semi-Fowler position. What is the rationale for this nursing intervention?
    1. Supports ventilation
    2. Promotes the passing of flatus
    3. Encourages urinary elimination
    4. Facilitates drainage in the portable wound drainage system

29. A nurse is teaching a group of nursing assistants about the administration of enemas. Which enema solution that works by irritating the intestinal mucosa should be included in the teaching?
    1. Oil
    2. Soap
    3. Tap water
    4. Normal saline

30. A nurse is administering oral medications to several patients. Which factor associated with the administration of medication will increase the absorption of oral medications?
    1. Given with water
    2. Taken on an empty stomach
    3. Administered in the morning
    4. Provided when the patient is resting

31. A nurse in the postanesthesia care unit is assessing several patients in pain. Patients in which age group should the nurse anticipate will be **most** sensitive to pain?
    1. Infants
    2. Adolescents
    3. Older adults
    4. Pregnant women

32. A nurse is caring for a patient who is practicing Orthodox Judaism. Which should the nurse consider about dietary regulations when assisting the patient to plan meals? **Select all that apply.**
    1. _____Coffee and tea are restricted during Passover.
    2. _____Meat from cloven-footed and cud-chewing animals is permitted.
    3. _____Dairy products and eggs are forbidden after sundown on Fridays.
    4. _____Dairy foods should not be ingested at the same meal as meat and meat products.
    5. _____Shellfish is permitted but must be prepared according to biblical religious rituals.

33. A newly admitted patient arrives on the unit. Which is **most** important for the nurse to do to help minimize the development of anxiety.
    1. Validate anxious feelings.
    2. Teach relaxation techniques.
    3. Minimize environmental stimuli.
    4. Explain procedures to the patient.

34. A home health-care nurse is helping a patient negotiate the health-care system within the community. Which word **best** reflects this role of the nurse?
1. Leader
2. Resource
3. Surrogate
4. Counselor

35. Which patient statement indicates to the nurse that an older adult understands the teaching about how to care for dry skin effectively?
1. "I will increase the amount of water that I drink."
2. "I can use baby powder on my skin rather than lotion."
3. "I should have a bath every day using a moisturizing soap."
4. "I ought to wear clothing made of wool rather than cotton."

36. A patient has a prescription for a vaginal suppository. Which actions should the nurse perform when administering this medication? **Select all that apply.**
1. _____Lubricate the suppository and the index finger of a gloved hand before insertion of the suppository.
2. _____Instruct the patient to remain flat in bed for twenty minutes after insertion of the suppository.
3. _____Irrigate the vagina with normal saline before inserting the suppository.
4. _____Place the patient in the dorsal recumbent position for the procedure.
5. _____Advance the suppository along the posterior vaginal wall.
6. _____Insert the suppository while wearing clean gloves.

37. A nurse is taking a patient's temperature using the instrument in the illustration. Place the following steps in the order in which they should be implemented.

1. While holding the button down and keeping the probe flat against the forehead, slide the instrument across the forehead, stopping when the hairline on the side of the face is reached.
2. Position the probe flat on the middle of the forehead halfway between the hairline and the eyebrow and hold the button down.
3. While continuing to hold the button, touch the probe to the soft area behind the earlobe and below the mastoid.
4. Clean the probe following the manufacturer's directions.
5. Release the button.
Answer: _____

38. A patient sustains soft tissue injuries from a motor vehicle collision. Which intervention is helpful in limiting the stress of both edema and bleeding into tissue?
1. Applying a cold compress
2. Exerting direct pressure
3. Performing effleurage
4. Providing massage

39. Which response by a patient in the postanesthesia care unit is the **priority** concern for the nurse?
1. Pain
2. Nausea
3. Reduced level of consciousness
4. Excessive loss of fluid through indwelling drains

40. Which should the nurse do when the vent of a patient's double-lumen nasogastric tube for decompression becomes obstructed?
1. Instill 10 mL of air into the vent lumen.
2. Place the patient in the high-Fowler position.
3. Position the vent below the level of the stomach.
4. Withdraw 30 mL of gastric contents from the drainage lumen.

41. In which situations is a nurse required to complete an incident report? **Select all that apply.**
1. _____Patient refused to go to physical therapy as ordered by a primary health-care provider.
2. _____Patient climbed over raised side rails and fell but was not injured.
3. _____Visitor ambulated a patient who should have been on bedrest.
4. _____Nurse left work early without reporting to the supervisor.
5. _____Patient did not receive a prescribed medication.
6. _____Nurse falls in the hall and breaks an arm.

42. A patient who has a transdermal analgesic patch for cancer experiences breakthrough pain with activity. Which is **most** important for the nurse to do?
1. Encourage the avoidance of moving around.
2. Seek a dose increase in the long-acting opioid.
3. Administer the prescribed shorter-acting opioid.
4. Obtain a prescription for an antianxiety medication.

43. A nurse must perform a procedure and is unsure of the exact steps of the procedure. Which should the nurse do **first**?
1. Refer to a fundamentals of nursing skills textbook.
2. Call the staff education department for assistance.
3. Check the nursing policy and procedure manual.
4. Refuse to do the nursing procedure.

44. A nurse is caring for a patient with a pressure ulcer. Which type of stressor is a pressure ulcer?
1. Microbiological
2. Developmental
3. Physiological
4. Physical

45. At which day and time did the patient have a respiratory rate of 15 breaths per minute?
1. 9-9 at 04
2. 9-9 at 08
3. 9-10 at 08
4. 9-10 at 16

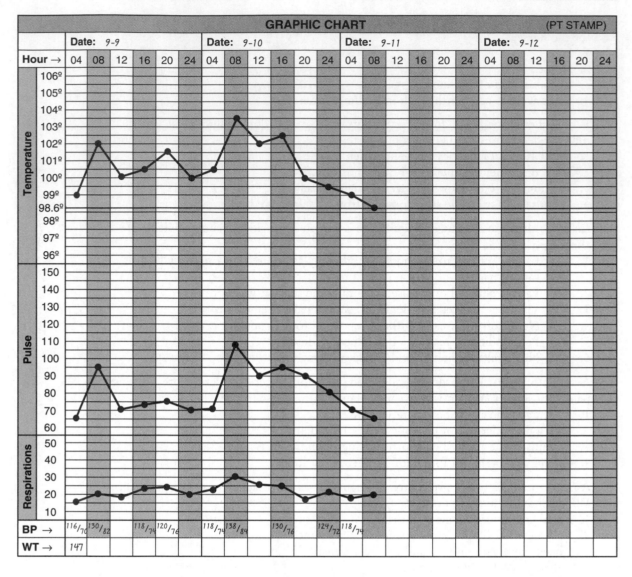

GRAPHIC CHART (PT STAMP)

		Date: 9-9						Date: 9-10						Date: 9-11						Date: 9-12					
Hour →		04	08	12	16	20	24	04	08	12	16	20	24	04	08	12	16	20	24	04	08	12	16	20	24

BP → 116/70 130/82 118/74 120/76 118/74 138/84 130/76 124/72 118/74

WT → 147

46. A patient appears agitated and states, "I'm not sure that I want to go through with this surgery." Which response by the nurse uses the technique of paraphrasing?
1. "Are you saying that you want to postpone the surgery?"
2. "You are undecided about having this surgery?"
3. "You seem upset about this surgery."
4. "Tell me more about your concerns."

47. A nurse is planning to apply a transdermal patch to a patient. Which actions should the nurse implement? **Select all that apply.**
1. _____ Use different sites each time to limit skin irritation and excoriation.
2. _____ Rub the area to promote comfort and vasodilation before applying the patch.
3. _____ Shave the area to facilitate adherence of the patch and medication absorption.
4. _____ Wear clean gloves to protect one's self from absorbing the medication through the hands.
5. _____ Remove the old patch an hour after applying the new patch to ensure a therapeutic blood level of the drug.

48. Which should the nurse do when providing a backrub for a patient?
1. Use continuous light gliding strokes with fingertips when finishing.
2. Concentrate deep circular motions across the scapulae and sacrum.
3. Knead firmly and quickly over the shoulders and the entire back.
4. Massage gently over the bony prominences of the vertebrae.

49. A patient is told by the primary health-care provider that the patient has metastatic lung cancer and is seriously ill. After the provider leaves the room, the patient has a severe episode of coughing and shortness of breath and says, "This is just a cold. I'll be fine once I get over it." How should the nurse respond?
    1. "What did you just find out about having a serious illness?"
    2. "Didn't you receive some bad news today?"
    3. "This is not a cold; it's lung cancer."
    4. "Tell me more about your illness."

50. A patient develops diarrhea after receiving several intermittent tube feedings. Which should the nurse consider is the cause of the diarrhea?
    1. A high osmolarity of the feeding
    2. An inadequate volume of the feeding
    3. Failure to test for a residual before the feeding
    4. Lying in the high-Fowler position during the feeding

51. While in a restaurant, a pregnant woman exhibits a total airway obstruction because of a bolus of food. How should the nurse modify the thrusts of the abdominal thrust (Heimlich) maneuver for this person?
    1. Perform them when the woman is in the supine, rather than standing, position.
    2. Use the pinkie finger side of the fist, rather than the thumb side, against the woman's body.
    3. Compress against the middle of the woman's sternum rather than between the umbilicus and xiphoid process.
    4. Initiate the procedure after the woman becomes unconscious, and discontinue it after six tries if unsuccessful.

52. A nurse is planning care to support a patient's ability to sleep. Which factor from among the options presented **most** commonly interferes with the sleep of hospitalized patients?
    1. Napping during the day
    2. Disrupted bedtime rituals
    3. Medication administration
    4. Difficulty finding a comfortable position

53. A nurse is providing dietary teaching for a patient who is a pure vegan. Which food combinations that are substitutes for a complete protein should the nurse include in the dietary teaching? **Select all that apply.**
    1. _____Pasta and peas
    2. _____Yogurt and fruit
    3. _____Bread and cheese
    4. _____Legumes and rice
    5. _____Peanut butter and jelly

54. A nurse is administering medication to an older adult. A decrease in which of the following increases the risk of drug toxicity in this patient?
    1. Serum calcium level
    2. Red blood cell count
    3. Glomerular filtration
    4. Frequency of urination

55. A nurse instills medicated drops into the ear of an adult. Which should the nurse do to ensure that the medication flows toward the eardrum?
    1. Pull the pinna of the ear backward and downward.
    2. Insert the drops into the center of the auditory canal.
    3. Press the tragus of the ear several times after insertion.
    4. Roll the patient from the side-lying to the supine position.

56. A nurse identifies that an adult patient is exhibiting antisocial behavior. According to Erikson, the negative resolution of which stage of development is **most** commonly associated with antisocial behavior?
1. Preschool age
2. Adolescence
3. School age
4. Infancy

57. Which nursing techniques will result in an accurate measurement when obtaining a patient's blood pressure? **Select all that apply.**
1. _____Positioning the arm at the level of the heart
2. _____Wrapping the lower edge of the cuff over the antecubital space
3. _____Pumping the cuff about 30 mm Hg above the point where the brachial pulse is lost on palpation
4. _____Releasing the valve on the cuff so that the pressure decreases at the rate of 2 to 3 mm Hg per second
5. _____Deflating the cuff completely and waiting 2 minutes before reinflating the blood pressure cuff to take the pressure again

58. Which should the nurse use to **best** provide oral care to an unconscious patient?
1. Gauze-wrapped tongue blades with a saline solution
2. Half-strength mouthwash and saline
3. Packaged glycerin swabs
4. Nonfoaming toothpaste

59. A patient is admitted to the hospital with a medical diagnosis of diverticulitis. Which is the **best** question the nurse should ask when obtaining an admission history from this patient?
1. "What did you eat yesterday?"
2. "How long have you had diverticulitis?"
3. "What led up to your coming to the hospital today?"
4. "Have you ever had any previous episodes of diverticulitis?"

60. A primary health-care provider orders peak and trough levels for a patient receiving an intravenous antibiotic. What time should the nurse obtain a blood sample to determine a trough level when the antibiotic was administered at 12 noon?
1. 11 a.m.
2. 11:30 a.m.
3. 12:30 p.m.
4. 1 p.m.

61. A nurse is planning care for a patient in the spiritual realm. Which age group generally is more involved with expanding and refining spiritual beliefs?
1. Adolescents
2. Older adults
3. Young adults
4. Middle-aged adults

62. Which actions are specifically related to the principle, *the greater the base of support, the more stable the body*? **Select all that apply.**
1. _____Assisting a patient to walk
2. _____Using a walker when ambulating
3. _____Locking the wheels of a wheelchair
4. _____Holding objects close to the body when walking
5. _____Keeping the back straight when lifting an object

63. Which is the **most** effective nursing intervention to promote sleep that is appropriate for a patient in any situation?
1. Providing a backrub
2. Playing relaxing music
3. Offering a glass of warm milk
4. Following a routine at bedtime

64. A nurse is performing an assessment of a patient. Place an X on the figure of the body where the nurse should place the stethoscope to assess for the presence of borborygmi.

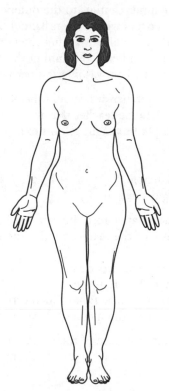

65. Which is the **most** important nursing intervention to help prevent falls from physical hazards in a hospital?
1. Positioning the telephone within easy reach
2. Storing belongings in a safe place
3. Ensuring adequate lighting
4. Using an over-bed table

66. A patient prefers and excessively maintains the supine position. For which potential problem associated with this position should the nurse assess the patient?
1. Pressure on the heels
2. Pressure on the trochanters
3. Internal rotation of the hips
4. Flexion contracture of the knees

67. A patient is using the call bell numerous times an hour and requesting assistance with activities that the patient is capable of achieving independently. Which should the nurse do to help this patient?
1. Set limits verbally.
2. Alternate care with another nurse.
3. Point out the behavior to the patient.
4. Attempt to see the situation from the patient's perspective.

68. A nurse going off duty is making rounds with the nurse coming on duty and provides a report on each patient in the district. Which information reported by the nurse is **most** complete?
    1. The patient was given an antiemetic and reports resolution of the nausea.
    2. The patient's family members just visited and the patient appears happy.
    3. The patient seems less anxious than earlier in the day.
    4. The patient's blood pressure is now stable.

69. A nurse is bathing a patient. Which nursing actions support a principle associated with medical asepsis? **Select all that apply.**
    1. _____Washing from the inner canthus to the outer canthus of the eye
    2. _____Replacing the top covers with a clean flannel bath blanket
    3. _____Changing the bath water after washing the perineal area
    4. _____Having the patient void before beginning the bed bath
    5. _____Wearing clean gloves when washing the perineum

70. Health teaching regarding a kitchen fire should include what to do if grease in a frying pan catches on fire. A nurse teaches that in this situation people should first call 911. Which should people be taught to do **next**?
    1. Pour water in the pan.
    2. Put the lid on the pan.
    3. Close the door to the kitchen.
    4. Use a class A fire extinguisher.

71. A patient who self-administers an aerosol medication by a metered-dose inhaler complains of "the nasty taste of the medication." Which should the nurse encourage the patient to do?
    1. Suck on a hard candy after the procedure.
    2. Shake the cartridge longer before using it.
    3. Perform oral hygiene before inhalation of medication.
    4. Attach an aerosol chamber to the metered-dose cartridge.

72. Which is the **most** important purpose of the orientation phase of a therapeutic relationship?
    1. Collect data.
    2. Build rapport.
    3. Identify problems.
    4. Establish priorities.

73. A patient has a temperature of 102°F and complains of feeling cold. Which additional responses should the nurse expect during this onset phase (cold or chill phase) of a fever? **Select all that apply.**
    1. _____Lethargy
    2. _____Pale skin
    3. _____Shivering
    4. _____Diaphoresis
    5. _____Dehydration

74. Which patient should the nurse identify will benefit the **most** from soaking the feet for several minutes as part of a bath?
    1. Has a personal preference for taking showers
    2. Has lower extremity arterial disease
    3. Is ambulating with paper slippers
    4. Is on bedrest

75. A nurse is assessing the skin of an older adult. Which assessment is the **greatest** concern?
    1. Flat, brown spots on the skin
    2. Thin, translucent skin
    3. Tenting of the skin
    4. Dry, flaky skin

76. A nurse is caring for a patient using an incentive spirometer. Which behaviors observed by the nurse indicate that further teaching is necessary? **Select all that apply.**
1. _____Inhales slowly and deeply using the spirometer
2. _____Tilts the incentive spirometer while breathing in
3. _____Raises the inspiratory goal on the spirometer once a day
4. _____Takes several regular breaths and then uses the spirometer again
5. _____Exhales while keeping the mouth sealed firmly around the mouthpiece

77. A nurse on a postpartum unit is teaching a class for new mothers about umbilical cord care. The nurse identifies that one mother does not become involved with the discussion and is withdrawn. Which is the **best** action by the nurse to help this new mother learn about umbilical cord care?
1. Give the mother written material about cord care.
2. Invite the mother to the next class about cord care.
3. Bring an audiovisual cassette into the mother's room about cord care.
4. Provide informal individual instruction for the mother about cord care.

78. A nurse is teaching a patient with dysphagia how to eat safely. Which should the nurse encourage the patient to do? **Select all that apply.**
1. _____Tilt the head backward when swallowing.
2. _____Drink fluids when eating bites of solid food.
3. _____Reduce environmental stimuli to a minimum.
4. _____Make sure that the mouth is empty after eating.
5. _____Keep food in the front of the mouth when chewing.

79. A patient consistently eats only 25% of every meal. Which should the nurse do to encourage the dietary intake of this patient?
1. Help the patient to select preferred foods.
2. Teach the patient to avoid fluids and foods that cause flatus.
3. Encourage the patient to engage in light exercise before meals.
4. Persuade the patient to drink between-meal supplements twice daily.

80. A charge nurse is delegating assignments to a Registered Nurse and Nursing Assistant on the nursing team. Which actions should be implemented only by a Registered Nurse? **Select all that apply.**
1. _____Evaluating a patient's response to activity
2. _____Taking the pulse of a patient with a dysrhythmia
3. _____Teaching a patient how to change a colostomy bag
4. _____Applying a condom catheter on a patient who is incontinent
5. _____Changing the linen on an occupied bed for a comatose patient

81. A nurse wants to influence a patient's beliefs so that new healthy behaviors are incorporated into the patient's lifestyle. Within which learning domain does the nurse need to direct teaching?
1. Affective
2. Cognitive
3. Psychomotor
4. Physiological

82. A nurse is teaching a family member how to perform range-of-motion exercises of the hand. Which motion occurs when the angle is reduced between the palm of the hand and forearm?
1. Hyperextension
2. Opposition
3. Abduction
4. Flexion

83. A patient with terminal cancer says to the nurse, "I've been fairly religious, but sometimes I wonder if the things I did were acceptable to God." How should the nurse respond?
    1. "Not knowing what the future brings can be a frightening thought."
    2. "God will appreciate that you went to religious services."
    3. "If you were good, you have nothing to fear."
    4. "In life, all we have to do is try to be good."

84. A nurse is administering a lozenge to a patient's buccal area of the mouth. Which should the nurse do? **Select all that apply.**
    1. _____Ensure the patient stays awake while the lozenge dissolves.
    2. _____Instruct the patient to take occasional sips of water.
    3. _____Place the medication under the patient's tongue.
    4. _____Alternate the cheeks from one dose to another.
    5. _____Administer the lozenge just before meals.

85. Which question by the nurse assesses a patient's pain tolerance?
    1. "At what point on a scale of 0 to 10 do you feel that you must have pain medication?"
    2. "What activities help distract you so that you don't feel the need for medication?"
    3. "How intense on a scale of 0 to 10 is the pain that you feel right now?"
    4. "Do you take pain medication frequently?"

86. An obese patient asks the nurse, "What should I do to help myself lose weight?" How should the nurse respond considering the **best** behavior modification strategy for controlling food intake?
    1. "Ask family members not to bring tempting food into the house."
    2. "Post piggy pictures on the refrigerator."
    3. "Avoid snacks between meals."
    4. "Maintain a daily food diary."

87. Which general concept related to growth and development should be considered by the nurse when caring for patients?
    1. Individuals experience growth and development at their own pace.
    2. Each task must be achieved before moving on to the next task.
    3. Family members provide safe and supportive environments.
    4. Once a task is achieved, regression is minimal.

88. A primary health-care provider orders the insertion of an indwelling urinary catheter (retention, Foley) as part of the patient's preoperative orders. Place the following steps of the procedure in the order in which they should be performed by the nurse.
    1. Don sterile gloves.
    2. Open the catheterization package.
    3. Place a fenestrated drape over the patient's perineal area.
    4. Maintain spread of labia while swiping directly over the urinary meatus.
    5. Maintain spread of labia while swiping each labium with a separate cotton ball.
    Answer: _____

89. A patient's vital signs are: apical heart rate—100 beats/min, radial heart rate—84 beats/min, respirations—20 breaths/min, blood pressure—140/84 mm Hg. What is the patient's pulse deficit? **Record your answer using a whole number.**
    Answer: _____

90. A patient is admitted to the emergency department after sustaining a crushing injury at work. Which characteristic of blood pressure should alert the nurse to impending shock?
    1. Rising diastolic
    2. Decreasing systolic
    3. Widening pulse pressure
    4. Robust Korotkoff's sounds

91. A primary health-care provider orders antiembolism stockings for a patient. Which is an important action the nurse should teach the patient?
1. Put them on after the legs have been dependent for 5 minutes.
2. Monitor the heels and toes for redness every 8 hours.
3. Apply body lotion before putting them on.
4. Remove and reapply them once a day.

92. Which is the important consequence of the use of Diagnosis Related Groups (DRGs) on the health-care system?
1. Increased quality of medical care
2. Increased reliability of research data
3. Decreased acuity of hospitalized patients
4. Decreased length of an average hospital stay

93. A primary health-care provider prescribes 1 g of an antibiotic to be administered via the intramuscular route twice a day. Which nursing action reflects the planning step of the nursing process?
1. Sending a copy of the order to the hospital pharmacy
2. Identifying body landmarks before giving the injection
3. Determining the times when the medication should be given
4. Verifying the patient's allergies in the chart and on the patient's allergy band

94. A nurse working in a nursing home routinely administers digoxin 0.125 mg by mouth to a patient every morning. Which patient responses should alert the nurse to withhold the medication? **Select all that apply.**
1. _____Diplopia
2. _____Vomiting
3. _____Tachypnea
4. _____Bradycardia
5. _____Dysrhythmias

95. A nurse is giving a patient a bed bath. Which should the nurse do to increase circulation?
1. Wash the extremities with firm strokes toward the heart.
2. Soak the feet in warm water for at least 20 minutes.
3. Expose just the areas that are being washed.
4. Ensure that the water is 120°F to 125°F.

96. A nurse is predicting the success of a teaching program regarding the learning of a skill. Which factor is **most** relevant?
1. Cognitive ability of the learner
2. Amount of reinforcement
3. Extent of family support
4. Interest of the learner

97. Which is **most** important for the nurse to do when assisting a female patient with care of the hair?
1. Use rubbing alcohol to remove tangles.
2. Ensure that the patient's hair is left dry, not wet.
3. Ask the patient what should be done with her hair.
4. Comb hair from the proximal to distal end of the hair shaft.

98. A patient who is secretly smoking in bed falls asleep and the cigarette ignites the patient's gown. Which should the nurse do **first** after discovering the fire?
1. Smother the flames with a blanket.
2. Roll the patient from side to side.
3. Activate the fire alarm.
4. Close the door.

99. A nurse discovers that a patient is taking natural herbal remedies. Which action is **most** important for the nurse to do?
    1. Learn about the supplements.
    2. Think of the supplements as drugs.
    3. Communicate the supplement use to the primary health-care provider.
    4. Include the details about supplement use in the patient's health history.

100. A patient sustained a traumatic brain injury resulting in neurological deficits after falling off a ladder at work. Which setting is **most** appropriate for assisting this patient to learn how to live with neurological limitations?
    1. Hospice program
    2. Acute-care setting
    3. Extended-care facility
    4. Assisted-living residence

COMPREHENSIVE FINAL BOOK EXAM: ANSWERS AND RATIONALES

1. 1. More than 100 beats per minute (tachycardia) is an early response to hypoxia. Hypoxia is insufficient oxygen anywhere in the body. To compensate for this lack of oxygen, the heart increases its rate to improve cardiac output, thereby increasing oxygen to all body cells.
   2. Difficulty breathing (dyspnea) is a late, not early, sign of hypoxia.
   3. Restlessness is an early sign of hypoxia. Restlessness occurs with hypoxia because of a decrease in oxygen to the brain.
   4. An increase in respirations more than 20 breaths per minute (tachypnea), not a decrease in respirations less than 12 breaths per minute (bradypnea), occurs as the body attempts to deliver more oxygen to body cells.
   5. Irritability is an early sign of hypoxia. Irritability occurs with hypoxia because of a decrease in oxygen to the brain.

CRITICAL-THINKING STRATEGY

Recognize keywords.	Which **early responses** indicate to the nurse that the patient is experiencing **hypoxia**?
Ask what the question is asking.	Which are early signs of hypoxia?
Critically analyze each option in relation to the question and the other options.	Examine each option from the perspective of whether or not the response is associated with reduced oxygenation in the body. This requires an understanding of physiological responses to reduced oxygenation and why each occurs.
Eliminate incorrect options.	Options 2 and 4 are late signs of hypoxia and can be eliminated.

2. 1. Persistent chronic pain becomes an unchanging part of life. As the duration of exposure increases, the individual may learn cognitive and behavioral strategies to cope with the pain.
   2. Chronic pain can markedly impair activities of daily living.
   3. Chronic pain may, or may not, have an identifiable cause.
   4. Acute pain and chronic pain both decrease the efficiency of the immune system.

CRITICAL-THINKING STRATEGY

Recognize keywords.	A patient has a history of **chronic pain** because of arthritis but dislikes taking large doses of analgesics. Which **concept unique to unrelieved chronic pain** should the nurse consider when caring for this patient?
Ask what the question is asking.	Which concept is related only to unrelieved chronic pain?
Critically analyze each option in relation to the question and the other options.	Compare and contrast the commonalities and differences between chronic and acute pain and then identify the one statement that is associated only with unrelieved chronic pain.
Eliminate incorrect options.	Options 2, 3, and 4 are inaccurate statements as indicated in their rationales and can be eliminated.

3. 1. A slight elevation of body temperature is expected after surgery because of the body's response to the stress of surgery.
   2. Dehiscence, separation of the wound edges, is more likely to occur between the fifth and eighth postoperative days, and it is not life-threatening.
   3. Dependent edema indicates problems, such as a fluid and electrolyte imbalance, impaired kidney function, or decreased cardiac output. All are serious but generally manageable.
   4. An acute onset of chest pain within 24 hours of surgery may indicate myocardial infarction in response to the stress of surgery. Also, it can be caused by a pulmonary embolus, although this is more likely to occur between the 7th and 10th postoperative days. Both of these complications are life-threatening.

CRITICAL-THINKING STRATEGY

Recognize keywords.	A nurse is assessing several patients who had **surgery the previous day**. Which **sudden patient response** should the nurse identify as a potential **life-threatening** event?
Ask what the question is asking.	Which clinical finding indicates a possible life-threatening event?
Critically analyze each option in relation to the question and the other options.	Critically review several expected or potential problems related to the stress of surgery. Then identify the one complication that is life-threatening.
Eliminate incorrect options.	Option 1 is an expected outcome; options 2 and 3 are complications that are not as life-threatening as chest pain. Chest pain may indicate a myocardial infarction, which is a life-threatening condition. Options 1, 2, and 3 can be eliminated.

4. 1. The passage of hard, dry stools supports the presence of constipation, not a concern with perceived constipation.
   2. **The expectation of a daily bowel movement at the same time every day with the resulting overuse of laxatives, enemas, and/or suppositories supports a concern with perceived constipation.**
   3. Abdominal distention supports the presence of constipation, not a concern with perceived constipation.
   4. Straining at stool supports the presence of constipation, not a concern with perceived constipation.

CRITICAL-THINKING STRATEGY

Recognize keywords.	A patient states, **"I like to have a bowel movement every morning."** Which **additional information** collected by the nurse **supports** a concern with **perceived constipation**?
Ask what the question is asking.	Which is a clinical finding associated with perceived constipation?

Critically analyze each option in relation to the question and the other options.	Analyze the differences between constipation and perceived constipation.
Eliminate incorrect options.	Perceived constipation has no relationship with the characteristics of stool but rather the fact that an enema or laxative is used to ensure a daily bowel movement. The clinical findings in options 1, 3, and 4 are associated with characteristics related to actual, not perceived, constipation. Options 1, 3, and 4 can be eliminated.

5. 1. Although checking the preoperative checklist is done, it is not the priority. It usually is done last before the intraoperative period.
   2. **The consent for surgery must be signed before preoperative medications are administered because they depress the central nervous system, impairing problem-solving and decision making.**
   3. Ensuring placement of an IV line is unnecessary. This can be done at any time during the preoperative phase or at the beginning of the intraoperative phase of surgery.
   4. Although assessing vital signs is done, it is not the priority.

CRITICAL-THINKING STRATEGY

Recognize keywords.	A nurse must **administer a sedative** to a patient before surgery. **Which should the nurse do first**?
Ask what the question is asking.	Which intervention is necessary before giving a preoperative sedative?
Critically analyze each option in relation to the question and the other options.	Review the components of a preoperative checklist and the legal implications of a preoperative consent form in relation to the administration of a sedative.

| Eliminate incorrect options. | Options 1, 3, and 4 are unrelated to when a presurgical sedative is administered; all these interventions can be done immediately before surgery and before or after the sedative is administered. Options 1, 3, and 4 can be eliminated. |

6. Answer: 5 mL. Use ratio and proportion to first convert 500 mg to its equivalent in grams as well as to solve the problem.

$$\frac{\text{Desire}}{\text{Have}} \frac{500 \text{ mg}}{1,000 \text{ mg}} = \frac{\text{x gram}}{1 \text{ gram}}$$

1,000x = 500
x = 500 ÷ 1,000
x = 0.5 gram (is equal to 500 mg)

Now proceed to solve the problem using ratio and proportion.

$$\frac{\text{Desire}}{\text{Have}} \frac{0.5 \text{ gram}}{1 \text{ gram}} = \frac{\text{x mL}}{10 \text{ mL}}$$

1x = 0.5 ÷ 10
x = 5 mL

CRITICAL-THINKING STRATEGY

Recognize keywords.	A primary health-care provider prescribes **500 mg** of an antibiotic to be administered IVPB every 6 hours for a patient with a systemic infection. The **vial dispensed** by the hospital pharmacist contains **1 g** of the prescribed antibiotic in powder form. The instructions on the vial state: "**Instill 9.6 mL to yield 10 mL.**" **How many milliliters** of the antibiotic should the nurse **add to the IVPB bag**?
Ask what the question is asking.	Compute the dose of the prescribed medication.
Critically analyze each option in relation to the question and the other options.	Use a mathematical formula to convert milligrams to grams. Then use a mathematical formula to compute the correct dose of medication prescribed. The information you need to insert into the formula is the Desired (prescribed: 500 mg [0.5 g]) dose and what you Have (how the medication is supplied: 1 g/10 mL).

| Eliminate incorrect options. | There is no need to eliminate options because this is a fill-in-the-blank question. |

7. 1. Primary nursing is not a cost-containment strategy in managed care but rather a nursing-care delivery system that ensures a comprehensive and consistent approach to identifying and meeting patients' needs. Primary nursing occurs when one nurse is assigned the 24-hour responsibility for the planning and delivery of nursing care to a specific patient for the duration of the patient's hospitalization.
2. Critical pathways are a case management system that identifies specific protocols and timetables for care and treatment by various disciplines designed to achieve expected patient outcomes within a specific time frame. The purpose is to discharge patients sooner, thereby reducing the cost of health care.
3. Functional method refers to a model of nursing-care delivery that assigns a specific task for a group of patients to one person. Although it is efficient, it is impersonal and contributes to fragmentation of care because it is task oriented rather than patient centered.
4. Quality management (also known as continuous quality improvement, total quality management, or persistent quality improvement) refers to a program designed to improve, not just ensure, the quality of care delivered to patients. Also, it includes an educational component to support growth and provide for corrective action.

CRITICAL-THINKING STRATEGY

| Recognize keywords. | **Which mechanism** is designed to facilitate **tracking a patient's progress** as a **cost-containment strategy** in managed care? |
| **A**sk what the question is asking. | Which cost-containment measure manages and documents a patient's progress through the health-care system? |

continued

continued

Critically analyze each option in relation to the question and the other options.	Recall the definition and components of each of the presented mechanisms. Determine which is a strategy that facilitates tracking a patient's progress as a cost-containment measure.
Eliminate incorrect options.	Options 1 and 3 are two different types of nursing-care delivery and are not strategies that track a patient's progress through the health-care system. Option 4 addresses ongoing activities designed to improve the quality of health care. Options 1, 3, and 4 can be eliminated.

8. 1. Explaining about the bath in detail may precipitate anxiety. The patient does not have the cognitive ability or attention span to comprehend a detailed explanation before a procedure.
   2. The patient has a problem with cognition, not vision.
   3. **When progressing through each aspect of the bath give simple, direct statements to limit the amount of incoming stimuli at one time. This will promote comprehension and self-care.**
   4. Patients with dementia do not have the cognitive ability to perform a procedure independently. The patient should be supervised.

CRITICAL-THINKING STRATEGY

Recognize keywords.	A nurse is **assisting** a patient who has **cognitive deficits with a bed bath**. Which is **important** for the nurse **to do**?
Ask what the question is asking.	Which must the nurse do to safely ensure that a patient with cognitive deficits receives an adequate bath?
Critically analyze each option in relation to the question and the other options.	Integrate what a patient with cognitive deficits can and cannot do, that daily-living activities must be accomplished adequately and safely, and that nursing care must address a patient's physical, emotional, and mental needs.

Eliminate incorrect options.	Options 1 and 4 are unrealistic for a patient with a cognitive deficit. Although option 2 should be done, it will not ensure an adequate bath. Options 1, 2, and 4 can be eliminated.

9. 1. **Episodes of sleep apnea begin with loud snoring followed by silence, during which the person struggles to breathe against a blocked airway. Decreasing oxygen levels cause the person to awaken abruptly with a loud snort.**
   2. Falling asleep abruptly describes narcolepsy, which is a sudden overwhelming sleepiness (hypersomnia) in the daytime.
   3. Kicking and thrashing describe restless legs syndrome, a feeling of creeping or itching sensation occurring in the lower extremities causing an irresistible urge to move and kick the legs.
   4. Dreams that cause fear describe nightmares. Nightmares are vivid frightening dreams that occur during REM sleep and awaken the sleeper.
   5. Patients with obstructive sleep apnea usually are not aware of awakening during an episode.

CRITICAL-THINKING STRATEGY

Recognize keywords.	When interviewing the wife of a patient, **which statements** about her husband **support** the presence of **obstructive sleep apnea**?
Ask what the question is asking.	Which statements describe clinical findings related to obstructive sleep apnea?
Critically analyze each option in relation to the question and the other options.	Distinguish among behaviors associated with obstructive sleep apnea versus other sleep disorders.
Eliminate incorrect options.	Options 2, 3, and 4 are descriptions of narcolepsy, restless legs syndrome, and nightmares, respectively. Options 2, 3, and 4 can be eliminated.

10. 1. A clear liquid diet will not relieve abdominal distention. A clear liquid diet is contraindicated in the presence of abdominal distention because gas has accumulated in the intestines as a result of a lack of intestinal motility.
2. A clear liquid diet will minimally stimulate digestive enzymes. A full-liquid diet or food will more likely stimulate gastric enzymes.
3. A clear liquid diet will not prevent postoperative ileus. A clear liquid diet is administered after a postoperative ileus resolves, not to prevent its occurrence.
4. **The molecules in clear liquids are less complex and easier to ingest, tolerate, and digest than those in a full-liquid diet or food.**

CRITICAL-THINKING STRATEGY

Recognize keywords.	A primary health-care provider orders a clear liquid diet for a patient who had **abdominal surgery** three days ago. Which does the nurse conclude is the **reason why a clear liquid diet was ordered** for this patient?
Ask what the question is asking.	Which is the benefit of a clear liquid diet after abdominal surgery?
Critically analyze each option in relation to the question and the other options.	Analyze the physiological responses to abdominal surgery, particularly complications such as abdominal distention and postoperative ileus and the benefits of a clear liquid diet after abdominal surgery.
Eliminate incorrect options.	A clear liquid diet is contraindicated with abdominal distention and postoperative ileus; therefore, options 1 and 3 can be eliminated. A clear liquid diet will minimally stimulate gastric secretions, and therefore option 2 can be eliminated.

11. 1. **Diarrhea is related directly to a risk for damage to epidermal and dermal tissue. The gastric and intestinal enzymes present in feces are acids capable of eroding the skin.**

2. Diarrhea is unrelated to the ability to provide self-care. The inability to care for self is the state in which the individual experiences an impaired motor or cognitive function, causing a decreased ability to perform self-care activities.
3. Diarrhea is not related directly to sexual dysfunction, which is the state in which an individual experiences or is at risk of experiencing a change in sexual function that is viewed as unrewarding or inadequate.
4. Diarrhea is not related directly to body image disturbance, which is the state in which an individual experiences, or is at risk of experiencing, a disruption in the way one perceives one's body image.

CRITICAL-THINKING STRATEGY

Recognize keywords.	For which **common problem associated with prolonged diarrhea** should the nurse assess a patient with this problem?
Ask what the question is asking.	Which common problem is caused by prolonged diarrhea?
Critically analyze each option in relation to the question and the other options.	Explore the consequences of diarrhea and identify the most common human response to diarrhea. Consider Maslow's Hierarchy of Needs when analyzing these options.
Eliminate incorrect options.	Preventing skin breakdown in option 1 is addressing a physiological need, which is a first-level need when compared with later level needs such as sexuality and body image. Options 3 and 4 can be eliminated. Just because a patient has diarrhea does not mean that the person cannot provide self-care. There are no data that indicate the patient is dependent. Option 2 can be eliminated.

12. 1. This situation is not an example of battery. Battery is the purposeful, angry, or negligent touching of a patient without consent.

2. This situation is not an example of assault. Assault is an attempt, or threat, to touch another person unjustly.

3. Although negligence occurs when a nurse's actions do not meet appropriate standards of care and result in injury to another, this term is not as specific as another term.

4. **Malpractice is misconduct, an act of commission or omission, performed in professional practice that results in harm to another. With malpractice the nurse and patient have a professional nurse-patient relationship.**

CRITICAL-THINKING STRATEGY

Recognize keywords.	A nurse causes harm to a hospitalized patient because of **improper use of medical equipment. Which is this tort specifically called?**
Ask what the question is asking.	Which is the name of the tort when a nurse caring for a patient causes harm to the patient?
Critically analyze each option in relation to the question and the other options.	Review the definitions and examples of situations that relate to a variety of intentional and unintentional torts. Use this information to assign a name of a tort to the situation presented.
Eliminate incorrect options.	Options 1 and 2 include intentional behaviors that are a threat to touch another unjustifiably (assault) or actual touching another unjustifiably (battery). Option 3 is a tort that does not address behaviors within a professional relationship. Options 1, 2, and 3 can be eliminated.

13. 1. The patient is not experiencing fluid retention. The urine output is almost twice the volume of the intake. With fluid retention the skin is taut and shiny, the mucous membranes are moist, and the patient will gain weight.

2. Kidney impairment can be ruled out because the 4,200 mL of urinary output indicates that the kidneys are functioning. Also, with kidney impairment, generally there is weight gain, not loss. The BUN and creatinine levels are within the normal range and indicate that the kidneys are not impaired.

3. **The serum glucose value of 350 mg/dL is excessive and indicates a hyperglycemic event; the acceptable range is less than 110 mg/dL. A hemoglobin A_{1c} level of 8% indicates inadequate glucose control over the past 90 to 120 days. The acceptable value for hemoglobin A_{1c} for a person with diabetes mellitus is less than 7% (American Diabetes Association) or less than 6.5% (American Association of Clinical Endocrinologists). The acceptable range for hemoglobin A_{1c} in a person without diabetes mellitus is 4.0% to 5.5%.**

4. There are no data to support the conclusion that this event is a hypertensive episode. With the degree of polyuria, poor skin turgor, and dry mucous membranes, hypotension resulting from dehydration, not hypertension, is expected.

CRITICAL-THINKING STRATEGY

Recognize keywords.	A patient with **type 2 diabetes** is experiencing **blurred vision, generalized weakness, and fatigue.** A nurse receives a report from the nurse on the previous shift and obtains additional information from the patient's clinical record. **Which should the nurse conclude that the patient is experiencing?**
Ask what the question is asking.	Which is the patient's problem based on the information presented?
Critically analyze each option in relation to the question and the other options.	Analyze the information presented in the laboratory results, I&O record, and nursing progress record in relation to the clinical manifestations associated with the four different clinical conditions.
Eliminate incorrect options.	The data presented do not support the problems in options 1, 2, and 4. Eliminate options 1, 2, and 4.

14. 1. Directive is not one of the four classic leadership styles.

2. The autocratic leadership style is probably the least effective style to use with a professionally mature and motivated staff. Autocratic leaders give orders and directions and make decisions for the group. There is little freedom and a large degree of control by the leader, which frustrates motivated and professionally mature staff members.

3. The democratic leadership style is the second best style to use when staff is motivated and professionally mature. The democratic style offers fewer opportunities for autonomy for staff members who are mature and motivated than a leadership style in another option.

4. **The laissez-faire leadership style is appropriate for a group of individuals who have an internal locus of control and desire autonomy and independence. Individuals who are professionally mature and motivated more often have an internal locus of control.**

CRITICAL-THINKING STRATEGY

Recognize keywords.	**Nurses** on a unit are personally and **professionally mature and motivated. Which classic leadership style should the nurse manager employ** when working with this group?
Ask what the question is asking.	Which classic leadership style works best when nurses are mature and motivated?
Critically analyze each option in relation to the question and the other options.	Review the descriptions of leadership styles and explore the situations in which each works best. Then you need to select the style that works best in the situation presented.
Eliminate incorrect options.	Option 1 is not a leadership style. Option 2 is too dictatorial for individuals with an internal locus of control. Although option 3 is more independent than an autocratic style, it is more restricted than a laissez-faire style. Eliminate options 1, 2, and 3.

15. 1. **Pressure on the popliteal areas can cause damage to nerves and interferes with circulation and must be avoided.**

2. The transfer belt should be removed after the transfer is totally completed.

3. A pillow will move the patient too close to the front of the seat and is unsafe.

4. The patient's feet should be positioned flat on the footrests of the wheelchair, not the floor, to protect the feet if the wheelchair is moved.

CRITICAL-THINKING STRATEGY

Recognize keywords.	A nurse transfers a patient from a bed to a wheelchair. Which is **an important nursing intervention after placing the patient in the wheelchair**?
Ask what the question is asking.	Which action is essential when a patient is in a wheelchair?
Critically analyze each option in relation to the question and the other options.	List the steps of the procedure—transferring a patient from a bed to a wheelchair. Then the behavior in each option must be compared with the steps in the transfer procedure. Finally, you must identify the option that reflects a safe, correct action by the nurse.
Eliminate incorrect options.	Options 3 and 4 are both unsafe interventions and may jeopardize the patient. Option 2 is unnecessary and may be uncomfortable for the patient. Eliminate options 2, 3, and 4.

16. 1. A patient's perceptions are only one part of the data that must be collected before the nurse can establish the priority of the patient's needs. Maslow's Hierarchy of Human Needs helps the nurse to determine the patient's needs in order of priority based on the collected data.

2. **Health perception reflects a person's knowledge, behavior, and attitudes regarding illness, disease prevention, health promotion, and what constitutes a healthy lifestyle. An assessment of these factors captures the uniqueness of each individual and provides essential data that must be considered**

before needs are identified and a plan formulated.

3. A healthy lifestyle can promote health and prevent some illness or even minimize complications; however, understanding a person's perceptions of health may not prevent human responses to disease.

4. Only a patient, not a nurse, can choose a patient's place along the health-illness continuum. How people perceive themselves is subjective and is influenced by their own attitudes, values, and beliefs.

CRITICAL-THINKING STRATEGY

Recognize keywords.	A nurse identifies a **patient's perception of health. Which can the nurse do as a result of obtaining this information**?
Ask what the question is asking.	Which can a nurse do after learning about the patient's beliefs about health?
Critically analyze each option in relation to the question and the other options.	Appreciate that health beliefs are specific to the individual. This concept must be analyzed in relation to the theories of Maslow's Hierarchy of Human Needs and the health-illness continuum.
Eliminate incorrect options.	Options 1, 3, and 4 are incorrect statements as indicated in their rationales and can be eliminated.

17. 1. Cantaloupe is an excellent source of vitamin A. A half cup of melon balls contains approximately 2,993 International Units of vitamin A.

2. Apricots are an excellent source of vitamin A. A 3½-ounce serving of apricots contains approximately 7,240 International Units of vitamin A.

3. Peaches are an excellent source of vitamin A. A 3½-ounce serving of peaches contains approximately 2,160 International Units of vitamin A.

4. Raisins are not high in vitamin A. A 3½-ounce serving of raisins contains approximately 10 International Units of vitamin A.

5. Prunes are an excellent source of vitamin A. A 3½-ounce serving of prunes contains approximately 1,990 International Units of vitamin A.

CRITICAL-THINKING STRATEGY

Recognize keywords.	An older adult asks the nurse, "I want to make sure I get enough vitamin A to keep my eyes healthy. Which fruits can I eat because I am not fond of vegetables?" **Which fruits** should the nurse explain **are excellent sources of vitamin A**?
Ask what the question is asking.	Which fruits have the highest vitamin A content?
Critically analyze each option in relation to the question and the other options.	Recall how much vitamin A is contained in each nutrient and then compare and contrast the nutrients among the options. The options with high vitamin A content are the correct answers.
Eliminate incorrect options.	Option 4 can be eliminated because raisins contain only small amounts of vitamin A versus larger amounts of vitamin A in the fruits in options 1, 2, 3, and 5.

18. 1. Nonverbal behavior is controlled more by the unconscious than by the conscious mind.

2. Nonverbal behavior carries more, not less, weight than verbal interactions because nonverbal behavior is influenced by the unconscious mind.

3. Transculturally, nonverbal communication varies widely. For example, gestures, facial expressions, eye contact, and touch may reflect opposite messages among cultures and among individuals within a culture.

4. The opposite is true. Nonverbal behaviors often directly reflect feelings.

CRITICAL-THINKING STRATEGY

Recognize keywords.	When caring for patients under stress, which is an **important concept** that nurses must consider **when making assessments about nonverbal behavior**?
Ask what the question is asking.	Which is important about nonverbal behavior that influences nursing assessments?

Critically analyze each option in relation to the question and the other options.	Review the variety of statements about nonverbal behavior, and determine their accuracy. Then select the option that is a true statement.
Eliminate incorrect options.	Options 1, 2, and 4 can be eliminated because the statements in the options are incorrect as indicated in the rationales.

19. 1. The lower edge of the acromion and the midpoint of the lateral aspect of the arm are anatomical landmarks that help to identify the deltoid muscle.
    2. **The line from the posterior superior iliac spine to the greater trochanter is an anatomical landmark that helps to identify the dorsogluteal site. This site contains the well-developed gluteus muscles, particularly the gluteus maximus, in the buttocks.**
    3. Placing the heel of the hand on the greater trochanter is the initial placement of the hand when identifying landmarks for the ventrogluteal site.
    4. Palpating the anterior lateral aspect of the thigh is associated with identifying the vastus lateralis site. It is between one handbreadth above the knee and one handbreadth below the greater trochanter on the anterior lateral aspect of the thigh.

CRITICAL-THINKING STRATEGY

Recognize keywords.	Which action should the nurse use to **landmark** the **left dorsogluteal site** for an **intramuscular injection** that is to be administered to a patient?
Ask what the question is asking.	What is the landmark for a dorsogluteal intramuscular injection?
Critically analyze each option in relation to the question and the other options.	List the steps in the procedure—landmarking the dorsogluteal injection site. Then identify the specific action included in one of the options that relates to the dorsogluteal site.
Eliminate incorrect options.	Options 1, 3, and 4 are options that present steps that are related to sites other than the dorsogluteal site and can be eliminated.

20. 1. **Taping a patient's get-well cards to the wall where the patient can see them supports the patient's need to feel loved and appreciated and meets love and belonging needs according to Maslow's Hierarchy of Needs.**
    2. Placing get-well cards where the patient can see them does not support a patient's safety and security needs. Safety and security needs are related to being and feeling protected in the physiological and interpersonal realms.
    3. Placing get-well cards where the patient can see them does not support a patient's self-actualization needs. Self-actualization involves the need to achieve the highest potential within abilities.
    4. Placing get-well cards where the patient can see them does not support a patient's physiological needs. Physiological needs are related to having adequate air, food, water, rest, shelter, and the ability to eliminate and regulate body temperature.

CRITICAL-THINKING STRATEGY

Recognize keywords.	Which level need in **Maslow's Hierarchy of Needs** is **supported** when the nurse places the patient's **get-well cards where the patient can see them**?
Ask what the question is asking.	Exhibiting cards is related to which level of Maslow's Hierarchy of Needs?
Critically analyze each option in relation to the question and the other options.	Recall behaviors related to each level of Maslow's Hierarchy of Needs. Then compare the situation presented with this recalled information.
Eliminate incorrect options.	Options 1, 3, and 4 can be eliminated because they are associated with needs on levels other than love and belonging.

21. 1. Rice, regardless of the type, is not high in calcium. One cup of rice contains approximately 5 to 33 mg of calcium.
    2. **Milk and products made with milk such as various forms of cheese are an excellent source of calcium. Eight ounces of 1% low-fat milk contain approximately 290 mg of calcium. Eight ounces of 2% reduced-fat milk contain approximately 285 mg of calcium.**

3. **Yogurt is an excellent source of calcium. Eight ounces of plain non-fat yogurt contains approximately 452 mg of calcium. Eight ounces of low-fat yogurt contains approximately 415 mg of calcium.**

4. **Sardines, which contain soft edible bones, are an excellent source of dietary calcium. Three ounces of sardines contain approximately 371 mg of calcium.**

5. **Almonds are an excellent source of calcium. One ounce of almonds (about 24) contains approximately 75 mg of calcium.**

6. Tomatoes are not high in calcium. One tomato (2¾ inches in diameter) contains approximately 9 mg of calcium.

CRITICAL-THINKING STRATEGY

Recognize keywords.	A patient has a diagnosis of **osteoporosis. Which nutrients** should the nurse encourage this patient to **eat**?
Ask what the question is asking.	Which foods facilitate bone maintenance?
Critically analyze each option in relation to the question and the other options.	Recall that osteoporosis is the reduction of bone mass and that an increase in calcium will support bone maintenance. Recall how much calcium is contained in each nutrient, and then compare and contrast the nutrients among the options. The options with the highest calcium content are the correct answers.
Eliminate incorrect options.	Options 1 and 6 can be eliminated because the nutrients in these options contain small amounts of calcium compared with the amounts of calcium in the nutrients in options 2, 3, 4, and 5.

22. 1. Cleansing the exit tube at the bottom of the drainage bag with an alcohol swab is unnecessary. When obtaining a specimen from a retention catheter, the aspiration port of the catheter (not the exit tube) is wiped with a disinfectant before inserting the syringe. Urine specimens from a retention catheter should come from the port, not the bag, because this urine is the most recently excreted.

2. Clamping the tubing immediately distal to the collection port should not be done until a step mentioned in another option is performed first. The drainage tubing should be clamped 1 to 2 inches below the aspiration port for 15 to 20 minutes to allow urine to accumulate.

3. Positioning the patient in a semi-Fowler position is done later in the procedure if necessary. This position moves urine toward the trigone (the triangular area at the base of the bladder where the ureters and urethra enter the bladder) where it is accessible to the catheter.

4. **Wearing personal protective equipment, such as clean gloves, is a medical asepsis practice. Gloves protect the nurse from the patient's body fluids because the catheter is close to the perineal area and there is a potential for exposure to urine during the procedure.**

CRITICAL-THINKING STRATEGY

Recognize keywords.	A nurse must obtain a **urine specimen** from a patient with a **urinary retention catheter** (Foley) and **drains urine in the tubing down into the urine collection bag. Which should the nurse do next?**
Ask what the question is asking.	When collecting a urine specimen from a urinary retention catheter, what should the nurse do after draining urine in the tubing into the collection bag?
Critically analyze each option in relation to the question and the other options.	List the step-by-step procedure for collecting a specimen from a urinary retention catheter. Then analyze the four options and select the option that reflects the next step of the procedure after urine in the tubing is drained into the collection bag.
Eliminate incorrect options.	Option 1 is not a step in this procedure. Options 2 and 3 are steps that are performed later in the procedure. Options 1, 2, and 3 can be eliminated.

23. 1. Clean gloves are adequate.
2. **A skin barrier protects the skin from the digestive enzymes in feces.**
3. Cranberry juice makes urine more alkaline; it does not influence bacteria and enzymes in stool.
4. Patients should attempt to have a bowel movement after a meal to take advantage of the gastrocolic reflex.

CRITICAL-THINKING STRATEGY

Recognize keywords.	Which nursing **action** is **appropriate in relation to** the concept, "**Bacteria and enzymes in stool are irritating to the skin?**"
Ask what the question is asking.	Which nursing intervention is necessitated by the fact that bacteria and enzymes are irritating to the skin?
Critically analyze each option in relation to the question and the other options.	This statement requires the integration of several concepts: bacteria are irritating to the skin; enzymes are irritating to the skin; and moisture barriers can protect the skin from irritating substances. To eliminate the other options, identify that they are either an inaccurate statement or are unrelated to the concept cited in the question.
Eliminate incorrect options.	The focus is on the connection between factors that irritate the skin and what can be done to prevent it. Option 1 is an inaccurate statement because sterile gloves are not necessary to obtain a stool specimen for culture and sensitivity and it does not relate to the concept cited in the question. Option 3 may help minimize the risk of a urinary tract infection but is unrelated to preventing irritation of the skin. Although option 4 is a true statement it is unrelated to preventing irritation of the skin. Options 1, 3, and 4 can be eliminated.

24. 1. The nurse does not need a primary health-care provider's order to provide nursing care that is within the realm of nursing practice.
2. **Providing hygiene, an activity of daily living, is within the scope of nursing practice.**
3. The nurse does not need to collaborate with other health-care professionals to provide nursing care.
4. The nurse does not need a primary health-care provider's order to implement nursing care that is within the realm of nursing practice.

CRITICAL-THINKING STRATEGY

Recognize keywords.	A nurse decides to give a **partial bath instead of a complete bath. How was the nurse working** when this decision was made?
Ask what the question is asking.	How is the nurse functioning in relation to the legal definition of nursing when giving a partial bed bath?
Critically analyze each option in relation to the question and the other options.	Each state has a nurse practice act that defines and describes the scope of nursing practice. You need to know that legally the nurse can work dependently, independently, collaboratively, and interdependently when implementing nursing care. Now analyze the situation and identify in what role the nurse is working.
Eliminate incorrect options.	Providing for a patient's hygiene needs is not a dependent, collaborative, or interdependent function of the nurse and therefore options 1, 3, and 4 can be eliminated.

25. 1. **Cocoa powder, containing non-fat dry milk, contains approximately 173 mg of sodium when mixed with 6 ounces of water and should be avoided when on a 2-g sodium diet.**
2. Seltzer contains no sodium and is permitted on a 2-g sodium diet.
3. Twelve fluid ounces of lemonade contains approximately 12 mg of sodium and is permitted on a 2-g sodium diet.

4. One cup of low-fat milk contains approximately 103 mg of sodium and should not be included in large amounts on a 2-g sodium diet.
5. One cup of tomato juice contains approximately 877 mg of sodium and should be avoided on a 2-g sodium diet.

CRITICAL-THINKING STRATEGY

Recognize keywords.	A primary health-care provider orders a **2-g sodium diet** for a patient. Which **fluids** should the nurse teach are **high in sodium**?
Ask what the question is asking.	Which fluids have the highest sodium content?
Critically analyze each option in relation to the question and the other options.	Identify the sodium content of a variety of fluids. Compare and contrast the fluids in the options presented, and identify the options with the highest sodium content.
Eliminate incorrect options.	Options 2 and 3 can be eliminated because these fluids contain no or small amounts of sodium versus the large amounts of sodium in fluids presented in options 1, 4, and 5.

26. 1. Although inflammation of the mouth (stomatitis) can occur from irritation caused by the tube used for delivering general anesthesia, it is uncommon and not life-threatening.
2. Although atelectasis is serious, it is not as serious as a response in another option. Anesthesia delivered by intubation can interfere with the action of surfactant, resulting in the collapse of alveoli (atelectasis).
3. Although the tube used for intubation commonly does irritate the posterior oropharynx, resulting in a sore throat, it is not as serious as a response in another option.
4. Laryngeal spasm is a potentially life-threatening complication because it prevents the exchange of gases between the lungs and the atmosphere. Laryngeal spasm can result from irritation caused by the presence of the intubation tube in the space between the vocal cords (glottis) during surgery.

CRITICAL-THINKING STRATEGY

Recognize keywords.	For which **most serious complication of intubation** associated with the administration of general anesthesia should the nurse assess a postoperative patient?
Ask what the question is asking.	What is the most serious potential consequence of intubation?
Critically analyze each option in relation to the question and the other options.	First define each problem and recall the cause of each. Then explore each problem in relation to the stress of intubation. Finally, compare and contrast the problems and determine which is most serious among the options. The concept of airway, breathing, and circulation can be applied when the question requires you to prioritize information.
Eliminate incorrect options.	All of the options can occur, but their consequences vary in severity. Options 1 and 3 can be eliminated first because they are similar and not life-threatening. Although atelectasis in option 2 will compromise respiratory function, it is not an obstruction of the airway and therefore can be eliminated.

27. 1. Intensity refers to the strength or amount of pain experienced, which often is rated from mild to excruciating. Pain scales (e.g., numerical scale, Wong-Baker FACES Rating Scale) can facilitate pain assessment.
2. The word "something" is too general to be related to the location of pain, which is the actual site where the pain is felt.
3. Quality refers to the description of the pain sensation. A total pain assessment is facilitated by the use of the mnemonic COLDERR (character, onset, location, duration, exacerbation, relief, and radiation).
4. The pattern of pain refers to time of onset, duration, recurrence, and remissions.

CRITICAL-THINKING STRATEGY

Recognize keywords.	A patient in pain tells the nurse, **"It feels like** something is on **fire." Which characteristic of pain** is associated with this statement?
Ask what the question is asking.	Which characteristic of pain is related to the statement, "It feels like something is on fire?"
Critically analyze each option in relation to the question and the other options.	First review the characteristics of pain. Use of the mnemonic COLDERR for pain assessment may be helpful for review of these characteristics. Then identify the characteristic that is reflected in the patient's statement.
Eliminate incorrect options.	Option 1 relates to the severity of the pain. Option 2 is related to location but the patient's statement is too general to identify the actual site of the pain. According to COLDERR, option 4 relates to onset, duration, exacerbation, and relief factors. Options 1, 2, and 4 can be eliminated because none of them refers to the character of the pain, which is reflective of the patient's statement.

28. 1. In the semi-Fowler position the abdominal organs drop by gravity, which permits maximum thoracic excursion. In addition, slight flexion of the hips reduces abdominal muscle tension, which limits pressure on the suture line and facilitates diaphragmatic (abdominal) breathing.
    2. Resting in bed in any position promotes flatus retention. Ambulation promotes intestinal motility, which promotes the passage of flatus.
    3. Inactivity results in decreased detrusor muscle tone, incomplete bladder emptying, and urinary stasis. The high-Fowler position and ambulation use gravity to promote urinary elimination.
    4. The semi-Fowler position does not facilitate drainage via a portable wound drainage system. Although negative pressure creates the vacuum that draws fluid into a portable wound drainage system, the collection container should be lower than the insertion site because its

negative pressure does not have to work against gravity.

CRITICAL-THINKING STRATEGY

Recognize keywords.	A nurse places a patient who had **abdominal surgery** in the **semi-Fowler position**. What is the **rationale** for this nursing intervention?
Ask what the question is asking.	Why is it beneficial to place a patient who had abdominal surgery in the semi-Fowler position?
Critically analyze each option in relation to the question and the other options.	First establish the relationship between abdominal surgery and the semi-Fowler position. Then explore nursing interventions that achieve the outcome identified in each option. Then connect the information among abdominal surgery, the semi-Fowler position, and each option.
Eliminate incorrect options.	For each option compare your list of nursing interventions that should accomplish the objective stated in the option. If the semi-Fowler position was not among your list, that option can be eliminated.

29. 1. Oil lubricates, not irritates, the intestinal mucosa.
    2. Soap irritates the intestinal mucosa and thus stimulates the circular and longitudinal muscles of the intestinal wall, which respond with wave-like movements (peristalsis) that propel intestinal contents toward the anus.
    3. Tap water is a hypotonic solution that exerts a lower osmotic pressure than the surrounding interstitial fluid, causing water to move from the colon into interstitial spaces. In addition, the volume of the fluid distends the lumen of the intestine. These processes stimulate peristalsis and defecation.
    4. Normal saline, a solution having the same osmotic pressure of surrounding interstitial fluid (isotonic), works by drawing fluid from interstitial spaces into the colon. This fluid, in addition to the original volume of saline instilled, exerts pressure against the intestinal mucosa, which stimulates peristalsis and defecation.

CRITICAL-THINKING STRATEGY

Recognize keywords.	A nurse is teaching a group of nursing assistants about the administration of enemas. **Which enema solution** that **works by irritating the intestinal mucosa** should be included in the teaching?
Ask what the question is asking.	Which enema solution promotes fecal elimination by irritating the intestinal mucosa?
Critically analyze each option in relation to the question and the other options.	Recall the physiological action of each type of enema presented in the question. Then make the connection between the type of enema and its action, whether or not it works by irritating the intestinal mucosa.
Eliminate incorrect options.	An oil-retention enema, a tap-water enema, and an enema that uses normal saline each work by another action than irritating the intestinal mucosa. Eliminate options 1, 3, and 4.

30. 1. Water will not increase the absorption of medications administered orally. Water will facilitate the swallowing and moving of medication down the esophagus to the stomach.
2. **Food can delay the dissolution and absorption of many drugs; therefore, most oral medications should be administered on an empty stomach. Oral medications should be administered with food only when indicated by the manufacturer's directions.**
3. The time of day does not influence the rate of absorption of medications administered orally.
4. Physical rest does not influence the rate of absorption of medications administered orally.

CRITICAL-THINKING STRATEGY

Recognize keywords.	A nurse is administering oral medications to several patients. **Which factor** associated with the administration of medication will **increase the absorption of oral medications**?
Ask what the question is asking.	Which factor promotes the absorption of oral medications?
Critically analyze each option in relation to the question and the other options.	Identify the absorption rate of medication in relation to each option presented. Then compare and contrast the absorption rates among the options to identify the one that promotes the absorption of oral medication.
Eliminate incorrect options.	Options 2 and 4 are related to the time of day and patient activity, respectively. Neither is concerned with an activity that takes place in the stomach or intestines where the process of absorption begins/occurs. Water in option 1 neither promotes nor hinders medication absorption. Food in the presence of medication inhibits/prolongs the process of absorption because both are competing for absorption. Recall that some medication should be taken with food to prevent gastric irritation, not to promote absorption. Options 1, 2, and 4 can be eliminated.

31. 1. **Infants react to pain in an intense way including physical resistance and lack of cooperation. Separation of an infant from the usual comforting contact with parents contributes to separation anxiety, which in turn lowers pain tolerance, which intensifies the pain experience. Infants express pain by irritability, rolling of the head, flexing the extremities, overreacting to common stimuli, an inability to be comforted by holding and rocking, and physical responses indicating stimulation of the sympathetic nervous system.**
2. Adolescents are less sensitive to pain than an age group in another option. Adolescents generally want to behave in an adult manner and therefore demonstrate a controlled behavioral response to pain.
3. Older adults have a decreased capacity to sense pain and pressure. Older adults often fail to notice situations that will cause acute pain in younger people.

4. Pregnant women generally are not more sensitive to pain than when not pregnant.

CRITICAL-THINKING STRATEGY

Recognize keywords.	A nurse in the postanesthesia care unit is assessing several patients in pain. Patients in **which age group** should the nurse anticipate **will be most sensitive to pain?**
Ask what the question is asking.	Which age patients are most sensitive to pain?
Critically analyze each option in relation to the question and the other options.	Recall the age groups most at risk for health-related issues, specifically pain. Compare and contrast the identified age groups to identify the one that is most sensitive to pain.
Eliminate incorrect options.	The age groups most at risk for health-related issues are children and older adults. Eliminate options 2 and 4. Review the physiological differences between infants and older adults. Infants have immature neurological systems and have limited experiential backgrounds to have learned to cope with pain. Older adults have declining physiological responses to stressors and the experiential background to have learned to cope with pain. Eliminate options 2, 3, and 4.

32. 1. Leavened bread and cake, not coffee and tea, are forbidden during Passover.
    2. **Meat from cloven-footed and cud-chewing animals is permitted as long as the animal is slaughtered and prepared following strict laws of Kashrut (Kosher diet).**
    3. There are no restrictions on dairy products and eggs after sundown on Fridays.
    4. **Dairy products and meat/poultry are never served at the same meal or on the same set of dishes. Dairy products are not permitted within 1 to 6 hours after eating meat/poultry. Meat/poultry cannot be eaten for 30 minutes after consuming dairy products. Historically, this was practiced so that one food did not contaminate the other.**

5. All crustaceans, shellfish, and fish-like mammals, such as crab, shrimp, and lobster, scallops, oysters, and clams are forbidden.

CRITICAL-THINKING STRATEGY

Recognize keywords.	A nurse is caring for a patient who is practicing **Orthodox Judaism.** Which should the nurse consider about **dietary regulations** when assisting the patient to plan meals?
Ask what the question is asking.	What are dietary regulations of Orthodox Judaism?
Critically analyze each option in relation to the question and the other options.	Recall beverages, dairy products, meat products, and shellfish that are influenced by dietary regulations of Orthodox Judaism. Compare the dietary regulations of Orthodox Judaism with the statements in the options.
Eliminate incorrect options.	Options 1, 3, and 5 have statements related to a specific factor (Passover, sundown on Friday, and rituals). After comparing your knowledge with the options and identifying that options 1, 3, and 5 have a factor as a focus and is different than options 2 and 4, which focuses just on food, you may use the test-taking skill of identifying which options are different. This technique may help you eliminate options 1, 3, and 5.

33. 1. Although validating a patient's feelings will help the patient feel accepted, understood, and credible, there is no information indicating that the patient is experiencing anxiety.
    2. Relaxation techniques are effective ways to reduce the autonomic nervous system response to a threat. However, it is not as effective as an intervention in another option.
    3. Minimizing environmental stimuli may support rest and sleep, which is an essential aspect of stress management in any setting. However, it is not as helpful as another option.

4. Anxiety is a response to an unknown threat to the self or self-esteem. Therefore, explaining what, how, why, when, and where of procedures to the patient will prevent and reduce anxiety by minimizing the unknown.

CRITICAL-THINKING STRATEGY

Recognize keywords.	A newly admitted patient arrives on the unit. Which is **most important** for the nurse to do to **help minimize the development of anxiety**?
Ask what the question is asking.	Which action will limit anxiety in a newly hospitalized patient?
Critically analyze each option in relation to the question and the other options.	The interventions in all the options may help reduce anxiety. The words *newly admitted* set a focus that must be addressed when analyzing the options. You are being asked to identify a priority action in relation to a parameter.
Eliminate incorrect options.	Options 2 and 3 are general interventions that address anxiety in any situation. Option 1 may minimize anxiety after it occurs, not before. Options 1, 2, and 3 can be eliminated.

34. 1. Although the leadership role is an important role and can be demonstrated in many different settings, a word in another option has a stronger relationship with the role of the nurse when helping a patient negotiate the health-care system.
2. The health-care delivery system in the United States is complex and can be confusing at a time when patients have the least energy to explore and negotiate intervention options. When functioning as a resource person, the nurse identifies resources, provides information, and makes referrals.
3. The surrogate role is not a professional role of the nurse. A surrogate role is assigned to a nurse when a patient believes that the nurse reminds them of another person and projects that role and the feelings he/she has for the other person onto the nurse.

4. The role of counselor is only one area of nursing practice and a word in another option has a stronger relationship with the role of the nurse when helping a patient negotiate the health-care system. Counseling is related only to helping a patient recognize and cope with emotional stressors, improve relationships, and promote personal growth.

CRITICAL-THINKING STRATEGY

Recognize keywords.	A home health-care nurse is **helping a patient negotiate the health-care system** within the **community**. Which **word best reflects this role** of the nurse?
Ask what the question is asking.	What is a significant role of the nurse who is working in the community?
Critically analyze each option in relation to the question and the other options.	Define the word in each option. Explore behaviors of a nurse who is functioning in the role in each option. Your list of behaviors should parallel behaviors in the correct option as they relate to *helping a patient negotiate the health-care system*.
Eliminate incorrect options.	The patient assumes the role of leader in the nurse-patient relationship. Being a surrogate is not a professional nursing role. Being a counselor relates to providing emotional and psychological support. A resource person provides information and facilitates movement through the multidisciplinary health-care system. Options 1, 3, and 4 can be eliminated.

35. 1. The percentage of body water dramatically decreases with age, and older adults have altered thirst mechanisms that place them at risk for inadequate fluid intake and dehydration. In addition, the skin of older adults is drier because of a decreased ability to sweat and a decreased production of sebum.
2. Lotion is preferable to baby powder because lotion lubricates the skin. Also, baby powder should be avoided because, when aerosolized, it is a respiratory irritant.

3. Having a bath daily, even when using a moisturizing soap, is drying to the skin of older adults. Two to three times a week is adequate for an older adult who is continent.
4. Wool fabrics are coarse and irritate the skin and therefore should be avoided.

CRITICAL-THINKING STRATEGY

Recognize keywords.	Which patient statement indicates to the nurse that an older adult understands the teaching about **how to care for dry skin effectively**?
Ask what the question is asking.	Which is the best intervention to treat dry skin?
Critically analyze each option in relation to the question and the other options.	Only one option is correct because you are not asked to identify a priority action. Explore interventions that can prevent or care for dry skin, particularly in the older adult. Compare your list to the options presented.
Eliminate incorrect options.	Having a daily bath is too drying for the skin of older adults. Eliminate option 3. Option 2 can be eliminated because lotion is preferable to baby powder. Eliminate option 4 because it is an incorrect statement.

36. 1. Lubricating the suppository and index finger of a gloved hand before insertion facilitates insertion and limits trauma to vaginal mucous membranes.
    2. Remaining flat in bed for 20 minutes will maintain the medication in place, which facilitates absorption.
    3. Perineal care, not a vaginal irrigation, should be performed before inserting a vaginal suppository.
    4. The patient should be placed in the supine position with the knees flexed (dorsal recumbent) to facilitate insertion of a vaginal suppository.
    5. Advancing the suppository along the posterior vaginal wall facilitates the placement of the vaginal suppository just outside the cervical os so that when it melts it will eventually disperse through the entire vaginal canal.

6. The vagina is not a sterile cavity. Only medical asepsis is required for the insertion of a vaginal suppository.

CRITICAL-THINKING STRATEGY

Recognize keywords.	A patient has a prescription for a **vaginal suppository. Which actions** should the nurse perform **when administering** this medication?
Ask what the question is asking.	Which are steps in the procedure for administering a vaginal suppository?
Critically analyze each option in relation to the question and the other options.	List the steps in the procedure for administering a vaginal suppository. Compare the statements in the options with your list.
Eliminate incorrect options.	Delete from consideration those options that do not correlate to your list of steps for administering a vaginal suppository. Eliminate option 3.

37. 4. Cleaning the probe minimizes cross contamination from one patient to another.
    2. Placing the temporal artery scanner in the middle of the forehead positions the instrument so that it is over the temporal artery as it is moved across the forehead and down toward the hairline on the side of the face.
    1. The temporal artery is a major artery close to the heart via the carotid artery, which directly leads from the aorta. The temporal artery is close to the skin and provides easy access to measure true body temperature accurately. Holding the probe flat against the forehead keeps the instrument in contact with the skin and provides for a more accurate reading.
    3. Touching the probe to the soft area just behind the earlobe helps to ensure an accurate reading if a person is sweating. Sweating causes cooling of the skin, and a reading given by a temporal scanner may be low. Research demonstrates that gently positioning the probe on the neck directly behind

the earlobe below the mastoid provides accurate results.

5. Releasing the button instructs the instrument to display the temperature reading on the LCD display screen on the instrument.

CRITICAL-THINKING STRATEGY

Recognize keywords.	A nurse is taking a patient's **temperature** using the **instrument in the illustration**. Place the following **steps in** the **order** in which they should be **implemented**.
Ask what the question is asking.	List the steps of using a temporal thermometer.
Critically analyze each option in relation to the question and the other options.	Identify the sequential steps when using a temporal thermometer. Refer to your list as you examine the options presented. Order the steps presented according to the order you identified.
Eliminate incorrect options.	There are no incorrect options.

38. 1. **Cold lowers the temperature of skin and underlying tissue, which causes vasoconstriction, reducing blood flow to the area. This controls bleeding and slows the passage of fluid from the intravascular to the interstitial compartment, which limits edema.**

2. Direct pressure may limit bleeding by compressing injured blood vessels, but it will not affect edema.

3. Long, smooth strokes sliding over the skin (effleurage) will not limit edema or bleeding into tissues. However, effleurage reduces pain by using the Gate-Control Theory of Pain. Peripheral stimuli transmitted via large-diameter nerves close the gate to painful stimuli that use small-diameter nerves, thereby blocking the perception of pain.

4. Cutaneous stimulation (massage) will not limit edema or bleeding into tissues. However, massage uses the Gate-Control Theory of Pain to limit pain.

CRITICAL-THINKING STRATEGY

Recognize keywords.	A patient sustains soft tissue injuries from a motor vehicle collision. **Which intervention** is helpful in **limiting** the stress of **both edema and bleeding** into tissue?
Ask what the question is asking.	What can be done to limit edema and bleeding?
Critically analyze each option in relation to the question and the other options.	Explore the purpose and outcomes of cold compresses, direct pressure, effleurage, and massage. Then consider this information in relation to just edema, just bleeding into tissue, and both edema and bleeding into tissue.
Eliminate incorrect options.	Pressure only limits bleeding. Eliminate option 2. Effleurage and massage do not influence bleeding or edema. However, they are similar in that both may limit pain. When options are similar (one is not better than the other), usually they both can be eliminated. Eliminate options 3 and 4.

39. 1. Although the physical trauma of surgery causes pain and it must be relieved, it is not the priority.

2. Although general anesthesia can cause nausea, it is not the priority problem in the postanesthesia care unit.

3. **With an altered level of consciousness the pharyngeal, laryngeal, and gag reflexes may be impaired. The inability to cough or swallow can result in aspiration of oral secretions. When considering the ABCs of nursing intervention, the airway has priority.**

4. Excessive fluid loss precipitates a deficient fluid volume, but the nurse generally has time to meet this need safely.

CRITICAL-THINKING STRATEGY

Recognize keywords.	**Which response** by a patient in the **postanesthesia care unit** is the **priority concern** for the nurse?

Ask what the question is asking.	Which patient response places a postoperative patient at the highest risk?
Critically analyze each option in relation to the question and the other options.	Explore the consequences of the patient responses in each option. Analyze the severity of each response in relation to the other responses. Identify the response that may be life-threatening. Analyze these options in relation to the ABCs (airway, breathing, and circulation) of patient assessment and needs.
Eliminate incorrect options.	Pain and nausea are not life-threatening issues in a postanesthesia care unit. Although fluid volume deficit has the potential to be a life-threatening problem if it is related to hemorrhage, it is a lower priority than another option because surgical patients are supported with IV fluids during and after surgery. Options 1, 2, and 4 can be eliminated.

40. 1. **The only way to reestablish patency of the air vent lumen of a double-lumen nasogastric tube is to instill air into the lumen. The injected air will push the secretions blocking the lumen back into the stomach, where the fluid can be removed by the drainage lumen. Keeping the end of the air vent lumen higher than the stomach prevents reflux of gastric contents into the air vent lumen.**
   2. Repositioning the patient will not reestablish patency of the air vent lumen. The patient is placed in this position as the tube is being inserted to facilitate its passage into the stomach.
   3. Placing the vent below the level of the stomach will draw fluid from the stomach into the air vent lumen by the principle of gravity.
   4. Withdrawing 30 mL of gastric contents from the drainage lumen will not reestablish patency of the air vent lumen. Withdrawing 30 mL of gastric contents via the drainage lumen is done to ensure that the catheter is in the correct anatomical location.

CRITICAL-THINKING STRATEGY

Recognize keywords.	Which should the nurse **do** when the **vent of** a patient's **double-lumen nasogastric tube** for decompression **becomes obstructed**?
Ask what the question is asking.	How do you correct an obstruction in a double-lumen gastric tube?
Critically analyze each option in relation to the question and the other options.	Distinguish between what the nurse should do regarding routine care of a double-lumen nasogastric tube versus what specifically should be done when the tube is clogged.
Eliminate incorrect options.	Options 2, 3, and 4 are nursing interventions that will not clear the air vent of gastric fluid, which will permit effective functioning of the system.

41. 1. An incident report is unnecessary when a patient refuses treatment. Patients have the right to refuse care; however, the patient's refusal of care and the reasons for the refusal should be documented in the patient's clinical record.
   2. **Any incident such as a fall that either results in harm to a patient, employee, or visitor or does not result in an injury must be documented in an incident report.**
   3. An incident report does not have to be completed when a visitor ambulates a patient who should have been on bedrest. The incident should be documented in the patient's clinical record.
   4. A nurse leaving work early without reporting to the supervisor does not require an incident report. The nurse manager should discuss this behavior with the nurse and may document it in the nurse's personnel file.
   5. **Not receiving a prescribed medication may have the potential to cause harm. Therefore, an incident or adverse occurrence report should be completed to document the incident to add to the data so that similar situations can be prevented in the future.**
   6. **Any incident such as a fall that either results in harm to a patient, employee,**

or visitor or does not result in an injury must be documented in an incident report.

CRITICAL-THINKING STRATEGY

Recognize keywords.	In **which situations** is a nurse **required** to complete **an incident report**?
Ask what the question is asking.	Identify situations that require an incident report.
Critically analyze each option in relation to the question and the other options.	Recall and make a list of the variety of situations that require an incident report. Compare the situations presented in the options to your identified list of situations. Identify the parallel situations.
Eliminate incorrect options.	Patients have a right to refuse care. Visitors violating a primary health-care provider's order should be documented in progress notes rather than an incident report. A nurse leaving work early without reporting to the supervisor is an ethical situation that does not require an incident report. Options 1, 3, and 4 can be eliminated.

42. 1. Encouraging the avoidance of moving will not promote absorption via the transdermal patch; it could result in the destructive effects of immobility and may interfere with the quality of life.
2. Seeking a dose increase in the long-acting opioid is not the priority. Although this may eventually be necessary, the patient's pain must be relieved immediately.
3. Intermittent episodes of pain that occur despite continued use of an analgesic (breakthrough pain) can be managed by administering an immediate-release analgesic to reduce pain (rescue dosing). This reduces pain during an unanticipated pain episode without unnecessarily raising the dosage of the long-acting analgesic.
4. Antianxiety medication will be ineffective in this situation. The patient has intractable (resistant to treatment) pain that requires an opioid at this time.

CRITICAL-THINKING STRATEGY

Recognize keywords.	A patient who has a transdermal **analgesic patch** for cancer experiences **breakthrough pain** with activity. Which is **most important** for the nurse **to do**?
Ask what the question is asking.	Which action will relieve intractable breakthrough pain?
Critically analyze each option in relation to the question and the other options.	Explore the outcome of the interventions in each option. Compare and contrast the benefits among the proposed interventions. Identify the priority nursing intervention that will relieve the patient's pain immediately.
Eliminate incorrect options.	Options 2 and 4 involve requesting additional medication. One is not better than the other, and it will take time to obtain a prescription. Options 2 and 4 can be eliminated. Transdermal patches are administered for the intractable pain associated with cancer; therefore, limiting movement will be ineffective to prevent severe pain. Eliminate option 1.

43. 1. Fundamental nursing textbooks are not the best source for a step-by-step review of a nursing skill. Generally, fundamental nursing textbooks do not address every nursing skill in a step-by-step approach, nor do they include intermediate or advanced skills.
2. Calling the staff education department for assistance should not be the first thing to do when unsure of the steps in a nursing procedure. Another action should be implemented first.
3. Checking the nursing policy and procedure manual is the first resource the nurse should use when unsure of the steps in a nursing procedure. A review of the procedure in the procedure manual may refresh the memory or support the confidence of the nurse so that it is safe to proceed.
4. Refusing to do the procedure is premature. Another action should be implemented first.

CRITICAL-THINKING STRATEGY

Recognize keywords.	A nurse must perform a procedure and is **unsure of** the exact **steps of the procedure. Which should the nurse do first?**
Ask what the question is asking.	Which should be done when unsure of the steps of a procedure?
Critically analyze each option in relation to the question and the other options.	All of the interventions in the options may eventually be done. Analyze each option in relation to the others to identify what should be done first. You are being asked to set a priority. If you cannot identify what should be done first, eliminate the option that would be done last. Repeat this process with the remaining three options. Make a final selection when you are down to two options.
Eliminate incorrect options.	Staff education personnel may not be immediately available. A fundamentals of nursing textbook does not provide comprehensive coverage of nursing procedures. Refusing to perform a procedure is a behavior of last resort. Options 1, 2, and 4 can be eliminated.

44. 1. A pressure ulcer is not a microbiological stressor. If an ulcer becomes infected, the organism causing the infection is a microbiological stressor.
    2. A pressure ulcer is not a developmental stressor. Developmental stressors are physiological changes or transitional life events that occur during the expected stages of growth and development.
    3. **A pressure ulcer is a physiological stressor because the change in structure or function causes further**

stressors (secondary stressors) in the body.
    4. Pressure is a physical stressor that stimulates responses that cause an ulcer.

CRITICAL-THINKING STRATEGY

Recognize keywords.	A nurse is caring for a patient with a pressure ulcer. Which **type of stressor** is a **pressure ulcer?**
Ask what the question is asking.	To which classification of stressor does a pressure ulcer belong?
Critically analyze each option in relation to the question and the other options.	Define the category of stressor in each option. Explore examples of stressors in each category. Compare your examples to a pressure ulcer. Identify a parallel between a pressure and an example from among those you identified in each option.
Eliminate incorrect options.	Microbiological stresses involve pathogens, and developmental stresses involve age-related issues. Options 1 and 2 can be eliminated. Physical stresses involve a stimulus from outside the body, whereas physiological stresses involve a stimulus from inside the body. Pressure ulcers occur within the body. Option 4 can be eliminated.

45. 1. **On 9-9 at 04 the respiratory rate was 15 breaths per minute.**
    2. On 9-9 at 08 the respiratory rate was 20 breaths per minute.
    3. On 9-10 at 08 the patient's respiratory rate was 30 breaths per minute.
    4. On 9-10 at 16 the patient's respiratory rate was 25 breaths per minute.

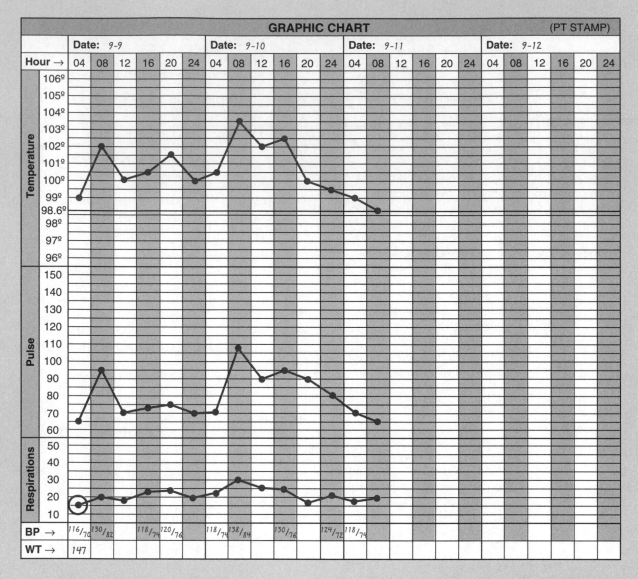

		GRAPHIC CHART																				(PT STAMP)	
	Date: 9-9						**Date:** 9-10						**Date:** 9-11						**Date:** 9-12					
Hour →	04	08	12	16	20	24	04	08	12	16	20	24	04	08	12	16	20	24	04	08	12	16	20	24

Temperature / Pulse / Respirations graphic chart.

| BP → | $116/70$ | $130/82$ | | $118/74$ | $120/76$ | | $118/74$ | $138/84$ | | $130/76$ | | | $124/72$ | $118/74$ | | | | | | | | | | |
| WT → | 147 | | | | | | | | | | | | | | | | | | | | | | | |

CRITICAL-THINKING STRATEGY

Recognize keywords.	At **which day and time** did the patient have a **respiratory rate of 15 breaths per minute**?
Ask what the question is asking.	Interpret a graphic record to identify the date and time at which a patient had a respiratory rate of 15 breaths per minute.
Critically analyze each option in relation to the question and the other options.	Identify the location of the date and time for each option at the top of the graphic chart, and carefully proceed down the column to identify the rate of respirations indicated by the position of the dot. Repeat this action for each date and time indicated in each option. Identify the option that has a dot on the line that indicates 15 respirations.

Eliminate incorrect options.	Eliminate the 3 options where the dot is located on a line that is more than 15 respirations.

46. 1. This response is clarifying, not paraphrasing. In addition, to respond more accurately when using clarification the nurse should have said, "Are you saying that you do not want to have this surgery?" Not wanting surgery and postponing surgery are two different concepts.
  2. **This response is an example of paraphrasing, which restates the content of the patient's message in similar words.**
  3. This response is an example of reflective technique, which focuses on feelings.
  4. This response is an example of an open-ended statement, which invites the patient to elaborate on the stated concern.

CRITICAL-THINKING STRATEGY

Recognize keywords.	A patient appears agitated and states, **"I'm not sure that I want to go through with this surgery." Which response** by the nurse uses the technique of **paraphrasing**?
Ask what the question is asking.	Which statement uses the technique of paraphrasing?
Critically analyze each option in relation to the question and the other options.	Define *paraphrasing*. Identify the communication technique being used in each nursing statement. Make a correlation between paraphrasing and the statement that restates what the patient said.
Eliminate incorrect options.	Option 1 uses clarification. Option 3 uses reflection. Option 4 is an open-ended statement. Eliminate options 1, 3, and 4.

47. 1. **Sites for a transdermal patch should be rotated because doing so limits skin irritation and excoriation. Also, it allows time for the site to recover if irritated.**
   2. Both irritation of the skin and vasodilation can result from rubbing the skin, which can alter absorption of the medication.
   3. **A hairless site will ensure that there is effective contact with the skin.**
   4. **When preparing and applying the patch, the nurse may be exposed to the medication on the patch. Clean gloves provide a barrier and protect the nurse from absorbing some of the medication.**
   5. The old patch should be removed at the same time that the new patch is applied.

CRITICAL-THINKING STRATEGY

Recognize keywords.	A nurse is planning to apply a **transdermal patch** to a patient. **Which actions should the nurse implement**?
Ask what the question is asking.	Which steps are associated with applying a transdermal patch?
Critically analyze each option in relation to the question and the other options.	List the steps of the procedure for applying a transdermal patch. Identify which options are among your list of interventions.
Eliminate incorrect options.	Option 2 may harm the patient and is contraindicated. Permitting two patches to remain on the skin concurrently may result in absorption of excessive medication, which may harm the patient. Eliminate options 2 and 5.

48. 1. **Effleurage involves long, smooth strokes sliding over the skin that have a relaxing, sedative effect. When performed slowly with light pressure at the end of a backrub, it is called "feathering off."**
   2. Firm, not deep, circular motions are used with backrub.
   3. Kneading (pétrissage) is not performed over the vertebrae because it is stimulating and traumatic for the vertebral column and spinal cord.
   4. Rubbing the back over the vertebrae is contraindicated because it is traumatic to the vertebral column and spinal cord. A backrub should be performed on either side of the vertebrae.

CRITICAL-THINKING STRATEGY

Recognize keywords.	Which **should** the nurse **do** when providing a **backrub** for a patient?
Ask what the question is asking.	Which action is part of a backrub?
Critically analyze each option in relation to the question and the other options.	List the steps associated with a backrub. Identify what will happen if each action in the options is implemented. Identify the option that reflects a safe, correct action by the nurse.
Eliminate incorrect options.	Actions in options 2, 3, and 4 are contraindicated when providing a backrub. Eliminate these options.

49. 1. This response is a challenging statement and is inappropriate. It may take away the patient's coping mechanism and cut off communication; the patient is using denial to cope with the diagnosis. Also, it does not address what the patient thinks or feels about the diagnosis.
2. This response may take away the patient's coping mechanism, is demeaning, and may cut off communication. The use of the word "bad" may increase the patient's anxiety. The patient is using denial to cope with the diagnosis.
3. This response is too direct and demeaning and may cut off communication. The patient is using denial to cope with the diagnosis.
4. **This provides an opportunity to discuss the illness; eventually a developing awareness will occur and the patient will move on to other coping mechanisms.**

CRITICAL-THINKING STRATEGY

Recognize keywords.	A **patient is told** by the primary health-care provider that the patient **has metastatic lung cancer** and is seriously ill. After the provider leaves the room, the patient has a severe episode of coughing and shortness of breath and says, **"This is just a cold, I'll be fine once I get over it." How should the nurse respond**?
Ask what the question is asking.	Which response will encourage a patient in denial to talk?
Critically analyze each option in relation to the question and the other options.	Review therapeutic communication skills and barriers to communication. Examine the options and identify the action that is therapeutic and the ones that are not therapeutic.
Eliminate incorrect options.	Options 1, 2, and 3 are challenging and should be avoided. Responses should not take away a patient's coping mechanism. Eliminate options 1, 2, and 3.

50. 1. **A tube feeding formula usually is hypertonic, which exerts an osmotic force that pulls fluid into the stomach** and intestine, resulting in intestinal cramping and diarrhea.
2. An inadequate volume of the feeding may result in fluid volume deficit and malnutrition, not diarrhea.
3. Failure to test for a residual before the feeding may result in vomiting, not diarrhea. If there is still fluid remaining from the previous feeding, failure to test for a residual before administering a tube feeding can result in adding more fluid than the patient's stomach can tolerate.
4. Placing a patient in the high-Fowler position during the administration of a tube feeding is done to prevent aspiration of the formula and will not cause diarrhea.

CRITICAL-THINKING STRATEGY

Recognize keywords.	A patient develops diarrhea after receiving several **intermittent tube feedings.** Which should the nurse consider is the **cause of** the **diarrhea?**
Ask what the question is asking.	Why can intermittent tube feedings cause diarrhea?
Critically analyze each option in relation to the question and the other options.	Review the physiological response of the body to a hypertonic solution and an inadequate volume of formula. Explore why testing for a residual is performed before and a high-Fowler position is used during an intermittent tube feeding. Compare and contrast the information you gathered in your review with the reasons for diarrhea presented in each option.
Eliminate incorrect options.	Options 1 and 2 address the formula (osmolarity and volume). Options 3 and 4 address nursing interventions during the procedure. Option 2 is related to fluid and nutritional deficiencies, not diarrhea. Failure to test for a residual in option 3 may result in vomiting, not diarrhea. A high-Fowler position in option 4 prevents aspiration, not diarrhea. Eliminate options 2, 3, and 4.

51. 1. Placing the patient in the supine position is unnecessary. This is done when the person is unconscious.
2. When attempting to clear an airway of an obstruction, the thumb side of the hand should always be against the person's body.
3. This is the appropriate modification of the abdominal thrust (Heimlich) maneuver for a pregnant woman. This provides thoracic compression while preventing pressure against the uterus that can result in trauma to the woman or the fetus.
4. Waiting until the person becomes unconscious wastes valuable time and is unsafe. Delaying or discontinuing the maneuver before the obstruction is cleared will result in death.

CRITICAL-THINKING STRATEGY

Recognize keywords.	While in a restaurant, a **pregnant woman** exhibits a **total airway obstruction** because of a bolus of food. How should the nurse **modify** the thrusts of the **abdominal thrust** (Heimlich) maneuver for this person?
Ask what the question is asking.	How should the abdominal thrust maneuver be adapted for a pregnant woman?
Critically analyze each option in relation to the question and the other options.	List the steps of the abdominal thrust maneuver. Recall the physiological changes in a woman's body when pregnant. Compare these physiological changes with the steps of the procedure, and determine what step may harm the woman or fetus. Identify the modification of the procedure that will help dislodge the obstruction while protecting the woman and fetus.
Eliminate incorrect options.	Options 1 and 4 delay the initiation of the procedure. Eliminate options 1 and 4. Option 2 will be physically difficult to perform and will still compress the woman's abdominal area, which may harm the woman or fetus. Eliminate option 2.

52. 1. The lights, noise, and activity in the hospital environment can interfere with napping during the day. However, naps when they do occur usually are short and rarely reach stage IV restorative sleep.
2. Hospitalized patients can follow their usual bedtime rituals.
3. Most medications are administered by 10 p.m. to 11 p.m. and should not interfere with sleep.
4. Studies support the fact that finding a comfortable position is one of the most common factors that interferes with sleep as reported by hospitalized patients. Patients frequently find hospital beds unfamiliar and uncomfortable. In addition, therapeutic regimens restrict movement or require patients to assume sleeping positions other than their preference.

CRITICAL-THINKING STRATEGY

Recognize keywords.	A nurse is planning care to support a patient's ability to sleep. Which **factor** from **among the options** presented **most commonly interferes with the sleep of hospitalized patients**?
Ask what the question is asking.	Which most hinders hospitalized patients' abilities to sleep?
Critically analyze each option in relation to the question and the other options.	Analyze each option in relation to a patient in the hospital environment. Then identify the option that most interferes with sleep.
Eliminate incorrect options.	The hospital environment impedes the ability to take naps. Eliminate option 1. Bedtime rituals can be maintained in a hospital. Eliminate option 2. Most medications are not administered between 11 p.m. and 6 a.m. Eliminate option 3.

53. 1. Pasta is made from grains, and peas are legumes, which together provide amino acids that make a complete protein. Complete proteins supply all eight essential amino acids. Essential amino acids are those that cannot be manufactured by the human body and must be obtained from food sources.

2. Yogurt and fruit together do not provide a complete protein. In addition, pure vegetarians (vegans) eat only plants. Lactovegetarians eat vegetables and milk products; lacto-ovovegetarians eat vegetables, milk products, and eggs (some may occasionally eat fish or poultry).

3. Bread and cheese together provide a complete protein. However, pure vegetarians (vegans) eat only plants (which includes grains), not dairy products.

4. **Grains and legumes lack different amino acids. When these foods are combined, they substitute for a complete protein. Complete proteins supply all eight essential amino acids. Essential amino acids are those that cannot be manufactured by the human body and must be obtained from food sources.**

5. Peanut butter combined with a grain, not jelly, is a substitute for a complete protein.

CRITICAL-THINKING STRATEGY

Recognize keywords.	A nurse is providing dietary teaching for a patient who is a **vegan. Which food combinations** that **are** substitutes for a **complete protein** should the nurse include in the dietary teaching?
Ask what the question is asking.	Which combination of food provides essential amino acids for a vegan?
Critically analyze each option in relation to the question and the other options.	Recall what a vegan does or does not eat. Identify the type of protein presented in each food combination. Analyze the food combinations presented, and conclude if they provide essential amino acids and are included in a vegan diet.
Eliminate incorrect options.	Eliminate options, 2, 3, and 5 because pure vegans eat only plants and the food combinations in the options do not provide essential amino acids.

54. 1. Calcium is essential for functioning, but it is unrelated to the risk for drug toxicity in the older adult. Calcium is essential for cell membrane structure, wound healing, synaptic transmission in nervous tissue, membrane excitability, muscle contraction, tooth and bone structure, blood clotting, and glycolysis.

2. Red blood cells are responsible for delivering oxygen to cells and are unrelated to the risk for drug toxicity in the older adult.

3. **The glomerular filtration rate is reduced by as much as 46% at 90 years of age. In addition, decreased cardiac output can reduce the amount of blood flow to the kidneys by as much as 50%. When the glomerular filtration rate declines, the time necessary for half of a drug to be excreted increases by as much as 40%, which places the older adult at risk for drug toxicity.**

4. Frequency of voiding is unrelated to the risk for drug toxicity in the older adult.

CRITICAL-THINKING STRATEGY

Recognize keywords.	A nurse is administering medication to an **older adult**. A **decrease in which** of the following **increases the risk of drug toxicity** in this patient?
Ask what the question is asking.	Which factor increases the risk for drug toxicity in older adults?
Critically analyze each option in relation to the question and the other options.	Analyze the relationship between the physiological changes associated with aging and drug toxicity while considering the factor in each option.
Eliminate incorrect options.	Consider that drug metabolism (biotransformation) occurs in the liver by microsomes that stimulate the enzymatic breakdown of drugs and that most medications are excreted via the kidneys. The efficiency of these organs decreases as people age. Eliminate options 1 and 2 because they are unrelated to the functioning of the liver or kidneys. Inadequate urinary output, not urinary frequency, is related to drug toxicity. Eliminate option 4.

55. 1. Pulling the pinna of the ear backward and downward is done to straighten the ear canal of an infant or a young child, not an adult.
2. Inserting the drops into the center of the auditory canal can injure the eardrum. Drops should be directed along the wall of the ear canal.
3. **Pressing gently on the tragus facilitates the flow of medication toward the eardrum.**
4. Rolling the patient from the side-lying position to the supine position can result in medication flowing out of the ear. The side-lying position with the involved ear on the uppermost side should be maintained for 2 to 3 minutes after the medication is instilled.

CRITICAL-THINKING STRATEGY

Recognize keywords.	A nurse instills medicated **drops into the ear** of an **adult.** Which should the nurse do to **ensure** that the **medication flows toward the eardrum**?
Ask what the question is asking.	Which action disperses medication in the ear canal of an adult?
Critically analyze each option in relation to the question and the other options.	List the steps of administering medicated drops into a patient's ear. Recall the difference in the procedure for an adult versus an infant/ young child. Compare the list and the difference identified to the options presented.
Eliminate incorrect options.	Option 1 is a technique used with infants and young children. Option 2 can harm the eardrum and is unsafe. Option 4 will result in fluid draining away from the eardrum. Eliminate options 1, 2, and 4.

56. 1. Preschoolers (age 3 to 5 years—Initiative versus Guilt) learn to separate from parents and develop a sense of initiative. Negative resolution will result in guilt, rigidity, and a hesitancy to explore new skills or challenge abilities.
2. **Adolescents (age 12 to 20 years— Identity versus Role Confusion) strive to develop a personal identity and** autonomy. **This is a turbulent time as the adolescent internalizes the dramatic physical changes and the psychological stressors of new social conflicts. It is common for adolescents to experience mood swings, make decisions without having all the facts, challenge authority, and assert the self. However, these behaviors are left behind when the developmental tasks of adolescence are positively resolved. Negative resolution results in assertive, rebellious, and antisocial behavior.**
3. School-aged children (age 6 to 12 years— Industry verses Inferiority) learn to compete, compromise, and cooperate; develop relationships with peers; and win recognition through productivity. Negative resolution results in feelings of inadequacy, low self-esteem, and a reluctance to explore the environment.
4. Infants (birth to 18 months—Trust versus Mistrust) learn to depend on others to meet their needs, thereby developing trust and a beginning sense of self. Negative resolution of this task results in mistrust, dependency, lack of self-confidence, and shallow relationships in later stages of development.

CRITICAL-THINKING STRATEGY

Recognize keywords.	A nurse identifies that an adult patient is exhibiting antisocial behavior. According to **Erikson**, the **negative resolution** of which **stage of development** is most commonly **associated with antisocial behavior**?
Ask what the question is asking.	To which stage of Erikson's theory of development is antisocial behavior most related?
Critically analyze each option in relation to the question and the other options.	Consider the developmental task and related behaviors associated with each age group presented. Recall the behaviors of a person with an antisocial personality disorder. Identify the stage that reflects behavior associated with behaviors of people with an antisocial personality disorder.

continued

continued

Eliminate incorrect options.	Infants are developing trust, preschoolers are developing initiative, and school-aged children are learning to compromise and cooperate. Usually infants, preschoolers, and school-aged children are not irresponsible and do not abuse substances, engage in illegal activities, or challenge authority. Eliminate options 1, 3, and 4.

57. 1. Positioning the arm at the level of the heart will result in an accurate blood pressure reading. If the arm is positioned higher than the level of the heart, the blood pressure will be inaccurately low. If the arm is positioned lower than the level of the heart, the blood pressure will be inaccurately high.
    2. Wrapping the lower edge of the cuff over the antecubital space will cover the brachial artery and interfere with the accurate assessment of blood pressure. The lower edge of the cuff should be approximately 1 inch (2.5 cm) above the antecubital space.
    3. The sphygmomanometer should be pumped up 20 to 30 mm Hg above the palpatory blood pressure reading. This ensures an accurate systolic reading without exerting undue pressure on the tissues of the arm.
    4. Releasing the valve slowly ensures that all five Korotkoff's sounds are heard accurately. Deflating the cuff too rapidly can result in a falsely low systolic reading, and deflating the cuff too slowly can result in a falsely high diastolic reading.
    5. When repeating a blood pressure the cuff should be completely deflated and the caregiver should wait 2 minutes before reinflating the blood pressure cuff. This action prevents congestion of the veins and an inaccurately high blood pressure reading.

CRITICAL-THINKING STRATEGY

Recognize keywords.	Which nursing **techniques** will result in an **accurate** measurement when obtaining a patient's **blood pressure**?

Ask what the question is asking.	Which are steps in obtaining a blood pressure measurement?
Critically analyze each option in relation to the question and the other options.	List the steps of the procedure for performing a blood pressure measurement. Compare and contrast the list with the options presented.
Eliminate incorrect options.	Inappropriate placement of the cuff and the sphygmomanometer will result in an inaccurate measurement. Eliminate option 2.

58. 1. Unconscious patients often bite down when something is placed in the mouth. Therefore, a padded tongue blade should be placed between the upper and lower teeth to help keep the mouth open during oral care. Other padded tongue blades, wetted with a small amount of saline, should be used to clean the oral cavity. This technique does not require flushing the oral cavity with fluid, which may compromise the airway.
    2. Although half-strength mouthwash and saline may be used, it is not the best intervention because mouthwash contains ingredients that can be irritating to the mucous membranes.
    3. Glycerin is not a cleansing agent and is not effective in cleaning the oral cavity.
    4. Toothpaste should be avoided because it requires flushing the mouth with adequate amounts of water to prevent leaving an irritating residue on the mucous membranes. An unconscious patient usually has a diminished gag reflex and is at risk for aspiration.

CRITICAL-THINKING STRATEGY

Recognize keywords.	Which should the nurse use to **best provide oral care** to an **unconscious patient**?
Ask what the question is asking.	What should be used to clean the oral cavity of an unconscious patient?

Critically analyze each option in relation to the question and the other options.	Consider the unique needs of a patient who is unconscious, particularly in relation to the ABCs (airway, breathing, and circulation). Analyze each option in relation to how it will impact on the patient's physical status.
Eliminate incorrect options.	Airway patency is always the priority. Options 2 and 4 require flushing the oral cavity with fluid, which may compromise the airway. Glycerin coats, rather than cleans, the oral mucosa. Eliminate options 2, 3, and 4.

59.
1. This question is too focused.
2. Although determining how long the patient has had diverticulitis is information that eventually may be obtained, it is not the immediate priority.
3. **This question invites the patient to expand on and develop a topic of importance that relates to the current problem.**
4. Although identifying previous episodes of diverticulitis is information that eventually may be obtained, it is not the immediate priority.

CRITICAL-THINKING STRATEGY

Recognize keywords.	A patient is admitted to the hospital with a medical diagnosis of **diverticulitis**. Which is the **best question** the nurse should ask when obtaining an **admission history** from this patient?
Ask what the question is asking.	Which question will obtain the patient's perspective of the situation?
Critically analyze each option in relation to the question and the other options.	Review the purpose of obtaining an admission history from a patient. Analyze each question to determine what information will be collected by the patient's response. Identify the most significant information the nurse should collect.

Eliminate incorrect options.	Options 1, 2, and 4 are direct questions that obtain limited information. Eliminate these options.

60.
1. 11 a.m. is too soon. The drug will not be at its lowest concentration in the blood.
2. **Thirty minutes before or closer to the next scheduled dose is the most appropriate time for a trough blood level to be obtained. The serum level of the drug will be at its lowest.**
3. Peak, not trough, levels are obtained 30 minutes after completion of drug administration.
4. The blood level of the drug increases after the drug is administered. A value taken at this time will not reflect the lowest serum level, which is the purpose of identifying a trough level.

CRITICAL-THINKING STRATEGY

Recognize keywords.	A primary health-care provider orders peak-and-trough levels for a patient receiving an intravenous antibiotic. **What time** should the nurse obtain a blood sample to determine a **trough level** when the **antibiotic was administered at 12 noon**?
Ask what the question is asking.	When should a blood specimen for a trough level of a drug be obtained?
Critically analyze each option in relation to the question and the other options.	Recall the parameters for obtaining a specimen for a trough level of a drug. Identify the interrelationship of when the drug was administered and the times offered in each of the options.
Eliminate incorrect options.	A specimen of blood for a trough level should be obtained when the drug is at its lowest level (about 30 minutes before the next dose). Options 3 and 4 are too soon after the drug was administered. Eliminate options 3 and 4. Option 1 is too early compared with option 2. Eliminate option 1.

61. 1. During adolescence, the individual is beginning to question life-guiding values such as spirituality. However, it is not uncommon for the adolescent to turn away from religious practices as part of dealing with role confusion and exploration of self-identity. Faith becomes centered around the peer group and away from the parents. This stage is called Synthetic-Conventional Faith by James Fowler.

    2. People expand and refine spiritual beliefs at an earlier stage of development than older adulthood.

    3. Young adults are just beginning to think about spirituality more introspectively at this age. Young adults generally enter a reflective period of time as discovery of values in relation to social goals are explored within their own frame of reference rather from the peer group frame of reference as during adolescence. This stage is called Individuative-Reflective Faith by James Fowler.

    4. **Middle-aged adults tend to engage in refining and expanding spiritual beliefs through questioning. Middle-aged adults are reported to have greater faith, have more reliance on personal spiritual strength, and be less inflexible in spiritual beliefs. Middle-aged adults integrate other viewpoints about faith, which introduces tension while working toward resolution of spiritual beliefs. This stage is called Conjunctive Faith by James Fowler.**

CRITICAL-THINKING STRATEGY

Recognize keywords.	A nurse is planning care for a patient in the spiritual realm. **Which age group generally is more involved with expanding and refining spiritual beliefs**?
Ask what the question is asking.	At what age are people more involved with expanding and refining spiritual beliefs?
Critically analyze each option in relation to the question and the other options.	Review the various age groups presented in relation to their concerns about spirituality. Use developmental and spiritual theories to place the beliefs and activities of the people in these age groups into perspective.
Eliminate incorrect options.	Generally adolescents are more concerned about peer relationships than spirituality. Eliminate option 1. Young adults are just beginning to explore spirituality, whereas older adults are refining previously explored beliefs. Eliminate options 2 and 3.

62. 1. **Assisting a patient to walk widens the patient's base of support because the base extends to include the nurse's feet on the floor in addition to the patient's feet on the floor.**

    2. **Walkers surround a person on three sides and provide four points of contact with the floor. This wide base provides the best support available for assisted ambulation.**

    3. Locking the wheels of a wheelchair follows the principle, *an object with wheels that are locked will remain stationary*.

    4. Holding objects close to the body when walking follows the principle, *the closer an object is held to the center of gravity, the greater the stability and the easier the object is to move*.

    5. Keeping the back straight when lifting an object follows the principle, *balance is maintained and muscle strain is limited as long as the line of gravity passes through the base of support*.

CRITICAL-THINKING STRATEGY

Recognize keywords.	Which **actions** are specifically **related to** the principle, *the greater the base of support, the more stable the body?*
Ask what the question is asking.	Which actions provide a wide base of support?
Critically analyze each option in relation to the question and the other options.	Identify the projected outcome for the behavior in each option. Then consider the principle that underlines the behavior and its outcome.
Eliminate incorrect options.	Option 3 relates to safety, not a wide base of support. Options 4 and 5 relate to principles associated with body mechanics, rather than a wide base of support. Eliminate options 3, 4, and 5.

63. 1. A backrub is the therapeutic manipulation of muscles and tissues that relaxes tense muscles, relieves muscle spasms, and induces rest or sleep. However, it may be contraindicated, and some people do not like a backrub or consider it an invasion of their personal space.

2. Music can be relaxing or stimulating depending on the music and the individual.

3. Although milk contains the amino acid L-tryptophan that promotes sleep, many people do not like milk or avoid fluids before bedtime to limit voiding during the night (nocturia).

4. **Following routines provides consistency and comfort in an unfamiliar environment. Bedtime rituals meet basic physiological needs and usually include physically and emotionally relaxing behaviors.**

CRITICAL-THINKING STRATEGY

Recognize keywords.	What is the **most effective** nursing **intervention** to **promote sleep** that is appropriate for a patient **in any situation**?
Ask what the question is asking.	Which is the best method to promote sleep?
Critically analyze each option in relation to the question and the other options.	Identify the commonalities and differences of nursing interventions that relate to promoting sleep. A commonality is an intervention that may work regardless of the patient situation. A difference is an intervention that may work for a patient in a specific situation.
Eliminate incorrect options.	Options 1, 2, and 3 may work for certain patients in specific situations. The nursing interventions in these options cannot be implemented for all patients. Eliminate options 1, 2, and 3.

64. An X in any part of the shaded area across the abdomen is a correct answer. A nurse should auscultate all four quadrants of the abdomen to determine the presence of borborygmi. Borborygmi are audible high-pitched, loud, gurgling sounds caused by the propulsion of gas through the intestine.

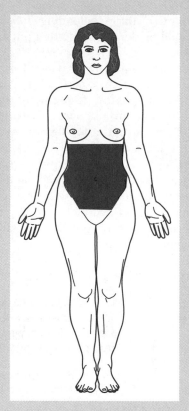

CRITICAL-THINKING STRATEGY

Recognize keywords.	A nurse is performing an assessment of a patient. Place an X on the figure of the body where the nurse should **place the stethoscope** to assess for the **presence of borborygmi.**
Ask what the question is asking.	Where on the body are borborygmi heard?
Critically analyze each option in relation to the question and the other options.	Define borborygmi. Consider where these sounds are produced within the body. Place an X where a stethoscope should be placed to auscultate these sounds.
Eliminate incorrect options.	Other areas of the body will be eliminated when an X is placed over the shaded area indicated in the answer.

65. 1. Although positioning the telephone within easy reach should be done, because it avoids reaching for a phone that can result in a loss of balance and a fall, it is not the most important intervention to prevent injury in a hospital.

2. Although storing belongings in a safe place should be done, this is not a physical hazard.

3. Adequate lighting provides for the safety of patients, staff, and visitors within a hospital. Inadequate lighting causes shadows, a dark environment, and the potential for misinterpreting stimuli (illusions) and is a major cause of accidents in the hospital setting.

4. An over-bed table has wheels and therefore cannot provide a firm base of support. Over-bed tables are physical hazards that may contribute to falls if used inappropriately.

CRITICAL-THINKING STRATEGY

Recognize keywords.	Which is the **most important** nursing **intervention** to help **prevent falls from physical hazards** in a hospital?
Ask what the question is asking.	How can the nurse best prevent falls in a hospital?
Critically analyze each option in relation to the question and the other options.	Analyze the outcome of each intervention in relation to safety. Compare and contrast options to eventually identify the best intervention.
Eliminate incorrect options.	Option 2 is unrelated to safety and option 4 is unsafe. Eliminate options 2 and 4. Options 1 and 3 both relate to safety. Option 1 relates to just one limited aspect of a safe environment. Option 2 relates to a more pervasive issue—inadequate lighting. Therefore, eliminate option 1.

66. 1. The supine position is a back-lying position that results in pressure on the heels (calcanei), which have minimal tissue between the bone and skin, making them vulnerable to the development of pressure ulcers.

2. There is no pressure on either greater trochanter when in the supine position. Pressure on a greater trochanter occurs when the patient is in a lateral (side-lying) position.

3. External, not internal, rotation of the hips tends to occur when a patient is in the supine position.

4. The knees are extended, not flexed, when in the supine position.

CRITICAL-THINKING STRATEGY

Recognize keywords.	A patient prefers and excessively maintains the **supine position**. For which **potential problem** associated with this position should the nurse assess the patient?
Ask what the question is asking.	Which problem is associated with the supine position?
Critically analyze each option in relation to the question and the other options.	Visualize a patient in the supine position. Examine each option in relation to the visualization. Identify the option that may place the patient at risk for a negative outcome.
Eliminate incorrect options.	Pressure on the trochanters does not occur in the supine position. External, not internal, rotation of the hips occurs with the supine position if trochanter rolls are not used to maintain functional alignment. Hyperextension of the knees, not flexion contractures of the knees, can occur in the supine position. Options 2, 3, and 4 can be eliminated.

67. 1. Setting limits will make the patient more anxious and demanding. Demanding behavior generally is an attempt to gain control over events in an effort to protect the self.

2. Alternating care with another nurse can be confusing to the patient and increase anxiety. Maintaining continuity in the nurse assignment will support the development of a trusting relationship and enable the nurse to explore the patient's feelings, as well as plan and implement interventions that encourage choices, all of which support feeling in control.

3. Pointing out demanding behavior is too confrontational at this time. Demanding behavior generally is a defense mechanism that reduces anxiety generated by powerlessness. To confront the behavior and take away the patient's coping mechanism will cause the patient to become more anxious.

4. Attempting to see the situation from the patient's perspective is an example of empathy, which is understanding a patient's emotional point of view. An empathic response communicates that the nurse is listening and cares.

CRITICAL-THINKING STRATEGY

Recognize keywords.	A patient is using the call bell **numerous times** an hour and **requesting assistance** with activities that the patient is **capable of achieving independently. Which should the nurse do** to help this patient?
Ask what the question is asking.	Which should the nurse do when a patient calls the nurse excessively?
Critically analyze each option in relation to the question and the other options.	Review concepts related to psychological responses to stress. Identify that the patient's behavior reflects anxiety. Explore nursing actions that support emotional needs and reduce anxiety. Then examine each option in light of whether the action will increase or decrease anxiety.
Eliminate incorrect options.	Options 1, 2, and 3 will increase, not decrease, anxiety and can be eliminated.

68. 1. This information includes a nursing intervention and an evaluation of the outcome, which is the most specific and complete of all the options.
    2. No data are given to support the assumption that the patient is happy.
    3. The words "less anxious" are relative and do not clearly evaluate the patient's status.
    4. Every patient has his or her own baseline. Indicating that a blood pressure is stable is incomplete and unclear.

CRITICAL-THINKING STRATEGY

Recognize keywords.	A nurse going off duty is making rounds with the nurse coming on duty and provides a report on each patient in the district. **Which information** reported by the nurse **is most complete?**

Ask what the question is asking.	Which information is most thorough?
Critically analyze each option in relation to the question and the other options.	Examine each option to determine if the information included is objective and comprehensive.
Eliminate incorrect options.	Options 2 and 3 use the terms "happy" and "less anxious," which are subjective and not measurable. Option 4 fails to provide the before and after blood pressures, making the information meaningless. Options 2, 3, and 4 can be eliminated.

69. 1. The eye should always be washed from the inner to the outer canthus to prevent secretions from entering the lacrimal ducts, which may result in an infection.
    2. A bath blanket promotes privacy and prevents heat loss during a bath and is unrelated to asepsis. If not soiled, a patient's bath blanket can be reused.
    3. Changing bath water after cleaning the perineum prevents transferring microorganisms from the perianal, urinary meatus, and vaginal area in women to subsequent areas of the body that are being washed. This action promotes medical asepsis.
    4. Having a patient void before beginning the bed bath is related to a patient's comfort and elimination needs, rather than asepsis.
    5. Clean gloves are required during this procedure to protect the nurse because the nurse may be exposed to body fluids.

CRITICAL-THINKING STRATEGY

Recognize keywords.	A nurse is bathing a patient. **Which** nursing **actions support** a principle associated with **medical asepsis?**
Ask what the question is asking.	Which actions are based on principles of medical asepsis?

continued

continued

Critically analyze each option in relation to the question and the other options.	Visualize the steps of the procedure for bathing a patient. Recall principles associated with maintaining medical asepsis. Integrate the principles of medical asepsis with the visualized steps of the procedure. Analyze the options in relation to this information.
Eliminate incorrect options.	Although options 2 and 4 are part of the procedure of bathing, they are unrelated to principles of medical asepsis. Eliminate options 2 and 4.

70. 1. Water is ineffective against a grease fire. It will scatter the flames and the fire will spread.
   2. The lid of the frying pan deprives the fire of oxygen. Without oxygen to support combustion the fire will go out.
   3. Although closing the door to the kitchen will help to contain the fire to the kitchen, there is a more appropriate intervention to contain the fire to the frying pan.
   4. Using a class A fire extinguisher is inappropriate. A class A fire extinguisher is designed for fires consisting of paper, wood, upholstery, rags, and ordinary rubbish.

CRITICAL-THINKING STRATEGY

Recognize keywords.	Health teaching regarding a kitchen fire should include what to do if **grease** in a frying pan catches on **fire**. A nurse teaches that in this situation people should **first call 911**. **Which** should people be taught **to do next**?
Ask what the question is asking.	Which should be done after calling 911 in the event of a grease fire?
Critically analyze each option in relation to the question and the other options.	Identify the steps to follow when confronted with a fire and integrate the concept "oxygen supports combustion." Refer to the mnemonic RACE (**R**escue patients in immediate danger, **A**ctivate the alarm, **C**onfine the fire, **E**xtinguish the fire).

Eliminate incorrect options.	No one needs to be rescued, and 911 was called. The next steps include confining and then extinguishing the fire. Placing a cover on the pan accomplishes both because it eliminates oxygen, which supports combustion. Eliminate options 1 and 4 because the actions are inappropriate and unsafe. Although the action in option 3 may confine the fire, it does not extinguish the fire. Eliminate options 1, 3, and 4.

71. 1. Sucking on a hard candy after the procedure addresses the problem after, rather than before, it occurs.
   2. Shaking the cartridge longer before using it will ensure that the medication is dispersed throughout solution in the cartridge. It will not change the taste of the medication.
   3. Oral hygiene should be performed after, not before, the procedure.
   4. The aerosolized medication enters the aerosol chamber, where the larger droplets fall to the bottom of the chamber. The smaller droplets are inhaled deep into the lungs rather than falling on the patient's tongue.

CRITICAL-THINKING STRATEGY

Recognize keywords.	A patient who self-administers an aerosol medication by a **metered-dose inhaler** complains of "the **nasty taste** of the medication." **Which should the nurse encourage the patient to do**?
Ask what the question is asking.	Which action will reduce the "nasty taste" of medication taken via a metered-dose inhaler?
Critically analyze each option in relation to the question and the other options.	Review the rationale for each step of the procedure when using a metered-dose inhaler. Identify the equipment that may be used when administering medication via a metered-dose inhaler. Compare and contrast this information in relation to resolution of the patient's problem.

Eliminate incorrect options.	The action in option 1 will not prevent the problem. The action in option 2 will not change the taste of the medication. The action in option 3 is done after, not before, the procedure. Options 1, 2, and 3 can be eliminated.

72. 1. Collecting data is not the most important purpose of the orientation phase of a therapeutic relationship.
    2. **The orientation phase (also called the introductory or pre-helping phase) of a therapeutic relationship sets the tone for the rest of the relationship. A rapport develops when the patient recognizes that the nurse is willing and able to help and can be trusted.**
    3. Problems are identified, explored, and dealt with during the working, not orientation, phase of a therapeutic relationship.
    4. Priority needs are identified and interventions planned and implemented during the working, not orientation, phase of a therapeutic relationship.

CRITICAL-THINKING STRATEGY

Recognize keywords.	Which is the **most important purpose** of the **orientation phase** of a therapeutic relationship?
Ask what the question is asking.	Which is the main function of the orientation phase of a therapeutic relationship?
Critically analyze each option in relation to the question and the other options.	Recall the phases of a therapeutic relationship. Determine what is significant about the orientation phase versus the other phases of the therapeutic relationship. Examine the options and identify which one accurately reflects the purposes of the orientation phase that you have identified.
Eliminate incorrect options.	Options 3 and 4 relate to the working phase of a therapeutic relationship and can be eliminated. Although data are collected during the orientation phase of the therapeutic relationship, this is not the most important purpose and therefore option 1 can be eliminated.

73. 1. Lethargy, weakness, and aching muscles occur during the course phase (plateau phase), not onset phase (cold or chill phase), of a fever.
    2. **Pale skin occurs as the peripheral blood vessels constrict in an attempt to increase the core body temperature.**
    3. **Feeling cold, chills, and shivering are adaptations associated with the onset phase (cold or chill phase) of a fever. During this phase the body responds to pyrogens by conserving heat to raise body temperature.**
    4. Profuse diaphoresis (sweating) occurs during the defervescence phase (fever abatement, flush phase) of a fever. During this phase the fever abates and body temperature returns to the expected range.
    5. Dehydration can occur during both the course phase (plateau phase) and defervescence phase (fever abatement, flush phase) of a fever.

CRITICAL-THINKING STRATEGY

Recognize keywords.	A patient has a temperature of 102°F and complains of **feeling cold**. Which **additional responses** should the nurse expect during this **onset phase (cold or chill phase) of a fever**?
Ask what the question is asking.	Which are signs associated with the onset phase (cold or chill phase) of a fever?
Critically analyze each option in relation to the question and the other options.	List the physiological responses associated with each phase of a fever. Compare the list with the options provided.
Eliminate incorrect options.	The response in option 1 is associated with the course phase (plateau phase) of a fever and can be eliminated. The responses in options 4 and 5 are associated with the defervescence phase (fever abatement, flush phase) of a fever and can be eliminated.

74. 1. The feet can be washed thoroughly when taking a shower.
    2. **The warm water used to soak the feet promotes vasodilation, which improves circulation to the most distal portions**

of the feet. Soaking the feet loosens dirt and limits scrubbing, which prevent trauma to the skin. Soaking the feet should be done for just several minutes because prolonged soaking removes natural skin oils, which dries the skin and makes it prone to cracking.

3. Extra care with the feet is unnecessary because paper slippers provide a barrier between the feet and the floor.

4. When on bedrest, the feet do not get soiled with dirt. Bedrest does not necessitate soaking the feet during a bed bath.

CRITICAL-THINKING STRATEGY

Recognize keywords.	**Which patient** should the nurse identify will **benefit the most** from **soaking the feet** for several minutes as part of a bath?
Ask what the question is asking.	Which patient will benefit the most from soaking the feet?
Critically analyze each option in relation to the question and the other options.	Identify that warm bath water will increase vasodilation and improve circulation. Then compare and contrast each patient situation and establish which patient will benefit most from increased peripheral circulation.
Eliminate incorrect options.	The patients in options 1, 3, and 4 do not require an intervention that will increase peripheral circulation. These options can be eliminated.

75. 1. Flat, brown spots on the skin are an expected integumentary change in older adults. Brown spots (*lentigo senilis*) on the skin are caused by a clustering of melanocytes, which are pigment-producing cells.

2. A loss of subcutaneous fat and a reduced thickness and vascularity of the dermis that occur with aging result in thin, translucent skin in the older adult.

3. Tenting occurs when the skin of a dehydrated person remains in a peak or tent position after the skin is pinched together. This is a sign of a fluid volume deficit. Care must be taken

when assessing an older person because some degree of tenting may occur, even when hydrated, because of the decrease in skin elasticity and decrease in tissue fluid associated with aging; however, in the hydrated patient tenting will slowly resolve.

4. A decrease in tissue fluid and sebaceous gland activity associated with aging commonly results in dry, flaky skin.

CRITICAL-THINKING STRATEGY

Recognize keywords.	A nurse is assessing the **skin** of an **older adult**. Which **assessment** is the **greatest concern**?
Ask what the question is asking.	Which skin condition in an older adult is most serious?
Critically analyze each option in relation to the question and the other options.	Explore the causes and consequences of the clinical finding presented in each option. Review the expected skin changes associated with aging. Compare and contrast the options in relation to this information to identify the most serious clinical finding.
Eliminate incorrect options.	The signs in options in 1, 2, and 4 are expected changes associated with aging and are not as serious as tenting of the skin, which indicates dehydration. Options 1, 2, and 4 can be eliminated.

76. 1. Inhaling slowly and deeply using the spirometer is the correct way to inhale when using an incentive spirometer; it helps to keep the airways open.

2. The patient is using the incentive spirometer incorrectly and needs further teaching. An incentive spirometer must be held in an upright position. A tilted flow-oriented device requires less effort to reach the desired inspiratory volume. A tilted volume-oriented device will not function correctly.

3. Inspiratory goals progressively should be increased daily or more frequently depending on the patient's ability to maximize the inspiratory volume continually, which promotes alveoli ventilation.

4. Taking several breaths using the spirometer and then breathing without using the spirometer and then using the spirometer again are desirable practices because they prevent hyperventilation and respiratory alkalosis.
5. **The patient should be taught to remove the mouthpiece from the mouth before exhalation. An incentive spirometer is designed to encourage inhalation, not exhalation.**

CRITICAL-THINKING STRATEGY

Recognize keywords.	A nurse is caring for a patient using an **incentive spirometer**. Which **behaviors** observed by the nurse **indicate** that **further teaching is necessary**?
Ask what the question is asking.	Which actions demonstrate incorrect use of an incentive spirometer?
Critically analyze each option in relation to the question and the other options.	List the steps of the procedure—use of an incentive spirometer. The behavior in each option must be compared with the steps in the procedure. This question has negative polarity and expects you to identify the action that demonstrates the incorrect use of an incentive spirometer.
Eliminate incorrect options.	Options 1, 3, and 4 are correct actions when using an incentive spirometer and can be eliminated.

77. 1. Giving the mother written material about cord care assumes that the patient can read at the reading level of the presented material. Also, it does not provide an opportunity for the nurse to communicate with the patient.
2. If the patient was not participating in the present formal class, it is unlikely that the patient will participate in the next class.
3. Although an audiovisual cassette is an excellent strategy to provide instruction, it does not provide the nurse an opportunity to individualize one-on-one instruction.
4. **The nurse identified that the patient was quiet and withdrawn in the group class. Individual instruction provides the nurse the opportunity to explore**

the patient's concerns and address the patient's individual needs in privacy.

CRITICAL-THINKING STRATEGY

Recognize keywords.	A nurse on a postpartum unit is teaching a class for new mothers about umbilical cord care. The nurse identifies that **one mother does not become involved** with the discussion and **is withdrawn**. Which is the **best action** by the nurse **to help this new mother learn** about umbilical cord care?
Ask what the question is asking.	Which teaching intervention is most helpful for a patient who is withdrawn?
Critically analyze each option in relation to the question and the other options.	This question requires the integration of several concepts: teaching-learning principles, strengths and weaknesses of various teaching strategies, and how best to teach a patient who is withdrawn. Examine the action presented in each option and determine if it will be effective for this patient considering what you explored about teaching-learning.
Eliminate incorrect options.	Options 1 and 3 support withdrawn behavior. Option 2 was not effective in the past and the teaching plan should be revised. Eliminate options 1, 2, and 3.

78. 1. Tilting the head backward increases the risk of aspiration because it straightens the trachea and anatomically makes it easier for food and fluid to enter the trachea rather than the esophagus.
2. Food and fluid should be consumed separately in the presence of dysphagia. Fluid is more difficult to control with dysphagia, and it may flush the solid food toward the trachea, where it can cause choking or a partial or total airway obstruction.
3. **A patient with dysphagia should concentrate on the acts of chewing and swallowing. Environmental stimuli can be distracting and can result in inadequate chewing or premature swallowing, which in turn can result in choking and aspiration.**

4. Ensuring that the mouth is empty after eating reduces the risk of aspiration.

5. Chewing food in the front of the mouth will increase the risk for aspiration. Food should be placed in the posterior, not anterior, part of the mouth toward the side. The molars in the back of the mouth are designed for chewing. Placing food to the side keeps it close to the molars for chewing and out of direct line with the trachea. Placing food in the posterior of the mouth limits the need for the tongue to manipulate the bolus of food toward the back of the mouth in preparation for swallowing (deglutition).

CRITICAL-THINKING STRATEGY

Recognize keywords.	A nurse is teaching a patient with **dysphagia how to eat safely**. Which should the nurse **encourage the patient to do**?
Ask what the question is asking.	Which should a patient with dysphagia do when eating?
Critically analyze each option in relation to the question and the other options.	Identify the major problem associated with dysphagia—risk for aspiration. Identify a patient's response to each of the actions presented in the options. Determine if the action in each option is safe or unsafe. Identify the option that will have a safe outcome.
Eliminate incorrect options.	Eliminate the options that increase the risk of aspiration. Options 1, 2, and 5 can be eliminated.

79. 1. A person's cultural, religious, educational, economic, and experiential background influences eating behaviors and food preferences. When familiar, preferred foods are available and personally selected, patients may feel that the care is individualized and that they are in more control, resulting in eating a greater percentage of the meal.

2. Teaching the patient to avoid fluids and foods that cause flatus assumes that the inadequate intake is related to discomfort associated with flatus. This must be validated before engaging in this teaching.

3. Research indicates that exercise decreases appetite and increases the need for calories. Exercise releases beta-endorphin, which results in a state of relaxation and satisfaction with less food.

4. Drinking between-meal supplements may further decrease the consumption of food at mealtimes. Supplements are given in addition to, not to replace, the nutrients that are consumed with meals.

CRITICAL-THINKING STRATEGY

Recognize keywords.	A patient consistently eats only 25% of every meal. Which should the nurse do to **encourage** the **dietary intake** of this patient?
Ask what the question is asking.	Which action will help increase food intake?
Critically analyze each option in relation to the question and the other options.	Determine the nursing actions that support nutritional intake. Compare and contrast the benefits among the proposed interventions in relation to this information. Eliminate those actions that are contraindicated and determine which is most effective of the remaining options.
Eliminate incorrect options.	Option 2 reads into the question and makes the assumption that the patient may have discomfort from flatus. Options 3 and 4 are inaccurate and contraindicated. Eliminate options 2, 3, and 4.

80. 1. Evaluating a patient's response to activity requires the knowledge and judgment of a Registered Nurse. This evaluation requires multiple assessments (e.g., breathing, heart rate, and fatigue) and may require immediate nursing intervention if an activity intolerance is identified.

2. A task of this complexity requires the knowledge and judgment of a Registered Nurse. This assessment requires more than just obtaining a pulse rate. It requires an additional assessment of rhythm and volume.

3. Patient teaching is a complex task. It requires knowledge of principles, such

as identifying readiness to learn, progressing from simple to complex information, using motivational theory, and evaluating outcomes. Also, it requires knowledge of principles related to colostomy care, such as the bag opening must be at least ⅛ inch larger than the stoma, a pale stoma may indicate ischemia, and what to include in an assessment of the characteristics of intestinal output.

4. Applying a condom catheter is not a complex task. It requires simple problem-solving skills, involves a predictable outcome, and employs a simple level of interaction with the patient. Although this task has the potential to cause harm if the critical elements of the skill are not implemented, it is within the scope of practice of a Nursing Assistant. It does not require the more advanced competencies of a Registered Nurse.

5. Making an occupied bed is not a complex task. It requires simple problem-solving skills, involves a predictable outcome, and employs a simple level of interaction with the patient. Although this task has the potential to cause harm if the critical elements of the skill are not implemented, it is within the scope of practice of a Nursing Assistant. It does not require the more advanced competencies of a Registered Nurse.

CRITICAL-THINKING STRATEGY

Recognize keywords.	A charge nurse is delegating assignments to a Registered Nurse and a Nursing Assistant on the nursing team. Which actions should be implemented only by a Registered Nurse?
Ask what the question is asking.	Which actions are within the legal scope of practice for a Registered Nurse.
Critically analyze each option in relation to the question and the other options.	In general terms contrast the responsibilities of a Registered Nurse and a Nursing Assistant. Assess each option and designate which member of the team can perform the assignment.

Eliminate incorrect options.	Health teaching and assessing patients experiencing complex problems or who are in high-risk situations are responsibilities of a Registered Nurse. Assignments that include the activities of daily living can be assigned to a Nursing Assistant. Eliminate options 4 and 5.

81. 1. **This is an example of learning in the affective domain. In the affective domain, learning is concerned with feelings, emotions, values, beliefs, and attitudes.**

2. Assuming new healthy behaviors is not an example of learning in the cognitive domain. In the cognitive domain, learning is concerned with intellectual understanding and includes thinking on many levels, with progressively increasing complexity.

3. Assuming new healthy behaviors is not an example of learning in the psychomotor domain. Learning in the psychomotor domain includes using motor and physical abilities to master a skill. It requires the learner to practice to improve coordination and dexterity manipulating the equipment associated with the skill.

4. There is no learning domain known as physiological.

CRITICAL-THINKING STRATEGY

Recognize keywords.	A nurse wants to **influence** a patient's **beliefs** so that **new healthy behaviors** are incorporated into the patient's lifestyle. Within **which learning domain** does the nurse need **to direct teaching**?
Ask what the question is asking.	Which learning domain is associated with influencing beliefs?
Critically analyze each option in relation to the question and the other options.	Explore what you know about the three domains of learning—affective, cognitive, and psychomotor. Identify examples of learning that occur in each domain. Determine the domain in which beliefs, attitudes, feelings, emotions, and values are addressed.

continued

continued

Eliminate incorrect options.	Option 2 reflects the cognitive domain. Option 3 reflects the psychomotor domain. Option 4 is not related to any learning domain. Eliminate options 2, 3, and 4.

82. 1. Hyperextension of the condyloid joint of the wrist is accomplished by bending the fingers and hand backward as far as possible.
    2. Opposition of the thumb, which is a saddle joint, occurs when the thumb touches the top of each finger on the same hand.
    3. Abduction of the fingers (metacarpophalangeal joints—condyloid) occurs when the fingers of each hand spread apart.
    4. **Flexion of the wrist, a condyloid joint, occurs when the fingers of the hand move toward the inner aspect of the forearm.**

CRITICAL-THINKING STRATEGY

Recognize keywords.	A nurse is teaching a family member how to perform range-of-motion exercises of the hand. **Which motion occurs when the angle is reduced between the palm of the hand and forearm?**
Ask what the question is asking.	Which range of motion is being described when the angle is reduced between the palm of the hand and forearm?
Critically analyze each option in relation to the question and the other options.	Review all the motions that are included when performing range-of-motion of the joints of the hand. Specifically recall the name of the motion associated with reducing the angle between the palm of the hand and forearm.
Eliminate incorrect options.	Options 1, 2, and 3 can be eliminated because they do not describe the action indicated in the question.

83. 1. **This response recognizes the patient's feelings.**
    2. This response denies the patient's feelings and gives false reassurance.
    3. This response denies the patient's feelings and gives false reassurance.
    4. This response denies the patient's feelings.

CRITICAL-THINKING STRATEGY

Recognize keywords.	A patient with terminal cancer says to the nurse, "I've been fairly religious, but sometimes **I wonder if the things I did were acceptable to God." How should the nurse respond?**
Ask what the question is asking.	Identify the therapeutic response by the nurse in this situation.
Critically analyze each option in relation to the question and the other options.	Review therapeutic communication techniques and barriers to communication. Examine the options and identify the response that promotes communication and the responses that are barriers to communication.
Eliminate incorrect options.	Options 2 and 3 are examples of false reassurance. Option 4 denies the patient's feelings. Options 2, 3, and 4 can be eliminated.

84. 1. **If the patient falls asleep the patient may aspirate the lozenge, which can cause an airway obstruction.**
    2. Fluid will interfere with the action and absorption of the lozenge. This action is unsafe because it can cause the patient to aspirate or swallow the lozenge.
    3. Medication that dissolves under the tongue is administered via the sublingual, not buccal, route.
    4. **Alternating cheeks when placing a lozenge will limit irritation to the mucous membranes in the buccal area.**
    5. A lozenge should be administered after, or between, meals. Food will interfere with the action and absorption of the medication.

CRITICAL-THINKING STRATEGY

Recognize keywords.	A nurse is administering a **lozenge** to a patient's **buccal area** of the mouth. **Which should the nurse do?**
Ask what the question is asking.	Which interventions are implemented when administering a lozenge?

Critically analyze each option in relation to the question and the other options.	List the steps of the procedure—administering a lozenge to a patient's buccal cavity. Examine the behavior in each option and compare it with the list.
Eliminate incorrect options.	Eliminate the options that have actions that are not on your identified list, which are associated with another route of administration, or are contraindicated. Options 2 and 5 are incorrect actions. Option 3 addresses the sublingual route. Eliminate options 2, 3, and 5.

85. 1. **Pain tolerance is the maximum amount and duration of pain that a person is willing to tolerate. It is influenced by psychosociocultural factors and usually increases with age.**
2. This question focuses on an alleviating factor, distraction, rather than on the concept of pain tolerance.
3. This question is determining the patient's perception of the intensity of pain, not pain tolerance.
4. This question focuses on an alleviating factor, medication, rather than on the concept of pain tolerance.

CRITICAL-THINKING STRATEGY

Recognize keywords.	**Which question** by the nurse **assesses** a patient's **pain tolerance**?
Ask what the question is asking.	Which statement assesses pain tolerance?
Critically analyze each option in relation to the question and the other options.	Several concepts must be explored: characteristics of pain, the difference between pain threshold and pain tolerance, and how the nurse can best assess each characteristic of pain. Use of the mnemonic COLDERR (character, onset, location, duration, exacerbation, relief, and radiation) and an intensity pain scale (e.g., numerical scale, Wong-Baker FACES Rating Scale) may help to answer this question.

Eliminate incorrect options.	Options 2 and 4 focus on alleviating factors. Option 3 focuses on intensity. Options 2, 3, and 4 can be eliminated.

86. 1. Asking family members not to bring tempting food into the house imposes on family members. A person must learn to cope with temptation regardless of where being exposed to desirable foods.
2. Posting piggy pictures on the refrigerator is degrading and should be avoided. Pictures that reflect a positive outcome are more desirable.
3. The rigidity and limitation of avoiding between-meal snacks may cause periods of hypoglycemia, overeating, and noncompliance. Between-meal snacks should be calculated into the weight-reduction program to meet both physical and emotional needs.
4. **Behavior modification strategies are most successful when the person has an internal locus of control and is actively involved in self-care. Research demonstrates that self-monitoring of food intake is the single most helpful strategy in weight reduction.**

CRITICAL-THINKING STRATEGY

Recognize keywords.	An obese patient asks the nurse, "What should I do to help myself lose weight?" How should the nurse respond considering the **best behavior modification strategy for controlling food intake**?
Ask what the question is asking.	Which is the best behavior modification strategy to control food intake?
Critically analyze each option in relation to the question and the other options.	Examine each option considering certain concepts: promote independence; avoid self-deprecation; physiological responses to dieting; and strategies to achieve dietary success.
Eliminate incorrect options.	Option 1 communicates to patients that they are unable to develop an internal locus of control. Option 2 is degrading. Option 3 will not meet the patient's psychological or physical needs. Options 1, 2, and 3 can be eliminated.

87. 1. Although there is a predictable sequence to growth and development, there are individual differences in the rate and pace in which developmental milestones are achieved. Therefore, achievement of milestones is measured in ranges of time to allow for individual differences.
2. Task achievement refers to Erikson's Theory of Personality Development, which is only one aspect of growth and development. Erikson believed that each stage of personality development is characterized by the need to achieve a specific developmental task and that achievement of each task is affected by the social environment and influence of significant others. The success or failure to achieve a task at one stage will influence task achievement in subsequent stages, but it does not have to be achieved before moving on to the next task.
3. Unfortunately, not all families provide safe and supportive environments. In addition, the family is only one of many factors that influence the stages of growth and development.
4. Thinking that once a task is achieved regression is minimal is untrue. Regression is possible at any stage when one attempts to cope with a threat to the self.

CRITICAL-THINKING STRATEGY

Recognize keywords.	Which **general concept related to growth and development** should be **considered** by the nurse **when caring for patients**?
Ask what the question is asking.	Which general principle related to growth and development should be considered when caring for patients?
Critically analyze each option in relation to the question and the other options.	Review the basic concepts associated with various growth and development theorists (e.g., Erikson, Freud, Gesell, Havighurst, and Piaget). Examine each option in light of the basic concepts you have identified. The word "general" must be addressed when analyzing the options.

Eliminate incorrect options.	Eliminate those options that are untrue or that are specific to a particular theorist rather than a general concept. Task achievement in option 2 is specific to Erikson. Not all families provide safe and supportive environments as indicated in option 3. Option 4 is untrue. Options 2, 3, and 4 can be eliminated.

88. 2. The outside of the catheterization package is contaminated and should be opened with hands that have been washed with soap and water.
1. The inside of the catheterization package is sterile. Sterile gloves are on the top of the supplies included because all subsequent equipment in the package must remain sterile.
3. The nurse's sterile gloved hands then place the fenestrated drape over the patient's perineal area to continue with the establishment of a sterile field.
5. Cleansing the labia moves from areas that are less likely to be contaminated than the urinary meatus as well as reduces the spread of microorganisms toward the urinary meatus.
4. Cleansing the urinary meatus last reduces the possibility of introducing microorganisms into the urinary meatus and bladder.

CRITICAL-THINKING STRATEGY

Recognize keywords.	A primary health-care provider orders the insertion of an **indwelling urinary catheter** (retention, Foley) as part of the patient's preoperative orders. Place the following **steps of the procedure in the order** in which they should be **performed** by the nurse.
Ask what the question is asking.	What is the progression of steps for inserting an indwelling urinary catheter?

Critically analyze each option in relation to the question and the other options.	List the sequential steps of inserting an indwelling urinary catheter. Refer to your list as you examine the options presented. Order the steps presented according to the order you identified.
Eliminate incorrect options.	There are no incorrect options.

89. Answer: 16.

The pulse deficit is the difference between the apical and radial pulse rates. Therefore, 100 (apical rate) minus 84 (radial rate) equals 16. The patient's pulse deficit is 16.

CRITICAL-THINKING STRATEGY

Recognize keywords.	A patient's vital signs are: apical heart rate—100 beats/min, radial heart rate—84 beats/min, respirations—20 breaths/min, blood pressure—140/84 mm Hg. **What is the patient's pulse deficit?** Record your answer using a whole number.
Ask what the question is asking.	Calculate a pulse deficit from the information provided.
Critically analyze each option in relation to the question and the other options.	Define a pulse deficit. Analyze the situation to extract the information needed to calculate the pulse deficit. Perform the calculation.
Eliminate incorrect options.	There are no incorrect options.

90. 1. The diastolic blood pressure decreases, not increases, during shock.
2. **The initial stage of shock begins when baroreceptors in the aortic arch and the carotid sinus detect a drop in the mean arterial pressure resulting in a decrease in the systolic blood pressure. The systolic pressure is the pressure in the arteries during ventricular contraction.**
3. During shock there will be a narrowing, not widening, of pulse pressure. Pulse pressure is the difference between the systolic and diastolic pressures.

4. Weak or absent, not robust, Korotkoff's sounds are associated with shock. Korotkoff's sounds are the five distinct sounds that are heard when auscultating a blood pressure (I—faint, clear tapping; II—swishing sound; III—intense, clear tapping; IV—muffled, blowing sounds; V—absence of sounds).

CRITICAL-THINKING STRATEGY

Recognize keywords.	A patient is admitted to the emergency department after sustaining a crushing injury at work. Which **characteristic of blood pressure** should **alert** the nurse to **impending shock**?
Ask what the question is asking.	Which abnormality in blood pressure is an early sign of shock?
Critically analyze each option in relation to the question and the other options.	Identify the physiological responses to impending shock (reduced oxygenation) and why each occurs. Compare and contrast the options and determine which option is a response to impending shock relative to the information you identified.
Eliminate incorrect options.	Options 1 and 4 are opposite of what will happen with impending shock. Korotkoff's sounds are expected and are not a sign of impending shock. Options 1, 3, and 4 can be eliminated.

91. 1. Putting the stockings on after the legs are dependent is unsafe because pressure injures fluid-filled tissue. They should be applied before the legs are dependent because there will be less fluid in the tissues.
2. **Elastic stockings provide external pressure on the patient's legs to prevent pooling of blood in the veins while not interfering with arterial circulation. However, if redness is observed the stockings may be too tight. Redness of the skin (erythema) is an early sign of tissue damage to skin resulting from a decrease in oxygen to cells.**
3. When applying elastic stockings, lotion increases friction that can injure tissue.

4. Removing and reapplying the stockings only once a day can lead to tissue damage because of impaired circulation. Elastic stockings should be removed for 30 minutes three times a day; some orders require elastic stockings to be worn only when the patient is out of bed.

CRITICAL-THINKING STRATEGY

Recognize keywords.	A primary health-care provider orders **antiembolism stockings** for a patient. Which is an **important action** the nurse should teach the patient?
Ask what the question is asking.	Which action is essential in relation to antiembolism hose?
Critically analyze each option in relation to the question and the other options.	Recall the steps and the rationale for each step in the procedure for applying and wearing antiembolism stockings. Identify the benefits and consequences of the action presented in each option. Compare and contrast the options relative to this information.
Eliminate incorrect options.	Eliminate options 1, 3, and 4 because these actions can injure tissue.

92. 1. The DRGs were not designed to increase the quality of medical care.
    2. DRGs are unrelated to increasing or decreasing reliability of research data. Reliability is the degree of consistency with which a research study measures a hypothesis and depends on how well the measurement tool and the research methods are designed.
    3. DRGs have increased, not decreased, the acuity of the hospitalized population. Patients who in the past were treated in the hospital are now treated in the home, in ambulatory care settings, or in less acute care settings, such as rehabilitation or extended-care centers.
    4. **The DRGs, pretreatment diagnoses reimbursement categories, were designed to decrease the average length of a hospital stay, which in turn reduces costs.**

CRITICAL-THINKING STRATEGY

Recognize keywords.	Which is the **important consequence** of the use **of Diagnosis Related Groups** (DRGs) **on the health-care system**?
Ask what the question is asking.	Which is the effect of DRGs on the health-care system?
Critically analyze each option in relation to the question and the other options.	List the purposes of the DRGs. Compare the list to the options presented in the question.
Eliminate incorrect options.	Identify those options that are either an inaccurate statement or are unrelated to the purpose of DRGs. The outcomes identified in options 1 and 2 are unrelated to the purpose of DRGs as indicated in the rationales. DRGs increase, not decrease, the acuity of hospitalized populations. Eliminate options 1, 2, and 3.

93. 1. Obtaining the medication is part of the procedure associated with giving medication, and therefore, this is an example of the implementation step of the nursing process.
    2. Identifying body landmarks before giving an injection is part of the procedure for administering an injection and, therefore, is an example of the implementation step of the nursing process.
    3. **Determining when medications should be administered requires planning and therefore is part of the planning step of the nursing process.**
    4. Collecting data from a patient involves assessment, and therefore, verifying a patient's allergies is an example of the assessment step of the nursing process.

CRITICAL-THINKING STRATEGY

Recognize keywords.	A primary health-care provider prescribes 1 g of an antibiotic to be administered via the intramuscular route twice a day. **Which nursing action reflects** the **planning step** of the **nursing process**?

Ask what the question is asking.	Identify the action that is part of the planning step of the nursing process.
Critically analyze each option in relation to the question and the other options.	Recall the steps in the nursing process—assessment, analysis, planning, implementation, and evaluation. Review nursing actions associated with each step. Examine each option and identify which step of the nursing process is reflected by the action presented.
Eliminate incorrect options.	Options 1 and 2 are examples of actions in the implementation phase of the nursing process. Collecting data in option 4 is related to the assessment phase. Options 1, 2, and 4 can be eliminated.

94. 1. Digoxin can cause sensory changes, such as diplopia (double vision), halos, colored vision, blind spots, and flashing lights. If any of these symptoms of toxicity occurs, the medication should be withheld and a serum digoxin level assessed to determine if the drug is exceeding its therapeutic range of 0.5 to 2 ng/mL.
  2. Nausea and vomiting are common clinical indicators of digoxin toxicity resulting from irritation of the gastrointestinal system caused by an excessive dose.
  3. A respiratory rate more than 20 breaths per minute (tachypnea) is not a sign of digoxin toxicity.
  4. Digoxin prolongs conduction through the SA and AV nodes, which slows the heart rate (negative chronotropic effect). When the heart rate is less than 60 beats per minute (bradycardia), the medication should be held to prevent a further decrease in the heart rate. Some primary health-care providers will stipulate the low and high levels of pulse rates at which the drug should be held.
  5. Dysrhythmias are a common sign of digoxin toxicity because of the negative effect of digoxin on cardiac tissue when a dose is excessive.

CRITICAL-THINKING STRATEGY

Recognize keywords.	A nurse working in a nursing home routinely administers **digoxin** 0.125 mg by mouth to a patient every morning. Which **patient responses** should alert the nurse to **withhold the medication**?
Ask what the question is asking.	Which patient responses indicate digoxin toxicity?
Critically analyze each option in relation to the question and the other options.	Review the physiological action of digoxin. Analyze each option to determine if the response is unrelated to digoxin or is a toxic effect (plasma concentration of the drug that causes serious/ life-threatening responses) of digoxin, requiring its discontinuation.
Eliminate incorrect options.	As indicated in the rationales, option 3 is unrelated to digoxin toxicity and can be eliminated.

95. 1. The pressure of firm strokes on the skin moving from distal to proximal areas increases venous return. When venous return increases, cardiac output increases.
  2. Prolonged soaking removes the protective oils on the skin; the result is dry, cracked skin that is prone to further injury.
  3. Exposing just the areas that are being washed prevents chilling, not increases circulation.
  4. A temperature of 120°F to 125°F is too hot for bath water because it may cause tissue injury. Bath water should be 110°F to 115°F.

CRITICAL-THINKING STRATEGY

Recognize keywords.	A nurse is giving a patient a **bed bath**. Which should the nurse **do to increase circulation**?
Ask what the question is asking.	Which action will increase circulation during a bed bath?

continued

continued

Critically analyze each option in relation to the question and the other options.	Identify the consequences of the action in each option. Then compare and contrast the options relative to whether the action will or will not increase circulation.
Eliminate incorrect options.	Options 2 and 4 may cause tissue injury. Option 3 does not increase circulation. Options 2, 3, and 4 can be eliminated.

96. 1. Although a teaching program must be designed within the patient's developmental and cognitive abilities, they are not the most relevant factors when predicting success of the options presented.
2. Although reinforcement is important, it is not the most relevant factor when predicting success of the options presented.
3. Although family support is important, it is not the most relevant factor when predicting success of the options presented. Not all patients have a family support system.
4. **The motivation of the learner to acquire new attitudes, information, or skills is the most important component for successful learning; motivation exists when the learner recognizes the future benefits of learning.**

CRITICAL-THINKING STRATEGY

Recognize keywords.	A nurse is **predicting** the **success of** a teaching program regarding the **learning** of a skill. Which **factor is most relevant**?
Ask what the question is asking.	Which factor is essential to the success of a teaching program?
Critically analyze each option in relation to the question and the other options.	Examine each option relative to its importance in facilitating learning. Compare and contrast the options.
Eliminate incorrect options.	Progressively eliminate the least important action until you arrive at a single option. Options 1, 2, and 3 can be eliminated because the factors in these options are not as important as motivation of the learner.

97. 1. A small amount of a lubricant, not alcohol, applied to the hair will facilitate the combing out of tangles.
2. After shampooing a patient's hair, it may be dried or just toweled dry until it is free of excess moisture.
3. **The appearance of one's hair is an extension of self-image. Therefore, the patient's personal preferences should be considered before grooming the hair.**
4. Combing or brushing should progress from the ends of the hair, then from the middle to the ends, and finally from the scalp to the ends (distal to proximal). This technique limits discomfort and prevents broken ends and damaged hair shafts.

CRITICAL-THINKING STRATEGY

Recognize keywords.	Which is **most important** for the nurse to do when assisting a **female** patient with **care of the hair**?
Ask what the question is asking.	Which is most essential when grooming a female patient's hair?
Critically analyze each option in relation to the question and the other options.	Identify the steps and rationales associated with caring for a patient's hair. Compare and contrast the options relative to these steps and rationales.
Eliminate incorrect options.	Eliminate the options that contain inaccuracies or that are not as important as another option. Options 1 and 4 present incorrect information. Option 2 is not as important as option 3. Options 1, 2, and 4 can be eliminated.

98. 1. **Smothering the flames with a blanket deprives the fire of oxygen. Without oxygen to support combustion, the fire will go out. Rescuing the patient is the first step of fire safety.**
2. Rolling the patient from side to side fans the flames, which will increase the intensity of the fire.
3. Activating the alarm is premature at this time, but it will be done eventually.
4. Closing the door will impede the evacuation of the patient from the room if it becomes necessary.

CRITICAL-THINKING STRATEGY

Recognize keywords.	A patient who is secretly smoking in bed falls asleep and the **cigarette ignites** the patient's **gown.** Which should the nurse **do first** after discovering the fire?
Ask what the question is asking.	What is the first action when a patient's gown is on fire?
Critically analyze each option in relation to the question and the other options.	Identify the steps to follow when confronted with a fire and integrate the concept "oxygen supports combustion." Refer to the mnemonic RACE (**R**escue patients in immediate danger, **A**ctivate the alarm, **C**onfine the fire, **E**xtinguish the fire). Identify the fact that to rescue the patient the nurse has to extinguish the fire. Identify ways in which the nurse can cut off oxygen that supports a fire. Examine options in light of the information you have explored.
Eliminate incorrect options.	Option 1 will impede departure from the room if it becomes necessary. Option 2 is premature. Option 3 is unsafe. Options 1, 2, and 3 can be eliminated.

99. 1. It is essential for the nurse to be an informed provider of care, but it is not the priority of care for this patient.
    2. Although thinking of supplements as drugs should be done, it is not the priority of care for this patient.
    3. **The primary health-care provider should be notified immediately because the herb may interact with prescribed medications or therapies.**
    4. Although including the details about supplement use in the patient's health history should be done, it is not the priority. Medications or therapies may interact with the herb before the primary health-care provider reads the information in the health history.

CRITICAL-THINKING STRATEGY

Recognize keywords.	A nurse **discovers** that a **patient is taking natural herbal remedies. Which action is most important** for the nurse to do?
Ask what the question is asking.	Which action is most important when the nurse identifies that the patient is taking natural herbal remedies?
Critically analyze each option in relation to the question and the other options.	Consider the significance of the word *discover* as it relates to the actions in the options—need for an immediate intervention. Identify the action that will protect the patient immediately. Although you first have to recognize that natural supplements are drugs, this will not protect the patient's safety. Analyze the other options and determine which action is most critical to ensure the patient's safety.
Eliminate incorrect options.	The actions in options 1 and 2 will not immediately provide for patient safety. Although documentation is important, it is not the priority. Eliminate options 1, 2, and 4.

100. 1. Hospice care is inappropriate for this patient because the patient is not dying. Hospice programs provide supportive care to dying patients and their family members to promote dying with dignity.
     2. An acute-care setting generally is not the best setting to provide extensive rehabilitation services. The acute-care setting provides services that medically and emotionally support the patient during the critical and acute phases right after the traumatic event and until the patient is stable and out of danger.
     3. **An extended-care facility is an inpatient setting where people live while receiving subacute medical, nursing, and rehabilitative care. Extended-care facilities that can meet the needs of this individual include intermediate-care facilities, nursing homes that provide subacute care/skilled nursing care, or rehabilitation centers.**
     4. Once stabilized and out of danger, the individual in this scenario needs intensive rehabilitation services that generally cannot be provided in an assisted-living

residence. An assisted-living residence provides limited assistance with activities of daily living, meal preparation, laundry services, transportation, and opportunities for socialization. Residents are relatively independent.

CRITICAL-THINKING STRATEGY

Recognize keywords.	A patient sustained a traumatic brain injury resulting in neurological deficits after falling off a ladder at work. Which **setting** is **most appropriate** for assisting this patient **to learn how to live with neurological limitations**?
Ask what the question is asking.	Which setting is best for learning how to live with neurological deficits?
Critically analyze each option in relation to the question and the other options.	Identify the types of services provided by each of the health-care settings presented in the options. Examine the situation in the question and determine which of the settings best provides services that meet the needs of a patient with neurological deficits.
Eliminate incorrect options.	Hospice services, hospitals, and assisted-living residences are not designed to meet the intense rehabilitation needs of a patient learning to live with neurological limitations. Options 1, 2, and 4 can be eliminated.

Glossary of English Words Commonly Encountered on Nursing Examinations

Abnormality — defect, irregularity, anomaly, oddity

Absence — nonappearance, lack, nonattendance

Abundant — plentiful, rich, profuse

Accelerate — go faster, speed up, increase, hasten

Accumulate — build up, collect, gather

Accurate — precise, correct, exact

Achievement — accomplishment, success, reaching, attainment

Acknowledge — admit, recognize, accept, reply

Activate — start, turn on, stimulate

Adequate — sufficient, ample, plenty, enough

Angle — slant, approach, direction, point of view

Application — use, treatment, request, claim

Approximately — about, around, in the region of, more or less, roughly speaking

Arrange — position, place, organize, display

Associated — linked, related

Attention — notice, concentration, awareness, thought

Authority — power, right, influence, clout, expert

Avoid — keep away from, evade, let alone

Balanced — stable, neutral, steady, fair, impartial

Barrier — barricade, blockage, obstruction, obstacle

Best — most excellent, most important, greatest

Capable — able, competent, accomplished

Capacity — ability, capability, aptitude, role, power, size

Central — middle, mid, innermost, vital

Challenge — confront, dare, dispute, test, defy, face up to

Characteristic — trait, feature, attribute, quality, typical

Circular — round, spherical, globular

Collect — gather, assemble, amass, accumulate, bring together

Commitment — promise, vow, dedication, obligation, pledge, assurance

Commonly — usually, normally, frequently, generally, universally

Compare — contrast, evaluate, match up to, weigh or judge against

Compartment — section, part, cubicle, booth, stall

Complex — difficult, multifaceted, compound, multipart, intricate

Complexity — difficulty, intricacy, complication

Component — part, element, factor, section, constituent

Comprehensive — complete, inclusive, broad, thorough

Conceal — hide, cover up, obscure, mask, suppress, secrete

Conceptualize — to form an idea

Concern — worry, anxiety, fear, alarm, distress, unease, trepidation

Concisely — briefly, in a few words, succinctly

Conclude — make a judgment, determine

Confidence — self-assurance, certainty, poise, self-reliance

Congruent — matching, fitting, going together well

Consequence — result, effect, outcome, end result

Constituents — elements, component, parts that make up a whole

Contain — hold, enclose, surround, include, control, limit

Continual — repeated, constant, persistent, recurrent, frequent

Continuous — constant, incessant, nonstop, unremitting, permanent

Contribute — be a factor, add, give

Convene — assemble, call together, summon, organize, arrange

Convenience — expediency, handiness, ease

Coordinate — organize, direct, manage, bring together

Create — make, invent, establish, generate, produce, fashion, build, construct

Creative — imaginative, original, inspired, inventive, resourceful, innovative

Critical — serious, grave, significant, dangerous, life-threatening

Cue — signal, reminder, prompt, sign, indication

Curiosity — inquisitiveness, interest, nosiness, snooping

Damage — injure, harm, hurt, break, wound

Deduct — subtract, take away, remove, withhold

Deficient — lacking, wanting, underprovided, scarce, faulty

Defining — important, crucial, major, essential, significant, central

Defuse — resolve, calm, soothe, neutralize, rescue, mollify

Delay — hold up, wait, hinder, postpone, slow down, hesitate, linger

Demand — insist, claim, require, command, stipulate, ask

Describe — explain, tell, express, illustrate, depict, portray

Design — plan, invent, intend, aim, propose, devise

Desirable — wanted, pleasing, enviable, popular, sought after, attractive, advantageous

Detail — feature, aspect, element, factor, facet

Deteriorate — worsen, decline, weaken

Determine — decide, conclude, resolve, agree on

Dexterity — skillfulness, handiness, agility, deftness

Dignity — self-respect, self-esteem, decorum, formality, poise

Dimension — aspect, measurement

Diminish — reduce, lessen, weaken, detract, moderate

Discharge — release, dismiss, set free

Discontinue — stop, cease, halt, suspend, terminate, withdraw

Disorder — complaint, problem, confusion, chaos

Display — show, exhibit, demonstrate, present, put on view

Dispose — get rid of, arrange, order, set out

Dissatisfaction — displeasure, discontent, unhappiness, disappointment

Distinguish — separate, classify, recognize differences

Distract — divert, sidetrack, entertain

Distress — suffering, trouble, anguish, misery, agony, concern, sorrow

Distribute — deliver, spread out, hand out, issue, dispense

Disturbed — troubled, unstable, concerned, worried, distressed, anxious, uneasy

Diversional — serving to distract

Don — put on, dress oneself in

Dramatic — spectacular

Drape — cover, wrap, dress, swathe

Dysfunction — abnormal, impaired

Edge — perimeter, boundary, periphery, brink, border, rim

Effective — successful, useful, helpful, valuable

Efficient — not wasteful, effective, competent, resourceful, capable

Elasticity — stretch, spring, suppleness, flexibility

Eliminate — get rid of, eradicate, abolish, remove, purge

Embarrass — make uncomfortable, make self-conscious, humiliate, mortify

Emerge — appear, come, materialize, become known

Emphasize — call attention to, accentuate, stress, highlight

Ensure — make certain, guarantee

Environment — setting, surroundings, location, atmosphere, milieu, situation

Episode — event, incident, occurrence, experience

Essential — necessary, fundamental, vital, important, crucial, critical, indispensable

Etiology — assigned cause, origin

Exaggerate — overstate, inflate

Excel — stand out, shine, surpass, outclass

Excessive — extreme, too much, unwarranted

Exertion — intense or prolonged physical effort

Exhibit — show signs of, reveal, display

Expand — get bigger, enlarge, spread out, increase, swell, inflate

Expect — wait for, anticipate, imagine

Expectation — hope, anticipation, belief, prospect, probability

Experience — knowledge, skill, occurrence, know-how

Expose — lay open, leave unprotected, allow to be seen, reveal, disclose, exhibit

External — outside, exterior, outer

Facilitate — make easy, make possible, help, assist

Factor — part, feature, reason, cause, think, issue

Focus — center, focal point, hub

Fragment — piece, portion, section, part, splinter, chip

Function — purpose, role, job, task

Furnish — supply, provide, give, deliver, equip

Further — additional, more, extra, added, supplementary

Generalize — take a broad view, simplify, to make inferences from particulars

Generate — make, produce, create

Gentle — mild, calm, tender

Girth — circumference, bulk, weight

Highest — uppermost, maximum, peak, main

Hinder — hold back, delay, hamper, obstruct, impede

Humane — caring, kind, gentle, compassionate, benevolent, civilized

Ignore — pay no attention to, disregard, overlook, discount

Imbalance — unevenness, inequality, disparity

Immediate — insistent, urgent, direct

Impair — damage, harm, weaken

Implantation — insertion

Implement — employ, execute, carry out

Impotent — powerless, weak, incapable, ineffective, unable

Inadvertent — unintentional, chance, unplanned, accidental

Include — comprise, take in, contain

Indicate — point out, sign of, designate, specify, show

Ineffective — unproductive, unsuccessful, useless, vain, futile

Inevitable — predictable, expected, unavoidable, foreseeable

Influence — power, pressure, sway, manipulate, affect, effect

Initiate — start, begin, open, commence, instigate

Insert — put in, add, supplement, introduce

Inspect — look over, check, examine

Inspire — motivate, energize, encourage, enthuse

Institutionalize — place in a facility for treatment

Integrate — put together, mix, add, combine, assimilate

Integrity — honesty

Interfere — get in the way, hinder, obstruct, impede, hamper

Interpret — explain the meaning of, make understandable

Intervention — action, activity

Intolerance — bigotry, prejudice, narrow-mindedness

Involuntary — instinctive, reflex, unintentional, automatic, uncontrolled

Irreversible — permanent, irrevocable, irreparable, unalterable

Irritability — sensitivity to stimuli, fretful, quick excitability

Justify — explain in accordance with reason

Likely — probably, possible, expected

Liquefy — change into or make more fluid

Logical — using reason

Longevity — long life

Lowest — inferior in rank

Maintain — continue, uphold, preserve, sustain, retain

Majority — the greater part of

Mention — talk about, refer to, state, cite, declare, point out

Minimal — least, smallest, nominal, negligible, token

Minimize — reduce, diminish, lessen, curtail, decrease to smallest possible

Mobilize — activate, organize, assemble, gather together, rally

Modify — change, adapt, adjust, revise, alter

Moist — slightly wet, damp

Multiple — many, numerous, several, various

Natural — normal, ordinary, unaffected

Negative — no, harmful, downbeat, pessimistic

Negotiate — bargain, talk, discuss, consult, cooperate, settle

Notice — become aware of, see, observe, discern, detect

Notify — inform, tell, alert, advise, warn, report

Nurture — care for, raise, rear, foster

Obsess — preoccupy, consume

Occupy — live in, inhabit, reside in, engage in

Occurrence — event, incident, happening

Odorous — scented, stinking, aromatic

Offensive — unpleasant, distasteful, nasty, disgusting

Opportunity — chance, prospect, break

Organize — put in order, arrange, sort, categorize, classify

Origin — source, starting point, cause, beginning, derivation, etiology

Pace — speed

Parameter — limit, factor, limitation, issue

Participant — member, contributor, partaker, applicant

Perspective — viewpoint, view, perception

Position — place, location, point, spot, situation

Practice — do, carry out, perform, apply, follow

Precipitate — cause to happen, bring on, hasten, abrupt, sudden

Predetermine — fix or set beforehand

Predictable — expected, knowable

Preference — favorite, liking, first choice

Prepare — get ready, plan, make, train, arrange, organize

Prescribe — set down, stipulate, order, recommend, impose

Previous — earlier, prior, before, preceding

Primarily — first, above all, mainly, mostly, largely, principally, predominantly

Primary — first, main, basic, chief, most important, key, prime, major, crucial

Priority — main concern, giving first attention to, order of importance

Production — making, creation, construction, assembly

Profuse — a lot of, plentiful, copious, abundant, generous, prolific, bountiful

Prolong — extend, delay, put off, lengthen, draw out

Promote — encourage, support, endorse, sponsor

Proportion — ratio, amount, quantity, part of, percentage, section of

Provide — give, offer, supply, make available

Rationalize — explain, reason

Realistic — practical, sensible, reasonable

Receive — get, accept, take delivery of, obtain

Recognize — acknowledge, appreciate, identify, aware of

Recovery — healing, mending, improvement, recuperation, renewal

Reduce — decrease, lessen, ease, moderate, diminish

Reestablish — reinstate, restore, return, bring back

Regard — consider, look upon, relate to, respect

Regular — usual, normal, ordinary, standard, expected, conventional

Relative — comparative, family member

Relevance — importance of

Reluctant — unwilling, hesitant, disinclined, indisposed, adverse

Reminisce — recall and review remembered experiences

Remove — take away, get rid of, eliminate, eradicate

Reposition — move, relocate, change position

Require — need, want, necessitate

Resist — oppose, defend against, keep from, refuse to go along with, defy

Resolution — decree, solution, decision, ruling, promise

Resolve — make up your mind, solve, determine, decide

Response — reply, answer, reaction, retort

Restore — reinstate, reestablish, bring back, return to, refurbish

Restrict — limit, confine, curb, control, contain, hold back, hamper

Retract — take back, draw in, withdraw, apologize

Reveal — make known, disclose, divulge, expose, tell, make public

Review — appraisal, reconsider, evaluation, assessment, examination, analysis

Ritual — custom, ceremony, formal procedure

Robust — sturdy, vigorous

Rotate — turn, go around, spin, swivel

Routine — usual, habit, custom, practice

Satisfaction — approval, fulfillment, pleasure, happiness

Satisfy — please, convince, fulfill, make happy, gratify

Secure — safe, protected, fixed firmly, sheltered, confident, obtain

Sequential — chronological, in order of occurrence

Significant — important, major, considerable, noteworthy, momentous

Slight — small, slim, minor, unimportant, insignificant, insult, snub

Source — basis, foundation, starting place, cause

Specific — exact, particular, detail, explicit, definite

Stable — steady, even, constant

Statistics — figures, data, information

Subtract — take away, deduct

Success — achievement, victory, accomplishment

Surround — enclose, encircle, contain

Suspect — think, believe, suppose, guess, deduce, infer, distrust, doubtful

Sustain — maintain, carry on, prolong, continue, nourish, suffer

Synonymous — same as, identical, equal, tantamount

Systemic — affecting the entire organism

Thorough — careful, detailed, methodical, systematic, meticulous, comprehensive, exhaustive

Tilt — tip, slant, slope, lean, angle, incline

Translucent — see-through, transparent, clear

Unique — one and only, sole, exclusive, distinctive

Universal — general, widespread, common, worldwide

Unoccupied — vacant, not busy, empty

Unrelated — unconnected, unlinked, distinct, dissimilar, irrelevant

Unresolved — unsettled, uncertain, unsolved, unclear, in doubt

Utilize — make use of, employ

Various — numerous, variety, range of, mixture of, assortment of

Verbalize — express, voice, speak, articulate

Verify — confirm, make sure, prove, attest to, validate, substantiate, corroborate, authenticate

Vigorous — forceful, strong, brisk, energetic

Volume — quantity, amount, size

Withdraw — remove, pull out, take out, extract

Bibliography

Ackley, BJ, and Ladwig, GB: *Nursing Diagnosis Handbook: An Evidence-Based Guide to Planning Care*, ed.10. St. Louis: Mosby Elsevier, 2014.

Aexaitus, I, and Broome, B: Implementation of a nurse-driven protocol to prevent catheter-associated urinary tract infections. *Journal of Nursing Care Quality 29*(3):245-252, 2014.

Ahern, J, and Kumar, C: Caring for a patient with mental illness in the acute care setting. *Nursing Made Incredibly Easy! 11*(3):18-23, 2013.

Alexander-Magalee, MA: Patient safety: Addressing pharmacology challenges in order adults. *Nursing 2013 43*(10):58-60, 2012.

Aschenbrenner, DS: Drug watch: Preventing injuries from OTC eyedrops and nasal sprays. *American Journal of Nursing 113*(2):23, 2013.

Aschenbrenner, DS: Overuse of certain OTC laxatives may be dangerous. *American Journal of Nursing 114*(5):25, 2014.

Association for Professionals in Infection Control and Epidemiology, Greene, L. (Ed.). (2014, April 1). APIC Guide to Prevent Catheter-Associated Urinary Tract Infections. Retrieved September 15, 2014, from http://bit.ly/1syFer5.

Association for the Advancement of Wound Care (AAWC). Education for the Generalist. http://aawconline.org/education-for-the-generalist/. Accessed 9/1/2014.

Association for the Advancement of Wound Care (AAWC). The ABC's of Skin and Wound Care. http://aawconline.org/wp-content/uploads/2011/04/ABCsPublic.pdf. Accessed 9/1/2014.

Babine, RL, Farrington, S, and Wierman, HR: Inspiring change: HELP© prevent falls by preventing delirium. *Nursing 2013 43*(5):17-20, 2013.

Black, BP: *Professional Nursing: Concepts & Challenges*, ed. 7. St. Louis: Elsevier, 2014.

Brous, E: Lessons learned from litigation: Maintaining professional boundaries. *American Journal of Nursing 114*(7):60-63, 2014.

Bryant, R, and Nix, D: *Acute and Chronic Wounds: Current Management Concepts*, ed. 4. St. Louis: Elsevier/Mosby, 2012.

Buck, HG: Transitions: Help patients and families choose end-of-life care "wisely." *Nursing 2013 43*(7):16-17, 2013.

Bulechek, G, Butcher, H, Dochterman, J, and Wagner, C (eds): *Nursing Interventions Classification (NIC)*, ed 6. St. Louis: Elsevier, 2012.

Burton, MA, and Ludwig, LJ: *Fundamentals of Nursing Care: Concepts, Connections & Skills*. Philadelphia: F.A. Davis, 2011.

Carter, D: In the News: The right balance between hand sanitizers and handwashing. *American Journal of Nursing 113*(7)13, 2013.

Castillo, SLM, and Werner-McCullough, M: *Calculating Drug Dosages: A Patient-Safe Approach to Nursing and Math*. Philadelphia: F.A. Davis, 2015.

Centers for Medicare & Medicaid Services (CMS.gov). National Health Expenditure Projections 2012-2022. http://www.cms.gov/Research-Statistics-Data-and-Systems/Statistics-Trends-and-Reports/NationalHealthExpendData/downloads/proj2012.pdf. Accessed 10/28/2014.

Center for Nursing Classification and Clinical Effectiveness. (CNC). www.nursing.uiowa. edu/center-for-nursing-classification-and-clinical-effectiveness. Accessed 8/29/2014.

Chaffee, J: *Thinking Critically*, ed. 11. Stamford: Cengage Learning, 2015.

Cherry, B, and Jacob, SR: *Contemporary Nursing: Issues, Trends, & Management*, ed.6. St. Louis: Elsevier, 2014.

Child Health USA 2013. Infant Mortality: An illustrated collection of current and historical data, published annually. http://mchb.hrsa.gov/chusa13/perinatal-health-status-indicators/p/infant-mortality.html. Accessed 11/1/2014.

Cohen, MR: Medication errors. *Nursing 2014 44*(9):72, 2014.

Cohen, NL: Patient safety: Using the ABCs of situational awareness for patient safety. *Nursing 2013 43*(4):64-65, 2013.

Costedio, E, Powers, J, and Stuart, TL: Student voices: Change-of-shift report: From hallways to the bedside. *Nursing 2013 43*(8):18-19, 2013.

Crusse, EP, and Kent, VP: Making SENSE of sensory changes in older adults. *Nursing Made Incredibly Easy! 11*(5):20-30, 2013.

Davis, D, Shuss, S, and Lockhart, L: Assessing suicide risk. *Nursing Made Incredibly Easy! 12*(1):22-29, 2014.

Doenges, ME: *Nursing Care Plans*, ed. 9. Philadelphia: F.A. Davis, 2014.

Fahlberg, B: Promoting patient dignity in nursing care. *Nursing 2014 44*(7):14, 2014.

Fleming, C: US health spending growth projected to average 5.8 percent annually through 2022. *Health Affairs Blog*. http://healthaffairs.org/blog/2013/09/18/us-health-spending-growth-projected-to-average-5-8-percent-annually-through-2022/. Accessed 10/28/1014.

Fowler, C: Caring for the caregiver. *Nursing 2014 44*(5):60-64, 2014.

Fronczek, M: Physical restraints: To use or not to use? *Nursing Made Incredibly Easy! 12*(2):54-55, 2014.

Fuchs, V: The gross domestic product and health care spending. *The New England Journal of Medicine*. 369:107-109 July 11, 2013. http://www.nejm.org/doi/full/10.1056/NEJMp1305298. Accessed 10/28/1014.

Gibson, M, and Keeling, A: Shaping family and community health: A historical perspective. *Family & Community Health 37*(3):168-169, 2014.

Goldsack, J, Cunningham, J, and Mascioli, S: Patient falls: Searching for the elusive "silver bullet." *Nursing 2014 44*(7):61-2, 2014.

Hale, A, and Hovey, J: *Fluid and Electrolyte Notes*. F.A. Davis, 2013.

Hargrove-Huttel, RA, and Colgrove, KC: *Pharmacology Success*, ed. 2. Philadelphia: F.A. Davis, 2014.

Hargrove-Huttel, RA, and Colgrove, KC: *Prioritization, Delegation, & Management of Care for the NCLEX-RN® Exam*. Philadelphia: F.A. Davis, 2014.

Harper, D: Infusion therapy: Much more than a simple task. *Nursing 2014 44*(7):66-67, 2014.

Heron, M. Deaths: Leading causes for 2010. *National Vital Statistics Report*. Vol. 62, No. 6, December 20, 2013. http://www.cdc.gov/nchs/data/nvsr/nvsr62/nvsr62_06.pdf. Accessed 11/1/2014.

Hislop, JO: fighting frailty in older patients. *Nursing 2014 44*(2):64-66, 2014.

Hopp, L: *Introduction to Evidence-Based Practice*. Philadelphia: F.A. Davis, 2012.

Huston, CJ: *Professional Issues in Nursing: Challenges and Opportunities*, ed. 3. Baltimore: Lippincott Williams & Wilkins, 2014.

Kelly, P, and Marthaler, M: Nursing Delegation, *Setting Priorities, and Making Patient Care Assignments*, ed. 2. Clifton Park, NY: Delmar Cengage Learning, 2011.

Kelton, D, and Davis, C: Ask an expert: The art of effective communication. *Nursing Made Incredibly Easy! 11*(1):55-56, 2013.

Kenneley, I: Clostridium difficile infection is on the rise. *American Journal of Nursing* *114*(3):62-67, 2014.

KHN Morning Briefing. Health care costs to reach nearly one-fifth of GDP by 2021. *KHN Morning Briefing.* http://kaiserhealthnews.org/morning-breakout/health-care-costs-4/. Accessed 10/28/1014.

Kirchner, RB: Introducing nursing informatics. *Nursing 2014* *44*(9):22-23, 2014.

Kübler-Ross, E: *On Death and Dying.* New York: Macmillan, 1969.

Lange, JW: *The Nurse's Role in Promoting Optimal Health of Older Adults.* Philadelphia: F.A. Davis, 2011.

Laskowski-Jones, L: The art of harmonious delegation. *Nursing 2014* *44*(5):6, 2014.

Leeuwen, AM, and Bladh, ML: *Davis's Comprehensive Handbook of Laboratory Tests With Nursing Implications,* ed. 6. Philadelphia: F.A. Davis, 2015.

Lutz, CA: *Nutrition and Diet Therapy,* ed. 6. Philadelphia: F.A. Davis, 2014.

MacDorman, MF, Hoyert, DL, and Mathews, TT: Recent declines in infant mortality in the United States, 2005–2011. *NCHS Data Brief,* No 120. April 2013. http://www.cdc.gov/nchs/data/databriefs/db120.pdf. Accessed 11/1/2014.

March of Dimes, March of Dimes 2013 Premature Birth Report Card. http://www.marchofdimes.org/materials/premature-birth-report-card-united-states.pdf. Accessed 10/27/2014.

Maslow, AH: Hierarchy of Needs: A Theory of Human Motivation. Eastford, CT: Martino Fine Books Publishers, 2013.

McCarron, K: Blood essentials. *Nursing Made Incredibly Easy!* *11*(2):16-24, 2013.

McCarron, K: Med check: Routine labs for common meds. *Nursing Made Incredibly Easy!* *11*(2):50-53, 2013.

Moorhead, S, Johnson, M, Maas, M, and Swanson, E: *Nursing Outcomes Classification (NOC),* ed. 5, St. Louis: Elsevier, 2012.

Murdock, A, and Griffin, B: How is patient education linked to patient satisfaction? *Nursing 2013* *43*(6):43-45, 2013.

Murphy, L., Xu, J, and Kochanek, K. Deaths: Final data for 2010. *National Vital Statistics Report.* Vol. 61, No 4, http://www.cdc.gov/nchs/data/nvsr/nvsr61/nvsr61_04.pdf. Accessed 10/30/2014. (most recent reported data as of 10/30/2014).

Nugent, PM, and Vitale, BA: *Fundamentals of Nursing: Content Review PLUS Practice Questions.* Philadelphia: F.A. Davis, 2014.

Nugent, PM, and Vitale, BA: *Test Success: Test-Taking Techniques for Beginning Nursing Students.* Philadelphia: F.A. Davis, 2016

O'Keeffe, M, and Saver, C (contributors): *Communication, Collaboration & You: Tools, Tips, and Techniques for Nursing Practice.* Silver Spring, MD: American Nurses Association, 2014.

Ortega, L, and Parash, B: Clinical queries: Improving change-of-shift report. *Nursing 3013* *43*(2):68, 2013.

Perry, SE: Hard of hearing. *American Journal of Nursing* *114*(8):13, 2014.

Pfeifer, GM: In the news: The top nursing news story of 2012: Health care reform goes hand in hand with expanded nursing roles. *American Journal of Nursing* *113*(1):15, 2013.

Phillips, J, Stinson, K, and Strickler, J: Avoiding eruptions: De-escalating agitated patients. *Nursing 2014* *44*(4):60-63, 2014.

Phillips, LD, and Gorski, L: *Manual of I.V. Therapeutics,* ed. 6. Philadelphia: F.A. Davis, 2014.

Primeau, MS, and Frith, KH: Clinical queries: Teaching patients with an intellectual disability. *Nursing 2013* *43*(6):68-69, 2013.

Purnell, LD: *Guide to Culturally Competent Health Care,* ed. 3. Philadelphia: F.A. Davis, 2014.

Purnell, LD: *Transcultural Health Care*, ed. 4. Philadelphia: F.A. Davis, 2012.

Queensland Government. Health care providers' handbook on Hindu patients. *Queensland Health*. http://www.health.qld.gov.au/multicultural/health_workers/hbook-hindu.asp. Accessed 11/1/2014.

Quinlan-Colwell, A: Controlling pain: Making an ethical plan for treating patients in pain. *Nursing 2013 43*(10):64-68, 2013.

Raines, V: *Davis's Basic Math Review for Nurses*. Philadelphia: F.A. Davis, 2009.

Rank, W: Performing a focused neurologic assessment. *Nursing 2013 43*(12):37-40, 2013.

Roe, E: Using evidence-based practice to prevent hospital-acquired pressure ulcers and promote wound healing. *American Journal of Nursing 114*(8):61-65, 2014.

Rogers, TL, and Darden, CD: How clinical nurse leaders can improve rural healthcare. *Nursing 2014 44*(9):52-55, 2014.

Saathoff, A, and Turnham, N: Stick it to me: The complexities of glucose testing. *Nursing Made Incredibly Easy 12*(5):50-53, 2014.

Said, AA, and Kautz, DD: Patient safety: Reducing restrint use for older adults in acute care. *Nursing 2013 43*(12):59-61, 2013.

Salladay, SA: Ethical problems. *Nursing 2014 44*(8):12-13, 2014.

Seckel, MA: Patient safety: Maintaining urinary catheters: What does the evidence say? *Nursing 2013 43*(2):63-65, 2013.

Segobiano, A, Waters, J, and Davis, C: All about acetaminophen—I.V.!. *Nursing Made Incredibly Easy! 12*(2):50-52, 2014.

Sukumaran, S: Hinduism and medicine: A guide for medical professionals. *Angelfire*, Copyright 1999. http://www.angelfire.com/az/ambersukumaran/medicine.html. Accessed 11/1/2014.

Tompson, GS: *Understanding Anatomy & Physiology: A Visual, Auditory, Interactive Approach*, ed. 2. Philadelphia: F.A. Davis, 2015.

Townsend, MC: *Psychiatric Nursing*, ed. 9. Philadelphia: F.A. Davis, 2014.

Treas, LS, and Wilkinson, JM: *Basic Nursing: Concepts, Skills & Reasoning*. Philadelphia: F.A. Davis, 2014.

United States Food and Drug Administration, How to Understand and Use the Nutrition Facts Label, http://www.fda.gov/Food/IngredientsPackagingLabeling/LabelingNutrition/ucm274593.htm, accessed 4/3/15.

United States Food and Drug Administration, Proposed Changes to the Nutrition Facts Label, http://www.fda.gov/Food/GuidanceRegulation/GuidanceDocumentsRegulatoryInformation/LabelingNutrition/ucm385663.htm, accessed 4/3/15.

Ulbricht, C: *Davis's Pocket Guide to Herbs and Supplements*. Philadelphia: F.A. Davis, 2010.

Vallerand, AH, and Sanoski, CA: *Davis's Drug Guide for Nurses®*, ed.14. Philadelphia: F.A. Davis, 2014.

Venes, D (ed): *Taber's Cyclopedic Medical Dictionary*, ed. 22. Philadelphia: F.A. Davis, 2013.

Vitale, BA: *NCLEX-RN: Core Review and Exam Prep*, ed. 2. Philadelphia: F.A. Davis, 2013.

Weiss, SA, and Tappen, RM: *Essentials of Nursing Leadership & Management*, ed. 6. Philadelphia: F.A. Davis, 2014.

Williams, W, Davis, C, and Brothers, K: I.V. essentials: Fluid management basics. *Nursing Made Incredibly Easy! 11*(4):48-51, 2013.

Woods, AD: Implementing evidence into practice. *Nursing 2013 43*(1-Supplement: Lippincott's 2013 Nursing Career & Education Directory):4-6, 2013.

Zerwekh, JA, and Garneau, AZ: *Nursing Today: Transition and Trends*, ed. 8. St. Louis: Elsevier/Saunders, 2015.

Index

Note: Page numbers followed by *f* indicate figures.